THE COMPLETE ILLUSTRATED NOVELS OF

Jane Austen

VOLUME 2

THE COMPLETE ILLUSTRATED NOVELS OF

Jane Austen

VOLUME 2

SENSE AND SENSIBILITY

EMMA

NORTHANGER ABBEY

Illustrated by
Hugh Thomson

CHANCELLOR
PRESS

Sense and Sensibility first appeared in Great Britain in 1811
Emma first appeared in Great Britain in 1915
Northanger Abbey first appeared in Great Britain in 1817

This collected edition published in Great Britain 1987 by
Chancellor Press, an imprint of Bounty Books,
a division of Octopus Publishing Group Ltd,
2-4 Heron Quays, London E14 4JP

Reprinted 1996, 2000

ISBN 1 85152 050 3

A CIP catalogue record for this title is available at the British Library

Printed and bound by Mackays of Chatham, England

Contents

Sense and Sensibility

CHAPTER ONE

THE FAMILY OF DASHWOOD had been long settled in Sussex. Their estate was large, and their residence was at Norland Park, in the centre of their property, where, for many generations, they had lived in so respectable a manner, as to engage the general good opinion of their surrounding acquaintance. The late owner of this estate was a single man, who lived to a very advanced age, and who for many years of his life, had a constant companion and housekeeper in his sister. But her death, which happened ten years before his own, produced a great alteration in his home; for to supply her loss, he invited and received into his house the family of his nephew Mr Henry Dashwood, the legal inheritor of the Norland estate, and the person to whom he intended to bequeath it. In the society of his nephew and niece, and their children, the old Gentleman's days were comfortably spent. His attachment to them all increased. The constant attention of Mr and Mrs Henry Dashwood to his wishes, which proceeded not merely from interest, but from goodness of heart, gave him every degree of solid comfort which his age could receive; and the cheerfulness of the children added a relish to his existence.

By a former marriage, Mr Henry Dashwood had one son: by his present lady, three daughters. The son, a steady respectable young man, was amply provided for by the fortune of his mother, which had been large, and half of which devolved on him on his coming of age. By his own marriage, likewise, which happened soon afterwards, he added to his wealth. To him therefore the succession to the Norland estate was not so really important as to his sisters; for their fortune, independent of what might arise to them from their father's inheriting that property, could be but small. Their mother had nothing, and their father only seven thousand pounds in his own disposal; for the remaining moiety of his first wife's fortune was also secured to her child, and he had only a life interest in it.

The old Gentleman died; his will was read, and like almost every other will, gave as much disappointment as pleasure. He was neither so unjust, nor so ungrateful, as to leave his estate from his nephew; – but he left it to him on such terms as destroyed half the value of the bequest. Mr Dashwood had wished for it more for the sake of his wife and daughters than for himself or his son: – but to his son,

His son's son, a child of four years old.

and his son's son, a child of four years old, it was secured, in such a way, as to leave to himself no power of providing for those who were most dear to him, and who most needed a provision, by any charge on the estate, or by any sale of its valuable woods. The whole was tied up for the benefit of this child, who, in occasional visits with his father and mother at Norland, had so far gained on the affections of his uncle, by such attractions as are by no means unusual in children of two or three years old; an imperfect articulation, an earnest desire of having his own way, many cunning tricks, and a great deal of noise, as to outweigh all the value of all the attention which, for years, he had received from his niece and her daughters. He meant not to be unkind however, and, as a mark of his affection for the three girls, he left them a thousand pounds a-piece.

Mr Dashwood's disappointment was, at first, severe; but his temper was cheerful and sanguine, and he might reasonably hope to live many years, and by living economically, lay by a considerable sum from the produce of an estate already large, and capable of almost immediate improvement. But the fortune, which had been so tardy in coming, was his only one twelvemonth. He survived his uncle no longer; and ten thousand pounds, including the late legacies, was all that remained for his widow and daughters.

His son was sent for, as soon as his danger was known, and to him Mr Dashwood recommended, with all the strength and urgency which illness could command, the interest of his mother-in-law and sisters.

Mr John Dashwood had not the strong feelings of the rest of the family; but he was affected by a recommendation of such a nature at such a time, and he promised to do every thing in his power to make them comfortable. His father was rendered easy by such an assurance, and Mr John Dashwood had then leisure to consider how much there might prudently be in his power to do for them.

He was not an ill-disposed young man, unless to be rather cold hearted, and rather selfish, is to be ill-disposed: but he was, in general, well respected; for he conducted himself with propriety in the discharge of his ordinary duties. Had he married a more amiable woman, he might have been made still more respectable than he was – he might even have been made amiable himself; for he was very young when he married, and very fond of his wife. But Mrs John Dashwood was a strong caricature of himself; – more narrow-minded and selfish.

When he gave his promise to his father, he meditated within himself to increase the fortunes of his sisters by the present of a thousand pounds a-piece. He then really thought himself equal to it. The prospect of four thousand a-year, in addition to his present income, besides the remaining half of his own mother's fortune, warmed his heart and made him feel capable of generosity. – 'Yes, he would give them three thousand pounds: it would be liberal and handsome! It would be enough to make them completely easy. Three thousand pounds! he could spare so considerable a sum with little inconvenience.' – He thought of it all day long, and for many days successively, and he did not repent.

No sooner was his father's funeral over, than Mrs John Dashwood, without sending any notice of her intention to her mother-in-law, arrived with her child and their attendants. No one could dispute her right to come; the house was her husband's from the moment of his father's decease; but the indelicacy of her conduct was so much the greater, and to a woman in Mrs Dashwood's situation, with only common feelings, must have been highly unpleasing: – but in *her* mind there was a sense of honour so keen, a generosity so romantic, that any offence of the kind, by whomsoever given or received, was to her a source of immoveable disgust. Mrs John Dashwood had never been a favourite with any of her husband's family; but she had had no opportunity, till the present, of shewing them with how little attention to the comfort of other people she could act when occasion required it.

So acutely did Mrs Dashwood feel this ungracious behaviour, and so earnestly did she despise her daughter-in-law for it, that, on the arrival of the latter, she would have quitted the house for ever, had not the entreaty of her eldest girl induced her first to reflect on the propriety of going, and her own tender love for all her three children determined her afterwards to stay, and for their sakes avoid a breach with their brother.

Elinor, this eldest daughter whose advice was so effectual, possessed a strength of understanding, and coolness of judgment, which qualified her, though only nineteen, to be the counsellor of her mother, and enabled her frequently to counteract, to the advantage of them all, that eagerness of mind in Mrs Dashwood which must generally have led to imprudence. She had an excellent heart; – her disposition was affectionate, and her feelings were strong; but she knew how to govern them: it was a knowledge which her mother had yet to learn, and which one of her sisters had resolved never to be taught.

Marianne's abilities were, in many respects, quite equal to Elinor's. She was sensible and clever; but eager in every thing; her sorrows, her joys, could have no moderation. She was generous, amiable, interesting: she was every thing but prudent. The resemblance between her and her mother was strikingly great.

Elinor saw, with concern, the excess of her sister's sensibility; but by Mrs Dashwood it was valued and cherished. They encouraged each other now in the violence of their affliction. The agony of grief which overpowered them at first, was voluntarily renewed, was sought for, was created again and again. They gave themselves up wholly to their sorrow, seeking increase of wretchedness in every reflection that could afford it, and resolved against ever admitting consolation in future. Elinor, too, was deeply afflicted; but still she could struggle, she could exert herself. She could consult with her brother, could receive her sister-in-law on her arrival, and treat her with proper attention; and could strive to rouse her mother to similar exertion, and encourage her to similar forbearance.

Margaret, the other sister, was a good-humoured well-disposed girl; but as she had already imbibed a good deal of Marianne's romance, without having much of her sense, she did not, at thirteen, bid fair to equal her sisters at a more advanced period of life.

CHAPTER TWO

Mrs John Dashwood now installed herself mistress of Norland; and her mother and sisters-in-law were degraded to the condition of visitors. As such, however, they were treated by her with quiet civility: and by her husband with as much kindness as he could feel towards any body beyond himself, his wife, and their child. He really pressed them, with some earnestness, to consider Norland as their home; and, as no plan appeared so eligible to Mrs Dashwood as remaining there till she could accommodate herself with a house in the neighbourhood, his invitation was accepted.

A continuance in a place where every thing reminded her of former delight, was exactly what suited her mind. In seasons of cheerfulness, no temper could be more cheerful than hers, or possess, in a greater degree, that sanguine expectation of happiness which is happiness itself. But in sorrow she must be equally carried away by her fancy, and as far beyond consolation as in pleasure she was beyond alloy.

Mrs John Dashwood did not at all approve of what her husband intended to do for his sisters. To take three thousand pounds from the fortune of their dear little boy, would be impoverishing him to the most dreadful degree. She begged him to think again on the subject. How could he answer it to himself to rob his child, and his only child too, of so large a sum? And what possible claim could the Miss Dashwoods, who were related to him only by half blood, which she considered as no relationship at all, have on his generosity to so large an amount. It was very well known that no affection was ever supposed to exist between the children of any man by different marriages; and why was he to ruin himself, and their poor little Harry, by giving away all his money to his half sisters?

'It was my father's last request to me,' replied her husband, 'that I should assist his widow and daughters.'

'He did not know what he was talking of, I dare say; ten to one but he was light-headed at the time. Had he been in his right senses, he could not have thought of such a thing as begging you to give away half your fortune from your own child.'

'He did not stipulate for any particular sum, my dear Fanny; he only requested me, in general terms, to assist them, and make their situation more comfortable than it was in his power to do. Perhaps it would have been as well if he had left it wholly to myself. He could hardly suppose I should neglect them. But as he required the promise, I could not do less than give it: at least I thought so at the time. The promise, therefore, was given, and must be performed. Something must be done for them whenever they leave Norland and settle in a new home.'

'Well, then *let* something be done for them; but *that* something need not be three thousand pounds. Consider,' she added, 'that when the money is once parted with, it never can return. Your sisters will marry, and it will be gone for ever. If, indeed, it could ever be restored to our poor little boy – '

'Why, to be sure,' said her husband, very gravely, 'that would make a great difference. The time may come when Harry will regret that so large a sum was parted with. If he should have a numerous family, for instance, it would be a very convenient addition.'

'To be sure it would.'

'Perhaps, then, it would be better for all parties if the sum were diminished one half – Five hundred pounds would be a prodigious increase to their fortunes!'

'Oh! beyond any thing great! What brother on earth would do half so much for his sisters, even if *really* his sisters! And as it is – only half blood! – But you have such a generous spirit!'

'I would not wish to do any thing mean,' he replied, 'One had rather, on such occasions, do too much than too little. No one, at least, can think I have not done enough for them: even themselves, they can hardly expect more.'

'There is no knowing what *they* may expect,' said the lady, 'but we are not to think of their expectations: the question is, what you can afford to do.'

'Certainly – and I think I may afford to give them five hundred pounds a-piece. As it is, without any addition of mine, they will each have above three thousand pounds on their mother's death – a very comfortable fortune for any young woman.'

'To be sure it is: and, indeed, it strikes me that they can want no addition at all. They will have ten thousand pounds divided amongst them. If they marry, they will be sure of doing well, and if they do not, they may all live very comfortably together on the interest of ten thousand pounds.'

'That is very true, and, therefore, I do not know whether, upon the whole, it would not be more advisable to do something for their mother while she lives rather than for them – something of the annuity kind I mean. – My sisters would feel the good effects of it as well as herself. A hundred a year would make them all perfectly comfortable.'

His wife hesitated a little, however, in giving her consent to this plan.

'To be sure,' said she, 'it is better than parting with fifteen hundred pounds at once. But then if Mrs Dashwood should live fifteen years we shall be completely taken in.'

'Fifteen years! my dear Fanny; her life cannot be worth half that purchase.'

'Certainly not; but if you observe, people always live for ever when there is any annuity to be paid them; and she is very stout and healthy, and hardly forty. An annuity is a very serious business; it comes over and over every year, and there is no getting rid of it. You are not aware of what you are doing. I have known a great deal of the trouble of annuities; for my mother was clogged with the payment of three to old superannuated servants by my father's will, and it is amazing how disagreeable she found it. Twice every year these annuities were to be paid; and there was the trouble of getting it to them; and then one of them was said to have died, and afterwards it turned out to be no such thing. My mother was quite sick of it. Her income was not her own, she said, with such perpetual claims on it; and it was the more unkind in my father, because, otherwise, the money would have been entirely at my mother's disposal, without any restriction whatever. It has given me such an abhorrence of annuities, that I am sure I would not pin myself down to the payment of one for all the world.'

'It is certainly an unpleasant thing,' replied Mr Dashwood, 'to have those kind of yearly drains on one's income. One's fortune, as your mother justly says, is *not* one's own. To be tied down to the regular payment of such a sum, on every rent day, is by no means desirable: it takes away one's independence.'

'Undoubtedly; and after all you have no thanks for it. They think themselves secure, you do no more than what is expected, and it raises no gratitude at all. If I were you, whatever I did should be done at my own discretion entirely. I would not bind myself to allow them any thing yearly. It may be inconvenient some years to spare a hundred, or even fifty pounds from our own expenses.'

'I believe you are right, my love; it will be better that there should be no annuity in the case; whatever I may give them occasionally will be of far greater assistance than a yearly allowance, because they would only enlarge their style of living if they felt sure of a larger income, and would not be sixpence the richer for it at the end of the year. It will certainly be much the best way. A present of fifty pounds, now and then, will prevent their ever being distressed for money, and will, I think, be amply discharging my promise to my father.'

'To be sure it will. Indeed, to say the truth, I am convinced within myself that your father had no idea of your giving them any money at all. The assistance he thought of, I dare say, was only such as might be reasonably expected of you; for instance, such as looking out for a comfortable small house for them, helping them to move their things, and sending them presents of fish and game, and so forth, whenever they are in season. I'll lay my life that he meant nothing farther; indeed, it would be very strange and unreasonable if he did. Do but consider, my dear Mr Dashwood, how excessively comfortable your mother-in-law and her daughters may live on the interest of seven thousand pounds, besides the thousand pounds belonging to each of the girls, which brings them in fifty pounds a-year a-piece, and, of course, they will pay their mother for their board out of it. Altogether, they will have five hundred a-year amongst them, and what on earth can four women want for more than that? – They will live so cheap! Their housekeeping will be nothing at all. They will have no carriage, no horses, and hardly any servants; they will keep no company, and can have no expences of any kind! Only conceive how comfortable they will be! Five hundred a-year! I am sure I cannot imagine how they will spend half of it; and as to your giving them more, it is quite absurd to think of it. They will be much more able to give *you* something.'

'Upon my word,' said Mr Dashwood, 'I believe you are perfectly right. My father certainly could mean nothing more by his request to me than what you say. I clearly understand it now, and I will strictly fulfil my engagement by such acts of assistance and kindness to them as you have described. When my mother removes into another house my services shall be readily given to accommodate her as far as I can. Some little present of furniture too may be acceptable then.'

'Certainly,' returned Mrs John Dashwood, 'But however, *one* thing must be considered. When your father and mother moved to

Norland, though the furniture of Stanhill was sold, all the china, plate, and linen was saved, and is now left to your mother. Her house will therefore be almost completely fitted up as soon as she takes it.'

'That is a material consideration undoubtedly. A valuable legacy indeed! And yet some of the plate would have been a very pleasant addition to our own stock here.'

'Yes; and the set of breakfast china is twice as handsome as what belongs to this house. A great deal too handsome, in my opinion, for any place *they* can ever afford to live in. But, however, so it is. Your father thought only of *them*. And I must say this: that you owe no particular gratitude to him, nor attention to his wishes, for we very well know that if he could, he would have left almost every thing in the world to *them*.'

'I cannot imagine how they will spend half of it.'

This argument was irresistible. It gave to his intentions whatever of decision was wanting before; and he finally resolved, that it would be absolutely unnecessary, if not highly indecorous, to do more for the widow and children of his father, than such kind of neighbourly acts as his own wife pointed out.

CHAPTER THREE

MRS DASHWOOD REMAINED at Norland several months; not from any disinclination to move when the sight of every well known spot ceased to raise the violent emotion which it produced for a while; for when her spirits began to revive, and her mind became capable of some other exertion than that of heightening its affliction by melancholy remembrances, she was impatient to be gone, and indefatigable in her inquiries for a suitable dwelling in the neighbourhood of Norland; for to remove far from that beloved spot was impossible. But she could hear of no situation that at once answered her notions of comfort and ease, and suited the prudence of her eldest daughter, whose steadier judgment rejected several houses as too large for their income, which her mother would have approved.

Mrs Dashwood had been informed by her husband of the solemn promise on the part of his son in their favour, which gave comfort to his last earthly reflections. She doubted the sincerity of this assurance no more than he had doubted it himself, and she thought of it for her daughters' sake with satisfaction, though as for herself she was persuaded that a much smaller provision than 70001. would support her in affluence. For their brother's sake too, for the sake of her own heart she rejoiced; and she reproached herself for being unjust to his merit before, in believing him incapable of generosity. His attentive behaviour to herself and his sisters convinced her that their welfare was dear to him, and, for a long time, she firmly relied on the liberality of his intentions.

The contempt which she had, very early in their acquaintance, felt for her daughter-in-law, was very much increased by the farther knowledge of her character, which half a year's residence in her family afforded; and perhaps in spite of every consideration of politeness or maternal affection on the side of the former, the two ladies might have found it impossible to have lived together so long, had not a particular circumstance occurred to give still greater eligibility, according to the opinions of Mrs Dashwood, to her daughters' continuance at Norland.

This circumstance was a growing attachment between her eldest girl and the brother of Mrs John Dashwood, a gentlemanlike and pleasing young man, who was introduced to their acquaintance soon after his sister's establishment at Norland, and who had since spent the greatest part of his time there.

Some mothers might have encouraged the intimacy from motives of interest, for Edward Ferrars was the eldest son of man who had died very rich; and some might have repressed it from motives of prudence, for, except a trifling sum, the whole of his fortune depended on the will of his mother. But Mrs Dashwood was alike uninfluenced by either consideration. It was enough for her that he appeared to be amiable, that he loved her daughter, and that Elinor returned the partiality. It was contrary to every doctrine of hers that difference of fortune should keep any couple asunder who were attracted by resemblance of disposition; and that Elinor's merit should not be acknowledged by every one who knew her, was to her comprehension impossible.

Edward Ferrars was not recommended to their good opinion by any peculiar graces of person or address. He was not handsome, and his manners required intimacy to make them pleasing. He was too diffident to do justice to himself; but when his natural shyness was overcome, his behaviour gave every indication of an open affectionate heart. His understanding was good, and his education had given it solid improvement. But he was neither fitted by abilities nor disposition to answer the wishes of his mother and sister, who longed to see him distinguished – as – they hardly knew what. They wanted him to make a fine figure in the world in some manner or other. His mother wished to interest him in political concerns, to get him into parliament, or to see him connected with some of the great men of the day. Mrs John Dashwood wished it likewise; but in the mean while, till one of these superior blessings could be attained, it would have quieted her ambition to see him driving a barouche. But Edward had no turn for great men or barouches. All his wishes centered in domestic comfort and the quiet of private life. Fortunately he had a younger brother who was more promising.

Edward had been staying several weeks in the house before he engaged much of Mrs Dashwood's attention; for she was, at that time, in such affliction, as rendered her careless of surrounding objects. She saw only that he was quiet and unobtrusive, and she liked him for it. He did not disturb the wretchedness of her mind by ill-timed conversation. She was first called to observe and approve him farther, by a reflection which Elinor chanced one day to make on the difference between him and his sister. It was a contrast which recommended him most forcibly to her mother.

'It is enough,' said she; 'to say that he is unlike Fanny is enough. It implies every thing amiable. I love him already.'

'I think you will like him,' said Elinor, 'when you know more of him.'

'Like him!' replied her mother with a smile. 'I can feel no sentiment of approbation inferior to love.'

'You may esteem him.'

'I have never yet known what it was to separate esteem and love.'

Mrs Dashwood now took pains to get acquainted with him. Her manners were attaching and soon banished his reserve. She speedily comprehended all his merits; the persuasion of his regard for Elinor perhaps assisted her penetration; but she really felt assured of his worth: and even that quietness of manner which militated against all her established ideas of what a young man's address ought to be, was no longer uninteresting when she knew his heart to be warm and his temper affectionate.

No sooner did she perceive any sympton of love in his behaviour to Elinor, than she considered their serious attachment as certain, and looked forward to their marriage as rapidly approaching.

'In a few months, my dear Marianne,' said she, 'Elinor will in all probability be settled for life. We shall miss her; but *she* will be happy.'

'Oh! mamma, how shall we do without her?'

'My love, it will be scarcely a separation. We shall live within a few miles of each other, and shall meet every day of our lives. You will gain a brother, a real affectionate brother. I have the highest opinion in the world of Edward's heart. But you look grave, Marianne; do you disapprove your sister's choice?'

'Perhaps,' said Marianne 'I may consider it with some surprise. Edward is very amiable, and I love him tenderly. But yet – he is not the kind of young man – there is a something wanting – his figure is not striking; it has none of that grace which I should expect in the man who could seriously attach my sister. His eyes want all that spirit, that fire, which at once announce virtue and intelligence. And besides all this, I am afraid, mama, he has no real taste. Music seems scarcely to attract him, and though he admires Elinor's drawings very much, it is not the admiration of a person who can understand their worth. It is evident, in spite of his frequent attention to her while she draws, that in fact he knows nothing of the matter. He admires as a lover, not as a connoisseur. To satisfy me, those characters must be united. I could not be happy with a man whose taste did not in every point coincide with my own. He must enter into all feelings; the same books, the same music must charm us both. Oh! mama, how spiritless, how tame was Edward's manner in reading to us last night! I felt for my sister most severely. Yet she bore it with so much composure, she seemed scarcely to notice. I could hardly keep my seat. To hear those beautiful lines which have frequently almost driven me wild, pronounced with such impenetrable calmness, such dreadful indifference!' –

'He would certainly have done more justice to simple and elegant prose. I thought so at the time; but you *would* give him Cowper.'

'Nay, mama, if he is not to be animated by Cowper! – but we must allow for difference of taste. Elinor has not my feelings, and therefore she may overlook it, and be happy with him. But it would have broke *my* heart had I loved him, to hear him read with so little sensibility. Mama, the more I know of the world, the more am I convinced that I shall never see a man whom I can really love. I require so much! He must have all Edward's virtues, and his person and manners must ornament his goodness with every possible charm.'

'Remember, my love, that you are not seventeen. It is yet too early in life to despair of such an happiness. Why should you be less fortunate than your mother? In one circumstance only, Marianne, may your destiny be different from her's!'

CHAPTER FOUR

'WHAT A PITY IT IS, ELINOR,' said Marianne, 'that Edward should have no taste for drawing.'

'No taste for drawing,' replied Elinor; 'why should you think so? He does not draw himself, indeed, but he has great pleasure in seeing the performances of other people, and I assure you he is by no means deficient in natural taste, though he has not had opportunities of improving it. Had he ever been in the way of learning, I think he would have drawn very well. He distrusts his own judgment in such matters so much, that he is always unwilling to give his opinion on any picture; but he has an innate propriety and simplicity of taste, which in general direct him perfectly right.'

Marianne was afraid of offending, and said no more on the subject; but the kind of approbation which Elinor described as excited in him by the drawings of other people, was very far from that rapturous delight, which, in her opinion, could alone be called taste. Yet, though smiling within herself at the mistake, she honoured her sister for that blind partiality to Edward which produced it.

'I hope, Marianne,' continued Elinor, 'you do not consider him as deficient in general taste. Indeed, I think I may say that you cannot, for your behaviour to him is perfectly cordial, and if *that* were your opinion, I am sure you could never be civil to him.'

Marianne hardly knew what to say. She would not wound the feelings of her sister on any account, and yet to say what she did not believe was impossible. At length she replied:

'Do not be offended, Elinor, if my praise of him is not in every thing equal to your sense of his merits. I have not had so many opportunities of estimating the minuter propensities of his mind, his inclinations and tastes as you have; but I have the highest opinion in the world of his goodness and sense. I think him every thing that is worthy and amiable.'

'I am sure,' replied Elinor with a smile, 'that his dearest friends could not be dissatisfied with such a commendation as that. I do not perceive how you could express yourself more warmly.'

Marianne was rejoiced to find her sister so easily pleased.

'Of his sense and his goodness,' continued Elinor, 'no one can, I think, be in doubt, who has seen him often enough to engage him in unreserved conversation. The excellence of his understanding and his principles can be concealed only by that shyness which too often keeps him silent. You know enough of him to do justice to his solid worth. But of his minuter propensities as you call them you have from peculiar circumstances been kept more ignorant than myself. He and I have been at times thrown a good deal together, while you have been wholly engrossed on the most affectionate principle by my mother. I have seen a great deal of him, have studied his sentiments and heard his opinion on subjects of literature and taste; and, upon the whole, I venture to pronounce that his mind is well-informed, his enjoyment of books exceedingly great, his imagination lively, his observation just and correct, and his taste delicate and pure. His abilities in every respect improve as much upon acquaintance as his manners and person. At first sight, his address is certainly not striking; and his person can hardly be called handsome, till the expression of his eyes, which are uncommonly good, and the general sweetness of his countenance, is perceived. At present, I know him so well, that I think him really handsome; or, at least, almost so. What say you, Marianne?'

'I shall very soon think him handsome, Elinor, if I do not now.

When you tell me to love him as a brother, I shall no more see imperfection in his face, than I now do in his heart.'

Elinor started at this declaration, and was sorry for the warmth she had been betrayed into, in speaking of him. She felt that Edward stood very high in her opinion. She believed the regard to be mutual; but she required greater certainty of it to make Marianne's conviction of their attachment agreeable to her. She knew that what Marianne and her mother conjectured one moment, they believed the next – that with them, to wish was to hope, and to hope was to expect. She tried to explain the real state of the case to her sister.

'I do not attempt to deny,' said she, 'that I think very highly of him – that I greatly esteem, that I like him.'

Marianne here burst forth with indignation –

'Esteem him! Like him! Cold-hearted Elinor! Oh! worse than cold-hearted! Ashamed of being otherwise. Use those words again and I will leave the room this moment.'

Elinor could not help laughing. 'Excuse me,' said she, 'and be assured that I meant no offence to you, by speaking, in so quiet a way, of my own feelings. Believe them to be stronger than I have declared; believe them, in short, to be such as his merit, and the suspicion – the hope of his affection for me may warrant, without imprudence or folly. But farther than this you must not believe. I am by no means assured of his regard for me. There are moments when the extent of it seems doubtful; and till his sentiments are fully known, you cannot wonder at my wishing to avoid any encouragement of my own partiality, by believing or calling it more than it is. In my heart I feel little – scarcely any doubt of his preference. But there are other points to be considered besides his inclination. He is very far from being independent. What his mother really is we cannot know; but, from Fanny's occasional mention of her conduct and opinions, we have never been disposed to think her amiable; and I am very much mistaken if Edward is not himself aware that there would be many difficulties in his way, if he were to wish to marry a woman who had not either a great fortune or high rank.'

Marianne was astonished to find how much the imagination of her mother and herself had outstripped the truth.

'And you really are not engaged to him!' said she. 'Yet it certainly soon will happen. But two advantages will proceed from this delay. I shall not lose you so soon, and Edward will have greater opportunity of improving that natural taste for your favourite pursuit which must be so indispensably necessary to your future felicity.

Oh! if he should be so far stimulated by your genius as to learn to draw himself, how delightful it would be!'

Elinor had given her real opinion to her sister. She could not consider her partiality for Edward in so prosperous a state as Marianne had believed it. There was, at times, a want of spirits about him which, if it did not denote indifference, spoke a something almost as unpromising. A doubt of her regard, supposing him to feel it, need not give him more than inquietude. It would not be likely to produce that dejection of mind which frequently attended him. A more reasonable cause might be found in the dependent situation which forbad the indulgence of his affection. She knew that his mother neither behaved to him so as to make his home comfortable at present, nor to give him any assurance that he might form a home for himself, without strictly attending to her views for his aggrandizement. With such a knowledge as this, it was impossible for Elinor to feel easy on the subject. She was far from depending on that result of his preference of her, which her mother and sister still considered as certain. Nay, the longer they were together the more doubtful seemed the nature of his regard; and sometimes, for a few painful minutes, she believed it to be no more than friendship.

But, whatever might really be its limits, it was enough, when perceived by his sister, to make her uneasy; and at the same time, (which was still more common,) to make her uncivil. She took the first opportunity of affronting her mother-in-law on the occasion, talking to her so expressively of her brother's great expectations, of Mrs Ferrars's resolution that both her sons should marry well, and of the danger attending any young woman who attempted to *draw him in*; that Mrs Dashwood could neither pretend to be unconscious, nor endeavour to be calm. She gave her an answer which marked her contempt, and instantly left the room, resolving that, whatever might be the inconvenience or expense of so sudden a removal, her beloved Elinor should not be exposed another week to such insinuations.

In this state of her spirits, a letter was delivered to her from the post, which contained a proposal particularly well timed. It was the offer of a small house, on very easy terms, belonging to a relation of her own, a gentleman of consequence and property in Devonshire. The letter was from this gentleman himself, and written in the true spirit of friendly accomodation. He understood that she was in need of a dwelling, and though the house he offered her was merely a cottage, he assured her that every thing should be done to it which she might think necessary, if the situation pleased her. He earnestly pressed her, after giving the particulars of the house and garden, to come with her daughters to Barton Park, the place of his own residence, from whence she might judge, herself, whether Barton Cottage, for the houses were in the same parish, could, by any alteration, be made comfortable to her. He seemed really anxious to accomodate them and the whole of his letter was written in so friendly a style as could not fail of giving pleasure to his cousin; more especially at a moment when she was suffering under the cold and unfeeling behaviour of her nearer connections. She needed no time for deliberation or inquiry. Her resolution was formed as she read. The situation of Barton, in a county so far distant from Sussex as Devonshire, which, but a few hours before, would have been a sufficient objection to outweigh every possible advantage belonging to the place, was now its first recommendation. To quit the neighbourhood of Norland was no longer an evil; it was an object of desire; it was a blessing, in comparison of the misery of continuing her daughter-in-law's guest: and to remove for ever from that beloved place would be less painful than to inhabit or visit it while such a woman was its mistress. She instantly wrote Sir John Middleton her acknowledgements of his kindness, and her acceptance of his proposal; and then hastened to shew both letters to her daughters, that she might be secure of their approbation before her answer were sent.

Elinor had always thought it would be more prudent for them to settle at some distance from Norland than immediately amongst their present acquaintance. On *that* head, therefore, it was not for her to oppose her mother's intention of removing into Devonshire. The house, too, as described by Sir John, was on so simple a scale, and the rent so uncommonly moderate, as to leave her no right of objection on either point; and, therefore, though it was not a plan which brought any charm to her fancy, though it was a removal from the vicinity of Norland beyond her wishes, she made no attempt to dissuade her mother from sending her letter of acquiescence.

CHAPTER FIVE

No sooner was her answer dispatched, than Mrs Dashwood indulged herself in the pleasure of announcing to her son-in-law and his wife that she was provided with an house, and should incommode them no longer than till every thing were ready for inhabiting it. They heard her with surprise. Mrs John Dashwood said nothing; but her husband civilly hoped that she would not be settled far from Norland. She had great satisfaction in replying that she was going into Devonshire. – Edward turned hastily towards her, on hearing this, and, in a voice of surprise and concern, which required no explanation to her, repeated, 'Devonshire! Are you, indeed, going there? So far from hence! And to what part of it?' She explained the situation. It was within four miles northward of Exeter.

'It is but a cottage,' she continued, 'but I hope to see many of my friends in it. A room or two can easily be added; and if my friends find no difficulty in travelling so far to see me, I am sure I will find none in accomodating them.'

She concluded with a very kind invitation to Mr and Mrs John Dashwood to visit her at Barton; and to Edward she gave one with still greater affection. Though her late conversation with her daughter-in-law had made her resolve on remaining at Norland no longer than was unavoidable, it had not produced the smallest effect on her in that point to which it principally tended. To separate Edward and Elinor was as far from being her object as ever; and she wished to shew Mrs John Dashwood by this pointed invitation to her brother, how totally she disregarded her disapprobation of the match.

Mr John Dashwood told his mother again and again how exceedingly sorry he was that she had taken a house at such a distance from Norland as to prevent his being of any service to her in removing her furniture. He really felt conscientiously vexed on the occasion; for the very exertion to which he had limited the performance of his promise to his father was by this arrangement rendered impracticable. – The furniture was all sent round by water. It chiefly consisted of household linen, plate, china, and books, with an handsome pianoforte of Marianne's. Mrs John Dashwood saw the packages depart with a sigh: she could not help feeling it hard that as

Mrs Dashwood's income would be so trifling in comparison with their own, she should have any handsome article of furniture.

Mrs Dashwood took the house for a twelvemonth; it was ready furnished, and she might have immediate possession. No difficulty arose on either side in the agreement; and she waited only for the disposal of her effects at Norland, and to determine her future household, before she set off for the west; and this, as she was exceedingly rapid in the performance of every thing that interested her, was soon done. – The horses which were left her by her husband, had been sold soon after his death, and an opportunity now offering of disposing of her carriage, she agreed to sell that likewise at the earnest advice of her eldest daughter. For the comfort of her children, had she consulted only her own wishes, she would have kept it; but the discretion of Elinor prevailed. *Her* wisdom too limited the number of their servants to three; two maids and a man, with whom they were speedily provided from amongst those who had formed their establishment at Norland.

The man and one of the maids were sent off immediately into Devonshire, to prepare the house for their mistress's arrival; for as Lady Middleton was entirely unknown to Mrs Dashwood, she preferred going directly to the cottage to being a visitor at Barton Park; and she relied so undoubtingly on Sir John's description of the house, as to feel no curiosity to examine it herself till she entered it as her own. He eagerness to be gone from Norland was preserved from diminution by the evident satisfaction of her daughter-in-law in the prospect of her removal; a satisfaction which was but feebly attempted to be concealed under a cold invitation to her to defer her departure. Now was the time when her son-in-law's promise to his father might with particular propriety be fulfilled. Since he had neglected to do it on first coming to the estate, their quitting his house might be looked on as the most suitable period for its accomplishment. But Mrs Dashwood began shortly to give over every hope of the kind, and to be convinced, from the general drift of his discourse, that his assistance extended no farther than their maintenance for six months at Norland. He so frequently talked of the increasing expenses of housekeeping, and of the perpetual demands upon his purse, which a man of any consequence in the world was beyond calculation exposed to, that he seemed rather to stand in need of more money himself than to have any design of giving money away.

In a very few weeks from the day which brought Sir John Middleton's first letter to Norland, every thing was so far settled in their future abode as to enable Mrs Dashwood and her daughters to begin their journey.

Many were the tears shed by them in their last adieus to a place so much beloved. 'Dear, dear Norland!' said Marianne, as she wandered alone before the house, on the last evening of their being there; 'when shall I cease to regret you! – when learn to feel a home elsewhere! – Oh! happy house, could you know what I suffer in now viewing you from this spot, from where perhaps I may view you no more! – And you, ye well-known trees! – but you will continue the same. – No leaf will decay because we are removed, nor any branch become motionless although we can observe you no longer! – No; you will continue the same; unconscious of the pleasure or the regret you occasion, and insensible of any change in those who walk under your shade! – But who will remain to enjoy you?'

CHAPTER SIX

THE FIRST PART OF THEIR journey was performed in too melancholy a disposition to be otherwise than tedious and unpleasant. But as they drew towards the end of it, their interest in the appearance of a country which they were to inhabit overcame their dejection, and a view of Barton Valley as they entered it gave them cheerfulness. It was a pleasant fertile spot, well wooded, and rich in pasture. After winding along it for more than a mile, they reached their own house. A small green court was the whole of its demesne in front; and a neat wicket gate admitted them into it.

As a house, Barton Cottage, though small, was comfortable and compact; but as a cottage it was defective, for the building was regular, the roof was tiled, the window shutters were not painted green, nor were the walls covered with honeysuckles. A narrow passage led directly through the house into the garden behind. On each side of the entrance was a sitting room, about sixteen feet square; and beyond them were the offices and the stairs. Four bedrooms and two garrets formed the rest of the house. It had not been built many years and was in good repair. In comparison of Norland, it was poor and small indeed! – but the tears which recollection called forth as they entered the house were soon dried away. They were cheered by the joy of the servants on their arrival, and each for the sake of the others resolved to appear happy. It was very early in September; the season was fine, and from first seeing the place under the advantage of good weather, they received an impression in its favour which was of material service in recommending it to their lasting approbation.

The situation of the house was good. High hills rose immediately behind, and at no great distance on each side; some of which were open downs, the others cultivated and woody. The village of Barton was chiefly on one of these hills, and formed a pleasant view from the cottage windows. The prospect in front was more extensive; it commanded the whole of the valley, and reached into the country beyond. The hills which surrounded the cottage terminated the valley in that direction; under another name, and in another course, it branched out again between two of the steepest of them.

With the size and furniture of the house Mrs Dashwood was upon the whole well satisfied; for though her former style of life rendered many additions to the latter indispensable, yet to add and improve was a delight to her; and she had at this time ready money enough to supply all that was wanted of greater elegance to the apartments. 'As for the house itself, to be sure,' she said, 'it is too small for our family, but we will make ourselves tolerably comfortable for the present, as it is too late in the year for improvements. Perhaps in the spring, if I have plenty of money, as I dare say I shall, we may think about building. These parlours are both too small for such parties of our friends as I hope to see often collected here; and I have some thoughts of throwing the passage into one of them with perhaps a part of the other, and so leave the remainder of that other for an entrance; this, with a new drawing room which may be easily added, and a bed-chamber and garret above, will make it a very snug little cottage. I could wish the stairs were handsome. But one must not expect every thing; though I suppose it would be no difficult matter to widen them. I shall see how much I am beforehand with the world in the spring, and we will plan our improvements accordingly.'

In the mean time, till all these alterations could be made from the savings of an income of five hundred a-year by a woman who never saved in her life, they were wise enough to be contented with the house as it was; and each of them was busy in arranging their particular concerns, and endeavouring, by placing around them their books and other possessions, to form themselves a home. Marianne's pianoforte was unpacked and properly disposed of; and Elinor's drawings were affixed to the walls of their sitting room.

In such employments as these they were interrupted soon after breakfast the next day by the entrance of their landlord, who called to welcome them to Barton, and to offer them every accommodation from his own house and garden in which their's might at present be deficient. Sir John Middleton was a good looking man about forty. He had formerly visited at Stanhill, but it was too long ago for his young cousins to remember him. His countenance was thoroughly good-humoured; and his manners were as friendly as the style of his letter. Their arrival seemed to afford him real satisfaction, and their comfort to be an object of real solicitude to him. He said much of his earnest desire of their living in the most sociable terms with his family, and pressed them so cordially to dine at Barton Park every day till they were better settled at home, that, though his entreaties were carried to a point of perseverance beyond civility, they could not give offence. His kindness was not confined to words; for within an hour after he left them, a large basket full of garden stuff and fruit arrived from the park, which was followed before the end of the day by a present of game. He insisted moreover on conveying all their letters to and from the post for them, and would not be denied the satisfaction of sending them his newspaper every day.

Lady Middleton had sent a very civil message by him, denoting her intention of waiting on Mrs Dashwood as soon as she could be assured that her visit would be no inconvenience; and as this message was answered by an invitation equally polite, her ladyship was introduced to them the next day.

They were of course very anxious to see a person on whom so much of their comfort at Barton must depend; and the elegance of her appearance was favourable to their wishes. Lady Middleton was not more than six or seven and twenty; her face was handsome, her figure tall and striking, and her address graceful. Her manners had all the elegance which her husband's wanted. But they would have been improved by some share of his frankness and warmth; and her visit was long enough to detract something from their first admiration, by shewing that though perfectly well-bred, she was reserved, cold, and had nothing to say for herself beyond the most common-place inquiry or remark.

Conversation however was not wanted, for Sir John was very chatty, and Lady Middleton had taken the wise precaution of bringing with her their eldest child, a fine little boy about six years old, by which means there was one subject always to be recurred to by the ladies in case of extremity, for they had to enquire his name and age, admire his beauty, and ask him questions which his mother answered for him, while he hung about her and held down his head, to the great surprise of her ladyship, who wondered at his

So shy before company.

being so shy before company as he could make noise enough at home. On every formal visit a child ought to be of the party, by way of provision for discourse. In the present case it took up ten minutes to determine whether the boy were most like his father or mother, and in what particular he resembled either, for of course every body differed, and every body was astonished at the opinion of the others.

An opportunity was soon to be given to the Dashwoods of debating on the rest of the children, as Sir John would not leave the house without securing their promise of dining at the park the next day.

CHAPTER SEVEN

Barton Park was about half a mile from the cottage. The ladies had passed near it in their way along the valley, but it was screened from their view at home by the projection of an hill. The house was large and handsome; and the Middletons lived in a style of equal hospitality and elegance. The former was for Sir John's gratification, the latter for that of his lady. They were scarcely ever without some friends staying with them in the house, and they kept more company of every kind than any other family in the neighbourhood. It was necessary to the happiness of both; for however dissimilar in temper and outward behaviour, they strongly resembled each other in that total want of talent and taste which confined their employments, unconnected with such as society produced, within a very narrow compass. Sir John was a sportsman, Lady Middleton a mother. He hunted and shot, and she humoured her children; and these were their only resources. Lady Middleton had the advantage of being able to spoil her children all the year round, while Sir John's independent employments were in existence only half the time. Continual engagements at home and abroad, however, supplied all the deficiencies of nature and education; supported the good spirits of Sir John, and gave exercise to the good-breeding of his wife.

Lady Middleton piqued herself upon the elegance of her table, and of all her domestic arrangements; and from this kind of vanity was her greatest enjoyment in any of their parties. But Sir John's satisfaction in society was much more real; he delighted in collecting about him more young people than his house would hold, and the noisier they were the better was he pleased. He was a blessing to all the juvenile part of the neighbourhood, for in summer he was for ever forming parties to eat cold ham and chicken out of doors, and in winter his private balls were numerous enough for any young lady who was not suffering under the insatiable appetite of fifteen.

The arrival of a new family in the country was always a matter of joy to him, and in every point of view he was charmed with the inhabitants he had now procured for his cottage at Barton. The Miss Dashwoods were young, pretty, and unaffected. It was enough to secure his good opinion; for to be unaffected was all that a pretty girl could want to make her mind as captivating as her person. The friendliness of his disposition made him happy in accommodating those, whose situation might be considered, in comparison with the past, as unfortunate. In shewing kindness to his cousins therefore he had the real satisfaction of a good heart; and in settling a family of females only in his cottage, he had all the satisfaction of a sportsman; for a sportsman, though he esteems only those of his sex who are sportsmen likewise, is not often desirous of encouraging their taste by admitting them to a residence within his own manor.

Mrs Dashwood and her daughters were met at the door of the house by Sir John, who welcomed them to Barton Park with unaffected sincerity; and as he attended them to the drawing room repeated to the young ladies the concern which the same subject had drawn from him the day before, at being unable to get any smart young men to meet them. They would see, he said, only one gentleman there besides himself; a particular friend who was staying at the park, but who was neither very young nor very gay. He hoped they would all excuse the smallness of the party, and could assure them it should never happen so again. He had been to several families that morning in hopes of procuring some addition to their number, but it was moonlight and every body was full of engagements. Luckily Lady Middleton's mother had arrived at Barton within the last hour, and as she was a very cheerful agreeable woman, he hoped the young ladies would not find it so very dull as they might imagine. The young ladies, as well as their mother, were perfectly satisfied with having two entire strangers of the party, and wished for no more.

Mrs Jennings, Lady Middleton's mother, was a good-humoured, merry, fat, elderly woman, who talked a great deal, seemed very happy, and rather vulgar. She was full of jokes and laughter, and before dinner was over had said many witty things on the subject of lovers and husbands; hoped they had not left their hearts behind them in Sussex, and pretended to see them blush whether they did or not. Marianne was vexed at it for her sister's sake, and turned her eyes towards Elinor to see how she bore these attacks, with an earnestness which gave Elinor far more pain than could arise from such commonplace raillery as Mrs Jennings's.

Colonel Brandon, the friend of Sir John, seemed no more adapted by resemblance of manner to be his friend, than Lady Middleton was to be his wife, or Mrs Jennings to be Lady Middleton's mother. He was silent and grave. His appearance however was not unpleasing, in spite of his being in the opinion of Marianne and Margaret an absolute old bachelor, for he was on the wrong side of five and thirty; but though his face was not handsome his countenance was sensible, and his address was particularly gentlemanlike.

There was nothing in any of the party which could recommend them as companions to the Dashwoods; but the cold insipidity of Lady Middleton was so particularly repulsive, that in comparison of it the gravity of Colonel Brandon, and even the boisterous mirth of Sir John and his mother-in-law was interesting. Lady Middleton seemed to be roused to enjoyment only by the entrance of her four noisy children after dinner, who pulled her about, tore her clothes, and put an end to every kind of discourse except what related to themselves.

In the evening, as Marianne was discovered to be musical, she was invited to play. The instrument was unlocked, every body prepared to be charmed, and Marianne, who sang very well, at their request went through the chief of the songs which Lady Middleton had brought into the family on her marriage, and which perhaps had lain ever since in the same position on the piano-forté, for her ladyship had celebrated that event by giving up music, although by her mother's account she had played extremely well, and by her own was very fond of it.

Marianne's performance was highly applauded. Sir John was loud in his admiration at the end of every song, and as loud in his conversation with the others while every song lasted. Lady Middleton frequently called him to order, wondered how any one's attention could be diverted from music for a moment, and asked Marianne to sing a particular song which Marianne had just finished. Colonel Brandon alone, of all the party, heard her without being in raptures. He paid her only the compliment of attention; and she felt a respect for him on the occasion, which the others had reasonably forfeited by their shameless want of taste. His pleasure in music, though it amounted not to that extatic delight which alone could sympathize with her own, was estimable when contrasted against the horrible insensibility of the others; and she was reasonable enough to allow that a man of five and thirty might well have outlived all acuteness of feeling and every exquisite power of enjoyment. She was perfectly disposed to make every allowance for the colonel's advanced state of life which humanity required.

CHAPTER EIGHT

Mrs Jennings was a widow, with an ample jointure. She had only two daughters, both of whom she had lived to see respectably married, and she had now therefore nothing to do but to marry all the rest of the world. In the promotion of this object she was zealously active, as far as her ability reached; and missed no opportunity of projecting weddings amongst all the young people of her acquaintance. She was remarkably quick in the discovery of attachments, and had enjoyed the advantage of raising the blushes and the vanity of many a young lady by insinuations of her power over such a young man; and this kind of discernment enabled her soon after her arrival at Barton decisively to pronounce that Colonel Brandon was very much in love with Marianne Dashwood. She rather suspected it to be so, on the very first evening of their being together, from his listening so attentively while she sang to them; and when the visit was returned by the Middletons' dining at the cottage, the fact was ascertained by his listening to her again. It must be so. She was perfectly convinced of it. It would be an excellent match, for *he* was rich and *she* was handsome. Mrs Jennings had been anxious to see Colonel Brandon well married, ever since her connection with Sir John first brought him to her knowledge; and she was always anxious to get a good husband for every pretty girl.

The immediate advantage to herself was by no means inconsiderable, for it supplied her with endless jokes against them both. At the park she laughed at the colonel, and in the cottage at Marianne. To the former her raillery was probably, as far as it regarded only himself, perfectly indifferent; but to the latter it was at first incomprehensible; and when its object was understood, she hardly knew whether most to laugh at its absurdity, or censure its impertinence, for she considered it as an unfeeling reflection on the colonel's advanced years, and on his forlorn condition as an old bachelor.

Mrs Dashwood, who could not think a man five years younger than herself, so exceedingly ancient as he appeared to the youthful fancy of her daughter, ventured to clear Mrs Jennings from the probability of wishing to throw ridicule on his age.

'But at least, mama, you cannot deny the absurdity of the accusation, though you may not think it intentionally illnatured. Colonel

Brandon is certainly younger than Mrs Jennings, but he is old enough to be *my* father; and if he were ever animated enough to be in love, must have long outlived every sensation of the kind. It is too ridiculous! When is a man to be safe from such wit, if age and infirmity will not protect him?'

'Infirmity!' said Elinor, 'do you call Colonel Brandon infirm? I can easily suppose that his age may appear much greater to you than to my mother; but you can hardly deceive yourself as to his having the use of his limbs!'

'Did not you hear him complain of the rheumatism? and is not that the commonest infirmity of declining life?'

'My dearest child,' said her mother laughing, 'at this rate you must be in continual terror of *my* decay; and it must seem to you a miracle that my life has been extended to the advanced age of forty.'

'Mama, you are not doing me justice. I know very well that Colonel Brandon is not old enough to make his friends yet apprehensive of losing him in the course of nature. He may live twenty years longer. But thirty-five has nothing to do with matrimony.'

'Perhaps,' said Elinor, 'thirty-five and seventeen had better not have any thing to do with matrimony together. But if there should by any chance happen to be a woman who is single at seven and twenty, I should not think Colonel Brandon's being thirty-five any objection to his marrying *her*.'

'A woman of seven and twenty,' said Marianne, after pausing a moment, 'can never hope to feel or inspire affection again, and if her home be uncomfortable, or her fortune small, I can suppose that she might bring herself to submit to the offices of a nurse, for the sake of the provision and security of a wife. In his marrying such a woman therefore there would be nothing unsuitable. It would be a compact of convenience, and the world would be satisfied. In my eyes it would be no marriage at all, but that would be nothing. To me it would seem only a commercial exchange, in which each wished to be benefited at the expence of the other.'

'It would be impossible, I know,' replied Elinor, 'to convince you that a woman of seven and twenty could feel for a man of thirty-five any thing near enough to love, to make him a desirable companion for her. But I must object to your dooming Colonel Brandon and his wife to the constant confinement of a sick chamber, merely because he chanced to complain yesterday (a very cold damp day) of a slight rheumatic feel in one of his shoulders.'

'But he talked of flannel waistcoats,' said Marianne, 'and with me a flannel waistcoat is invariably connected with aches, rheumatisms, and every species of ailment that can afflict the old and the feeble.'

'Had he been only in a violent fever, you would not have despised him half so much. Confess, Marianne, is not there something interesting to you in the flushed cheek, hollow eye, and quick pulse of a fever?'

Soon after this, upon Elinor's leaving the room, 'Mama,' said Marianne, 'I have an alarm on the subject of illness, which I cannot conceal from you. I am sure Edward Ferrars is not well. We have now been here almost a fortnight, and yet he does not come. Nothing but real indisposition could occasion this extraordinary delay. What else can detain him at Norland?'

'Had you any idea of his coming so soon?' said Mrs Dashwood. '*I* had none. On the contrary, if I have felt any anxiety at all on the subject, it has been in recollecting that he sometimes shewed a want of pleasure and readiness in accepting my invitation, when I talked of his coming to Barton. Does Elinor expect him already?'

'I have never mentioned it to her, but of course she must.'

'I rather think you are mistaken, for when I was talking to her yesterday of getting a new grate for the spare bedchamber, she observed that there was no immediate hurry for it, as it was not likely that the room would be wanted for some time.'

'How strange this is! what can be the meaning of it! But the whole of their behaviour to each other has been unaccountable! How cold, how composed were their last adieus! How languid their conversation the last evening of their being together! In Edward's farewell there was no distinction between Elinor and me: it was the good wishes of an affectionate brother to both. Twice did I leave them purposely together in the course of the last morning, and each time did he most unaccountably follow me out of the room. And Elinor, in quitting Norland and Edward, cried not as I did. Even now her self-command is invariable. When is she dejected or melancholy? When does she try to avoid society, or appear restless and dissatisfied in it?'

CHAPTER NINE

THE DASHWOODS WERE now settled at Barton with tolerable comfort to themselves. The house and the garden, with all the objects surrounding them, were now become familiar, and the ordinary pursuits which had given to Norland half its charms, were engaged in again with far greater enjoyment than Norland had been able to afford, since the loss of their father. Sir John Middleton, who called on them every day for the first fortnight, and who was not in the habit of seeing much occupation at home, could not conceal his amazement on finding them always employed.

Their visitors, except those from Barton Park, were not many; for, in spite of Sir John's urgent entreaties that they would mix more in the neighbourhood, and repeated assurances of his carriage being always at their service, the independence of Mrs Dashwood's spirit overcame the wish of society for her children; and she was resolute in declining to visit any family beyond the distance of a walk. There were but few who could be so classed; and it was not all of them that were attainable. About a mile and a half from the cottage, along the narrow winding valley of Allenham, which issued from that of Barton, as formerly described, the girls had, in one of their earliest walks, discovered an ancient respectable looking mansion which, by reminding them a little of Norland, interested their imagination and made them wish to be better acquainted with it. But they learnt, on inquiry, that its possessor, an elderly lady of very good character, was unfortunately too infirm to mix with the world, and never stirred from home.

The whole country about them abounded in beautiful walks. The high downs which invited them from almost every window of the cottage to seek the exquisite enjoyment of air on their summits, were an happy alternative when the dirt of the valleys beneath shut up their superior beauties; and towards one of these hills did Marianne and Margaret one memorable morning direct their steps, attracted by the partial sunshine of a showery sky, and unable longer to bear the confinement which the settled rain of the two preceding days had occasioned. The weather was not tempting enough to draw the two others from their pencil and their book, in spite of Marianne's declaration that the day would be lastingly fair, and that every threatening cloud would be drawn off from their hills; and the two girls set off together.

They gaily ascended the downs, rejoicing in their own penetration at every glimpse of blue sky; and when they caught in their faces the animating gales of an high south-westerly wind, they pitied the fears which had prevented their mother and Elinor from sharing such delightful sensations.

'Is there a felicity in the world,' said Marianne, 'superior to this? – Margaret, we will walk here at least two hours.'

Margaret agreed, and they pursued their way against the wind, resisting it with laughing delight for about twenty minutes longer, when suddenly the clouds united over their heads, and a driving rain set full in their face. – Chagrined and surprised, they were obliged, though unwillingly, to turn back, for no shelter was nearer than their own house. One consolation however remained for them, to which the exigence of the moment gave more than usual propriety; it was that of running with all possible speed down the steep side of the hill which led immediately to their garden gate.

They set off. Marianne had at first the advantage, but a false step brought her suddenly to the ground, and Margaret, unable to stop herself to assist her, was involuntarily hurried along, and reached the bottom in safety.

A gentleman carrying a gun, with two pointers playing round him, was passing up the hill and within a few yards of Marianne, when her accident happened. He put down his gun and ran to her assistance. She had raised herself from the ground, but her foot had been twisted in the fall, and she was scarcely able to stand. The gentleman offered his services, and perceiving that her modesty declined what her situation rendered necessary, took her up in his arms without farther delay, and carried her down the hill. Then passing through the garden, the gate of which had been left open by Margaret, he bore her directly into the house, whither Margaret was just arrived, and quitted not his hold till he had seated her in a chair in the parlour.

Elinor and her mother rose up in amazement at their entrance, and while the eyes of both were fixed on him with an evident wonder and a secret admiration which equally sprung from his appearance, he apologized for his intrusion by relating its cause, in a manner so frank and so graceful, that his person, which was uncommonly handsome, received additional charms from his voice and expression. Had he been even old, ugly, and vulgar, the gratitude and kindness of Mrs Dashwood would have been secured by any act of attention to her child; but the influence of youth, beauty, and elegance, gave an interest to the action which came home to her feelings.

She thanked him again and again; and with a sweetness of address which always attended her, invited him to be seated. But this he declined, as he was dirty and wet. Mrs Dashwood then begged to know to whom she was obliged. His name, he replied, was Willoughby, and his present home was at Allenham, from whence he hoped she would allow him the honour of calling tomorrow to inquire after Miss Dashwood. The honour was readily granted, and he then departed, to make himself still more interesting, in the midst of an heavy rain.

His manly beauty and more than common gracefulness were

instantly the theme of general admiration, and the laugh which his gallantry raised against Marianne, received particular spirit from his exterior attractions – Marianne herself had seen less of his person than the rest, for the confusion which crimsoned over her face, on his lifting her up, had robbed her of the power of regarding him after their entering the house. But she had seen enough of him to join in all the admiration of the others, and with an energy which always adorned her praise. His person and air were equal to what her fancy had ever drawn for the hero of a favourite story; and in his carrying her into the house with so little previous formality, there was a rapidity of thought which particularly recommended the action to her. Every circumstance belonging to him was interesting. His name was good, his residence was in their favourite village, and she soon found out that of all manly dresses a shooting-jacket was the most becoming. Her imagination was busy, her reflections were pleasant, and the pain of a sprained ancle was disregarded.

Sir John called on them as soon as the next interval of fair weather that morning allowed him to get out of doors; and Marianne's accident being related to him, he was eagerly asked whether he knew any gentleman of the name of Willoughby at Allenham.

'Willoughby!' cried Sir John; 'what, is *he* in the country? That is good news however; I will ride over tomorrow, and ask him to dinner on Thursday.'

'You know him then,' said Mrs Dashwood.

'Know him! to be sure I do. Why, he is down here every year.'

'And what sort of a young man is he?'

'As good a kind of fellow as ever lived, I assure you. A very decent shot, and there is not a bolder rider in England.'

'And is *that* all you can say for him?' cried Marianne, indignantly. 'But what are his manners on more intimate acquaintance? What his pursuits, his talents and genius?'

Sir John was rather puzzled.

'Upon my soul,' said he, 'I do not know much about him as to all *that*. But he is a pleasant, good humoured fellow, and has got the nicest little black bitch of a pointer I ever saw. Was she out with him today?'

But Marianne could no more satisfy him as to the colour of Mr Willoughby's pointer, than he could describe to her the shades of his mind.

'But who is he?' said Elinor. 'Where does he come from? Has he a house at Allenham?'

On this point Sir John could give more certain intelligence; and he told them that Mr Willoughby had no property of his own in the country; that he resided there only while he was visiting the old lady at Allenham Court, to whom he was related, and whose possessions he was to inherit; adding, 'Yes, yes, he is very well worth catching, I can tell you, Miss Dashwood; he has a pretty little estate of his own in Somersetshire besides; and if I were you, I would not give him up to my younger sister in spite of all this tumbling down hills. Miss Marianne must not expect to have all the men to herself. Brandon will be jealous, if she does not take care.'

'I do not believe,' said Mrs Dashwood, with a good humoured smile, 'that Mr Willoughby will be incommoded by the attempts of either of *my* daughters towards what you call *catching* him. It is not an employment to which they have been brought up. Men are very safe with us, let them be ever so rich. I am glad to find, however, from what you say, that he is a respectable young man, and one whose acquaintance will not be ineligible.'

'He is as good a sort of fellow, I believe, as ever lived,' repeated Sir John. 'I remember last Christmas at a little hop at the park, he danced from eight o'clock till four, without once sitting down.'

'Did he indeed?' cried Marianne with sparkling eyes, 'and with elegance, with spirit?'

'Yes; and he was up again at eight to ride to covert.'

'That is what I like; that is what a young man ought to be. Whatever be his pursuits, his eagerness in them should know no moderation, and leave him no sense of fatigue.'

'Aye, aye, I see how it will be,' said Sir John, 'I see how it will be. You will be setting your cap at him now, and never think of poor Brandon.'

'That is an expression, Sir John,' said Marianne, warmly, 'which I particularly dislike. I abhor every common-place phrase by which wit is intended; and "setting one's cap at a man," or "making a conquest," are the most odious of all. Their tendency is gross and illiberal; and if their construction could ever be deemed clever, time has long ago destroyed all its ingenuity.'

Sir John did not much understand this reproof; but he laughed as heartily as if he did, and then replied,

'Aye, you will make conquests enough, I dare say, one way or other. Poor Brandon! he is quite smitten already, and he is very well worth setting your cap at, I can tell you, in spite of all this tumbling about and spraining of ancles.'

CHAPTER TEN

Marianne's preserver, as Margaret, with more elegance than precision, stiled Willoughby, called at the cottage early the next morning to make his personal inquiries. He was received by Mrs Dashwood with more than politeness; with a kindness which Sir John's account of him and her own gratitude prompted; and every thing that passed during the visit, tended to assure him of the sense, elegance, mutual affection, and domestic comfort of the family to whom accident had now introduced him. Of their personal charms he had not required a second interview to be convinced.

Miss Dashwood had a delicate complexion, regular features and a remarkably pretty figure. Marianne was still handsomer. Her form, though not so correct as her sister's, in having the advantage of height, was more striking; and her face was so lovely, that when in the common cant of praise she was called a beautiful girl, truth was less violently outraged than usually happens. Her skin was very brown, but from its transparency, her complexion was uncommonly brilliant; her features were all good; her smile was sweet and attractive, and in her eyes, which were very dark, there was a life, a spirit, an eagerness which could hardly be seen without delight. From Willoughby their expression was at first held back, by the embarrassment which the remembrance of his assistance created. But when this passed away, when her spirits became collected, when she saw that to the perfect good-breeding of the gentleman, he united frankness and vivacity, and above all, when she heard him declare that of music and dancing he was passionately fond, she gave him such a look of approbation as secured the largest share of his discourse to herself for the rest of his stay.

It was only necessary to mention any favourite amusement to engage her to talk. She could not be silent when such points were introduced, and she had neither shyness nor reserve in their discussion. They speedily discovered that their enjoyment of dancing and music was mutual, and that it arose from a general conformity of judgment in all that related to either. Encouraged by this to a further examination of his opinions, she proceeded to question him on the subject of books; her favourite authors were brought forward and dwelt upon with so rapturous a delight, that any young man of five and twenty must have been insensible indeed, not to become an immediate convert to the excellence of such works, however disregarded before. Their taste was strikingly alike. The same books, the same passages were idolized by each – or if any difference appeared, any objection arose, it lasted no longer than till the force of her arguments and the brightness of her eyes could be displayed. He acquiesced in all her decisions, caught all her enthusiasm; and long before his visit concluded, they conversed with the familiarity of a long-established acquaintance.

'Well, Marianne,' said Elinor, as soon as he had left them, 'for *one* morning I think you have done pretty well. You have already ascertained Mr Willoughby's opinion in almost every matter of importance. You know what he thinks of Cowper and Scott; you are certain of his estimating their beauties as he ought, and you have received every assurance of his admiring Pope no more than is proper. But how is your acquaintance to be long supported, under such extraordinary dispatch of every subject for discourse? You will soon have exhausted each favourite topic. Another meeting will suffice to explain his sentiments on picturesque beauty, and second marriages, and then you can have nothing farther to ask.' –

'Elinor,' cried Marianne, 'is this fair? is this just? are my ideas so scanty? But I see what you mean. I have been too much at my ease, too happy, too frank. I have erred against every common-place notion of decorum; I have been open and sincere where I ought to have been reserved, spiritless, dull, and deceitful: – had I talked only of the weather and the roads, and had I spoken only once in ten minutes, this reproach would have been spared.'

'My love,' said her mother, 'you must not be offended with Elinor – she was only in jest. I should scold her myself, if she were capable of wishing to check the delight of your conversation with our new friend.' – Marianne was softened in a moment.

Willoughby, on his side, gave every proof of his pleasure in their acquaintance, which an evident wish of improving it could offer. He came to them every day. To inquire after Marianne was at first his excuse; but the encouragement of his reception, to which every day gave greater kindness, made such an excuse unnecessary before it had ceased to be possible, by Marianne's perfect recovery. She was confined for some days to the house; but never had any confinement been less irksome. Willoughby was a young man of good abilities, quick imagination, lively spirits, and open, affectionate manners. He was exactly formed to engage Marianne's heart, for with all this, he joined not only a captivating person, but a natural ardour of mind which was now roused and increased by the example of her own, and which recommended him to her affection beyond every thing else.

His society became gradually her most exquisite enjoyment. They read, they talked, they sang together; his musical talents were considerable; and he read with all the sensibility and spirit which Edward had unfortunately wanted.

In Mrs Dashwood's estimation, he was as faultless as in Marianne's; and Elinor saw nothing to censure in him but a propensity, in which he strongly resembled and peculiarly delighted her sister, of saying too much what he thought on every occasion, without attention to persons or circumstances. In hastily forming and giving

They sang together.

his opinion of other people, in sacrificing general politeness to the enjoyment of undivided attention where his heart was engaged, and in slighting too easily the forms of worldly propriety, he displayed a want of caution which Elinor could not approve, in spite of all that he and Marianne could say in its support.

Marianne began now to perceive that the desperation which had seized her at sixteen and a half, of ever seeing a man who could satisfy her ideas of perfection, had been rash and unjustifiable. Willoughby was all that her fancy had delineated in that unhappy hour and in every brighter period, as capable of attaching her; and his behaviour declared his wishes to be in that respect as earnest, as his abilities were strong.

Her mother too, in whose mind not one speculative thought of their marriage had been raised, by his prospect of riches, was led before the end of a week to hope and expect it; and secretly to congratulate herself on having gained two such sons-in-law as Edward and Willoughby.

Colonel Brandon's partiality for Marianne, which had so early been discovered by his friends, now first became perceptible to Elinor, when it ceased to be noticed by them. Their attention and wit were drawn off to his more fortunate rival; and the raillery which the other had incurred before any partiality arose, was removed when his feelings began really to call for the ridicule so justly annexed to sensibility. Elinor was obliged, though unwillingly, to believe that the sentiments which Mrs Jennings had assigned him for her own satisfaction, were now actually excited by her sister; and that however a general resemblance of disposition between the parties might forward the affection of Mr Willoughby, an equally striking opposition of character was no hindrance to the regard of Colonel Brandon. She saw it with concern; for what could a silent man of five and thirty hope, when opposed by a very lively one of five and twenty? and as she could not even wish him successful, she heartily wished him indifferent. She liked him – in spite of his gravity and reserve, she beheld in him an object of interest. His manners, though serious, were mild; and his reserve appeared rather the result of some oppression of spirits, than of any natural gloominess of temper. Sir John had dropt hints of past injuries and disappointments, which justified her belief of his being an unfortunate man, and she regarded him with respect and compassion.

Perhaps she pitied and esteemed him the more because he was slighted by Willoughby and Marianne, who, prejudiced against him for being neither lively nor young, seemed resolved to undervalue his merits.

'Brandon is just the kind of man,' said Willoughby one day, when they were talking of him together, 'whom every body speaks well of, and nobody cares about; whom all are delighted to see, and nobody remembers to talk to.'

'That is exactly what I think of him,' cried Marianne.

'Do not boast of it, however,' said Elinor, 'for it is injustice in both of you. He is highly esteemed by all the family at the park, and I never see him myself without taking pains to converse with him.'

'That he is patronized by *you*,' replied Willoughby, 'is certainly in his favour; but as for the esteem of the others, it is a reproach in itself. Who would submit to the indignity of being approved by such women as Lady Middleton and Mrs Jennings, that could command the indifference of any body else?'

'But perhaps the abuse of such people as yourself and Marianne, will make amends for the regard of Lady Middleton and her mother. If their praise is censure, your censure may be praise, for they are not more undiscerning, than you are prejudiced and unjust.'

'In defence of your protégé you can even be saucy.'

'My protégé, as you call him, is a sensible man; and sense will always have attractions for me. Yes, Marianne, even in a man between thirty and forty. He has seen a great deal of the world; has been abroad; has read, and has a thinking mind. I have found him capable of giving me much information on various subjects, and he has always answered my inquiries with the readiness of good-breeding and good nature.'

'That is to say,' cried Marianne contemptuously, 'he has told you that in the East Indies the climate is hot, and the mosquitoes are troublesome.'

'He *would* have told me so, I doubt not, had I made any such inquiries, but they happened to be points on which I had been previously informed.'

'Perhaps,' said Willoughby, 'his observations may have extended to the existence of nabobs, gold mohrs, and palanquins.'

'I may venture to say that *his* observations have stretched much farther than your candour. But why should you dislike him?'

'I do not dislike him. I consider him, on the contrary, as a very respectable man, who has every body's good word and nobody's notice; who has more money than he can spend, more time than he knows how to employ, and two new coats every year.'

'Add to which,' cried Marianne, 'that he has neither genius, taste, nor spirit. That his understanding has no brilliancy, his feelings no ardour, and his voice no expression.'

'You decide on his imperfections so much in the mass,' replied Elinor, 'and so much on the strength of your own imagination, that the commendation I am able to give of him is comparatively cold and insipid. I can only pronounce him to be a sensible man, well-bred, well-informed, of gentle address, and I believe possessing an amiable heart.'

'Miss Dashwood,' cried Willoughby, 'you are now using me unkindly. You are endeavouring to disarm me by reason, and to convince me against my will. But it will not do. You shall find me as stubborn as you can be artful. I have three unanswerable reasons for disliking Colonel Brandon: he has threatened me with rain when I wanted it to be fine; he has found fault with the hanging of my curricle, and I cannot persuade him to buy my brown mare. If it will be any satisfaction to you, however, to be told, that I believe his character to be in other respects irreproachable, I am ready to confess it. And in return for an acknowledgment, which must give me some pain, you cannot deny me the privilege of disliking him as much as ever.'

CHAPTER ELEVEN

LITTLE HAD MRS DASHWOOD or her daughters imagined when they first came into Devonshire, that so many engagements would arise to occupy their time as shortly presented themselves, or that they should have such frequent invitations and such constant visitors as to leave them little leisure for serious employment. Yet such was the case. When Marianne was recovered, the schemes of amusement at home and abroad, which Sir John has been previously forming, were put in execution. The private balls at the park then began; and parties on the water were made and accomplished as often as a showery October would allow. In every meeting of the kind Willoughby was included; and the ease and familiarity which naturally attended these parties were exactly calculated to give increasing intimacy to his acquaintance with the Dashwoods, to afford him opportunity of witnessing the excellencies of Marianne, of marking his animated admiration of her, and of receiving, in her behaviour to himself, the most pointed assurance of her affection.

Elinor could not be surprised at their attachment. She only wished that it were less openly shewn; and once or twice did venture to suggest the propriety of some self-command to Marianne. But

Marianne abhorred all concealment where no real disgrace could attend unreserve; and to aim at the restraint of sentiments which were not in themselves illaudable, appeared to her not merely an unnecessary effort, but a disgraceful subjection of reason to common-place and mistaken notions. Willoughby thought the same; and their behaviour, at all times, was an illustration of their opinions.

When he was present she had no eyes for any one else. Every thing he did, was right. Every thing he said, was clever. If their evenings at the park were concluded with cards, he cheated himself and all the rest of the party to get her a good hand. If dancing formed the amusement of the night, they were partners for half the time; and when obliged to separate for a couple of dances, were careful to stand together and scarcely spoke a word to any body else. Such conduct made them of course most exceedingly laughed at; but ridicule could not shame, and seemed hardly to provoke them.

Mrs Dashwood entered into all their feelings with a warmth which left her no inclination for checking this excessive display of them. To her it was but the natural consequence of a strong affection in a young and ardent mind.

This was the season of happiness to Marianne. Her heart was devoted to Willoughby, and the fond attachment to Norland, which she brought with her from Sussex, was more likely to be softened than she had thought it possible before, by the charms which his society bestowed on her present home.

Elinor's happiness was not so great. Her heart was not so much at ease, nor her satisfaction in their amusements so pure. They afforded her no companion that could make amends for what she had left behind, nor that could teach her to think of Norland with less regret than ever. Neither Lady Middleton nor Mrs Jennings could supply to her the conversation she missed; although the latter was an everlasting talker, and from the first had regarded her with a kindness which ensured her a large share of her discourse. She had already repeated her own history to Elinor three or four times; and had Elinor's memory been equal to her means of improvement, she might have known very early in their acquaintance all the particulars of Mr Jenning's last illness, and what he said to his wife a few minutes before he died. Lady Middleton was more agreeable than her mother, only in being more silent. Elinor needed little observation to perceive that her reserve was a mere calmness of manner with which sense had nothing to do. Towards her husband and mother she was the same as to them; and intimacy was therefore neither to be looked for nor desired. She had nothing to say one day that she had not said the day before. Her insipidity was invariable, for even her spirits were always the same; and though she did not oppose the parties arranged by her husband, provided every thing were conducted in style and her two eldest children attended her, she never appeared to receive more enjoyment from them, than she might have experienced in sitting at home; – and so little did her presence add to the pleasure of the others, by any share in their conversation, that they were sometimes only reminded of her being amongst them by her solicitude about her troublesome boys.

In Colonel Brandon alone, of all her new acquaintance, did Elinor find a person who could in any degree claim the respect of abilities, excite the interest of friendship, or give pleasure as a companion. Willoughby was out of the question. Her admiration and regard, even her sisterly regard, was all his own; but he was a lover; his attentions were wholly Marianne's, and a far less agreeable man might have been more generally pleasing. Colonel Brandon, unfortunately for himself, had no such encouragement to think only of Marianne, and in conversing with Elinor he found the greatest consolation for the total indifference of her sister.

Elinor's compassion for him increased, as she had reason to suspect that the misery of disappointed love had already been known by him. This suspicion was given by some words which accidentally dropt from him one evening at the park, when they were sitting down together by mutual consent, while the others were dancing. His eyes were fixed on Marianne, and, after a silence of some minutes, he said with a faint smile. 'Your sister, I understand, does not approve of second attachments.'

'No,' replied Elinor, 'her opinions are all romantic.'

'Or rather, as I believe, she considers them impossible to exist.'

'I believe she does. But how she contrives it without reflecting on the character of her own father, who had himself two wives, I know not. A few years however will settle her opinions on the reasonable basis of common sense and observation; and then they may be more easy to define and to justify than they now are, by any body but herself.'

'This will probably be the case,' he replied; 'and yet there is something so amiable in the prejudices of a young mind, that one is sorry to see them give way to the reception of more general opinions.'

'I cannot agree with you there,' said Elinor. 'There are inconveniences attending such feelings as Marianne's, which all the charms of enthusiasm and ignorance of the world cannot atone for. Her systems have all the unfortunate tendency of setting propriety at nought; and a better acquaintance with the world is what I look forward to as her greatest possible advantage.'

After a short pause he resumed the conversation by saying –

'Does your sister make no distinction in her objections against a second attachment? or is it equally criminal in every body? Are those who have been disappointed in their first choice, whether from the inconstancy of its object, or the perverseness of circumstances, to be equally indifferent during the rest of their lives?'

'Upon my word, I am not acquainted with the minutia of her principles. I only know that I never yet heard her admit any instance of a second attachment's being pardonable.'

'This,' said he, 'cannot hold; but a change, a total change of sentiments – No, no, do not desire it, – for when the romantic refinements of a young mind are obliged to give way, how frequently are they succeeded by such opinions as are but too common, and too dangerous! I speak from experience. I once knew a lady who in temper and mind greatly resembled your sister, who thought and judged like her, but who from an inforced change – from a series of unfortunate circumstances' – Here he stopt suddenly; appeared to think that he had said too much, and by his countenance gave rise to conjectures, which might not otherwise have entered Elinor's head. The lady would probably have passed without suspicion, had he not convinced Miss Dashwood that what concerned her ought not to escape his lips. As it was, it required but a slight effort of fancy to connect his emotion with the tender recollection of past regard. Elinor attempted no more. But Marianne, in her place, would not have done so little. The whole story would have been speedily formed under her active imagination; and every thing established in the most melancholy order of disastrous love.

CHAPTER TWELVE

As Elinor and Marianne were walking together the next morning the latter communicated a piece of news to her sister, which in spite of all that she knew before of Marianne's imprudence and want of thought, surprised her by its extravagant testimony of both. Marianne told her, with the greatest delight, that Willoughby had given her a horse, one that he had bred himself on his estate in Somersetshire, and which was exactly calculated to carry a woman. Without considering that it was not in her mother's plan to keep any horse, that if she were to alter her resolution in favour of this gift, she must buy another for the servant, and keep a servant to ride it, and after all, build a stable to receive them, she had accepted the present without hesitation, and told her sister of it in raptures.

'He intends to send his groom into Somersetshire immediately for it,' she added, 'and when it arrives, we will ride every day. You shall share its use with me. Imagine to yourself, my dear Elinor, the delight of a gallop on some of these downs.'

Most unwilling was she to awaken from such a dream of felicity, to comprehend all the unhappy truths which attended the affair; and for some time she refused to submit to them. As to an additional servant, the expence would be a trifle; mama she was sure would never object to it; and any horse would do for *him*; he might always get one at the park; as to a stable, the merest shed would be sufficient. Elinor then ventured to doubt the propriety of her receiving such a present from a man so little, or at least so lately known to her. This was too much.

'You are mistaken, Elinor,' said she warmly, 'in supposing I know very little of Willoughby. I have not known him long indeed, but I am much better acquainted with him, than with any other creature in the world, except yourself and mama. It is not time or opportunity that is to determine intimacy; – it is disposition alone. Seven years would be insufficient to make some people acquainted with each other, and seven days are more than enough for others. I should hold myself guilty of greater impropriety in accepting a horse from my brother, than from Willoughby. Of John I know very little, though we have lived together for years; but of Willoughby my judgment has long been formed.'

Elinor thought it wisest to touch that point no more. She knew her sister's temper. Opposition on so tender a subject would only attach her the more to her own opinion. But by an appeal to her affection for her mother, by representing the inconveniences which that indulgent mother must draw on herself, if (as would probably be the case) she consented to this increase of establishment, Marianne was shortly subdued; and she promised not to tempt her mother to such imprudent kindness by mentioning the offer, and to tell Willoughby when she saw him next, that it must be declined.

She was faithful to her word; and when Willoughby called at the cottage, the same day, Elinor heard her express her disappointment to him in a low voice, on being obliged to forego the acceptance of his present. The reasons for this alteration were at the same time related, and they were such as to make further entreaty on his side impossible. His concern however was very apparent; and after expressing it with earnestness, he added in the same low voice – 'But, Marianne, the horse is still yours, though you cannot use it now. I shall keep it only till you can claim it. When you leave Barton to form your own establishment in a more lasting home, Queen Mab shall receive you.'

This was all overheard by Miss Dashwood; and in the whole of the sentence, in his manner of pronouncing it, and in his addressing her sister by her christian name alone, she instantly saw an intimacy so decided, a meaning so direct, as marked a perfect agreement between them. From that moment she doubted not of their being engaged to each other; and the belief of it created no other surprise, than that she, or any of their friends, should be left by tempers so frank, to discover it by accident.

Margaret related something to her the next day, which placed this matter in a still clearer light. Willoughby had spent the preceding evening with them, and Margaret, by being left some time in the parlour with only him and Marianne, had had opportunity for observations, which, with a most important face, she communicated to her eldest sister, when they were next by themselves.

'Oh! Elinor,' she cried, 'I have such a secret to tell you about Marianne. I am sure she will be married to Mr Willoughby very soon.'

'You have said so,' replied Elinor, 'almost every day since they first met on Highchurch Down; and they had not known each other a week, I believe, before you were certain that Marianne wore his picture round her neck; but it turned out to be only the miniature of our great uncle.'

'But indeed this is quite another thing. I am sure they will be married very soon, for he has got a lock of her hair.'

'Take care, Margaret. It may be only the hair of some great uncle of *his*.'

'But indeed, Elinor, it is Marianne's. I am almost sure it is, for I saw him cut it off. Last night after tea, when you and mama went out of the room, they were whispering and talking together as fast as could be, and he seemed to be begging something of her, and presently he took up her scissors and cut off a long lock of her hair, for it was all tumbled down her back; and he kissed it, and folded it up in a piece of white paper, and put it into his pocket-book.'

From such particulars, stated on such authority, Elinor could not withhold her credit: nor was she disposed to it, for the circumstance was in perfect unison with what she had heard and seen herself.

He cut off a long lock of her hair.

Margaret's sagacity was not always displayed in a way so satisfactory to her sister. When Mrs Jennings attacked her one evening at the park, to give the name of the young man who was Elinor's particular favourite, which had been long a matter of great curiosity to her, Margaret answered by looking at her sister, and saying, 'I must not tell, may I, Elinor?'

This of course made every body laugh; and Elinor tried to laugh too. But the effort was painful. She was convinced that Margaret had fixed on a person, whose name she could not bear with composure to become a standing joke with Mrs Jennings.

Marianne felt for her most sincerely; but she did more harm than good to the cause, by turning very red, and saying in an angry manner to Margaret,

'Remember that whatever your conjectures may be, you have no right to repeat them.'

'I never had any conjectures about it,' replied Margaret; 'it was you who told me of it yourself.'

This increased the mirth of the company, and Margaret was eagerly pressed to say something more.

'Oh! pray, Miss Margaret, let us know all about it,' said Mrs Jennings. 'What is the gentleman's name?'

'I must not tell, ma'am. But I know very well what it is; and I know where he is too.'

'Yes, yes, we can guess where he is; at his own house at Norland to be sure. He is the curate of the parish I dare say.'

'No, *that* he is not. He is of no profession at all.'

'Margaret,' said Marianne with great warmth, 'you know that all this is an invention of your own, and that there is no such person in existence.'

'Well then he is lately dead, Marianne, for I am sure there was such a man once, and his name begins with an F.'

Most grateful did Elinor feel to Lady Middleton for observing at this moment, 'that it rained very hard,' though she believed the interruption to proceed less from any attention to her than from her ladyship's great dislike of all such inelegant subjects of raillery as delighted her husband and mother. The idea however started by her, was immediately pursued by Colonel Brandon, who was on every occasion mindful of the feelings of others; and much was said on the subject of rain by both of them. Willoughby opened the piano-forte, and asked Marianne to sit down to it; and thus amidst the various endeavours of different people to quit the topic, it fell to the ground. But not so easily did Elinor recover from the alarm into which it had thrown her.

A party was formed this evening for going on the following day to see a very fine place about twelve miles from Barton, belonging to a brother-in-law of Colonel Brandon, without whose interest it could not be seen, as the proprietor, who was then abroad, had left strict orders on that head. The grounds were declared to be highly beautiful, and Sir John, who was particularly warm in their praise, might be allowed to be a tolerable judge, for he had formed parties to visit them, at least, twice every summer for the last ten years. They contained a noble piece of water; a sail on which was to form a great part of the morning's amusement; cold provisions were to be taken, open carriages only to be employed, and every thing conducted in the usual style of a complete party of pleasure.

To some few of the company, it appeared rather a bold undertaking, considering the time of year, and that it had rained every day for the last fortnight; – and Mrs Dashwood, who had already a cold, was persuaded by Elinor to stay at home.

CHAPTER THIRTEEN

THEIR INTENDED EXCURSION to Whitwell turned out very different from what Elinor had expected. She was prepared to be wet through, fatigued, and frightened; but the event was still more unfortunate, for they did not go at all.

By ten o'clock the whole party were assembled at the park, where they were to breakfast. The morning was rather favourable, though it had rained all night, as the clouds were then dispersing across the sky, and the sun frequently appeared. They were all in high spirits and good humour, eager to be happy, and determined to submit to the greatest inconveniences and hardships rather than be otherwise.

While they were at breakfast the letters were brought in. Among the rest there was one for Colonel Brandon; – he took it, looked at the direction, changed colour, and immediately left the room.

'What is the matter with Brandon?' said Sir John.

Nobody could tell.

'I hope he has had no bad news,' said Lady Middleton. 'It must be something extraordinary that could make Colonel Brandon leave my breakfast table so suddenly.'

In about five minutes he returned.

'No bad news, Colonel, I hope;' said Mrs Jennings, as soon as he entered the room.

'None at all, ma'am, I thank you.'

'Was it from Avignon? I hope it is not to say that your sister is worse.'

'No, ma'am. It came from town, and is merely a letter of business.'

'But how came the hand to discompose you so much, if it was only a letter of business? Come, come, this won't do, Colonel; so let us hear the truth of it.'

'My dear Madam,' said Lady Middleton, 'recollect what you are saying.'

'Perhaps it is to tell you that your cousin Fanny is married?' said Mrs Jennings, without attending to her daughter's reproof.

'No, indeed, it is not.'

'Well, then, I know who it is from, Colonel. and I hope she is well.'

'Whom do you mean, ma'am?' said he, colouring a little.

'Oh! you know who I mean.'

'I am particularly sorry, ma'am,' said he, addressing Lady Middleton, 'that I should receive this letter today, for it is on business which requires my immediate attendance in town.'

'In town!' cried Mrs Jennings. 'What can you have to do in town at this time of year?'

'My own loss is great,' he continued, 'in being obliged to leave so agreeable a party; but I am the more concerned, as I fear my presence is necessary to gain your admittance at Whitwell.'

What a blow upon them all was this!

'But if you write a note to the housekeeper, Mr Brandon,' said Marianne eagerly, 'will it not be sufficient?'

He shook his head.

'We must go,' said Sir John. – 'It shall not be put off when we are so near it. You cannot go to town till tomorrow, Brandon, that is all.'

'I wish it could be so easily settled. But it is not in my power to delay my journey for one day!'

'If you would but let us know what your business is,' said Mrs Jennings, 'we might see whether it could be put off or not.'

'You would not be six hours later,' said Willoughby, 'if you were to defer your journey till our return.'

'I cannot afford to lose *one* hour.' –

Elinor then heard Willoughby say in a low voice to Marianne, 'There are some people who cannot bear a party of pleasure. Brandon is one of them. He was afraid of catching cold I dare say, and invented this trick for getting out of it. I would lay fifty guineas the letter was of his own writing.'

'I have no doubt of it.' replied Marianne.

'There is no persuading you to change your mind, Brandon, I know of old,' said Sir John, 'when once you are determined on any thing. But, however, I hope you will think better of it. Consider, here are the two Miss Careys come over from Newton, the three Miss Dashwoods walked up from the cottage, and Mr Willoughby got up two hours before his usual time, on purpose to go to Whitwell.'

Colonel Brandon again repeated his sorrow at being the cause of disappointing the party; but at the same time declared it to be unavoidable.

'Well then, when will you come back again?'

'I hope we shall see you at Barton,' added her ladyship, 'as soon as you can conveniently leave town; and we must put off the party to Whitwell till you return.'

'You are very obliging. But it is so uncertain, when I may have it in my power to return, that I dare not engage for it at all.'

'Oh! he must and shall come back,' cried Sir John. 'If he is not here by the end of the week, I shall go after him.'

'Aye, so do, Sir John,' cried Mrs Jennings, 'and then perhaps you may find out what his business is.'

'I do not want to pry into other men's concerns. I suppose it is something he is ashamed of.'

Colonel Brandon's horses were announced.

'You do not go to town on horseback, do you?' added Sir John.

'No. Only to Honiton. I shall then go post.'

'Well, as you are resolved to go, I wish you a good journey. But you had better change your mind.'

'I assure you it is not in my power.'

He then took leave of the whole party.

'Is there no chance of my seeing you and your sisters in town this winter, Miss Dashwood?'

'I am afraid, none at all.'

'Then I must bid you farewell for a longer time than I should wish to do.'

To Marianne, he merely bowed and said nothing.

'Come, Colonel,' said Mrs Jennings, 'before you go, do let us know what you are going about.'

He wished her a good morning, and attended by Sir John, left the room.

The complaints and lamentations which politeness had hitherto restrained, now burst forth universally; and they all agreed again and again how provoking it was to be so disappointed.

'I can guess what his business is, however,' said Mrs Jennings exultingly.

'Can you ma'am?' said almost every body.

'Yes; it is about Miss Williams, I am sure.'

'And who is Miss Williams?' asked Marianne.

'What! do not you know who Miss Williams is? I am sure you must have heard of her before. She is a relation of the Colonel's, my dear; a very near relation. We will not say how near, for fear of shocking the young ladies.' Then lowering her voice a little, she said to Elinor. 'She is his natural daughter.'

'Indeed!'

'Oh! yes; and as like him as she can stare. I dare say the Colonel will leave her all his fortune.'

When Sir John returned, he joined most heartily in the general regret on so unfortunate an event; concluding however by observing, that as they were all got together, they must do something by way of being happy; and after some consultation it was agreed, that although happiness could only be enjoyed at Whitwell, they might procure a tolerable composure of mind by driving about the country. The carriages were then ordered; Willoughby's was first, and Marianne never looked happier than when she got into it. He drove through the park very fast, and they were soon out of sight; and nothing more of them was seen till their return, which did not happen till after the return of all the rest. They both seemed delighted with their drive, but said only in general terms that they had kept in the lanes, while the others went on the downs.

It was settled that there should be a dance in the evening, and that every body should be extremely merry all day long. Some more

'I have found you out in spite of all your tricks.'

of the Careys came to dinner, and they had the pleasure of sitting down nearly twenty to table, which Sir John observed with great contentment. Willoughby took his usual place between the two elder Miss Dashwoods. Mrs Jennings sat on Elinor's right hand; and they had not been long seated, before she leant behind her and Willoughby and said to Marianne, loud enough for them both to hear, 'I have found you out in spite of all your tricks. I know where you spent the morning.'

Marrianne coloured, and replied very hastily, 'Where, pray?' –

'Did not you know,' said Willoughby, 'that we had been out in my curricle?'

'Yes, yes, Mr Impudence, I know that very well, and I was determined to find out *where* you had been to. – I hope you like your house, Miss Marianne. It is a very large one I know, and when I come to see you, I hope you will have new-furnished it, for it wanted it very much, when I was there six years ago.'

Marianne turned away in great confusion. Mrs Jennings laughed heartily; and Elinor found that in her resolution to know where they had been, she had actually made her own woman enquire of Mr Willoughby's groom, and that she had by that method been informed that they had gone to Allenham, and spent a considerable time there in walking about the garden and going all over the house.

Elinor could hardly believe this to be true, as it seemed very unlikely that Willoughby should propose, or Marianne consent, to enter the house while Mrs Smith was in it, with whom Marianne had not the smallest acquaintance.

As soon as they left the dining-room, Elinor enquired of her about it; and great was her surprise when she found that every circumstance related by Mrs Jennings was perfectly true. Marianne was quite angry with her for doubting it.

'Why should you imagine, Elinor, that we did not go there, or that we did not see the house? Is not it what you have often wished to do yourself?'

'Yes, Marianne, but I would not go while Mrs Smith was there, and with no other companion than Mr Willoughby.'

'Mr Willoughby however is the only person who can have a right to shew that house; and as we went in an open carriage, it was impossible to have any other companion. I never spent a pleasanter morning in my life.'

'I am afraid,' replied Elinor, 'that the pleasantness of an employment does not always evince its propriety.'

'On the contrary, nothing can be stronger proof of it, Elinor; for if there had been any real impropriety in what I did, I should have been sensible of it at the time, for we always know when we are acting wrong, and with such a conviction I could have had no pleasure.'

'But, my dear Marianne, as it has already exposed you to some very impertinent remarks, do you not now begin to doubt the discretion of your own conduct?'

'If the impertinent remarks of Mrs Jennings are to be the proof of impropriety in conduct, we are all offending every moment of all our lives. I value not her censure any more than I should do her commendation. I am not sensible of having done any thing wrong in walking over Mrs Smith's grounds, or in seeing her house. They will one day be Mr Willoughby's, and . . .'

'If they were one day to be your own, Marianne, you would not be justified in what you have done.'

She blushed at this hint; but it was even visibly gratifying to her; and after a ten minutes' interval of earnest thought, she came to her sister again, and said with great good humour, 'Perhaps, Elinor, it *was* rather ill-judged in me to go to Allenham; but Mr Willoughby wanted particularly to shew me the place; and it is a charming house I assure you. – There is one remarkably pretty sitting room up stairs; of a nice comfortable size for constant use, and with modern furniture it would be delightful. It is a corner room, and has windows on two sides. On one side you look across the bowling-green, behind the house, to a beautiful hanging wood, and on the other you have a view of the church and village, and, beyond them, of those fine bold hills that we have so often admired. I did not see it to advantage, for nothing could be more forlorn than the furniture, – but if it were newly fitted up – a couple of hundred pounds. Willoughby says, would make it one of the pleasantest summer-rooms in England.'

Could Elinor have listened to her without interruption from the others, she would have described every room in the house with equal delight.

CHAPTER FOURTEEN

THE SUDDEN TERMINATION of Colonel Brandon's visit at the park, with his steadiness in concealing its cause, filled the mind and raised the wonder of Mrs Jennings for two or three days; she was a great wonderer, as every one must be who takes a very lively interest in all the comings and goings of all their acquaintance. She wondered with little intermission what could be the reason of it; was sure there must be some bad news, and thought over every kind of distress that could have befallen him, with a fixed determination that he should not escape them all.

'Something very melancholy must be the matter, I am sure,' she said. 'I could see it in his face. Poor man! I am afraid his circumstances may be bad. The estate at Delaford was never reckoned more than two thousand a year, and his brother left every thing sadly involved. I do think he must have been sent for about money matters, for what else can it be? I wonder whether it is so. I would give any thing to know the truth of it. Perhaps it is about Miss Williams and, by the bye, I dare say it is, because he looked so conscious when I mentioned her. May be she is ill in town; nothing in the world more likely, for I have a notion she is always rather sickly. I would lay any wager it is about Miss Williams. It is not so very likely he should be distressed in his circumstances *now*, for he is a very prudent man, and to be sure must have cleared the estate by this time. I wonder what it can be! May be his sister is worse at Avignon, and has sent for him over. His setting off in such a hurry seems very like it. Well, I wish him out of all his trouble with all my heart, and a good wife into the bargain.'

So wondered, so talked Mrs Jennings. Her opinion varying with every fresh conjecture, and all seeming equally probable as they arose. Elinor, though she felt really interested in the welfare of Colonel Brandon, could not bestow all the wonder of his going so suddenly away, which Mrs Jennings was desirous of her feeling; for besides that the circumstance did not in her opinion justify such lasting amazement or variety of speculation, her wonder was otherwise disposed of. It was engrossed by the extraordinary silence of her sister and Willoughby on the subject, which they must know to be peculiarly interesting to them all. As this silence continued, every day made it appear more strange and more incompatible with the disposition of both. Why they should not openly acknowledge to her mother and herself, what their constant behaviour to each other declared to have taken place, Elinor could not imagine.

She could easily conceive that marriage might not be immediately in their power; for though Willoughby was independent, there was no reason to believe him rich. His estate had been rated by Sir John at about six or seven hundred a year; but he lived at an expense to which that income could hardly be equal, and he had himself often complained of his poverty. But for this strange kind of secrecy maintained by them relative to their engagement, which in fact concealed nothing at all, she could not account; and it was so wholly contradictory to their general opinions and practice, that a doubt sometimes entered her mind of their being really engaged, and this doubt was enough to prevent her making any inquiry of Marianne.

Nothing could be more expressive of attachment to them all, than Willoughby's behaviour. To Marianne it had all the distinguishing tenderness which a lover's heart could give, and to the rest of the family it was the affectionate attention of a son and a brother. The cottage seemed to be considered and loved by him as his home; many more of his hours were spent there than at Allenham; and if no general engagement collected them at the park, the exercise which called him out in the morning was almost certain of ending there, where the rest of the day was spent by himself at the side of Marianne, and by his favourite pointer at her feet.

One evening in particular, about a week after Colonel Brandon had left the country, his heart seemed more than usually open to every feeling of attachment to the objects around him; and on Mrs Dashwood's happening to mention her design of improving the cottage in the spring, he warmly opposed every alteration of a place which affection had established as perfect with him.

'What!' he exclaimed – 'Improve this dear cottage! No. *That* I will never consent to. Not a stone must be added to its walls, not an inch to its size, if my feelings are regarded.'

'Do not be alarmed,' said Miss Dashwood, 'nothing of the kind will be done; for my mother will never have money enough to attempt it.'

'I am heartily glad of it,' he cried. 'May she always be poor, if she can employ her riches no better.'

'Thank you, Willoughby. But you may be assured that I would not sacrifice one sentiment of local attachment of yours, or of any one whom I loved, for all the improvements in the world. Depend upon it that whatever unemployed sum may remain, when I make up my accounts in the spring, I would even rather lay it uselessly by than dispose of it in a manner so painful to you. But are you really so attached to this place as to see no defect in it?'

'I am,' said he. 'To me it is faultless. Nay, more, I consider it as the only form of building in which happiness is attainable, and were I rich enough, I would instantly pull Combe down, and build it up again in the exact plan of this cottage.'

'With dark narrow stairs, and a kitchen that smokes, I suppose,' said Elinor.

'Yes,' cried he in the same eager tone, 'with all and every thing belonging to it; – in no one convenience or *in*convenience about it, should the least variation be perceptible. Then, and then only, under such a roof, I might perhaps be as happy at Combe as I have been at Barton.'

'I flatter myself,' replied Elinor, 'that even under the disadvantage of better rooms and a broader staircase, you will hereafter find your own house as faultless as you now do this.'

'There certainly are circumstances,' said Willoughby, 'which might greatly endear it to me; but this place will always have one claim on my affection, which no other can possibly share.'

Mrs Dashwood looked with pleasure at Marianne, whose fine eyes were fixed so expressively on Willoughby, as plainly denoted how well she understood him.

'How often did I wish,' added he, 'when I was at Allenham this time twelvemonth, that Barton cottage was inhabited! I never passed within view of it without admiring its situation, and grieving that no one should live in it. How little did I then think that the very first news I should hear from Mrs Smith, when I next came into the country, would be that Barton cottage was taken: and I felt an immediate satisfaction and interest in the event, which nothing but a kind of prescience of what happiness I should experience from it, can account for. Must it not have been so, Marianne?' speaking to her in a lowered voice. Then continuing his former tone, he said, 'And yet this house you would spoil, Mrs Dashwood? You would rob it of its simplicity by imaginary improvement! and this dear parlour, in which our acquaintance first began, and in which so many happy hours have been since spent by us together, you would degrade to the condition of a common entrance, and every body would be eager to pass through the room which has hitherto contained within itself, more real accommodation and comfort than any other apartment of the handsomest dimensions in the world could possibly afford.'

Mrs Dashwood again assured him that no alteration of the kind should be attempted.

'You are a good woman,' he warmly replied. 'Your promise makes me easy. Extend it a little farther, and it will make me happy. Tell me that not only your house will remain the same, but that I shall ever find you and yours as unchanged as your dwelling; and that you will always consider me with the kindness which has made every thing belonging to you so dear to me.'

The promise was readily given, and Willoughby's behaviour during the whole of the evening declared at once his affection and happiness.

'Shall we see you tomorrow to dinner?' said Mrs Dashwood when he was leaving them. 'I do not ask you to come in the morning, for we must walk to the park, to call on Lady Middleton.'

He engaged to be with them by four o'clock.

CHAPTER FIFTEEN

MRS DASHWOOD'S VISIT to Lady Middleton took place the next day, and two of her daughters went with her; but Marianne excused herself from being of the party under some trifling pretext of employment; and her mother, who concluded that a promise had been made by Willoughby the night before of calling on her while they were absent, was perfectly satisfied with her remaining at home.

On thier return from the park they found Willoughby's curricle and servant in waiting at the cottage, and Mrs Dashwood was convinced that her conjecture had been just. So far it was all as she had foreseen; but on entering the house she beheld what no foresight had taught her to expect. They were no sooner in the passage than Marianne came hastily out of the parlour apparently in violent affliction, with her handkerchief at her eyes; and without noticing them ran up stairs. Surprised and alarmed they proceeded directly into the room she had just quitted, where they found only Willoughby, who was leaning against the mantle-piece with his back towards them. He turned round on their coming in, and his countenance shewed that he strongly partook of the emotion which overpowered Marianne.

'Is any thing the matter with her?' cried Mrs Dashwood as she entered – 'is she ill?'

'I hope not,' he replied, trying to look cheerful; and with a forced smile presently added, 'It is I who may rather expect to be ill – for I am now suffering under a very heavy disappointment!'

'Disappointment!'

'Yes, for I am unable to keep my engagement with you. Mrs Smith has this morning exercised the privilege of riches upon a poor dependant cousin, by sending me on business to London. I have just received my dispatches, and taken my farewel of Allenham; and by way of exhilaration I am now come to take my farewell of you.'

'To London! – and are you going this morning?'

'Almost this moment.'

Apparently in violent affliction.

'This is very unfortunate. But Mrs Smith must be obliged; – and her business will not detain you from us long I hope.'

He coloured as he replied, 'You are very kind, but I have no idea of returning into Devonshire immediately. My visits to Mrs Smith are never repeated within the twelvemonth.'

'And is Mrs Smith your only friend? Is Allenham the only house in the neighbourhood to which you will be welcome? For shame, Willoughby. Can you wait for an invitation here?'

His colour increased; and with his eyes fixed on the ground he only replied, 'You are too good.'

Mrs Dashwood looked at Elinor with surprise. Elinor felt equal amazement. For a few moments every one was silent. Mrs Dashwood first spoke.

'I have only to add, my dear Willoughby, that at Barton cottage you will always be welcome; for I will not press you to return here immediately, because you only can judge how far *that* might be pleasing to Mrs Smith; and on this head I shall be no more disposed to question your judgment than to doubt your inclination.'

'My engagements at present,' replied Willoughby confusedly, 'are of such a nature – that – I dare not flatter myself – '

He stopt. Mrs Dashwood was too much astonished to speak, and another pause succeeded. This was broken by Willoughby, who said with a faint smile, 'It is folly to linger in this manner. I will not torment myself any longer by remaining among friends whose society it is impossible for me now to enjoy.'

He then hastily took leave of them all and left the room. They saw him step into his carriage, and in a minute it was out of sight.

Mrs Dashwood felt too much for speech, and instantly quitted the parlour to give way in solitude to the concern and alarm which this sudden departure occasioned.

Elinor's uneasiness was at least equal to her mother's. She thought of what had just passed with anxiety and distrust. Willoughby's behaviour in taking leave of them, his embarrassment, and affection of cheerfulness, and, above all, his unwillingness to accept her mother's invitation, a backwardness so unlike a lover, so unlike himself, greatly disturbed her. One moment she feared that no serious design had ever been formed on his side; and the next that some unfortunate quarrel had taken place between him and her sister; – the distress in which Marianne had quitted the room was such as a serious quarrel could most reasonably account for, though when she considered what Marianne's love for him was, a quarrel seemed almost impossible.

But whatever might be the particulars of their separation, her sister's affliction was indubitable; and she thought with the tenderest compassion of that violent sorrow which Marianne was in all probability not merely giving way to as a relief, but feeding and encouraging as a duty.

In about half an hour her mother returned, and though her eyes were red, her countenance was not uncheerful.

'Our dear Willoughby is now some miles from Barton, Elinor,' said she, as she sat down to work, 'and with how heavy a heart does he travel?'

'It is all very strange. So suddenly to be gone! It seems but the work of a moment. And last night he was with us so happy, so cheerful, so affectionate? And now after only ten minutes notice – Gone too without intending to return! – Something more than what he owned to us must have happened. He did not speak, he did not behave like himself. *You* must have seen the difference as well as I. What can it be? Can they have quarrelled? Why else should he have shewn such unwillingness to accept your invitation here?' –

'It was not inclination that he wanted, Elinor; I could plainly see *that*. He had not the power of accepting it. I have thought it all over I assure you, and I can perfectly account for every thing that at first seemed strange to me as well as to you.'

'Can you indeed?'

'Yes. I have explained it to myself in the most satisfactory way; – but you, Elinor, who love to doubt where you can – It will not satisfy *you*, I know; but you shall not talk *me* out of my trust in it. I am persuaded that Mrs Smith suspects his regard for Marianne, disapproves of it, (perhaps because she has other views for him,) and on that account is eager to get him away; – and that the business which she sends him off to transact, is invented as an excuse to dismiss him. This is what I believe to have happened. He is moreover aware that she *does* disapprove the connection, he dares not therefore at present confess to her his engagement with Marianne, and he feels himself obliged, from his dependent situation, to give into her schemes, and absent himself from Devonshire for a while. You will tell me, I know, that this may, or may *not* have happened; but I will listen to no cavil, unless you can point out any other method of understanding the affair as satisfactory as this. And now, Elinor, what have you to say?'

'Nothing, for you have anticipated my answer.'

'Then you would have told me, that it might or might not have happened. Oh! Elinor, how incomprehensible are your feelings! You had rather take evil upon credit than good. You had rather look out for misery for Marianne and guilt for poor Willoughby, than an apology for the latter. You are resolved to think him blameable, because he took leave of us with less affection than his usual behaviour has shewn. And is no allowance to be made for inadvertence, or for spirits depressed by recent disappointment? Are no probabilities to be accepted, merely because they are not certainties? Is nothing due to the man whom we have all so much reason to love, and no reason in the world to think ill of? To the possibility of motives unanswerable in themselves, though unavoidably secret for a while? And, after all, what is it you suspect him of?'

'I can hardly tell you myself. – But suspicion of something unpleasant is the inevitable consequence of such an alteration as we have just witnessed in him. There is great truth, however, in what you have now urged of the allowances which ought to be made for him, and it is my wish to be candid in my judgment of every body.

Willoughby may undoubtedly have very sufficient reasons for his conduct, and I will hope that he has. But it would have been more like Willoughby to acknowledge them at once. Secrecy may be advisable; but still I cannot help wondering at its being practised by him.'

'Do not blame him, however, for departing from his character, where the deviation is necessary. But you really do admit the justice of what I have said in his defence? – I am happy – and he is acquitted.'

'Not entirely. It may be proper to conceal their engagement (if they *are* engaged) from Mrs Smith – and if that is the case, it must be highly expedient for Willoughby to be but little in Devonshire at present. But this is no excuse for their concealing it from us.'

'Concealing it from us! my dear child, do you accuse Willoughby and Marianne of concealment? This is strange indeed, when your eyes have been reproaching them every day for incautiousness.'

'I want no proof of their affection,' said Elinor; 'but of their engagement I do.'

'I am perfectly satisfied of both.'

'Yet not a syllable has been said to you on the subject, by either of them.'

'I have not wanted syllables where actions have spoken so plainly. Has not his behaviour to Marianne and to all of us, for at least the last fortnight, declared that he loved and considered her as his future wife, and that he felt for us the attachment of the nearest relation? Have we not perfectly understood each other? Has not my consent been daily asked by his looks, his manner, his attentive and affectionate respect? My Elinor, is it possible to doubt their engagement? How could such a thought occur to you? How is it to be supposed that Willoughby, persuaded as he must be of your sister's love, should leave her, and leave her perhaps for months, without telling her of his affection; – that they should part without a mutual exchange of confidence?'

'I confess,' replied Elinor, 'that every circumstance except *one* is in favour of their engagement; but that *one* is the total silence of both on the subject, and with me it almost outweighs every other.'

'How strange this is! You must think wretchedly indeed of Willoughby, if after all that has openly passed between them, you can doubt the nature of the terms on which they are together. Has he been acting a part in his behaviour to your sister all this time? Do you suppose him really indifferent to her?'

'No, I cannot think that. He must and does love her I am sure.'

'But with a strange kind of tenderness, if he can leave her with such indifference, such carelessness of the future, as you attribute to him.'

'You must remember, my dear mother, that I have never considered this matter as certain. I have had my doubts, I confess; but they are fainter than they were, and they may soon be entirely done away. If we find they correspond, every fear of mine will be removed.'

'A mighty concession indeed! If you were to see them at the altar, you would suppose they were going to be married. Ungracious girl! But *I* require no such proof. Nothing in my opinion has ever passed to justify doubt; no secrecy has been attempted; all has been uniformly open and unreserved. You cannot doubt your sister's wishes. It must be Willoughby therefore who you suspect. But why? Is he not a man of honour and feeling? Has there been any inconsistency on his side to create alarm? can he be deceitful?'

'I hope not, I believe not,' cried Elinor. 'I love Willoughby, sincerely love him; and suspicion of his integrity cannot be more painful to yourself than to me. It has been involuntary, and I will not encourage it. I was startled, I confess, by the alteration in his manners this morning; – he did not speak like himself, and did not return your kindness with any cordiality. But all this may be explained by such a situation of his affairs as you have supposed. He had just parted from my sister, had seen her leave him in the greatest affliction; and if he felt obliged, from a fear of offending Mrs Smith, to resist the temptation of returning here soon, and yet aware that by declining your invitation, by saying that he was going away for some time, he should seem to act an ungenerous, a suspicious part by our family, he might well be embarrassed and disturbed. In such a case, a plain and open avowal of his difficulties would have been more to his honour I think, as well as more consistent with his general character; – but I will not raise objections against any one's conduct on so illiberal a foundation, as a difference in judgment from myself, or a deviation from what I may think right and consistent.'

'You speak very properly. Willoughby certainly does not deserve to be suspected. Though *we* have not known him long, he is no stranger in this part of the world; and who has ever spoken to his disadvantage? Had he been in a situation to act independently and marry immediately, it might have been odd that he should leave us without acknowledging every thing to me at once: but this is not the case. It is an engagement in some respects not prosperously begun, for their marriage must be at a very uncertain distance;

and even secrecy, as far as it can be observed, may now be very advisable.'

They were interrupted by the entrance of Margaret; and Elinor was then at liberty to think over the representations of her mother, to acknowledge the probability of many, and hope for the justice of all.

They saw nothing of Marianne till dinner time, when she entered the room and took her place at the table without saying a word. Her eyes were red and swollen; and it seemed as if her tears were even then restrained with difficulty. She avoided the looks of them all, could neither eat nor speak, and after some time, on her mother's silently pressing her hand with tender compassion, her small degree of fortitude was quite overcome, she burst into tears and left the room.

This violent oppression of spirits continued the whole evening. She was without any power, because she was without any desire of command over herself. The slightest mention of any thing relative to Willoughby overpowered her in an instant; and though her family were most anxiously attentive to her comfort, it was impossible for them, if they spoke at all, to keep clear of every subject which her feelings connected with him.

CHAPTER SIXTEEN

MARIANNE WOULD HAVE thought herself very inexcusable had she been able to sleep at all the first night after parting from Willoughby. She would have been ashamed to look her family in the face the next morning, had she not risen from her bed in more need of repose than when she lay down in it. But the feelings which made such composure a disgrace, left her in no danger of incurring it. She was awake the whole night, and she wept the greatest part of it. She got up with an headache, was unable to talk, and unwilling to take any nourishment; giving pain every moment to her mother and sisters, and forbidding all attempt at consolation from either. Her sensibility was potent enough!

When breakfast was over she walked out by herself, and wandered about the village of Allenham, indulging the recollection of past enjoyment and crying over the present reverse for the chief of the morning.

The evening passed off in the equal indulgence of feeling. She played over every favourite song that she had been used to play to Willoughby, every air in which their voices had been oftenest joined, and sat at the instrument gazing on every line of music that he had written out for her, till her heart was so heavy that no farther sadness could be gained; and this nourishment of grief was every day applied. She spent whole hours at the piano-forté alternately singing and crying; her voice often totally suspended by her tears. In books too, as well as in music, she courted the misery which a contrast between the past and present was certain of giving. She read nothing but what they had been used to read together.

Such violence of affliction indeed could not be supported for ever; it sunk within a few days into a calmer melancholy; but these employments, to which she daily recurred, her solitary walks and silent meditations, still produced occasional effusions of sorrow as lively as ever.

No letter from Willoughby came; and none seemed expected by Marianne. Her mother was surprised, and Elinor again became uneasy. But Mrs Dashwood could find explanations whenever she wanted them, which at least satisfied herself.

'Remember, Elinor,' said she, 'how very often Sir John fetches our letters himself from the post, and carries them to it. We have already agreed that secrecy may be necessary, and we must acknowledge that it could not be maintained if their correspondence were to pass through Sir John's hands.'

Elinor could not deny the truth of this, and she tried to find in it a motive sufficient for their silence. But there was one method so direct, so simple, and in her opinion so eligible of knowing the real state of the affair, and of instantly removing all mystery, that she could not help suggesting it to her mother.

'Why do you not ask Marianne at once,' said she, 'whether she is or is not engaged to Willoughby? From you, her mother, and so kind, so indulgent a mother, the question could not give offence. It would be the natural result of your affection for her. She used to be all unreserve, and to you more especially.'

'I would not ask such a question for the world. Supposing it possible that they are not engaged, what distress would not such an inquiry inflict! At any rate it would be most ungenerous. I should never deserve her confidence again, after forcing from her a confession of what is meant at present to be unacknowledged to any one. I know Marianne's heart: I know that she dearly loves me, and that I shall not be the last to whom the affair is made known, when circumstances make the revealment of it eligible. I would not attempt to force the confidence of any one; of a child much less;

because a sense of duty would prevent the denial which her wishes might direct.'

Elinor thought this generosity overstrained, considering her sister's youth, and urged the matter farther, but in vain; common sense, common care, common prudence, were all sunk in Mrs Dashwood's romantic delicacy.

It was several days before Willoughby's name was mentioned before Marianne by any of her family; Sir John and Mrs Jennings, indeed, were not so nice; their witticisms added pain to many a painful hour; – but one evening, Mrs Dashwood, accidentally taking up a volume of Shakespeare, exclaimed,

'We have never finished Hamlet, Marianne; our dear Willoughby went away before we could get through it. We will put it by, and when he comes again . . . But it may be months, perhaps, before *that* happens.'

'Months!' cried Marianne, with strong surprise. 'No – nor many weeks.'

Mrs Dashwood was sorry for what she had said; but it gave Elinor pleasure, as it produced a reply from Marianne so expressive of confidence in Willoughby and knowledge of his intentions.

One morning, about a week after his leaving the country, Marianne was prevailed on to join her sisters in their usual walk, instead of wandering away by herself. Hitherto she had carefully avoided every companion in her rambles. If her sisters intended to walk on the downs, she directly stole away towards the lanes; if they talked of the valley, she was as speedy in climbing the hills, and could never be found when the others set off. But at length she was secured by the exertions of Elinor, who greatly disapproved such continual seclusion. They walked along the road through the valley, and chiefly in silence, for Marianne's *mind* could not be controlled, and Elinor, satisfied with gaining one point, would not then attempt more. Beyond the entrance of the valley, where the country, though still rich, was less wild and more open, a long stretch of the road which they had travelled on first coming to Barton, lay before them; and on reaching that point, they stopped to look around them, and examine a prospect which formed the distance of their view from the cottage, from a spot which they had never happened to reach in any of their walks before.

Amongst the objects in the scene, they soon discovered an animated one; it was a man on horseback riding towards them. In a few minutes they could distinguish him to be a gentleman; and in a moment afterwards Marianne rapturously exclaimed,

'It is he; it is indeed; – I know it is!' – And was hastening to meet him, when Elinor cried out,

'Indeed, Marianne, I think you are mistaken. It is not Willoughby. The person is not tall enough for him, and has not his air.'

'He has, he has,' cried Marianne, 'I am sure he has. His air, his coat, his horse. I knew how soon he would come.'

She walked eagerly on as she spoke; and Elinor, to screen Marianne from particularity, as she felt almost certain of its not being Willoughby, quickened her pace and kept up with her. They were soon within thirty yards of the gentleman. Marianne looked again; her heart sunk within her; and abruptly turning round, she was hurrying back, when the voices of both her sisters were raised to detain her, a third, almost as well known as Willoughby's, joined them in begging her to stop, and she turned round with surprise to see and welcome Edward Ferrars.

He was the only person in the world who could at that moment

Begging her to stop.

be forgiven for not being Willoughby; the only one who could have gained a smile from her; but she dispersed her tears to smile on *him*, and in her sister's happiness forgot for a time her own disappointment.

He dismounted, and giving his horse to his servant, walked back with them to Barton, whither he was purposely coming to visit them.

He was welcomed by them all with great cordiality, but especially by Marianne, who shewed more warmth of regard in her reception of him than even Elinor herself. To Marianne, indeed, the meeting between Edward and her sister was but a continuation of that unaccountable coldness which she had often observed at Norland in their mutual behaviour. On Edward's side, more particularly, there was a deficiency of all that a lover ought to look and say on such an occasion. He was confused, seemed scarcely sensible of pleasure in seeing them, looked neither rapturous nor gay, said little but what was forced from him by questions, and distinguished Elinor by no mark of affection. Marianne saw and listened with increasing surprise. She began almost to feel a dislike of Edward; and it ended, as every feeling must end with her, by carrying back her thoughts to Willoughby, whose manners formed a contrast sufficiently striking to those of his brother elect.

After a short silence which succeeded the first surprise and inquiries of meeting, Marianne asked Edward if he came directly from London. No, he had been in Devonshire a fortnight.

'A fortnight!' she repeated, surprised at his being so long in the same county with Elinor without seeing her before.

He looked rather distressed as he added, that he had been staying with some friends near Plymouth.

'Have you been lately in Sussex?' said Elinor.

'I was at Norland about a month ago.'

'And how does dear, dear Norland look?' cried Marianne.

'Dear, dear Norland,' said Elinor, 'probably looks much as it always does at this time of year. The woods and walks thickly covered with dead leaves.'

'Oh!' cried Marianne, 'with what transporting sensations have I formerly seen them fall! How have I delighted, as I walked, to see them driven in showers about me by the wind! What feelings have they, the season, the air altogether inspired! Now there is no one to regard them. They are seen only as a nuisance, swept hastily off, and driven as much as possible from the sight.'

'It is not every one,' said Elinor, 'who has your passion for dead leaves.'

'No; my feelings are not often shared, not often understood. But *sometimes* they are.' – As she said this, she sunk into a reverie for a few moments; – but rousing herself again, 'Now, Edward,' said she, calling his attention to the prospect, 'here is Barton valley. Look up to it, and be tranquil if you can. Look at those hills! Did you ever see their equals? To the left is Barton park, amongst those woods and plantations. You may see one end of the house. And there, beneath that farthest hill, which rises with such grandeur, is our cottage.'

'It is a beautiful country,' he replied; 'but these bottoms must be dirty in winter.'

'How can you think of dirt, with such objects before you?'

'Because,' replied he, smiling, 'among the rest of the objects before me, I see a very dirty lane.'

'How strange!' said Marianne to herself as she walked on.

'Have you an agreeable neighbourhood here? Are the Middletons pleasant people?'

'No, not at all,' answered Marianne, 'we could not be more unfortunately situated.'

'Marianne,' cried her sister, 'how can you say so? How can you be so unjust? They are a very respectable family, Mr Ferrars; and towards us have behaved in the friendliest manner. Have you forgot, Marianne, how many pleasant days we have owed to them?'

'No,' said Marianne in a low voice, 'nor how many painful moments.'

Elinor took no notice of this, and directing her attention to their visitor, endeavoured to support something like discourse with him by talking of their present residence, its conveniences, &c. extorting from him occasional questions and remarks. His coldness and reserve mortified her severely; she was vexed and half angry; but resolving to regulate her behaviour to him by the past rather than the present, she avoided every appearance of resentment or displeasure, and treated him as she thought he ought to be treated from the family connection.

CHAPTER SEVENTEEN

MRS DASHWOOD WAS surprised only for a moment at seeing him; for his coming to Barton was, in her opinion, of all things the most natural. Her joy and expressions of regard long outlived her wonder. He received the kindest welcome from her; and shyness, coldness, reserve could not stand against such a reception. They had begun to fail him before he entered the house, and they were quite overcome by the captivating manners of Mrs Dashwood. Indeed a man could not very well be in love with either of her daughters, without extending the passion to her, and Elinor had the satisfaction of seeing him soon become more like himself. His affections seemed to reanimate towards them all, and his interest in their welfare again became perceptible. He was not in spirits however; he praised their house, admired its prospects, was attentive, and kind; but still he was not in spirits. The whole family perceived it, and Mrs Dashwood, attributing it to some want of liberality in his mother, sat down to table indignant against all selfish parents.

'What are Mrs Ferrars's views for you at present, Edward?' said she, when dinner was over and they had drawn round the fire; 'are you still to be a great orator in spite of yourself?'

'No. I hope my mother is now convinced that I have no more talents than inclination for a public life!'

'But how is your fame to be established? for famous you must be to satisfy all your family, and with no inclination for expence, no affection for strangers, no profession, and no assurance, you may find it a difficult matter.'

'I shall not attempt it. I have no wish to be distinguished; and I have every reason to hope I never shall. Thank Heaven! I cannot be forced into genius and eloquence.'

'You have no ambition, I well know. Your wishes are all moderate.'

'As moderate as those of the rest of the world, I believe. I wish as well as every body else to be perfectly happy; but like every body else it must be in my own way. Greatness will not make me so.'

'Strange if it would!' cried Marianne. 'What have wealth or grandeur to do with happiness?'

'Grandeur has but little,' said Elinor, 'but wealth has much to do with it.'

'Elinor, for shame!' said Marianne; 'money can only give happiness where there is nothing else to give it. Beyond a competence, it can afford no real satisfaction, as far as mere self is concerned.'

'Perhaps,' said Elinor, smiling, 'we may come to the same point. *Your* competence and *my* wealth are very much alike, I dare say, and without them, as the world goes now, we shall both agree that every kind of external comfort must be wanting. Your ideas are only more noble than mine. Come, what is your competence?'

'About eighteen hundred or two thousand a-year; not more than *that.*'

Elinor laughed. '*Two* thousand a-year! *One* is my wealth! I guessed how it would end.'

'And yet two thousand a-year is a very moderate income,' said Marianne. 'A family cannot well be maintained on a smaller. I am sure I am not extravagant in my demands. A proper establishment of servants, a carriage, perhaps two, and hunters, cannot be supported on less.'

Elinor smiled again, to hear her sister describing so accurately their future expences at Combe Magna.

'Hunters' repeated Edward – 'But why must you have hunters? Every body does not hunt.'

Marianne coloured as she replied, 'But most people do.'

'I wish,' said Margaret, striking out a novel thought, 'that somebody would give us all a large fortune apiece!'

'Oh that they would!' cried Marianne, her eyes sparkling with animation, and her cheeks glowing with the delight of such imaginary happiness.

'We are all unanimous in that wish, I suppose,' said Elinor, 'in spite of the insufficiency of wealth.'

'Oh dear!' cried Margaret, 'how happy I should be! I wonder what I should do with it!'

Marianne looked as if she had no doubt on that point.

'I should be puzzled to spend a large fortune myself,' said Mrs Dashwood, 'if my children were all to be rich without my help.'

'You must begin your improvements on this house,' observed Elinor, 'and your difficulties will soon vanish.'

'What magnificent orders would travel from this family to London,' said Edward, 'in such an event! What a happy day for booksellers, music-sellers, and print-shops! You, Mrs Dashwood, would give a general commission for every new print of merit to be sent you – and as for Marianne, I know her greatness of soul, there would not be music enough in London to content her. And books! – Thomson, Cowper, Scott – she would buy them all over and over again; she would buy up every copy, I believe, to prevent their falling into unworthy hands; and she would have every book that tells her how to admire an old twisted tree. Should not you, Marianne? Forgive me, if I am very saucy. But I was willing to shew you that I had not forgot our old disputes.'

'I love to be reminded of the past, Edward – whether it be melancholy or gay, I love to recall it – and you will never offend me by talking of former times. You are very right in supposing how my money would be spent – some of it, at least – my loose cash would certainly be employed in improving my collection of music and books.'

'And the bulk of your fortune would be laid out in annuities on the authors or their heirs.'

'No, Edward, I should have something else to do with it.'

'Perhaps then you would bestow it as a reward on that person who wrote the ablest defence of your favourite maxim, that no one can ever be in love more than once in their life – for your opinion on that point is unchanged, I presume?'

'Undoubtedly. At my time of life opinions are tolerably fixed. It is not likely that I should now see or hear anything to change them.'

'Marianne is as steadfast as ever, you see,' said Elinor, 'she is not at all altered.'

'She is only grown a little more grave than she was.'

'Nay, Edward,' said Marianne, '*you* need not reproach me. You are not very gay yourself.'

'Why should you think so!' replied he, with a sigh. 'But gaiety never was a part of *my* character.'

'Nor do I think it a part of Marianne's,' said Elinor, 'I should hardly call her a lively girl – she is very earnest, very eager in all she does – sometimes talks a great deal and always with animation – but she is not often really merry.'

'I believe you are right,' he replied, 'and yet I have always set her down as a lively girl.'

'I have frequently detected myself in such kind of mistakes,' said Elinor, 'in a total misapprehension of character in some point or other: fancying people so much more gay or grave, or ingenious or stupid than they really are, and I can hardly tell why or in what the deception originated. Sometimes one is guided by what they say of themselves, and very frequently by what other people say of them, without giving oneself time to deliberate and judge.'

'But I thought it was right, Elinor,' said Marianne, 'to be guided wholly by the opinion of other people. I thought our judgments were given us merely to be subservient to those of our neighbours. This has always been your doctrine, I am sure.'

'No, Marianne, never. My doctrine has never aimed at the subjection of the understanding. All I have ever attempted to influence has been the behaviour. You must not confound my meaning. I am guilty, I confess, of having often wished you to treat our acquaintance in general with greater attention; but when have I advised you to adopt their sentiments or conform to their judgment in serious matters?'

'You have not been able to bring your sister over to your plan of general civility,' said Edward to Elinor. 'Do you gain no ground?'

'Quite the contrary,' replied Elinor, looking expressively at Marianne.

'My judgment,' he returned, 'is all on your side of the question; but I am afraid my practice is much more on your sister's. I never wish to offend, but I am so foolishly shy, that I often seem negligent, when I am only kept back by my natural awkwardness. I have frequently thought that I must have been intended by nature to be fond of low company, I am so little at my ease among strangers of gentility!'

'Marianne has not shyness to excuse any inattention of hers,' said Elinor.

'She knows her own worth too well for false shame,' replied Edward. 'Shyness is only the effect of a sense of inferiority in some way or other. If I could persuade myself that my manners were perfectly easy and graceful, I should not be shy.'

'But you would still be reserved,' said Marianne, 'and that is worse.'

Edward stared – 'Reserved! Am I reserved, Marianne?'

'Yes, very.'

'I do not understand you,' replied he, colouring. 'Reserved! – how, in what manner? What am I to tell you? What can you suppose?'

Elinor looked surprised at his emotion, but trying to laugh off the subject, she said to him, 'Do not you know my sister well enough to understand what she means? Do not you know she calls every one reserved who does not talk fast, and admire what she admires as rapturously as herself?'

Edward made no answer. His gravity and thoughtfulness returned on him in their fullest extent – and he sat for some time silent and dull.

CHAPTER EIGHTEEN

ELINOR SAW, WITH great uneasiness, the low spirits of her friend. His visit afforded her but a very partial satisfaction, while his own enjoyment in it appeared so imperfect. If was evident that he was unhappy; she wished it were equally evident that he still distinguished her by the same affection which once she had felt no doubt of inspiring; but hitherto the continuance of his preference seemed very uncertain; and the reservedness of his manner towards her contradicted one moment what a more animated look had intimated the preceding one.

He joined her and Marianne in the breakfast-room the next morning before the others were down; and Marianne, who was always eager to promote their happiness as far as she could, soon left them to themselves. But before she was half way upstairs she heard the parlour door open, and, turning round, was astonished to see Edward himself come out.

'I am going into the village to see my horses,' said he, 'as you are not ready for breakfast; I shall be back again presently.'

Edward returned to them with fresh admiration of the surrounding country; in his walk to the village, he had seen many parts of the valley to advantage; and the village itself, in a much higher situation than the cottage, afforded a general view of the whole, which had exceedingly pleased him. This was a subject which ensured Marianne's attention, and she was beginning to describe her own admiration of these scenes, and to question him more minutely on the objects that had particularly struck him, when Edward interrupted her by saying, 'You must not inquire too far, Marianne – remember I have no knowledge in the picturesque, and I shall offend you by my ignorance and want of taste if we come to particulars. I shall call hills steep, which ought to be bold; surfaces strange and uncouth, which ought to be irregular and rugged; and distant objects out of sight, which ought only to be indistinct through the soft medium of a hazy atmosphere. You must be satisfied with such admiration as I can honestly give. I call it a very fine country – the hills are steep, the woods seem full of fine timber, and the valley looks comfortable and snug – with rich meadows and several neat farm houses scattered here and there. It exactly answers my idea of a fine country, because it unites beauty with utility – and I dare say it is a picturesque one too, because you admire it; I can easily believe it to be full of rocks and promontories, grey moss and brush wood, but these are all lost on me. I know nothing of the picturesque.'

'I am afraid it is but too true,' said Marianne; 'but why should you boast of it?'

'I suspect,' said Elinor, 'that to avoid one kind of affectation, Edward here falls into another. Because he believes many people pretend to more admiration of the beauties of nature than they really feel, and is disgusted with such pretensions, he affects greater indifference and less discrimination in viewing them himself than he possesses. He is fastidious and will have an affectation of his own.'

'It is very true,' said Marianne, 'that admiration of landscape scenery is become a mere jargon. Every body pretends to feel and tries to describe with the taste and elegance of him who first defined what picturesque beauty was. I detest jargon of every kind, and sometimes I have kept my feelings to myself, because I could find no language to describe them in but what was worn and hackneyed out of all sense and meaning.'

'I am convinced,' said Edward, 'that you really feel all the delight in a fine prospect which you profess to feel. But, in return, your sister must allow me to feel no more than I profess. I like a fine prospect, but not on picturesque principles. I do not like crooked, twisted, blasted trees. I admire them much more if they are tall, straight and flourishing. I do not like ruined, tattered cottages. I am not fond of nettles, or thistles, or heath blossoms. I have more pleasure in a snug farm-house than a watch-tower – and a troop of tidy, happy villagers please me better than the finest banditti in the world.'

Marianne looked with amazement at Edward, with compassion at her sister. Elinor only laughed.

The subject was continued no farther; and Marianne remained thoughtfully silent, till a new object suddenly engaged her attention. She was sitting by Edward, and in taking his tea from Mrs Dashwood, his hand passed so directly before her, as to make a ring, with a plait of hair in the centre, very conspicuous on one of his fingers.

'I never saw you wear a ring before, Edward,' she cried. 'Is that Fanny's hair? I remember her promising to give you some. But I should have thought her hair had been darker.'

Marianne spoke inconsiderately what she really felt – but when she saw how much she had pained Edward, her own vexation at

Came to take a survey of the guest.

her want of thought could not be surpassed by his. He coloured very deeply, and giving a momentary glance at Elinor, replied, 'Yes; it is my sister's hair. The setting always casts a different shade on it you know.'

Elinor had met his eye, and looked conscious likewise. That the hair was her own, she instantaneously felt as well satisfied as Marianne; the only difference in their conclusions was, that what Marianne considered as a free gift from her sister, Elinor was conscious must have been procured by some theft or contrivance unknown to herself. She was not in a humour, however, to regard it as an affront, and affecting to take no notice of what passed, by instantly talking of something else, she internally resolved henceforward to catch every opportunity of eyeing the hair and of satisfying herself, beyond all doubt, that it was exactly the shade of her own.

Edward's embarrassment lasted some time, and it ended in an absence of mind still more settled. He was particularly grave the whole morning. Marianne severely censured herself for what she had said; but her own forgiveness might have been more speedy, had she known how little offence it had given her sister.

Before the middle of the day, they were visited by Sir John and Mrs Jennings, who, having heard of the arrival of a gentleman at the cottage, came to take a survey of the guest. With the assistance of his mother-in-law, Sir John was not long in discovering that the name of Ferrars began with an F. and this prepared a future mine of raillery against the devoted Elinor, which nothing but the newness of their acquaintance with Edward could have prevented from being immediately sprung. But, as it was, she only learned from some very significant looks, how far their penetration, founded on Margaret's instructions, extended.

Sir John never came to the Dashwoods without either inviting them to dine at the park the next day, or to drink tea with them that evening. On the present occasion, for the better entertainment of their visitor, towards whose amusement he felt himself bound to contribute, he wished to engage them for both.

'You *must* drink tea with us tonight,' said he, 'for we shall be quite alone – and tomorrow you must absolutely dine with us, for we shall be a large party.'

Mrs Jennings enforced the necessity. 'And who knows but you may raise a dance,' said she. 'And that will tempt *you*, Miss Marianne.'

'A dance!' cried Marianne. 'Impossible! Who is to dance?'

'Who! why yourselves, and the Careys, and the Whitakers to be sure – What! you thought nobody could dance because a certain person that shall be nameless is gone!'

'I wish with all my soul,' cried Sir John, 'that Willoughby were among us again.'

This, and Marianne's blushing, gave new suspicions to Edward. 'And who is Willoughby?' said he, in a low voice, to Miss Dashwood, by whom he was sitting.

She gave him a brief reply. Marianne's countenance was more communicative. Edward saw enough to comprehend, not only the meaning of others, but such of Marianne's expressions as had puzzled him before; and when their visitors left them, he went immediately round to her and said, in a whisper, 'I have been guessing. Shall I tell you my guess?'

'What do you mean?'

'Shall I tell you?'

'Certainly.'

'Well then; I guess that Mr Willoughby hunts.'

Marianne was surprised and confused, yet she could not help smiling at the quiet archness of his manner, and, after a moment's silence, said,

'Oh! Edward! How can you? – But the time will come I hope . . . I am sure you will like him.'

'I do not doubt it,' replied he, rather astonished at her earnestness and warmth; for had he not imagined it to be a joke for the good of her acquaintance in general, founded only on a something or a nothing between Mr Willoughby and herself, he would not have ventured to mention it.

CHAPTER NINETEEN

EDWARD REMAINED A week at the cottage; he was earnestly pressed by Mrs Dashwood to stay longer; but as if he were bent only on self-mortification, he seemed resolved to be gone when his enjoyment among his friends was at the height. His spirits, during the last two or three days, though still very unequal, were greatly improved – he grew more and more partial to the house and environs – never spoke of going away without a sigh – declared his time to be wholly disengaged – even doubted to what place he should go when he left them – but still, go he must. Never had any week passed so quickly – he could hardly believe it to be gone. He said so repeatedly; other things he said too, which marked the turn of his feelings and gave the lie to his actions. He had no pleasure at Norland; he detested being in town; but either to Norland or London, he must go. He valued their kindness beyond any thing, and his greatest happiness was in being with them. Yet he must leave them at the end of a week, in spite of their wishes and his own, and without any restraint on his time.

Elinor placed all that was astonishing in this way of acting to his mother's account; and it was happy for her that he had a mother whose character was so imperfectly known to her, as to be the general excuse for every thing strange on the part of her son. Disappointed, however, and vexed as she was, and sometimes displeased with his uncertain behaviour to herself, she was very well disposed on the whole to regard his actions with all the candid allowances and generous qualifications, which had been rather more painfully extorted from her, for Willoughby's service, by her mother. His want of spirits, of openness, and of consistency, were most usually attributed to his want of independence, and his better knowledge of Mrs Ferrars's disposition and designs. The shortness of his visit, the steadiness of his purpose in leaving them, originated in the same fettered inclination, the same inevitable necessity of temporizing with his mother. The old, well-established grievance of duty against will, parent against child, was the cause of all. She would have been glad to know when these difficulties were to cease, this opposition was to yield, – when Mrs Ferrars would be reformed, and her son be at liberty to be happy. But from such vain wishes, she was forced to turn for comfort to the renewal of her confidence in Edward's affection, to the remembrance of every mark of regard in look or word which fell from him while at Barton, and above all to that flattering proof of it which he constantly wore round his finger.

'I think, Edward,' said Mrs Dashwood, as they were at breakfast the last morning, 'you would be a happier man if you had any profession to engage your time and give an interest to your plans and actions. Some inconvenience to your friends, indeed, might result from it – you would not be able to give them so much of your time. But (with a smile) you would be materially benefited in one particular at least – you would know where to go when you left them.'

'I do assure you,' he replied, 'that I have long thought on this point, as you think now. It has been, and is, and probably will always be a heavy misfortune to me, that I have had no necessary business to engage me, no profession to give me employment, or afford me any thing like independence. But unfortunately my own nicety, and the nicety of my friends, have made me what I am, an idle, helpless being. We never could agree in our choice of a profession. I always preferred the church, as I still do. But that was not smart enough for my family. They recommended the army. That was a great deal too smart for me. The law was allowed to be genteel enough; many young men, who had chambers in the Temple, made a very good appearance in the first circles, and drove about town in very knowing gigs. But I had no inclination for the law, even in this less abstruse study of it, which my family approved. As for the navy, it had fashion on its side, but I was too old when the subject was first started to enter it – and, at length, as there was no necessity for my having any profession at all, as I might be as dashing and expensive without a red coat on my back as with one, idleness was pronounced on the whole to be the most advantageous and honourable, and a young man of eighteen is not in general so earnestly bent on being busy as to resist the solicitations of his friends to do nothing I was therefore entered at Oxford and have been properly idle ever since.'

'The consequence of which, I suppose, will be,' said Mrs Dashwood, 'since leisure has not promoted your own happiness, that your sons will be brought up to as many pursuits, employments, professions, and trades as Columella's.'

'They will be brought up,' said he, in a serious accent, 'to be as unlike myself as is possible. In feeling, in action, in condition, in every thing.'

'Come, come; this is all an effusion of immediate want of spirits, Edward. You are in a melancholy humour, and fancy that any one unlike yourself must be happy. But remember that the pain of parting from friends will be felt by every body at times, whatever be their education or state. Know your own happiness. You want nothing but patience – or give it a more fascinating name, call it hope. Your mother will secure to you, in time, that independence you are so anxious for; it is her duty, and it will, it must ere long become her happiness to prevent your whole youth from being wasted in discontent. How much may not a few months do?'

'I think,' replied Edward, 'that I may defy many months to produce any good to me.'

This desponding turn of mind, though it could not be communicated to Mrs Dashwood, gave additional pain to them all in the parting, which shortly took place, and left an uncomfortable impression on Elinor's feelings especially, which required some trouble and time to subdue. But as it was her determination to subdue it, and to prevent herself from appearing to suffer more than what all her family suffered on his going away, she did not adopt the method so judiciously employed by Marianne, on a similar occasion, to augment and fix her sorrow, by seeking silence, solitude and idleness. Their means were as different as their objects, and equally suited to the advancement of each.

Elinor sat down to her drawing-table as soon as he was out of the house, busily employed herself the whole day, neither sought nor avoided the mention of his name, appeared to interest herself almost as much as ever in the general concerns of the family, and if, by this conduct, she did not lessen her own grief, it was at least prevented from unnecessary increase, and her mother and sisters were spared much solicitude on her account.

Such behaviour as this, so exactly the reverse of her own, appeared no more meritorious to Marianne, than her own had seemed faulty to her. The business of self-command she settled very easily – with strong affections it was impossible, with calm ones it could have no merit. That her sister's affections *were* calm, she dared not deny, though she blushed to acknowledge it; and of the strength of her own, she gave a very striking proof, by still loving and respecting that sister, in spite of this mortifying conviction.

Without shutting herself up from her family, or leaving the house in determined solitude to avoid them, or laying awake the whole night to indulge meditation, Elinor found every day afforded her leisure enough to think of Edward, and of Edward's behaviour, in every possible variety which the different state of her spirits at different times could produce, – with tenderness, pity, approbation, censure and doubt. There were moments in abundance, when, if not by the absence of her mother and sisters, at least by the nature of their employments, conversation was forbidden among them, and every effect of solitude was produced. Her mind was inevitably at liberty; her thoughts could not be chained elsewhere; and the past and the future, on a subject so interesting, must be before her, must force her attention, and engross her memory, her reflection, and her fancy.

From a reverie of this kind, as she sat at her drawing-table, she was roused one morning, soon after Edward's leaving them, by the arrival of company. She happened to be quite alone. The closing of the little gate, at the entrance of the green court in front of the house, drew her eyes to the window, and she saw a large party walking up to the door. Amongst them were Sir John and Lady Middleton and Mrs Jennings, but there were two others, a gentleman and lady, who were quite unknown to her. She was sitting near the window, and as soon as Sir John perceived her, he left the rest of the party to the ceremony of knocking at the door, and stepping across the turf, obliged her to open the casement to speak to him, though the space was so short between the door and the window, as to make it hardly possible to speak at one without being heard at the other.

'Well,' said he, 'we have brought you some strangers. How do you like them?'

'Hush! they will hear you.'

'Never mind if they do. It is only the Palmers. Charlotte is very pretty, I can tell you. You may see her if you look this way.'

As Elinor was certain of seeing her in a couple of minutes, without taking that liberty, she begged to be excused.

'Where is Marianne? Has she run away because we are come? I see her instrument is open.'

'She is walking, I believe.'

They were now joined by Mrs Jennings, who had not patience enough to wait till the door was opened before she told *her* story. She came hallooing to the window, 'How do you do, my dear? How does Mrs Dashwood do? And where are your sisters? What! all alone! you will be glad of a little company to sit with you. I have brought my other son and daughter to see you. Only think of their coming so suddenly! I thought I heard a carriage last night, while we were drinking our tea, but it never entered my head that it could be them. I thought of nothing but whether it might not be Colonel Brandon come back again; so I said to Sir John, I do think I hear a carriage; perhaps it is Colonel Brandon come back again – '

Elinor was obliged to turn from her, in the middle of her story, to receive the rest of the party; Lady Middleton introduced the two strangers; Mrs Dashwood and Margaret came down stairs at the same time, and they all sat down to look at one another, while Mrs Jennings continued her story as she walked through the passage into the parlour, attended by Sir John.

Mrs Palmer was several years younger than Lady Middleton, and totally unlike her in every respect. She was short and plump, had a very pretty face, and the finest expression of good humour in it that could possibly be. Her manners were by no means so elegant as her sister's, but they were much more prepossessing. She came in with a smile, smiled all the time of her visit, except when she laughed, and smiled when she went away. Her husband was a grave looking young man of five or six and twenty, with an air of more fashion and sense than his wife, but of less willingness to please or be pleased. He entered the room with a look of self-consequence, slightly bowed to the ladies, without speaking a word, and, after briefly surveying them and their apartments, took up a newspaper from the table and continued to read it as long as he stayed.

Mrs Palmer, on the contrary, who was strongly endowed by nature with a turn for being uniformly civil and happy, was hardly seated before her admiration of the parlour and every thing in it burst forth.

'Well! what a delightful room this is! I never saw anything so charming! Only think, mama, how it is improved since I was here last! I always thought it such a sweet place, ma'am! (turning to Mrs Dashwood,) but you have made it so charming! Only look, sister, how delightful every thing is! How I should like such a house for myself! Should not you, Mr Palmer?'

Mr Palmer made her no answer, and did not even raise his eyes from the newspaper.

'Mr Palmer does not hear me,' said she, laughing, 'he never does sometimes. It is so ridiculous!'

This was quite a new idea to Mrs Dashwood, she had never been used to find wit in the inattention of any one, and could not help looking with surprise at them both.

Mrs Jennings in the mean time, talked on as loud as she could, and continued her account of their surprise the evening before, on seeing their friends, without ceasing till every thing was told. Mrs Palmer laughed heartily at the recollection of their astonishment, and every body agreed, two or three times over, that it had been quite an agreeable surprise.

'You may believe how glad we all were to see them,' added Mrs Jennings, leaning forwards towards Elinor, and speaking in a low voice as if she meant to be heard by no one else, though they were seated on different sides of the room; 'but, however, I can't help

'I declare they are quite charming.'

wishing they had not travelled quite so fast, nor made such a long journey of it, for they came all round by London upon account of some business, for you know (nodding significantly and pointing to her daughter) it was wrong in her situation. I wanted her to stay at home and rest this morning, but she would come with us; she longed so much to see you all!'

Mrs Palmer laughed, and said it would not do her any harm.

'She expects to be confined in February,' continued Mrs Jennings.

Lady Middleton could no longer endure such a conversation, and therefore exerted herself to ask Mr Palmer if there was any news in the paper.

'No, none at all,' he replied, and read on.

'Here comes Marianne,' cried Sir John. 'Now, Palmer, you shall see a monstrous pretty girl.'

He immediately went into the passage, opened the front door, and ushered her in himself. Mrs Jennings asked her, as soon as she appeared, if she had not been to Allenham; and Mrs Palmer laughed so heartily at the question, as to shew she understood it. Mr Palmer looked up on her entering the room, stared at her some minutes, and then returned to his newspaper. Mrs Palmer's eye was now caught by the drawings which hung round the room. She got up to examine them.

'Oh! dear, how beautiful these are! Well! how delightful! Do but look, mama, how sweet! I declare they are quite charming; I could look at them for ever.' And then sitting down again, she very soon forgot that there were any such things in the room.

When Lady Middleton rose to go away, Mr Palmer rose also, laid down the newspaper, stretched himself, and looked at them all round.

'My love, have you been asleep?' said his wife, laughing.

He made her no answer; and only observed, after again examining the room, that it was very low pitched, and that the ceiling was crooked. He then made his bow and departed with the rest.

Sir John had been very urgent with them all to spend the next day at the park. Mrs Dashwood, who did not chuse to dine with them oftener than they dined at the cottage, absolutely refused on her own account; her daughters might do as they pleased. But they had no curiosity to see how Mr and Mrs Palmer ate their dinner, and no expectation of pleasure from them in any other way. They attempted, therefore, likewise to excuse themselves; the weather was uncertain and not likely to be good. But Sir John would not be satisfied – the carriage should be sent for them and they must come. Lady Middleton too, though she did not press their mother, pressed them. Mrs Jennings and Mrs Palmer joined their entreaties, all seemed equally anxious to avoid a family party; and the young ladies were obliged to yield.

'Why should they ask us?' said Marianne, as soon as they were gone. 'The rent of this cottage is said to be low, but we have it on very hard terms, if we are to dine at the park whenever any one is staying either with them, or with us.'

'They mean no less to be civil and kind to us now,' said Elinor, 'by these frequent invitations than by those which we received from them a few weeks ago. The alteration is not in them, if their parties are grown tedious and dull. We must look for the change elsewhere.'

CHAPTER TWENTY

As the Miss Dashwoods entered the drawing-room of the park the next day, at one door, Mrs Palmer came running in at the other, looking as good humoured and merry as before. She took them all most affectionately by the hand, and expressed great delight in seeing them again.

'I am so glad to see you!' said she, seating herself between Elinor and Marianne, 'for it is so bad a day I was afraid you might not come, which would be a shocking thing, as we go away again tomorrow. We must go, for the Westons come to us next week you know. It was quite a sudden thing our coming at all, and I knew nothing of it till the carriage was coming to the door, and then Mr Palmer asked me if I would go with him to Barton. He is so droll! He never tells me any thing! I am so sorry we cannot stay longer; however we shall meet again in town very soon, I hope.'

They were obliged to put an end to such an expectation.

'Not go to town!' cried Mrs Palmer, with a laugh, 'I shall be quite disappointed if you do not. I could get the nicest house in the world for you, next door to our's, in Hanover-square. You must come, indeed. I am sure I shall be very happy to chaperon you at any time till I am confined, if Mrs Dashwood should not like to go into public.'

They thanked her; but were obliged to resist all her entreaties.

'Oh! my love,' cried Mrs Palmer to her husband, who just then entered the room – 'You must help me persuade the Miss Dashwoods to go to town this winter.'

Her love made no answer; and after slightly bowing to the ladies, began complaining of the weather.

'How horrid all this is!' said he. 'Such weather makes every thing and every body disgusting. Dulness is as much produced within doors as without, by rain. It makes one detest all one's acquaintance. What the devil does Sir John mean by not having a billiards room in his house? How few people know what comfort is! Sir John is as stupid as the weather.'

The rest of the company soon dropt in.

'I am afraid, Miss Marianne,' said Sir John, 'you have not been able to take your usual walk to Allenham today.'

Marianne looked very grave and said nothing.

'Oh! don't be so sly before us,' said Mrs Palmer; 'for we know all about it, I assure you; and I admire your taste very much, for I think he is extremely handsome. We do not live a great way from him in the country, you know. Not above ten miles, I dare say.'

'Much nearer thirty,' said her husband.

'Ah! well! there is not much difference. I never was at his house; but they say it is a sweet pretty place.'

'As vile a spot as I ever saw in my life,' said Mr Palmer.

Marianne remained perfectly silent, though her countenance betrayed her interest in what was said.

'Is it very ugly?' continued Mrs Palmer – 'then it must be some other place that is so pretty I suppose.'

When they were seated in the dining room, Sir John observed with regret that they were only eight altogether.

'My dear,' said he to his lady, 'it is very provoking that we should be so few. Why did you not ask the Gilberts to come to us today?'

'Did not I tell you, Sir John, when you spoke to me about it before, that it could not be done? They dined with us last.'

'You and I, Sir John,' said Mrs Jennings, 'should not stand upon such ceremony.'

'Then you would be very ill-bred,' cried Mr Palmer.

'My love, you contradict every body,' – said his wife with her usual laugh. 'Do you know that you are quite rude?'

'I did not know I contradicted any body in calling your mother ill-bred.'

'Aye, you may abuse me as you please,' said the good-natured old lady, 'you have taken Charlotte off my hands, and cannot give her back again. So there I have the whip hand of you.'

Charlotte laughed heartily to think that her husband could not get rid of her; and exultingly said, she did not care how cross he was to her, as they must live together. It was impossible for any one to be more thoroughly good-natured, or more determined to be happy than Mrs Palmer. The studied indifference, insolence, and discontent of her husband gave her no pain: and when he scolded or abused her, she was highly diverted.

'Mr Palmer is so droll!' said she, in a whisper, to Elinor. 'He is always out of humour.'

Elinor was not inclined, after a little observation, to give him credit for being so genuinely and unaffectedly ill-natured or ill-bred as he wished to appear. His temper might perhaps be a little soured by finding, like many others of his sex, that through some unaccountable bias in favour of beauty, he was the husband of a very silly woman, – but she knew that this kind of blunder was too common for any sensible man to be lastingly hurt by it. – It was rather a wish of distinction she believed, which produced his contemptuous treatment of every body, and his general abuse of every thing before him. It was the desire of appearing superior to other people. The motive was too common to be wondered at; but the means, however they might succeed by establishing his superiority in ill-breeding, were not likely to attach any one to him except his wife.

'Oh! my dear Miss Dashwood,' said Mrs Palmer soon afterwards, 'I have got such a favour to ask of you and your sister. Will you come and spend some time at Cleveland this Christmas? Now, pray do, – and come while the Westons are with us. You cannot think how happy I shall be! It will be quite delightful! – My love,' applying to her husband, 'don't you long to have the Miss Dashwoods come to Cleveland?'

'Certainly,' – he replied with a sneer – 'I came into Devonshire with no other view.'

'There now' – said his lady, 'you see Mr Palmer expects you; so you cannot refuse to come.'

They both eagerly and resolutely declined her invitation.

'But indeed you must and shall come. I am sure you will like it of all things. The Westons will be with us, and it will be quite delightful. You cannot think what a sweet place Cleveland is; and we are so gay now, for Mr Palmer is always going about the country canvassing against the election; and so many people come to dine with us that I never saw before, it is quite charming! But, poor fellow! it is very fatiguing to him! for he is forced to make every body like him.'

Elinor could hardly keep her countenance as she assented to the hardship of such an obligation.

'How charming it will be,' said Charlotte, 'when he is in Parliament! – won't it? How I shall laugh! It will be so ridiculous to see all his letters directed to him with an M.P. – But do you know, he says, he will never frank for me? He declares he won't. Don't you, Mr Palmer?'

Mr Palmer took no notice of her.

'He cannot bear writing, you know,' she continued – 'he says it is quite shocking.'

'No;' said he, 'I never said any thing so irrational. Don't palm all your abuses of language upon me.'

'There now; you see how droll he is. This is always the way with him! Sometimes he won't speak to me for half a day together, and then he comes out with something so droll – all about any thing in the world.'

She surprised Elinor very much as they returned into the drawing-room by asking her whether she did not like Mr Palmer excessively.

'Certainly;' said Elinor, 'he seems very agreeable.'

'Well – I am so glad you do. I thought you would, he is so pleasant; and Mr Palmer is excessively pleased with you and your sisters I can tell you, and you can't think how disappointed he will be if you don't come to Cleveland – I can't imagine why you should object to it.'

Elinor was again obliged to decline her invitation; and by changing the subject, put a stop to her entreaties. She thought it probable that as they lived in the same county, Mrs Palmer might be able to give some more particular account of Willoughby's general character, than could be gathered from the Middletons' partial acquaintance with him; and she was eager to gain from any one, such a confirmation of his merits as might remove the possibility of fear for Marianne. She began by inquiring if they saw much of Mr Willoughby at Cleveland, and whether they were intimately acquainted with him.

'Oh! dear, yes; I know him extremely well,' replied Mrs Palmer – 'Not that I ever spoke to him indeed; but I have seen him for ever in town. Somehow or other I never happened to be staying at Barton while he was at Allenham. Mama saw him here once before; – but I was with my uncle at Weymouth. However, I dare say we should have seen a great deal of him in Somersetshire, if it had not happened very unluckily that we should never have been in the country together. He is very little at Combe, I believe; but if he were ever so much there, I do not think Mr Palmer would visit him, for he is in the opposition you know, and besides it is such a way off. I know why you inquire about him, very well; your sister is to marry him. I am monstrous glad of it, for then I shall have her for a neighbour you know.'

'Upon my word,' replied Elinor, 'you know much more of the matter than I do, if you have any reason to expect such a match.'

'Don't pretend to deny it, because you know it is what every body talks of. I assure you I heard of it in my way through town.'

'My dear Mrs Palmer!'

'Upon my honour I did – I met Colonel Brandon Monday morning in Bond-street, just before we left town, and he told me of it directly.'

'You surprise me very much. Colonel Brandon tell you of it! Surely you must be mistaken. To give such intelligence to a person who could not be interested in it, even if it were true, is not what I should expect Colonel Brandon to do.'

'But I do assure you it was so, for all that, and I will tell you how it happened. When we met him, he turned back and walked with us; and so we began talking of my brother and sister, and one thing and another, and I said to him, "So, Colonel, there is a new family come to Barton cottage, I hear, and mama sends me word they are very pretty, and that one of them is going to be married to Mr Willoughby of Combe Magna. Is it true, pray? for of course you must know, as you have been in Devonshire so lately.'

'And what did the Colonel say?'

'Oh! – he did not say much; but he looked as if he knew it to be true, so from that moment I set it down as certain. It will be quite delightful, I declare! When is it to take place?'

'Mr Brandon was very well I hope.'

'Oh! yes, quite well; and so full of your praises, he did nothing but say fine things of you.'

'I am flattered by his commendation. He seems an excellent man; and I think him uncommonly pleasing.'

'So do I. – He is such a charming man, that it is quite a pity he should be so grave and so dull. Mama says *he* was in love with your sister too. – I assure you it was a great compliment if he was, for he hardly ever falls in love with any body.'

'Is Mr Willoughby much known in your part of Somersetshire?' said Elinor.

'Oh! yes, extremely well; that is, I do not believe many people are acquainted with him, because Combe Magna is so far off; but they all think him extremely agreeable I assure you. Nobody is more liked than Mr Willoughby wherever he goes, and so you may tell your sister. She is a monstrous lucky girl to get him, upon my honour; not but that he is much more lucky in getting her, because she is so very handsome and agreeable, that nothing can be good enough for her. However I don't think her hardly at all handsomer than you, I assure you; for I think you both excessively pretty, and so does Mr Palmer too I am sure, though we could not get him to own it last night.'

Mrs Palmer's information respecting Willoughby was not very material; but any testimony in his favour, however small, was pleasing to her.

'I am so glad we are got acquainted at last,' continued Charlotte. – 'And now I hope we shall always be great friends. You can't think how much I longed to see you! It is so delightful that you should live at the cottage! Nothing can be like it to be sure! And I am so glad your sister is going to be well married! I hope you will be a great deal at Combe Magna. It is a sweet place by all accounts.'

'You have been long acquainted with Colonel Brandon, have not you?'

'Yes, a great while; ever since my sister married. – He was a particular friend of Sir John's. I believe,' she added in a low voice, 'he would have been very glad to have had me, if he could. Sir John and Lady Middleton wished it very much. But mama did not think the match good enough for me, otherwise Sir John would have mentioned it to the Colonel, and we should have been married immediately.'

'Did not Colonel Brandon know of Sir John's proposal to your mother before it was made? Had he never owned his affection to yourself?'

'Oh! no; but if mama had not objected to it, I dare say he would have liked it of all things. He had not seen me then above twice, for it was before I left school. However I am much happier as I am. Mr Palmer is just the kind of man I like.'

CHAPTER TWENTY-ONE

The Palmers returned to Cleveland the next day, and the two families at Barton were again left to entertain each other. But this did not last long; Elinor had hardly got their last visitors out of her head, had hardly done wondering at Charlotte's being so happy without a cause, at Mr Palmer's acting so simply, with good abilities, and at the strange unsuitableness which often existed between husband and wife, before Sir John's and Mrs Jennings's active zeal in the cause of society, procured her some other new acquaintance to see and observe.

In a morning's excursion to Exeter, they had met with two young ladies, whom Mrs Jennings had the satisfaction of discovering to be her relations, and this was enough for Sir John to invite them directly to the park, as soon as their present engagements at Exeter were over. Their engagements at Exeter instantly gave way before such an invitation, and Lady Middleton was thrown into no little alarm on the return of Sir John, by hearing that she was very soon to receive a visit from two girls whom she had never seen in her life, and of whose elegance, – whose tolerable gentility even, she could have no proof; for the assurances of her husband and mother on that subject went for nothing at all. Their being her relations too made it so much the worse; and Mrs Jennings's attempts at consolation were therefore unfortunately founded, when she advised her daughter not to care about their being so fashionable; because they were all cousins and must put up with one another. As it was impossible however now to prevent their coming, Lady Middleton resigned herself to the idea of it, with all the philosophy of a well-bred woman, contenting herself with merely giving her husband a gentle reprimand on the subject five or six times every day.

The young ladies arrived, their appearance was by no means ungenteel or unfashionable. Their dress was very smart, their manners very civil, they were delighted with the house, and in raptures with the furniture, and they happened to be so doatingly fond of children that Lady Middleton's good opinion was engaged in their favour before they had been an hour at the Park. She declared them to be very agreeable girls indeed, which for her ladyship was enthusiastic admiration. Sir John's confidence in his own judgment rose with this animated praise, and he set off directly for the cottage to tell the Miss Dashwoods of the Miss Steeles' arrival, and to assure them of their being the sweetest girls in the world. From such commendation as this, however, there was not much to be learned; Elinor well knew that the sweetest girls in the world were to be met with in every part of England, under every possible variation of form, face, temper and understanding. Sir John wanted the whole family to walk to the Park directly and look at his guests. Benevolent, philanthropic man! It was painful to him even to keep a third cousin to himself.

'Do come now,' said he – 'pray come – you must come – I declare you shall come – You can't think how you will like them. Lucy is monstrous pretty, and so good humoured and agreeable! The children are all hanging about her already, as if she was an old acquaintance. And they both long to see you of all things, for they have heard at Exeter that you are the most beautiful creatures in the world; and I have told them it is all very true, and a great deal more. You will be delighted with them I am sure. They have brought the whole coach full of playthings for the children. How can you be so cross as not to come? Why they are your cousins, you know, after a fashion. *You* are my cousins, and they are my wife's, so you must be related.'

But Sir John could not prevail. He could only obtain a promise of their calling at the Park within a day or two, and then left them in amazement at their indifference, to walk home and boast anew of their attractions to the Miss Steeles, as he had been already boasting of the Miss Steeles to them.

When their promised visit to the Park and consequent introduction to these young ladies took place, they found in the appearance of the eldest, who was nearly thirty, with a very plain and not a sensible face, nothing to admire; but in the other, who was not more than two or three and twenty, they acknowledged considerable beauty; her features were pretty, and she had a sharp quick eye, and a smartness of air, which though it did not give actual elegance or grace, gave distinction to her person. – Their manners were particularly civil, and Elinor soon allowed them credit for some kind of sense, when she saw with what constant and judicious attentions they were making themselves agreeable to Lady Middleton. With her children they were in continual raptures, extolling their beauty, courting their notice, and humouring all their whims; and such of their time as could be spared from the importunate demands which this politeness made on it, was spent in admiration of whatever her ladyship was doing, if she happened to be doing any thing, or in taking patterns of some elegant new dress, in which her appearance the day before had thrown them into unceasing delight. Fortunately for those who pay their court through such foibles, a fond mother, though, in pursuit of praise for her children, the most rapacious of human beings, is likewise the most credulous; her demands are exorbitant; but she will swallow any thing; and the excessive affection and endurance of the Miss Steeles towards her offspring, were viewed therefore by Lady Middleton without the smallest surprise or distrust. She saw with maternal complacency all the impertinent incroachments and mischievous tricks to which her cousins submitted. She saw their sashes untied, their hair pulled about their ears, their work-bags searched, and their knives and scissors stolen away, and felt no doubt of its being a reciprocal enjoyment. It

Mischievous tricks.

suggested no other surprise than that Elinor and Marianne should sit so composedly by, without claiming a share in what was passing.

'John is in such spirits today!' said she, on his taking Miss Steele's pocket handkerchief, and throwing it out of window – 'He is full of monkey tricks.'

And soon afterwards, on the second boy's violently pinching one of the same lady's fingers, she fondly observed, 'How playful William is!'

'And here is my sweet little Annamaria,' she added, tenderly caressing a little girl of three years old, who had not made a noise for the last two minutes; 'And she is always so gentle and quiet – Never was there such a quiet little thing!'

But unfortunately in bestowing these embraces, a pin in her ladyship's head dress slightly scratching the child's neck, produced from this pattern of gentleness, such violent screams, as could hardly be outdone by any creature professedly noisy. The mother's consternation was excessive; but it could not surpass the alarm of the Miss Steeles, and every thing was done by all three, in so critical an emergency, which affection could suggest as likely to assuage the agonies of the little sufferer. She was seated in her mother's lap, covered with kisses, her wound bathed with lavender-water, by one of the Miss Steeles, who was on her knees to attend her, and her mouth stuffed with sugar plums by the other. With such a reward for her tears, the child was too wise to cease crying. She still screamed and sobbed lustily, kicked her two brothers for offering to touch her, and all their united soothings were ineffectual till Lady Middleton luckily remembering that in a sense of similar distress last week, some apricot marmalade had been successfully applied for a bruised temple, the same remedy was eagerly proposed for this unfortunate scratch, and a slight intermission of screams in the young lady on hearing it, gave them reason to hope that it would not be rejected. – She was carried out of the room therefore in her mother's arms, in quest of this medicine, and as the two boys chose to follow, though earnestly entreated by their mother to stay behind, the four young ladies were left in a quietness which the room had not known for many hours.

'Poor little creature!' said Miss Steele, as soon as they were gone. 'It might have been a very sad accident.'

'Yet I hardly know how,' cried Marianne, 'unless it had been under totally different circumstances. But this is the usual way of heightening alarm, where there is nothing to be alarmed at in reality.'

'What a sweet woman Lady Middleton is!' said Lucy Steele.

Marianne was silent; it was impossible for her to say what she did not feel, however trivial the occasion, and upon Elinor therefore the whole task of telling lies when politeness required it, always fell. She did her best when thus called on, by speaking of Lady Middleton with more warmth than she felt, though with far less than Miss Lucy.

'And Sir John too,' cried the elder sister, 'what a charming man he is!'

Here too, Miss Dashwood's commendation, being only simple and just, came in without any eclat. She merely observed that he was perfectly good humoured and friendly.

'And what a charming little family they have! I never saw such fine children in my life – I declare I quite doat upon them already, and indeed I am always distractedly fond of children.'

'I should guess so,' said Elinor with a smile, 'from what I have witnessed this morning.'

'I have a notion,' said Lucy, 'you think the little Middletons rather too much indulged; perhaps they may be the outside of enough; but it is so natural in Lady Middleton; and for my part, I love to see children full of life and spirits; I cannot bear them if they are tame and quiet.'

'I confess,' replied Elinor, 'that while I am at Barton Park, I never think of tame and quiet children with any abhorrence.'

A short pause succeeded this speech, which was first broken by Miss Steele, who seemed very much disposed for conversation, and who now said rather abruptly, 'And how do you like Devonshire, Miss Dashwood? I suppose you were very sorry to leave Sussex.'

In some surprise at the familiarity of this question, or at least of the manner in which it was spoken, Elinor replied that she was.

'Norland is a prodigious beautiful place, is not it?' added Miss Steele.

'We have heard Sir John admire it excessively,' said Lucy, who seemed to think some apology necessary for the freedom of her sister.

'I think every one *must* admire it,' replied Elinor, 'who ever saw the place; though it is not to be supposed that any one can estimate its beauties as we do.'

'And had you a great many smart beaux there? I suppose you have not so many in this part of the world; for my part, I think they are a vast addition always.'

'But why should you think,' said Lucy, looking ashamed of her sister, 'that there are not as many genteel young men in Devonshire as Sussex?'

'Nay, my dear, I'm sure I don't pretend to say that there an't. I'm sure there's a vast many smart beaux in Exeter; but you know, how could I tell what smart beaux there might be about Norland; and I was only afraid the Miss Dashwoods might find it dull at Barton, if they had not so many as they used to have. But perhaps you young ladies may not care about the beaux, and had as lief be without them as with them. For my part, I think they are vastly agreeable, provided they dress smart and behave civil. But I can't bear to see them dirty and nasty. Now there's Mr Rose at Exeter, a prodigious smart young man, quite a beau, clerk to Mr Simpson you know, and yet if you do but meet him of a morning, he is not fit to be seen. – I suppose your brother was quite a beau, Miss Dashwood, before he married, as he was so rich?'

'Upon my word,' replied Elinor, 'I cannot tell you, for I do not perfectly comprehend the meaning of the word. But this I can say, that if he ever was a beau before he married, he is one still, for there is not the smallest alteration in him.'

'Oh! dear! one never thinks of married mens' being beaux – they have something else to do.'

'Lord! Anne,' cried her sister, 'you can talk of nothing but beaux; – you will make Miss Dashwood believe you think of nothing else.' And then to turn the discourse, she began admiring the house and the furniture.

This specimen of the Miss Steeles was enough. The vulgar freedom and folly of the eldest left her no recommendation, and as Elinor was not blinded by the beauty, or the shrewd look of the youngest, to her want of real elegance and artlessness, she left the house without any wish of knowing them better.

Not so, the Miss Steeles. – They came from Exeter, well provided with admiration for the use of Sir John Middleton, his family, and all his relations, and no niggardly proportion was now dealt out to his fair cousins, whom they declared to be the most beautiful, elegant, accomplished, and agreeable girls they had ever beheld, and with whom they were particularly anxious to be better acquainted. – And to be better acquainted therefore, Elinor soon found was their inevitable lot, for as Sir John was entirely on the side of the Miss Steeles, their party would be too strong for opposition, and that kind of intimacy must be submitted to, which consists of sitting an hour or two together in the same room almost every day. Sir John could do no more; but he did not know that any more was required; to be together was, in his opinion, to be intimate, and while his continual schemes for their meeting were effectual, he had not a doubt of their being established friends.

To do him justice, he did every thing in his power to promote their unreserve, by making the Miss Steeles acquainted with whatever he knew or supposed of his cousins' situations in the most delicate particulars, – and Elinor had not seen them more than twice, before the eldest of them wished her joy on her sister's having been so lucky as to make a conquest of a very smart beau since she came to Barton.

' 'Twill be a fine thing to have her married so young to be sure,' said she, 'and I hear he is quite a beau, and prodigious handsome. And I hope you may have as good luck yourself soon, – but perhaps you may have a friend in the corner already.'

Elinor could not suppose that Sir John would be more nice in proclaiming his suspicions of her regard for Edward, than he had been with respect to Marianne; indeed it was rather his favourite joke of the two, as being somewhat newer and more conjectural; and since Edward's visit, they had never dined together, without his drinking to her best affections with so much significancy and so many nods and winks, as to excite general attention. The letter F— had been likewise invariably brought forward, and found productive of such countless jokes, that its character as the wittiest letter in the alphabet had been long established with Elinor.

The Miss Steeles, as she expected, had now all the benefit of these

Drinking to her best affections.

jokes, and in the eldest of them they raised a curiosity to know the name of the gentleman alluded to, which, though often impertinently expressed, was perfectly of a piece with her general inquisitiveness into the concerns of their family. But Sir John did not sport long with the curiosity which he delighted to raise, for he had at least as much pleasure in telling the name, as Miss Steele had in hearing it.

'His name is Ferrars,' said he, in a very audible whisper; 'but pray do not tell it, for it's a great secret.'

'Ferrars!' repeated Miss Steele; 'Mr Ferrars is the happy man, is he? What! your sister-in-law's brother, Miss Dashwood? a very agreeable young man to be sure; I know him very well.'

'How can you say so, Anne?' cried Lucy, who generally made an amendment to all her sister's assertions. 'Though we have seen him once or twice at my uncle's, it is rather too much to pretend to know him very well.'

Elinor heard all this with attention and surprise. 'And who was this uncle? Where did he live? How came they acquainted?' She wished very much to have the subject continued, though she did not chuse to join in it herself; but nothing more of it was said, and for the first time in her life, she thought Mrs Jennings deficient either in curiosity after petty information, or in a disposition to communicate it. The manner in which Miss Steele had spoken of Edward, increased her curiosity; for it struck her as being rather ill-natured and suggested the suspicion of that lady's knowing, or fancying herself to know something to his disadvantage. – But her curiosity was unavailing, for no farther notice was taken of Mr Ferrars's name by Miss Steele when alluded to, or even openly mentioned by Sir John.

CHAPTER TWENTY-TWO

MARIANNE, WHO HAD never much toleration for any thing like impertinence, vulgarity, inferiority of parts, or even difference of taste from herself, was at this time particularly ill-disposed, from the state of her spirits, to be pleased with the Miss Steeles, or to encourage their advances; and to the invariable coldness of her behaviour towards them, which checked every endeavour at intimacy on their side, Elinor principally attributed that preference of herself which soon became evident in the manners of both, but especially of Lucy, who missed no opportunity of engaging her in conversation, or of striving to improve their acquaintance by an easy and frank communication of her sentiments.

Lucy was naturally clever; her remarks were often just and amusing; and as a companion for half an hour Elinor frequently found her agreeable; but her powers had received no aid from education, she was ignorant and illiterate, and her deficiency of all mental improvement, her want of information in the most common particulars, could not be concealed from Miss Dashwood, in spite of her constant endeavour to appear to advantage. Elinor saw, and pitied her for, the neglect of abilities which education might have rendered so respectable; but she saw, with less tenderness of feeling, the thorough want of delicacy, of rectitude, and integrity of mind, which her attentions, her assiduities, her flatteries at the Park betrayed; and she could have no lasting satisfaction in the company of a person who joined insincerity with ignorance; whose want of instruction prevented their meeting in conversation on terms of equality, and whose conduct towards others, made every shew of attention and deference towards herself perfectly valueless.

'You will think my question an odd one, I dare say,' said Lucy to her one day as they were walking together from the park to the cottage – 'pray, are you personally acquainted with your sister-in-law's mother, Mrs Ferrars?'

Elinor *did* think the question a very odd one, and her countenance expressed it, as she answered that she had never seen Mrs Ferrars.

'Indeed!' replied Lucy; 'I wonder at that, for I thought you must have seen her at Norland sometimes. Then perhaps you cannot tell me what sort of a woman she is?'

'No;' returned Elinor, cautious of giving her real opinion of Edward's mother, and not very desirous of satisfying, what seemed impertinent curiosity – 'I know nothing of her.'

'I am sure you think me very strange, for inquiring about her in such a way;' said Lucy, eyeing Elinor attentively as she spoke; 'but perhaps there may be reasons – I wish I might venture; but however I hope you will do me the justice of believing that I do not mean to be impertinent.'

Elinor made her a civil reply, and they walked on for a few minutes in silence. It was broken by Lucy, who renewed the subject again by saying with some hesitation,

'I cannot bear to have you think me impertinently curious. I am sure I would rather do any thing in the world than be thought so by a person whose good opinion is so well worth having as yours. And I am sure I should not have the smallest fear of trusting *you*;

Amiably bashful.

indeed I should be very glad of your advice how to manage in such an uncomfortable situation as I am; but however there is no occasion to trouble *you*. I am sorry you do not happen to know Mrs Ferrars.'

'I am sorry I do *not*,' said Elinor, in great astonishment, 'if it could be of any use to *you* to know my opinion of her. But really, I never understood that you were at all connected with that family, and therefore I am a little surprised, I confess, at so serious an inquiry into her character.'

'I dare say you are, and I am sure I do not at all wonder at it. But if I dared tell you all, you would not be so much surprised. Mrs Ferrars is certainly nothing to me at present, – but the time *may* come – how soon it will come must depend upon herself – when we may be very intimately connected.'

She looked down as she said this, amiably bashful, with only one side glance at her companion to observe its effect on her.

'Good heavens!' cried Elinor, 'what do you mean? Are you acquainted with Mr Robert Ferrars? Can you be?' And she did not feel much delighted with the idea of such a sister-in-law.

'No;' replied Lucy, 'not to Mr *Robert* Ferrars – I never saw him in my life; but,' fixing her eyes upon Elinor, 'to his elder brother.'

What felt Elinor at that moment? Astonishment, that would have been as painful as it was strong, had not an immediate disbelief of the assertion attended it. She turned towards Lucy in silent amazement, unable to divine the reason or object of such a declaration, and though her complexion varied, she stood firm in incredulity and felt in no danger of an hysterical fit, or a swoon.

'You may well be surprised,' continued Lucy; 'for to be sure you could have had no idea of it before; for I dare say he never dropped the smallest hint of it to you or any of your family; because it was always meant to be a great secret, and I am sure has been faithfully kept so by me to this hour. Not a soul of all my relations know of it but Anne and I never should have mentioned it to you, if I had not felt the greatest dependance in the world upon your secrecy; and I really thought my behaviour in asking so many questions about Mrs Ferrars, must seem so odd, that it ought to be explained. And I do not think Mr Ferrars can be displeased, when he knows I have trusted you, because I know he had the highest opinion in the world of all your family, and looks upon yourself and the other Miss Dashwoods, quite as his own sisters.' – She paused.

Elinor for a few moments remained silent. Her astonishment at what she heard was at first too great for words; but at length forcing herself to speak, and to speak cautiously, she said with a calmness of manner, which tolerably well concealed her surprise and solicitude – 'May I ask if your engagement is of long standing?'

'We have been engaged these four years.'

'Four years!'

'Yes.'

Elinor, though greatly shocked, still felt unable to believe it.

'I did not know,' said she, 'that you were even acquainted till the other day.'

'Our acquaintance, however, is of many years date. He was under my uncle's care, you know, a considerable while.'

'Your uncle!'

'Yes; Mr Pratt. Did you never hear him talk of Mr Pratt?'

'I think I have,' replied Elinor, with an exertion of spirits, which increased with her increase of emotion.

'He was four years with my uncle, who lives at Longstaple, near Plymouth. It was there our acquaintance begun, for my sister and me was often staying with my uncle, and it was there our engagement was formed, though not till a year after he had quitted as a pupil; but he was almost always with us afterwards. I was very unwilling to enter into it, as you may imagine, without the knowledge and approbation of his mother; but I was too young and loved him too well to be so prudent as I ought to have been. – Though you do not know him so well as me, Miss Dashwood, you must have seen enough of him to be sensible he is very capable of making a woman sincerely attached to him.'

'Certainly,' answered Elinor, without knowing what she said; but after a moment's reflection, she added with revived security of Edward's honour and love, and her companion's falsehood – 'Engaged to Mr Edward Ferrars! – I confess myself so totally surprised at what you tell me, that really – I beg your pardon; but surely there must be some mistake of person or name. We cannot mean the same Mr Ferrars.'

'We can mean no other,' cried Lucy smiling. 'Mr Edward Ferrars, the eldest son of Mrs Ferrars of Park-street, and brother of your sister-in-law, Mrs John Dashwood, is the person I mean; you must allow that *I* am not likely to be deceived, as to the name of the man on who all my happiness depends.'

'It is strange,' replied Elinor in a most painful perplexity, 'that I should never have heard him even mention your name.'

'No; considering our situation, it was not strange. Our first care has been to keep the matter secret. – You knew nothing of me, or my family, and therefore there could be no *occasion* for ever mentioning my name to you, and as he was always particularly afraid of his sister's suspecting any thing, *that* was reason enough for his not mentioning it.'

She was silent. – Elinor's security sunk; but her self-command did not sink with it.

'Four years you have been engaged,' said she with a firm voice.

'Yes; and heaven knows how much longer we may have to wait. Poor Edward! It puts him quite out of heart.' Then taking a small miniature from her pocket, she added, 'To prevent the possibility of mistake, be so good as to look at this face. It does not do him justice to be sure, but yet I think you cannot be deceived as to the person it was drew for. – I have had it above these three years.'

She put it into her hands as she spoke, and when Elinor saw the painting, whatever other doubts her fear of a too hasty decision, or her wish of detecting falsehood might suffer to linger in her mind, she could have none of its being Edward's face. She returned it almost instantly, acknowledging the likeness.

'I have never been able,' continued Lucy, 'to give him my picture in return, which I am very much vexed at, for he has been always so anxious to get it! But I am determined to set for it the very first opportunity.'

'You are quite in the right;' replied Elinor calmly. They then proceeded a few paces in silence. Lucy spoke first.

'I am sure,' said she, 'I have no doubt in the world of your faithfully keeping this secret, because you must know of what importance it is to us, not to have it reach his mother; for she would never approve of it, I dare say. I shall have no fortune, and I fancy she is an exceeding proud woman.'

'I certainly did not seek your confidence,' said Elinor; 'but you do me nor more than justice in imagining that I may be depended on. Your secret is safe with me; but pardon me if I express some surprise at so unnecessary a communication. You must at least have felt that my being acquainted with it could not add to its safety.'

As she said this, she looked earnestly at Lucy, hoping to discover something in her countenance; perhaps the falsehood of the greatest part of what she had been saying; but Lucy's countenance suffered no change.

'I was afraid you would think I was taking a great liberty with you,' said she, 'in telling you all this. I have not known you long to be sure, personally at least, but I have known you and all your family by description a great while; and as soon as I saw you, I felt almost as if you was an old acquaintance. Besides in the present case, I really thought some explanation was due to you after my making such particular inquiries about Edward's mother; and I am so unfortunate, that I have not a creature whose advice I can ask. Anne is the only person that knows of it, and she has no judgment at all; indeed she does me a great deal more harm than good, for I am in constant fear of her betraying me. She does not know how to hold her tongue, as you must perceive, and I am sure I was in the greatest fright in the world t'other day, when Edward's name was mentioned by Sir John, lest she should out with it all. You can't think how much I go through in my mind from it altogether. I only wonder that I am alive after what I have suffered for Edward's sake these last four years. Every thing in such suspense and uncertainty; and seeing him so seldom – we can hardly meet above twice a-year. I am sure I wonder my heart is not quite broke.'

Here she took out her handkerchief; but Elinor did not feel very compassionate.

'Sometimes,' continued Lucy, after wiping her eyes, 'I think whether it would not be better for us both, to break off the matter entirely.' As she said this, she looked directly at her companion. 'But then at other times I have not resolution enough for it. – I cannot bear the thoughts of making him so miserable, as I know the very mention of such a thing would do. And on my own account too – so dear as he is to me – I don't think I could be equal to it. What would you advise me to do in such a case, Miss Dashwood? What would you do yourself?'

'Pardon me,' replied Elinor, startled by the question; 'but I can give you no advice under such circumstances. Your own judgment must direct you.'

'To be sure,' continued Lucy, after a few minutes silence on both sides, 'his mother must provide for him sometime or other; but poor Edward is *so* cast down about it! Did not you think him dreadful low-spirited when he was at Barton? He was so miserable when he left us at Longstaple, to go to you, that I was afraid you would think him quite ill.'

'Did he come from your uncle's then, when he visited us?'

'Oh! yes; he had been staying a fortnight with us. Did you think he came directly from town?'

'No,' replied Elinor, most feelingly sensible of every fresh circumstance in favour of Lucy's veracity; 'I remember he told us, that he had been staying a fortnight with some friends near Plymouth.' She remembered too, her own surprise at the time, at his mentioning nothing farther of those friends, at his total silence with respect even to their names.

'Did not you think him sadly out of spirits?' repeated Lucy.

'We did indeed, particularly so when he first arrived.'

'I begged him to exert himself for fear you should suspect what was the matter; but it made him so melancholy, not being able to stay more than a fortnight with us, and seeing me so much affected. – Poor fellow! – I am afraid it is just the same with him now; for he writes in wretched spirits. I heard from him just before I left Exeter;' taking a letter from her pocket and carelessly showing the direction to Elinor. 'You know his hand, I dare say, a charming one it is; but that is not written so well as usual. – He was tired, I dare say, for he had just filled the sheet to me as full as possible.'

Elinor saw that it *was* his hand, and she could doubt no longer. The picture, she had allowed herself to believe, might have been accidentally obtained; it might not have been Edward's gift; but a correspondence between them by letter, could subsist only under a positive engagement, could be authorized by nothing else; for a few moments, she was almost overcome – her heart sunk within her, and she could hardly stand; but exertion was indispensably necessary, and she struggled so resolutely against the oppression of her feelings, that her success was speedy, and for the time complete.

'Writing to each other,' said Lucy, returning the letter into her pocket, 'is the only comfort we have in such long separations. Yes, *I* have one other comfort in his picture; but poor Edward has not even *that*. If he had but my picture, he says he should be easy. I gave him a lock of my hair set in a ring when he was at Longstaple last, and that was some comfort to him, he said, but not equal to a picture. Perhaps you might notice the ring when you saw him?'

'I did,' said Elinor, with a composure of voice, under which was concealed an emotion and distress beyond any thing she had ever felt before. She was mortified, shocked, confounded.

Fortunately for her, they had now reached the cottage, and the conversation could be continued no farther. After sitting with them a few minutes, the Miss Steeles returned to the Park, and Elinor was then at liberty to think and be wretched.

CHAPTER TWENTY-THREE

HOWEVER SMALL ELINOR'S general dependance on Lucy's veracity might be, it was impossible for her on serious reflection to suspect it in the present case, where no temptation could be answerable to the folly of inventing a falsehood of such a description. What Lucy had asserted to be true, therefore, Elinor could not, dared not longer doubt; supported as it was too on every side by such probabilities and proofs, and contradicted by nothing but her own wishes. Their opportunity of acquaintance in the house of Mr Pratt was a foundation for the rest, at once indisputable and alarming; and Edward's visit near Plymouth, his melancholy state of mind, his dissatisfaction at his own prospects, his uncertain behaviour towards herself, the intimate knowledge of the Miss Steeles as to Norland and their family connections, which had often surprised her, the picture, the letter, the ring, formed altogether such a body of evidence, as overcame every fear of condemning him unfairly, and established as a fact, which no partiality could set aside, his ill-treatment of herself. – Her resentment of such behaviour, her indignation at having been its dupe, for a short time made her feel only for herself; but other ideas, other considerations soon arose. Had Edward been intentionally deceiving her? Had he feigned a regard for her which he did not feel? Was his engagement to Lucy, an engagement of the heart? No; whatever it might once have been, she could not believe it such at present. His affection was all her own. She could not be deceived in that. Her mother, sisters, Fanny, all had been conscious of his regard for her at Norland; it was not an illusion of her own vanity. He certainly loved her. What a softener of the heart was this persuasion! How much could it not tempt her to forgive! He had been blameable, highly blameable, in remaining at Norland after he first felt her influence over him to be more than it ought to be. In fact, he could not be defended; but if he had injured her, how much more had he injured himself; if her case were pitiable, his was hopeless. His imprudence had made her miserable for a while; but it seemed to have deprived himself of all chance of ever being otherwise. She might in time regain tranquillity, but *he*, what had he to look forward to? Could he ever be tolerably happy with Lucy Steele; could he, were his affection for herself out of the question, with is integrity, his delicacy, and well-informed mind, be satisfied with a wife like her – illiterate, artful, and selfish?

The youthful infatuation of nineteen would naturally blind him to everything but her beauty and good nature; but the four succeeding years – years, which if rationally spent, give such improvement ot the understanding, must have opened his eyes to her defects of education, while the same period of time, spent on her side in inferior society and more frivolous pursuits, had perhaps robbed her of that simplicity, which might once have given an interesting character to her beauty.

If in the supposition of his seeking to marry herself, his difficulties from his mother had seemed great, how much greater were they now likely to be, when the object of his engagement was undoubtedly inferior in connections, and probably inferior in fortune to herself. These difficulties, indeed, with an heart so alienated from Lucy, might not press very hard upon his patience; but melancholy was the state of the person, by whom the expectation of family opposition and unkindness, could be felt as a relief!

As these considerations occurred to her in painful succession, she wept for him, more than for herself. Supported by the conviction of having done nothing to merit her present unhappiness, and consoled by the belief that Edward had done nothing to forfeit her esteem, she thought she could even now, under the first smart of the heavy blow, command herself enough to guard every suspicion of the truth from her mother and sisters. And so well was she able to answer her own expectations, that when she joined them at dinner only two hours after she had first suffered the extinction of all her dearest hopes, no one would have supposed from the appearance of the sisters, that Elinor was mourning in secret over obstacles which must divide her for ever from the object of her love, and that Marianne was internally dwelling on the perfections of a man, of whose whole heart she felt thoroughly possessed, and whom she expected to see in every carriage which drove near their house.

The necessity of concealing from her mother and Marianne, what had been entrusted in confidence to herself, though it obliged her to unceasing exertion, was no aggravation of Elinor's distress. On the contrary it was a relief to her, to be spared the communication of what would give such affliction to them, and to be saved likewise from hearing that condemnation of Edward, which would probably flow from the excess of their partial affection for herself, and which was more than she felt equal to support.

From their counsel, or their conversation she knew she could receive no assistance, their tenderness and sorrow must add to her distress, while her self-command would neither receive encouragement from their example nor from their praise. She was stronger alone, and her own good sense so well supported her, that her firmness was as unshaken, her appearance of cheerfulness as invariable, as with regrets so poignant and so fresh, it was possible for them to be.

Much as she had suffered from her first conversation with Lucy on the subject, she soon felt an earnest wish of renewing it; and this for more reasons than one. She wanted to hear many particulars of their engagement repeated again, she wanted more clearly to understand what Lucy really felt for Edward, whether there were any sincerity in her declaration of tender regard for him, and she particularly wanted to convince Lucy, by her readiness to enter on the matter again, and her calmness in conversing on it, that she was no otherwise interested in it than as a friend, which she very much feared her involuntary agitation, in their morning discourse, must have left at least doubtful. That Lucy was disposed to be jealous of her, appeared very probable; it was plain that Edward had always spoken highly in her praise, not merely from Lucy's assertion, but from her venturing to trust her on so short a personal acquaintance, with a secret, so confessedly and evidently important. And even Sir John's joking intelligence must have had some weight. But indeed, while Elinor remained so well assured within herself of being really beloved by Edward, it required no other consideration of probabilities to make it natural that Lucy should be jealous; and that she was so, her very confidence was a proof. What other reason for the disclosure of the affair could there be, but that Elinor might be informed by it of Lucy's superior claims on Edward, and be taught to avoid him in future? She had little difficulty in understanding thus much of her rival's intentions, and while she was firmly resolved to act by her as every principle of honour and honesty directed, to combat her own affection for Edward and to see him as little as possible; she could not deny herself the comfort of endeavouring to convince Lucy that her heart was unwounded. And as she could now have nothing more painful to hear on the subject than had already been told, she did not mistrust her own ability of going through a repetition of particulars with composure.

But it was not immediately that an opportunity of doing so could be commanded, though Lucy was as well disposed as herself to take advantage of any that occurred; for the weather was not often fine enough to allow of their joining in a walk, where they might most easily separate themselves from the others; and though they met at least every other evening either at the park or cottage, and chiefly at the former, they could not be supposed to meet for the sake of conversation. Such a thought would never enter either Sir John or Lady Middleton's head, and therefore very little leisure was ever given for general chat, and none at all for particular discourse. They met for the sake of eating, drinking, and laughing together, playing at cards, or consequences, or any other game that was sufficiently noisy.

One or two meetings of this kind had taken place, without affording Elinor any chance of engaging Lucy in private, when Sir John called at the cottage one morning, to beg in the name of charity, that they would all dine with Lady Middleton that day, as he was obliged to attend the club at Exeter, and she would otherwise be quite alone, except her mother and the two Miss Steeles. Elinor, who foresaw a fairer opening for the point she had in view, in such a party as this was likely to be, more at liberty among themselves under the tranquil and well-bred direction of Lady Middleton than when her husband united them together in one noisy purpose, immediately accepted the invitation; Margaret, with her mother's permission, was equally compliant, and Marianne, though always unwilling to join any of their parties, was persuaded by her mother, who could not bear to have her seclude herself from any chance of amusement, to go likewise.

The young ladies went, and Lady Middleton was happily preserved from the frightful solitude which had threatened her. The insipidity of the meeting was exactly such as Elinor had expected; it produced not one novelty of thought or expression, and nothing could be less interesting than the whole of their discourse both in the dining parlour and the drawing room: to the latter, the children accompanied them, and while they remained there, she was too well convinced of the impossibility of engaging Lucy's attention to attempt it. They quitted it only with the removal of the tea-things. The card-table was then placed, and Elinor began to wonder at herself for having ever entertained a hope of finding time for conversation at the park. They all rose up in preparation for a round game.

'I am glad,' said Lady Middleton to Lucy, 'you are not going to finish poor little Annamaria's basket this evening; for I am sure it must hurt your eyes to work fillagree by candlelight. And we will make the dear little love some amends for her disappointment tomorrow, and then I hope she will not much mind it.'

This hint was enough, Lucy recollected herself instantly and replied, 'Indeed you are very much mistaken, Lady Middleton; I am only waiting to know whether you can make your party without me, or I should have been at my fillagree already. I would not disappoint the little angel for all the world, and if you want me at the card-table now, I am resolved to finish the basket after supper.'

'You are very good, I hope it won't hurt your eyes – will you ring the bell for some working candles? My poor little girl would be sadly disappointed, I know, if the basket was not finished tomorrow, for though I told her it certainly would not, I am sure she depends upon having it done.'

Lucy directly drew her work table near her and reseated herself with an alacrity and cheerfulness which seemed to infer that she could taste no greater delight than in making a fillagree basket for a spoilt child.

Lady Middleton proposed a rubber of Casino to the others. No one made any objection but Marianne, who, with her usual inattention to the forms of general civility, exclaimed, 'Your ladyship will have the goodness to excuse *me* – you know I detest cards. I shall go to the piano-forté; I have not touched it since it was tuned.' And without farther ceremony, she turned away and walked to the instrument.

Lady Middleton looked as if she thanked heaven that *she* had never made so rude a speech.

'Marianne can never keep long from that instrument you know, ma'am,' said Elinor, endeavouring to smooth away the offence; 'and I do not much wonder at it; for it is the very best toned piano-forté I ever heard.'

The remaining five were now to draw their cards.

'Perhaps,' continued Elinor, 'if I should happen to cut out, I may be of some use to Miss Lucy Steele, in rolling her papers for her; and there is so much still to be done to the basket, that it must be impossible I think for her labour singly, to finish it this evening. I should like the work exceedingly, if she would allow me a share in it.'

'Indeed I shall be very much obliged to you for your help,' cried Lucy, 'for I find there is more to be done to it than I thought there was; and it would be a shocking thing to disappoint dear Annamaria after all.'

'Oh! that would be terrible indeed,' said Miss Steele – 'Dear little soul, how I do love her!'

'You are very kind' said Lady Middleton to Elinor; 'and as you really like the work, perhaps you will be as well pleased not to cut in till another rubber, or will you take your chance now?'

Elinor joyfully profited by the first of these proposals, and thus by a little of that address, which Marianne could never condescend to practise, gained her own end, and pleased Lady Middleton at the same time. Lucy made room for her with ready attention, and the two fair rivals were thus seated side by side at the same table, and with the utmost harmony engaged in forwarding the same work. The piano-forté, at which Marianne, wrapt up in her own music and her own thoughts, had by this time forgotten that any body was in the room besides herself, was luckily so near them that Miss Dashwood now judged, she might safely, under the shelter of its noise, introduce the interesting subject, without any risk of being heard at the card-table.

CHAPTER TWENTY-FOUR

In a firm, though cautious tone, Elinor thus began.

'I should be undeserving of the confidence you have honoured me with, if I felt no desire for its continuance, or no farther curiosity on its subject. I will not apologize therefore for bringing it forward again.'

'Thank you,' cried Lucy warmly, 'for breaking the ice; you have set my heart at ease by it; for I was somehow or other afraid I had offended you by what I told you that Monday.'

'Offended me! How could you suppose so? Believe me,' and Elinor spoke it with the truest sincerity, 'nothing could be farther from my intention, than to give you such an idea. Could you have a motive for the trust, that was not honourable and flattering to me?'

'And yet I do assure you,' replied Lucy, her little sharp eyes full of meaning, 'there seemed to me to be a coldness and displeasure in your manner, that made me quite uncomfortable. I felt sure that you was angry with me; and have been quarrelling with myself ever since, for having took such a liberty as to trouble you with my affairs. But I am very glad to find it was only my own fancy, and that you do not really blame me. If you knew what a consolation it was to me to relieve my heart by speaking to you of what I am always thinking of every moment of my life, your compassion would make you overlook every thing else I am sure.'

'Indeed I can easily believe that it was a very great relief to you, to acknowledge your situation to me, and be assured that you shall never have reason to repent it. Your case is a very unfortunate one; you seem to me to be surrounded with difficulties, and you will have need of all your mutual affection to support you under them. Mr Ferrars, I believe, is entirely dependent on his mother.'

'He has only two thousand pounds of his own; it would be madness to marry upon that, though for my own part, I could give up every prospect of more without a sigh. I have been always used to a very small income, and could struggle with any poverty for him; but I love him too well to be the selfish means of robbing him, perhaps, of all that his mother might give him if he married to please her. We must wait, it may be for many years. With almost every other man in the world, it would be an alarming prospect; but Edward's affection and constancy nothing can deprive me of I know.'

'That conviction must be every thing to you; and he is undoubtedly supported by the same trust in yours. If the strength of your reciprocal attachment had failed, as between many people and under many circumstances it naturally would during a four years' engagement, your situation would have been pitiable indeed.'

Lucy here looked up; but Elinor was careful in guarding her countenance from every expression that could give her words a suspicious tendency.

'Edward's love for me,' said Lucy, 'has been pretty well put to the test, by our long, very long absence since we were first engaged, and it has stood the trial so well, that I should be unpardonable to doubt it now. I can safely say that he has never gave me one moment's alarm on that account from the first.'

Elinor hardly knew whether to smile or sigh at this assertion.

Lucy went on. 'I am rather of a jealous temper too by nature, and from our different situations in life, from his being so much more in the world than me, and our continual separation, I was enough inclined for suspicion, to have found out the truth in an instant, if there had been the slightest alteration in his behaviour to me when we met, or any lowness of spirits that I could not account for, or if he had talked more of one lady than another, or seemed in any respect less happy at Longstaple than he used to be. I do not mean to say that I am particularly observant or quick-sighted in general, but in such a case I am sure I could not be deceived.'

'All this,' thought Elinor, 'is very pretty; but it can impose upon neither of us.'

'But what,' said she after a short silence, 'are your views? or have you none but that of waiting for Mrs Ferrars' death, which is a melancholy and shocking extremity? – Is her son determined to submit to this, and to all the tediousness of the many years of suspense in which it may involve you, rather than run the risk of her displeasure for a while by owning the truth?'

'If we could be certain that it would be only for a while! But Mrs Ferrars is a very headstrong proud woman, and in her first fit of anger upon hearing it, would very likely secure every thing to Robert, and the idea of that, for Edward's sake, frightens away all my inclination for hasty measures.'

'And for your own sake too, or you are carrying your disinterestedness beyond reason.'

Lucy looked at Elinor again, and was silent.

'Do you know Mr Robert Ferrars?' asked Elinor.

'Not at all – I never saw him; but I fancy he is very unlike his brother – silly and a great coxcomb.'

'A great coxcomb!' repeated Miss Steele, whose ear had caught those words by a sudden pause in Marianne's music. – 'Oh! they are talking of their favourite beaux, I dare say.'

'No, sister,' cried Lucy, 'you are mistaken there, our favourite beaux are *not* great coxcombs.'

'I can answer for it that Miss Dashwood's is not,' said Mrs Jennings, laughing heartily; 'for he is one of the modestest, prettiest behaved young men I ever saw; but as for Lucy, she is such a sly little creature, there is no finding out who *she* likes.'

'Oh!' cried Miss Steele, looking significantly round at them, 'I dare say Lucy's beau is quite as modest and pretty as Miss Dashwood's.'

Elinor blushed in spite of herself. Lucy bit her lip, and looked angrily at her sister. A mutual silence took place for some time. Lucy first put an end to it by saying in a lower tone, though

Marianne was then giving them the powerful protection of a very magnificent concerto –

'I will honestly tell you of one scheme which has lately come into my head, for bringing matters to bear; indeed I am bound to let you into the secret, for you are a party concerned. I dare say you have seen enough of Edward to know that he would prefer the church to every other profession; now my plan is that he should take orders as soon as he can, and then through your interest, which I am sure you would be kind enough to use out of friendship for him, and I hope out of some regard to me, your brother might be persuaded to give him Norland living; which I understand is a very

'I can answer for it,' said Mrs Jennings.

good one, and the present incumbent not likely to live a great while. That would be enough for us to marry upon, and we might trust to time and chance for the rest.'

'I should be always happy,' replied Elinor, 'to shew any mark of my esteem and friendship for Mr Ferrars; but do not you perceive that my interest on such an occasion would be perfectly unnecessary? He is brother to Mrs John Dashwood – *that* must be recommendation enough to her husband.'

'But Mrs John Dashwood would not much approve of Edward's going into orders.'

'Then I rather suspect that my interest would do very little.'

They were again silent for many minutes. At length Lucy exclaimed with a deep sigh,

'I believe it would be the wisest way to put an end to the business at once by dissolving the engagement. We seem so beset with difficulties on every side, that though it would make us miserable for a time, we should be happier perhaps in the end. But you will not give me your advice, Miss Dashwood?'

'No;' answered Elinor, with a smile, which concealed very agitated feelings, 'on such a subject I certainly will not. You know very well that my opinion would have no weight with you, unless it were on the side of your wishes.'

'Indeed you wrong me,' replied Lucy with great solemnity; 'I know nobody of whose judgment I think so highly as I do of yours; and I do really believe, that if you was to say to me, "I advise you by all means to put an end to your engagement with Edward Ferrars, it will be more for the happiness of both of you," I should resolve upon doing it immediately.'

Elinor blushed for the insincerity of Edward's future wife, and replied, 'this compliment would effectually frighten me from giving any opinion on the subject had I formed one. It raises my influence much too high; the power of dividing two people so tenderly attached is too much for an indifferent person.'

' 'Tis because you are an indifferent person,' said Lucy, with some pique, and laying a particular stress on those words, 'that your judgment might justly have such weight with me. If you could be supposed to be biassed in any respect by your own feelings, your opinion would not be worth having.'

Elinor thought it wisest to make no answer to this, lest they might provoke each other to an unsuitable increase of ease and unreserve; and was even partly determined never to mention the subject again. Another pause therefore of many minutes' duration, succeeded this speech, and Lucy was still the first to end it.

'Shall you be in town this winter, Miss Dashwood?' said she with all her accustomary complacency.

'Certainly not.'

'I am sorry for that,' returned the other, while her eyes brightened at the information, 'it would have gave me such pleasure to meet you there! But I dare say you will go for all that. To be sure, your brother and sister will ask you to come to them.'

'It will not be in my power to accept their invitation if they do.'

'How unlucky that is! I had quite depended upon meeting you there. Anne and me are to go the latter end of January to some relations who have been wanting us to visit them these several years! But I only go for the sake of seeing Edward. He will be there in February, otherwise London would have no charms for me; I have not spirits for it.'

Elinor was soon called to the card-table by the conclusion of the first rubber, and the confidential discourse of the two ladies was therefore at an end, to which both of them submitted without any reluctance, for nothing had been said on either side, to make them dislike each other less than they had done before; and Elinor sat down to the card-table with the melancholy persuasion that Edward was not only without affection for the person who was to be his wife; but that he had not even the chance of being tolerably happy in marriage, which sincere affection on *her* side would have given, for self-interest alone could induce a woman to keep a man to an engagement, of which she seemed so thoroughly aware that he was weary.

From this time the subject was never revived by Elinor, and when entered on by Lucy, who seldom missed an opportunity of introducing it, and was particularly careful to inform her confidante, of her happiness whenever she received a letter from Edward, it was treated by the former with calmness and caution, and dismissed as soon as civility would allow; for she felt such conversations to be an indulgence which Lucy did not deserve, and which were dangerous to herself.

The visit of the Miss Steeles at Barton Park was lengthened far beyond what the first invitation implied. Their favour increased, they could not be spared; Sir John would not hear of their going; and in spite of their numerous and long arranged engagements in Exeter, in spite of the absolute necessity of their returning to fulfil them immediately, which was in full force at the end of every week, they were prevailed on to stay nearly two months at the park, and to assist in the due celebration of that festival which requires a more than ordinary share of private balls and large dinners to proclaim its importance.

CHAPTER TWENTY-FIVE

THOUGH MRS JENNINGS was in the habit of spending a large portion of the year at the houses of her children and friends, she was not without a settled habitation of her own. Since the death of her husband, who had traded with success in a less elegant part of the town, she had resided every winter in a house in one of the streets near Portman-square. Towards this home, she began on the approach of January to turn her thoughts, and thither she one day abruptly, and very unexpectedly by them, asked the elder Miss Dashwoods to accompany her. Elinor, without observing the varying complexion of her sister, and the animated look which spoke no indifference to the plan, immediately gave a grateful but absolute denial for both, in which she believed herself to be speaking their united inclinations. The reason alleged was their determined resolution of not leaving their mother at that time of the year. Mrs Jennings received the refusal with some surprize, and repeated her invitation immediately.

'Oh! Lord, I am sure your mother can spare you very well, and I *do* beg you will favour me with your company, for I've quite set my heart upon it. Don't fancy that you will be any inconvenience to me, for I shan't put myself at all out of my way for you. It will only be sending Betty by the coach, and I hope I can afford *that*. We three shall be able to go very well in my chaise; and when we are in town, if you do not like to go wherever I do, well and good, you may always go with one of my daughters. I am sure your mother will not object to it; for I have had such good luck in getting my own children off my hands, that she will think me a very fit person to have the charge of you; and if I don't get one of you at least well married before I have done with you, it shall not be my fault. I shall speak a good word for you to all the young men, you may depend upon it.'

'I have a notion,' said Sir John, 'that Miss Marianne would not object to such a scheme, if her elder sister would come into it. It is very hard indeed that she should not have a little pleasure, because Miss Dashwood does not wish it. So I would advise you two, to set off for town, when you are tired of Barton, without saying a word to Miss Dashwood about it.'

'Nay,' cried Mrs Jennings, 'I am sure I shall be monstrous glad of Miss Marianne's company, whether Miss Dashwood will go or not, only the more the merrier say I, and I thought it would be more comfortable for them to be together; because if they got tired of me, they might talk to one another, and laugh at my odd ways behind my back. But one or the other, if not both of them, I must have. Lord bless me! how do you think I can live poking by myself, I who have been always used till this winter to have Charlotte with me. Come, Miss Marianne, let us strike hands upon the bargain, and if Miss Dashwood will change her mind by and bye, why so much the better.'

'I thank you, ma'am, sincerely thank you,' said Marianne, with warmth; 'your invitation has insured my gratitude for ever, and it would give me such happiness, yes almost the greatest happiness I am capable of, to be able to accept it. But my mother, my dearest, kindest mother, – I feel the justice of what Elinor has urged, and if she were to be made less happy, less comfortable by our absence – Oh! no nothing should tempt me to leave her. It should not, must not be a struggle.'

Mrs Jennings repeated her assurance that Mrs Dashwood could spare them perfectly well; and Elinor, who now understood her sister, and saw to what indifference to almost every thing else, she was carried by her eagerness to be with Willoughby again, made no farther direct opposition to the plan, and merely referred it to her mother's decision, from whom however she scarcely expected to receive any support in her endeavour to prevent a visit, which she could not approve of for Marianne, and which on her own account she had particular reasons to avoid. Whatever Marianne was desirous of, her mother would be eager to promote – she could not expect to influence the latter to cautiousness of conduct in an affair, respecting which she had never been able to inspire her with distrust; and she dared not explain the motive of her own disinclination for going to London. That Marianne, fastidious as she was, thoroughly acquainted with Mrs Jennings' manners, and invariably disgusted by them, should overlook every inconvenience of that kind, should disregard whatever must be most wounding to her irritable feelings, in her pursuit of one object, was such a proof, so strong, so full, of the importance of that object to her, as Elinor, in spite of all that had passed, was not prepared to witness.

On being informed of the invitation, Mrs Dashwood, persuaded that such an excursion would be productive of much amusement to both her daughters, and perceiving through all her affectionate attention to herself, how much the heart of Marianne was in it, would not hear of their declining the offer upon *her* account; insisted on their both accepting it directly, and then began to foresee with her usual cheerfulness, a variety of advantages that would accrue to them all, from this separation.

'I am delighted with the plan,' she cried, 'it is exactly what I could wish. Margaret and I shall be as much benefited by it as yourselves. When you and the Middletons are gone, we shall go on so quietly and happily together with our books and our music! You will find Margaret so improved when you come back again! And I have a little plan of alteration for your bedrooms too, which may now be performed without inconvenience to any one. It is very right that you *should* go to town; I would have every young woman of your condition in life, acquainted with the manners and amusements of London. You will be under the care of a motherly good sort of woman, of whose kindness to you I can have no doubt. And in all probability you will *see* your brother, and whatever may be his faults, or the faults of his wife, when I consider whose son he is, I cannot bear to have you so wholly estranged from each other.'

'Though with your usual anxiety for our happiness,' said Elinor, 'you have been obviating every impediment to the present scheme which occurred to you, there is still one objection which, in my opinion, cannot be so easily removed.'

Marianne's countenance sunk.

'And what,' said Mrs Dashwood, 'is my dear prudent Elinor going to suggest? What formidable obstacle is she now to bring forward? Do not let me hear a word about the expence of it.'

'My objection is this; though I think very well of Mrs Jennings's heart, she is not a woman whose society can afford us pleasure, or whose protection will give us consequence.'

'That is very true,' replied her mother; 'but of her society, separately from that of other people, you will scarcely have any thing at all, and you will almost always appear in public with Lady Middleton.'

'If Elinor is frightened away by her dislike of Mrs Jennings,' said Marianne, 'at least it need not prevent *my* accepting her invitation. I have no such scruples, and I am sure, I could put up with every unpleasantness of that kind with very little effort.'

Elinor could not help smiling at this display of indifference towards the manners of a person, to whom she had often had difficulty in persuading Marianne to behave with tolerable politeness: and resolved within herself, that if her sister persisted in going, she would go likewise, as she did not think it proper that Marianne should be left to the sole guidance of her own judgment, or that Mrs Jennings should be abandoned to the mercy of Marianne for all the comfort of her domestic hours. To this determination she was the more easily reconciled, by recollecting, that Edward Ferrars, by Lucy's account, was not to be in town before February; and that their visit, without any unreasonable abridgment, might be previously finished.

'I will have you *both* go,' said Mrs Dashwood; 'these objections are nonsensical. You will have much pleasure in being in London, and especially in being together; and if Elinor would ever condescend to anticipate enjoyment, she would foresee it there from a variety of sources; she would perhaps expect some from improving her acquaintance with her sister-in-law's family.'

Elinor had often wished for an opportunity of attempting to weaken her mother's dependence on the attachment of Edward and herself, that the shock might be the less when the whole truth were revealed, and now on this attack, though almost hopeless of success, she forced herself to begin her design by saying, as calmly as she could, 'I like Edward Ferrars very much, and shall always be glad to see him; but as to the rest of the family, it is a matter of perfect indifference to me, whether I am ever known to them or not.'

Mrs Dashwood smiled and said nothing. Marianne lifted up her eyes in astonishment, and Elinor conjectured that she might as well have held her tongue.

After very little farther discourse, it was finally settled that the invitation should be fully accepted. Mrs Jennings received the information with a great deal of joy, and many assurances of kindness and care; nor was it a matter of pleasure merely to her. Sir John was delighted; for to a man, whose prevailing anxiety was the dread of being alone, the acquisition of two, to the number of inhabitants in London, was something. Even Lady Middleton took the trouble of being delighted, which was putting herself rather out of her way; and as for the Miss Steeles, especially Lucy, they had never been so happy in their lives as this intelligence made them.

Elinor submitted to the arrangement which counter-acted her wishes, with less reluctance than she had expected to feel. With regard to herself, it was now a matter of unconcern whether she went to town or not, and when she saw her mother so thoroughly pleased with the plan, and her sister exhilarated by it in look, voice, and manner, restored to all her usual animation, and elevated to more than her usual gaiety, she could not be dissatisfied with the cause, and would hardly allow herself to distrust the consequence.

Marianne's joy was almost a degree beyond happiness, so great was the perturbation of her spirits and her impatience to be gone. Her unwillingness to quit her mother was her only restorative to calmness; and at the moment of parting, her grief on that score was excessive. Her mother's affliction was hardly less, and Elinor was the only one of the three, who seemed to consider the separation as any thing short of eternal.

Their departure took place in the first week in January. The Middletons were to follow in about a week. The Miss Steeles kept their station at the park, and were to quit it only with the rest of the family.

CHAPTER TWENTY-SIX

ELINOR COULD NOT FIND herself in the carriage with Mrs Jennings, and beginning a journey to London under her protection, and as her guest, without wondering at her own situation, so short had their acquaintance with that lady been, so wholly unsuited were they in age and disposition, and so many had been her objections against such a measure only a few days before! But these objections had all, with that happy ardour of youth which Marianne and her mother equally shared, been overcome or overlooked; and Elinor, in spite of every occasional doubt of Willoughby's constancy, could not witness the rapture of delightful expectation which filled the whole soul and beamed in the eyes of Marianne, without feeling how blank was her own prospect, how cheerless her own state of mind in the comparison, and how gladly she would engage in the solicitude of Marianne's situation to have the same animating object in view, the same possibility of hope. A short, a very short time however must now decide what Willoughby's intentions were; in all probability he was already in town. Marianne's eagerness to be gone declared her dependance on finding him there; and Elinor was resolved not only upon gaining every new light as to his character which her own observation or the intelligence of others could give her, but likewise upon watching his behaviour to her sister with such zealous attention, as to ascertain what he was and what he meant, before many meetings had taken place. Should the result of her observations be unfavourable, she was determined at all events to open the eyes of her sister; should it be otherwise, her exertions would be of a different nature – she must then learn to avoid every selfish comparison, and banish every regret which might lessen her satisfaction in the happiness of Marianne.

They were three days on their journey, and Marianne's behaviour as they travelled was a happy specimen of what her future complaisance and companionableness to Mrs Jennings might be expected to be. She sat in silence almost all the way, wrapt in her own meditations, and scarcely ever voluntarily speaking, except when any object of picturesque beauty within their view drew from her an exclamation of delight exclusively addressed to her sister. To atone for this conduct therefore, Elinor took immediate possession of the post of civility which she had assigned herself, behaved with the greatest attention to Mrs Jennings, talked with her, laughed with her, and listened to her whenever she could; and Mrs Jennings on her side treated them both with all possible kindness, was solicitous on every occasion for their ease and enjoyment, and only disturbed that she could not make them choose their own dinners at the inn, nor extort a confession of their preferring salmon to cod, or boiled fowls to veal cutlets. They reached town by three o'clock the third day, glad to be released, after such a journey, from the confinement of a carriage, and ready to enjoy all the luxury of a good fire.

The house was handsome and handsomely fitted up, and the young ladies were immediately put in possession of a very comfortable apartment. It had formerly been Charlotte's, and over the mantelpiece still hung a landscape in coloured silks of her performance, in proof of her having spent seven years at a great school in town to some effect.

As dinner was not to be ready in less than two hours from their arrival, Elinor determined to employ the interval in writing to her mother, and sat down for that purpose. In a few moments Marianne did the same. '*I* am writing home, Marianne,' said Elinor; 'had not you better defer your letter for a day or two?'

'I am *not* going to write to my mother,' replied Marianne hastily, and as if wishing to avoid any farther inquiry. Elinor said no more; it immediately struck her that she must then be writing to Willoughby, and the conclusion which as instantly followed was, that however mysteriously they might wish to conduct the affair, they must be engaged. This conviction, though not entirely satisfactory, gave her pleasure, and she continued her letter with greater alacrity. Marianne's was finished in a very few minutes; in length it could be no more than a note; it was then folded up, sealed and directed with eager rapidity. Elinor thought she could distinguish a large W. in the direction, and no sooner was it complete than Marianne, ringing the bell, requested the footman who answered it, to get that letter conveyed for her to the two-penny post. This decided the matter at once.

Her spirits still continued very high, but there was a flutter in them which prevented their giving much pleasure to her sister, and this agitation increased as the evening drew on. She could scarcely eat any dinner, and when they afterwards returned to the drawing room, seemed anxiously listening to the sound of every carriage.

It was a great satisfaction to Elinor that Mrs Jennings, by being much engaged in her own room, could see little of what was passing. The tea things were brought in, and already had Marianne been disappointed more than once by a rap at a neighbouring door, when a loud one was suddenly heard which could not be mistaken for one at any other house, Elinor felt secure of its announcing Willoughby's approach, and Marianne starting up moved towards the door. Every thing was silent; this could not be borne many seconds, she opened the door, advanced a few steps towards the stairs, and after listening half a minute, returned into the room in all the agitation which a conviction of having heard him would naturally produce; in the extasy of her feelings at that instant she could not help exclaiming, 'Oh! Elinor, it is Willoughby, indeed it is!' and seemed almost ready to throw herself into his arms, when Colonel Brandon appeared.

It was too great a shock to be borne with calmness, and she immediately left the room. Elinor was disappointed too; but at the same time her regard for Colonel Brandon ensured his welcome with her, and she felt particularly hurt that a man so partial to her sister should perceive that she experienced nothing but grief and disappointment in seeing him. She instantly saw that it was not unnoticed by him, that he even observed Marianne as she quitted the room, with such astonishment and concern, as hardly left him the recollection of what civility demanded towards herself.

'Is your sister ill?' said he.

Elinor answered in some distress that she was, and then talked of head-aches, low spirits, and over fatigues; and of every thing to which she could decently attribute her sister's behaviour.

He heard her with the most earnest attention, but seeming to recollect himself, said no more on the subject, and began directly to speak of his pleasure at seeing them in London, making the usual inquiries about their journey and the friends they had left behind.

In this calm kind of way, with very little interest on either side, they continued to talk, both of them out of spirits, and the thoughts of both engaged elsewhere. Elinor wished very much to ask whether Willoughby were then in town, but she was afraid of giving him pain by any inquiry after his rival; and at length by way of saying something, she asked if he had been in London ever since she had seen him last. 'Yes,' he replied, with some embarrassment, 'almost ever since; I have been once or twice at Delaford for a few days, but it has never been in my power to return to Barton.'

This, and the manner in which it was said, immediately brought back to her remembrance, all the circumstances of his quitting that place, with the uneasiness and suspicions they had caused to Mrs Jennings, and she was fearful that her question had implied much more curiosity on the subject than she had ever felt.

Mrs Jennings soon came in. 'Oh! Colonel,' said she, with her usual noisy cheerfulness, 'I am monstrous glad to see you – sorry I could not come before – beg your pardon, but I have been forced to look about me a little, and settle my matters; for it is a long while since I have been at home, and you know one has always a world of little odd things to do after one has been away for any time; and then I have had Cartwright to settle with – Lord, I have been as busy as a bee ever since dinner! But pray, Colonel, how came you to conjure out that I should be in town today?'

'I had the pleasure of hearing it at Mr Palmer's, where I have been dining.'

'Oh! you did; well, and how do they all do at their house? How does Charlotte do? I warrant you she is a fine size by this time.'

'Mrs Palmer appeared quite well, and I am commissioned to tell you, that you will certainly see her to-morrow.'

'Aye, to be sure, I thought as much. Well, Colonel, I have brought two young ladies with me, you see – that is, you see but one of them now, but there is another somewhere. Your friend Miss Marianne, too – which you will not be sorry to hear. I do not know what you and Mr Willoughby will do between you about her. Aye, it is a fine thing to be young and handsome. Well! I was young once, but I never was very handsome – worse luck for me. However I got a very good husband, and I don't know what the greatest beauty can do more. Ah! poor man! he has been dead these eight years and better. But Colonel, where have you been to since we parted? And how does your business go on? Come, come, let's have no secrets among friends.'

He replied with his accustomary mildness to all her inquiries, but without satisfying her in any. Elinor now began to make the tea, and Marianne was obliged to appear again.

After her entrance, Colonel Brandon became more thoughtful and silent than he had been before, and Mrs Jennings could not prevail on him to stay long. No other visitor appeared that evening, and the ladies were unanimous in agreeing to go early to bed.

Marianne rose the next morning with recovered spirits and happy looks. The disappointment of the evening before seemed forgotten in the expectation of what was to happen that day. They had not long finished their breakfast before Mrs Palmer's barouche stopt at the door, and in a few minutes she came laughing into the room; so delighted to see them all, that it was hard to say whether she received most pleasure from meeting her mother or the Miss Dashwoods again. So surprised at their coming to town, though it was what she had rather expected all along; so angry at their accepting her mother's invitation after having declined her own, though at the same time she would never have forgiven them if they had not come!

'Mr Palmer will be so happy to see you,' said she; 'what do you think he said when he heard of your coming with mama? I forget what it was now, but it was something so droll!'

After an hour or two spent in what her mother called comfortable chat, or in other words, in every variety of inquiry concerning all their acquaintance on Mrs Jennings's side, and in laughter without cause on Mrs Palmer's, it was proposed by the latter that they should all accompany her to some shops where she had business that morning, to which Mrs Jennings and Elinor readily consented, as having likewise some purchases to make themselves; and Marianne, though declining it at first, was induced to go likewise.

Wherever they went, she was evidently always on the watch. In Bond-street especially, where much of their business lay, her eyes were in constant inquiry; and in whatever shop the party were engaged, her mind was equally abstracted from every thing actually before them, from all that interested and occupied the others. Restless and dissatisfied every where, her sister could never obtain her opinion of any article of purchase, however it might equally concern them both; she received no pleasure from any thing; was only impatient to be at home again, and could with difficulty govern her vexation at the tediousness of Mrs Palmer, whose eye was caught by every thing pretty, expensive, or new; who was wild to buy all, could determine on none, and dawdled away her time in rapture and indecision.

It was late in the morning before they returned home; and no sooner had they entered the house than Marianne flew eagerly up stairs, and when Elinor followed she found her turning from the table with a sorrowful countenance, which declared that no Willoughby had been there.

'Has no letter been left here for me since we went out?' said she to the footman who then entered with the parcels. She was answered in the negative. 'Are you quite sure of it?' she replied. 'Are you certain that no servant, no porter has left any letter or note?'

The man replied that none had.

'How very odd!' said she in a low and disappointed voice, as she turned away to the window.

'How odd indeed!' repeated Elinor within herself, regarding her sister with uneasiness. 'If she had not known him to be in town she would not have written to him, as she did; she would have written to Combe Magna; and if he is in town, how odd that he should neither come nor write! Oh! my dear mother, you must be wrong in permitting an engagement between a daughter so young, a man so little known, to be carried on in so doubtful, so mysterious a manner? *I* long to inquire; but how will *my* interference be borne!'

She determined after some consideration, that if appearances continued many days longer, as unpleasant as they now were, she would represent in the strongest manner to her mother the necessity of some serious inquiry into the affair.

Mrs Palmer and two elderly ladies of Mrs Jennings's intimate acquaintance, whom she had met and invited in the morning, dined with them. The former left them soon after tea to fulfil her evening engagements; and Elinor was obliged to assist in making a whist table for the others. Marianne was of no use on these occasions, as she would never learn the game, but though her time was therefore at her own disposal, the evening was by no means more productive of pleasure to her than to Elinor, for it was spent in all the anxiety of expectation and the pain of disappointment. She sometimes endeavoured for a few minutes to read; but the book was soon thrown aside, and she returned to the more interesting employment of walking backwards and forwards across the room, pausing for a moment whenever she came to the window, in hopes of distinguishing the long-expected rap.

CHAPTER TWENTY-SEVEN

'IF THIS OPEN WEATHER holds much longer,' said Mrs Jennings, when they met at breakfast the following morning, 'Sir John will not like leaving Barton next week; 'tis a sad thing for sportsmen to lose a day's pleasure. Poor souls! I always pity them when they do; they seem to take it so much to heart.'

'That is true,' cried Marianne in a cheerful voice, and walking to the window as she spoke, to examine the day. 'I had not thought of *that*. This weather will keep many sportsmen in the country.'

It was a lucky recollection, all her good spirits were restored by it. 'It is charming weather for *them* indeed,' she continued, as she sat down to the breakfast table with a happy countenance. 'How much they must enjoy it! But' (with a little return of anxiety) 'it cannot be expected to last long. At this time of year, and after such a series of rain, we shall certainly have very little more of it. Frosts will soon set in, and in all probability with severity. In another day or two perhaps; this extreme mildness can hardly last longer – nay, perhaps, it may freeze tonight!'

'At any rate,' said Elinor, wishing to prevent Mrs Jennings from seeing her sister's thoughts as clearly as she did, 'I dare say we shall have Sir John and Lady Middleton in town by the end of next week.'

'Aye, my dear, I'll warrant you we do. Mary always has her own way.'

'And now,' silently conjectured Elinor, 'she will write to Combe by this day's post.'

But if she *did*, the letter was written and sent away with a privacy which eluded all her watchfulness to ascertain the fact. Whatever the truth of it might be, and far as Elinor was from feeling thorough contentment about it, yet while she saw Marianne in spirits, she could not be very uncomfortable herself. And Marianne was in spirits; happy in the mildness of the weather, and still happier in her expectation of a frost.

The morning was chiefly spent in leaving cards at the houses of Mrs Jennings's acquaintance to inform them of her being in town; and Marianne was all the time busy in observing the direction of the wind, watching the variations of the sky and imagining an alteration in the air.

'Don't you find it colder than it was in the morning, Elinor? There seems to me a very decided difference. I can hardly keep my hands warm even in my muff. It was not so yesterday, I think. The clouds seem parting too, the sun will be out in a moment; and we shall have a clear afternoon.'

Elinor was alternately diverted and pained; but Marianne persevered, and saw every night in the brightness of the fire, and every morning in the appearance of the atmosphere, the certain symptoms of approaching frost.

The Miss Dashwoods had no greater reason to be dissatisfied with Mrs Jennings's style of living, and set of acquaintance, than with her behaviour to themselves, which was invariably kind. Every thing in her household arrangements was conducted on the most liberal plan, and excepting a few old city friends, whom, to Lady Middleton's regret, she had never dropped, she visited no one, to whom an introduction could at all discompose the feelings of her young companions. Pleased to find herself more comfortably situated in that particular than she had expected, Elinor was very willing to compound for the want of much real enjoyment from any of their evening parties, which, whether at home or abroad, formed only for cards, could have little to amuse her.

Colonel Brandon, who had a general invitation to the house, was with them almost every day; he came to look at Marianne and talk to Elinor, who often derived more satisfaction from conversing with him than from any other daily occurrence, but who saw at the same time with much concern his continued regard for her sister. She feared it was a strengthening regard. It grieved her to see the earnestness with which he often watched Marianne, and his spirits were certainly worse than when at Barton.

About a week after their arrival it became certain that Willoughby was also arrived. His card was on the table, when they came in from the morning's drive.

'Good God!' said Marianne, 'he has been here while we were out.' Elinor, rejoiced to be assured of his being in London, now ventured to say, 'depend upon it he will call again tomorrow.' But Marianne seemed hardly to hear her, and on Mrs Jennings's entrance escaped with the precious card.

This event, while it raised the spirits of Elinor, restored to those of her sister, all, and more than all, their former agitation. From this moment her mind was never quiet; the expectation of seeing him every hour of the day, made her unfit for anything. She insisted on being left behind, the next morning, when the others went out.

Elinor's thoughts were full of what might be passing in Berkeley-street during their absence; but a moment's glance at her sister when they returned was enough to inform her, that Willoughby had paid no second visit there. A note was just then brought in, and laid on the table.

'For me!' cried Marianne, stepping hastily forward.

'No, ma'am, for my mistress.'

But Marianne, not convinced, took it instantly up.

'It is indeed for Mrs Jennings; how provoking!'

'You are expecting a letter then?' said Elinor, unable to be longer silent.

'Yes, a little – not much.'

After a short pause, 'you have no confidence in me, Marianne.'

'Nay, Elinor, this reproach from *you* – you who have confidence in no one!'

'Me!' returned Elinor in some confusion; 'indeed, Marianne, I have nothing to tell.'

'Nor I,' answered Marianne with energy, 'our situations then are alike. We have neither of us any thing to tell; you, because you do not communicate, and I, because I conceal nothing.'

Elinor, distressed by this charge of reserve in herself, which she was not at liberty to do away, knew not how, under such circumstances, to press for greater openness in Marianne.

Mrs Jennings soon appeared, and the note being given her, she read it aloud. It was from Lady Middleton, announcing their arrival in Conduit-street the night before, and requesting the company of her mother and cousins the following evening. Business on Sir John's part, and a violent cold on her own, prevented their calling in Berkeley-street. The invitation was accepted: but when the hour of appointment drew near, necessary as it was in common civility to Mrs Jennings, that they should both attend her on such a visit, Elinor had some difficulty in persuading her sister to go, for still she had seen nothing of Willoughby; and therefore was not more indisposed for amusement abroad, than unwilling to run the risk of his calling again in her absence.

Elinor found, when the evening was over, that disposition is not materially altered by a change of abode, for although scarcely settled in town, Sir John had contrived to collect around him, nearly twenty young people, and to amuse them with a ball. This was an affair, however, of which Lady Middleton did not approve. In the country, an unpremeditated dance was very allowable; but in London, where the reputation of elegance was more important and less easily attained, it was risking too much for the gratification of a few girls, to have it known that Lady Middleton had given a small dance of eight or nine couple, with two violins, and a mere side-board collation.

Mr and Mrs Palmer were of the party; from the former, whom they had not seen before since their arrival in town, as he was careful to avoid the appearance of any attention to his mother-in-law, and therefore never came near her, they received no mark of recognition on their entrance. He looked at them slightly, without seeming to know who they were, and merely nodded to Mrs Jennings from the other side of the room. Marianne gave one glance round the apartment as she entered;; it was enough, *he* was not there – and she sat down, equally ill-disposed to receive or communicate pleasure. After they had been assembled about an hour, Mr Palmer sauntered towards the Miss Dashwoods to express his surprise on seeing them in town, though Colonel Brandon had been first informed of their arrival at his house, and he had himself said something very droll on hearing that they were to come.

'I thought you were both in Devonshire,' said he.

'Did you?' replied Elinor.

'When do you go back again?'

'I do not know.' And thus ended their discourse.

Never had Marianne been so unwilling to dance in her life, as she was that evening, and never so much fatigued by the exercise. She complained of it as they returned to Berkeley-street.

'Aye, aye,' said Mrs Jennings, 'we know the reason of all that very well; if a certain person who shall be nameless, had been there, you would not have been a bit tired: and to say the truth it was not very pretty of him not to give you the meeting when he was invited.'

'Invited!' cried Marianne.

'So my daughter Middleton told me, for it seems Sir John met him somewhere in the street this morning.' Marianne said no more, but looked exceedingly hurt. Impatient in this situation to be doing something that might lead to her sister's relief, Elinor resolved to write the next morning to her mother, and hoped by awakening her fears for the health of Marianne, to procure those inquiries which had been so long delayed; and she was still more eagerly bent on this measure by perceiving after breakfast on the morrow, that Marianne was again writing to Willoughby, for she could not suppose it to be to any other person.

About the middle of the day, Mrs Jennings went out by herself on business, and Elinor began her letter directly, while Marianne, too restless for employment, too anxious for conversation, walked from one window to the other, or sat down by the fire in melancholy meditation. Elinor was very earnest in her application to her mother, relating all that had passed, her suspicions of Willoughby's inconstancy, urging her by every plea of duty and affection to demand from Marianne, an account of her real situation with respect to him.

Her letter was scarcely finished, when a rap foretold a visitor, and Colonel Brandon was announced. Marianne, who had seen him from the window, and who hated company of any kind, left the room before he entered it. He looked more than usually grave, and though expressing satisfaction at finding Miss Dashwood alone, as if he had somewhat in particular to tell her, sat for some time without saying a word. Elinor, persuaded that he had some communication to make in which her sister was concerned, impatiently expected its opening. It was not the first time of her feeling the same kind of conviction; for more than once before, beginning with the observation of 'your sister looks unwell today,' or 'your sister seems out of spirits,' he had appeared on the point, either of disclosing, or of inquiring, something particular about her. After a pause of several minutes, their silence was broken, by his asking her in a voice of some agitation, when he was to congratulate her on the acquisition of a brother? Elinor was not prepared for such a question, and having no answer ready, was obliged to adopt the simple and common expedient, of asking what he meant? He tried to smile as he replied, 'your sister's engagement to Mr Willoughby is very generally known.'

'It cannot be generally known,' returned Elinor, 'for her own family do not know it.'

He looked surprised and said, 'I beg your pardon, I am afraid my inquiry has been impertinent; but I had not supposed any secrecy intended, as they openly correspond, and their marriage is universally talked of.'

'How can that be? By whom can you have heard it mentioned?'

'By many – by some of whom you know nothing, by others with whom you are most intimate, Mrs Jennings, Mrs Palmer, and the Middletons. But still I might not have believed it, for where the mind is perhaps rather unwilling to be convinced, it will always find something to support its doubts, if I had not, when the servant let me in today, accidentally seen a letter in his hand, directed to Mr Willoughby in your sister's writing. I came to inquire, but I was convinced before I could ask the question. Is every thing finally settled? Is it impossible to – ? But I have no right, and I could have no chance of succeeding. Excuse me, Miss Dashwood. I believe I have been wrong in saying so much, but I hardly know what to do, and on your prudence I have the strongest dependence. Tell me that it is all absolutely resolved on, that any attempt, that in short concealment, if concealment be possible, is all that remains.'

These words, which conveyed to Elinor a direct avowal of his love for her sister, affected her very much. She was not immediately able to say any thing, and even when her spirits were recovered, she debated for a short time, on the answer it would be most proper to give. The real state of things between Willoughby and her sister was so little known to herself, that in endeavouring to explain it, she might be as liable to say too much as too little. Yet as she was convinced that Marianne's affection for Willoughby, could leave no hope of Colonel Brandon's success, whatever the event of that affection might be, and at the same time wished to shield her conduct from censure, she thought it most prudent and kind, after some consideration, to say more than she really knew or believed. She acknowledged, therefore, that though she had never been informed by themselves of the terms on which they stood with each other, of their mutual affection she had no doubt, and of their correspondence she was not astonished to hear.

He listened to her with silent attention, and on her ceasing to speak, rose directly from his seat, and after saying in a voice of emotion, 'to your sister I wish all imaginable happiness; to Willoughby that he may endeavour to deserve her,' – took leave, and went away.

Elinor derived no comfortable feelings from this conversation, to lessen the uneasiness of her mind on other points; she was left, on the contrary, with a melancholy impression of Colonel Brandon's unhappiness, and was prevented even from wishing it removed, by her anxiety for the very event that must confirm it.

CHAPTER TWENTY-EIGHT

Nothing occurred during the next three or four days, to make Elinor regret what she had done, in applying to her mother; for Willoughby neither came nor wrote. They were engaged about the end of that time to attend Lady Middleton to a party, from which Mrs Jennings was kept away by the indisposition of her youngest daughter; and for this party, Marianne, wholly dispirited, careless of her appearance, and seeming equally indifferent whether she went or staid, prepared, without one look of hope, or one expression of pleasure. She sat by the drawing-room fire after tea, till the moment of Lady Middleton's arrival, without once stirring from her seat, or altering her attitude, lost in her own thoughts and insensible of her sister's presence; and when at last they were told that Lady Middleton waited for them at the door, she started as if she had forgotten that any one was expected.

They arrived in due time at the place of destination, and as soon as the string of carriages before them would allow, alighted, ascended the stairs, heard their names announced from one landing-place to another in an audible voice, and entered a room splendidly lit up, quite full of company, and insufferably hot. When they had paid their tribute of politeness by curtsying to the lady of the house, they were permitted to mingle in the crowd, and take their share

At that moment she first perceived him.

of the heat and inconvenience, to which their arrival must necessarily add. After some time spent in saying little and doing less, Lady Middleton sat down to Casino, and as Marianne was not in spirits for moving about, she and Elinor luckily succeeding to chairs, placed themselves at no great distance from the table.

They had not remained in this manner long, before Elinor perceived Willoughby, standing within a few yards of them, in earnest conversation with a very fashionable looking young woman. She soon caught his eye, and he immediately bowed, but without attempting to speak to her, or to approach Marianne, though he could not but see her; and then continued his discourse with the same lady. Elinor turned involuntarily to Marianne, to see whether it could be unobserved by her. At that moment she first perceived him, and her whole countenance glowing with sudden delight, she would have moved towards him instantly, had not her sister caught hold of her.

'Good heavens!' she exclaimed, 'he is there – he is there – Oh! why does he not look at me? why cannot I speak to him?'

'Pray, pray be composed,' cried Elinor, 'and do not betray what you feel to every body present. Perhaps he has not observed you yet.'

This however was more than she could believe herself; and to be composed at such a moment was not only beyond the reach of Marianne, it was beyond her wish. She sat in an agony of impatience, which affected every feature.

At last he turned round again, and regarded them both; she started up, and pronouncing his name in a tone of affection, held out her hand to him. He approached and addressing himself rather to Elinor than Marianne, as if wishing to avoid her eye, and determined not to observe her attitude, inquired in a hurried manner after Mrs Dashwood, and asked how long they had been in town. Elinor was robbed of all presence of mind by such an address, and was unable to say a word. But the feelings of her sister were instantly expressed. Her face was crimsoned over, and she exclaimed in a voice of the greatest emotion, 'Good God! Willoughby, what is the meaning of this? Have you not received my letters? Will you not shake hands with me?'

He could not then avoid it, but her touch seemed painful to him, and he held her hand only for a moment. During all this time he was evidently struggling for composure. Elinor watched his countenance and saw its expression becoming more tranquil. After a moment's pause, he spoke with calmness.

'I did myself the honour of calling in Berkeley-street last Tuesday, and very much regretted that I was not fortunate enough to find yourselves and Mrs Jennings at home. My card was not lost, I hope.'

'But have you not received my notes?' cried Marianne in the wildest anxiety. 'Here is some mistake I am sure – some dreadful mistake. What can be the meaning of it? Tell me, Willoughby; for heaven's sake tell me, what is the matter?'

He made no reply; his complexion changed and all his embarrassment returned; but as if, on catching the eye of the young lady with whom he had been previously talking, he felt the necessity of instant exertion, he recovered himself again, and after saying, 'Yes, I had the pleasure of receiving the information of your arrival in town, which you were so good as to send me,' turned hastily away with a slight bow and joined his friend.

Marianne, now looking dreadfully white, and unable to stand, sunk into her chair, and Elinor, expecting every moment to see her faint, tried to screen her from the observation of others, while reviving her with lavender water.

'Go to him, Elinor,' she cried, as soon as she could speak, 'and force him to come to me. Tell him I must see him again – must speak to him instantly – I cannot rest – I shall not have a moment's peace till this is explained – some dreadful misapprehension or other – Oh go to him this moment.'

'How can that be done? No, my dearest Marianne, you must wait. This is not a place for explanations. Wait only till to-morrow.'

With difficulty however could she prevent her from following him herself; and to persuade her to check her agitation, to wait, at least, with the appearance of composure, till she might speak to him with more privacy and more effect, was impossible; for Marianne continued incessantly to give way in a low voice to the misery of her feelings, by exclamations of wretchedness. In a short time Elinor saw Willoughby quit the room by the door towards the staircase, and telling Marianne that he was gone, urged the impossibility of speaking to him again that evening, as a fresh argument for her to be calm. She instantly begged her sister would entreat Lady Middleton to take them home, as she was too miserable to stay a minute longer.

Lady Middleton, though in the middle of a rubber, on being informed that Marianne was unwell, was too polite to object for a moment to her wish of going away, and making over her cards to a friend, they departed as soon as the carriage could be found. Scarcely a word was spoken during their return to Berkeley-street. Marianne was in a silent agony, too much oppressed even for tears; but as Mrs Jennings was luckily not come home, they could go directly to their own room, where hartshorn restored her a little to herself. She was soon undressed and in bed, and as she seemed desirous of being alone, her sister then left her, and while she waited the return of Mrs Jennings, had leisure enough for thinking over the past.

That some kind of engagement had subsisted between Willoughby and Marianne she could not doubt; and that Willoughby was weary of it, seemed equally clear; for however Marianne might still feed her own wishes, *she* could not attribute such behaviour to mistake or misapprehension of any kind. Nothing but a thorough change of sentiment could account for it. Her indignation would have been still stronger than it was, had she not witnessed that embarrassment which seemed to speak a consciousness of his own misconduct, and prevented her from believing him so unprincipled as to have been sporting with the affections of her sister from the first, without any design that would bear investigation. Absence might have weakened his regard, and convenience might have determined him to overcome it, but that such a regard had formerly existed she could not bring herself to doubt.

As for Marianne, on the pangs which so unhappy a meeting must already have given her, and on those still more severe which might await her in its probable consequence, she could not reflect without the deepest concern. Her own situation gained in the comparison; for while she could *esteem* Edward as much as ever, however they might be divided in future, her mind might be always supported. But every circumstance that could embitter such an evil seemed uniting to heighten the misery of Marianne in a final separation from Willoughby – in an immediate and irreconcilable rupture with him.

CHAPTER TWENTY-NINE

BEFORE THE HOUSE-MAID had lit their fire the next day, or the sun gained any power over a cold, gloomy morning in January, Marianne, only half-dressed, was kneeling against one of the window-seats for the sake of all the light she could command from it, and writing as fast as a continual flow of tears would permit her. In this situation, Elinor, roused from sleep by her agitation and sobs, first perceived her; and after observing her for a few moments with silent anxiety, said, in a tone of the most considerate gentleness,

'Marianne, may I ask?' –

'No, Elinor,' she replied, 'ask nothing; you will soon know all.'

The sort of desperate calmness with which this was said, lasted no longer than while she spoke, and was immediately followed by a return of the same excessive affliction. It was some minutes before she could go on with her letter, and the frequent bursts of grief which still obliged her, at intervals, to withhold her pen, were proofs enough of her feeling how more than probable it was that she was writing for the last time to Willoughby.

Elinor paid her every quiet and unobtrusive attention in her power, and she would have tried to soothe and tranquillize her still more, had not Marianne entreated her, with all the eagerness of the most nervous irritability, not to speak to her for the world. In such circumstances, it was better for both that they should not be long together; and the restless state of Marianne's mind not only prevented her from remaining in the room a moment after she was dressed, but requiring at once solitude and continual change of place, made her wander about the house till breakfast time, avoiding the sight of every body.

At breakfast she neither ate, nor attempted to eat any thing; and Elinor's attention was then all employed, not in urging her, not in pitying her, nor in appearing to regard her, but in endeavouring to engage Mrs Jennings's notice entirely to herself.

As this was a favourite meal with Mrs Jennings, it lasted a considerable time, and they were just setting themselves, after it, round the common working table, when a letter was delivered to Marianne, which she eagerly caught from the servant, and, turning of a death-like paleness, instantly ran out of the room. Elinor, who saw as plainly by this, as if she had seen the direction, that it must come from Willoughby, felt immediately such a sickness at heart as made her hardly able to hold up her head, and sat in such a general tremor as made her fear it impossible to escape Mrs Jennings's notice. That good lady, however, saw only that Marianne had received a letter from Willoughby, which appeared to her a very good joke, and which she treated accordingly, by hoping, with a laugh, that she would find it to her liking. Of Elinor's distress, she was too busily employed in measuring lengths of worsted for her rug, to see any thing at all; and calmly continuing her talk, as soon as Marianne disappeared, she said,

'Upon my word I never saw a young woman so desperately in love in my life! My girls were nothing to her, and yet they used to be foolish enough; but as for Miss Marianne, she is quite an altered creature. I hope, from the bottom of my heart, he won't keep her waiting much longer, for it is quite grievous to see her look so ill and forlorn. Pray, when are they to be married?'

Elinor, though never less disposed to speak than at that moment, obliged herself to answer such an attack as this, and, therefore, trying to smile, replied, 'And have you really, Ma'am, talked yourself into a persuasion of my sister's being engaged to Mr Willoughby? I thought it had been only a joke, but so serious a question seems to imply more; and I must beg, therefore, that you will not deceive yourself any longer. I do assure you that nothing would surprise me more than to hear of their being going to be married.'

'For shame, for shame, Miss Dashwood! how can you talk so! Don't we all know that it must be a match, that they were over head and ears in love with each other from the first moment they met? Did not I see them together in Devonshire every day, and all day long; and did not I know that your sister came to town with me on purpose to buy wedding clothes? Come, come, this won't do. Because you are so sly about it yourself, you think nobody else has any senses; but it is no such thing, I can tell you, for it has been known all over town this ever so long. I tell everybody of it and so does Charlotte.'

'Indeed, Ma'am,' said Elinor, very seriously, 'you are mistaken. Indeed, you are doing a very unkind thing in spreading the report, and you will find that you have, though you will not believe me now.'

Mrs Jennings laughed again, but Elinor had not spirits to say more, and eager at all events to know what Willoughby had written, hurried away to their room, where, on opening the door, she saw Marianne stretched on the bed, almost choked by grief, one letter in her hand, and two or three others lying by her. Elinor drew near, but without saying a word; and seating herself on the bed, took her hand, kissed her affectionately several times, and then gave way to a burst of tears, which at first was scarcely less violent than Marianne's. The latter, though unable to speak, seemed to feel all the tenderness of this behaviour, and after some time thus spent in joint affliction, she put all the letters into Elinor's hands; and then covering her face with her handkerchief, almost screamed with agony. Elinor, who knew that such grief, shocking as it was to witness it, must have its course, watched by her till this excess of suffering had somewhat spent itself, and then turning eagerly to Willoughby's letter, read as follows:

Bond Street, January.

My Dear Madam,

I have just had the honour of receiving your letter, for which I beg to return my sincere acknowledgments. I am much concerned to find there was any thing in my behaviour last night that did not meet your approbation; and though I am quite at a loss to discover in what point I could be so unfortunate as to offend you, I entreat your forgiveness of what I can assure you to have been perfectly unintentional. I shall never reflect on my former acquaintance with your family in Devonshire without the most grateful pleasure, and flatter myself it will not be broken by an mistake or misapprehension of my actions. My esteem for your whole family is very sincere; but if I have been so unfortunate as to give rise to a belief of more than I felt, or meant to express, I shall reproach myself for not having been more guarded in my professions of that esteem. That I should ever have meant more you will allow to be impossible, when you understand that my affections have been long engaged elsewhere, and it will not be many weeks, I believe, before this engagement is fulfilled. It is with great regret that I obey your commands of returning the letters, with which I have been honoured from you, and the lock of hair, which you so obligingly bestowed on me.

I am, dear Madam,
Your most obedient
humble Servant,
JOHN WILLOUGHBY.

With what indignation such a letter as this must be read by Miss Dashwood, may be imagined. Though aware, before she began it, that it must bring a confession of his inconstancy, and confirm their separation for ever, she was not aware that such language could be suffered to announce it; nor could she have supposed Willoughby capable of departing so far from the appearance of every honourable and delicate feeling – so far from the common decorum of a gentleman, as to send a letter so impudently cruel: a letter which, instead of bringing with his desire of a release any professions of regret, acknowledged no breach of faith, denied all peculiar affection whatever – a letter of which every line was an insult, and which proclaimed its writer to be deep in hardened villany.

She paused over it for some time with indignant astonishment; then read it again and again; but every perusal only served to increase her abhorrence of the man, and so bitter were her feelings against him, that she dared not trust herself to speak, lest she might wound Marianne still deeper by treating their disengagement, not as a loss to her of any possible good but as an escape from the worst and most irremediable of all evils, a connection, for life, with an unprincipled man, as a deliverance the most real, a blessing the most important.

In her earnest meditations on the contents of the letter, on the depravity of that mind which could dictate it, and, probably, on the very different mind of a very different person, who had no other connection whatever with the affair than what her heart gave him with every thing that passed, Elinor forgot the immediate distress of her sister, forgot that she had three letters on her lap yet unread, and so entirely forgot how long she had been in the room, that when on hearing a carriage drive up to the door, she went to the window to see who could be coming so unreasonably early, she was all astonishment to perceive Mrs Jennings's chariot, which she knew had not been ordered till one. Determined not to quit Marianne, though hopeless of contributing, at present, to her ease, she hurried away to excuse herself from attending Mrs Jennings, on account of her sister being indisposed. Mrs Jennings, with a thoroughly good-humoured concern for its cause, admitted the excuse most readily, and Elinor, after seeing her safe off, returned to Marianne, whom she found attempting to rise from the bed, and whom she reached just in time to prevent her from falling on the floor, faint and giddy, from a long want of proper rest and food; for it was many days since she had any appetite, and many nights since she had really slept; and now, when her mind was no longer supported by the fever of suspense, the consequence of all this was felt in an aching head, a weakened stomach, and a general nervous faintness. A glass of wine, which Elinor procured for her directly, made her more comfortable, and she was at last able to express some sense of her kindness, by saying,

'Poor Elinor! how unhappy I make you!'

'I only wish,' replied her sister, 'there were any thing I *could* do, which might be of comfort to you.'

This, as every thing else would have been, was too much for Marianne, who could only exclaim, in the anguish of her heart, 'Oh! Elinor, I am miserable indeed,' before her voice was entirely lost in sobs.

Elinor could no longer witness this torrent of unresisted grief in silence.

'Exert yourself, dear Marianne,' she cried, 'if you would not kill yourself and all who love you. Think of your mother; think of her misery while *you* suffer, for her sake you must exert yourself.'

'I cannot, I cannot,' cried Marianne; 'leave me, leave me, if I distress you; leave me, hate me, forget me! but do not torture me so. Oh! how easy for those who have no sorrow of their own to talk of exertion! Happy, happy Elinor, *you* cannot have an idea of what I suffer.'

'Do you call *me* happy, Marianne? Ah! if you knew! – And can you believe me to be so, while I see you so wretched!'

'Forgive me, forgive me,' throwing her arms round her sister's neck; I know you feel for me; I know what a heart you have; but yet you are – you must be happy; Edward loves you – what, oh! what can do away such happiness as that?'

'Many, many circumstances,' said Elinor, solemnly.

'No, no, no,' cried Marianne wildly, 'he loves you, and only you. You *can* have no grief.'

'I can have no pleasure while I see you in this state.'

'And you will never see me otherwise. Mine is a misery which nothing can do away.'

'You must not talk so, Marianne. Have you no comforts? no friends? Is your loss such as leaves no opening for consolation? Much as you suffer now, think of what you would have suffered if the discovery of his character had been delayed to a later period – if your engagement had been carried on for months and months, as it might have been, before he chose to put an end to it. Every additional day of unhappy confidence, on your side, would have made the blow more dreadful.'

'Engagement!' cried Marianne, 'there has been no engagement.'

'No engagement?'

'No, he is not so unworthy as you believe him. He has broken no faith with me.'

'But he told you that he loved you?'

'Yes – no – never absolutely. It was every day implied, but never professedly declared. Sometimes I thought it had been – but it never was.'

'Yet you wrote to him?' –

'Yes – could that be wrong after all that had passed? – But I cannot talk.'

Elinor said no more, and turning again to the three letters which now raised a much stronger curiosity than before, directly ran over the contents of all. The first, which was what her sister had sent him on their arrival in town, was to this effect.

Berkeley Street, January.

How surprised you will be, Willoughby, on receiving this; and I think you will feel something more than surprise, when you know that I am in town. An opportunity of coming hither, though with Mrs Jennings, was a temptation we could not resist. I wish you may receive this in time to come here to-night, but I will not depend on it. At any rate I shall expect you to-morrow. For the present, adieu.

M.D.

Her second note, which had been written on the morning after the dance at the Middletons', was in these words: –

I cannot express my disappointment in having missed you the day before yesterday, nor my astonishment at not having received any answer to a note which I sent you above a week ago. I have been expecting to hear from you, and still more to see you, every hour of the day. Pray call again as soon as possible, and explain the reason of my having expected this in vain. You had better come earlier another time, because we are generally out by one. We were last night at Lady Middleton's, where there was a dance. I have been told that you were asked to be one of the party. But could it be so? You must be very much altered indeed since we parted, if that could be the case, and you not there. But I will not suppose this possible, and I hope very soon to receive your personal assurance of its being otherwise.

M.D.

The contents of her last note to him were these: –

What am I to imagine, Willoughby, by your behaviour last night? Again I demand an explanation of it. I was prepared to meet you with the pleasure which our separation naturally produced, with the familiarity which our intimacy at Barton appeared to me to justify. I was repulsed indeed! I have passed a wretched night in endeavouring to excuse a conduct which can scarcely be called less than insulting; but though I have not yet been able to form any reasonable apology for your behaviour, I am perfectly ready to hear your justification of it. You have perhaps been misinformed, or purposely deceived, in something concerning me, which may have lowered me in your opinion. Tell me what it is, explain the grounds on which you acted, and I shall be satisfied, in being able to satisfy you. It would grieve me indeed to be obliged to think ill of you; but if I am to do it, if I am to learn that you are not what we have hitherto believed you, that your regard for us all was insincere, that your behaviour to me was intended only to deceive, let it be told as soon as possible. My feelings are at present in a state of dreadful indecision; I wish to acquit you, but certainty on either side will be ease to what I now suffer. If your sentiments are no longer what they were, you will return my notes, and the lock of my hair which is in your possession.

M.D.

That such letters, so full of affection and confidence, could have been so answered, Elinor, for Willoughby's sake, would have been unwilling to believe. But her condemnation of him did not blind her to the impropriety of their having been written at all; and she was silently grieving over the imprudence which had hazarded such unsolicited proofs of tenderness, not warranted by anything preceding, and most severely condemned by the event, when Marianne, perceiving that she had finished the letters, observed to her that they contained nothing but what any one would have written in the same situation.

'I felt myself,' she added, 'to be as solemnly engaged to him, as if the strictest legal covenant had bound us to each other.'

'I can believe it,' said Elinor, 'but unfortuantely he did not feel the same.'

'He *did* feel the same, Elinor – for weeks and weeks he felt it. I know he did. Whatever may have changed him now, (and nothing but the blackest art employed against me can have done it,) I was once as dear to him as my own soul could wish. This lock of hair, which now he can so readily give up, was begged of me with the most earnest supplication. Had you seen his look, his manner, had you heard his voice at that moment! Have you forgot the last evening of our being together at Barton! The morning that we parted too! When he told me that it might be many weeks before we meet again – his distress – can I ever forget his distress!'

For a moment or two she could say no more; but when this emotion had passed away, she added, in a firmer tone,

'Elinor, I have been cruelly used; but not by Willoughby.'

'Dearest Marianne, who but himself? By whom can he have been instigated?'

'By all the world, rather than by his own heart. I could rather believe every creature of my acquaintance leagued together to ruin me in his opinion, than believe his nature capable of such cruelty. This woman of whom he writes – whoever she be – or any one, in short, but your own dear self, mama, and Edward, may have been so barbarous to belie me. Beyond you three, is there a creature in the world whom I would not rather suspect of evil than Willoughby, whose heart I know so well?'

Elinor would not contend, and only replied, 'Whoever may have been so detestably your enemy, let them be cheated of their malignant triumph, my dear sister, by seeing how nobly the consciousness of your own innocence and good intentions supports your spirits. It is a reasonable and laudable pride which resists such malevolence.'

'No, no,' cried Marianne, 'misery such as mine has no pride. I care not who knows that I am wretched. The triumph of seeing me so may be open to all the world. Elinor, Elinor, they who suffer little may be proud and independent as they like – may resist insult, or return mortification – but I cannot. I must feel – I must be wretched – and they are welcome to enjoy the consciousness of it that can.'

'But for my mother's sake and mine' –

'I would do more than for my own. But to appear happy when I am so miserable – Oh! who can require it?'

Again they were both silent. Elinor was employed in walking thoughtfully from the fire to the window, from the window to the fire, without knowing that she received warmth from one, or discerning objects through the other; and Marianne, seated at the foot of the bed, with her head leaning against one of its posts, again took up Willoughby's letter, and after shuddering over every sentence, exclaimed –

'It is too much! Oh! Willoughby, Willoughby, could this be yours! Cruel, cruel – nothing can acquit you. Elinor, nothing can. Whatever he might have heard against me – ought he not to have suspended his belief? ought he not to have told me of it, to have given me the power of clearing myself? "The lock of hair, (repeating it from the letter,) which you so obligingly bestowed on me" – That is unpardonable. Willoughby, where was your heart, when you wrote those words? Oh! barbarously insolent! – Elinor, can he be justified?'

'No, Marianne, in no possible way.'

'And yet this woman – who knows what her art may have been – how long it may have been premeditated, and how deeply contrived by her! – Who is she? – Who can she be? – Whom did I ever hear him talk of as young and attractive among his female acquaintance? – Oh! no one, no one – he talked to me only of myself.'

Another pause ensued; Marianne was greatly agitated, and it ended thus.

'Elinor, I must go home. I must go and comfort mama. Cannot we be gone to-morrow?'

'To-morrow, Marianne!'

'Yes; why should I stay here? I came only for Willoughby's sake – and now who cares for me? Who regards me?'

'It would be impossible to go to-morrow. We owe Mrs Jennings much more than civility; and civility of the commonest kind must prevent such a hasty removal as that.'

'Well, then, another day or two, perhaps; but I cannot stay here long, I cannot stay to endure the questions and remarks of all these people. The Middletons and Palmers – how am I to bear their pity? The pity of such a woman as Lady Middleton! Oh! what would *he* say to that!'

Elinor advised her to lie down again, and for a moment she did so; but no attitude could give her ease; and in restless pain of mind and body she moved from one posture to another, till growing more and more hysterical, her sister could with difficulty keep her on the bed at all, and for some time was fearful of being constrained to call for assistance. Some lavender drops, however, which she was at length persuaded to take, were of use; and from that time till Mrs Jennings returned, she continued on the bed quiet and motionless.

CHAPTER THIRTY

Mrs Jennings came immediately to their room on her return, and without waiting to have her request of admittance answered, opened the door and walked in with a look of real concern.

'How do you do my dear?' – said she in a voice of great compassion to Marianne, who turned away her face without attempting to answer.

'How is she, Miss Dashwood? – Poor thing! she looks very bad. – No wonder. Aye, it is but too true. He is to be married very soon – a good-for-nothing fellow! I have no patience with him. Mrs Taylor told me of it half an hour ago, and she was told it by a particular friend of Miss Grey herself, else I am sure I should not have believed it; and I was almost ready to sink as it was. Well, said I, all I can say is, that if it is true, he has used a young lady of my acquaintance abominably ill, and I wish with all my soul his wife may plague his heart out. And so I shall always say, my dear, you may depend on it. I have no notion of men's going on in this way: and if ever I meet him again, I will give him such a dressing as he has not had this many a day. But there is one comfort, my dear Miss Marianne; he is not the only young man in the world worth having; and with your pretty face you will never want admirers. Well, poor thing! I won't disturb her any longer, for she had better have her cry out at once and have done with it. The Parrys and Sandersons luckily are coming tonight you know, and that will amuse her.'

She then went away, walking on tiptoe out of the room, as if she supposed her young friend's affliction could be increased by noise.

Marianne, to the surprise of her sister, determined on dining with them. Elinor even advised her against it. But 'no, she would go down; she could bear it very well, and the bustle about her would be less.' Elinor, pleased to have her governed for a moment by such a motive, though believing it hardly possible that she could sit out the dinner, said no more; and adjusting her dress for her as well as she could, while Marianne still remained on the bed, was ready to assist her into the dining room as soon as they were summoned to it.

When there, though looking most wretchedly, she ate more and was calmer than her sister had expected. Had she tried to speak, or had she been conscious of half Mrs Jennings's well-meant but ill-judged attentions to her, this calmness could not have been maintained; but not a syllable escaped her lips, and the abstraction of her thoughts preserved her in ignorance of every thing that was passing before her.

Elinor, who did justice to Mrs Jennings's kindness, though its effusions were often distressing, and sometimes almost ridiculous, made her those acknowledgments, and returned her those civilities, which her sister could not make or return for herself. Their good friend saw that Marianne was unhappy, and felt that every thing was due to her which might make her at all less so. She treated her therefore, with all the indulgent fondness of a parent towards a favourite child on the last day of its holidays. Marianne was to have the best place by the fire, was to be tempted to eat by every delicacy in the house, and to be amused by the relation of all the news of the day. Had not Elinor, in the sad countenance of her sister, seen a check to all mirth, she could have been entertained by Mrs Jennings's endeavours to cure a disappointment in love, by a variety of sweetmeats and olives, and a good fire. As soon, however, as the consciousness of all this was forced by continual repetition on Marianne, she could stay no longer. With an hasty exclamation of misery, and a sign to her sister not to follow her, she directly got up and hurried out of the room.

'Poor soul!' cried Mrs Jennings, as soon as she was gone, 'how it grieves me to see her! And I declare if she is not gone away without finishing her wine! And the dried cherries too! Lord! nothing seems to do her any good. I am sure if I knew of any thing she would like, I would send all over the town for it. Well, it is the oddest thing to me, that a man should use such a pretty girl so ill! But when there is plenty of money on one side, and next to none on the other, Lord bless you! they care no more about such things! – '

'The lady then – Miss Grey I think you called her – is very rich?'

'Fifty thousand pounds, my dear. Did you ever see her? a smart, stilish girl they say, but not handsome. I remember her aunt very well, Biddy Henshawe; she married a very wealthy man. But the family are all rich together. Fifty thousand pounds! and by all accounts it won't come before it's wanted; for they say he is all to pieces. No wonder! dashing about with his curricle and hunters! Well, it don't signify talking, but when a young man, be he who he will, comes and makes love to a pretty girl, and promises marriage, he has no business to fly off from his word only because he grows poor, and a richer girl is ready to have him. Why don't he, in such a case, sell his horses, let his house, turn off his servants, and make a thorough reform at once? I warrant you, Miss Marianne would have been ready to wait till matters came round. But that won't do, now-a-days; nothing in the way of pleasure can ever be given up by the young men of this age.'

'Do you know what kind of a girl Miss Grey is? Is she said to be amiable?'

'I never heard any harm of her; indeed I hardly ever heard her mentioned; except that Mrs Taylor did say this morning, that one day Miss Walker hinted to her, that she believed Mr and Mrs Ellison would not be sorry to have Miss Grey married, for she and Mrs Ellison could never agree.' –

'And who are the Ellisons?'

'Her guardians, my dear. But now she is of age and may choose for herself; and a pretty choice she has made! – What now,' after pausing a moment – 'your poor sister is gone to her own room I suppose to moan by herself. Is there nothing one can get to comfort her? Poor dear, it seems quite cruel to let her be alone. Well, by-an-by we shall have a few friends, and that will amuse her a little. What shall we play at? She hates whist I know; but is there no round game she cares for?'

'Dear Ma'am, this kindness is quite unnecessary. Marianne I dare say will not leave her room again this evening. I shall persuade her if I can to go early to bed, for I am sure she wants rest.'

'Aye, I believe that will be best for her. Let her name her own supper, and go to bed. Lord! no wonder she has been looking so bad and so cast down this last week or two, for this matter I suppose has been hanging over her head as long as that. And so the letter that came today finished it! Poor soul! I am sure if I had had a notion of it, I would not have joked her about it for all my money. But then you know, how should I guess such a thing? I made sure of its being nothing but a common love letter, and you know young people like to be laughed at about them. Lord! how concerned Sir John and my daughters will be when they hear it! If I had had my senses about me I might have called in Conduit-street in my way home, and told them of it. But I shall see them tomorrow.'

'It would be unnecessary I am sure, for you to caution Mrs Palmer and Sir John against ever naming Mr Willoughby, or making the slightest allusion to what has passed, before my sister. Their own good-nature must point out to them the real cruelty of appearing to know any thing about it when she is present; and the less that may ever be said to myself on the subject, the more my feelings will be spared, as you my dear madam will easily believe.'

'Oh! Lord! yes, that I do indeed. It must be terrible for you to hear it talked of; and as for your sister, I am sure I would not mention a word about it to her for the world. You saw I did not all dinner time. No more would Sir John nor my daughters, for they are all very thoughtful and considerate; especially if I give them a hint, as I certainly will. For my part, I think the less that is said about such things, the better, the sooner 'tis blown over and forgot. And what good does talking ever do you know?'

'In this affair it can only do harm; more so perhaps than in many cases of a similar kind, for it has been attended by circumstances which, for the sake of every one concerned in it, make it unfit to become the public conversation. I must do *this* justice to Mr Willoughby – he has broken no positive engagement with my sister.'

'Law, my dear! Don't pretend to defend him. No positive engagement indeed! after taking her all over Allenham House, and fixing on the very rooms they were to live in hereafter!'

Elinor, for her sister's sake, could not press the subject farther, and she hoped it was not required of her for Willoughby's; since, though Marianne might lose much, he could gain very little by the enforcement of the real truth. After a short silence on both sides, Mrs Jennings, with all her natural hilarity, burst forth again.

'Well, my dear, 'tis a true saying about an ill wind, for it will be all the better for Colonel Brandon. He will have her at last; aye, that he will. Mind me, now, if they an't married by Midsummer. Lord! how he'll chuckle over this news! I hope he will come tonight. It will be all to one a better match for your sister. Two thousand a year without debt or drawback – except the little love-child, indeed; aye, I had forgot her; but she may be 'prenticed out at small cost, and then what does it signify? Delaford is a nice place, I can tell you; exactly what I call a nice old fashioned place, full of comforts and conveniences; quite shut in with great garden walls that are covered with the best fruit-trees in the country: and such a mulberry tree in one corner! Lord! how Charlotte and I did stuff the only time we were there!Then, there is a dove-cote, some delightful stewponds, and a very pretty canal; and every thing, in short, that one could wish for: and, moreover, it is close to the church, and only a quarter of a mile from the turnpike-road, so 'tis never dull, for if you only go and sit up in an old yew arbour behind the house, you may see all the carriages that pass along. Oh! 'tis a nice place! A butcher hard by in the village, and the parsonage-house within a stone's throw. To my fancy, a thousand times prettier than Barton Park, where they are forced to send three miles for their meat, and have not a neighbour nearer than your mother. Well, I shall spirit up the Colonel as soon as I can. One shoulder of mutton, you know, drives another down. If we *can* but put Willoughby out of her head!'

'Aye, if we can do *that*, Ma'am,' said Elinor, 'we shall do very well with or without Colonel Brandon.' And then rising, she went away to join Marianne, whom she found, as she expected, in her own room, leaning, in silent misery, over the small remains of a fire, which, till Elinor's entrance, had been her only light.

'You had better leave me,' was all the notice that her sister received from her.

'I will leave you,' said Elinor 'if you will go to bed.' But this, from the momentary perverseness of impatient suffering, she at first refused to do. Her sister's earnest, though gentle persuasion, however, soon softened her to compliance, and Elinor saw her lay her aching head on the pillow, and saw her, as she hoped, in a way to get some quiet rest before she left her.

In the drawing-room, whither she then repaired, she was soon joined by Mrs Jennings, with a wine-glass, full of something, in her hand.

'My dear,' said she, entering, 'I have just recollected that I have some of the finest old Constantia wine in the house, that ever was tasted, so I have brought a glass of it for your sister. My poor husband! how fond he was of it! Whenever he had a touch of his old cholicky gout, he said it did him more good than any thing else in the world. Do take it to your sister.'

'Dear Ma'am,' replied Elinor, smiling at the difference of the complaints for which it was recommended, 'how good you are! But I have just left Marianne in bed, and, I hope, almost asleep; and as I think nothing will be of so much service to her as rest, if you will give me leave, I will drink the wine myself.'

Mrs Jennings, though regretting that she had not been five minutes earlier, was satisfied with the compromise; and Elinor, as she swallowed the chief of it, reflected that, though its good effects on a cholicky gout were, at present, of little importance to her, its healing powers on a disappointed heart might be as reasonably tried on herself as on her sister.

Colonel Brandon came in while the party were at tea, and by his manner of looking round the room for Marianne, Elinor immedi-

'How fond he was of it!'

ately fancied that he neither expected, nor wished to see her there, and, in short, that he was already aware of what occasioned her absence. Mrs Jennings was not struck by the same thought; for, soon after his entrance, she walked across the room to the tea-table where Elinor presided, and whispered – 'The Colonel looks as grave as ever you see. He knows nothing of it; do tell him my dear.'

He shortly afterwards drew a chair close to her's, and, with a look which perfectly assured her of his good information, inquired after her sister.

'Marianne is not well,' said she. 'She has been indisposed all day, and we have persuaded her to go to bed.'

'Perhaps, then,' he hesitatingly replied, 'what I heard this morning may be – there may be more truth in it than I could believe possible at first.'

'What did you hear?'

'That a gentleman, whom I had reason to think – in short, that a man, whom I *knew* to be engaged – but how shall I tell you? If you know it already, as surely you must, I may be spared.'

'You mean,' answered Elinor with forced calmness, 'Mr Willoughby's marriage with Miss Grey. Yes, we *do* know it all. This seems to have been a day of general elucidation, for this very morning first unfolded it to us. Mr Willoughby is unfathomable! Where did you hear it?'

'In a stationer's shop in Pall Mall, where I had business. Two ladies were waiting for their carriage, and one of them was giving the other an account of the intended match, in a voice so little attempting concealment, that it was impossible for me not to hear all. The name of Willoughby, John Willoughby, frequently repeated, first caught my attention, and what followed was a positive assertion that every thing was now finally settled respecting his marriage with Miss Grey – it was no longer to be a secret – it would take place even within a few weeks, with many particulars of preparations and other matters. One thing, especially, I remember, because it served to identify the man still more: – as soon as the ceremony was over, they were to go to Combe Magna, his seat in Somersetshire. My astonishment! – but it would be impossible to describe what I felt. The communicative lady I learnt, on inquiry, for I staid in the shop till they were gone, was a Mrs Ellison, and that, as I have been since informed, is the name of Miss Grey's guardian.'

'It is. But have you likewise heard that Miss Grey has fifty thousand pounds? In that, if in anything, we may find an explanation.'

'It may be so; but Willoughby is capable – at least I think' – he stopped a moment; then added in a voice which seemed to distrust itself, 'And your sister – how did she – '

'Her sufferings have been very severe. I have only to hope that they may be proportionately short. It has been, it is a most cruel affliction. Till yesterday, I believe she never doubted his regard; and even now, perhaps – but *I* am almost convinced that he never was really attached to her. He has been very deceitful! and in some points, there seems a hardness of heart about him.'

'Ah!' said Colonel Brandon, 'there is, indeed! But your sister does not – I think you said so – she does not consider it quite as you do?'

'You know her disposition, and may believe how eagerly she would still justify him if she could.'

He made no answer; and soon afterwards, by the removal of the tea-things, and the arrangement of the card parties, the subject was necessarily dropped. Mrs Jennings, who had watched them with pleasure while they were talking, and who expected to see the effect of Miss Dashwood's communication, in such an instantaneous gaiety on Colonel Brandon's side, as might have become a man in the bloom of youth, of hope and happiness, saw him, with amazement, remain the whole evening more serious and thoughtful than usual.

CHAPTER THIRTY-ONE

From a night of more sleep than she had expected, Marianne awoke the next morning to the same consciousness of misery in which she had closed her eyes.

Elinor encouraged her as much as possible to talk of what she felt; and before breakfast was ready, they had gone through the subject again and again; with the same steady conviction and affectionate counsel on Elinor's side, the same impetuous feelings and varying opinions on Marianne's, as before. Sometimes she could believe Willoughby to be as unfortunate and as innocent as herself, and at others, lost every consolation in the impossibility of acquitting him. At one moment she was absolutely indifferent to the observation of all the world, at another she would seclude herself from it for ever, and at a third could resist it with energy. In one thing, however, she was uniform, when it came to the point, in avoiding, where it was possible, the presence of Mrs Jennings, and in a determined silence when obliged to endure it. Her heart was hardened against the belief of Mrs Jennings's entering into her sorrows with any compassion.

'No, no, no, it cannot be,' she cried; 'she cannot feel. Her kindness is not sympathy; her good nature is not tenderness. All that she wants is gossip, and she only likes me now because I supply it.'

Elinor had not needed this to be assured of the injustice to which her sister was often led in her opinion of others, by the irritable refinement of her own mind, and the too great importance placed by her on the delicacies of a strong sensibility, and the graces of a polished manner. Like half the rest of the world, if more than half there be that are clever and good, Marianne, with excellent abilities and an excellent disposition, was neither reasonable nor candid. She expected from other people the same opinions and feelings as her own, and she judged of their motives by the immediate effect of their actions on herself. Thus a circumstance occurred, while the sisters were together in their own room after breakfast, which sunk the heart of Mrs Jennings still lower in her estimation; because, through her own weakness, it chanced to prove a source of fresh pain to herself, though Mrs Jennings was governed in it by an impulse of the utmost goodwill.

With a letter in her outstretched hand, and countenance gaily smiling, from the persuasion of bringing comfort, she entered their room, saying,

'Now, my dear, I bring you something that I am sure will do you good.'

Marianne heard enough. In one moment her imagination placed before her a letter from Willoughby, full of tenderness and contrition, explanatory of all that had passed, satisfactory, convincing, and instantly followed by Willoughby himself, rushing eagerly into the room to inforce, at her feet, by the eloquence of his eyes, the assurances of his letter. The work of one moment was destroyed by the next. The hand writing of her mother, never till then unwelcome, was before her; and, in the acuteness of the disappointment which followed such an extasy of more than hope, she felt as if, till that instant, she had never suffered.

The cruelty of Mrs Jennings no language, within her reach in her moments of happiest eloquence, could have expressed; and now she could reproach her only by the tears which streamed from her eyes with passionate violence – a reproach, however, so entirely lost on its object, that after many expressions of pity, she withdrew, still referring her to the letter for comfort. But the letter, when she was calm enough to read it, brought little comfort. Willoughby filled every page. Her mother, still confident of their engagement, and relying as warmly as ever on his constancy, had only been roused by Elinor's application, to intreat from Marianne greater openness towards them both; and this, with such tenderness towards her, such affection for Willoughby, and such a conviction of their future happiness in each other, that she wept with agony through the whole of it.

All her impatience to be at home again now returned; her mother was dearer to her than ever; dearer through the very excess of her mistaken confidence in Willoughby, and she was wildly urgent to be gone. Elinor, unable herself to determine whether it were better for Marianne to be in London or at Barton, offered no counsel of her own except of patience till their mother's wishes could be known; and at length she obtained her sister's consent to wait for that knowledge.

Mrs Jennings left them earlier than usual; for she could not be easy till the Middletons and Palmers were able to grieve as much as herself; and positively refusing Elinor's offered attendance, went out alone for the rest of the morning. Elinor, with a very heavy heart, aware of the pain she was going to communicate, and perceiving by Marianne's letter how ill she had succeeded in laying any foundation for it, then sat down to write her mother an account of what had passed, and intreat her directions for the future; while Marianne, who came into the drawing-room on Mrs Jennings's going away, remained fixed at the table where Elinor wrote, watching the advancement of her pen, grieving over her for the hardship of such a task, and grieving still more fondly over its effect on her mother.

In this manner they had continued about a quarter of an hour, when Marianne, whose nerves could not then bear any sudden noise, was startled by a rap at the door.

'Who can this be?' cried Elinor. 'So early too! I thought we *had* been safe.'

Marianne moved to the window –

'It is Colonel Brandon!' said she, with vexation. 'We are never safe from *him*.'

'He will not come in, as Mrs Jennings is from home.'

'I will not trust to *that*,' retreating to her own room. 'A man who has nothing to do with his own time has no conscience in his intrusion on that of others.'

The event proved her conjecture right, though it was founded on injustice and error; for Colonel Brandon *did* come in; and Elinor, who was convinced that solicitude for Marianne brought him thither, and who saw *that* solicitude in his disturbed and melancholy look, and in his anxious though brief enquiry after her, could not forgive her sister for esteeming him so lightly.

'I met Mrs Jennings in Bond-street,' said he, after the first salutation, 'and she encouraged me to come on; and I was the more easily encouraged, because I thought it probable that I might find you alone, which I was very desirous of doing. My object – my wish – my sole wish in desiring it – I hope, I believe it is – is to be a means of giving comfort; – no, I must not say comfort – not present comfort – but conviction, lasting conviction to your sister's mind. My regard for her, for yourself, for your mother – will you allow me to prove it, by relating some circumstances, which nothing but a *very* sincere regard – nothing but an earnest desire of being useful – I think I am justified – though where so many hours have been spent in convincing myself that I am right, is there not some reason to fear I may be wrong?' He stopped.

'I understand you,' said Elinor, 'You have something to tell me of Mr Willoughby, that will open his character farther. Your telling it will be the greatest act of friendship that can be shewn Marianne. *My* gratitude will be insured immediately by any information tending to that end, and *her's* must be granted by it in time. Pray, pray let me hear it.'

'You shall; and, to be brief, when I quitted Barton last October, – but this will give you no idea – I must go farther back. You will find me a very awkward narrator, Miss Dashwood; I hardly know where to begin. A short account of myself, I believe, will be necessary, and it *shall* be a short one. On such a subject,' sighing heavily, 'I can have little temptation to be diffuse.'

He stopt a moment for recollection, and then, with another sigh, went on.

'You have probably entirely forgotten a conversation – (it is not to be supposed that it could make any impression on you) – a conversation between us one evening at Barton Park – it was the evening of a dance – in which I alluded to a lady I had once known, as resembling, in some measure, your sister Marianne.'

'Indeed,' answered Elinor, 'I have *not* forgotten it.' He looked pleased by this remembrance, and added,

'If I am not deceived by the uncertainty, the partiality of tender recollection, there is a very strong resemblance between them, as well in mind as person. The same warmth of heart, the same eagerness of fancy and spirits. This lady was one of my nearest relations, an orphan from her infancy, and under the guardianship of my father. Our ages were nearly the same, and from our earliest years we were playfellows and friends. I cannot remember the time when I did not love Eliza; and my affection for her, as we grew up, was such, as perhaps, judging from my present forlorn and cheerless gravity, you might think me incapable of having ever felt. Her's, for me, was I believe, fervent as the attachment of your sister to Mr Willoughby and it was, though from a different cause, no less unfortunate. At seventeen, she was lost to me for ever. She was married – married against her inclination to my brother. Her fortune was large, and our family estate much encumbered. And this, I fear, is all that can be said for the conduct of one, who was at once her uncle and guardian. My brother did not deserve her; he did not even love her. I had hoped that her regard for me would support her under any difficulty, and for some time it did; but at last the misery of her situation, for she experienced great unkindness, overcame all her resolution, and though she had promised me that nothing – but how blindly I relate! I have never told you how this was brought on. We were within a few hours of eloping together for Scotland. The treachery, or the folly, of my cousin's maid betrayed us. I was banished to the house of a relation far distant, and she was allowed no liberty, no society, no amusement, till my father's point was gained. I had depended on her fortitude too far, and the blow was a severe one – but had her marriage been happy, so young as I then was, a few months must have reconciled me to it, or at least I should not have now to lament it. This however was not the case. My brother had no regard for her; his pleasures were not what they ought to have been, and from the first he treated her unkindly. The consequence of this, upon a mind so young, so lively, so inexperienced as Mrs Brandon's, was but too natural. She resigned herself at first to all the misery of her situation; and happy had it been if she had not lived to overcome those regrets which the remembrance of me occasioned. But can we wonder that with such a husband to provoke inconstancy, and without a friend to advise or restrain her, (for my father lived only a few months after their marriage, and I was with my regiment in the East Indies) she should fall? Had I remained in England, perhaps – but I meant to promote the happiness of both by removing from her for years, and for that purpose had procured my exchange. The shock which her marriage had given me,' he continued, in a voice of great agitation, 'was of trifling weight – was nothing – to what I felt when I heard, about two years afterwards, of her divorce. It was *that* which threw this gloom, – even now the recollection of what I suffered – '

He could say no more, and rising hastily walked for a few minutes about the room. Elinor, affected by his relation, and still more by his distress, could not speak. He saw her concern, and coming to her, took her hand, pressed it, and kissed it with grateful respect. A few minutes more of silent exertion enabled him to proceed with composure.

'It was nearly three years after this unhappy period before I returned to England. My first care, when I *did* arrive, was of course to seek for her; but the search was as fruitless as it was melancholy. I could not trace her beyond her first seducer, and there was every reason to fear that she had removed from him only to sink deeper in a life of sin. Her legal allowance was not adequate to her fortune, nor sufficient for her comfortable maintenance, and I learnt from my brother, that the power of receiving it had been made over some months before to another person. He imagined, and calmly could he imagine it, that her extravagance and consequent distress had obliged her to dispose of it for some immediate relief. At last, however, and after I had been six months in England, I *did* find her. Regard for a former servant of my own, who had since fallen into misfortune, carried me to visit him in a spunging-house, where he was confined for debt; and there, in the same house, under a similar confinement, was my unfortunate sister. So altered – so faded – worn down by acute suffering of every kind! hardly could I believe the melancholy and sickly figure before me, to be the remains of the lovely, blooming, healthful girl, on whom I had once doated. What I endured in so beholding her – but I have no right to wound your feelings by attempting to describe it – I have pained you too much already. That she was, to all appearance, in the last stage of consumption, was – yes, in such a situation it was my greatest comfort. Life could do nothing for her, beyond giving time for a better preparation for death; and that was given. I saw her placed in comfortable lodgings, and under proper attendants; I visited her every day during the rest of her short life; I was with her in her last moments.'

Again he stopped to recover himself; and Elinor spoke her feelings in an exclamation of tender concern, at the fate of his unfortunate friend.

'Your sister, I hope, cannot be offended,' said he, 'by the resemblance I have fancied between her and my poor disgraced relation. Their fates, their fortunes cannot be the same; and had the natural sweet disposition of the one been guarded by a firmer mind, or an happier marriage, she might have been all that you will live to see the other be. But to what does all this lead? I seem to have been distressing you for nothing. Ah! Miss Dashwood – a subject such as this – untouched for fourteen years – it is dangerous to handle it at all! I *will* be more collected – more concise. She left to my care her only child, a little girl, the offspring of her first guilty connection, who was then about three years old. She loved the child, and had always kept it with her. It was valued, a precious trust to me; and gladly would I have discharged it in the strictest sense, by watching over her education myself, had the nature of our situations allowed it; but I had no family, no home; and my little Eliza was therefore placed at school. I saw her there whenever I could, and after the death of my brother, (which happened about five years ago, and which left to me the possession of the family property,) she frequently visited me at Delaford. I called her a distant relation; but I am well aware that I have in general been suspected of a much nearer connection with her. It is now three years ago, (she had just reached her fourteenth year,) that I removed her from school, to place her under the care of a very respectable woman, residing in Dorsetshire, who had the charge of four or five other girls of about the same time of life; and for two years I had every reason to be pleased with her situation. But last February, almost a twelvemonth back, she suddenly disappeared. I had allowed her, (imprudently, as it has since turned out,) at her earnest desire, to go to Bath with one of her young friends, who was attending her father there for his health. I knew him to be a very good sort of man, and I thought well of his daughter – better than she deserved, for, with a most obstinate and ill-judged secrecy, she would tell nothing, would give no clue, though she certainly knew. He, her father, a well-meaning, but not a quick-sighted man, could really, I believe, give no information; for he had been generally confined to the house, while the girls were ranging over the town and making what acquaintance they chose, and he tried to convince me, as thoroughly as he was convinced himself, of his daughter's being entirely unconcerned in the business. In short, I could learn nothing but that she was gone; all the rest, for eight long months, was left to conjecture. What I thought, what I feared, may be imagined; and what I suffered too.'

'Good heavens!' cried Elinor, 'could it be – could Willoughby!' –

'The first news that reached me of her,' he continued, 'came in a letter from herself, last October. It was forwarded to me from Delaford, and I received it on the very morning of our intended party to Whitwell; and this was the reason of my leaving Barton so suddenly, which I am sure must at the time have appeared strange to every body, and which I believe gave offence to some. Little did Mr Willoughby imagine, I suppose, when his looks censured me for incivility in breaking up the party, that I was called away to the relief of one, whom he had made poor and miserable; but *had* he known it, what would it have availed? Would he have been less gay or less happy in the smiles of your sister? No, he had already done that, which no man who *can* feel for another, would do. He had left the girl whose youth and innocence he had seduced, in a situation of the utmost distress, with no creditable home, no help, no friends, ignorant of his address! He had left her promising to return; he neither returned, nor wrote, nor relieved her.'

'This is beyond every thing!' exclaimed Elinor.

'His character is now before you; expensive, dissipated, and worse than both. Knowing all this, as I have now known it many weeks, guess what I must have felt on seeing your sister as fond of him as ever, and on being assured that she was to marry him; guess what I must have felt for all your sakes. When I came to you last week and found you alone, I came determined to know the truth; though irresolute what to do when it *was* known. My behaviour must have seemed strange to you then; but now you will comprehend it. To suffer you all to be so deceived; to see your sister – but what could I do? I had no hope of interfering with success; and sometimes I thought your sister's influence might yet reclaim him. But now, after such dishonourable usage, who can tell what were his designs on her? Whatever they may have been, however, she may now, and hereafter doubtless *will*, turn with gratitude towards her own condition, when she compares it with that of my poor Eliza, when she considers the wretched and hopeless situation of this poor girl, and pictures her to herself, with an affection for him as strong, still as strong as her own, and with a mind tormented by self-reproach, which must attend her through life. Surely this comparison must have its use with her. She will feel her own sufferings to be nothing. They proceed from no misconduct, and can bring no disgrace. On the contrary, every friend must be made still more her friend by them. Concern for her unhappiness, and respect for her fortitude under it, must strengthen every attachment. Use your own discretion, however, in communicating to her what I have told you. You must know best what will be its effect; but had I not seriously, and from my heart believed it might be of service, might lessen her regrets, I would not have suffered myself to trouble you with this account of my family afflictions, with a recital which may seem to have been intended to raise myself at the expense of others.'

Elinor's thanks followed this speech with grateful earnestness; attended too with the assurance of her expecting material advantage to Marianne, from the communication of what had passed.

'I have been more pained,' said she, 'by her endeavours to acquit him than by all the rest; for it irritates her mind more than the most perfect conviction of his unworthiness can do. Now, though at first she will suffer much, I am sure she will soon become easier. Have you,' she continued, after a short silence, 'ever seen Mr Willoughby since you left him at Barton?'

'Yes,' he replied gravely, 'once I have. One meeting was unavoidable.'

Elinor, startled by his manner, looked at him anxiously, saying, 'What? have you met him to – '

'I could meet him in no other way. Eliza confessed to me, though most reluctantly, the name of her lover; and when he returned to town, which was within a fortnight after myself, we met by appointment, he to defend, I to punish his conduct. We returned unwounded, and the meeting, therefore, never got abroad.'

Elinor sighed over the fancied necessity of this; but to a man and a soldier, she presumed not to censure it.

'Such,' said Colonel Brandon, after a pause, 'has been the unhappy resemblance between the fate of mother and daughter! and so imperfectly have I discharged my trust!'

'Is she still in town?'

'No; as soon as she recovered from her lying-in, for I found her near her delivery, I removed her and her child into the country, and there she remains.'

Recollecting, soon afterwards, that he was probably dividing Elinor from her sister, he put an end to his visit, receiving from her again the same grateful acknowledgments, and leaving her full of compassion and esteem for him.

CHAPTER THIRTY-TWO

WHEN THE PARTICULARS of this conversation were repeated by Miss Dashwood to her sister, as they very soon were, the effect on her was not entirely such as the former had hoped to see. Not that Marianne appeared to distrust the truth of any part of it, for she listened to it all with the most steady and submissive attention, made neither objection nor remark, attempted no vindication of Willoughby, and seemed to shew by her tears that she felt it to be impossible. But though this behaviour assured Elinor that the conviction of his guilt *was* carried home to her mind, though she saw with satisfaction the effect of it, in her no longer avoiding Colonel Brandon when he called, in her speaking to him, even voluntarily speaking, with a kind of compassionate respect, and though she saw her spirits less violently irritated than before, she did not see her less wretched. Her mind did become settled, but it was settled in a gloomy dejection. She felt the loss of Willoughby's character yet more heavily than she had felt the loss of his heart; his seduction and desertion of Miss Williams, the misery of that poor girl, and the doubt of what his designs might *once* have been on herself, preyed altogether so much on her spirits, that she could not bring herself to speak of what she felt even to Elinor; and brooding over her sorrows in silence, gave more pain to her sister than could have been communicated by the most open and most frequent confession of them.

To give the feelings or the language of Mrs Dashwood on receiving and answering Elinor's letter, would be only to give a repetition of what her daughters had already felt and said; of a disappointment hardly less painful than Marianne's, and an indignation even greater than Elinor's. Long letters from her, quickly succeeding each other, arrived to tell all that she suffered and thought; to express her anxious solicitude for Marianne, and entreat she would bear up with fortitude under this misfortune. Bad indeed must the nature of Marianne's affliction be, when her mother could talk of fortitude! mortifying and humiliating must be the origin of those regrets, which *she* could wish her not to indulge!

Against the interests of her own individual comfort, Mrs Dashwood had determined that it would be better for Marianne to be anywhere, at that time, than at Barton, where every thing within her view would be bringing back the past in the strongest and most afflicting manner, by constantly placing Willoughby before her, such as she had always seen him there. She recommended it to her daughters, therefore, by all means not to shorten their visit to Mrs Jennings; the length of which, though never exactly fixed, had been expected by all to comprise at least five or six weeks. A variety of occupations, of objects, and of company, which could not be procured at Barton, would be inevitable there, and might yet, she hoped, cheat Marianne, at times, into some interest beyond herself, and even into some amusement, much as the idea of both might now be spurned by her.

From all danger of seeing Willoughby again, her mother considered her to be at least equally safe in town as in the country, since his acquaintance must now be dropped by all who called themselves her friends. Design could never bring them in each other's way; negligence could never leave them exposed to a surprise; and chance had less in its favour in the crowd of London than even in the retirements of Barton, where it might force him before her while paying that visit at Allenham on his marriage, which Mrs Dashwood, from foreseeing at first as a probable event, had brought herself to expect as a certain one.

She had yet another reason for wishing her children to remain where they were; a letter from her son-in-law had told her that he and his wife were to be in town before the middle of February, and she judged it right that they should sometimes see their brother.

Marianne had promised to be guided by her mother's opinion,

and she submitted to it therefore without opposition, though it proved perfectly different from what she wished and expected, though she felt it to be entirely wrong, formed on mistaken grounds; and that by requiring her long continuance in London it deprived her of the only possible alleviation of her wretchedness, the personal sympathy of her mother, and doomed her to such society and such scenes as must prevent her ever knowing a moment's rest.

But it was a matter of great consolation to her, that what brought evil to herself would bring good to her sister; and Elinor, on the other hand, suspecting that it would not be in her power to avoid Edward entirely, comforted herself by thinking, that though their long stay would therefore militate against her own happiness, it would be better for Marianne than an immediate return into Devonshire.

Her carefulness in guarding her sister from ever hearing Willoughby's name mentioned, was not thrown away. Marianne, though without knowing it herself, reaped all its advantage; for neither Mrs Jennings, nor Sir John, nor even Mrs Palmer herself, ever spoke of him before her. Elinor wished that the same forbearance could have extended towards herself, but that was impossible, and she was obliged to listen day after day to the indignation of them all.

Sir John could not have thought it possible. 'A man of whom he had always had such reason to think well! Such a good natured fellow! He did not believe there was a bolder rider in England! It was an unaccountable business. He wished him at the devil with all his heart. He would not speak another word to him, meet him where he might, for all the world! No, not if it were to be by the side of Barton covert, and they were kept waiting for two hours together. Such a scoundrel of a fellow! such a deceitful dog! It was only the last time they met that he had offered him one of Folly's puppies! and this was the end of it!'

Mrs Palmer, in her way, was equally angry. 'She was determined to drop his acquaintance immediately, and she was very thankful that she had never been acquainted with him at all. She wished with all her heart Combe Magna was not so near Cleveland; but it did not signify, for it was a great deal too far off to visit; she hated him so much that she was resolved never to mention his name again, and she should tell everybody she saw, how good-for-nothing he was.'

The rest of Mrs Palmer's sympathy was shewn in procuring all the particulars in her power of the approaching marriage, and communicating them to Elinor. She could soon tell at what coach-

Offered him one of Folly's puppies.

maker's the new carriage was building, by what painter Mr Willoughby's portrait was drawn, and at what warehouse Miss Grey's clothes might be seen.

The calm and polite unconcern of Lady Middleton on the occasion was an happy relief to Elinor's spirits, oppressed as they often were by the clamorous kindness of the others. It was a great comfort to her, to be sure of exciting no interest in *one* person at least among their circle of friends; a great comfort to know that there was *one* who would meet her without feeling any curiosity after particulars, or any anxiety for her sister's health.

Every qualification is raised at times, by the circumstances of the moment, to more than its real value; and she was sometimes worried down by officious condolence to rate good-breeding as more indispensable to comfort than good-nature.

Lady Middleton expressed her sense of the affair about once every day, or twice, if the subject occurred very often, by saying, 'It is very shocking indeed!' and by the means of this continual though gentle vent, was able not only to see the Miss Dashwoods from the first without the smallest emotion, but very soon to see them without recollecting a word of the matter; and having thus supported the dignity of her own sex, and spoken her decided censure of what was wrong in the other, she thought herself at liberty to attend to the interest of her own assemblies, and therefore determined (though rather against the opinion of Sir John) that as Mrs Willoughby would at once be a woman of elegance and fortune, to leave her card with her as soon as she married.

Colonel Brandon's delicate unobtrusive inquiries were never unwelcome to Miss Dashwood. He had abundantly earned the privilege of intimate discussion of her sister's disappointment, by the friendly zeal with which he had endeavoured to soften it, and they always conversed with confidence. His chief reward for the painful exertion of disclosing past sorrows and present humiliations, was given in the pitying eye with which Marianne sometimes observed him, and the gentleness of her voice when ever (though it did not often happen) she was obliged, or could oblige herself to speak to him. *These* assured him that his exertion had produced an increase of good-will towards himself, and *these* gave Elinor hopes of its being farther augmented hereafter; but Mrs Jennings, who knew nothing of all this, who knew only that the Colonel continued as grave as ever, and that she could neither prevail on him to make the offer himself, nor commission her to make it for him, began, at the end of two days, to think that, instead of Midsummer, they would not be married till Michaelmas, and by the end of a week that it would not be a match at all. The good understanding between the Colonel and Miss Dashwood seemed rather to declare that the honours of the mulberry-tree, the canal, and the yew arbour, would all be made over to *her*; and Mrs Jennings had for some time ceased to think at all of Mr Ferrars.

Early in February, within a fortnight from the receipt of Willoughby's letter, Elinor had the painful office of informing her sister that he was married. She had taken care to have the intelligence conveyed to herself, as soon as it was known that the ceremony was over, as she was desirous that Marianne should not receive the first notice of it from the public papers, which she saw her eagerly examining every morning.

She received the news with resolute composure; made no observation on it, and at first shed no tears; but after a short time they would burst out, and for the rest of the day, she was in a state hardly less pitiable than when she first learnt to expect the event.

The Willoughbys left town as soon as they were married; and Elinor now hoped, as there could be no danger of her seeing either of them, to prevail on her sister, who had never yet left the house since the blow first fell, to go out again by degrees as she had done before.

About this time, the two Miss Steeles, lately arrived at their cousin's house in Bartlett's Buildings, Holborn, presented themselves again before their more grand relations in Conduit and Berkeley-street; and were welcomed by them all with great cordiality.

Elinor only was sorry to see them. Their presence always gave her pain, and she hardly knew how to make a very gracious return to the overpowering delight of Lucy in finding her *still* in town.

'I should have been quite disappointed if I had not found you here *still*,' said she repeatedly, with a strong emphasis on the word. 'But I always thought I *should*. I was almost sure you would not leave London yet awhile; though you *told* me, you know, at Barton, that you should not stay above a *month*. But I thought, at the time, that you would most likely change your mind when it came to the point. It would have been such a great pity to have went away before your brother and sister came. And now to be sure you will be in no hurry to be gone. I am amazingly glad you did not keep to *your word*.'

Elinor perfectly understood her, and was forced to use all her self-command to make it appear that she did *not*.

'Well, my dear,' said Mrs Jennings, 'and how did you travel?'

'Not in the stage, I assure you,' replied Miss Steele, with quick exultation; 'we came post all the way and had a very smart beau to attend us. Dr Davies was coming to town, and so we thought we'd join him in a post-chaise; and he behaved very genteelly, and paid ten or twelve shillings more than we did.'

'Oh, oh!' cried Mrs Jennings; 'very pretty, indeed! and the Doctor is a single man, I warrant you.'

'There now,' said Miss Steele, affectedly simpering, 'every body laughs at me so about the Doctor, and I cannot think why. My cousins say they are sure I have made a conquest; but for my part I declare I never think about him from one hour's end to another. "Lord! here comes your beau, Nancy," my cousin said t'other day, when she saw him crossing the street to the house. My beau, indeed! said I – I cannot think who you mean. The Doctor is no beau of mine.'

'Aye, aye, that is very pretty talking – but it won't do – the Doctor is the man, I see.'

A very smart beau.

'No, indeed!' replied her cousin, with affected earnestness, 'and I beg you will contradict it, if you ever hear it talked of.'

Mrs Jennings directly gave her the gratifying assurance that she certainly would *not*, and Miss Steele was made completely happy.

'I suppose you will go and stay with your brother and sister, Miss Dashwood, when they come to town,' said Lucy, returning, after a cessation of hostile hints, to the charge.

'No, I do not think we shall.'

'Oh, yes, I dare say you will.'

Elinor would not humour her by farther opposition.

'What a charming thing it is that Mrs Dashwood can spare you both for so long a time together!'

'Long a time, indeed!' interposed Mrs Jennings. 'Why, their visit is but just begun!'

Lucy was silenced.

'I am sorry we cannot see your sister, Miss Dashwood,' said Miss Steele. 'I am sorry she is not well;' for Marianne had left the room on their arrival.

'You are very good. My sister will be equally sorry to miss the pleasure of seeing you; but she has been very much plagued lately with nervous head-aches, which make her unfit for company or conversation.'

'Oh, dear, that is a great pity! but such old friends as Lucy and me! – I think she might see *us*; and I am sure we would not speak a word.'

Elinor, with great civility, declined the proposal. Her sister was perhaps laid down upon the bed, or in her dressing gown, and therefore not able to come to them.

'Oh, if that's all,' cried Miss Steele, 'we can just as well go and see *her*.'

Elinor began to find this impertinence too much for her temper; but she was saved the trouble of checking it, by Lucy's sharp reprimand, which now, as on many occasions, though it did not give much sweetness to the manners of one sister, was of advantage in governing those of the other.

CHAPTER THIRTY-THREE

After some opposition, Marianne yielded to her sister's entreaties, and consented to go out with her and Mrs Jennings one morning for half an hour. She expressly conditioned, however, for paying no visits, and would do no more than accompany them to Gray's in Sackville-street, where Elinor was carrying on a negociation for the exchange of a few old-fashioned jewels of her mother.

When they stopped at the door, Mrs Jennings recollected that there was a lady at the other end of the street, on whom she ought to call; and as she had no business at Gray's, it was resolved, that while her young friends transacted their's, she should pay her visit and return for them.

On ascending the stairs, the Miss Dashwoods found so many people before them in the room, that there was not a person at liberty to attend to their orders; and they were obliged to wait. All that could be done was, to sit down at that end of the counter which seemed to promise the quickest succession; one gentleman only was standing there, and it is probable that Elinor was not without hope of exciting his politeness to a quicker dispatch. But the correctness of his eye, and the delicacy of his taste, proved to be beyond his politeness. He was giving orders for a toothpick-case for himself, and till its size, shape, and ornaments were determined, all of which, after examining and debating for a quarter of an hour over every toothpick-case in the shop, were finally arranged by his own inventive fancy, he had no leisure to bestow any other attention on the two ladies, than what was comprised in three or four very broad stares; a kind of notice which served to imprint on Elinor the remembrance of a person and face, of strong, natural, sterling insignificance, though adorned in the first style of fashion.

Marianne was spared from the troublesome feelings of contempt and resentment, on this impertinent examination of their features, and on the puppyism of his manner in deciding on all the different horrors of the different toothpick-cases presented to his inspection, by remaining unconscious of it all; for she was as well able to collect her thoughts within herself, and be as ignorant of what was passing around her, in Mr Gray's shop, as in her own bed-room.

At last the affair was decided. The ivory, the gold, and the pearls all received their appointment, and the gentleman having named the last day on which his existence could be continued without the possession of the toothpick-case, drew on his gloves with leisurely care, and bestowing another glance on the Miss Dashwoods, but such a one as seemed rather to demand than express admiration, walked off with an happy air of real conceit and affected indifference.

Elinor lost no time in bringing her business forward, and was on the point of concluding it, when another gentleman presented himself at her side. She turned her eyes towards his face, and found him with some surprise to be her brother.

Their affection and pleasure in meeting, was just enough to make a very creditable appearance in Mr Gray's shop. John Dashwood was really far from being sorry to see his sisters again; it rather gave him satisfaction; and his inquiries after their mother were respectful and attentive.

Elinor found that he and Fanny had been in town two days.

'I wished very much to call upon you yesterday,' said he, 'but it was impossible, for we were obliged to take Harry to see the wild beasts at Exeter Exchange: and we spent the rest of the day with Mrs Ferrars. Harry was vastly pleased. *This* morning I had fully intended to call on you, if I could possible find a spare half hour, but one has always so much to do on first coming to town. I am come here to bespeak Fanny a seal. But tomorrow I think I shall certainly be able to call in Berkeley-street, and be introduced to your friend Mrs Jennings. I understand she is a woman of very good fortune. And the Middletons too, you must introduce me to *them*. As my mother-in-law's relations, I shall be happy to shew them every respect. They are excellent neighbours to you in the country, I understand.'

'Excellent indeed. Their attention to our comfort, their friendliness in every particular, is more than I can express.'

'I am extremely glad to hear it, upon my word; extremely glad indeed. But so it ought to be; they are people of large fortune, they are related to you, and every civility, and accommodation that can serve to make your situation pleasant, might be reasonably expected. And so you are most comfortably settled in your little cottage and want for nothing! Edward brought us a most charming account of the place; the most complete thing of its kind, he said, that ever was, and you all seemed to enjoy it beyond any thing. It was a great satisfaction to us to hear it, I assure you.'

Elinor did feel a little ashamed of her brother; and was not sorry to be spared the necessity of answering him, by the arrival of Mrs Jennings's servant, who came to tell her that his mistress waited for them at the door.

Mr Dashwood attended them down stairs, was introduced to Mrs Jennings at the door of her carriage, and repeating his hope of being able to call on them the next day, took leave.

His visit was duly paid. He came with a pretence at an apology from their sister-in-law, for not coming too; 'but she was so much engaged with her mother, that really she had no leisure for going any where.' Mrs Jennings, however, assured him directly, that she should not stand upon ceremony, for they were all cousins, or something like it, and she should certainly wait on Mrs John Dashwood very soon, and bring her sisters to see her. His manners to *them*, though calm, were perfectly kind; to Mrs Jennings most attentively civil; and on Colonel Brandon's coming in soon after himself, he eyed him with a curiosity which seemed to say, that he only wanted to know him to be rich, to be equally civil to *him*.

After staying with them half an hour, he asked Elinor to walk with him to Conduit-street, and introduce him to Sir John and Lady Middleton. The weather was remarkably fine, and she readily consented. As soon as they were out of the house, his enquiries began.

'Who is Colonel Brandon? Is he a man of fortune?'

Introduced to Mrs Jennings.

'Yes; he has a very good property in Dorsetshire.'

'I am glad of it. He seems a most gentlemanlike man; and I think Elinor, I may congratulate you on the prospect of a very respectable establishment in life.'

'Me, brother! what do you mean?'

'He likes you. I observed him narrowly, and am convinced of it. What is the amount of his fortune?'

'I believe about two thousand a-year.'

'Two thousand a-year;' and then working himself up to a pitch of enthusiastic generosity, he added, 'Elinor, I wish, with all my heart, it were *twice* as much, for your sake.'

'Indeed I believe you,' replied Elinor; 'but I am very sure that Colonel Brandon has not the smallest wish of marrying *me.*'

'You are mistaken, Elinor; you are very much mistaken. A very little trouble on your side secures him. Perhaps just at present he may be undecided; the smallness of your fortune may make him hang back; his friends may all advise him against it. But some of those little attentions and encouragements which ladies can so easily give, will fix him, in spite of himself. And there can be no reason why you should not try for him. It is not to be supposed that any prior attachment on your side – in short, you know as to an attachment of that kind, it is quite out of the question, the objections are

Mrs Jennings assured him directly that she should not stand upon ceremony.

insurmountable – you have too much sense not to see all that. Colonel Brandon must be the man; and no civility shall be wanting on my part, to make him pleased with you and your family. It is a match that must give universal satisfaction. In short, it is a kind of thing that' – lowering his voice to an important whisper – 'will be exceedingly welcome to *all parties*.' Recollecting himself, however, he added, 'That is, I mean to say – your friends are all truly anxious to see you well settled; Fanny particularly, for she has your interest very much at heart, I assure you. And her mother too, Mrs Ferrars, a very good-natured woman, I am sure it would give her great pleasure; she said as much the other day.'

Elinor would not vouchsafe any answer.

'It would be something remarkable now,' he continued, 'something droll, if Fanny should have a brother and I a sister settling at the same time. And yet it is not very unlikely.'

'Is Mr Edward Ferrars,' said Elinor, with resolution, 'going to be married?'

'It is not actually settled, but there is such a thing in agitation. He has a most excellent mother. Mrs Ferrars, with the utmost liberality, will come forward, and settle on him a thousand a year, if the match takes place. The lady is the Hon. Miss Morton, only daughter of the late Lord Morton, with thirty thousand pounds. A very desirable connection on both sides, and I have not a doubt of its taking place in time. A thousand a-year is a great deal for a mother to give away, to make over for ever; but Mrs Ferrars has a noble spirit. To give you another instance of her liberality: – The other day, as soon as we came to town, aware that money could not be very plenty with us just now, she put bank-notes into Fanny's hands to the amount of two hundred pounds. And extremely acceptable it is, for we must live at a great expence while we are here.'

He paused for her assent and compassion; and she forced herself to say,

'Your expences both in town and country must certainly be considerable, but your income is a large one.'

'Not so large, I dare say, as many people suppose. I do not mean to complain, however; it is undoubtedly a comfortable one, and I hope will in time be better. The inclosure of Norland Common, now carrying on, is a most serious drain. And then I have made a little purchase within this half year; East Kingham Farm, you must remember the place, where old Gibson used to live. The land was so very desirable for me in every respect, so immediately adjoining my own property, that I felt it my duty to buy it. I could not have answered it to my conscience to let it fall into any other hands. A man must pay for his convenience; and it *has* cost me a vast deal of money.'

'More than you think it really and intrinsically worth.'

'Why, I hope not that. I might have sold it again the next day, for more than I gave: but with regard to the purchase-money, I might have been very unfortunate indeed; for the stocks were at that time so low, that if I had not happened to have the necessary sum in my banker's hands, I must have sold out to very great loss.'

Elinor could only smile.

'Other great and inevitable expences too we have had on first coming to Norland. Our respected father, as you well know, bequeathed all the Stanhill effects that remained at Norland (and very valuable they were) to your mother. Far be it from me to repine at his doing so; he had an undoubted right to dispose of his own property as he chose, but, in consequence of it, we have been obliged to make large purchases of linen, china, &c. to supply the place of what was taken away. You may guess, after all these expenses, how very far we must be from being rich, and how acceptable Mrs Ferrar's kindness is.'

'Certainly,' said Elinor; 'and assisted by her liberality, I hope you may yet live to be in easy circumstances.'

'Another year or two may do much towards it,' he gravely replied; 'but however there is still a great deal to be done. There is not a stone laid of Fanny's greenhouse, and nothing but the plan of the flower-garden marked out.'

'Where is the green-house to be?'

'Upon the knoll behind the house. The old walnut trees are all come down to make room for it. It will be a very fine object from many parts of the park, and the flower-garden will slope down just before it, and be exceedingly pretty. We have cleared away all the old thorns that grew in patches over the brow.'

Elinor kept her concern and her censure to herself; and was very thankful that Marianne was not present, to share the provocation.

Having now said enough to make his poverty clear, and to do away the necessity of buying a pair of ear-rings for each of his sisters, in his next visit at Gray's, his thoughts took a cheerfuller turn, and he began to congratulate Elinor on having such a friend as Mrs Jennings.

'She seems a most valuable woman indeed – Her house, her style of living, all bespeak an exceeding good income; and it is an acquaintance that has not only been of great use to you hitherto, but in the end may prove materially advantageous. – Her inviting you to town is certainly a vast thing in your favour; and indeed, it speaks altogether so great a regard for you, that in all probability when she dies you will not be forgotten. – She must have a great deal to leave.'

'Nothing at all, I should rather suppose; for she has only her jointure, which will descend to her children.'

'But it is not to be imagined that she lives up to her income. Few people of common prudence will do *that*; and whatever she saves, she will be able to dispose of.'

'And do you not think it more likely that she should leave it to her daughters, than to us?'

'Her daughters are both exceedingly well married, and therefore I cannot perceive the necessity of her remembering them farther. Whereas, in my opinion, by her taking so much notice of you, and treating you in this kind of way, she has given you a sort of claim on her future consideration, which a conscientious woman would not disregard. Nothing can be kinder than her behaviour; and she can hardly do all this, without being aware of the expectation she raises.'

'But she raises none in those most concerned. Indeed, brother, your anxiety for our welfare and prosperity carries you too far.'

'Why to be sure,' said he, seeming to recollect himself, 'people who have little, have very little in their power. But, my dear Elinor, what is the matter with Marianne? – she looks very unwell, has lost her colour, and is grown quite thin. Is she ill?'

'She is not well, she has had a nervous complaint on her for several weeks.'

'I am sorry for that. At her time of life, any thing of an illness destroys the bloom for ever! Her's has been a very short one! She was as handsome a girl last September, as any I ever saw; and as likely to attract the men. There was something in her style of beauty, to please them particularly. I remember Fanny used to say that she would marry sooner and better than you did; not but what she is exceedingly fond of *you*, but so it happened to strike her. She will be mistaken, however. I question whether Marianne *now*, will marry a man worth more than five or six hundred a-year, at the utmost, and I am very much deceived if *you* do not do better. Dorsetshire! I know very little of Dorsetshire; but, my dear Elinor, I shall be exceedingly glad to know more of it; and think I can answer for your having Fanny and myself among the earliest and best pleased of your visitors.'

Elinor tried very seriously to convince him that there was no likelihood of her marrying Colonel Brandon; but it was an expectation of too much pleasure to himself to be relinquished, and he was really resolved on seeking an intimacy with that gentleman, and promoting the marriage by every possible attention. He had just compunction enough for having done nothing for his sisters himself, to be exceedingly anxious that everybody else should do a great deal; and an offer from Colonel Brandon, or a legacy from Mrs Jennings, was the easiest means of atoning for his own neglect.

They were lucky enough to find Lady Middleton at home, and Sir John came in before their visit ended. Abundance of civilities passed on all sides. Sir John was ready to like any body, and though Mr Dashwood did not seem to know much about horses, he soon set him down as a very good-natured fellow: while Lady Middleton saw enough of fashion in his appearance, to think his acquaintance worth having; and Mr Dashwood went away delighted with both.

'I shall have a charming account to carry to Fanny,' said he, as he walked back with his sister. 'Lady Middleton is really a most elegant woman! Such a woman as I am sure Fanny will be glad to know. And Mrs Jennings too, an exceedingly well-behaved woman, though not so elegant as her daughter. Your sister need not have any scruple even of visiting *her*, which, to say the truth, has been a little the case, and very naturally; for we only knew that Mrs Jennings was the widow of a man who had got all his money in a low way; and Fanny and Mrs Ferrars were both strongly prepossessed that neither she nor her daughters were such kind of women as Fanny would like to associate with. But now I can carry her a most satisfactory account of both.'

CHAPTER THIRTY-FOUR

Mrs John Dashwood had so much confidence in her husband's judgment that she waited the very next day both on Mrs Jennings and her daughter; and her confidence was rewarded by finding even the former, even the woman with whom her sisters were staying, by no means unworthy her notice; and as for Lady Middleton, she found her one of the most charming women in the world!

Lady Middleton was equally pleased with Mrs Dashwood. There was a kind of cold hearted selfishness on both sides, which mutually attracted them; and they sympathised with each other in an insipid propriety of demeanour, and a general want of understanding.

The same manners however, which recommended Mrs John Dashwood to the good opinion of Lady Middleton, did not suit the fancy of Mrs Jennings, and to *her* she appeared nothing more than a little proud-looking woman of uncordial address, who met her husband's sisters without any affection and almost without having any thing to say to them; for of the quarter of an hour bestowed on Berkeley-street, she sat at least seven minutes and a half in silence.

Elinor wanted very much to know, though she did not chuse to ask, whether Edward was then in town; but nothing would have induced Fanny voluntarily to mention his name before her, till able to tell her that his marriage with Miss Morton was resolved on, or till her husband's expectations on Colonel Brandon were answered; because she believed them still so very much attached to each other, that they could not be too sedulously divided in word and deed on every occasion. The intelligence however, which *she* would not give, soon flowed from another quarter. Lucy came very shortly to claim Elinor's compassion on being unable to see Edward, though he had arrived in town with Mr and Mrs Dashwood. He dared not come to Bartlett's Buildings for fear of detection, and though their mutual impatience to meet, was not to be told, they could do nothing at present but write.

Edward assured them himself of his being in town, within a very short time, by twice calling in Berkeley-street. Twice was his card found on the table, when they returned from their morning's engagements. Elinor was pleased that he had called; and still more pleased that she had missed him.

The Dashwoods were so prodigiously delighted with the Middletons, that though not much in the habit of giving any thing, they determined to give them – a dinner; and soon after their acquaintance began, invited them to dine in Harley-street, where they had taken a very good house for three months. Their sisters and Mrs Jennings were invited likewise, and John Dashwood was careful to secure Colonel Brandon, who always glad to be where the Miss Dashwoods were, received his eager civilities with some surprise, but much more pleasure. They were to meet Mrs Ferrars; but Elinor could not learn whether her sons were to be of the party. The expectation of seeing *her*, however, was enough to make her interested in the engagement; for though she could not meet Edward's mother without that strong anxiety which had once promised to attend such an introduction, though she could now see her with perfect indifference as to her opinion of herself, her desire of being in company with Mrs Ferrars, her curiosity to know what she was like, was as lively as ever.

The interest with which she thus anticipated the party, was soon afterwards increased, more powerfully than pleasantly, by her hearing that the Miss Steeles were also to be at it.

So well had they recommended themselves to Lady Middleton, so agreeable had their assiduities made them to her, that though Lucy was certainly not elegant, and her sister not even genteel, she was as ready as Sir John to ask them to spend a week or two in Conduit-street: and it happened to be particularly convenient to the Miss Steeles, as soon as the Dashwoods' invitation was known, that their visit should begin a few days before the party took place.

Their claims to the notice of Mrs John Dashwood, as the nieces of the gentleman who for many years had had the care of her brother, might not have done much, however, towards procuring them seats at her table; but as Lady Middleton's guests they must be welcome; and Lucy, who had long wanted to be personally known to the family, to have a nearer view of their characters and her own difficulties, and to have an opportunity of endeavouring to please them, had seldom been happier in her life than she was on receiving Mrs John Dashwood's card.

On Elinor its effect was very different. She began immediately to determine that Edward who lived with his mother, must be asked as his mother was, to a party given by his sister; and to see him for the first time after all that passed, in the company of Lucy! – she hardly knew how she could bear it!

These apprehensions perhaps were not founded entirely on reason, and certainly not at all on truth. They were relieved however, not by her own recollection, but by the good will of Lucy, who believed herself to be inflicting a severe disappointment when she told her that Edward certainly would not be in Harley-street on Tuesday, and even hoped to be carrying the pain still farther by persuading her, that he was kept away by that extreme affection for herself, which he could not conceal when they were together.

The important Tuesday came that was to introduce the two young ladies to this formidable mother-in-law.

'Pity me, dear Miss Dashwood!' said Lucy, as they walked up the stairs together – for the Middletons arrived so directly after Mrs Jennings, that they all followed the servant at the same time – 'There is nobody here but you, that can feel for me. – I declare I can hardly stand. Good gracious! – In a moment I shall see the person that all my happiness depends on – that is to be my mother!' –

Elinor could have given her immediate relief by suggesting the possibility of its being Miss Morton's mother, rather than her own, whom they were about to behold; but instead of doing that, she assured her, and with great sincerity, that she did pity her, – to the

Mrs Ferrars.

utter amazement of Lucy, who, though really uncomfortable herself, hoped at least to be an object of irrepressible envy to Elinor.

Mrs Ferrars was a little, thin woman, upright, even to formality, in her figure, and serious, even to sourness, in her aspect. Her complexion was sallow; and her features small, without beauty, and naturally without expression; but a lucky contraction of the brow had rescued her countenance from the disgrace of insipidity, by giving it the strong characters of pride and ill nature. She was not a woman of many words: for, unlike people in general, she proportioned them to the number of her ideas; and of the few syllables that did escape her, not one fell to the share of Miss

Dashwood, whom she eyed with the spirited determination of disliking her at all events.

Elinor could not *now* be made unhappy by this behaviour. – A few months ago it would have hurt her exceedingly; but it was not in Mrs Ferrars's power to distress her by it now; – and the difference of her manners to the Miss Steeles, a difference which seemed purposely made to humble her more, only amused her. She could not but smile to see the graciousness of both mother and daughter towards the very person – for Lucy was particularly distinguished – whom of all others, had they known as much as she did, they would have been most anxious to mortify; while she herself, who had comparatively no power to wound them, sat pointedly slighted by both. But while she smiled at a graciousness so misapplied, she could not reflect on the mean-spirited folly from which it sprung, nor observe the studied attentions with which the Miss Steeles courted its continuance, without thoroughly despising them all four.

Lucy was all exultation on being so honourably distinguished; and Miss Steele wanted only to be teazed about Dr Davis to be perfectly happy.

The dinner was a grand one, the servants were numerous, and every thing bespoke the Mistress's inclination for shew, and the Master's ability to support it. In spite of the improvements and additions which were making to the Norland estate, and in spite of its owner having once been within some thousand pounds of being obliged to sell out at a loss, nothing gave any symptom of that indigence which he had tried to infer from it; – no poverty of any kind, except of conversation, appeared – but there, the deficiency was considerable. John Dashwood had not much to say for himself that was worth hearing, and his wife had still less. But there was no peculiar disgrace in this, for it was very much the case with the chief of their visitors, who almost all laboured under one or other of these disqualifications for being agreeable – Want of sense, either natural or improved – want of elegance – want of spirits – or want of temper.

When the ladies withdrew to the drawing-room after dinner, this poverty was particularly evident, for the gentlemen *had* supplied the discourse with some variety – the variety of politics, inclosing land, and breaking horses – but then it was all over; one subject only engaged the ladies till coffee came in, which was the comparative heights of Harry Dashwood, and Lady Middleton's second son William, who were nearly of the same age.

Had both the children been there, the affair might have been determined too easily by measuring them at once; but as Harry only was present, it was all conjectural assertion on both sides, and every body had a right to be equally positive in their opinion, and to repeat it over and over again as often as they liked.

The parties stood thus:

The two mothers, though each really convinced that her own son was the tallest, politely decided in favour of the other.

The two grandmothers, with not less partiality, but more sincerity, were equally earnest in support of their own descendant.

Lucy, who was hardly less anxious to please one parent than the other, thought the boys were both remarkably tall for their age, and could not conceive that there could be the smallest difference in the world between them; and Miss Steele, with yet greater address gave it, as fast as she could, in favour of each.

Elinor, having once delivered her opinion on William's side, by which she offended Mrs Ferrars and Fanny still more, did not see the necessity of enforcing it by any farther assertion; and Marianne, when called on for her's, offended them all, by declaring that she had no opinion to give, as she had never thought about it.

Before her removing from Norland, Elinor had painted a very pretty pair of screens for her sister-in-law, which being now just mounted and brought home, ornamented her present drawing room; and these screens, catching the eye of John Dashwood on his following the other gentlemen into the room, were officiously handed by him to Colonel Brandon for his admiration.

'These are done by my eldest sister,' said he; 'and you, as a man of taste, will, I dare say, be pleased with them. I do not know whether you ever happened to see any of her performances before, but she is in general reckoned to draw extremely well.'

The Colonel, though disclaiming all pretensions to connoisseurship, warmly admired the screens, as he would have done any thing painted by Miss Dashwood; and the curiosity of the others being of course excited, they were handed round for general inspection. Mrs Ferrars, not aware of their being Elinor's work, particularly requested to look at them; and after they had received the gratifying testimony of Lady Middleton's approbation, Fanny presented them to her mother, considerately informing her at the same time, that they were done by Miss Dashwood.

'Hum' – said Mrs Ferrars – 'very pretty,' – and without regarding them at all, returned them to her daughter.

Perhaps Fanny thought for a moment that her mother had been quite rude enough, – for, colouring a little, she immediately said,

'They are very pretty, ma'am – an't they?' But then again, the dread of having been too civil, too encouraging herself, probably came over her, for she presently added,

'Do you not think they are something in Miss Morton's style of painting, Ma'am? – *She does* paint most delightfully! – How beautifully her last landscape is done!'

'Beautifully indeed! But *she* does every thing well.'

Marianne could not bear this. – She was already greatly displeased with Mrs Ferrars; and such ill-timed praise of another, at Elinor's expense, though she had not any notion of what was principally meant by it, provoked her immediately to say with warmth,

'This is admiration of a very particular kind! – what is Miss Morton to us? – who knows, or who cares, for her? – it is Elinor of whom *we* think and speak.'

And so saying, she took the screens out of her sister-in-law's hands, to admire them herself as they ought to be admired.

Mrs Ferrars looked exceedingly angry, and drawing herself up more stiffly than ever, pronounced in retort this bitter phillippic; 'Miss Morton is Lord Morton's daughter.'

Fanny looked very angry too, and her husband was all in a fright at his sister's audacity. Elinor was much more hurt by Marianne's warmth, than she had been by what produced it; but Colonel Brandon's eyes, as they were fixed on Marianne, declared that he noticed only what was amiable in it, the affectionate heart which could not bear to see a sister slighted in the smallest point.

Marianne's feelings did not stop here. The cold insolence of Mrs Ferrars's general behaviour to her sister, seemed, to her, to foretell such difficulties and distresses to Elinor, as her own wounded heart taught her to think of with horror; and urged by a strong impulse of affectionate sensibility, she moved, after a moment, to her sister's chair, and putting one arm round her neck, and one cheek close to hers, said in a low, but eager, voice.

'Dear, dear Elinor, don't mind them. Don't let them make *you* unhappy.'

She could say no more; her spirits were quite overcome, and hiding her face on Elinor's shoulder, she burst into tears. – Every body's attention was called, and almost every body was concerned. – Colonel Brandon rose up and went to them without knowing what he did. – Mrs Jennings, with a very intelligent 'Ah! poor dear,' immediately gave her, her salts; and Sir John felt so desperately enraged against the author of this nervous distress, that he instantly changed his seat to one close by Lucy Steele, and gave her, in a whisper, a brief account of the whole shocking affair.

In a few minutes, however, Marianne was recovered enough to

put an end to the bustle, and sit down among the rest; though her spirits retained the impression of what had passed, the whole evening.

'Poor Marianne!' said her brother to Colonel Brandon in a low voice, as soon as he could secure his attention, – 'She has not such good health as her sister, – she is very nervous, – she has not Elinor's constitution; – and one must allow that there is something very trying to a young woman who *has been* a beauty, in the loss of her personal attractions. You would not think it perhaps, but Marianne *was* remarkably handsome a few months ago; quite as handsome as Elinor. – Now you see it is all gone.'

CHAPTER THIRTY-FIVE

ELINOR'S CURIOSITY to see Mrs Ferrars was satisfied. – She had found in her every thing that could tend to make a farther connection between the families, undesirable. – She had seen enough of her pride, her meanness, and her determined prejudice against herself, to comprehend all the difficulties that must have perplexed the engagement, and retarded the marriage, of Edward and herself, had he been otherwise free; – and she had seen almost enough to be thankful for her *own* sake, that one greater obstacle preserved her from suffering under any other of Mrs Ferrars's creation, preserved her from all dependence upon her caprice, or any solicitude for her good opinion. Or at least, if she did not bring herself quite to rejoice in Edward's being fettered to Lucy, she determined, that had Lucy been more amiable, she *ought* to have rejoiced.

She wondered that Lucy's spirits could be so very much elevated by the civility of Mrs Ferrars; – that her interest and her vanity should so very much blind her, as to make the attention which seemed only paid her because she was *not Elinor*, appear a compliment to herself – or to allow her to derive encouragement from a preference only given her, because her real situation was unknown. But that it was so, had not only been declared by Lucy's eyes at the time, but was declared over again the next morning more openly, for at her particular desire, Lady Middleton set her down in Berkeley-street on the chance of seeing Elinor alone, to tell her how happy she was.

The chance proved a lucky one, for a message from Mrs Palmer soon after she arrived, carried Mrs Jennings away.

'My dear friend,' cried Lucy as soon as they were by themselves, 'I come to talk to you of my happiness. Could any thing be so flattering as Mrs Ferrars's way of treating me yesterday? So exceeding affable as she was! – You know how I dreaded the thoughts of seeing her; – but the very moment I was introduced, there was such an affability in her behaviour as really should seem to say, she had quite took a fancy to me. Now was not it so? – You saw it all; and was not you quite struck with it?'

'She was certainly very civil to you.'

'Civil! – Did you see nothing but only civility? – I saw a vast deal more. Such kindness as fell to the share of nobody but me! – No pride, no hauteur, and your sister just the same – all sweetness and affability!'

Elinor wished to talk of something else, but Lucy still pressed her to own that she had reason for her happiness; and Elinor was obliged to go on. –

'Undoubtedly, if they had known your engagement,' said she, 'nothing could be more flattering than their treatment of you; – but as that was not the case' –

'I guessed you would say so' – replied Lucy quickly – 'but there was no reason in the world why Mrs Ferrars should seem to like me, if she did not, and her liking me is every thing. You shan't talk me out of my satisfaction. I am sure it will all end well, and there will be no difficulties at all, to what I used to think. Mrs Ferrars is a charming woman, and so is your sister. They are both delightful women indeed! – I wonder I should never hear you say how agreeable Mrs Dashwood was!'

To this, Elinor had no answer to make, and did not attempt any.

'Are you ill, Miss Dashwood? – you seem low – you don't speak; – sure you an't well.'

'I never was in better health.'

'I am glad of it with all my heart, but really you did not look it. I should be so sorry to have *you* ill; you, that have been the greatest comfort to me in the world! – Heaven knows what I should have done without your friendship.' –

Elinor tried to make a civil answer, though doubting her own success. But it seemed to satisfy Lucy, for she directly replied.

'Indeed I am perfectly convinced of your regard for me, and next to Edward's love, it is the greatest comfort I have. – Poor Edward! – But now, there is one good thing, we shall be able to meet, and meet pretty often, for Lady Middleton's delighted with Mrs Dashwood, so we shall be a good deal in Harley-street, I dare say, and Edward spends half his time with his sister – besides, Lady

Middleton and Mrs Ferrars will visit now; – and Mrs Ferrars and your sister were both so good to say more than once, they should always be glad to see me. – They are such charming women! – I am sure if ever you tell your sister what I think of her, you cannot speak too high.'

But Elinor would not give her any encouragement to hope that she *should* tell her sister. Lucy continued.

'I am sure I should have seen it in a moment, if Mrs Ferrars had took a dislike to me. If she had only made me a formal curtsey, for instance, without saying a word, and never after had took any notice of me, and never looked at me in a pleasant way – you know what I mean, – if I had been treated in that forbidding sort of way, I should have gave it all up in despair. I could not have stood it. For where she *does* dislike, I know it is most violent.'

Elinor was prevented from making any reply to this civil triumph, by the door's being thrown open, the servant's announcing Mr Ferrars, and Edward's immediately walking in.

It was a very awkward moment; and the countenance of each shewed that it was so. They all looked exceedingly foolish; and Edward seemed to have as great an inclination to walk out of the room again, as to advance further into it. The very circumstance, in its unpleasantest form, which they would each have been most anxious to avoid, had fallen on them – They were not only all three together, but were together without the relief of any other person. The ladies recovered themselves first. It was not Lucy's business to put herself forward, and the appearance of secrecy must still be kept up. She could therefore only *look* her tenderness, and after slightly addressing him, said no more.

But Elinor had more to do; and so anxious was she, for his sake and her own, to do it well, that she forced herself, after a moment's recollection, to welcome him, with a look and manner that were almost easy, and almost open; and another struggle, another effort still improved them. She would not allow the presence of Lucy, nor the consciousness of some injustice towards herself, to deter her from saying that she was happy to see him, and that she had very much regretted being from home, when he called before in Berkeley-street. She would not be frightened from paying him those attentions which, as a friend and almost a relation, were his due, by the observant eyes of Lucy, though she soon perceived them to be narrowly watching her.

Her manners gave some re-assurance to Edward, and he had courage enough to sit down; but his embarrassment still exceeded that of the ladies in a proportion, which the case rendered reasonable, though his sex might make it rare; for his heart had not the indifference of Lucy's, nor could his conscience have quite the ease of Elinor's.

Lucy, with a demure and settled air, seemed determined to make no contribution to the comfort of the others, and would not say a word; and almost every thing that *was* said, proceeded from Elinor, who was obliged to volunteer all the information about her mother's health, their coming to town, &c. which Edward ought to have inquired about, but never did.

Her exertions did not stop here; for she soon afterwards felt herself so heroically disposed as to determine, under pretence of fetching Marianne, to leave the others by themselves: and she really did it, and *that* in the handsomest manner, for she loitered away several minutes on the landing-place, with the most highminded fortitude, before she went to her sister. When that was once done, however, it was time for the raptures of Edward to cease; for Marianne's joy hurried her into the drawing-room immediately. Her pleasure in seeing him was like every other of her feelings, strong in itself, and strongly spoken. She met him with a hand that would be taken, and a voice that expressed the affection of a sister.

'Dear Edward!' she cried, 'this is a moment of great happiness! – This would almost make amends for every thing!'

Edward tried to return her kindness as it deserved, but before such witnesses he dared not say half what he really felt. Again they all sat down, and for a moment or two all were silent; while Marianne was looking with the most speaking tenderness, sometimes at Edward and sometimes at Elinor, regretting only that their delight in each other should be checked by Lucy's unwelcome presence. Edward was the first to speak, and it was to notice Marianne's altered looks, and express his fear of her not finding London agree with her.

'Oh! don't think of me!' she replied, with spirited earnestness, though her eyes were filled with tears as she spoke, 'don't think of *my* health. Elinor is well, you see. That must be enough for us both.'

This remark was not calculated to make Edward or Elinor more easy, nor to conciliate the good will of Lucy, who looked up at Marianne with no very benignant expression.

'Do you like London?' said Edward, willing to say any thing that might introduce another subject.

'Not at all. I expected much pleasure in it, but I have found none. The sight of you, Edward, is the only comfort it has afforded; and thank Heaven! you are what you always were!'

She paused – no one spoke.

'I think, Elinor,' she presently added, 'we must employ Edward to take care of us in our return to Barton. In a week or two, I suppose, we shall be going; and, I trust, Edward will not be very unwilling to accept the charge.'

Poor Edward muttered something, but what it was, nobody knew, not even himself. But Marianne, who saw his agitation, and could easily trace it to whatever cause best pleased herself, was perfectly satisfied, and soon talked of something else.

'We spent such a day, Edward, in Harley-street yesterday! So dull, so wretchedly dull! – But I have much to say to you on that head, which cannot be said now.'

And with this admirable discretion did she defer the assurance of her finding their mutual relatives more disagreeable than ever, and of her being particularly disgusted with his mother, till they were more in private.

'But why were you not there, Edward? – Why did you not come?'

'I was engaged elsewhere.'

'Engaged! But what was that, when such friends were to be met?'

'Perhaps, Miss Marianne,' cried Lucy, eager to take some revenge on her, 'you think young men never stand upon engagements, if they have no mind to keep them, little as well as great.'

Elinor was very angry, but Marianne seemed entirely insensible of the sting; for she calmly replied.

'Not so, indeed; for seriously speaking, I am very sure that conscience only kept Edward from Harley-street. And I really believe he *has* the most delicate conscience in the world; the most scrupulous in performing every engagement however minute, and however it may make against his interest or pleasure. He is the most fearful of giving pain, of wounding expectation, and the most incapable of being selfish, of any body I ever saw. Edward, it is so and I will say it. What! are you never to hear yourself praised! – Then, you must be no friend of mine; for those who will accept of my love and esteem, must submit to my open commendation.'

The nature of her commendation, in the present case, however, happened to be particularly ill-suited to the feelings of two thirds of her auditors, and was so very unexhilarating to Edward, that he very soon got up to go away.

'Going so soon!' said Marianne; 'my dear Edward, this must not be.'

And drawing him a little aside, she whispered her persuasion that Lucy could not stay much longer. But even this encouragement failed, for he would go; and Lucy, who would have outstaid him had his visit lasted two hours, soon afterwards went away.

'What can bring her here so often!' said Marianne, on her leaving them. 'Could she not see that we wanted her gone! – how teazing to Edward!'

'Why so? – we were all his friends, and Lucy has been the longest known to him of any. It is but natural that he should like to see her as well as ourselves.'

Marianne looked at her steadily, and said, 'You know, Elinor, that this is a kind of talking which I cannot bear. If you only hope

Drawing him a little aside.

to have your assertion contradicted, as I must suppose to be the case, you ought to recollect that I am the last person in the world to do it. I cannot descend to be tricked out of assurances, that are not really wanted.'

She then left the room; and Elinor dared not follow her to say more, for bound as she was by her promise of secrecy to Lucy, she could give no information that would convince Marianne; and painful as the consequences of her still continuing in an error might be, she was obliged to submit to it. All that she could hope, was that Edward would not often expose her or himself to the distress of hearing Marianne's mistaken warmth, nor to the repetition of any other part of the pain that had attended their recent meeting – and this she had every reason to expect.

CHAPTER THIRTY-SIX

WITHIN A FEW DAYS after this meeting, the newspapers announced to the world, that the Lady of Thomas Palmer, Esq. was safely delivered of a son and heir; a very interesting and satisfactory paragraph, at least to all those intimate connections who knew it before.

This event, highly important to Mrs Jennings's happiness, produced a temporary alteration in the disposal of her time, and influenced, in a like degree, the engagements of her young friends; for as she wished to be as much as possible with Charlotte, she went thither every morning as soon as she was dressed, and did not return till late in the evening; and the Miss Dashwoods, at the particular request of the Middletons, spent the whole of every day in Conduit-street. For their own comfort, they would much rather have remained, at least all the morning, in Mrs Jennings's house; but it was not a thing to be urged against the wishes of every body. Their hours were therefore made over to Lady Middleton and the two Miss Steeles, by whom their company was in fact as little valued, as it was professedly sought.

They had too much sense to be desirable companions to the former; and by the latter they were considered with a jealous eye, as intruding on *their* ground, and sharing the kindness which they wanted to monopolize. Though nothing could be more polite than Lady Middleton's behaviour to Elinor and Marianne, she did not really like them at all. Because they neither flattered herself nor her children, she could not believe them good-natured; and because they were fond of reading, she fancied them satirical: perhaps without exactly knowing what it was to be satirical; but *that* did not signify. It was censure in common use, and easily given.

Their presence was a restraint both on her and on Lucy. It checked the idleness of one, and the business of the other. Lady Middleton was ashamed of doing nothing before them, and the flattery which Lucy was proud to think of and administer at other times, she feared they would despise her for offering. Miss Steele was the least discomposed of the three, by their presence; and it was in their power to reconcile her to it entirely. Would either of them, only have given her a full and minute account of the whole affair between Marianne and Mr Willoughby, she would have thought herself amply rewarded for the sacrifice of the best place by the fire after dinner, which their arrival occasioned. But this conciliation was not granted; for though she often threw out expressions of pity for her sister to Elinor, and more than once dropt a reflection on the inconstancy of beaux before Marianne, no effect was produced, but a look of indifference from the former, or of disgust in the latter. An effort even yet lighter might have made her their friend. Would they only have laughed at her about the Doctor! But so little were they, anymore than the others, inclined to oblige her, that if Sir John dined from home, she might spend a whole day without hearing any other raillery on the subject, than what she was kind enough to bestow on herself.

All these jealousies and discontents, however, were so totally unsuspected by Mrs Jennings, that she thought it a delightful thing for the girls to be together; and generally congratulated her young friends every night, on having escaped the company of a stupid old woman so long. She joined them sometimes at Sir John's, and sometimes at her own house; but wherever it was, she always came in excellent spirits, full of delight and importance, attributing Charlotte's well doing to her own care, and ready to give so exact, so minute a detail of her situation, as only Miss Steele had curiosity enough to desire. One thing *did* disturb her; and of that she made her daily complaint. Mr Palmer maintained the common, but unfatherly opinion among his sex, of all infants being alike; and though she could plainly perceive at different times, the most striking resemblance between this baby and every one of his relations on both sides, there was no convincing his father of it; no persuading him to believe that it was not exactly like every other baby of the same age; nor could he even be brought to acknowledge the simple proposition of its being the finest child in the world.

I come now to the relation of a misfortune, which about this time befell Mrs John Dashwood. It so happened that while her two sisters with Mrs Jennings were first calling on her in Harley-street, another of her acquaintance had dropt in – a circumstance in itself not apparently likely to produce evil to her. But while the imaginations of other people will carry them away to form wrong judgments of our conduct, and to decide on it by slight appearances, one's happiness must in some measure be always at the mercy of chance. In the present instance, this last-arrived lady allowed her fancy so far to outrun truth and probability, that on merely hearing the name of the Miss Dashwoods, and understanding them to be Mr Dashwood's sisters, she immediately concluded them to be staying in Harley-street; and this misconstruction produced within a day or two afterwards, cards of invitation for them as well as for their brother and sister, to a small musical party at her house. The consequence of which was, that Mrs John Dashwood was obliged to submit not only to the exceedingly great inconvenience of sending her carriage for the Miss Dashwoods; but, what was still worse, must be subject to all the unpleasantness of appearing to treat them with attention: and who could tell that they might not expect to go out with her a second time? The power of disappointing them, it was true, must always be her's. But that was not enough; for when people are determined on a mode of conduct which they know to be wrong, they feel injured by the expectation of any thing better from them.

Marianne had now been brought by degrees, so much into the habit of going out every day, that it was become a matter of indifference to her, whether she went or not: and she prepared quietly and mechanically for every evening's engagement, though without expecting the smallest amusement from any, and very often without knowing till the last moment, where it was to take her.

To her dress and appearance she was grown so perfectly indifferent, as not to bestow half the consideration on it, during the whole of her toilette, which it received from Miss Steele in the first five minutes of their being together, when it was finished. Nothing escaped *her* minute observation and general curiosity; she saw every thing, and asked every thing; was never easy till she knew the price of every part of Marianne's dress; could have guessed the number of her gowns altogether with better judgment than Marianne herself, and was not without hopes of finding out before they parted, how much her washing cost per week, and how much she had every year to spend upon herself. The impertinence of these kind of scrutinies, moreover, was generally concluded with a compliment, which though meant as its douceur, was considered by Marianne as the greatest impertinence of all; for after undergoing an examination into the value and make of her gown, the colour of her shoes, and the arrangement of her hair, she was almost sure of being told that upon 'her word she looked vastly smart, and she dared to say would make a great many conquests.'

With such encouragement as this, was she dismissed on the present occasion to her brother's carriage; which they were ready to enter five minutes after it stopped at the door, a punctuality not very agreeable to their sister-in-law, who had preceded them to the house of her acquaintance, and was there hoping for some delay on their part that might inconvenience either herself or her coachman.

The events of the evening were not very remarkable. The party, like other musical parties, comprehended a great many people who had real taste for the performance, and a great many more who had none at all; and the performers themselves were, as usual, in their own estimation, and that of their immediate friends, the first private performers in England.

As Elinor was neither musical nor affecting to be so, she made no scruple of turning away her eyes from the grand pianoforté, whenever it suited her, and unrestrained even by the presence of a harp, and a violoncello, would fix them at pleasure on any other object in the room. In one of these excursive glances she perceived among a group of young men, the very he, who had given them a lecture on toothpick-cases at Gray's. She perceived him soon afterwards looking at herself, and speaking familiarly to her brother; and had just determined to find out his name from the latter, when they both came towards her, and Mr Dashwood introduced him to her as Mr Robert Ferrars.

He addressed her with easy civility, and twisted his head into a bow which assured her as plainly as words could have done, that he was exactly the coxcomb she had heard him described to be by Lucy. Happy had it been for her, if her regard for Edward had depended less on his own merit, than on the merit of his nearest relations! For then his brother's bow must have given the finishing stroke to what the ill-humour of his mother and sister would have begun. But while she wondered at the difference of the two young men, she did not find that the emptiness and conceit of the one, put her at all out of charity with the modesty and worth of the other. Why they *were* different, Robert exclaimed to her himself in the course of a quarter of an hour's conversation; for, talking of his brother, and lamenting the extreme *gaucherie* which he really believed kept him from mixing in proper society, he candidly and generously attributed it much less to any natural deficiency, than to the misfortune of a private education; while he himself, though

Mr Dashwood introduced him.

probably without any particular, any material superiority by nature, merely from the advantage of a public school, was as well fitted to mix in the world as any other man.

'Upon my soul,' he added, 'I believe it is nothing more; and so I often tell my mother, when she is grieving about it. "My dear Madam," I always say to her, "you must make yourself easy. The evil is now irremediable, and it has been entirely your own doing. Why would you be persuaded by my uncle, Sir Robert, against your own judgment, to place Edward under private tuition, at the most critical time of his life? If you had only sent him to Westminster as well as myself, instead of sending him to Mr Pratt's, all this would have been prevented." This is the way in which I always consider the matter, and my mother is perfectly convinced of her error.'

Elinor would not oppose his opinion, because, whatever might be her general estimation of the advantage of a public school, she could not think of Edward's abode in Mr Pratt's family, with any satisfaction.

'You reside in Devonshire, I think' – was his next observation, 'in a cottage near Dawlish.'

Elinor set him right as to its situation, and it seemed rather surprising to him that anybody could live in Devonshire, without living near Dawlish. He bestowed his hearty approbation however on their species of house.

'For my own part,' said he, 'I am excessively fond of a cottage; there is always so much comfort, so much elegance about them. And I protest, if I had any money to spare, I should buy a little land and build one myself, within a short distance of London, where I might drive myself down at any time, and collect a few friends about me, and be happy. I advise every body who is going to build, to build a cottage. My friend Lord Courtland came to me the other day on purpose to ask my advice, and laid before me three different plans of Bonomi's. I was to decide on the best of them. "My dear Courtland," said I, immediately throwing them all into the fire, "do not adopt either of them, but by all means build a cottage." And that, I fancy, will be the end of it.'

'Some people imagine that there can be no accommodations, no space in a cottage; but this is all a mistake. I was last month at my friend Elliott's near Dartford. Lady Elliott wished to give a dance. "But how can it be done?" said she; "my dear Ferrars, do tell me how it is to be managed. There is not a room in this cottage that will hold ten couple, and where can the supper be?" I immediately saw that there could be no difficulty in it, so I said, "My dear Lady Elliott, do not be uneasy. The dining parlour will admit eighteen couple with ease; card-tables may be placed in the drawing-room; the library may be open for tea and other refreshments; and let the supper be set out in the saloon." Lady Elliott was delighted with the thought. We measured the dining-room, and found it would hold exactly eighteen couple, and the affair was arranged precisely after my plan. So that, in fact, you see, if people do but know how to set about it, every comfort may be as well enjoyed in a cottage as in the most spacious dwelling.'

Elinor agreed to it all, for she did not think he deserved the compliment of rational opposition.

As John Dashwood had no more pleasure in music than his eldest sister, his mind was equally at liberty to fix on any thing else; and a thought struck him during the evening, which he communicated to his wife, for her approbation, when they got home. The consideration of Mrs Dennison's mistake, in supposing his sisters their guests, had suggested the propriety of their being really invited to become such, while Mrs Jennings's engagements kept her from home. The expence would be nothing, the inconvenience not more; and it was altogether an attention, which the delicacy of his conscience pointed out to be requisite to its complete enfranchisement from his promise to his father. Fanny was startled at the proposal.

'I do not see how it can be done,' said she, 'without affronting Lady Middleton, for they spend every day with her; otherwise I should be exceedingly glad to do it. You know I am always ready to pay them any attention in my power, as my taking them out this evening shews. But they are Lady Middleton's visitors. How can I ask them away from her?'

Her husband, but with great humility, did not see the force of her objection. 'They had already spent a week in this manner in Conduit-street, and Lady Middleton could not be displeased at their giving the same number of days to such near relations.'

Fanny paused a moment, and then, with fresh vigour, said,

'My love, I would ask them with all my heart, if it was in my power. But I had just settled within myself to ask the Miss Steeles to spend a few days with us. They are very well behaved, good kind of girls; and I think the attention is due to them, as their uncle did so very well by Edward. We can ask your sisters some other year, you know; but the Miss Steeles may not be in town any more. I am sure you will like them; indeed, you *do* like them, you know, very much already, and so does my mother; and they are such favourites with Harry!'

Mr Dashwood was convinced. He saw the necessity of inviting the Miss Steeles immediately, and his conscience was pacified by the resolution of inviting his sisters another year; at the same time, however, slyly suspecting that another year would make the invitation needless, by bringing Elinor to town as Colonel Brandon's wife, and Marianne as *their* visitor.

Fanny, rejoicing in her escape, and proud of the ready wit that had procured it, wrote the next morning to Lucy, to request her company and her sister's, for some days, in Harley-street, as soon as Lady Middleton could spare them. This was enough to make Lucy really and reasonably happy. Mrs Dashwood seemed actually working for her, herself; cherishing all her hopes, and promoting all her views! Such an opportunity of being with Edward and his family was, above all things, the most material to her interest, and such an invitation the most gratifying to her feelings! It was an advantage that could not be too gratefully acknowledged, nor too speedily made use of; and the visit to Lady Middleton, which had not before had any precise limits, was instantly discovered to have been always meant to end in two days' time.

When the note was shewn to Elinor, as it was within ten minutes after its arrival, it gave her, for the first time, some share in the expectations of Lucy; for such a mark of uncommon kindness, vouchsafed on so short an acquaintance, seemed to declare that the good will towards her arose from something more than merely malice against herself; and might be brought, by time and address, to do every thing that Lucy wished. Her flattery had already subdued the pride of Lady Middleton, and made an entry into the close heart of Mrs John Dashwood; and these were effects that laid open the probability of greater.

The Miss Steeles removed to Harley-street, and all that reached Elinor of their influence there, strengthened her expectation of the event. Sir John, who called on them more than once, brought home such accounts of the favour that they were in, as must be universally striking. Mrs Dashwood had never been so much pleased with any young women in her life, as she was with them; had given each of them a needle book, made by some emigrant; called Lucy by her Christian name; and did not know whether she should ever be able to part with them.

CHAPTER THIRTY-SEVEN

Mrs Palmer was so well at the end of a fortnight, that her mother felt it no longer necessary to give up the whole of her time to her; and contenting herself with visiting her once or twice a day, returned from that period to her own home, and her own habits, in which she found the Miss Dashwoods very ready to reassume their former share.

About the third or fourth morning after their being thus resettled in Berkeley-street, Mrs Jennings, on returning from her ordinary visit to Mrs Palmer, entered the drawing-room, where Elinor was sitting by herself, with an air of such hurrying importance as prepared her to hear something wonderful; and giving her time only to form that idea, began directly to justify it by saying,

'Lord! my dear Miss Dashwood! have you heard the news!'

'No, ma'am. What is it?'

'Something so strange! But you shall hear it all. – When I got to

Mr Palmer's, I found Charlotte quite in a fuss about the child. She was sure it was very ill – it cried, and fretted, and was all over pimples. So I looked at it directly, and, "Lord! my dear," says I, "it is nothing in the world but the red-gum;" and nurse said just the same. But Charlotte, she would not be satisfied, so Mr Donavan was sent for; and luckily he happened to be just come in from Harley-street, so he stepped over directly, and as soon as ever he saw the child, he said just as we did, that it was nothing in the world but the red-gum, and then Charlotte was easy. And so, just as he was going away again, it came into my head, I am sure I do not know how I happened to think of it, but it came into my head to ask him if there was any news. So upon that, he smirked, and simpered, and looked grave, and seemed to know something or

In a whisper.

other, and at last he said in a whisper, "For fear any unpleasant report should reach the young ladies under your care as to their sister's indisposition, I think it advisable to say, that I believe there is no great reason for alarm; I hope Mrs Dashwood will do very well." '

'What! is Fanny ill?'

'That is exactly what I said, my dear. "Lord!" says I, "is Mrs Dashwood ill?" So then it all came out; and the long and the short of the matter, by all I can learn, seems to be this. Mr Edward Ferrars, the very young man I used to joke with you about (but however, as it turns out, I am monstrous glad there never was any thing in it), Mr Edward Ferrars, it seems, has been engaged above this twelvemonth to my cousin Lucy! – There's for you, my dear! – And not a creature knowing a syllable of the matter except Nancy! – Could you have believed such a thing possible? – There is no great wonder in their liking one another; but that matters should be brought so forward between them, and nobody suspect it! *That* is strange! – I never happened to see them together, or I am sure I should have found it out directly. Well, and so this was kept a great secret, for fear of Mrs Ferrars, and neither she nor your brother or sister suspected a word of the matter; – till this very morning, poor Nancy, who, you know, is a well-meaning creature, but no conjurer, popt it all out. "Lord!" thinks she to herself, "they are all so fond of Lucy, to be sure they will make no difficulty about it;" and so, away she went to your sister, who was sitting all alone at her carpet-work, little suspecting what was to come – for she had just been saying to your brother, only five minutes before, that she thought to make a match between Edward and some Lord's daughter or other, I forget who. So you may think what a blow it was to all her vanity and pride. She fell into violent hysterics immediately, with such screams as reached your brother's ears, as he was sitting in his own dressing-room down stairs, thinking about writing a letter to his steward in the country. So up he flew directly, and a terrible scene took place, for Lucy was come to them by that time, little dreaming what was going on. Poor soul! I pity *her*. And I must say, I think she was used very hardly; for your sister scolded like any fury, and soon drove her into a fainting fit. Nancy, she fell upon her knees, and cried bitterly; and your brother, he walked about the room, and said he did not know what to do. Mrs Dashwood declared they should not stay a minute longer in the house, and your brother was forced to go down upon *his* knees too, to persuade her to let them stay till they had packed up their clothes. *Then* she fell into hysterics again, and he was so frightened that he would send for Mr Donavan, and Mr Donavan found the house in all this uproar. The carriage was at the door ready to take my poor cousins away, and they were just stepping in as he came off; poor Lucy in such a condition, he says, she could hardly walk; and Nancy, she was almost as bad. I declare, I have no patience with your sister; and I hope, with all my heart, it will be a match in spite of her. Lord! what a taking poor Mr Edward will be in when he hears of it! To have his love used so scornfully! for they say he is monstrous fond of her, as well he may. I should not wonder, if he was to be in the greatest of a passion! – and Mr Donavan thinks just the same. He and I had a great deal of talk about it; and the best of all is, that he is gone back again to Harley-street, that he may be within call when Mrs Ferrars is told of it, for she was sent for as soon as ever my cousin left the house, for your sister was sure *she* would be in hysterics too; and so she may, for what I care. I have no pity for either of them. I have no notion of people's making such a to-do about money and greatness. There is no reason on earth why Mr Edward and Lucy should not marry; for I am sure Mrs Ferrars may afford to do very well by her son, and though Lucy has next to nothing herself, she knows better than any body how to make the most of every thing; and I dare say, if Mrs Ferrars would only allow him five hundred a-year, she would make as good an appearance with it as any body else would with eight. Lord! how snug they might live in such another cottage as yours – or a little bigger – with two maids and two men; and I believe I could help them to a housemaid, for my Betty has a sister out of place, that would fit them exactly.'

Here Mrs Jennings ceased, and as Elinor had had time enough to collect her thoughts, she was able to give such an answer, and make such observations, as the subject might naturally be supposed to produce. Happy to find that she was not suspected of any extraordinary interest in it; that Mrs Jennings (as she had of late often hoped might be the case) had ceased to imagine her at all attached to Edward; and happy above all the rest, in the absence of Marianne, she felt very well able to speak of the affair without embarrassment, and to give her judgment, as she believed, with impartiality on the conduct of every one concerned in it.

She could hardly determine what her own expectation of its event really was; though she earnestly tried to drive away the notion of its being possible to end otherwise at last, than in the marriage of Edward and Lucy. What Mrs Ferrars would say and do, though there could not be a doubt of its nature, she was anxious to hear; and still more anxious to know how Edward would conduct himself. For *him* she felt much compassion; – for Lucy very little – and it cost her some pains to procure that little; – for the rest of the party none at all.

As Mrs Jennings could talk on no other subject, Elinor soon saw the necessity of preparing Marianne for its discussion. No time was to be lost in undeceiving her, in making her acquainted with the real truth, and in endeavouring to bring her to hear it talked of by others, without betraying that she felt any uneasiness for her sister, or any resentment against Edward.

Elinor's office was a painful one. – She was going to remove what she really believed to be her sister's chief consolation, – to give such particulars of Edward, as she feared would ruin him for ever in her good opinion, – and to make Marianne, by a resemblance in their situations, which to *her* fancy would seem strong, feel all her own disappointment over again. But unwelcome as such a task must be, it was necessary to be done, and Elinor therefore hastened to perform it.

She was very far from wishing to dwell on her own feelings, or to represent herself as suffering much, any otherwise than as the self-command she had practised since her first knowledge of Edward's engagement, might suggest a hint of what was practicable to Marianne. Her narration was clear and simple; and though it could not be given without emotion, it was not accompanied by violent agitation, nor impetuous grief. – *That* belonged rather to the hearer, for Marianne listened with horror, and cried excessively. Elinor was to be the comforter of others in her own distresses, no less than in theirs; and all the comfort that could be given by assurances of her own composure of mind, and a very earnest vindication of Edward from every charge but of imprudence, was readily offered.

But Marianne for some time would give credit to neither. Edward seemed a second Willoughby; and acknowledging as Elinor did, that she *had* loved him most sincerely, could she feel less than herself! As for Lucy Steele, she considered her so totally unamiable, so absolutely incapable of attaching a sensible man, that she could not be persuaded at first to believe, and afterwards to pardon, any former affection of Edward for her. She would not even admit it to have been natural; and Elinor left her to be convinced that it was so, by that which only could convince her, a better knowledge of mankind.

Her first communication had reached no farther than to state the fact of the engagement, and the length of time it had existed. – Marianne's feelings had then broken in, and put an end to all regularity of detail; and for some time all that could be done was to sooth her distress, lessen her alarms, and combat her resentment. The first question on her side, which led to farther particulars, was,

'How long has this been known to you, Elinor? has he written to you?'

'I have known it these four months. When Lucy first came to Barton-park last November, she told me in confidence of her engagement.'

At these words, Marianne's eyes expressed the astonishment, which her lips could not utter. After a pause of wonder, she exclaimed,

'Four months! – Have you known of this four months?' –

Elinor confirmed it.

'What! – while attending me in all my misery, has this been on your heart? – and I have reproached you for being happy!' –

'It was not fit that you should then know how much I was the reverse!' –

'Four months!' – cried Marianne again. – 'So calm! – so cheerful! – how have you been supported?' –

'By feeling that I was doing my duty. – My promise to Lucy, obliged me to be secret. I owed it to her, therefore, to avoid giving any hint of the truth; and I owed it to my family and friends, not to create in them a solicitude about me, which it could not be in my power to satisfy.'

Marianne seemed much struck. –

'I have very often wished to undeceive yourself and my mother,' added Elinor; 'and once or twice I have attempted it; – but without betraying my trust, I never could have convinced you.'

'Four months! – and yet you loved him!' –

'Yes. But I did not love only him; – and while the comfort of others was dear to me, I was glad to spare them from knowing how much I felt. Now, I can think and speak of it with little emotion. I would not have you suffer on my account; for I assure you I no longer suffer materially myself. I have many things to support me. I am not conscious of having provoked the disappointment by any imprudence of my own, and I have borne it as much as possible without spreading it farther. I acquit Edward of all essential misconduct. I wish him very happy; and I am so sure of his always doing his duty, that though now he may harbour some regret, in the end he must become so. Lucy does not want sense, and that is the foundation on which every thing good may be built. – And after all, Marianne, after all that is bewitching in the idea of a single and constant attachment, and all that can be said of one's happiness depending entirely on any particular person, it is not meant – it is not fit – it is not possible that it should be so. – Edward will marry Lucy; he will marry a woman superior in person and understanding to half her sex; and time and habit will teach him to forget that he ever thought another superior to *her*.' –

'If such is your way of thinking,' said Marianne, 'if the loss of what is most valued is so easily to be made up by something else, your resolution, your self-command, are, perhaps, a little less to be wondered at. – They are brought more within my comprehension.'

'I understand you. – You do not suppose that I have ever felt much. – For four months, Marianne, I have had all this hanging on my mind, without being at liberty to speak of it to a single creature; knowing that it would make you and my mother most unhappy whenever it were explained to you, yet unable to prepare you for it in the least. – It was told me, – it was in a manner forced on me by the very person herself, whose prior engagement ruined all my prospects; and told me, as I thought, with triumph. – This person's suspicions, therefore, I have had to oppose, by endeavouring to appear indifferent where I have been most deeply interested; – and it has not been only once; – I have had her hopes and exultation to listen to again and again. – I have known myself to be divided from Edward for ever, without hearing one circumstance that could make me less desire the connection. – Nothing has proved him unworthy; nor has any thing declared him indifferent to me. – I have had to contend against the unkindness of his sister, and the insolence of his mother; and have suffered the punishment of an attachment, without enjoying its advantages. – And all this has been going on at a time, when, as you too well know, it has not been my only unhappiness. – If you can think me capable of ever feeling – surely you may suppose that I have suffered *now*. The composure of mind with which I have brought myself at present to consider the matter, the consolation that I have been willing to admit, have been the effect of constant and painful exertion; – they did not spring up of themselves; – they did not occur to relieve my spirits at first – No, Marianne. – *Then*, if I had not been bound to silence, perhaps nothing could have kept me entirely – not even what I owed to my dearest friends – from openly shewing that I was *very* unhappy.' –

Marianne was quite subdued. –

'Oh! Elinor,' she cried, 'you have made me hate myself for ever. – How barbarous have I been to you! – you, who have been my only comfort, who have borne with me in all my misery, who have seemed to be only suffering for me! – Is this my gratitude! – Is this the only return I can make you? – Because you merit cries out upon myself, I have been trying to do it away.'

The tenderest caresses followed this confession. In such a frame of mind as she was now in, Elinor had no difficulty in obtaining from her whatever promise she required; and at her request, Marianne engaged never to speak of the affair to any one with the least appearance of bitterness; – to meet Lucy without betraying the smallest increase of dislike to her; – and even to see Edward himself, if chance should bring them together, without any diminution of her usual cordiality. – These were great concessions; – but where Marianne felt that she had injured, no reparation could be too much for her to make.

She performed her promise of being discreet, to admiration. – She attended to all that Mrs Jennings had to say upon the subject, with an unchanging complexion, dissented from her in nothing, and was heard three times to say, 'Yes, ma'am.' – She listened to her praise of Lucy with only moving from one chair to another, and when Mrs Jennings talked of Edward's affection, it cost her only a spasm in her throat. – Such advances towards heroism in her sister, made Elinor feel equal to any thing herself.

The next morning brought a farther trial of it, in a visit from their brother, who came with a most serious aspect to talk over the dreadful affair, and bring them news of his wife.

'You have heard, I suppose,' said he with great solemnity, as soon as he was seated, 'of the very shocking discovery that took place under our roof yesterday.'

They all looked their assent; it seemd too awful a moment for speech.

'Your sister,' he continued, 'has suffered dreadfully. Mrs Ferrars too – in short it has been a scene of such complicated distress – but I will hope that the storm may be weathered without our being any of us quite overcome. Poor Fanny! she was in hysterics all yesterday. But I would not alarm you too much. Donavan says there is nothing materially to be apprehended; her constitution is a good one, and her resolution equal to any thing. She has borne it all, with the fortitude of an angel! She says she never shall think well of anybody again; and one cannot wonder at it, after being so deceived! – meeting with such ingratitude, where so much kindness had been shewn, so much confidence had been placed! It was quite out of the benevolence of her heart, that she had asked these young women to her house; merely because she thought they deserved some attention, were harmless, well-behaved girls, and would be pleasant companions; for otherwise we both wished very much to have invited you and Marianne to be with us, while your kind friend there, was attending her daughter. And now to be so rewarded! "I

'You have heard, I suppose.'

wish with all my heart," says poor Fanny in her affectionate way, "that we had asked your sisters instead of them." '

Here he stopped to be thanked; which being done, he went on.

'What poor Mrs Ferrars suffered, when first Fanny broke it to her, is not to be described. While she with the truest affection had been planning a most eligible connection for him, was it to be supposed that he could be all the time secretly engaged to another person! – such a suspicion could never have entered her head! If she suspected *any* prepossession elsewhere, it could not be in *that* quarter. "*There*, to be sure," said she, "I might have thought myself safe." She was quite in an agony. We consulted together, however, as to what should be done, and at last she determined to send for Edward.

He came. But I am sorry to relate what ensued. All that Mrs Ferrars could say to make him put an end to the engagement, assisted too as you may well suppose by my arguments, and Fanny's entreaties, was of no avail. Duty, affection, every thing was disregarded. I never thought Edward so stubborn, so unfeeling before. His mother explained to him her liberal designs, in case of his marrying Miss Morton; told him she would settle on him the Norfold estate, which, clear of land-tax, brings in a good thousand a-year; offered even, when matters grew desperate, to make twelve hundred; and in opposition to this, if he still persisted in this low connection, represented to him the certain penury that must attend the match. His own two thousand pounds she protested should be his all, she would never see him again; and so far would she be from affording him the smallest assistance, that if he were to enter into any profession with a view of better support, she would do all in her power to prevent his advancing in it.'

Here Marianne, in an ecstacy of indignation, clapped her hands together, and cried, 'Gracious God! can this be possible!'

'Well may you wonder, Marianne,' replied her brother, 'at the obstinacy which could resist such arguments as these. Your exclamation is very natural.'

Marianne was going to retort, but she remembered her promises, and forbore.

'All this, however,' he continued, 'was urged in vain. Edward said very little; but what he did say, was in the most determined manner. Nothing should prevail on him to give up his engagement. He would stand to it, cost him what it might.'

'Then,' cried Mrs Jennings with blunt sincerity, no longer able to be silent, 'he has acted like an honest man! I beg your pardon, Mr Dashwood, but if he had done otherwise, I should have thought him a rascal. I have some little concern in the business, as well as yourself, for Lucy Steele is my cousin, and I believe there is not a better kind of girl in the world, nor one who more deserves a good husband.'

John Dashwood was greatly astonished; but his nature was calm, not open to provocation, and he never wished to offend anybody, especially anybody of good fortune. He therefore replied, without any resentment,

'I would by no means speak disrespectfully of any relation of yours, madam. Miss Lucy Steele is, I dare say, a very deserving young woman, but in the present case you know, the connection must be impossible. And to have entered into a secret engagement with a young man under her uncle's care, the son of a woman especially of such very large fortune as Mrs Ferrars, is perhaps altogether a little extraordinary. In short, I do not mean to reflect upon the behaviour of any person whom you have a regard for, Mrs Jennings. We all wish her extremely happy, and Mrs Ferrars's conduct throughout the whole, has been such as every conscientious good mother, in like circumstances, would adopt. It has been dignified and liberal. Edward has drawn his own lot, and I fear it will be a bad one.'

Marianne sighed out her similar apprehension; and Elinor's heart wrung for the feelings of Edward, while braving his mother's threats, for a woman who could not reward him.

'Well, sir,' said Mrs Jennings, 'and how did it end?'

'I am sorry to say, ma'am, in a most unhappy rupture: – Edward is dismissed for ever from his mother's notice. He left her house yesterday, but where he is gone, or whether he is still in town, I do not know; for *we* of course can make no inquiry.'

'Poor young man! – and what is to become of him?'

'What, indeed, ma'am! It is a melancholy consideration. Born to the prospect of such affluence! I cannot conceive a situation more deplorable. The interest of two thousand pounds – how can a man live on it! – and when to that is added the recollection, that he might, but for his own folly, within three months have been in the receipt of two thousand, five hundred a-year, (for Miss Morton has thirty thousand pounds,) I cannot picture to myself a more wretched condition. We must all feel for him; and the more so, because it is totally out of our power to assist him.'

'Poor young man!' cried Mrs Jennings, 'I am sure he should be very welcome to bed and board at my house; and so I would tell him if I could see him. It is not fit that he should be living about at his own charge now, at lodgings and taverns.'

Elinor's heart thanked her for such kindness towards Edward, though she could not forbear smiling at the form of it.

'If he would only have done as well by himself,' said John Dashwood, 'as all his friends were disposed to do by him, he might now have been in his proper situation, and would have wanted for nothing. But as it is, it must be out of anybody's power to assist him. And there is one thing more preparing against him, which must be worse than all – his mother has determined, with a very natural kind of spirit, to settle *that* estate upon Robert immediately, which might have been Edward's, on proper conditions. I left her this morning with her lawyer, talking over the business.'

'Well!' said Mrs Jennings, 'that is *her* revenge. Everybody has a way of their own. But I don't think mine would be, to make one son independent, because another had plagued me.'

Marianne got up, and walked about the room.

'Can any thing be more galling to the spirit of a man,' continued John, 'than to see his younger brother in possession of an estate which might have been his own? Poor Edward! I feel for him sincerely.'

A few minutes more spent in the same kind of effusion, concluded his visit; and with repeated assurances to his sisters that he really believed there was no material danger in Fanny's indisposition, and that they need not therefore be very uneasy about it, he went away; leaving the three ladies unanimous in their sentiments on the present occasion, as far at least as it regarded Mrs Ferrars's conduct, the Dashwoods' and Edward's.

Marianne's indignation burst forth as soon as he quitted the room;

Talking over the business.

and as her vehemence made reserve impossible in Elinor, and unnecessary in Mrs Jennings, they all joined in a very spirited critique upon the party.

CHAPTER THIRTY-EIGHT

MRS JENNINGS WAS very warm in her praise of Edward's conduct, but only Elinor and Marianne understood its true merit. *They* only knew how little he had had to tempt him to be disobedient, and how small was the consolation, beyond the consciousness of doing right, that could remain to him in the loss of friends and fortune. Elinor gloried in his integrity; and Marianne forgave all his offences in compassion for his punishment. But though confidence between them was, by this public discovery, restored to its proper state, it was not a subject on which either of them were fond of dwelling when alone. Elinor avoided it upon principle, as tending to fix still more upon her thoughts, by the too warm, too positive assurances of Marianne, that belief of Edward's continued affection for herself which she rather wished to do away; and Marianne's courage soon failed her, in trying to converse upon a topic which always left her more dissatisfied with herself than ever, by the comparision it necessarily produced between Elinor's conduct and her own.

She felt all the force of that comparison; but not as her sister had hoped, to urge her to exertion now; she felt it with all the pain of continual self-reproach, regretted most bitterly that she had never exerted herself before; but it brought only the torture of penitence, without the hope of amendment. Her mind was so much weakened that she still fancied present exertion impossible, and therefore it only dispirited her more.

Nothing new was heard by them, for a day or two afterwards, of affairs in Harley-street, or Bartlett's Buildings. But though so much of the matter was known to them already, that Mrs Jennings might have had enough to do in spreading that knowledge farther, without seeking after more, she had resolved from the first to pay a visit of comfort and inquiry to her cousins as soon as she could; and nothing but the hindrance of more visitors than usual, had prevented her going to them within that time.

The third day succeeding their knowledge of the particulars, was so fine, so beautiful a Sunday as to draw many to Kensington Gardens, though it was only the second week in March. Mrs

Jennings and Elinor were of the number; but Marianne, who knew that the Willoughbys were again in town, and had a constant dread of meeting them, chose rather to stay at home, than venture into so public a place.

An intimate acquaintance of Mrs Jennings joined them soon after they entered the Gardens, and Elinor was not sorry that by her continuing with them, and engaging all Mrs Jennings's conversation, she was herself left to quiet reflection. She saw nothing of the Willoughbys, nothing of Edward, and for some time nothing of any body who could by any chance whether grave or gay, be interesting to her. But at last she found herself with some surprise, accosted by Miss Steele, who, though looking rather shy, expressed great satisfaction in meeting them, and on receiving encouragement from the particular kindness of Mrs Jennings, left her own party for a short time, to join their's. Mrs Jennings immediately whispered to Elinor,

'Get it all out of her, my dear. She will tell you any thing if you ask. You see I cannot leave Mrs Clarke.'

It was lucky, however, for Mrs Jenning's curiosity and Elinor's too, that she would tell any thing *without* being asked, for nothing would otherwise have been learnt.

'I am so glad to meet you;' said Miss Steele, taking her familiarly by the arm – 'for I wanted to see you of all things in the world.' And then lowering her voice, 'I suppose Mrs Jennings has heard all about it. Is she angry?'

'Not at all, I believe, with you.'

'That is a good thing. And Lady Middleton, is *she* angry?'

'I cannot suppose it possible that she should.'

'I am monstrous glad of it. Good gracious! I have had such a time of it! I never saw Lucy in such a rage in my life. She vowed at first she would never trim me up a new bonnet, nor do any thing for me again, so long as she lived, but now she is quite come to, and we are as good friends as ever. Look, she made me this bow to my hat, and put in the feather last night. There now, *you* are going to laugh at me too. But why should not I wear pink ribbons? I do not care it is *is* the Doctor's favourite colour. I am sure, for my part, I should never have known he *did* like it better than any other colour, if he had not happened to say so. My cousins have been so plaguing me! – I declare sometimes I do not know which way to look before them.'

She had wandered away to a subject on which Elinor had nothing to say, and therefore soon judged it expedient to find her way back again to the first.

'She put in the feather last night.'

'Well, but Miss Dashwood,' speaking triumphantly, 'people may say what they chuse about Mr Ferrars's declaring he would not have Lucy, for it's no such a thing I can tell you; and it's quite a shame for such ill-natured reports to be spread abroad. Whatever Lucy might think about it herself, you know, it was no business of other people to set it down for certain.'

'I never heard anything of the kind hinted at before, I assure you,' said Elinor.

'Oh! did not you? But it *was* said, I know, very well, and by more than one; for Miss Godby told Miss Sparks, that nobody in their senses could expect Mr Ferrars to give up a woman like Miss Morton, with thirty thousand pounds to her fortune, for Lucy Steele that had nothing at all; and I had it from Miss Sparks myself. And besides that, my cousin Richard said himself, that when it came to the point, he was afraid Mr Ferrars would be off; and when Edward did not come near us for three days, I could not tell what to think myself; and I believe in my heart Lucy gave it up all for lost; for we came away from your brother's Wednesday, and we saw nothing of him not all Thursday, Friday, and Saturday, and did not know what was become with him. Once Lucy thought to write to him, but then her spirit rose against that. However this morning he came just as we came home from church; and then it all came out, how he had been sent for Wednesday to Harley-street, and been talked to by his mother and all of them, and how he had declared before them all that he loved nobody but Lucy, and nobody but Lucy would he have. And how he had been so worried by what passed, that as soon as he had went away from his mother's house, he had got upon his horse, and rid into the country some where or other; and how he had staid about at an inn all Thursday and Friday, on purpose to get the better of it. And after thinking it all over and over again, he said, it seemed to him as if, now he had no fortune, and no nothing at all, it would be quite unkind to keep her on to the engagement, because it must be for her loss, for he had nothing but two thousand pounds, and no hope of any thing else; and if he was to go into orders, as he had some thoughts, he could get nothing but a curacy, and how was they to live upon that? – He could not bear to think of her doing no better, and so he begged, if she had the least mind for it, to put an end to the matter directly, and leave him to shift for himself. I heard him say all this as plain as could possibly be. And it was entirely for *her* sake, and upon *her* account, that he said a word about being off, and not upon his own. I will take my oath he never dropt a syllable of being tired of her, or of wishing to marry Miss Morton, or anything like it. But, to be sure, Lucy would not give ear to such kind of talking; so she told him directly (with a great deal about sweet and love, you know, and all that – Oh, la! one can't repeat such kind of things you know) – she told him directly, she had not the least mind in the world to be off, for she could live with him upon a trifle, and how little so ever he might have, she should be very glad to have it all, you know, or something of the kind. So then he was monstrous happy, and talked on some time about what they should do, and they agreed he should take orders directly, and they must wait to be married till he got a living. And just then I could not hear any more, for my cousin called from below to tell me Mrs Richardson was come in her coach, and would take one of us to Kensington Gardens; so I was forced to go into the room and interrupt them, to ask Lucy if she would like to go, but she did not care to leave Edward; so I just run up stairs and put on a pair of silk stockings, and came off with the Richardsons.'

'I do not understand what you mean by interrupting them,' said Elinor; 'you were all in the same room together, were not you?'

'No, indeed, not us. La! Miss Dashwood, do you think people make love when any body else is by? Oh for shame! – To be sure, you must know better than that. (Laughing affectedly.) – No, no; they were shut up in the drawing-room together, and all I heard was only by listening at the door.'

'How!' cried Elinor; 'have you been repeating to me what you

Listening at the door.

only learnt yourself by listening at the door? I am sorry I did not know it before; for I certainly would not have suffered you to give me particulars of a conversation which you ought not to have known yourself. How could you behave so unfairly by your sister?'

'Oh, la! there is nothing in *that.* I only stood at the door, and heard what I could. And I am sure Lucy would have done just the same by me; for a year or two back, when Martha Sharpe and I had so many secrets together, she never made any bones of hiding in a closet, or behind a chimney-board, on purpose to hear what we said.'

Elinor tried to talk of something else; but Miss Steele could not be kept beyond a couple of minutes, from what was uppermost in her mind.

'Edward talks of going to Oxford soon,' said she, 'but now he is lodging at No. –, Pall Mall. What an ill-natured woman his mother is, an't she? And your brother and sister were not very kind! However, I shan't say anything against them to *you*; and to be sure they did send us home in their own chariot, which was more than I looked for. And for my part, I was all in a fright for fear your sister should ask us for the huswifes she had gave us a day or two before; but however, nothing was said about them, and I took care to keep mine out of sight. Edward have got some business at Oxford, he says; so he must go there for a time; and after *that*, as soon as he can light upon a Bishop, he will be ordained. I wonder what curacy he will get! – Good gracious! (giggling as she spoke) I'd lay my life I know what my cousins will say, when they hear of it. They will tell me I should write to the Doctor, to get Edward the curacy of his new living. I know they will; but I am sure I would not do such a thing for all the world. – "La!" I shall say directly, "I wonder how you could think of such a thing. *I* write to the Doctor, indeed!" '

'Well,' said Elinor, 'it is a comfort to be prepared against the worst. You have got your answer ready.'

Miss Steele was going to reply on the same subject but the approach of her own party made another more necessary.

'Oh, la! here come the Richardsons. I had a vast deal more to say to you, but I must not stay away from them any longer. I assure you they are very genteel people. He makes a monstrous deal of money, and they keep their own coach. I have not time to speak to Mrs Jennings about it myself, but pray tell her I am quite happy to hear she is not in anger against us, and Lady Middleton the same; and if any thing should happen to take you and your sister away, and Mrs Jennings should want company, I am sure we should be very glad to come and stay with her for as long as a time as she likes. I suppose Lady Middleton won't ask us any more this bout. Good bye; I am sorry Miss Marianne was not here. Remember me kindly to her. La! If you have not got your spotted muslin on! – I wonder you was not afraid of its being torn.'

Such was her parting concern; for after this, she had time only to pay her farewell compliments to Mrs Jennings, before her company was claimed by Mrs Richardson; and Elinor was left in possession of knowledge which might feed her powers of reflection some time, though she had learnt very little more than what had been already foreseen and foreplanned in her own mind. Edward's marriage with Lucy was as firmly determined on, and the time of its taking place remained as absolutely uncertain, as she had concluded it would be; – every thing depended, exactly after her expectation, on his getting that preferment, of which, at present, there seemed not the smallest chance.

As soon as they returned to the carriage, Mrs Jennings was eager for information; but as Elinor wished to spread as little as possible intelligence that had in the first place been so unfairly obtained, she confined herself to the brief repetition of such simple particulars, as she felt assured that Lucy, for the sake of her own consequence, would chuse to have known. The continuance of their engagement, and the means that were to be taken for promoting its end, was all her communication; and this produced from Mrs Jennings the following natural remark.

'Wait for his having a living! – aye, we all know how *that* will end; – they will wait a twelvemonth, and finding no good comes of it, will set down upon a curacy of fifty pounds a-year, with the interest of his two thousand pounds, and what little matter Mr Steele and Mr Pratt can give her. – Then they will have a child every year! and Lord help 'em! how poor they will be! – I must see what I can give them towards furnishing their house. Two maids and two men indeed! – as I talked of t'other day. – No, no, they must get a stout girl of all works. – Betty's sister would never do for them *now*.'

The next morning brought Elinor a letter by the two-penny post from Lucy herself. It was as follows:

Bartlett's Buildings, March.

I hope my dear Miss Dashwood will excuse the liberty I take of writing to her; but I know your friendship for me will make you pleased to hear such a good account of myself and my dear Edward, after all the troubles we have went through lately, therefore will make no more apologies, but proceed to say that, thank God! though we have suffered dreadfully, we are both quite well now, and as happy as we must always be in one another's love. We have had great trials, and great persecutions, but however, at the same time, gratefully acknowledge many friends, yourself not the least among them, whose great kindness I shall always thankfully remember, as will Edward too, who I have told of it. I am sure you will be glad to hear, as likewise dear Mrs Jennings, I spent two happy hours with him yesterday afternoon, he would not hear of our parting, though earnestly did I, as I thought my duty required, urge him to it for prudence sake, and would have parted for ever on the spot, would he consent to it; but he said it should never be, he did not regard his mother's anger, while he could have my affections; our prospects are not very bright, to be sure, but we must wait, and hope for the best; he will be ordained shortly, and should it ever be in your power to recommend him to any body that has a living to bestow, am very sure you will not forget us, and dear Mrs Jennings too, trust she will speak a good word for us to Sir John, or Mr Palmer, or any friend that may be able to assist us. – Poor Anne was much to blame for what she did, but she did it for the best, so I say nothing; hope Mrs Jennings won't think it too much trouble to give us a call, should she come this way any morning, 'twould be a great kindness, and my cousins would be proud to know her. – My paper reminds me to conclude, and begging to be most gratefully and respectfully remembered to her, and to Sir John and Lady Middleton, and the dear children, when you chance to see them, and love to Miss Marianne,

I am, &c. &c.

As soon as Elinor finished it, she performed what she concluded to be its writer's real design, by placing it in the hands of Mrs Jennings, who read it aloud with many comments of satisfaction and praise.

'Very well indeed! – how prettily she writes! – aye, that was quite proper to let him be off if he would. That was just like Lucy. – Poor soul! I wish I *could* get him a living with all my heart. – She calls me dear Mrs Jennings, you see. She is a good-hearted girl as ever lived. – Very well upon my word. That sentence is very prettily turned. Yes, yes, I will go and see her, sure enough. How attentive she is, to think of everybody! – Thank you, my dear, for shewing it me. It is as pretty a letter as ever I saw, and does Lucy's head and heart great credit.'

CHAPTER THIRTY-NINE

THE MISS DASHWOODS had now been rather more than two months in town, and Marianne's impatience to be gone increased every day. She sighed for the air, the liberty, the quiet of the country; and fancied that if any place could give her ease, Barton must do it. Elinor was hardly less anxious than herself for their removal, and only so much less bent on its being effected immediately, as that she was conscious of the difficulties of so long a journey, which Marianne could not be brought to acknowledge. She began, however, seriously to turn her thoughts towards its accomplishment, and had already mentioned their wishes to their kind hostess, who resisted them with all the eloquence of her good-will, when a plan was suggested, which, though detaining them from home yet a few weeks longer, appeared to Elinor together much more eligible than any other. The Palmers were to remove to Cleveland about the end of March, for the Easter holidays; and Mrs Jennings, with both her friends, received a very warm invitation from Charlotte to go with them. This would not, in itself, have been sufficient for the delicacy of Miss Dashwood; – but it was inforced with so much real politeness by Mr Palmer himself, as joined to the very great amendment of his manners towards them since her sister had been known to be unhappy, induced her to accept it with pleasure.

When she told Marianne what she had done, however, her first reply was not very auspicious.

'Cleveland!' – she cried, with great agitation. 'No, I cannot go to Cleveland.' –

'You forget,' said Elinor, gently, 'that its situation is not . . . that it is not in the neighbourhood of . . .'

'But it is in Somersetshire. – I cannot go into Somersetshire. – There, where I looked forward to going . . . No, Elinor, you cannot expect me to go there.'

Elinor would not argue upon the propriety of overcoming such feelings; – she only endeavoured to counteract them by working on others; – and represented it, therefore, as a measure which would fix the time of her returning to that dear mother, whom she so much wished to see, in a more eligible, more comfortable manner, than any other plan could do, and perhaps without any greater delay. From Cleveland, which was within a few miles of Bristol, the distance to Barton was not beyond one day, though a long day's journey; and their mother's servant might easily come there to attend them down; and as there could be no occasion for their staying above a week at Cleveland, they might now be at home in little more than three weeks' time. As Marianne's affection for her mother was sincere, it must triumph, with little difficulty, over the imaginary evils she had started.

Mrs Jennings was so far from being weary of her guests, that she pressed them very earnestly to return with her again from Cleveland. Elinor was grateful for the attention, but it could not alter their design; and their mother's concurrence being readily gained, every thing relative to their return was arranged as far as it could be; – and Marianne found some relief in drawing up a statement of the hours, that were yet to divide her from Barton.

'Ah! Colonel, I do not know what you and I shall do without the Miss Dashwoods;' – was Mrs Jennings's address to him when he first called on her, after their leaving her was settled – 'for they are quite resolved upon going home from the Palmers; – and how forlorn we shall be, when I come back! – Lord! we shall sit and gape at one another as dull as two cats.'

Perhaps Mrs Jennings was in hopes, by this vigorous sketch of their future ennnui, to provoke him to make that offer, which might give himself an escape from it; – and if so, she had soon afterwards good reason to think her object gained; for, on Elinor's moving to the window to take more expeditiously the dimensions of a print, which she was going to copy for her friend, he followed her to it with a look of particular meaning, and conversed with her there for several minutes. The effect of his discourse on the lady too, could not escape her observation, for though she was too honourable to listen, and had even changed her seat, on purpose that she might *not* hear, to one close by the piano forté on which Marianne was playing, she could not keep herself from seeing that Elinor changed colour, attended with agitation, and was too intent on what he said, to pursue her employment. – Still farther in confirmation of her hopes, in the interval of Marianne's turning from one lesson to another, some words of the Colonel's inevitably reached her ear, in which he seemed to be apologizing for the badness of his house. This set the matter beyond a doubt. She wondered indeed at his thinking it necessary to do so; – but supposed to to be the proper etiquette. What Elinor said in reply she could not distinguish, but judged from the motion of her lips that she did not think *that* any material objection; – and Mrs Jennings commended her in her heart for being so honest. They then talked on for a few mintues longer without her catching a syllable, when another lucky stop in Marianne's performance brought her these words in the Colonel's calm voice,

'I am afraid it cannot take place very soon.'

Astonished and shocked at so unlover-like a speech, she was almost ready to cry out, 'Lord! what should hinder it?' – but checking her desire, confined herself to this silent ejaculation.

'This is very strange! – sure he need not wait to be older.' –

This delay on the Colonel's side, however, did not seem to offend or mortify his fair companion in the least, for on their breaking up the conference soon afterwards, and moving different ways, Mrs Jennings very plainly heard Elinor say, and with a voice which shewed her to feel what she said,

'I shall always think myself very much obliged to you.'

Mrs Jennings was delighted with her gratitude, and only wondered that after hearing such a sentence, the Colonel should be able to take leave of them, as he immediately did, with the utmost sang-froid, and go away without making her any reply! She had not thought her old friend could have made so indifferent a suitor.

What had really passed between them was to this effect.

'I have heard,' said he, with great compassion, 'of the injustice your friend Mr Ferrars has suffered from his family; for if I understand the matter right, he has been entirely cast off by them for persevering in his engagement with a very deserving young woman – Have I been rightly informed? – Is it so?' –

Elinor told him that it was.

'The cruelty, the impolitic cruelty,' – he replied, with great feeling – 'of dividing, or attempting to divide, two young people long attached to each other, is terrible – Mrs Ferrars does not know what she may be doing – what she may drive her son to. I have seen Mr Ferrars two or three times in Harley-street, and am much pleased with him. He is not a young man with whom one can be intimately acquainted in a short time, but I have seen enough of him to wish him well for his own sake, and as a friend of yours, I wish it still more. I understand that he intends to take orders. Will you be so good as to tell him that the living of Delaford, now just vacant, as I am informed by this day's post, is his, if he think it worth his acceptance – but *that*, perhaps, so unfortunately circumstanced as he is now, it may be nonsense to appear to doubt; I only wish it were more valuable. – It is a rectory, but a small one; the late incumbent, I believe, did not make more than 200*l*. per annum, and though it is certainly capable of improvement, I fear, not to such an amount as to afford him a very comfortable income. Such as it is, however, my pleasure in presenting him to it, will be very great. Pray assure him of it.'

Elinor's astonishment at this commission could hardly have been greater, had the Colonel been really making an offer of his hand. The preferment, which only two days before she had considered as hopeless for Edward, was already provided to enable him to marry; – and *she*, of all people in the world, was fixed on to bestow it! – Her emotion was such as Mrs Jennings had attributed to a very different cause; – but whatever minor feelings less pure, less pleasing, might have a share in that emotion, her esteem for the general benevolence, and her gratitude for the particular friendship, which together prompted Colonel Brandon to this act, were strongly felt, and warmly expressed. She thanked him for it with all her heart, spoke of Edward's principles and disposition with that praise which she knew them to deserve; and promised to undertake the commission with pleasure, if it were really his wish to put off so agreeable an office to another. But at the same time, she could not help thinking that no one could so well perform it as himself. It was an office in short, from which, unwilling to give Edward the pain of receiving an obligation from *her*, she would have been very glad to be spared herself; – but Colonel Brandon, on motives of equal delicacy, declining it likewise, still seemed so desirous of its being given through her means, that she would not on any account make farther opposition. Edward, she believed, was still in town, and fortunately she had heard his address from Miss Steele. She could undertake therefore to inform him of it, in the course of the day. After this had been settled, Colonel Brandon began to talk of his own advantage in securing so respectable and agreeable a neighbour, and *then* it was that he mentioned with regret, that the house was small and indifferent; – an evil which Elinor, as Mrs Jennings had supposed her to do, made very light of, at least as far as regarded its size.

'The smallness of the house,' said she, 'I cannot imagine any inconvenience to them, for it will be in proportion to their family and income.'

By which the Colonel was surprised to find that *she* was considering Mr Ferrars's marriage as the certain consequence of the presentation; for he did not suppose it possible that Delaford living could supply such an income, as any body in his style of life would venture to settle on – and he said so.

'This little rectory *can* do no more than make Mr Ferrars comfortable as a bachelor; it cannot enable him to marry. I am sorry to say that my patronage ends with this; and my interest is hardly more extensive. If, however, by any unforseen chance it should be in my power to serve him farther, I must think very differently of him from what I now do, if I am not as ready to be useful to him then, as I sincerely wish I could be at present. What I am now doing indeed, seems nothing at all, since it can advance him so little towards what must be his principal, his only object of happiness. His marriage must still be a distant good; – at least, I am afraid it cannot take place very soon. – '

Such was the sentence which, when misunderstood, so justly offended the delicate feelings of Mrs Jennings; but after this narration of what really passed between Colonel Brandon and Elinor, while they stood at the window, the gratitude expressed by the latter on their parting, may perhaps appear in general, not less reasonably excited, nor less properly worded than if it had arisen from an offer of marriage.

CHAPTER FORTY

'WELL, MISS DASHWOOD,' said Mrs Jennings, sagaciously smiling, as soon as the gentleman had withdrawn, 'I do not ask you what the Colonel has been saying to you; for though, upon my honour, I *tried* to keep out of hearing, I could not help catching enough to understand his business. And I assure you I never was better pleased in my life, and I wish you joy of it will all my heart.'

'Thank you, ma'am,' said Elinor, 'It is a matter of great joy to me; and I feel the goodness of Colonel Brandon most sensibly. There are not many men who would act as he had done. Few people who have so compassionate an heart! I never was more astonished in my life.'

'Lord! my dear, you are very modest! I an't the least astonished at it in the world, for I have often thought of late, there was nothing more likely to happen.'

'You judged from your knowledge of the Colonel's general benevolence; but at least you could not foresee that the opportunity would so very soon occur.'

'Opportunity!' repeated Mrs Jennings – 'Oh! as to that, when a man has once made up his mind to such a thing, somehow or other he will soon find an opportunity. Well, my dear, I wish you joy of it again and again; and if ever there was a happy couple in the world, I think I shall soon know where to look for them.'

'You mean to go to Delaford after them I suppose,' said Elinor, with a faint smile.

'Aye, my dear, that I do, indeed. And as to the house being a bad one, I do not know what the Colonel would be at, for it is as good a one as ever I saw.'

'He spoke of its being out of repair.'

'Well, and whose fault is that? why don't he repair it? – who should do it but himself?'

They were interrupted by the servant's coming in to announce the carriage being at the door; and Mrs Jennings immediately preparing to go, said –

'Well, my dear, I must be gone before I have had half my talk out. But, however, we may have it all over in the evening, for we shall be quite alone. I do not ask you to go with me, for I dare say your mind is too full of the matter to care for company; and besides, you must long to tell your sister about it.'

Marianne had left the room before the conversation began.

'Certainly, ma'am, I shall tell Marianne of it; but I shall not mention it at present to any body else.'

'Oh! very well,' said Mrs Jennings rather disappointed. 'Then you would not have me tell it Lucy, for I think of going as far as Holborn today.'

'No, ma'am, not even Lucy if you please. One day's delay will not be very material; and till I have written to Mr Ferrars, I think it ought not to be mentioned to any body else. I shall do *that* directly. It is of importance that no time should be lost with him, for he will of course have much to do relative to his ordination.'

This speech at first puzzled Mrs Jennings exceedingly. Why Mr Ferrars was to be written to about it in such a hurry, she could not immediately comprehend. A few moments' reflection, however, produced a very happy idea, and she exclaimed; –

'Oh ho! – I understand you. Mr Ferrars is to be the man. Well, so much the better for him. Aye, to be sure, he must be ordained in readiness; and I am very glad to find things are so forward between you. But, my dear, is not this rather out of character? Should not the Colonel write himself? – sure, he is the proper person.'

Elinor did not quite understand the beginning of Mrs Jennings's speech; neither did she think it worth inquiring into; and therefore only replied to its conclusion.

'Colonel Brandon is so delicate a man, that he rather wished any one to announce his intentions to Mr Ferrars than himself.'

'And so *you* are forced to do it. Well, *that* is an odd kind of delicacy! However, I will not disturb you (sseing her preparing to write.) You know your own concerns best. So good bye, my dear. I have not heard of any thing to please me so well since Charlotte was brought to bed.'

And away she went; but returning again in a moment,

'I have just been thinking of Betty's sister, my dear. I should be very glad to get her so good a mistress. But whether she would do for a lady's maid, I am sure I can't tell. She is an excellent housemaid, and works very well at her needle. However, you will think of all that at your leisure.'

'Certainly, ma'am,' replied Elinor, not hearing much of what she said, and more anxious to be alone, than to be mistress of the subject.

How she should begin – how she should express herself in her note to Edward, was now all her concern. The particular circumstances between them made a difficulty of that which to any other person would have been the easiest thing in the world; but she equally feared to say too much or too little, and sat deliberating over her paper, with the pen in her hand, till broken in on by the entrance of Edward himself.

He had met Mrs Jennings at the door in her way to the carriage, as he came to leave his farewell card; and she, after apologizing for not returning herself, had obliged him to enter, by saying that Miss Dashwood was above, and wanted to speak with him on very particular business.

Elinor had just been congratulating herself, in the midst of her perplexity, that however difficult it might be to express herself properly by letter, it was at least preferable to giving the information by word of mouth, when her visitor entered, to force her upon this greatest exertion of all. Her astonishment and confusion were very great on his so sudden appearance. She had not seen him before since his engagement became public, and therefore not since his knowing her to be acquainted with it; which, with the consciousness of what she had been thinking of, and what she had to tell him, made her feel particularly uncomfortable for some minutes. He too was much distressed, and they sat down together in a most promising state of embarrassment. – Whether he had asked her pardon for his intrusion on first coming into the room, he could not recollect; but determining to be on the safe side, he made his apology in form as soon as he could say any thing, after taking a chair.

'Mrs Jennings told me,' said he, 'that you wished to speak with me, at least I understood her so – or I certainly should not have intruded on you in such a manner; though at the same time, I should have been extremely sorry to leave London without seeing you and your sister; especially as it will most likely be some time – it is not probable that I should soon have the pleasure of meeting you again. I go to Oxford tomorrow.'

'You would not have gone, however,' said Elinor, recovering herself, and determined to get over what she so much dreaded as soon as possible, 'without receiving our good wishes, even if we had not been able to give them in person. Mrs Jennings was quite right in what she said. I have something of consequence to inform you of, which I was on the point of communicating by paper. I am charged with a most agreeable office, (breathing rather faster than usual as she spoke.) Colonel Brandon, who was here only ten minutes ago, has desired me to say that, understanding you mean to take orders, he has great pleasure in offering you the living of Delaford, now just vacant, and only wishes it were more valuable. Allow me to congratulate you on having so respectable and well-judging a friend, and to join in his wish that the living – it is about two hundred a-year – were much more considerable, and such as might better enable you to – as might be more than a temporary accommodation to yourself – such, as might establish all your views of happiness.'

What Edward felt, as he could not say it himself, it cannot be expected that any one else should say for him. He *looked* all the astonishment which such unexpected, such unthought-of information could not fail of exciting; but he said only these two words.

'Colonel Brandon!'

'Yes,' continued Elinor, gathering more resolution, as some of the worst was over; 'Colonel Brandon means it as a testimony of his concern for what has lately passed – for the cruel situation in which the unjustifiable conduct of your family has placed you – a concern which I am sure Marianne, myself and all your friends must share; and likewise as a proof of his high esteem for your general character, and his particular approbation of your behaviour on the present occasion.'

'Colonel Brandon give *me* a living! – Can it be possible?'

'The unkindness of your own relations has made you astonished to find friendship any where.'

'No,' replied he, with sudden consciousness, 'not to find it in *you*; for I cannot be ignorant that to you, to your goodness I owe it all. – I feel it – I would express it if I could – but, as you well know, I am no orator.'

'You are very much mistaken. I do assure you that you owe it entirely, at least almost entirely, to your own merit, and Colonel

Brandon's discernment of it. I have had no hand in it. I did not even know, till I understood his design, that the living was vacant; nor had it occurred to me that he might have had such a living in his gift. As a friend of mine, of my family, he may perhaps – indeed I know he *has*, still greater pleasure in bestowing it; but, upon my word, you owe nothing to my solicitation.'

Truth obliged her to acknowledge some small share in the action, but she was at the same time so unwilling to appear as the benefactress of Edward, that she acknowledged it with hesitation; which probably contributed to fix that suspicion in his mind which had recently entered it. For a short time he sat deep in thought, after Elinor had ceased to speak; – at last, and as if it were rather an effort, he said,

'Colonel Brandon seems a man of great worth and respectability. I have always heard him spoken of as such, and your brother I know esteems him highly. He is undoubtedly a sensible man, and in his manners perfectly the gentleman.'

'Indeed,' replied Elinor, 'I believe that you will find him, on farther acquaintance, all that you have heard him to be, and as you will be such very near neighbours, (for I understand the parsonage is almost close to the mansion-house,) it is particularly important that he *should* be all this.'

Edward made no answer; but when she had turned away her head, gave her a look so serious, so earnest, so uncheerful, as seemed to say, that he might hereafter wish the distance between the parsonage and the mansion-house much greater.

'Colonel Brandon, I think, lodges in St James's-street,' said he, soon afterwards rising from his chair.

Elinor told him the number of the house.

'I must hurry away then, to give him those thanks which you will not allow me to give *you*; to assure him that he had made me a very – an exceedingly happy man.'

Elinor did not offer to detain him; and they parted, with a very earnest assurance on *her* side of unceasing good wishes for his happiness in every change of situation that might befall him; on *his*, with rather an attempt to return the same good will, than the power of expressing it.

'When I see him again,' said Elinor to herself, as the door shut him out, 'I shall see him the husband of Lucy.'

And with this pleasing anticipation, she sat down to re-consider the past, recall the words and endeavour to comprehend all the feelings of Edward; and, of course to reflect on her own with discontent.

When Mrs Jennings came home, though she returned from seeing people whom she had never seen before, and of whom therefore she must have a great deal to say, her mind was so much more occupied by the important secret in her possession, than by anything else, that she reverted to it again as soon as Elinor appeared.

'Well, my dear,' she creid, 'I sent you up the young man. Did not I do right? – And I suppose you had no great difficulty – You did not find him very unwilling to accept your proposal?'

'No, ma'am; *that* was not very likely.'

'Well, and how soon will he be ready? – For it seems all to depend upon that.'

'Really,' said Elinor, 'I know so little of these kind of forms, that I can hardly even conjecture as to the time, or the preparation necessary; but I suppose two or three months will complete his ordination.'

'Two or three months!' cried Mrs Jennnigs; 'Lord! my dear, how calmly you talk of it; and can the Colonel wait two or three months! Lord bless me! – I am sure it would put *me* quite out of patience! – And though one would be very glad to do a kindness by poor Mr Ferrars, I do think it is not worth while to wait two or three months for him. Sure, somebody else might be found that would do as well; somebody that is in orders already.'

'My dear ma'am,' said Elinor, 'what can you be thinking of? – Why, Colonel Brandon's only object is to be of use to Mr Ferrars.'

'Lord bless you, my dear! – Sure you do not mean to persuade me that the Colonel only marries you for the sake of giving ten guineas to Mr Ferrars!'

The deception could not continue after this; and an explanation immediately took place, by which both gained considerable amusement for the moment, without any material loss of happiness to either, for Mrs Jennings only exchanged one form of delight for another, and still without forfeiting her expectation of the first.

'Aye, aye, the parsonage is but a small one,' said she, after the first ebullition of surprise and satisfaction was over, 'and very likely *may* be out of repair; but to hear a man apologising, as I thought, for a house that to my knowledge has five sitting rooms on the ground-floor, and I think the housekeeper told me, could make up fifteen beds! – and to you too, that had been used to live in Barton cottage! – It seemed quite ridiculous. But, my dear, we must touch up the Colonel to do something to the parsonage, and make it comfortable for them, before Lucy goes to it.'

'But Colonel Brandon does not seem to have any idea of the living's being enough to allow them to marry.'

Both gained considerable amusement.

'The Colonel is a ninny, my dear; because he has two thousand a-year himself, he thinks that nobody else can marry on less. Take my word for it, that, if I am alive, I shall be paying a visit at Delaford Parsonage before Michaelmas; and I am sure I sha'nt go if Lucy an't there.'

Elinor was quite of her opinion, as to the probability of their not waiting for any thing more.

CHAPTER FORTY-ONE

EDWARD, HAVING CARRIED his thanks to Colonel Brandon, proceeded with his happiness to Lucy; and such was the excess of it by the time he reached Bartlett's Buildings, that she was able to assure Mrs Jennings, who called on her again the next day with her congratulations, that she had never seen him in such spirits before in her life.

Her own happiness, and her own spirits, were at least very certain; and she joined Mrs Jennings most heartily in her expectation of their being all comfortably together in Delaford Parsonage before Michaelmas. So far was she, at the same time, from any backwardness to give Elinor that credit which Edward *would* give her, that she spoke of her friendship for them both with the most grateful warmth, was ready to own all their obligation to her, and openly decalred that no exertion for their good on Miss Dashwood's part, either present or future, would ever surprise her, for she believed her capable of doing anything in the world for those she really valued. As for Colonel Brandon, she was not only ready to worship him as a saint, but was moreover truly anxious that he should be treated as one in all wordly concerns; anxious that his tythes should be raised to the utmost; and secretly resolved to avail herself, at Delaford, as far as she possibly could, of his servants, his carriage, his cows and his poultry.

It was now above a week since John Dashwood had called in Berkeley-street, and as since that time no notice had been taken of them by his wife's indisposition, beyond one verbal enquiry, Elinor began to feel it necessary to pay her a visit. – This was an obligation, however, which not only opposed her own inclination, but which had not the assistance of any encouragement from her companions. Marianne, not contented with absolutely refusing to go herself, was very urgent to prevent her sister's going at all; and Mrs Jennings, though her carriage was always at Elinor's service, so very much disliked Mrs John Dashwood, that not even her curiosity to see how she looked after the late discovery, nor her strong desire to affront her by taking Edward's part, could overcome her unwillingness to be in her company again. The consequence was, that Elinor set out by herself to pay a visit, for which no one could really have less inclination, and to run the risk of a tête-à-tête with a woman, whom neither of the others had so much reason to dislike.

Mrs Dashwood was denied; but before the carriage could turn from the house, her husband accidentally came out. He expressed great pleasure in meeting Elinor, told her that he had been just going to call in Berkeley-street, and assuring her that Fanny would be very glad to see her, invited her to come in.

They walked up stairs into the drawing-room. – Nobody was there.

'Fanny is in her own room, I suppose,' said he; – 'I will go to her presently, for I am sure she will not have the least objection in the world to seeing *you*. – Very far from it indeed. Now especially there cannot be – but however, you and Marianne were always great favourites. Why would not Marianne come?'

Elinor made what excuse she could for her.

'I am not sorry to see you alone,' he replied, 'for I have a good deal to say to you. This living of Colonel Brandon's – can it be true? – has he really given it to Edward? – I heard it yesterday by chance, and was coming to you on purpose to inquire farther about it.'

'It is perfectly true. – Colonel Brandon has given the living of Delaford to Edward.'

'Really! – Well, this is very astonishing! – no relationship! – no connection between them! – and now that livings fetch such a price! – what was the value of this?'

'About two hundred a-year.'

'Very well – and for the next presentation to a living of that value – supposing the late incumbent to have been old and sickly, and likely to vacate it soon – he might have got I dare say – fourteen hundred pounds. And how came he not to have settled that matter before this person's death? – *Now* indeed it would be too late to sell it, but a man of Colonel Brandon's sense! – I wonder he should be so improvident in a point of such common, such natural, concern! – Well, I am convinced that there is a vast deal of inconsistency in almost every human character. I suppose, however – on recollection – that the case may probably be *this*. Edward is only to hold the living till the person to whom the Colonel has really sold the presentation, is old enough to take it. – Aye, aye, that is the fact, depend upon it.'

Elinor contradicted it, however, very positively; and by relating that she had herself been employed in conveying the offer from Colonel Brandon to Edward, and therefore must understand the terms on which it was given, obliged him to submit to her authority.

'It is truly astonishing!' – he cried, after hearing what she said – 'what could be the Colonel's motive?'

'A very simple one – to be of use to Mr Ferrars.'

'Well, well; whatever Colonel Brandon may be, Edward is a very lucky man! – You will not mention the matter to Fanny, however, for though I have broke it to her, and she bears it vastly well – she will not like to hear it much talked of.'

Elinor had some difficulty here to refrain from observing, that she thought Fanny might have borne with composure, an acquisition of wealth to her brother, by which neither she nor her child could be possibly impoverished.

'Mrs Ferrars,' added he, lowering his voice to the tone becoming so important a subject, 'knows nothing about it at present, and I believe it will be best to keep it entirely concealed from her as long as may be. – When the marriage takes place, I fear she must hear of it all.'

'But why should such precaution be used? – Though it is not to be supposed that Mrs Ferrars can have the smallest satisfaction in knowing that her son has money enough to live upon, – for *that* must be quite out of the question; yet why, after her late behaviour is she supposed to feel at all? – she has done with her son, she has cast him off for ever, and has made all those over whom she had any influence, cast him off likewise. Surely, after doing so, she cannot be imagined liable to any impression of sorrow or of joy on his account – she cannot be interested in any thing that befalls him. – She would not be so weak as to throw away the comfort of a child, and yet retain the anxiety of a parent!'

'Ah! Elinor,' said John, 'your reasoning is very good, but it is founded on ignorance of human nature. When Edward's unhappy match takes place, depend upon it his mother will feel as much as if she had never discarded him; and therefore every circumstance that may accelerate that dreadful event, must be concealed from her as much as possible. Mrs Ferrars can never forget that Edward is her son.'

'You surprise me; I should think it must nearly have escaped her memory by *this* time.'

'You wrong her exceedingly. Mrs Ferrars is one of the most affectionate mothers in the world.'

Elinor was silent.

'We think *now*' – said Mr Dashwood, after a short pause, 'of *Robert's* marrying Miss Morton.'

Elinor, smiling at the grave and decisive importance of her brother's tone, calmly replied,

'The lady, I suppose, has no choice in the affair.'

'Choice! – how do you mean?' –

'I only mean, that I suppose from your manner of speaking, it must be the same to Miss Morton whether she marry Edward or Robert.'

'Certainly, there can be no difference, for Robert will now to all intents and purposes be considered as the eldest son; – and as to any thing else, they are both very agreeable young men, I do not know that one is superior to the other.'

Elinor said no more, and John was also for a short time silent. – His reflections ended thus.

'Of *one* thing, my dear sister,' kindly taking her hand, and speaking in an awful whisper – 'I may assure you; – and I *will* do it, because I know it must gratify you. I have good reason to think – indeed I have it from the best authority, or I should not repeat it,

'Of one thing I may assure you.'

for otherwise it would be very wrong to say any thing about it – but I have it from the very best authority – not that I ever precisely heard Mrs Ferrars say it herself – but her daughter *did*, and I have it from her – That in short, whatever objections there might be against a certain – a certain connection – you understand me – it would have been far preferable to her, it would not have given her half the vexation that *this* does. I was exceedingly pleased to hear that Mrs Ferrars considered it in that light – a very gratifying circumstance you know to us all. "It would have been beyond comparison" she said, "the least evil of the two, and she would be glad to compound *now* for nothing worse." But however, all that is quite out of the question – not to be thought of or mentioned – as to any attachment you know – it never could be – all that is gone by. But I thought I would just tell you of this, because I knew how much it must please you. Not that you have any reason to regret, my dear Elinor. There is no doubt of your doing exceedingly well – quite as well, or better, perhaps, all things considered. Has Colonel Brandon been with you lately?'

Elinor had heard enough, if not to gratify her vanity, and raise her self-importance, to agitate her nerves and fill her mind; – and she was therefore glad to be spared from the necessity of saying much in reply herself, and from the danger of hearing any thing more from her brother, by the entrance of Mr Robert Ferrars. After a few moments' chat, John Dashwood, recollecting that Fanny was yet uninformed of his sister's being there, quitted the room in quest of her; and Elinor was left to improve her acquaintance with Robert, who, by the gay unconcern, the happy self-complacency of his manner while enjoying so unfair a division of his mother's love and liberality, to the prejudice of his banished brother, earned only by his own dissipated course of life, and that brother's integrity, was confirming her most unfavourable opinion of his head and heart.

They had scarcely been two minutes by themselves, before he began to speak of Edward; for he too had heard of the living and was very inquisitive on the subject. Elinor repeated the particulars of it, as she had given them to John; and their effect on Robert, though very different, was not less striking than it had been on *him*. He laughed most immoderately. The idea of Edward's being a clergyman, and living in a small parsonage-house, diverted him beyond measure; – and when to that was added the fanciful imagery of Edward reading prayers in a white surplice, and publishing the banns of marriage between John Smith and Mary Brown, he could conceive nothing more ridiculous.

Elinor, while she waited in silence, and immovable gravity, the conclusion of such folly, could not restrain her eyes from being fixed on him with a look that spoke all the contempt it excited. It was a look, however, very well bestowed, for it relieved her own feelings, and gave no intelligence to him. He was recalled from wit to wisdom, not by any reproof of her's, but by his own sensibility.

'We may treat it as a joke,' said he at last, recovering from the affected laugh which had considerably lengthened out the genuine gaiety of the moment – 'but upon my soul, it is a most serious business. Poor Edward! he is ruined for ever. I am extremely sorry for it – for I know him to be a very good-hearted creature; as well-meaning a fellow perhaps, as any in the world. You must not judge of him, Miss Dashwood, from *your* slight acquaintance. – Poor Edward! – His manners are certainly not the happiest in nature. – But we are not all born, you know, with the same powers – the same address. – Poor fellow! – to see him in a circle of strangers! – to be sure it was pitiable enough! – but, upon my soul, I believe he has as good a heart as any in the kingdom; and I declare and protest to you I never was so shocked in my life, as when it all burst forth. I could not believe it. – My mother was the first person who told me of it, and I, feeling myself called on to act with resolution, immediately said to her, "My dear madam, I do not know what you may intend to do on the occasion, but as for myself, I must say, that if Edward does marry this young woman, *I* never will see him again." That was what I said immediately, – I was most uncommonly shocked indeed! – Poor Edward! – he has done for himself completely – shut himself out for ever from all decent society! – but, as I directly said to my mother, I am not in the least surprised at it; from his style of education it was always to be expected. My poor mother was half frantic.'

'Have you ever seen the lady?'

'Yes; once, while she was staying in the house, I happened to drop in for ten minutes; and I saw quite enough of her. The merest awkward country girl; without style or elegance, and almost without beauty. – I remember her perfectly. Just the kind of girl I should suppose likely to captivate poor Edward. I offered immediately, as soon as my mother related the affair to me, to talk to him myself, and dissuade him from the match; but it was too late *then*, I found, to do any thing, for unluckily, I was not in the way at first, and knew nothing of it till after the breach had taken place, when it was not for me, you know, to interfere. But had I been informed of it a few hours earlier – I think it is most probable – that something might have been hit on. I certainly should have represented it to Edward in a very strong light. "My dear fellow,"

I should have said, "consider what you are doing. You are making a most disgraceful connection, and such a one as your family are unanimous in disapproving," I cannot help thinking, in short, that means might have been found. But now it is all too late. He must be starved, you know, – that is certain; absolutely starved.'

He had just settled this point with great composure, when the entrance of Mrs John Dashwood put an end to the subject. But though *she* never spoke of it out of her own family. Elinor could see its influence on her mind, in the something like confusion of countenance with which she entered, and an attempt at cordiality in her behaviour to herself. She even proceeded so far as to be concerned to find that Elinor and her sister were so soon to leave town, as she had hoped to see more of them; – an exertion in which her husband, who attended her into the room and hung enamoured over her accents, seemed to distinguish every thing that was most affectionate and graceful.

CHAPTER FORTY-TWO

One other short call in Harley-street, in which Elinor received her brother's congratulations on their travelling so far towards Barton without any expense, and on Colonel Brandon's being to follow them to Cleveland in a day or two, completed the intercourse of the brother and sisters in town; – and a faint invitation from Fanny, to come to Norland whenever it should happen to be in their way, which of all things was the most unlikely to occur, with a more warm, though less public, assurance, from John to Elinor, of the promptitude with which he should come to see her at Delaford, was all that foretold any meeting in the country.

It amused her to observe that all her friends seemed determined to send her to Delaford; – a place, in which, of all others, she would now least chuse to visit, or wish to reside; for not only was it considered as her future home by her brother and Mrs Jennings, but even Lucy, when they parted, gave her a pressing invitation to visit her there.

Very early in April, and tolerably early in the day, the two parties from Hanover-square and Berkeley-street set out from their respective homes, to meet, by appointment, on the road. For the convenience of Charlotte and her child, they were to be more than two days on their journey, and Mr Palmer, travelling more expeditiously with Colonel Brandon, was to join them at Cleveland soon after their arrival.

Marianne, few as had been her hours of comfort in London, and eager as she had long been to quit it, could not, when it came to the point, bid adieu to the house in which she had for the last time enjoyed those hopes, and that confidence, in Willoughby, which were now extinguished for ever, without great pain. Nor could she leave the place in which Willoughby remained, busy in new engagements, and new schemes, in which *she* could have no share, without shedding many tears.

Elinor's satisfaction at the moment of removal, was more positive. She had no such object for her lingering thoughts to fix on, she left no creature behind, from whom it would give her a moment's regret to be divided for ever, she was pleased to be free herself from the persecution of Lucy's friendship, she was grateful for bringing her sister away unseen by Willoughby since his marriage, and she looked forward with hope to what a few months of tranquility at Barton might do towards restoring Marianne's peace of mind, and confirming her own.

Their journey was safely performed. The second day brought them into the cherished, or the prohibited, county of Somerset, for as such was it dwelt on by turns in Marianne's imagination; and in the forenoon of the third they drove up to Cleveland.

Cleveland was a spacious, modern-built house, situated on a sloping lawn. It had no park, but the pleasure-grounds were tolerably extensive; and like every other place of the same degree of importance, it had its open shrubbery, and closer wood walk, a road of smooth gravel winding round a plantation, led to the front, the lawn was dotted over with timber, the house itself was under the guardianship of the fir, the mountain-ash, and the acacia, and a thick screen of them altogether, interspersed with tall Lombardy poplars, shut out the offices.

Marianne entered the house with an heart swelling with emotion from the consciousness of being only eighty miles from Barton, and not thirty from Combe Magna; and before she had been five minutes within its walls, while the others were busily helping Charlotte shew her child to the housekeeper, she quitted it again, stealing away through the winding shrubberies, now just beginning to be in beauty, to gain a distant eminence; where, from its Grecian temple, her eye, wandering over a wide tract of country to the south-east, could fondly rest on the farthest ridge of hills in the horizon, and fancy that from their summits Combe Magna might be seen.

Shewing her child to the housekeeper.

In such moments of precious, invaluable misery, she rejoiced in tears of agony to be at Cleveland; and as she returned by a different circuit to the house, feeling all the happy privilege of country liberty, of wandering from place to place in free and luxurious solitude, she resolved to spend almost every hour of every day while she remained with the Palmers, in the indulgence of such solitary rambles.

She returned just in time to join the others as they quitted the house, on an excursion through its more immediate premises; and the rest of the morning was easily whiled away, in lounging round the kitchen garden, examining the bloom upon its walls, and listening to the gardener's lamentations upon blights, – in dawdling through the greenhouse, where the loss of her favourite plants, unwarily exposed, and nipped by the lingering frost, raised the laughter of Charlotte, – and in visiting her poultry-yard, where, in the disappointed hopes of her dairy-maid, by hens forsaking their nests, or being stolen by a fox, or in the rapid decrease of a promising young brood, she found fresh sources of merriment.

The morning was fine and dry, and Marianne, in her plan of enjoyment abroad, had not calculated for any change of weather during their stay at Cleveland. With great surprise therefore, did she find herself prevented by a settled rain from going out again after dinner. She had depended on a twilight walk to the Grecian temple, and perhaps all over the grounds, and an evening merely

The gardener's lamentations.

cold or damp would not have deterred her from it; but an heavy and settled rain even *she* could not fancy dry or pleasant weather for walking.

Their party was small, and the hours passed quietly away. Mrs Palmer had her child, and Mrs Jennings her carpet-work; they talked of the friends they had left behind, arranged Lady Middleton's engagements, and wondered whether Mr Palmer and Colonel Brandon would get farther than Reading that night. Elinor, however little concerned in it, joined in their discourse, and Marianne, who had the knack of finding her way in every house to the library, however it might be avoided by the family in general, soon procured herself a book.

Nothing was wanting on Mrs Palmer's side that constant and friendly good-humour could do, to make them feel themselves welcome. The openness and heartiness of her manner, more than atoned for want of recollection and elegance, which made her often deficient in the forms of politeness; her kindness, recommended by so pretty a face, was engaging; her folly, though evident, was not disgusting, because it was not conceited; and Elinor could have forgiven every thing but her laugh.

The two gentlemen arrived the next day to a very late dinner, affording a pleasant enlargement of the party, and a very welcome variety to their conversation, which a long morning of the same continued rain had reduced very low.

Elinor had seen so little of Mr Palmer, and in that little had seen so much variety in his address to her sister and herself, that she knew not what to expect to find him in his own family. She found him, however, perfectly the gentleman in his behaviour to all his visitors, and only occasionally rude to his wife and her mother; she found him very capable of being a pleasant companion, and only prevented from being so always, by too great an aptitude to fancy himself as much superior to people in general, as he must feel himself to be to Mrs Jennings and Charlotte. For the rest of his character and habits, they were marked, as far as Elinor could perceive, with no traits at all unusual in his sex and time of life. He was nice in his eating, uncertain in his hours; fond of his child, though affecting to slight it; and idled away the mornings at billiards, which ought to have been devoted to business. She liked him, however, upon the whole much better than she had expected, and in her heart was not sorry that she could like him no more; – not sorry to be driven by the observation of his Epicurism, his selfishness, and his conceit, to rest with complacency on the remembrance of Edward's generous temper, simple taste, and diffident feelings.

Of Edward, or at least of some of his concerns, she now received intelligence from Colonel Brandon, who had been into Dorsetshire lately; and who, treating her at once as the disinterested friend of Mr Ferrars, and the kind confidante of himself, talked to her a great deal of the Parsonage of Delaford, described its deficiencies, and told her what he meant to do himself towards removing them. – His behaviour to her in this, as well as in every other particular, his open pleasure in meeting her after an absence of only ten days, his readiness to converse with her, and his deference for her opinion, might very well justify Mrs Jennings's persuasion of his attachment, and would have been enough, perhaps, had not Elinor still, as from the first, believed Marianne his real favourite, to make her suspect it herself. But as it was, such a notion had scarcely ever entered her head, except by Mrs Jennings's suggestion; and she could not help believing herself the nicest observer of the two; – she watched his eyes, while Mrs Jennings thought only of his behaviour; – and while his looks of anxious solicitude on Marianne's feeling, in her head and throat, the beginnings of an heavy cold, because unexpressed by words, entirely escaped the latter lady's observation; – *she* could discover in them the quick feelings, and needless alarm of a lover.

Two delightful twilight walks on the third and fourth evenings of her being there, not merely on the dry gravel of the shrubbery, but all over the grounds, and especially in the most distant parts of them, where there was something more of wildness than in the rest, where the trees were the oldest, and the grass was the longest and wettest, had – assisted by the still greater imprudence of sitting in her wet shoes and stockings – give Marianne a cold so violent, as, though for a day or two trifled with or denied, would force itself by increasing ailments, on the concern of every body, and the notice of herself. Prescriptions poured in from all quarters, and as usual, were all declined. Though heavy and feverish, with a pain in her limbs, a cough, and a sore throat, a good night's rest was to cure her entirely; and it was with difficulty that Elinor prevailed on her, when she went to bed, to try one or two of the simplest of the remedies.

CHAPTER FORTY-THREE

MARIANNE GOT UP THE next morning at her usual time; to every inquiry replied that she was better, and tried to prove herself so, by engaging in her accustomary employments. But a day spent in sitting shivering over the fire with a book in her hand, which she was unable to read, or in lying, weary and languid, on a sofa, did not speak much in favour of her amendment; and when, at last, she went early to bed, more and more indisposed, Colonel Brandon was only astonished at her sister's composure, who, though attending and nursing her the whole day, against Marianne's inclination, and forcing proper medicines on her at night, trusted, like Marianne, to the certainty and efficacy of sleep, and felt no real alarm.

A very restless and feverish night, however, disappointed the expectation of both; and when Marianne, after persisting in rising, confessed herself unable to sit up, and returned voluntarily to her bed, Elinor was very ready to adopt Mrs Jennings's advice, of sending for the Palmers' apothecary.

He came, examined his patient, and though encouraging Miss Dashwood to expect that a very few days would restore her sister to health, yet, by pronouncing her disorder to have a putrid tendency, and allowing the word 'infection' to pass his lips, gave instant alarm to Mrs Palmer on her baby's account. Mrs Jennings, who had been inclined from the first to think Marianne's complaint more serious than Elinor, now looked very grave on Mr Harris's report, and confirming Charlotte's fears and caution, urged the necessity of her immediate removal with her infant; and Mr Palmer, though treating their apprehensions as idle, found the anxiety and importunity of his wife too great to be withstood. Her departure therefore was fixed on; and, within an hour after Mr Harris's arrival, she set off, with her little boy and his nurse, for the house of a near relation of Mr Palmer's, who lived a few miles on the other side of Bath; whither her husband promised, at her earnest entreaty, to join her in a day or two; and whither she was almost equally urgent with her mother to accompany her. Mrs Jennings, however, with a kindness of heart which made Elinor really love her, declared her resolution of not stirring from Cleveland as long as Marianne remained ill, and of endeavouring, by her own attentive care, to supply to her the place of the mother she had taken her from; and Elinor found her on every occasion a most willing and active helpmate, desirous to share in all her fatigues, and often by her better experience in nursing, of material use.

Poor Marianne, languid and low from the nature of her malady, and feeling herself universally ill, could no longer hope that tomorrow would find her recovered; and the idea of what tomorrow would have produced, but for this unlucky illness, made every ailment more severe; for on that day they were to have begun their journey home; and, attended the whole way by a servant of Mrs Jennings, were to have taken their mother by surprise on the following forenoon. The little that she said, was all in lamentation of this inevitable delay; though Elinor tried to raise her spirits, and make her believe, as she *then* really believed herself, that it would be a very short one.

The next day produced little or no alteration in the state of the patient; she certainly was not better, and except that there was no amendment, did not appear worse. Their party was now farther reduced; for Mr Palmer, though very unwilling to go, as well from real humanity and good-nature, as from a dislike of appearing to be frightened away by his wife, was persuaded at last by Colonel Brandon to perform his promise of following her; and while he was preparing to go, Colonel Brandon himself, with a much greater exertion, began to talk of going likewise. – Here, however, the kindness of Mrs Jennings interposed most acceptably; for to send the Colonel away while his love was in so much uneasiness on her sister's account, would be to deprive them both, she thought, of every comfort; and therefore telling him at once that his stay at Cleveland was necessary to herself, that she should want him to play at piquet of an evening, while Miss Dashwood was above with her sister, &c. she urged him so strongly to remain, that he, who was gratifying the first wish of his own heart by a compliance, could not long even affect to demur; especially as Mrs Jennings's entreaty was warmly seconded by Mr Palmer, who seemed to feel a relief to himself, in leaving behind him a person so well able to assist or advise Miss Dashwood in any emergency.

Marianne was of course kept in ignorance of all these arrangements. She knew not that she had been the means of sending the owners of Cleveland away, in about seven days from the time of their arrival. It gave her no surprise that she saw nothing of Mrs Palmer; and as it gave her likewise no concern, she never mentioned her name.

Two days passed away from the time of Mr Palmer's departure, and her situation continued, with little variation, the same. Mr Harris, who attended her every day, still talked boldly of a speedy recovery, and Miss Dashwood was equally sanguine; but the expectation of the others was by no means so cheerful. Mrs Jennings had determined very early in the seisure that Marianne would never get over it, and Colonel Brandon, who was chiefly of use in listening to Mrs Jennings's forebodings, was not in a state of mind to resist their influence. He tried to reason himself out of fears, which the different judgment of the apothecary seemed to render absurd; but the many hours of each day in which he was left entirely alone, were but too favourable for the admission of every melancholy idea, and he could not expel from his mind the persuasion that he should see Marianne no more.

On the morning of the third day however, the gloomy anticipations of both were almost done away; for when Mr Harris arrived, he declared his patient materially better. Her pulse was much stronger, and every symptom more favourable than on the preceding visit. Elinor, confirmed in every pleasant hope, was all cheerfulness; rejoicing that in her letters to her mother, she had pursued her own judgment rather than her friend's, in making very light of the indisposition which delayed them at Cleveland; and almost fixing on the time when Marianne would be able to travel.

But the day did not close so auspiciously as it began. – Towards the evening, Marianne became ill again, growing more heavy, restless, and uncomfortable than before. Her sister, however, still sanguine, was willing to attribute the change to nothing more than the fatigue of having sat up to have her bed made; and carefully administering the cordials prescribed, saw her with satisfaction sink at last into a slumber, from which she expected the most beneficial effects. Her sleep, though not so quiet as Elinor wished to see it, lasted a considerable time; and anxious to observe the result of it herself, she resolved to sit with her during the whole of it. Mrs Jennings, knowing nothing of any change in the patient, went unusually early to bed; her maid, who was one of the principal nurses, was recreating herself in the housekeeper's room, and Elinor remained alone with Marianne.

The repose of the latter became more and more disturbed; and her sister, who watched with unremitting attention her continual change of posture, and heard the frequent but inarticulate sounds of complaint which passed her lips, was almost wishing to rouse her from so painful a slumber, when Marianne, suddenly awakened by some accidental noise in the house, started hastily up, and with feverish wildness, cried out –

'Is mama coming? – '

'Not yet,' replied the other, concealing her terror, and assisting Marianne to lie down again, 'but she will be here, I hope, before it is long. It is a great way, you know, from hence to Barton.'

'But she must not go round by London,' cried Marianne, in the same hurried manner, 'I shall never see her, if she goes by London.'

Elinor perceived with alarm that she was not quite herself, and while attempting to sooth her, eagerly felt her pulse. It was lower and quicker than ever! and Marianne, still talking wildly of mama, her alarm increased so rapidly, as to determine her on sending instantly for Mr Harris, and dispatching a messenger to Barton for her mother. To consult with Colonel Brandon on the best means of effecting the latter, was a thought which immediately followed the resolution of its performance; and as soon as she had rung up the maid to take her place by her sister, she hastened down to the drawing-room, where she knew he was generally to be found at a much later hour than the present.

It was no time for hesitation. Her fears and her difficulties were immediately before him. Her fears, he had no courage, no confidence to attempt the removal of; – he listened to them in silent despondence; – but her difficulties were instantly obviated, for with a readiness that seemed to speak the occasion, and the service pre-arranged in his mind, he offered himself as the messenger who should fetch Mrs Dashwood. Elinor made no resistance that was not easily overcome. She thanked him with brief, though fervent gratitude, and while he went to hurry off his servant with a message to Mr Harris, and an order for post-horses directly, she wrote a few lines to her mother.

The comfort of such a friend at that moment as Colonel Brandon – of such a companion for her mother, – how gratefully was it felt! – a companion whose judgment would guide, whose attendance must relieve, and whose friendship might sooth her! – as far as the shock of such a summons *could* be lessened to her, his presence, his manners, his assistance, would lessen it.

He, meanwhile, whatever he might feel, acted with all the firmness of a collected mind, made every necessary arrangement with the utmost dispatch, and calculated with exactness the time in which she might look for his return. Not a moment was lost in delay of any kind. The horses arrived, even before they were expected, and Colonel Brandon only pressing her hand with a look of solemnity, and a few words spoken too low to reach her ear, hurried into the carriage. It was then about twelve o'clock, and she returned to her sister's apartment to wait for the arrival of the apothecary, and to watch by her the rest of the night. It was a night of almost equal suffering to both. Hour after hour passed away in sleepless pain and delirium on Marianne's side, and in the most cruel anxiety on Elinor's, before Mr Harris appeared. Her apprehensions once raised, paid by their excess for all her former security; and the servant who sat up with her, for she would not allow Mrs Jennings to be called, only tortured her more, by hints of what her mistress had always thought.

Marianne's ideas were still, at intervals, fixed incoherently on her mother, and whenever she mentioned her name, it gave a pang to the heart of poor Elinor, who, reproaching herself for having trifled with so many days of illness, and wretched for some immediate relief, fancied that all relief might soon be in vain, that every thing had been delayed too long, and pictured to herself her suffering mother arriving too late to see this darling child, or to see her rational.

She was on the point of sending again for Mr Harris, or if *he* could not come, for some other advice, when the former – but not till after five o'clock – arrived. His opinion, however, made some little amends for his delay, for though acknowledging a very unexpected and unpleasant alteration in his patient, he would not allow the danger to be material, and talked of the relief which a fresh mode of treatment must procure, with a confidence which, in a lesser degree, was communicated to Elinor. He promised to call again in the course of three or four hours, and left both the patient and her anxious attendant more composed than he had found them.

With strong concern, and with many reproaches for not being called to their aid, did Mrs Jennings hear in the morning of what had passed. Her former apprehensions, now with greater reason restored, left her no doubt of the event; and though trying to speak comfort to Elinor, her conviction of her sister's danger would not allow her to offer the comfort of hope. Her heart was really grieved. The rapid decay, the early death of a girl so young, so lovely as Marianne, must have struck a less interested person with concern. On Mrs Jennings's compassion she had other claims. She had been for three months her companion, was still under her care, and she was known to have been greatly injured, and long unhappy. The distress of her sister too, particularly a favourite, was before her; – and as for their mother, when Mrs Jennings considered that Marianne might probably be to *her* what Charlotte was to herself, her sympathy in *her* sufferings was very sincere.

Mr Harris was punctual in his second visit; – but he came to be disappointed in his hopes of what the last would produce. His medicines had failed; – the fever was unabated; and Marianne only more quiet – not more herself – remained in an heavy stupor. Elinor, catching all, and more than all, his fears in a moment, proposed to call in farther advice. But he judged it unnecessary; he had still something more to try, some fresh application, of whose success he was almost as confident as the last, and his visit concluded with encouraging assurances which reached the ear, but could not enter the heart, of Miss Dashwood. She was calm, except when she thought of her mother, but she was almost hopeless; and in this state she continued till noon, scarcely stirring from her sister's bed, her thoughts wandering from one image of grief, one suffering friend to another, and her spirits oppressed to the utmost by the conversation of Mrs Jennings, who scrupled not to attribute the severity and danger of this attack, to the many weeks of previous indisposition which Marianne's disappointment had brought on. Elinor felt all the reasonableness of the idea, and it gave fresh misery to her reflections.

About noon, however, she began – but with a caution – a dread of disappointment, which for some time kept her silent, even to her friend – to fancy, to hope she could perceive a slight amendment in her sister's pulse; – she waited, watched, and examined it again and again; – and at last, with an agitation more difficult to bury under exterior calmness, than all her foregoing distress, ventured to communicate her hopes. Mrs Jennings, though forced, on examination, to acknowledge a temporary revival, tried to keep her young friend from indulging a thought of its continuance; – and Elinor, conning over every injuction of distrust, told herself likewise not to hope. But it was too late. Hope had already entered; and feeling all its anxious flutter, she bent over her sister to watch – she hardly knew for what. Half an hour passed away, and the favourable symptom yet blessed her. Others even arose to confirm it. Her breath, her skin, her lips, all flattered Elinor with signs of amendment, and Marianne fixed her eyes on her with a rational, though languid, gaze. Anxiety and hope now oppressed her in equal degrees, and left her no moment of tranquillity till the arrival of Mr Harris at four o'clock; – when his assurances, his felicitations on a recovery in her sister even surpassing his expectation, gave her confidence, comfort, and tears of joy.

Marianne was in every respect materially better, and he declared her entirely out of danger. Mrs Jennings, perhaps satisfied with the partial justification of her forebodings which had been found in their late alarm, allowed herself to trust in his judgment, and admitted with unfeigned joy, and soon with unequivocal cheerfulness, the probability of an entire recovery.

Elinor could not be cheerful. Her joy was of a different kind, and led to anything rather than to gaiety. Marianne restored to life, health, friends, and to her doating mother, was an idea to fill her heart with sensations of exquisite comfort, and expand it in fervent gratitude; – but it led to no outward demonstrations of joy, no words, no smiles. All within Elinor's breast was satisfaction, silent and strong.

She continued by the side of her sister with little intermission the whole afternoon, calming every fear, satisfying every enquiry of her enfeebled spirits, supplying every succour, and watching almost every look and every breath. The possibility of a relapse would of course, in some moments, occur to remind her of what anxiety was – but when she saw, on her frequent and minute examination, that every symptom of recovery continued, and saw Marianne at six o'clock sink into a quiet, steady, and to all appearance comfortable, sleep, she silenced every doubt.

The time was now drawing on, when Colonel Brandon might be expected back. At ten o'clock, she trusted, or at least not much later her mother would be relieved from the dreadful suspense in which she must now be travelling towards them. The Colonel too! – perhaps scarcely less an object of pity! – Oh! – how slow was the progress of time which yet kept them in ignorance!

At seven o'clock, leaving Marianne still sweetly asleep, she joined Mrs Jennings in the drawing-room to tea. Of breakfast she had been kept by her fears, and of dinner by their sudden reverse, from eating much; – and the present refreshment, therefore, with such feelings of content as she brought to it, was particularly welcome. Mrs Jennings would have persuaded her at its conclusion to take some rest before her mother's arrival, and allow *her* to take her place by Marianne; but Elinor had no sense of fatigue, no capability of sleep at that moment about her, and she was not to be kept away from her sister an unnecessary instant. Mrs Jennings therefore attending her up stairs into the sick chamber, to satisfy herself that all continued right, left her there again to her charge and her thoughts, and retired to her own room to write letters and sleep.

The night was cold and stormy. The wind roared round the house, and the rain beat against the windows; but Elinor, all happiness within, regarded it not. Marianne slept through every blast, and the travellers – they had a rich reward in store, for every present inconvenience.

The clock struck eight. Had it been ten, Elinor would have been

Opened a window-shutter.

convinced that at that moment she heard a carriage driving up to the house; and so strong was the persuasion that she *did*, in spite of the *almost* impossibility of their being already come, that she moved into the adjoining dressing-closet and opened a window-shutter, to be satisfied of the truth. She instantly saw that her ears had not deceived her. The flaring lamps of a carriage were immediately in view. By their uncertain light she thought she could discern it to be drawn by four horses; and this, while it told the excess of her poor mother's alarm, gave some explanation to such unexpected rapidity.

Never in her life had Elinor found it so difficult to be calm, as at that moment. The knowledge of what her mother must be feeling as the carriage stopt at the door, – of her doubt – her dread – perhaps her despair! – and of what *she* had to tell! – with such knowledge it was impossible to be calm. All that remained to be done, was to be speedy; and therefore staying only till she could leave Mrs Jennings's maid with her sister, she hurried down stairs.

The bustle in the vestibule, as she passed along an inner lobby, assured her that they were already in the house. She rushed forwards towards the drawing-room, – she entered it, – and saw only Willoughby.

CHAPTER FORTY-FOUR

ELINOR, STARTING BACK with a look of horror at the sight of him, obeyed the first impulse of her heart in turning instantly to quit the room, and her hand was already on the lock, when its action was suspended by his hastily advancing, and saying, in a voice rather of command than supplication,

'Miss Dashwood, for half an hour – for ten minutes – I entreat you stay.'

'No, sir,' she replied with firmness, 'I shall *not* stay. Your business cannot be with *me*. The servants, I suppose, forgot to tell you that Mr Palmer was not in the house.'

'Had they told me,' he cried with vehemence, 'that Mr Palmer and all his relations were at the devil, it would not have turned me from the door. My business is with you, and only you.'

'With me!' – in the utmost amazement – 'well, sir – be quick – and if you can – less violent.'

'Sit down, and I will be both.'

She hesitated; she knew not what to do. The possibility of Colonel Brandon's arriving and finding him there, came across her. But she had promised to hear him, and her curiosity no less than her honour was engaged. After a moment's recollection, therefore, concluding that prudence required dispatch, and that her acquiescence would best promote it, she walked silently towards the table and sat down. He took the opposite chair, and for half a minute not a word was said by either.

'Pray be quick, sir' – said Elinor impatiently – 'I have no time to spare.'

He was sitting in an attitude of deep meditation, and seemed not to hear her.

'Your sister,' said he, with abruptness, a moment afterwards – 'is out of danger. I heard it from the servant. God be praised! – But is it true? is it really true?'

Elinor would not speak. He repeated the inquiry with yet greater eagerness.

'I entreat you to stay.'

'For God's sake tell me, is she out of danger, or is she not?'

'We hope she is.'

He rose up, and walked across the room.

'Had I known as such half an hour ago – But since I *am* here' – speaking with a forced vivacity as he returned to his seat – 'what does it signify? – For once, Miss Dashwood – it will be the last time, perhaps – let us be cheerful together. – I am in a fine mood for gaiety. – Tell me honestly' – a deeper glow overspreading his cheeks – 'do you think me most a knave or a fool?'

Elinor looked at him with greater astonishment than ever. She began to think that he must be in liquor; – the strangeness of such a visit, and of such manners, seemed no otherwise intelligible; and with this impression she immediately rose, saying,

'Mr Willoughby, I advise you at present to return to Combe – I am not at leisure to remain with you longer. – Whatever your business may be with me, it will be better recollected and explained to-morrow.'

'I understand you,' he replied, with an expressive smile, and a voice perfectly calm, 'yes, I am very drunk. – A pint of porter with my cold beef at Marlborough was enough to over-set me.'

'At Marlborough!' – cried Elinor, more and more at a loss to understand what he would be at.

'Yes – I left London this morning at eight o'clock, and the only ten minutes I have spent out of my chaise since that time, procured me a luncheon at Marlborough.'

The steadiness of his manner, and the intelligence of his eye as he spoke, convincing Elinor, that whatever other unpardonable folly might bring him to Cleveland, he was not brought there by intoxication, she said, after a moment's recollection,

'Mr Willoughby, you *ought* to feel, and I certainly *do* – that after what has passed – your coming here in this manner, and forcing yourself upon my notice, requires a very particular excuse. – What is it, that you mean by it?' –

'I mean' – said he, with serious energy – 'if I can, to make you hate me one degree less than you do *now*. I mean to offer some kind of explanation, some kind of apology, for the past; to open my whole heart to you, and by convincing you, that though I have been always a blockhead, I have not been always a rascal, to obtain something like forgiveness from Ma – from your sister.'

'Is this the real reason of your coming?'

'Upon my soul it is,' – was his answer, with a warmth which brought all the former Willoughby to her remembrance, and in spite of herself made her think him sincere.

'If that is all, you may be satisfied already, – for Marianne *does* – she has *long* forgiven you.'

'Has she!' – he cried, in the same eager tone. – 'Then she has forgiven me before she ought to have done it. But she shall forgive me again, and on more reasonable grounds. – *Now* will you listen to me?'

Elinor bowed her assent.

'I do not know,' said he, after a pause of expectation on her side, and thoughtfulness on his own, – 'how *you* may have accounted for my behaviour to your sister, or what diabolical motive you may have imputed to me. – Perhaps you will hardly think the better of me, – it is worth the trial however, and you shall hear every thing. When I first became intimate in your family, I had no other intention, no other view in the acquaintance than to pass my time pleasantly while I was obliged to remain in Devonshire, more pleasantly than I had ever done before. Your sister's lovely person and interesting manners could not but please me; and her behaviour to me almost from the first, was of a kind – It is astonishing, when I reflect on what it was, and what *she* was, that my heart should have been so insensible! But at first I must confess, my vanity only was elevated by it. Careless of her happiness, thinking only of my own amusement, giving way to feelings which I had always been too much in the habit of indulging, I endeavoured, by every means in my power, to make myself pleasing to her, without any design of returning her affection.'

Miss Dashwood at this point, turning her eyes on him with the most angry contempt, stopped him, by saying,

'It is hardly worth while, Mr Willoughby, for you to relate, or for me to listen any longer. Such a beginning as this cannot be followed by any thing. – Do not let me be pained by hearing any thing more on the subject.'

'I insist on your hearing the whole of it,' he replied. 'My fortune was never large, and I had always been expensive, always in the habit of associating with people of better income than myself. Every year since my coming of age, or even before, I believe, had added to my debts; and though the death of my old cousin, Mrs Smith, was to set me free; yet that event being uncertain, and possibly far distant, it had been for some time my intention to re-establish my circumstances by marrying a woman of fortune. To attach myself to your sister, therefore, was not a thing to be thought of; – and with a meanness, selfishness, cruelty – which no indignant, no contemptuous look, even of yours, Miss Dashwood, can ever reprobate too much – I was acting in this manner, trying to engage her regard, without a thought of returning it. – But one thing may be said for me, even in that horrid state of selfish vanity, I did not know the extent of the injury I meditated, because I did not *then* know what it was to love. But have I ever known it? – Well may it be doubted; for, had I really loved, could I have sacrificed my feelings to vanity, to avarice? – or, what is more, could I have sacrificed her's? – But I have done it. To avoid a comparative poverty, which her affection and her society would have deprived of all its horrors, I have, by raising myself to affluence, lost every thing that could make it a blessing.'

'You did then,' said Elinor, a little softened, 'believe yourself at one time attached to her.'

'To have resisted such attractions, to have withstood such tenderness! – Is there a man on earth who could have done it! – Yes, I found myself, by insensible degrees, sincerely fond of her; and the happiest hours of my life were what I spent with her, when I felt my intentions were strictly honourable, and my feelings blameless. Even *then*, however, when fully determined on paying my addresses to her, I allowed myself most improperly to put off, from day to day, the moment of doing it, from an unwillingness to enter into an engagement while my circumstances were so greatly embarrassed. I will not reason here – nor will I stop for *you* to expatiate on the absurdity, and the worse than absurdity, of scrupling to engage my faith where my honour was already bound. The event has proved, that I was a cunning fool, providing with great circumspection for a possible opportunity of making myself contemptible and wretched for ever. At last, however, my resolution was taken, and I had determined, as soon as I could engage her alone, to justify the attentions I had so invariably paid her, and openly assure her of an affection which I had already taken such pains to display. But in the interim – in the interim of the very few hours that were to pass, before I could have an opportunity of speaking with her in private – a circumstance occurred – an unlucky circumstance, to ruin all my resolution, and with it all my comfort. A discovery took place,' – here he hesitated and looked down. – 'Mrs Smith had somehow or other been informed, I imagine by some distant relation, whose interest it was to deprive me of her favour, of an affair, a connection – but I need not explain myself farther,' he added, looking at her with an heightened colour and an enquiring eye, – 'your particular intimacy – you have probably heard the whole story long ago.'

'I have,' returned Elinor, colouring likewise, and hardening her heart anew against any compassion for him, 'I have heard it all. And how you will explain away any part of your guilt in that dreadful business, I confess is beyond my comprehension.'

'Remember,' cried Willoughby, 'from whom you received the account. Could it be an impartial one? I acknowledge that her situation and her character ought to have been respected by me. I do not mean to justify myself, but at the same time cannot leave you to suppose that I have nothing to urge – that because she was injured she was irreproachable, and because *I* was a libertine, *she* must be a saint. If the violence of her passions, the weakness of her understanding – I do not mean, however, to defend myself. Her affection for me deserved better treatment, and I often, with great self-reproach, recall the tenderness which, for a very short time, had the power of creating any return. I wish – I heartily wish it had never been. But I have injured more than herself; and I have injured one, whose affection for me – (may I say it?) was scarcely less warm than her's; and whose mind – Oh! how infinity superior!' –

'Your indifference, however, towards that unfortunate girl – I must say it, unpleasant to me as the discussion of such a subject may well be – your indifference is no apology for your cruel neglect of her. Do not think yourself excused by any weakness, any natural defect of understanding on her side, in the wanton cruelty so evident on yours. You must have known, that while you were enjoying yourself in Devonshire pursuing fresh schemes, always gay, always happy, she was reduced to the extremest indigence.'

'But, upon my soul, I did *not* know it,' he warmly replied; 'I did not recollect that I had omitted to give her my direction; and common sense might have told her how to find it out.'

'Well, sir, and what said Mrs Smith?'

'She taxed me with the offence at once, and my confusion may be guessed. The purity of her life, the formality of her notions, her ignorance of the world – every thing was against me. The matter itself I could not deny, and vain was every endeavour to soften it. She was previously disposed, I believe, to doubt the morality of my conduct in general, and was moreover discontented with the very little attention, the very little portion of my time that I had bestowed on her, in my present visit. In short, it ended in a total breach. By one measure I might have saved myself. In the height of her morality, good woman! she offered to forgive the past, if I would marry Eliza. That could not be – and I was formally dismissed from her favour and her house. The night following this affair – I was to go the next morning – was spent by me in deliberating on what my future conduct should be. The struggle was great – but it ended too soon. My affection for Marianne, my thorough conviction of her

'I was formally dismissed.'

attachment to me – it was all insufficient to outweigh that dread of poverty, or get the better of those false ideas of the necessity of riches, which I was naturally inclined to feel, and expensive society had increased. I had reason to believe myself secure of my present wife, if I chose to address her, and I persuaded myself to think that nothing else in common prudence remained for me to do. An heavy scene however awaited me, before I could leave Devonshire; – I was engaged to dine with you on that very day; some apology was therefore necessary for my breaking the engagement. But whether I should write this apology, or deliver it in person, was a point of long debate. To see Marianne, I felt, would be dreadful, and I even doubted whether I could see her again, and keep to my resolution. In that point, however, I undervalued my own magnanimity, as the event declared; for I went, I saw her, and saw her miserable and left her miserable – and left her hoping never to see her again.'

'Why did you call, Mr Willoughby?' said Elinor, reproachfully;

'a note would have answered every purpose. – Why was it necessary to call?'

'It was necessary to my own pride. I could not bear to leave the country in a manner that might lead you, or the rest of the neighbourhood, to suspect any part of what had really passed between Mrs Smith and myself – and I resolved therefore on calling at the cottage, in my way to Honiton. The sight of your dear sister, however, was really dreadful; and to heighten the matter, I found her alone. You were all gone I do not know where. I had left her only the evening before, so fully, so firmly resolved within myself on doing right! A few hours were to have engaged her to me for ever; and I remember how happy, how gay were my spirits, as I walked from the cottage to Allenham, satisfied with myself, delighted with every body! But in this, our last interview of friendship, I approached her with a sense of guilt that almost took from me the power of dissembling. Her sorrow, her disappointment, her deep regret, when I told her that I was obliged to leave Devonshire so immediately – I never shall forget it – united too with such reliance, such confidence in me! – Oh, God! – what an hard-hearted rascal I was!'

They were both silent for a few moments. Elinor first spoke.

'Did you tell her that you should soon return?'

'I do not know what I told her,' he replied, impatiently; 'less than was due to the past, beyond a doubt, and in all likelihood much more than was justified by the future. I cannot think of it. – It won't do – Then came your dear mother to torture me farther, with all her kindness and confidence. Thank Heaven! it *did* torture me. I was miserable. Miss Dashwood, you cannot have an idea of the comfort it gives me to look back on my own misery. I owe such a grudge to myself for the stupid, rascally folly of my own heart, that all my past sufferings under it are only triumph and exultation to me now. Well, I went, left all that I loved, and went to those to whom, at best, I was only indifferent. My journey to town – travelling with my own horses, and therefore so tediously – no creature to speak to – my own reflections so cheerful – when I looked forward everything so inviting! – when I looked back at Barton, the picture so soothing! – oh! it was a blessed journey!'

He stopt.

'Well, sir,' said Elinor, who, though pitying him, grew impatient for his departure, 'and this is all?'

'All! – no, – have you forgot what passed in town? – That infamous letter – Did she shew it you?'

'Yes, I saw every note that passed.'

'When the first of her's reached me, (as it immediately did, for I was in town the whole time,) what I felt is – in the common phrase, not to be expressed; in a more simple one – perhaps too simple to raise any emotion – my feelings were very, very painful. – Every line, every word was – in the hackneyed metaphor which their dear writer, were she here, would forbid – a dagger to my heart. To know that Marianne was in town was – in the same language – a thunderbolt – Thunderbolts and daggers! – what a reproof would she have given me! – her taste, her opinions – I believe they are better known to me than my own, – and I am sure they are dearer.'

Elinor's heart, which had undergone many changes in the course of this extraordinary conversation, was now softened again; – yet she felt it her duty to check such ideas in her companion as the last.

'This is not right, Mr Willoughby. – Remember that you are married. Relate only what in your conscience you think necessary for me to hear.'

'Marianne's note, by assuring me that I was still as dear to her as in former days, that in spite of the many, many weeks we had been separated, she was as constant in her own feelings, and as full of faith in the constancy of mine as ever, awakened all my remorse. I say awakened, because time and London, business and dissipation, had in some measure quieted it, and I had been growing a fine hardened villain, fancying myself indifferent to her, and chusing to fancy that she too must have become indifferent to me; talking to myself of our past attachment as a mere idle, trifling, business, shrugging up my shoulders in proof of its being so, and silencing every reproach, overcoming every scruple, by secretly saying now and then, "I shall be heartily glad to hear she is well married." – But this note made me know myself better. I felt that she was infinitely dearer to me than any other woman in the world, and that I was using her infamously. But everything was then just settled between Miss Grey and me. To retreat was impossible. All that I had to do, was to avoid you both. I sent no answer to Marianne, intending by that means to preserve myself from her farther notice; and for some time I was even determined not to call in Berkeley-street; – but at last, judging it wiser to affect the air of a cool, common acquaintance than anything else, I watched you all safely out of the house one morning, and left my name.'

'Watched us out of the house!'

'Even so. You would be surprised to hear how often I watched you, how often I was on the point of falling in with you. I have entered many a shop to avoid your sight, as the carriage drove by. Lodging as I did in Bond-street, there was hardly a day in which I did not catch a glimpse of one or other of you; and nothing but the most constant watchfulness on my side, a most invariably prevailing desire to keep out of your sight, could have separated us so long. I avoided the Middletons as much as possible, as well as everybody else who was likely to prove an acquaintance in common. Not aware of their being in town, however, I blundered on Sir John, I believe, the first day of his coming, and the day after I had called at Mrs Jennings's. He asked me to a party, a dance at his house in

'I have entered many a shop to avoid your sight.'

the evening. – Had he *not* told me as an inducement that you and your sister were to be there, I should have felt it too certain a thing, to trust myself near him. The next morning brought another short note from Marianne – still affectionate, open, artless, confiding – everything that could make *my* conduct most hateful. I could not answer it. I tried – but could not frame a sentence. But I thought of her, I believe, every moment of the day. If you *can* pity me, Miss Dashwood, pity my situation as it was *then*. With my head and heart full of your sister, I was forced to play the happy lover to another woman! – Those three or four weeks were worse than all. Well, at last, as I need not tell you, you were forced on me; and what a sweet figure I cut! – what an evening of agony it was! – Marianne, beautiful as an angel on one side, calling me Willoughby in such a tone! – Oh! God! – holding out her hand to me, asking for an explanation with those bewitching eyes fixed in such speaking solicitude on my face! – and Sophia, jealous as the devil on the other hand, looking all that was – Well, it does not signify; it is over now. – Such an evening! – I ran away from you all as soon as I could; but not before I had seen Marianne's sweet face as white as death. – *That* was the last, last look I ever had of her; – the last manner in which she appeared to me. It was a horrid sight! – Yet when I thought of her to-day as really dying, it was a kind of comfort to me to imagine that I knew exactly how she would appear to those, who saw her last in this world. She was before me, constantly before me, as I travelled, in the same look and hue.'

A short pause of mutual thoughtfulness succeeded. Willoughby first rousing himself, broke it thus:

'Well, let me make haste and be gone. Your sister is certainly better, certainly out of danger?'

'We are assured of it.'

'Your poor mother too! – doting on Marianne.'

'But the letter, Mr Willoughby, your own letter; have you anything to say about that?'

'Yes, yes, *that* in particular. Your sister wrote to me again, you know, the very next morning. You saw what she said. I was breakfasting at the Ellisons, – and her letter, with some others, was brought to me there from my lodgings. It happened to catch Sophia's eye before it caught mine – and its size, the elegance of the paper, the handwriting altogether, immediately gave her a suspicion. Some vague report had reached her before of my attachment to some young lady in Devonshire, and what had passed within her observation the preceding evening had marked who the young lady was, and made her more jealous than ever. Affecting that air of playfulness, therefore, which is delightful in a woman one loves, she opened the letter directly, and read its contents. She was well paid for her impudence. She read what made her wretched. Her wretchedness I could have borne, but her passion – her malice – At all events it must be appeased. And in short – what do you think of my wife's style of letter-writing? – delicate – tender – truly feminine – was it not?'

'Your wife! – The letter was in your own hand-writing.'

'Yes, but I had only the credit of servilely copying such sentences as I was ashamed to put my name to. The original was all her own – her own happy thoughts and gentle diction. But what could I do! – we were engaged, every thing in preparation, the day almost fixed – But I am talking like a fool. Preparation! – day! – In honest words, her money was necessary to me, and in a situation like mine, any thing was to be done to prevent a rupture. And after all, what did it signify to my character in the opinion of Marianne and her friends, in what language my answer was couched? – It must have been only to one end. My business was to declare myself a scoundrel, and whether I did it with a bow or a bluster was of little importance. – "I am ruined for ever in their opinion – said I to myself – I am shut out for ever from their society, they already think me an unprincipled fellow, this letter will only make them think me a blackguard one." Such were my reasonings, as, in a sort of desperate carelessness, I copied my wife's words, and parted with the last relics of Marianne. Her three notes – unluckily they were all in my pocket-book, or I should have denied their existence, and hoarded them for ever – I was forced to put them up, and could not even kiss them. And the lock of hair – that too I had always carried about me in the same pocket-book, which was now searched by Madam with the most ingratiating virulence, – the dear lock – all, every memento was torn from me.'

'You are very wrong, Mr Willoughby, very blameable,' said Elinor, while her voice, in spite of herself, betrayed her compassionate emotion; 'you ought not to speak in this way, either of Mrs Willoughby or my sister. You have made your choice. It was not forced on you. Your wife has a claim to your politeness, to your respect, at least. She must be attached to you, or she would not have married you. To treat her with unkindness, to speak of her slightingly is no atonement to Marianne – nor can I suppose it a relief to your own conscience.'

'Do not talk to me of my wife,' said he with an heavy sigh. – 'She does not deserve your compassion. – She knew I had no regard for her when we married. – Well, married we were, and came down to Combe Magna to be happy, and afterwards returned to town to be gay. – And now do you pity me, Miss Dashwood? – or have I said all this to no purpose? – Am I – be it only one degree – am I less guilty in your opinion than I was before? – My intentions were not always wrong. Have I explained away any part of my guilt?'

'Yes, you have certainly removed something – a little. – You have proved yourself, on the whole, less faulty than I had believed you. You have proved your heart less wicked, much less wicked. But I hardly know – the misery that you have inflicted – I hardly know what could have made it worse.'

'Will you repeat to your sister when she is recovered, what I have been telling you? – Let me be a little lightened too in her opinion as well as in yours. You tell me that she has forgiven me already. Let me be able to fancy that a better knowledge of my heart, and of my present feelings, will draw from her a more spontaneous, more natural, more gentle, less dignified, forgiveness. Tell her of my misery and my penitence – tell her that my heart was never inconstant to her, and if you will, that at this moment she is dearer to me than ever.'

'I will tell her all that is necessary to what may comparatively be called, your justification. But you have not explained to me the particular reason of your coming now, nor how you heard of her illness.'

'Last night, in Drury-lane lobby, I ran against Sir John Middleton, and when he saw who I was – for the first time these two months – he spoke to me. – That he had cut me ever since my marriage, I had seen without surprise or resentment. Now, however, his good-natured, honest, stupid soul, full of indignation against me, and concern for your sister, could not resist the temptation of telling me what he knew ought to – though probably he did not think it *would* – vex me horridly. – As bluntly as he could speak it, therefore, he told me that Marianne Dashwood was dying of a putrid fever at Cleveland – a letter that morning received from Mrs Jennings declared her danger most imminent – the Palmers all gone off in a fright, &c. – I was too shocked to be able to pass myself off as insensible even to the undiscerning Sir John. His heart was softened in seeing mine suffer; and so much of his ill-will was done away, that when we parted, he almost shook me by the hand while he reminded me of an old promise about a pointer puppy. What I felt on hearing that your sister was dying – and dying too, believing me the greatest villain upon earth, scorning, hating me in her latest moments – for how could I tell what horrid projects might not have been imputed? *One* person I was sure would represent me as capable of anything – What I felt was dreadful! – My resolution was soon made, and at eight o'clock this morning I was in my carriage. Now you know all.'

Elinor made no answer. Her thoughts were silently fixed on the irreparable injury which too early an independence and its consequent habits of idleness, dissipation, and luxury, had made in the mind, the character, the happiness, of a man who, to every advantage of person and talents, united a disposition naturally open and honest, and a feeling affectionate temper. The world had made him extravagant and vain – Extravagance and vanity had made him cold-hearted and selfish. Vanity, while seeking its own guilty triumph at the expense of another, had involved him in a real attachment, which extravagance, or at least its offspring, necessity, had required to be sacrificed. Each faulty propensity in leading him to evil, had led him likewise to punishment. The attachment, from which against honour, against feeling, against every better interest he had outwardly torn himself, now, when no longer allowable, governed every thought; and the connection, for the sake of which he had, with little scruple, left her sister to misery, was likely to prove a source of unhappiness to himself of a far more incurable nature. From a reverie of this kind she was recalled at the end of some minutes by Willoughby, who, rousing himself from a reverie at least equally painful, started up in preparation for going, and said,

'There is no use in staying here; I must be off.'

'Are you going back to town?'

'No – to Combe Magna. I have business there; from thence to town in a day or two. Good bye.'

He held out his hand. She could not refuse to give him her's; – he pressed it with affection.

'And you *do* think something better of me than you did?' – said he, letting it fall, and leaning against the mantle-piece as if forgetting he was to go.

Elinor assured him that she did; – that she forgave, pitied, wished him well – was even interested in his happiness – and added some gentle counsel as to the behaviour most likely to promote it. His answer was not very encouraging.

'As to that,' said he, 'I must rub through the world as well as I can. Domestic happiness is out of the question. If, however, I am allowed to think that you and yours feel an interest in my fate and actions, it may be the means – it may put me on my guard – at least, it will be something to live for. Marianne to be sure is lost to me for ever. Were I even by any blessed chance at liberty again' –

Elinor stopped him with a reproof.

'Well' – he replied – 'once more good bye. I shall now go away and live in dread of one event.'

'What do you mean?'

'Your sister's marriage.'

'You are very wrong. She can never be more lost to you than she is now.'

'But she will be gained by some one else. And if that some one should be the very he whom, of all others, I could least bear – But I will not stay to rob myself of all your compassionate goodwill, by shewing that where I have most injured I can least forgive. Good bye, – God bless you!'

And with these words, he almost ran out of the room.

CHAPTER FORTY-FIVE

ELINOR, FOR SOME TIME after he left her, for some time even after the sound of his carriage had died away, remained too much oppressed by a croud of ideas, widely differing in themselves, but of which sadness was the general result, to think even of her sister.

Willoughby, he, whom only half an hour ago she had abhorred as the most worthless of men, Willoughby, in spite of all his faults, excited a degree of commiseration for the sufferings produced by them, which made her think of him as now separated for ever from her family with a tenderness, a regret, rather in proportion, as she soon acknowledged within herself – to his wishes than to his merits. She felt that his influence over her mind was heightened by circumstances which ought not in reason to have weight; by that person of uncommon attraction, that open, affectionate, and lively manner which it was no merit to possess; and by that still ardent love for Marianne, which it was not even innocent to indulge. But she felt that it was so, long, long before she could feel his influence less.

When at last she returned to the unconscious Marianne, she found her just awaking, refreshed by so long and sweet a sleep to the extent of her hopes. Elinor's heart was full. The past, the present, the future, Willoughby's visit, Marianne's safety, and her mother's expected arrival, threw her altogether into an agitation of spirits which kept off every indication of fatigue, and made her only fearful of betraying herself to her sister. Short was the time, however, in which that fear could affect her, for within half an hour after Willoughby's leaving the house, she was again called down stairs by the sound of another carriage. – Eager to save her mother from every unnecessary moment's horrible suspense, she ran immediately into the hall, and reached the outward door just in time to receive and support her as she entered it.

Mrs Dashwood, whose terror as they drew near the house had produced almost the conviction of Marianne's being no more, had no voice to enquire after her, no voice even for Elinor; but *she*, waiting neither for salutation nor inquiry, instantly gave the joyful relief; – and her mother, catching it with all her usual warmth, was in a moment as much overcome by her happiness, as she had been before by her fears. She wassupportewas supported into the drawing-room between her daughter and her friend; – and there, shedding tears of joy, though still unable to speak, embraced Elinor again and again, turning from her at intervals to press Colonel Brandon's hand, with a look which spoke at once her gratitude, and her conviction of his sharing with herself in the bliss of the moment. He shared it, however, in a silence even greater than her own.

As soon as Mrs Dashwood had recovered herself, to see Marianne was her first desire; and in two minutes she was with her beloved child, rendered dearer to her than ever by absence, unhappiness, and danger. Elinor's delight, as she saw what each felt in the meeting, was only checked by an apprehension of its robbing Marianne of farther sleep; – but Mrs Dashwood could be calm, could be even prudent, when the life of a child was at stake, and Marianne, satisfied in knowing her mother was near her, and conscious of being too weak for conversation, submitted readily to the silence and quiet prescribed by every nurse around her. Mrs Dashwood *would* sit up with her all night, and Elinor, in compliance with her mother's entreaty, went to bed. But the rest, which one night entirely sleepless, and many hours of the most wearing anxiety seemed to make requisite, was kept off by irritation of spirits. Willoughby, 'poor Willoughby,' as she now allowed herself to call him, was constantly in her thoughts; she would not but have heard his vindication for the world, and now blamed, now acquitted herself for having judged him so harshly before. But her promise of relating to her sister was invariably painful. She dreaded the performance of it, dreaded what its effect on Marianne might be; doubted whether after such an explanation she could ever be happy with another; and for a moment wished Willoughby a widower. Then, remembering Colonel Brandon, reproved herself, felt that to *his* sufferings and his constancy far more than to his rival's, the reward of her sister was due, and wished any thing rather than Mrs Willoughby's death.

The shock of Colonel Brandon's errand at Barton had been much softened to Mrs Dashwood by her own previous alarm; for so great was her uneasiness about Marianne, that she had already determined to set out for Cleveland on that very day, without waiting for any farther intelligence, and had so far settled her journey before his arrival, that the Careys were then expected every moment to fetch Margaret away, as her mother was unwilling to take her where there might be infection.

Marianne continued to mend every day, and the brilliant cheerfulness of Mrs Dashwood's looks and spirits proved her to be, as she repeatedly declared herself, one of the happiest women in the world. Elinor could not hear the declaration, nor witness its proofs without sometimes wondering whether her mother ever recollected Edward. But Mrs Dashwood, trusting to the temperate account of her own disappointment which Elinor had sent her, was led away by the exuberance of her joy to think only of what would increase it. Marianne was restored to her from a danger in which, as she now began to feel, her own mistaken judgment in encouraging the unfortunate attachment to Willoughby, had contributed to place her; – and in her recovery she had yet another source of joy unthought of by Elinor. It was thus imparted to her, as soon as any opportunity of private conference between them occurred.

'At last we are alone. My Elinor, you do not yet know all my happiness. Colonel Brandon loves Marianne. He has told me so himself.'

Her daughter, feeling by turns both pleased and pained, surprised and not surprised, was all silent attention.

'You are never like me, dear Elinor, or I should wonder at your composure now. Had I sat down to wish for any possible good to my family, I should have fixed on Colonel Brandon's marrying one of you as the object most desirable. And I believe Marianne will be the most happy with him of the two.'

Elinor was half inclined to ask her reason for thinking so, because satisfied that none founded on an impartial consideration of their age, characters, or feelings, could be given; – but her mother must always be carried away by her imagination on any interesting subject, and therefore instead of an inquiry, she passed it off with a smile.

'He opened his whole heart to me yesterday as we travelled. It came out quite unawares, quite undesignedly. I, you may well believe, could talk of nothing but my child; – he could not conceal his distress; I saw that it equalled my own, and he perhaps, thinking that mere friendship, as the world now goes, would not justify so warm a sympathy – or rather not thinking at all, I suppose – giving way to irresistible feelings, made me acquainted with his earnest, tender, constant, affection for Marianne. He has loved her, my Elinor, ever since the first moment of seeing her.'

Here, however, Elinor perceived, – not the language, not the professions of Colonel Brandon, but the natural embellishments of her mother's active fancy, which fashioned every thing delightful to her, as it chose.

'His regard for her, infinitely surpassing anything that Willoughby ever felt or feigned, as much more warm, as more sincere or constant – which ever we are to call it – has subsisted through all the knowledge of dear Marianne's unhappy prepossession for that worthless young man! – and without selfishness – without encouraging a hope! – could he have seen her happy with another – Such a noble mind! – such openness, such sincerity! – no one can be deceived in *him*.'

'Colonel Brandon's character,' said Elinor, 'as an excellent man, is well established.'

'I know it is' – replied her mother seriously, 'or after such a warning, I should be the last to encourage such affection, or even to be pleased by it. But his coming for me as he did, with such active, such ready friendship, is enough to prove him one of the worthiest of men.'

'His character, however,' answered Elinor, 'does not rest on *one* act of kindness, to which his affection for Marianne, were humanity out of the case, would have prompted him. To Mrs Jennings, to the Middletons, he has been long and intimately known; they equally love and respect him; and even my own knowledge of him, though lately acquired, is very considerable; and so highly do *I* value and esteem him, that if Marianne can be happy with him, I shall be as ready as yourself to think our connection the greatest blessing to us in the world. What answer did you give him? – Did you allow him to hope?'

'Oh! my love, I could not then talk of hope to him or to myself. Marianne might at that moment be dying. But he did not ask for hope or encouragement. His was an involuntary confidence, an irrepressible effusion to a soothing friend – not an application to a parent. Yet after a time I *did* say, for at first I was quite overcome – that if she lived, as I trusted she might, my greatest happiness would lie in promoting their marriage; and since our arrival, since our delightful security I have repeated it to him more fully, have given him every encouragement in my power. Time, a very little time, I tell him, will do everything; – Marianne's heart is not to be wasted for ever on such a man as Willoughby. – His own merits must soon secure it.'

'To judge from the Colonel's spirits, however, you have not yet made him equally sanguine.'

'No. – He thinks Marianne's affection too deeply rooted for any change in it under a great length of time, and even supposing her heart again free, is too diffident of himself to believe, that with such a difference of age and disposition, he could ever attach her. There, however, he is quite mistaken. His age is only so much beyond her's, as to be an advantage, as to make his character and principles fixed; – and his disposition, I am well convinced, is exactly the very one to make your sister happy. And his person, his manners too, are all in his favour. My partiality does not blind me; he certainly is not so handsome as Willoughby – but at the same time, there is something much more pleasing in his countenance. – There was always a something, – if you remember, – in Willoughby's eyes at times, which I did not like.'

Elinor could *not* remember it; – but her mother, without waiting for her assent, continued,

'And his manners, the Colonel's manners are not only more pleasing to me than Willoughby's ever were, but they are of a kind I well know to be more solidly attaching to Marianne. Their gentleness, their genuine attention to other people, and their manly unstudied simplicity is much more accordant with her real disposition, than the liveliness – often artificial, and often ill-timed of the other. I am very sure myself, that had Willoughby turned out as really amiable, as he has proved himself the contrary, Marianne would yet never have been so happy with *him*, as she will be with Colonel Brandon.'

She paused. – Her daughter could not quite agree with her, but her dissent was not heard, and therefore gave no offence.

'At Delaford, she will be within an easy distance of me,' added Mrs Dashwood, 'even if I remain at Barton; and in all probability, – for I hear it is a large village, – indeed there certainly *must* be some small house or cottage close by, that would suit us quite as well as our present situation.'

Poor Elinor! – here was a new scheme for getting her to Delaford! – but her spirit was stubborn.

'His fortune too! – for at my time of life you know, everybody cares about *that*; – and though I neither know, nor desire to know, what it really is, I am sure it must be a good one.'

Here they were interrupted by the entrance of a third person, and Elinor withdrew to think it all over in private, to wish success to her friend, and yet in wishing it, to feel a pang for Willoughby.

CHAPTER FORTY-SIX

Marianne's illness, though weakening in its kind, had not been long enough to make her recovery slow; and with youth, natural strength, and her mother's presence in aid, it proceeded so smoothly as to enable her to remove, within four days after the arrival of the latter, into Mrs Palmer's dressing-room. When there, at her own particular request, for she was impatient to pour forth her thanks to him for fetching her mother, Colonel Brandon was invited to visit her.

His emotion in entering the room, in seeing her altered looks, and in receiving the pale hand which she immediately held out to him, was such, as, in Elinor's conjecture, must arise from something more than his affection for Marianne, or the consciousness of its being known to others; and she soon discovered in his melancholy eye and varying complexion as he looked at her sister, the probable recurrence of many past scenes of misery to his mind, brought back by that resemblance between Marianne and Eliza already acknowledged, and now strengthened by the hollow eye, the sickly skin, the posture of reclining weakness, and the warm acknowledgment of peculiar obligation.

Mrs Dashwood, not less watchful of what passed than her daughter, but with a mind very differently influenced, and therefore watching to very different effect, saw nothing in the Colonel's behaviour but what arose from the most simple and self-evident sensations, while in the actions and words of Marianne she persuaded herself to think that something more than gratitude already dawned.

At the end of another day or two, Marianne growing visibly stronger every twelve hours, Mrs Dashwood, urged equally by her own and her daughter's wishes, began to talk of removing to Barton. On *her* measures depended those of her two friends; Mrs Jennings could not quit Cleveland during the Dashwoods' stay, and Colonel Brandon was soon brought, by their united request, to consider his own abode there as equally determinate, if not equally indispensable. At his and Mrs Jennings's united request in return, Mrs Dashwood was prevailed on to accept the use of his carriage on her journey back, for the better accommodation of her sick child; and the Colonel, at the joint invitation of Mrs Dashwood and Mrs Jennings, whose active good-nature made her friendly and hospitable for other people as well as herself, engaged with pleasure to redeem it by a visit at the cottage, in the course of a few weeks.

The day of separation and departure arrived; and Marianne, after taking so particular and lengthened a leave of Mrs Jennings, one so earnestly grateful, so full of respect and kind wishes as seemed due to her own heart from a secret acknowledgment of past inattention, and bidding Colonel Brandon farewell with the cordiality of a friend, was carefully assisted by him into the carriage, of which he seemed anxious that she should engross at least half. Mrs Dashwood and Elinor then followed, and the others were left by themselves, to talk of the travellers, and feel their own dulness, till Mrs Jennings was summoned to her chaise to take comfort in the gossip of her maid for the loss of her two young companions; and Colonel Brandon immediately afterwards took his solitary way to Delaford.

The Dashwoods were two days on the road, and Marianne bore her journey on both, without essential fatigue. Every thing that the most zealous affection, the most solicitous care could do to render her comfortable, was the office of each watchful companion, and each found their reward in her bodily ease, and her calmness of spirits. To Elinor, the observation of the latter was particularly grateful. She, who had seen her week after week so constantly suffering, oppressed by anguish of heart which she had neither courage to speak of, nor fortitude to conceal, now saw with a joy, which no other could equally share, an apparent composure of mind, which, in being the result as she trusted of serious reflection, must eventually lead her to contentment and cheerfulness.

As they approached Barton, indeed, and entered on scenes, of which every field and every tree brought some peculiar, some painful recollection, she grew silent and thoughtful, and turning away her face from their notice, sat earnestly gazing through the window. But here, Elinor could neither wonder nor blame; and when she saw, as she assisted Marianne from the carriage, that she had been crying, she saw only an emotion too natural in itself to raise anything less tender than pity, and in its unobtrusiveness entitled to praise. In the whole of her subsequent manner, she traced the direction of a mind awakened to reasonable exertion; for no sooner had they entered their common sitting-room, than Marianne turned her eyes around it with a look of resolute firmness, as if determined at once to accustom herself to the sight of every object with which the remembrance of Willoughby could be connected. – She said little, but every sentence aimed at cheerfulness, and though a sigh sometimes escaped her, it never passed away without the atonement of a smile. After dinner she would try her piano-forté. She went to it;

'And see how the children go on.'

but the music on which her eye first rested was an opera, procured for her by Willoughby, containing some of their favourite duets, and bearing on its outward leaf her own name in his hand writing. – That would not do. – She shook her head, put the music aside, and after running over the keys for a minute complained of feebleness in her fingers, and closed the instrument again; declaring however with firmness as she did so, that she should in future practise much.

The next morning produced no abatement in these happy symptoms. On the contrary, with a mind and body alike strengthened by rest, she looked and spoke with more genuine spirit, anticipating the pleasure of Margaret's return, and talking of the dear family party which would then be restored, of their mutual pursuits and cheerful society as the only happiness worth a wish.

'When the weather is settled, and I have recovered my strength,' said she, 'we will take long walks together every day. We will walk to the farm at the edge of the down, and see how the children go on; we will walk to Sir John's new plantations at Barton-Cross, and the Abbeyland; and we will often go to the old ruins of the Priory, and try to trace its foundations as far as we are told they once reached. I know we shall be happy. I know the summer will pass happily away. I mean never to be late in rising than six, and from that time till dinner I shall divide every moment between music and reading. I have formed my plan, and am determined to enter on a course of serious study. Our own library is too well known to me, to be resorted to for anything beyond mere amusement. But there are many works well worth reading, at the Park; and there are others of more modern production which I know I can borrow of Colonel Brandon. By reading only six hours a-day, I shall gain in the course of a twelve-month a great deal of instruction which I now feel myself to want.'

Elinor honoured her for a plan which originated so nobly as this; though smiling to see the same eager fancy which had been leading her to the extreme of languid indolence and selfish repining, now at work in introducing excess into a scheme of such rational employment and virtuous self-control. Her smile however changed to a sigh when she remembered that her promise to Willoughby was yet unfulfilled, and feared she had that to communicate which might again unsettle the mind of Marianne, and ruin at least for a time this fair prospect of busy tranquillity. Willing therefore to delay the evil hour, she resolved to wait till her sister's health were more secure, before she appointed it. But the resolution was made only to be broken.

Marianne had been two or three days at home, before the weather was fine enough for an invalid like herself to venture out. But at last a soft, genial morning appeared; such as might tempt the daughter's wishes and the mother's confidence; and Marianne, leaning on Elinor's arm, was authorised to walk as long as she could without fatigue, in the lane before the house.

The sisters set out at a pace, slow as the feebleness of Marianne in an exercise hitherto untried since her illness required; – and they had advanced only so far beyond the house as to admit a full view of the hill, the important hill behind, when pausing with her eyes turned towards it, Marianne calmly said,

'There, exactly there' – pointing with one hand, 'on that projecting mound, – there I fell; and there I first saw Willoughby.'

Her voice sunk with the word, but presently reviving she added,

'I am thankful to find that I can look with so little pain on the spot! – shall we ever talk on that subject, Elinor?' – hesitatingly it was said, – 'Or will it be wrong? – I *can* talk of it now, I hope, as I ought to do.' –

Elinor tenderly invited her to be open.

'As for regret,' said Marianne, 'I have done with that, as far as *he* is concerned. I do not mean to talk to you of what my feelings have been for him, but what they are *now*. – At present, if I could be satisfied on one point, if I could be allowed to think that he was not *always* acting a part, not *always* deceiving me; – but above all, if I could be assured that he never was so *very* wicked as my fears have sometimes fancied him, since the story of that unfortunate girl' –

She stopt. – Elinor joyfully treasured her words as she answered,

'If you could be assured of that, you think you should be easy.'

'Yes. My peace of mind is doubly involved in it; – for not only is it horrible to suspect a person, who has been what *he* has been to *me*, of such designs, – but what must it make me appear to myself? – What in a situation like mine, but a most shamefully unguarded affection could expose me to' –

'How then,' asked her sister, 'would you account for his behaviour?'

'I would suppose him, – Oh! how gladly would I suppose him, only fickle, very, very fickle.'

Elinor said no more. She was debating within herself on the eligibility of beginning her story directly, or postponing it till Marianne were in stronger health; – and they crept on for a few minutes in silence.

'I am not wishing him too much good,' said Marianne at last with a sigh, 'when I wish his secret reflections may be no more unpleasant than my own. He will suffer enough in them.'

'Do you compare your conduct with his?'

'No. I compare it with what it ought to have been; I compare it with yours.'

'Our situations have borne little resemblance.'

'They have borne more than our conduct. – Do not, my dearest Elinor, let your kindness defend what I know your judgment must censure. My illness has made me think – It has given me leisure and calmness for serious recollection. Long before I was enough recovered to talk, I was perfectly able to reflect. I considered the past; I saw in my own behaviour since the beginning of our acquaintance with him last autumn, nothing but a series of imprudence towards myself, and want of kindness to others. I saw that my own feelings had prepared my sufferings, and that my want of fortitude under them had almost led me to the grave. My illness, I well knew, had been entirely brought on by myself, by such negligence of my own health, as I had felt even at the time to be wrong. Had I died, – it would have been self-destruction. I did not know my danger till the danger was removed; but with such feelings as these reflections gave me, I wonder at my recovery, – wonder that the very eagerness of my desire to live, to have time for atonement to my God, and to you all, did not kill me at once. Had I died, – in what peculiar misery should I have left you, my nurse, my friend, my sister! – You, who had seen all the fretful selfishness of my latter days; who had known all the murmurings of my heart! – How should I have lived in *your* remembrance! – My mother too! How could you have consoled her! – I cannot express my own abhorrence of myself. Whenever I looked towards the past, I saw some duty neglected, or some failing indulged. Every body seemed injured by me. The kindness, the unceasing kindness of Mrs Jennings, I had repaid with ungrateful contempt. To the Middletons, the Palmers, the Steeles, to every common acquaintance even, I had been insolent and unjust; with an heart hardened against their merits, and a temper irritated by their very attention. – To John, to Fanny, – yes, even to them, little as they deserve, I had given less than their due. But you, – you above all, above my mother, had been wronged by me. I, and only I, knew your heart and its sorrows; yet, to what did it influence me? – not to any compassion that could benefit you or myself. – Your example was before me: but to what avail? – Was I more considerate of you and your comfort? Did I imitate your forbearance, or lessen your restraints, by taking any part in those offices of general complaisance or particular gratitude which you had hitherto been left to discharge alone? – No; – not less when I knew you to be unhappy, than when I had believed you at ease, did I turn away from every exertion of duty or friendship; scarcely allowing sorrow to exist but with me, regretting only *that* heart which had deserted and wronged me, and leaving you, for whom I professed an unbounded affection, to be miserable for my sake.'

Here ceased the rapid flow of her self-reproving spirit; and Elinor, impatient to sooth, though too honest to flatter, gave her instantly that praise and support which her frankness and her contrition so well deserved. Marianne pressed her hand and replied,

'You are very good. – The future must be my proof. I have laid down my plan, and if I am capable of adhering to it – my feelings shall be governed and my temper improved. They shall no longer worry others, nor torture myself. I shall now live solely for my family. You, my mother, and Margaret, must henceforth be all the world to me; you will share my affections entirely between you. From you, from my home, I shall never again have the smallest incitement to move; and if I do mix in other society it will be only to shew that my spirit is humbled, my heart amended, and that I can practise the civilities, the lesser duties of life, with gentleness, and forbearance. As for Willoughby – to say that I shall soon or that I shall ever forget him, would be idle. His remembrance can be overcome by no change of circumstances or opinions. But it shall be regulated, it shall be checked by religion, by reason, by constant employment.'

She paused – and added in a lower voice, 'If I could but know *his* heart, everything would become easy.'

Elinor, who had now been for some time reflecting on the propriety or impropriety of speedily hazarding her narration, without feeling at all nearer decision than at first, heard this; and perceiving that as reflection did nothing, resolution must do all, soon found herself leading to the fact.

She managed the recital, as she hoped, with address; prepared her anxious listener with caution; related simply and honestly the chief points on which Willoughby grounded his apology; did justice to his repentance, and softened only his protestations of present regard. Marianne said not a word. – She trembled, her eyes were fixed on the ground, and her lips became whiter than even sickness had left them. A thousand inquiries sprung up from her heart, but she dared not urge one. She caught every syllable with panting eagerness; her hand, unknowingly to herself, closely pressed her sister's, and tears covered her cheeks.

Elinor, dreading her being tired, led her towards home; and till they reached the door of the cottage, easily conjecturing what her curiosity must be though no question was suffered to speak it, talked of nothing but Willoughby, and their conversation together; and was carefully minute in every particular of speech and look, where minuteness could be safely indulged. As soon as they entered the house, Marianne with a kiss of gratitude and these two words just articulate through her tears, 'Tell mama,' withdrew from her sister and walked slowly up stairs. Elinor would not attempt to disturb a solitude so reasonable as what she now sought; and with a mind anxiously pre-arranging its result, and a resolution of reviving the subject again, should Marianne fail to do it, she turned into the parlour to fulfil her parting injunction.

CHAPTER FORTY-SEVEN

MRS DASHWOOD DID NOT hear unmoved the vindication of her former favourite. She rejoiced in his being cleared from some part of his imputed guilt; – she was sorry for him; – she wished him happy. But the feelings of the past could not be recalled. – Nothing could restore him with a faith unbroken – a character unblemished, to Marianne. Nothing could do away the knowledge of what the latter had suffered through his means, nor remove the guilt of his conduct towards Eliza. Nothing could replace him, therefore, in her former esteem, nor injure the interests of Colonel Brandon.

Had Mrs Dashwood, like her daughter, heard Willoughby's story from himself – had she witnessed his distress, and been under the influence of his countenance and his manner, it is probable that her compassion would have been greater. But it was neither in Elinor's power, nor in her wish, to rouse such feelings in another, by her retailed explanation, as had at first been called forth in herself. Reflection had given calmness to her judgment, and sobered her own opinion of Willoughby's deserts; – she wished, therefore, to declare only the simple truth, and lay open such facts as were really due to his character, without any embellishments of tenderness to lead the fancy astray.

In the evening, when they were all three together, Marianne began voluntarily to speak of him again; – but not without an effort, the restless, unquiet thoughtfulness in which she had been for some time previously sitting – her rising colour, as she spoke – and her unsteady voice, plainly shewed.

'I wish to assure you both,' said she, 'that I see every thing – as you can desire me to do.'

Mrs Dashwood would have interrupted her instantly with soothing tenderness, had not Elinor, who really wished to hear her sister's unbiassed opinion, by an eager sign, engaged her silence. Marianne slowly continued –

'It is a great relief to me – what Elinor told me this morning – I have now heard exactly what I wished to hear.' – For some moments her voice was lost; but recovering herself, she added, and with greater calmness than before – 'I am now perfectly satisfied, I wish for no change. I never could have been happy with him, after knowing, as sooner or later I must have known, all this. – I should have had no confidence, no esteem. Nothing could have done it away to my feelings.'

'I know it – I know it,' cried her mother. 'Happy with a man of libertine practices! – With one who had so injured the peace of the dearest of our friends, and the best of men! – No – my Marianne has not a heart to be made happy with such a man! – Her conscience, her sensitive conscience, would have felt all that the conscience of her husband ought to have felt.'

Marianne sighed, and repeated – 'I wish for no change.'

'You consider the matter,' said Elinor, 'exactly as a good mind and a sound understanding must consider it; and I dare say, your perceive, as well as myself, not only in this, but in many other circumstances, reason enough to be convinced that your marriage must have involved you in many certain troubles and disappointments, in which you would have been poorly supported by an affection, on his side, much less certain. Had you married, you must have been always poor. His expensiveness is acknowledged even by himself, and his whole conduct declares that self-denial is a word hardly understood by him. His demands and your inexperience together on a small, very small income, must have brought on distress which would not be the *less* grievous to you, from having been entirely unknown and unthought of before. Your sense of honour and honesty would have led you I know, when aware of your situation, to attempt all the economy that would appear to you possible; and perhaps, as long as your frugality retrenched only on your own comfort, you might have been suffered to practise it, but beyond that – and how little could the utmost of your single management do to stop the ruin which had begun before your marriage? – Beyond *that*, had you endeavoured, however reasonably, to abridge *his* enjoyments, is it not to be feared, that instead of prevailing on feelings so selfish to consent to it, you would have lessened your own influence on his heart, and made him regret the connection which had involved him in such difficulties?'

Marianne's lips quivered, and she repeated the word 'Selfish?' in a tone that implied – 'do you really think him selfish?'

'The whole of his behaviour,' replied Elinor, 'from the beginning to the end of the affair, has been grounded on selfishness. It was selfishness which first made him sport with your affections; which afterwards, when his own were engaged, made him delay the confession of it, and which finally carried him from Barton. His own enjoyment, or his own ease, was, in every particular, his ruling principle.'

'It is very true. *My* happiness never was his object.'

'At present,' continued Elinor, 'he regrets what he has done. And why does he regret it? – Because he finds it has not answered towards himself. It has not made him happy. His circumstances are now unembarrassed – he suffers from no evil of that kind; and he thinks only that he has married a woman of a less amiable temper than yourself. But does it thence follow that had he married you, he would have been happy? – The inconveniences would have been different. He would then have suffered under the pecuniary distresses which, because they are removed, he now reckons as nothing. He would have had a wife of whose temper he could make no complaint, but he would have been always necessitous – always poor; and probably would soon have learnt to rank the innumerable comforts of a clear estate and good income as of far more importance, even to domestic happiness, than the mere temper of a wife.'

'I have not a doubt of it,' said Marianne, 'and I have nothing to regret – nothing but my own folly.'

'Rather say your mother's imprudence, my child,' said Mrs Dashwood; '*she* must be answerable.'

Marianne would not let her proceed; – and Elinor, satisfied that each felt their own error, wished to avoid any survey of the past that might weaken her sister's spirits; she therefore, pursuing the first subject, immediately continued,

'*One* observation may, I think, be fairly drawn from the whole of the story – that all Willoughby's difficulties have arisen from the first offence against virtue, in his behaviour to Eliza Williams. That crime has been the origin of every lesser one, and of all his present discontents.'

Marianne assented most feelingly to the remark; and her mother was led by it to an enumeration of Colonel Brandon's injuries and merits, warm as friendship and design could unitedly dictate. Her daughter did not look, however, as if much of it were heard by her.

Elinor, according to her expectation, saw on the two or three following days, that Marianne did not continue to gain strength as she had done; but while her resolution was unsubdued, and she still tried to appear cheerful and easy, her sister could safely trust to the effect of time upon her health.

Margaret returned, and the family were again all restored to each other, again quietly settled at the cottage, and if not pursuing their usual studies with quite so much vigour as when they first came to Barton, at least planning a vigorous prosecution of them in future.

Elinor grew impatient for some tidings of Edward. She had heard nothing of him since her leaving London, nothing new of his plans, nothing certain even of his present abode. Some letters had passed between her and her brother, in consequence of Marianne's illness; and in the first of John's there had been this sentence: – 'We know nothing of our unfortunate Edward, and can make no enquiries on so prohibited a subject, but conclude him to be still at Oxford;' which was all the intelligence of Edward afforded her by the correspondence, for his name was not even mentioned in any of the succeeding letters. She was not doomed, however, to be long in ignorance of his measures.

Their man-servant had been sent one morning to Exeter on business; and when, as he waited at table, he had satisfied the enquiries of his mistress as to the event of his errand, this was his voluntary communication –

'I suppose you know, ma'am, that Mr Ferrars is married.'

Marianne gave a violent start, fixed her eyes upon Elinor, saw

'I suppose you know, that Mr Ferrars is married.'

her turning pale, and fell back in her chair in hysterics. Mrs Dashwood, whose eyes, as she answered the servant's inquiry, had intuitively taken the same direction, was shocked to perceive by Elinor's countenance how much she really suffered, and in a moment afterwards, alike distressed by Marianne's situation, knew not on which child to bestow her principal attention.

The servant, who saw only that Miss Marianne was taken ill, had sense enough to call one of the maids, who, with Mrs Dashwood's assistance, supported her into the other room. By that time, Marianne was rather better, and her mother leaving her to the care of Margaret and the maid, returned to Elinor, who, though still much disordered, had so far recovered the use of her reason and voice as to be just beginning an inquiry of Thomas, as to the source of his intelligence. Mrs Dashwood immediately took all that trouble on herself; and Elinor had the benefit of the information without the exertion of seeking it.

'Who told you that Mr Ferrars was married, Thomas?'

'I see Mr Ferrars myself, ma'am this morning in Exeter, and his lady too, Miss Steele as was. They was shopping in a chaise at the door of the New London Inn, as I went there with a message from Sally at the Park to her brother, who is one of the post-boys. I happened to look up as I went by the chaise, and so I see directly it was the youngest Miss Steele; so I took off my hat, and she knew me and called to me, and inquired after you, ma'am, and the young ladies, especially Miss Marianne, and bid me I should give her compliments and Mr Ferrars's, their best compliments and service, and how sorry they was they had not time to come on and see you, but they was in a great hurry to go forwards, for they was going further down for a little while, but howsever, when they come back, they'd make sure to come and see you.'

'But did she tell you she was married, Thomas?'

'Yes, ma'am. She smiled, and said how she had changed her name since she was in these parts. She was always a very affable and free-spoken young lady, and very civil behaved. So, I made free to wish her joy.'

'Was Mr Ferrars in the carriage with her?'

'Yes, ma'am, I just see him leaning back in it, but he did not look up; – he never was a gentleman much for talking.'

Elinor's heart could easily account for his not putting himself forward; and Mrs Dashwood probably found the same explanation.

'Was there no one else in the carriage?'

'No, ma'am, only they two.'

'Do you know where they came from?'

'They come straight from town, as Miss Lucy – Mrs Ferrars told me.'

'And are going farther westward?'

'Yes, ma'am – but not to bide long. They will soon be back again, and then they'd be sure and call here.'

Mrs Dashwood now looked at her daughter, but Elinor knew better than to expect them. She recognised the whole of Lucy in the message, and was very confident that Edward would never come near them. She observed, in a low voice, to her mother, that they were probably going down to Mr Pratt's, near Plymouth.

Thomas's intelligence seemed over. Elinor looked as if she wished to hear more.

'Did you see them off, before you came away?'

'No, ma'am – the horses was just coming out, but I could not bide any longer; I was afraid of being late.'

'Did Mrs Ferrars look well?'

'Yes, ma'am, she said how she was very well; and to my mind she was always a very handsome young lady – and she seemed vastly contented.'

Mrs Dashwood could think of no other question, and Thomas and the table-cloth, now alike needless, were soon afterwards dismissed. Marianne had already sent to say that she should eat nothing more. Mrs Dashwood's and Elinor's appetites were equally lost, and Margaret might think herself very well off, that with so much uneasiness as both her sisters had lately experienced, so much reason as they had often had to be careless of their meals, she had never been obliged to go without her dinner before.

When the dessert and the wine were arranged, and Mrs Dashwood and Elinor were left by themselves, they remained long together in a similarity of thoughtfulness and silence. Mrs Dashwood feared to hazard any remark, and ventured not to offer consolation. She now found that she had erred in relying on Elinor's representation of herself; and justly concluded that every thing had been expressly softened at the time, to spare her from an increase of unhappiness, suffered as she then had suffered for Marianne. She found that she had been misled by the careful, the considerate attention of her daughter, to think the attachment, which once she had so well understood, much slighter in reality, than she had been wont to believe, or than it was now proved to be. She feared that under this persuasion she had been unjust, inattentive, nay, almost unkind, to her Elinor; – that Marianne's affliction, because more acknowledged, more immediately before her, had too much engrossed her tenderness, and led her away to forget than in Elinor she might have a daughter suffering almost as much, certainly with less self-provocation, and greater fortitude.

CHAPTER FORTY-EIGHT

ELINOR NOW FOUND THE difference between the expectation of an unpleasant event, however certain the mind may be told to consider it, and certainty itself. She now found, that in spite of herself, she had always admitted a hope, while Edward remained single, that something would occur to prevent his marrying Lucy; that some resolution of his own, some mediation of friends, or some more eligible opportunity of establishment for the lady, would arise to assist the happiness of all, but he was now married, and she condemned her heart for the lurking flattery, which so much heightened the pain of the intelligence.

That he should be married so soon, before (as she imagined) he could be in orders, and consequently before he could be in possession of the living, surprised her a little at first. But she soon saw how likely it was that Lucy, in her self-provident care, in her haste to secure him, should overlook every thing but the risk of delay. They were married, married in town, and now hastening down to her uncle's. What had Edward felt on being within four miles of Barton, on seeing her mother's servant, on hearing Lucy's message!

They would soon, she supposed, be settled at Delaford. – Delaford, – that place in which so much conspired to give her an interest; which she wished to be acquainted with, and yet desired to avoid. She saw them in an instant in their parsonage-house; saw in Lucy, the active, contriving manager, uniting at once a desire of smart appearance, with the utmost frugality, and ashamed to be suspected of half her economical practices; – pursuing her own interest in every thought, courting the favour of Colonel Brandon, of Mrs Jennings, and of every wealthy friend. In Edward – she knew not what she saw, nor what she wished to see; – happy or unhappy, – nothing pleased her; she turned away her head from every sketch of him.

Elinor flattered herself that some one of their connection in London would write to them to announce the event, and give farther particulars, – but day after day passed off, and brought no letter, no tidings. Though uncertain that any one were to blame, she found fault with every absent friend. They were all thoughtless or indolent.

It was *Edward.*

'When do you write to Colonel Brandon, ma'am?' was an enquiry which sprung from the impatience of her mind to have something going on.

'I wrote to him, my love, last week, and rather expected to see, than to hear from him again. I earnestly pressed his coming to us, and should not be surprised to see him walk in today or tomorrow, or any day.'

This was gaining something, something to look forward to. Colonel Brandon *must* have some information to give.

Scarcely had she so determined it, when the figure of a man on horseback drew her eyes to the window. He stopt at their gate. It was a gentleman, it was Colonel Brandon himself. Now she should hear more; and she trembled in expectation of it. But – it was *not* Colonel Brandon – neither his air – nor his height. Were it possible, she should say it must be Edward. She looked again. He had just dismounted; – she could not be mistaken; – it *was* Edward. She moved away and sat down. 'He comes from Mr Pratt's purposely to see us. I *will* be calm; I *I will* be mistress of myself.'

In a moment she perceived that the others were likewise aware of the mistake. She saw her mother and Marianne change colour; saw them look at herself, and whisper a few sentences to each other. She would have given the world to be able to speak – and to make them understand that she hoped no coolness, no slight, would appear in their behaviour to him; – but she had no utterance, and was obliged to leave all to their own discretion.

Not a syllable passed aloud. They all waited in silence for the appearance of their visitor. His footsteps were heard along the gravel path; in a moment he was in the passage; and in another, he was before them.

His countenance, as he entered the room, was not too happy, even for Elinor. His complexion was white with agitation, and he looked as if fearful of his reception, and conscious that he merited no kind one. Mrs Dashwood, however, conforming, as she trusted, to the wishes of that daughter, by whom she then meant in the warmth of her heart to be guided in everything, met him with a look of forced complacency, gave him her hand, and wished him joy.

He coloured, and stammered out an unintelligible reply. Elinor's lips had moved with her mother's, and when the moment of action was over, she wished that she had shaken hands with him too. But it was then too late, and with a countenance meaning to be open, she sat down again and talked of the weather.

Marianne had retreated as much as possible out of sight, to conceal her distress, and Margaret, understanding some part, but not the whole, of the case, thought it incumbent on her to be dignified, and therefore took a seat as far from him as she could, and maintained a strict silence.

When Elinor had ceased to rejoice in the dryness of the season, a very awful pause took place. It was put an end to by Mrs Dashwood, who felt obliged to hope that he had left Mrs Ferrars very well. In a hurried manner, he replied in the affirmative.

Another pause.

Elinor, resolving to exert herself, though fearing the sound of her own voice, now said,

'Is Mrs Ferrars at Longstaple?'

'At Longstaple!' he replied, with an air of surprise – 'No, my mother is in town.'

'I meant,' said Elinor, taking up some work from the table, 'to inquire after Mrs *Edward* Ferrars.'

She dared not look up; – but her mother and Marianne both turned their eyes on him. He coloured, seemed perplexed, looked doubtingly, and after some hesitation, said,

'Perhaps you mean – my brother – you mean Mrs – Mrs *Robert* Ferrars.'

'Mrs Robert Ferrars!' – was repeated by Marianne and her mother, in an accent of the utmost amazement; – and though Elinor could not speak, even *her* eyes were fixed on him with the same impatient wonder. He rose from his seat and walked to the window, apparently from not knowing what to do; took up a pair of scissars that lay there, and while spoiling both them and their sheath by cutting the latter to pieces as he spoke, said, in an hurried voice,

'Perhaps you do not know – you may not have heard that my brother is lately married to – to the youngest – to Miss Lucy Steele.'

His words were echoed with unspeakable astonishment by all but Elinor, who sat with her head leaning over her work, in a state of such agitation as made her hardly know where she was.

'Yes,' said he, 'they were married last week, and are now at Dawlish.'

Elinor could sit no longer. She almost ran out of the room, and as soon as the door was closed, burst into tears of joy, which at first she thought would never cease. Edward, who had till then looked any where, rather than at her, saw her hurry away, and perhaps saw – or even heard, her emotion; for immediately afterwards he fell into a reverie, which no remarks, no inquiries, no affectionate address of Mrs Dashwood could penetrate, and at last, without saying a word, quitted the room, and walked out towards the village – leaving the others in the greatest astonishment and perplexity on a change in his situation, so wonderful and so sudden; – a perplexity which they had no means of lessening but by their own conjectures.

CHAPTER FORTY-NINE

UNACCOUNTABLE, HOWEVER, AS the circumstances of his release might appear to the whole family, it was certain that Edward was free: and to what purpose that freedom would be employed was easily pre-determined by all; – for after experiencing the blessing of *one* imprudent engagement, contracted without his mother's consent, as he had already done for more than four years, nothing less could be expected of him in the failure of *that*, than the immediate contraction of another.

His errand at Barton, in fact, was a simple one. It was only to ask Elinor to marry him; – and considering that he was not altogether inexperienced in such a question, it might be strange that he should feel so uncomfortable in the present case as he really did, so much in need of encouragement and fresh air.

How soon he had walked himself into the proper resolution, however, how soon an opportunity of exercising it occurred, in what manner he expressed himself, and how he was received, need not be particularly told. This only need be said; – that when they all sat down to table at four o'clock, about three hours after his arrival, he had secured his lady, engaged her mother's consent, and was not only in the rapturous profession of the lover, but in the reality of reason and truth, one of the happiest of men. His situation indeed was more than commonly joyful. He had more than the ordinary triumph of accepted love to swell his heart, and raise his spirits. He was released without any reproach to himself from an entanglement which had long formed his misery, from a woman whom he had long ceased to love; – and elevated at once to that security with another, which he must have thought of almost with despair, as soon as he had learnt to consider it with desire. He was brought, not from doubt or suspense, but from misery to happiness; – and the change was openly spoken in such a genuine, flowing, grateful cheerfulness, as his friends had never witnessed in him before.

His heart was now open to Elinor, all its weaknesses, all its errors confessed, and his first boyish attachment to Lucy treated with all the philosophic dignity of twenty-four.

'It was a foolish, idle inclination on my side,' said he, 'the consequence of ignorance of the world – and want of employment. Had my mother given me some active profession when I was removed at eighteen from the care of Mr Pratt, I think – nay, I am sure, it would never have happened; for though I left Longstaple with what I thought, at the time, a most unconquerable preference for his niece, yet had I then had any pursuit, any object to engage my time and keep me at a distance from her for a few months, I should very soon have outgrown the fancied attachment, especially by mixing more with the world, as in such a case I must have done. But instead of having anything to do, instead of having any profession chosen for me, or being allowed to chuse any myself, I returned home to be completely idle; and for the first twelvemonth afterwards, I had not even the nominal employment, which belonging to the university would have given me, for I was not entered at Oxford till I was nineteen. I had therefore nothing in the world to do, but to fancy myself in love; and as my mother did not make my home in every respect comfortable, as I had no friend, no companion in my brother, and disliked new acquaintance, it was not unnatural for me to be very often at Longstaple, where I always felt myself at home, and was always sure of a welcome; and accordingly I spent the greatest part of my time there from eighteen to nineteen: Lucy appeared everything that was amiable and obliging. She was pretty too – at least I thought so *then*, and I had seen so little of other women, that I could make no comparisons, and see no defects. Considering everything, therefore, I hope, foolish as our engagement was, foolish as it has since in every way been proved, it was not at the time an unnatural, or an inexcusable piece of folly.'

The change which a few hours had wrought in the minds and the happiness of the Dashwoods, was such – so great – as promised them all, the satisfaction of a sleepless night. Mrs Dashwood, too happy to be comfortable, knew not how to love Edward, nor praise Elinor enough, how to be enough thankful for his release without wounding his delicacy, nor how at once to give them leisure for unrestrained conversation together, and yet enjoy, as she wished, the sight and society of both.

Marianne could speak *her* happiness only by tears. Comparisons would occur – regrets would arise; – and her joy, though sincere as her love for her sister, was of a kind to give her neither spirits nor language.

But Elinor – How are *her* feelings to be described? – From the moment of learning that Lucy was married to another, that Edward was free, to the moment of his justifying the hopes which had so instantly followed, she was everything by turns but tranquil. But when the second moment had passed, when she found every doubt, every solicitude removed, compared her situation with what so lately it had been, – saw him honourably released from his former engagement, saw him instantly profiting by the release, to address herself and declare an affection as tender, as constant as she had ever supposed it to be, – she was oppressed, she was overcome by her own felicity; – and happily disposed as is the human mind to be easily familiarized with any change for the better, it required several hours to give sedateness to her spirits, or any degree of tranquillity to her heart.

Edward was now fixed at the cottage at least for a week; – for whatever other claims might be made on him, it was impossible that less than a week should be given up to the enjoyment of Elinor's company, or suffice to say half that was to be said of the past, the present, and the future; – for though a very few hours spent in the hard labour of incessant talking will dispatch more subjects than can really be in common between any two rational creatures, yet with lovers it is different. Between *them* no subject is finished, no communication is even made, till it has been made at least twenty times over.

Lucy's marriage, the unceasing and reasonable wonder among them all, formed of course one of the earliest discussions of the lovers; – and Elinor's particular knowledge of each party made it appear to her in every view, as one of the most extraordinary and unaccountable circumstances she had ever heard. How they could be thrown together, and by what attraction Robert could be drawn on to marry a girl, of whose beauty she had herself heard him speak without any admiration, – a girl too already engaged to his brother, and on whose account that brother had been thrown off by his family – it was beyond her comprehension to make out. To her own heart it was a delightful affair, to her imagination it was even a ridiculous one, but to her reason, her judgment, it was completely a puzzle.

Edward could only attempt an explanation by supposing, that perhaps at first accidentally meeting, the vanity of the one had been so worked on by the flattery of the other, as to lead by degrees to all the rest. Elinor remembered what Robert had told her in Harley-street, of his opinion of what his own mediation in his brother's affairs might have done, if applied to in time. She repeated it to Edward.

'*That* was exactly like Robert,' – was his immediate observation. – 'And *that*,' he presently added, 'might perhaps be in *his* head when the acquaintance between them first began. And Lucy perhaps at first might think only of procuring his good offices in my favour. Other designs might afterwards arise.'

How long it had been carrying on between them however, he was equally at a loss with herself to make out; for at Oxford, where he had remained by choice ever since his quitting London, he had no means of hearing of her but from herself, and her letters to the very last were neither less frequent, nor less affectionate than usual. Not the smallest suspicion, therefore, had ever occurred to prepare him for what followed; – and when at last it burst on him in a letter from Lucy herself, he had been for some time, he believed, half stupified between the wonder, the horror, and the joy of such a deliverance. He put the letter into Elinor's hands.

Dear Sir

Being very sure I have long lost your affections, I have thought myself at liberty to bestow my own on another, and have no doubt of being as happy with him as I once used to think I might be with you; but I scorn to accept a hand while the heart was another's. Sincerely wish you happy in your choice, and it shall not be my fault if we are not always good friends, as our near relationship now makes proper. I can safely say I owe you no ill-will, and am sure you will be too generous to do us any ill offices. Your brother has gained my affections entirely, and as we could not live without one another, we are just returned from the altar, and are now on our way to Dawlish for a few weeks, which place your dear brother has great curiosity to see, but thought I would first trouble you with these few lines, and shall always remain,

Your sincere well-wisher, friend, and sister,

Lucy Ferrars.

I have burnt all your letters, and will return your picture the first opportunity. Please to destroy my scrawls – but the ring with my hair you are very welcome to keep.

Elinor read and returned it without any comment.

'I will not ask your opinion of it as a composition,' said Edward. – 'For worlds would not I have had a letter of her's seen by *you* in former days. – In a sister it is bad enough, but in a wife! – how I have blushed over the pages of her writing! – and I believe I may say that since the first half year of our foolish – business – this is the only letter I ever received from her, of which the substance made me any amends for the defect of the style.'

'However it may have come about,' said Elinor, after a pause –

'they are certainly married. And your mother has brought on her a most appropriate punishment. The independence she settled on Robert, through resentment against you, has put it in his power to make his own choice; and she has actually been bribing one son with a thousand a-year, to do the very deed which she disinherited the other for intending to do. She will hardly be less hurt, I suppose, by Robert's marrying Lucy, than she would have been by your marrying her.'

'She will be more hurt by it, for Robert always was her favourite. – She will be more hurt by it, and on the same principle will forgive him much sooner.'

In what state the affair stood at present between them, Edward knew not, for no communication with any of his family had yet been attempted by him. He had quitted Oxford within four and twenty hours after Lucy's letter arrived, and with only one object before him, the nearest road to Barton, had had no leisure to form any scheme of conduct, with which that road did not hold the most intimate connection. He could do nothing till he were assured of his fate with Miss Dashwood; and by his rapidity in seeking *that* fate, it is to be supposed, in spite of the jealousy with which he had once thought of Colonel Brandon, in spite of the modesty with which he rated his own deserts, and the politeness with which he talked of his doubts, he did not, upon the whole, expect a very cruel reception. It was his business, however, to say that he *did*, and he said it very prettily. What he might say on the subject a twelvemonth after, must be referred to the imagination of husbands and wives.

That Lucy had certainly meant to deceive, to go off with a flourish of malice against him in her message by Thomas, was perfectly clear to Elinor; and Edward himself, now thoroughly enlightened on her character, had no scruple in believing her capable of the utmost meanness of wanton ill-nature. Though his eyes had been long opened, even before his acquaintance with Elinor began, to her ignorance and a want of liberality in some of her opinions – they had been equally imputed, by him, to her want of education; and till her last letter reached him, he had always believed her to be a well-disposed, good-hearted girl, and thoroughly attached to himself. Nothing but such a persuasion could have prevented his putting an end to an engagement, which, long before the discovery of it laid him open to his mother's anger, had been a continual source of disquiet and regret to him.

'I thought it my duty,' said he, 'independent of my feelings, to give her the option of continuing the engagement or not, when I was renounced by my mother, and stood to all appearance without a friend in the world to assist me. In such a situation as that, where there seemed nothing to tempt the avarice of the vanity of any living creature, how could I suppose, when she so earnestly, so warmly insisted on sharing my fate, whatever it might be, that any thing but the most disinterested affection was her inducement? And even now, I cannot comprehend on what motive she acted, or what fancied advantage it could be to her, to be fettered to a man for whom she had not the smallest regard, and who had only two thousand pounds in the world. She could not foresee that Colonel Brandon would give me a living.'

'No, but she might suppose that something would occur in your favour, that your own family might in time relent. And at any rate, she lost nothing by continuing the engagement, for she has proved that it fettered neither her inclination or her actions. The connection was certainly a respectable one, and probably gained her consideration among her friends; and, if nothing more advantageous occurred, it would be better for her to marry *you* than be single.'

Edward was of course immediately convinced that nothing could have been more natural than Lucy's conduct, nor more self-evident than the motive of it.

Elinor scolded him, harshly as ladies always scold the imprudence which compliments themselves, for having spent so much time with them at Norland, when he must have felt his own inconstancy.

'Your behaviour was certainly very wrong,' said she, 'because – to say nothing of my own conviction, our relations were all led away by it to fancy and expect *what*, as you were *then* situated, could never be.'

He could only plead an ignorance of his own heart, and a mistaken confidence in the force of his engagement.

'I was simple enough to think, that because my *faith* was plighted to another, there could be no danger in my being with you; and that the consciousness of my engagement was to keep my heart as safe and sacred as my honour. I felt that I admired you, but I told myself it was only friendship; and till I began to make comparisons between yourself and Lucy, I did not know how far I was got. After that, I suppose, I *was* wrong in remaining so much in Sussex, and the arguments with which I reconciled myself to the expediency of it, were no better than these: – The danger is my own; I am doing no injury to anybody but myself.'

Elinor smiled, and shook her head.

Edward heard with pleasure of Colonel Brandon's being expected at the Cottage, as he really wished not only to be better acquainted with him, but to have an opportunity of convincing him that he no longer resented his giving him the living of Delaford – 'Which, at present,' said he, 'after thanks so ungraciously delivered as mine were on the occasion, he must think I have never forgiven him for offering.'

Now he felt astonished himself that he had never yet been to the place. But so little interest had he taken in the matter, that he owed all his knowledge of the house, garden, and glebe, extent of the parish, condition of the land, and rate of the tythes, to Elinor herself, who had heard so much of it from Colonel Brandon, and heard it with so much attention, as to be entirely mistress of the subject.

One question after this only remained undecided, between them, one difficulty only was to be overcome. They were brought together by mutual affection, with the warmest approbation of their real friends, their intimate knowledge of each other seemed to make their happiness certain – and they only wanted something to live upon. Edward had two thousand pounds, and Elinor one, which, with Delaford living, was all that they could call their own; for it was impossible that Mrs Dashwood should advance anything, and they were neither of them quite enough in love to think that three hundred and fifty pounds a-year would supply them with the comforts of life.

Edward was not entirely without hopes of some favourable change in his mother towards him; and on *that* he rested for the residue of their income. But Elinor had no such dependance, for since Edward would still be unable to marry Miss Morton, and his chusing herself had been spoken of in Mrs Ferrar's flattering language as only a lesser evil than his chusing Lucy Steele, she feared that Robert's offence would serve no other purpose than to enrich Fanny.

About four days after Edward's arrival, Colonel Brandon appeared, to complete Mrs Dashwood's satisfaction, and to give her the dignity of having, for the first time since her living at Barton, more company with her than the house would hold. Edward was allowed to retain the privilege of first comer, and Colonel Brandon therefore walked every night to his old quarters at the Park; from whence he usually returned in the morning, early enough to interrupt the lovers' first tête-à-tête before breakfast.

A three weeks' residence at Delaford, where, in his evening hours at least, he had little to do but to calculate the disproportion between thirty-six and seventeen, brought him to Barton in a temper of mind which needed all the improvement in Marianne's looks, all the kindness of her welcome, and all the encouragement of her mother's language, to make it cheerful. Among such friends, however, and such flattery, he did revive. No rumour of Lucy's marriage had yet reached him; – he knew nothing of what had passed; and the first hours of his visit were consequently spent in hearing and in wondering. Every thing was explained to him by Mrs Dashwood, and he found fresh reason to rejoice in what he had done for Mr Ferrars, since eventually it promoted the interest of Elinor.

It would be needless to say, that the gentlemen advanced in the good opinion of each other, as they advanced in each other's acquaintance, for it could not be otherwise. Their resemblance in good principles and good sense, in disposition and manner of thinking, would probably have been sufficient to unite them in friendship, without any other attraction; but their being in love with two sisters, and two sisters fond of each other, made that mutual regard inevitable and immediate, which might otherwise have waited the effect of time and judgment.

The letters from town, which a few days before would have made every nerve in Elinor's body thrill with transport, now arrived to be read with less emotion than mirth. Mrs Jennings wrote to tell the wonderful tale, to vent her honest indignation against the jilting girl, and pour forth her compassion towards poor Mr Edward, who, she was sure, had quite doted upon the worthless hussey, and was now, by all accounts, almost broken-hearted, at Oxford. – 'I do think,' she continued, 'nothing was ever carried on so sly; for it was but two days before Lucy called and sat a couple of hours with me. Not a soul suspected anything of the matter, not even Nancy, who, poor soul! came crying to me the day after, in a great fright for fear of Mrs Ferrars, as well as not knowing how to get to Plymouth; for Lucy it seems borrowed all her money before she went off to be married, on purpose we suppose to make a shew with, and poor Nancy had not seven shillings in the world; – so I was very glad to give her five guineas to take her down to Exeter, where she thinks of staying three or four weeks with Mrs Burgess, in hopes, as I tell her, to fall in with the Doctor again. And I must say that Lucy's crossness not to take her along with them in the chaise is worse than all. Poor Mr Edward! I cannot get him out of my head, but you must send for him to Barton, and Miss Marianne must try to comfort him.'

Mr Dashwood's strains were more solemn. Mrs Ferrars was the most unfortunate of women – poor Fanny had suffered agonies of sensibility – and he considered the existence of each, under such a blow, with grateful wonder. Robert's offence was unpardonable, but Lucy's was infinitely worse. Neither of them was ever again to be mentioned to Mrs Ferrars; and even, if she might hereafter be induced to forgive her son, his wife should never be acknowledged as her daughter, nor be permitted to appear in her presence. The secrecy with which every thing had been carried on between them, was rationally treated as enormously heightening the crime, because, had any suspicion of it occurred to the others, proper measures would have been taken to prevent the marriage; and he called on Elinor to join with him in regretting that Lucy's engagement with Edward had not rather been fulfilled, than that she should thus be the means of spreading misery farther in the family. – He thus continued:

'Mrs Ferrars has never yet mentioned Edward's name, which does not surprise us; but to our great astonishment, not a line has been received from him on the occasion. Perhaps, however, he is kept silent by his fear of offending, and I shall, therefore, give him a hint, by a line to Oxford, that his sister and I both think a letter of proper submission from him, addressed perhaps to Fanny, and by her shewn to her mother, might not be taken amiss; for we all know the tenderness of Mrs Ferrars's heart, and that she wishes for nothing so much as to be on good terms with her children.'

This paragraph was of some importance to the prospects and conduct of Edward. It determined him to attempt a reconciliation, though not exactly in the manner pointed out by their brother and sister.

'A letter of proper submission!' repeated he; 'would they have me beg my mother's pardon for Robert's ingratitude to *her*, and breach of honour to *me*? – I can make no submission – I am grown neither humble nor penitent by what has passed. – I am grown very happy, but that would not interest. – I know of no submission that *is* proper for me to make.'

'You may certainly ask to be forgiven,' said Elinor, 'because you have offended; – and I should think you might *now* venture so far as to profess some concern for having ever formed the engagement which drew on you your mother's anger.'

He agreed that he might.

'And when she has forgiven you, perhaps a little humility may be convenient while acknowledging a second engagement, almost as imprudent in *her* eyes, as the first.'

He had nothing to urge against it, but still resisted the idea of a letter of proper submission; and therefore, to make it easier to him, as he declared a much greater willingness to make mean concessions by word of mouth than on paper, it was resolved that, instead of writing to Fanny, he should go to London, and personally intreat her good offices in his favour. – 'And if they really *do* interest themselves,' said Marianne, in her new character of candour, 'in bringing about a reconciliation, I shall think that even John and Fanny are not entirely without merit.'

After a visit on Colonel Brandon's side of only three or four days, the two gentlemen quitted Barton together. – They were to go immediately to Delaford, that Edward might have some personal knowledge of his future home, and assist his patron and friend in deciding on what improvements were needed to it; and from thence, after staying there a couple of nights, he was to proceed on his journey to town.

CHAPTER FIFTY

AFTER A PROPER RESISTANCE on the part of Mrs Ferrars, just so violent and so steady as to preserve her from that reproach while she always seemed fearful of incurring, the reproach of being too amiable, Edward was admitted to her presence, and pronounced to be again her son.

Her family had of late been exceedingly fluctuating. For many years of her life she had had two sons; but the crime and annihilation of Edward a few weeks ago, had robbed her of one; the similar annihilation of Robert had left her for a fortnight without any; and now, by the resuscitation of Edward, she had one again.

In spite of his being allowed once more to live, however, he did not feel the continuance of his existence secure, till he had revealed his present engagement; for the publication of that circumstance, he feared, might give a sudden turn to his constitution, and carry him off as rapidly as before. With apprehensive caution therefore it was revealed, and he was listened to with unexpected calmness. Mrs Ferrars at first reasonably endeavoured to dissuade him from marrying Miss Dashwood, by every argument in her power; – told him, that in Miss Morton he would have a woman of higher rank and larger fortune; – and enforced the assertion, by observing that Miss Morton was the daughter of a nobleman with thirty thousand pounds, while Miss Dashwood was only the daughter of a private gentleman, with no more than *three*; but when she found that, though perfectly admitting the truth of her representation, he was by no means inclined to be guided by it, she judged it wisest, from the experience of the past, to submit – and therefore, after such an ungracious delay as she owed to her own dignity, and as served to prevent every suspicion of good-will, she issued her decree of consent to the marriage of Edward and Elinor.

What she would engage to do towards augmenting their income, was next to be considered; and here it plainly appeared, that though Edward was now her only son, he was by no means her eldest; for while Robert was inevitably endowed with a thousand pounds a-year, not the smallest objection was made against Edward's taking orders for the sake of two hundred and fifty at the utmost; nor was anything promised either for the present or in future, beyond the ten thousand pounds, which had been given with Fanny.

It was as much, however, as was desired, and more than was expected by Edward and Elinor; and Mrs Ferrars herself, by her shuffling excuses, seemed the only person surprised at her not giving more.

With an income quite sufficient to their wants thus secured to them, they had nothing to wait for after Edward was in possession of the living, but the readiness of the house, to which Colonel Brandon, with an eager desire for the accommodation of Elinor, was making considerable improvements; and after waiting some time for their completion, after experiencing, as usual, a thousand disappointments and delays, from the unaccountable dilatoriness of the workmen, Elinor, as usual, broke through the first positive resolution of not marrying till every thing was ready, and the ceremony took place in Barton church early in the autumn.

The first month after their marriage was spent with their friend at the Mansion-house, from whence they could superintend the progress of the Parsonage, and direct every thing as they liked on the spot; – could chuse papers, project shrubberies, and invent a sweep. Mrs Jennings's prophecies, though rather jumbled together, were chiefly fulfilled; for she was able to visit Edward and his wife in their Parsonage by Michaelmas, and she found in Elinor and her husband, as she really believed, one of the happiest couple in the world. They had in fact nothing to wish for, but the marriage of Colonel Brandon and Marianne, and rather better pasturage for their cows.

They were visited on their first settling by almost all their relations and friends. Mrs Ferrars came to inspect the happiness which she was almost ashamed of having authorised; and even the Dashwoods were at the expense of a journey from Sussex to do them honour.

'I will not say that I am disappointed, my dear sister,' said John, as they were walking together one morning before the gates of Delaford House, '*that* would be saying too much, for certainly you have been one of the most fortunate young women in the world, as it is. But, I confess, it would give me great pleasure to call Colonel Brandon brother. His property here, his place, his house, every thing in such respectable and excellent condition! – and his woods! – I have not seen such timber any where in Dorsetshire, as there is now standing in Delaford Hanger! – And though, perhaps, Marianne may not seem exactly the person to attract him – yet I think it would altogether be adviseable for you to have them now frequently staying with you, for as Colonel Brandon seems a great deal at home, nobody can tell what may happen – for, when people are much thrown together, and see little of any body else – and it will always be in your power to set her off to advantage, and so forth; – in short, you may as well give her a chance – You understand me' –

'Everything in such respectable condition.'

But though Mrs Ferrars *did* come to see them, and always treated them with the make-believe of decent affection, they were never insulted by her real favour and preference. *That* was due to the folly of Robert, and the cunning of his wife; and it was earned by them before many months had passed away. The selfish sagacity of the latter, which had at first drawn Robert into the scrape, was the principal instrument of his deliverance from it; for her respectful humility, assiduous attentions, and endless flatteries, as soon as the smallest opening was given for their exercise, reconciled Mrs Ferrars to his choice, and re-established him completely in her favour.

The whole of Lucy's behaviour in the affair, and the prospertiy which crowned it, therefore, may be held forth as a most encouraging instance of what an earnest, an unceasing attention to self-interest, however its progress may be apparently obstructed, will do in securing every advantage of fortune, with no other sacrifice than that of time and conscience. When Robert first sought her acquaintance, and privately visited her in Bartlett's Buildings, it was only with the view imputed to him by his brother. He merely meant to persuade her to give up the engagement; and as there could be nothing to overcome but the affection of both, he naturally expected that one or two interviews would settle the matter. In that point, however, and that only, he erred; – for though Lucy soon gave him hopes that his eloquence would convince her in *time*, another visit, another conversation, was always wanted to produce this conviction. Some doubts always lingered in her mind when they parted, which could only be removed by another half hour's discourse with himself. His attendance was by this means secured, and the rest followed in course. Instead of talking of Edward, they came gradually to talk only of Robert, – a subject on which he had always more to say than on any other, and in which she soon betrayed an interest even equal to his own; and in short, it became speedily evident to both, that he had entirely supplanted his brother. He was proud of his conquest, proud of tricking Edward, and very proud of marrying privately without his mother's consent. What immediately followed is known. They passed some months in great happiness at Dawlish; for she had many relations and old acquaintance to cut – and he drew several plans for magnificent cottages; – and from thence returning to town, procured the forgiveness of Mrs Ferrars, by the simple expedient of asking it, which, at Lucy's instigation, was adopted. The forgiveness at first, indeed, as was reasonable, comprehended only Robert; and Lucy, who had owed his mother no duty, and therefore could have transgressed none, still remained some weeks longer unpardoned. But perseverance in humility of conduct and messages, in self-condemnation for Robert's offence, and gratitude for the unkindness she was treated with, procured her in time the haughty notice which overcame her by its graciousness, and led soon afterwards, by rapid degrees, to the highest state of affection and influence. Lucy became as necessary to Mrs Ferrars, as either Robert or Fanny; and while Edward was never cordially forgiven for having once intended to marry her, and Elinor, though superior to her in fortune and birth, was spoken of as an intruder, *she* was in every thing considered, and always openly acknowledged, to be a favourite child. They settled in town, received very liberal assistance from Mrs Ferrars, were on the best terms imaginable with the Dashwoods; and setting aside the jealousies and ill-will continually subsisting between Fanny and Lucy, in which their husbands of course took a part, as well as the frequent domestic disagreements between Robert and Lucy themselves, nothing could exceed the harmony in which they all lived together.

What Edward had done to forfeit the right of eldest son, might have puzzled many people to find out; and what Robert had done to succeed to it, might have puzzled them still more. It was an arrangement, however, justified in its effects, if not in its cause, for nothing ever appeared in Robert's style of living or of talking, to give a suspicion of his regretting the extent of his income, as either leaving his brother too little, or bringing himself too much; – and if Edward might be judged from the ready discharge of his duties in every particular, from an increasing attachment to his wife and his home, and from the regular cheerfulness of his spirits, he might be supposed no less contented with his lot, no less free from every wish of an exchange.

Elinor's marriage divided her as little from her family as could well be contrived, without rendering the cottage at Barton entirely useless, for her mother and sisters spent much more than half their time with her. Mrs Dashwood was acting on motives of policy as well as pleasure in the frequency of her visits at Delaford; for her wish of bringing Marianne and Colonel Brandon together was hardly less earnest, though rather more liberal than what John had expressed. It was now her darling object. Precious as was the company of her daughter to her, she desired nothing so much as to give up its constant enjoyment to her valued friend; and to see Marianne settled at the mansion-house was equally the wish of Edward and Elinor. They each felt his sorrows, and their own obligations, and Marianne, by general consent, was to be the reward of all.

With such a confederacy against her – with a knowledge so intimate of his goodness – with a conviction of his fond attachment to herself, which at last, though long after it was observable to everybody else – burst on her – what could she do?

Marianne Dashwood was born to an extraordinary fate. She was born to discover the falsehood of her own opinions, and to counteract, by her conduct, her most favourite maxims. She was born to overcome an affection formed so late in life as at seventeen, and with no sentiment superior to strong esteem and lively friendship, voluntarily to give her hand to another! – and *that* other, a man who had suffered no less than herself under the event of a former attachment, whom, two years before, she had considered too old to be married, – and who still sought the constitutional safeguard of a flannel waistcoat!

But so it was. Instead of falling a sacrifice to an irresistible passion, as once she had fondly flattered herself with expecting, – instead of remaining even for ever with her mother, and finding her only pleasures in retirement and study, as afterwards in her more calm and sober judgment she had determined on, – she found herself at nineteen, submitting to new attachments, entering on new duties, placed in a new home, a wife, the mistress of a family, and the patroness of a village.

Colonel Brandon was now as happy, as all those who best loved him, believed he deserved to be; – in Marianne he was consoled for every past affliction; – her regard and her society restored his mind to animation, and his spirits to cheerfulness; and that Marianne found her own happiness in forming his, was equally the persuasion and delight of each observing friend. Marianne could never love by halves, and her whole heart became, in time, as much devoted to her husband, as it had once been to Willoughby.

Willoughby could not hear of her marriage without a pang; and his punishment was soon afterwards complete in the voluntary forgiveness of Mrs Smith, who, by stating his marriage with a woman of character, as the source of her clemency, gave him reason for believing that had he behaved with honour towards Marianne, he might at once have been happy and rich. That his repentance of misconduct, which thus brought its own punishment, was sincere, need not be doubted; – nor that he long thought of Colonel Brandon with envy, and of Marianne with regret. But that he was for ever inconsolable, that he fled from society, or contracted an habitual gloom of temper, or died of a broken heart, must not be depended on – for he did neither. He lived to exert, and frequently to enjoy himself. His wife was not always out of humour, nor his home always uncomfortable; and in his breed of horses and dogs, and in sporting of every kind, he found no inconsiderable degree of domestic felicity.

For Marianne, however – in spite of his incivility in surviving her loss – he always retained that decided regard which interested him in everything that befell her, and made her his secret standard of perfection in woman; – and many a rising beauty would be slighted by him in after-days as bearing no comparison with Mrs Brandon.

Mrs Dashwood was prudent enough to remain at the cottage, without attempting a removal to Delaford; and fortunately for Sir John and Mrs Jennings, when Marianne was taken from them, Margaret had reached an age highly suitable for dancing, and not very ineligible for being supposed to have a lover.

Between Barton and Delaford, there was that constant communication which strong family affection would naturally dictate; – and among the merits and the happiness of Elinor and Marianne, let it not be ranked as the least considerable, that though sisters, and living almost within sight of each other, they could live without disagreement between themselves, or producing coolness between their husbands.

Emma

CHAPTER ONE

Emma Woodhouse, handsome, clever, and rich, with a comfortable home and happy disposition, seemed to unite some of the best blessings of existence; and had lived nearly twenty-one years in the world with very little to distress or vex her.

She was the youngest of the two daughters of a most affectionate, indulgent father, and had, in consequence of her sister's marriage, been mistress of his house from a very early period. Her mother had died too long ago for her to have more than an indistinct remembrance of her caresses, and her place had been supplied by an excellent woman as governess, who had fallen little short of a mother in affection.

Sixteen years had Miss Taylor been in Mr Woodhouse's family, less as a governess than a friend, very fond of both daughters, but particularly of Emma. Between *them* it was more the intimacy of sisters. Even before Miss Taylor had ceased to hold the nominal office of governess, the mildness of her temper had hardly allowed her to impose any restraint; and the shadow of authority being now long passed away, they had been living together as friend and friend very mutually attached, and Emma doing just what she liked; highly esteeming Miss Taylor's judgment, but directed chiefly by her own.

The real evils indeed of Emma's situation were the power of having rather too much of her own way, and a disposition to think a little too well of herself; these were the disadvantages which threatened alloy to her many enjoyments. The danger, however, was at present so unperceived, that they did not by any means rank as misfortunes with her.

Sorrow came – a gentle sorrow – but not all in the shape of any disagreeable consciousness. – Miss Taylor married. It was Miss Taylor's loss which first brought grief. It was on the wedding-day of this beloved friend that Emma first sat in mournful thought of any continuance. The wedding over and the bride-people gone, her father and herself were left to dine together, with no prospect of a third to cheer a long evening. Her father composed himself to sleep after dinner, as usual, and she had then only to sit and think of what she had lost.

The event had every promise of happiness for her friend. Mr Weston was a man of unexceptionable character, easy fortune, suitable age and pleasant manners; and there was some satisfaction in considering with what self-denying, generous friendship she had always wished and promoted the match; but it was a black morning's work for her. The want of Miss Taylor would be felt every hour of every day. She recalled her past kindness – the kindness, the affection of sixteen years – how she had taught and how she had played with her from five years old – how she had devoted all her powers to attach and amuse her in health – and how nursed her through the various illnesses of childhood. A large debt of gratitude was owing here; but the intercourse of the last seven years, the equal footing and perfect unreserve which had soon followed Isabella's marriage on their being left to each other, was yet a dearer, tenderer recollection. It had been a friend and companion such as few possessed, intelligent, well-informed, useful, gentle, knowing all the ways of the family, interested in all its concerns, and peculiarly interested in herself, in every pleasure, every scheme of her's; – one to whom she could speak every thought as it arose, and who had such an affection for her as could never find fault.

How was she to bear the change? – It was true that her friend was going only half a mile from them; but Emma was aware that great must be the difference between a Mrs Weston only half a mile from them, and a Miss Taylor in the house; and with all her advantages, natural and domestic, she was now in great danger of suffering from intellectual solitude. She dearly loved her father, but he was no companion for her. He could not meet her in conversation, rational or playful.

The evil of the actual disparity in their ages (and Mr Woodhouse had not married early) was much increased by his constitution and habits; for having been a valetudinarian all his life, without activity of mind or body, he was a much older man in ways than in years; and though everywhere beloved for the friendliness of his heart and his amiable temper, his talents could not have recommended him at any time.

Her sister, though comparatively but little removed by matrimony, being settled in London, only sixteen miles off, was much beyond her daily reach; and many a long October and November evening must be struggled through at Hartfield, before Christmas brought the next visit from Isabella and her husband and their little children to fill the house and give her pleasant society again.

Highbury, the large and populous village almost amounting to a town, to which Hartfield, in spite of its separate lawn and shrubberies and name, did really belong, afforded her no equals. The Woodhouses were first in consequence here. All looked up to them.

She had many acquaintance in the place, for her father was universally civil, but not one among them who could be accepted in lieu of Miss Taylor for even half a day. It was a melancholy change; and Emma could not but sigh over it and wish for impossible things, till her father awoke, and made it necessary to be cheerful. His spirits required support. He was a nervous man, easily depressed; fond of every body that he was used to, and hating to part with them; hating change of every kind. Matrimony, as the origin of change, was always disagreeable; and he was by no means yet reconciled to his own daughter's marrying, nor could ever speak of her but with compassion, though it had been entirely a match of affection, when he was now obliged to part with Miss Taylor too; and from his habits of gentle selfishness and of being never able to suppose that other people could feel differently from himself, he was very much disposed to think Miss Taylor had done as sad a thing for herself as for them, and would have been a great deal happier if she had spent all the rest of her life at Hartfield. Emma smiled and chatted as cheerfully as she could, to keep him from such thoughts; but when tea came, it was impossible for him not to say exactly as he had said at dinner.

'Poor Miss Taylor! – I wish she were here again. What a pity it is that Mr Weston ever thought of her!'

'I cannot agree with you, papa; you know I cannot. Mr Weston is such a good-humoured, pleasant, excellent man that he thoroughly deserves a good wife; – and you would not have had Miss Taylor live with us for ever and bear all my odd humours, when she might have a house of her own?'

'A house of her own! – but where is the advantage of a house of her own? This is three times as large. – And you have never any odd humours, my dear.'

'How often we shall be going to see them and they coming to see us! – We shall be always meeting! *We* must begin, we must go and pay our wedding-visit very soon.'

'My dear, how am I to get so far? Randalls is such a distance. I could not walk half so far.'

'No papa, nobody thought of your walking. We must go in the carriage to be sure.'

'The carriage! But James will not like to put the horses to for such a little way; – and where are the poor horses to be while we are paying our visit?'

'They are to be put into Mr Weston's stable, papa. You know we have settled all that already. We talked it all over with Mr Weston last night. And as for James, you may be very sure he will always like going to Randalls, because of his daughter's being housemaid there. I only doubt whether he will ever take us anywhere else. That was your doing, papa. You got Hannah that good place. Nobody thought of Hannah till you mentioned her – James is so obliged to you!'

'I am very glad I did think of her. It was very lucky, for I would not have had poor James think himself slighted upon any account; and I am sure she will make a very good servant; she is a civil, pretty-spoken girl; I have a great opinion of her. Whenever I see her, she always curtseys and asks me how I do, in a very pretty manner; and when you have had her here to do needlework, I observe she always turns the lock of the door the right way and never bangs it. I am sure she will be an excellent servant; and it will be a great comfort to poor Miss Taylor to have somebody about her that she is used to see. Whenever James goes over to see his daughter you know, she will be hearing of us. He will be able to tell her how we all are.'

Emma spared no exertions to maintain this happier flow of ideas, and hoped, by the help of backgammon, to get her father tolerably through the evening, and be attacked by no regrets but her own. The backgammon-table was placed; but a visitor immediately afterwards walked in and made it unnecessary.

Mr Knightley, a sensible man about seven or eight-and-thirty, was not only a very old and intimate friend of the family, but particularly connected with it as the elder brother of Isabella's husband. He lived about a mile from Highbury, was a frequent visitor and always welcome, and at this time more welcome than usual, as coming directly from their mutual connections in London. He had returned to a later dinner after some days absence, and now walked up to Hartfield to say that all were well in Brunswick-square. It was a happy circumstance and animated Mr Woodhouse for some time. Mr Knightley had a cheerful manner which always did him good; and his many inquiries after 'poor Isabella' and her children were answered most satisfactorily. When this was over, Mr Woodhouse gratefully observed,

'It is very kind of you, Mr Knightley, to come out at this late hour to call upon us. I am afraid you must have had a shocking walk.'

'Not at all, sir. It is a beautiful, moonlight night; and so mild that I must draw back from your great fire.'

'But you must have found it very damp and dirty. I wish you may not catch cold.'

'Dirty, sir! Look at my shoes. Not a speck on them.'

'Well! that is quite surprizing for we have had a vast deal of rain here. It rained dreadfully hard for half an hour, while we were at breakfast. I wanted them to put off the wedding.'

'By the bye – I have not wished you joy. Being pretty well aware of what sort of joy you must both be feeling, I have been in no hurry with my congratulations. But I hope it all went off tolerably well. How did you all behave? Who cried most?'

'Ah! poor Miss Taylor! 'tis a sad business.'

'Poor Mr and Miss Woodhouse, if you please; but I cannot possibly say "poor Miss Taylor." I have a great regard for you and Emma; but when it comes to the question of dependence or independence! – At any rate, it must be better to have only one to please, than two.'

'Especially when *one* of those two is such a fanciful, troublesome creature!' said Emma playfully. 'That, is what you have in your head, I know – and what you would certainly say if my father were not by.'

'I believe it is very true, my dear, indeed,' said Mr Woodhouse with a sigh. 'I am afraid I am sometimes very fanciful and troublesome.'

'My dearest papa! You do not think I could mean *you*, or suppose Mr Knightley to mean *you*. What a horrible idea! Oh, no! I meant only myself. Mr Knightley loves to find fault with me you know – in a joke – it is all a joke. We always say what we like to one another.'

Mr Knightley, in fact, was one of the few people who could see faults in Emma Woodhouse, and the only one who ever told her of them: and though this was not particularly agreeable to Emma herself, she knew it would be so much less so to her father, that she would not have him really suspect such a circumstance as her not being thought perfect by every body.

'Emma knows I never flatter her,' said Mr Knightley; 'but I meant no reflection on any body. Miss Taylor has been used to have two persons to please; she will now have but one. The chances are that she must be a gainer.'

'Well,' said Emma, willing to let it pass – 'you want to hear about the wedding, and I shall be happy to tell you, for we all behaved charmingly. Every body was punctual, every body in their best looks. Not a tear, and hardly a long face to be seen. Oh! no, we all felt that we were going to be only half a mile apart, and were sure of meeting every day.'

'Dear Emma bears every thing so well,' said her father. 'But, Mr Knightley, she is really very sorry to lose poor Miss Taylor, and I am sure she *will* miss her more than she thinks for.'

Emma turned away her head, divided between tears and smiles.

'It is impossible that Emma should not miss such a companion,' said Mr Knightley. 'We should not like her so well as we do, sir, if we could suppose it. But she knows how much the marriage is to Miss Taylor's advantage; she knows how very acceptable it must be at Miss Taylor's time of life to be settled in a home of her own, and how important to her to be secure of a comfortable provision, and therefore cannot allow herself to feel so much pain as pleasure. Every friend of Miss Taylor must be glad to have her so happily married.'

'And you have forgotten one matter of joy to me,' said Emma, 'and a very considerable one – that I made the match myself. I made the match, you know, four years ago; and to have it take place, and be proved in the right, when so many people said Mr Weston would never marry again, may comfort me for any thing.'

Mr Knightley shook his head at her. Her father fondly replied, 'Ah! my dear, I wish you would not make matches and foretell things, for whatever you say always comes to pass. Pray do not make any more matches.'

'I promise you to make none for myself, papa; but I must, indeed, for other people. It is the greatest amusement in the world! And after such success you know! – Every body said that Mr Weston would nevery marry again. Oh dear, no! Mr Weston, who had been a widower so long, and who seemed so perfectly comfortable without a wife, so constantly occupied either in his business in town or among his friends here, always acceptable wherever he went, always cheerful – Mr Weston need not spend a single evening in the year alone if he did not like it. Oh, no! Mr Weston certainly would never marry again. Some people even talked of a promise to his wife on her death-bed, and others of the son and the uncle not letting him. All manner of solemn nonsense was talked on the subject, but I believe none of it. Ever since the day (about four years ago) that Miss Taylor and I met with him in Broadway-lane, when, because it began to mizzle; he darted away with so much gallantry, and borrowed two umbrellas for us from Farmer Mitchell's, I made up my mind on the subject. I planned the match from that hour; and when such success has blessed me in this instance, dear papa, you cannot think that I shall leave off match-making.'

'I do not understand what you mean by "success;" ' said Mr Knightley. 'Success supposes endeavour. Your time has been properly and delicately spent, if you have been endeavouring for the last four years to bring about this marriage. A worthy employment for a young lady's mind! But if, which I rather imagine, your making

'Two umbrellas for us.'

the match, as you call it, means only your planning it, your saying to yourself one idle day, "I think it would be a very good thing for Miss Taylor if Mr Weston were to marry her," and saying it again to yourself every now and then afterwards, – why do you talk of success? where is your merit? – what are you proud of? – you made a lucky guess; and *that* is all that can be said.'

'And have you ever known the pleasure and triumph of a lucky guess? – I pity you. – I thought you cleverer – for depend upon it, a lucky guess is never merely luck. There is always some talent in it. And as to my poor word "success," which you quarrel with, I do not know that I am so entirely without any claim to it. You have drawn two pretty pictures – but I think there may be a third

– a something between the do-nothing and the do-all. If I had not promoted Mr Weston's visits here, and given many little encouragements, and smoothed many little matters, it might not have come to any thing after all. I think you must know Hartfield enough to comprehend that.'

'A straight-forward, open-hearted man, like Weston, and a rational unaffected woman, like Miss Taylor, may be safely left to manage their own concerns. You are more likely to have done harm to yourself, than good to them, by interference.'

'Emma never thinks of herself, if she can do good to others;' rejoined Mr Woodhouse, understanding but in part. 'But, my dear, pray do not make any more matches, they are silly things, and break up one's family circle grievously.'

'Only one more, papa; only for Mr Elton. Poor Mr Elton! You like Mr Elton, papa, – I must look about for a wife for him. There is nobody in Highbury who deserves him – and he has been here a whole year, and has fitted up his house so comfortably that it would be a shame to have him single any longer – and I thought when he was joining their hands to-day, he looked so very much as if he would like to have the same kind office done for him! I think very well of Mr Elton, and this is the only way I have of doing him a service.'

'Mr Elton is a very pretty young man to be sure, and a very good young man, and I have great regard for him. But if you want to shew him any attention, my dear, ask him to come and dine with us some day. That will be a much better thing. I dare say Mr Knightley wil be so kind as to meet him.

'With a great deal of pleasure, sir, at any time,' said Mr Knightley laughing; 'and I agree with you entirely that it will be a much better thing. Invite him to dinner, Emma, and help him to the best of the fish and chicken, but leave him to chuse his own wife. Depend upon it, a man of six or seven-and-twenty can take care of himself.'

CHAPTER TWO

MR WESTON WAS A NATIVE of Highbury, and born of a respectable family, which for the last two or three generations had been rising into gentility and property. He had recieved a good education, but on succeeding early in life to a small independence, had become indisposed for any of the more homely pursuits in which his brothers were engaged; and had satisfied an active cheerful mind and social temper by entering into the militia of his county, then embodied.

Captain Weston was a general favourite; and when the chances of his military life had introduced him to Miss Churchill, of a great Yorkshire family, and Miss Churchill fell in love with him, nobody was surprised except her brother and his wife, who had never seen him, and who were full of pride and importance, which the connection would offend.

Miss Churchill, however, being of age, and with the full command of her fortune – though her fortune bore no proportion to the family-estate – was not to be dissuaded from the marriage, and it took place to the infinite mortification of Mr & Mrs Churchill, who threw her off with due decorum. It was an unsuitable connection, and did not produce much happiness. Mrs Weston ought to have found more in it, for she had a husband whose warm heart and sweet temper made him think every thing due to her in return for the great goodness of being in love with him; but though she had one sort of spirit, she had not the best. She had resolution enough to pursue her own will in spite of her brother, but not enough to refrain from unreasonable regrets at that brother's unreasonable anger, nor from missing the luxuries of her former home. They lived beyond their income, but still it was nothing in comparison of Enscombe: she did not cease to love her husband, but she wanted at once to be the wife of Captain Weston, and Miss Churchill of Enscombe.

Captain Weston, who had been considered, especially by the Churchills, as making such an amazing match, was proved to have much the worst of the bargain; for when his wife died after a three years' marriage, he was rather a poorer man than at first, and with a child to maintain. From the expence of the child, however, he was soon relieved. The boy had, with the additional softening claim of a lingering illness of his mother's, been the means of a sort of reconciliation; and Mr and Mrs Churchill, having no children of their own, nor any other young creature of equal kindred to care for, offered to take the whole charge of little Frank soon after her decease. Some scruples and some reluctance the widower-father may be supposed to have felt; but as they were overcome by other considerations, the child was given up to the care and the wealth of the Churchills, and he had only his own comfort to seek and his own situation to improve as he could.

A complete change of life became desirable. He quitted the militia and engaged in trade, having brothers already established in a good way in London, which afforded him a favourable opening. It was a concern which brought just employment enough. He had still a small house in Highbury, where most of his leisure days were spent; and between useful occupation and the pleasures of society, the next eighteen or twenty years of his life passed cheerfully away. He had, by that time, realized an easy competence – enough to secure the purchase of a little estate adjoining Highbury, which he had always longed for – enough to marry a woman as portionless even as Miss Taylor, and to live according to the wishes of his own family and social disposition.

It was now some time since Miss Taylor had begun to influence his schemes; but as it was not the tyrannic influence of youth on youth, it had not shaken his determination of never settling till he could purchase Randalls, and the sale of Randalls was long looked forward to: but he had gone steadily on, with these objects in view, till they were accomplished. He had made his fortune, bought his house, and obtained his wife; and was beginning a new period of existence with every probability of greater happiness than in any yet passed through. He had never been an unhappy man; his own temper had secured him from that, even in his first marriage; but his second must shew him how delightful a well-judging and truly amiable woman could be, and must give him the pleasantest proof of its being a great deal better to chuse than to be chosen, to excite gratitude than to feel it.

He had only himself to please in his choice: his fortune was his own; for as to Frank, it was more than being tacitly brought up as his uncle's heir, it had become so avowed an adoption as to have him assume the name of Churchill on coming of age. It was most unlikely, therefore, that he should ever want his father's assistance. His father had no apprehension of it. The aunt was a capricious woman, and governed her husband entirely; but it was not in Mr Weston's nature to imagine that any caprice could be strong enough to affect one so dear, and, as he believed, so deservedly dear. He saw his son every year in London, and was proud of him; and his fond report of him as a very fine young man had made Highbury feel a sort of pride in him too. He was looked on as sufficiently belonging to the place to make his merit and prospects a kind of common concern.

Mr Frank Churchill was one of the boasts of Highbury, and a lively curiosity to see him prevailed, though the compliment was so little returned that he had never been there in his life. His coming to visit his father had been often talked of but never achieved.

Now, upon his father's marriage, it was very generally proposed, as a most proper attention, that the visit should take place. There was not a dissentient voice on the subject, either when Mrs Perry drank tea with Mrs and Miss Bates, or when Mrs and Miss Bates returned the visit. Now was the time for Mr Frank Churchill to come among them; and the hope strengthened when it was understood that he had written to his new mother on the occasion. For a few days every morning visit in Highbury included some mention of the handsome letter Mrs Weston had received. 'I suppose you have heard of the handsome letter Mr Frank Churchill had written to Mrs Weston? I understand it was a very handsome letter, indeed. Mr Woodhouse told me of it. Mr Woodhouse saw the letter, and he says he never saw such a handsome letter in his life.'

It was, indeed, a highly-prized letter. Mrs Weston had, of course, formed a very favourable idea of the young man, and such a pleasing attention was an irresistible proof of his great good sense, and a most welcome addition to every source and every expression of congratulation which her marriage had already secured. She felt herself a most fortunate woman; and she had lived long enough to know how fortunate she might well be thought, where the only regret was for a partial separation from friends, whose friendship for her had never cooled, and who could ill bear to part with her!

She knew that at times she must be missed; and could not think, without pain, of Emma's losing a single pleasure, or suffering an hour's ennui, from the want of her companionableness: but dear Emma was of no feeble character; she was more equal to her situation than most girls would have been, and had sense and energy and spirits that might be hoped would bear her well and happily through its little difficulties and privations. And then there was such comfort in the very easy distance of Randalls from Hartfield, so convenient for even solitary female walking, and in Mr Weston's disposition and circumstances, which would make the approaching season no hindrance to their spending half the evenings in the week together.

Her situation was altogether the subject of hours of gratitude to Mrs Weston, and of moments only of regret; and her satisfaction – her more than satisfaction – her cheerful enjoyment was just and so apparent, that Emma, well as she knew her father, was sometimes taken by surprise at his being still able to pity 'poor Miss Taylor,' when they left her at Randalls in the centre of every domestic comfort, or saw her go away in the evening attended by her pleasant husband to a carriage of her own. But never did she go without Mr Woodhouse's giving a gentle sigh, and saying:

'Ah! poor Miss Taylor. She would be very glad to stay.'

There was no recovering Miss Taylor – nor much likelihood of ceasing to pity her: but a few weeks brought some alleviation to Mr Woodhouse. The compliments of his neighbours were over; he was no longer teased by being wished joy of so sorrowful an event; and the wedding-cake, which had been a great distress to him, was all eat up. His own stomach could bear nothing rich, and he could never believe other people to be different from himself. What was unwholesome to him, he regarded as unfit for any body; and he had, therefore, earnestly tried to dissuade them from having any wedding-cake at all, and when that proved vain, as earnestly tried to prevent any body's eating it. He had been at the pains of

With a slice of Mrs Weston's wedding-cake.

consulting Mr Perry, the apothecary, on the subject. Mr Perry was an intelligent, gentlemanlike man, whose frequent visits were one of the comforts of Mr Woodhouse's life; and, upon being applied to, he could not but acknowledge, (though it seemed rather against the bias of inclination,) that wedding-cake might certainly disagree with many – perhaps with most people, unless taken moderately. With such an opinion, in confirmation of his own, Mr Woodhouse hoped to influence every visitor of the new-married pair; but still the cake was eaten; and there was no rest for his benevolent nerves till it was all gone.

There was a strange rumour in Highbury of all the little Perrys being seen with a slice of Mrs Weston's wedding-cake in their hands: but Mr Woodhouse would never believe it.

CHAPTER THREE

Mr Woodhouse was fond of society in his own way. He liked very much to have his friends come and see him; and from various united causes, from his long residence at Hartfield, and his good nature, from his fortune, his house, and his daughter, he could command the visits of his own little circle, in a great measure as he liked. He had not much intercourse with any families beyond that circle; his horror of late house and large dinner-parties made him unfit for any acquaintance, but such as would visit him on his own terms. Fortunately for him, Highbury, including Randalls in the same parish, and Donwell Abbey in the parish adjoining, the seat of Mr Knightley, comprehended many such. Not unfrequently, through Emma's persuasion, he had some of the chosen and the best to dine with him, but evening-parties were what he preferred, and, unless he fancied himself at any time unequal to company, there was scarcely an evening in the week in which Emma could not make up a card-table for him.

Real, long-standing regard brought the Westons and Mr Knightley; and by Mr Elton, a young man living alone without liking it, the privilege of exchanging any vacant evening of his own blank solitude for the elegancies and society of Mr Woodhouse's drawing-room and the smiles of his lovely daughter, was in no danger of being thrown away.

After these came a second set; among the most come-at-able of whom were Mrs and Miss Bates and Mrs Goddard, three ladies almost always at the service of an invitation from Hartfield, and who were fetched and carried home so often that Mr Woodhouse thought it no hardship for either James or the horses. Had it taken place only once a year, it would have been a grievance.

Mrs Bates, the widow of a former vicar of Highbury, was a very old lady, almost past every thing but tea and quadrille. She lived with her single daughter in a very small way, and was considered with all the regard and respect which a harmless old lady, under such untoward circumstances, can excite. Her daughter enjoyed a most uncommon degree of popularity for a woman neither young, handsome, rich, nor married. Miss Bates stood in the very worst predicament in the world for having much of the public favour; and she had no intellectual superiority to make atonement to herself, or frighten those who might hate her, into outward respect. She had never boasted either beauty or cleverness. Her youth had passed without distinction, and her middle of life was devoted to the care of a failing mother, and the endeavour to make a small income go as far as possible. And yet she was a happy woman, and a woman whom no one named without good-will. It was her own universal good-will and contented temper which worked such wonders. She loved every body, was interested in every body's happiness, quick-sighted to every body's merits; thought herself a most fortunate creature, and surrounded with blessings in such an excellent mother and so many good neighbours and friends, and a home that wanted for nothing. The simplicity and cheerfulness of her nature, her contented and grateful spirit, were a recommendation to every body and a mine of felicity to herself. She was a great talker upon little matters, which exactly suited Mr Woodhouse, full of trivial communications and harmless gossip.

Mrs Goddard was the mistress of a School – not of a seminary, or an establishment, or any thing which professed, in long sentences of refined nonsense, to combine liberal acquirements with elegant morality upon new principles and new systems – and where young ladies for enormous pay might be screwed out of health and into vanity – but a real, honest, old-fashioned Boarding-school, where a reasonable quantity of accomplishments were sold at a reasonable price, and where girls might be sent to be out of the way and scramble themselves into a little education, without any danger of coming back prodigies. Mrs Goddard's school was in high repute – and very deservedly; for Highbury was reckoned a particularly healthy spot; she had an ample house and garden, gave the children plenty of wholesome food, let them run about a great deal in the summer, and in winter dressed their chilblains with her own hands.

It was no wonder that a train of twenty young couple now walked after her to church. She was a plain, motherly kind of woman, who had worked hard in her youth, and now thought herself entitled to the occasional holiday of a tea-visit; and having formerly owed much to Mr Woodhouse's kindness, felt his particular claim on her to leave her neat parlour hung round with fancy-work whenever she could, and win or lose a few sixpences by his fireside.

These were the ladies whom Emma found herself very frequently able to collect; and happy was she, for her father's sake, in the power; though, as far as she was herself concerned, it was no remedy for the absence of Mrs Weston. She was delighted to see her father look comfortable, and very much pleased with herself for contriving things so well; but the quiet prosings of three such women made her feel that every evening so spent, was indeed one of the long evenings she had fearfully anticipated.

As she sat one morning, looking forward to exactly such a close of the present day, a note was brought from Mrs Goddard, requesting, in most respectful terms, to be allowed to bring Miss Smith with her; a most welcome request: for Miss Smith was a girl of seventeen whom Emma knew very well by sight and had long felt an interest in, on account of her beauty. A very gracious invitation was returned, and the evening no longer dreaded by the fair mistress of the mansion.

Harriet Smith was the natural daughter of somebody. Somebody had placed her, several years back, at Mrs Goddard's school, and somebody had lately raised her from the condition of scholar to that of parlour-boarder. This was all that was generally known of her history. She had no visible friends but what had been acquired at Highbury, and was now just returned from a long visit in the country to some young ladies who had been at school there with her.

She was a very pretty girl, and her beauty happened to be of a sort which Emma particularly admired. She was short, plump and fair, with a fine bloom, blue eyes, light hair, regular features, and a look of great sweetness; and before the end of the evening, Emma was as much pleased with her manners as her person, and quite determined to continue the acquaintance.

She was not struck by any thing remarkably clever in Miss Smith's conversation, but she found her altogether engaging – not inconveniently shy, not unwilling to talk – and yet so far from pushing, shewing so proper and becoming a deference, seeming so pleasantly grateful for being admitted to Hartfield, and so artlessly impressed by the appearance of every thing in so superior a style to what she had been used to, that she must have good sense and deserve encouragement. Encouragement should be given. Those soft blue eyes and all those natural graces should not be wasted on the inferior society of Highbury and its connections. The acquaintance she had already formed were unworthy of her. The friends from whom she had just parted, though very good sort of people, must be doing her harm. They were a family of the name of Martin, whom Emma well knew by character, as renting a large farm of Mr Knightley, and residing in the parish of Donwell – very creditably she believed – she knew Mr Knightley thought highly of them – but they must be coarse and unpolished, and very unfit to be the intimates of a girl who wanted only a little more knowledge and elegance to be quite perfect. *She* would notice her; she would improve her; she would detach her from her bad acquaintance, and introduce her into good society; she would inform her opinions and her manners. It would be an interesting, and certainly a very kind undertaking; highly becoming her own situation in life, her leisure, and powers.

She was so busy in admiring those soft blue eyes, in talking and listening, and forming all these schemes in the in-betweens, that the evening flew away at a very unusual rate; and the supper-table, which always closed such parties, and for which she had been used to sit and watch the due time, was all set out and ready, and moved forwards to the fire, before she was aware. With an alacrity beyond the common impulse of a spirit which yet was never indifferent to the credit of doing every thing well and attentively, with the real good-will of a mind delighted with its own ideas, did she then do all the honours of the meal, and help and recommend the minced chicken and scalloped oysters with an urgency which she knew would be acceptable to the early hours and civil scruples of their guests.

Upon such occasions poor Mr Woodhouse's feelings were in sad warfare. He loved to have the cloth laid, because it had been the fashion of his youth; but this conviction of suppers being very unwholesome made him rather sorry to see any thing put on it; and while his hospitality would have welcomed his visitors to every thing, his care for their health made him grieve that they would eat.

Such another small basin of thin gruel as his own, was all that he could, with thorough self-approbation, recommend, though he might constrain himself, while the ladies were comfortably clearing the nicer things, to say:

'Mrs Bates, let me propose your venturing on one of these eggs. An egg boiled very soft is not unwholesome. Serle understands boiling an egg better than anybody. I would not recommend an egg boiled by any body else – but you need not be afraid – they are very small, you see – one of our small eggs will not hurt you. Miss Bates, let Emma help you to a *little* bit of tart – a *very* little bit. Ours are all apple tarts. You need not be afraid of unwholesome preserves here. I do not advise the custard. Mrs Goddard, what say you to *half* a glass of wine? A *small* half glass – put into a tumbler of water? I do not think it could disagree with you.'

Emma allowed her father to talk – but supplied her visitors in a much more satisfactory style, and on the present evening had particular pleasure in sending them away happy. The happiness of Miss Smith was quite equal to her intentions. Miss Woodhouse was so great a personage in Highbury, that the prospect of the introduction had given as much panic as pleasure – but the humble, grateful, little girl went off with highly gratified feelings, delighted with the affability with which Miss Woodhouse had treated her all the evening, and actually shaken hands with her at last!

CHAPTER FOUR

HARRIET SMITH'S INTIMACY at Hartfield was soon a settled thing. Quick and decided in her ways, Emma lost no time in inviting, encouraging, and telling her to come very often; and as their acquaintance increased, so did their satisfaction in each other. As a walking companion, Emma had very early forseen how useful she might find her. In that respect Mrs Weston's loss had been important. Her father never went beyond the shrubbery, where two divisions of the grounds sufficed him for his long walk, or his short, as the year varied; and since Mrs Weston's marriage her exercise had been too much confined. She had ventured once alone to Randalls, but it was not pleasant; and a Harriet Smith, therefore, one whom she could summon at any time to a walk, would be a valuable addition to her privileges. But in every respect as she saw more of her, she approved her, and was confirmed in all her kind designs.

Harriet certainly was not clever, but she had a sweet, docile, grateful disposition; was totally free from conceit; and only desiring to be guided by any one she looked up to. Her early attachment to herself was very amiable; and her inclination for good company, and power of appreciating what was elegant and clever, shewed that there was no want of taste, though strength of understanding must not be expected. Altogether she was quite convinced of Harriet

Smith's being exactly the young friend she wanted – exactly the something which her home required. Such a friend as Mrs Weston was out of the question. Two such could never be granted. Two such she did not want. It was quite a different sort of thing – a sentiment distinct and independent. Mrs Weston was the object of a regard, which had its basis in gratitude and esteem. Harriet would be loved as one to whom she could be useful. For Mrs Weston there was nothing to be done; for Harriet every thing.

Her first attempts at usefulness were in an endeavour to find out who were the parents; but Harriet could not tell. She was ready to tell every thing in her power, but on this subject questions were vain. Emma was obliged to fancy what she liked – but she could never believe that in the same situation *she* should not have discovered the truth. Harriet had no penetration. She had been satisfied to hear and believe just what Mrs Goddard chose to tell her; and looked no farther.

Mrs Goddard, and the teachers, and the girls, and the affairs of the school in general, formed naturally a great part of her conversation – and but for her acquaintance with the Martins of Abbey-Mill-Farm, it must have been the whole. But the Martins occupied her thoughts a good deal; she had spent two very happy months with them, and now loved to talk of the pleasures of her visit, and describe the many comforts and wonders of the place. Emma encouraged her talkativeness – amused by such a picture of another set of beings, and enjoying the youthful simplicity which could speak with so much exultation of Mrs Martin's having '*two* parlours, two very good parlours indeed; one of them quite as large as Mrs Goddard's drawing-room; and of her having an upper maid who had lived five-and-twenty years with her; and of their having eight cows, two of them Alderneys, and one a little Welch cow, a very pretty little Welch cow, indeed; and of Mrs Martin's saying, as she was so fond of it, it should be called *her* cow; and of their having a very handsome summer-house in their garden, where some day next year they were all to drink tea: – a very handsome summer-house, large enough to hold a dozen people.'

For some time she was amused, without thinking beyond the immediate cause; but as she came to understand the family better, other feelings arose. She had taken up a wrong idea, fancying it was a mother and daughter, a son and son's wife, who all lived together; but when it appeared that the Mr Martin, who bore a part in the narrative, and was always mentioned with approbation for his great good-nature in doing something or other, was a single man; that there was no young Mrs Martin, no wife in the case; she did suspect danger to her poor little friend from all this hospitality and kindness – and that if she were not taken care of, she might be required to sink herself for ever.

With this inspiriting notion, her questions increased in number and meaning; and she particularly led Harriet to talk more of Mr Martin, – and there was evidently no dislike to. Harriet was very ready to speak of the share he had had in their moonlight walks and merry evening games; and dwelt a good deal upon his being so very good-humoured and obliging. 'He had gone three miles round one day, in order to bring her some walnuts, because she had said how fond she was of them – and in every thing else he was so very obliging! He had his shepherd's son into the parlour one night on purpose to sing to her. She was very fond of singing. He could sing a little himself. She believed he was very clever, and understood every thing. He had a very fine flock, and while she was with them, he had been bid more for his wool than any body in the country. She believed every body spoke well of him. His mother and sisters were very fond of him. Mrs Martin had told her one day, (and there was a blush as she said it,) that it was impossible for any body to be a better son; and therefore she was sure whenever he married he would make a good husband. Not that she *wanted* him to marry. She was in no hurry at all.'

'Well done, Mrs Martin!' thought Emma. 'You know what you are about.'

'And when she had come away, Mrs Martin was so very kind as to send Mrs Goddard a beautiful goose: the finest goose Mrs Goddard had ever seen. Mrs Goddard had dressed it on a Sunday, and asked all the three teachers, Miss Nash, and Miss Prince, and Miss Richardson, to sup with her.'

'Mr Martin, I suppose, is not a man of information beyond the line of his own business. He does not read?'

'Oh, yes! – that is, no – I do not know – but I believe he has read a good deal – but not what you would think any thing of. He reads the Agricultural Reports and some other books, that lay in one of the window seats – but he reads all *them* to himself. But sometimes of an evening, before we went to cards, he would read something aloud out of the Elegant Extracts – very entertaining. And I know he has read the Vicar of Wakefield. He never read the Romance of the Forest, nor the Children of the Abbey. He had never heard of such books before I mentioned them, but he is determined to get them now as soon as ever he can.'

The next question was:

'What sort of looking man is Mr Martin?'

'Oh! not handsome – not at all handsome. I thought him very plain at first, but I do not think him so plain now. One does not, you know, after a time. But, did you never see him? He is in Highbury every now and then, and he is sure to ride through every week in his way to Kingston. He has passed you very often.'

'That may be – and I may have seen him fifty times, but without having any idea of his name. A young farmer, whether on horseback or on foot, is the very last sort of person to raise my curiosity. The yeomanry are precisely the order of people with whom I feel I can have nothing to do. A degree or two lower, and a creditable appearance might interest me; I might hope to be useful to their families in some way or other. But a farmer can need none of my help, and is therefore in one sense as much above my notice as in every other he is below it.'

'To be sure. Oh! yes, it is not likely you should ever have observed him – but he knows you very well indeed – I mean by sight.'

'I have no doubt of his being a very respectable young man. I know indeed that he is so; and as such wish him well. What do you imagine his age to be?'

'He was four-and twenty the 8th of last June, and my birth-day is the 23rd – just a fortnight and a day's difference! which is very odd!'

'Only four-and-twenty. That is too young to settle. His mother is perfectly right not to be in a hurry. They seem very comfortable as they are, and if she were to take any pains to marry him, she would probably repent it. Six years hence, if he could meet with a good sort of young woman in the same rank as his own, with a little money, it might be very desirable.'

'Six years hence! dear Miss Woodhouse, he would be thirty years old!'

'Well, and that is as early as most men can afford to marry, who are not born to an independence. Mr Martin, I imagine, has his fortune entirely to make – cannot be at all beforehand with the world. Whatever money he might come into when his father died, whatever his share of the family property, it is, I dare say, all afloat, all employed in his stock, and so forth; and though, with diligence and good luck, he may be rich in time, it is next to impossible that he should have realised any thing yet.'

'To be sure, so it is. But they live very comfortably. They have no in-doors man – else they do not want for any thing; and Mrs Martin talks of taking a boy another year.'

'I wish you may not get into a scrape, Harriet, whenever he does marry; – I mean as to being acquainted with his wife – for though his sisters, from a superior education, are not to be altogether objected to, it does not follow that he might marry any body at all fit for you to notice. The misfortune of your birth ought to make you particularly careful as to your associates. There can be no doubt of your being a gentleman's daughter, and you must support your claim to that station by every thing within your own power, or there will be plenty of people who would take pleasure in degrading you.'

'Yes, to be sure – I suppose there are. But while I visit at Hartfield, and you are so kind to me, Miss Woodhouse, I am not afraid of what any body can do.'

'You understand the force of influence pretty well, Harriet; but I would have you so firmly established in good society, as to be independent even of Hartfield and Miss Woodhouse. I want to see you permanently well connected – and to that end it will be advisable to have as few odd acquaintance as may be; and, therefore, I say that if you should still be in this country when Mr Martin marries, I wish you may not be drawn in, by your intimacy with the sisters, to be acquainted with the wife, who will probably be some mere farmer's daughter, without education.'

'To be sure. Yes. Not that I think Mr Martin would ever marry any body but what had had some education – and been very well brought up. However, I do not mean to set up my opinion against your's – and I am sure I shall not wish for the acquaintance of his wife. I shall always have a great regard for the Miss Martins, especially Elizabeth, and should be very sorry to give them up, for they are quite as well educated as me. But if he married a very ignorant, vulgar woman, certainly I had better not visit her, if I can help it.'

Emma watched her through the fluctuations of this speech, and saw no alarming symptoms of love. The young man had been the first admirer, but she trusted there was no other hold, and that there would be no serious difficulty on Harriet's side to oppose any friendly arrangement of her own.

They met Mr Martin the very next day, as they were walking on the Donwell Road. He was on foot, and after looking very respectfully at her, looked with most unfeigned satisfaction at her companion. Emma was not sorry to have such an opportunity of survey; and walking a few yards forward, while they talked together, soon made her quick eye sufficiently acquainted with Mr Robert Martin. His appearance was very neat, and he looked like a sensible young man, but his person had no other advantage; and when he came to be contrasted with gentlemen, she thought he

Emma was not sorry to have such an opportunity of survey.

must lose all the ground he had gained in Harriet's inclination. Harriet was not insensible of manner; she had voluntarily noticed her father's gentleness with admiration as well as wonder. Mr Martin looked as if he did not know what manner was.

They remained but a few minutes together, as Miss Woodhouse must not be kept waiting; and Harriet then came running to her with a smiling face, and in a flutter of spirits, which Miss Woodhouse hoped very soon to compose.

'Only think of our happening to meet him! – How very odd! It was quite a chance, he said, that he had not gone round by Randalls. He did not think we ever walked this road. He thought we walked towards Randalls most days. He has not been able to get the Romance of the Forest yet. He was so busy the last time he was at Kingston that he quite forgot it, but he goes again to-morrow. So very odd we should happen to meet! Well, Miss Woodhouse, is he like what you expected? What do you think of him? Do you think him so very plain?'

'He is very plain, undoubtedly – remarkably plain: – but that is nothing, compared with his entire want of gentility. I had no right to expect much, and I did not expect much; but I had no idea that he could be so very clownish, so totally without air. I had imagined him, I confess, a degree or two nearer gentility.'

'To be sure,' said Harriet, in a mortified voice, 'he is not so genteel as real gentlemen.'

'I think, Harriet, since your acquaintance with us, you have been repeatedly in the company of some, such very real gentlemen, that you must yourself be struck with the difference in Mr Martin. At Hartfield you have had very good specimens of well educated, well bred men. I should be surprized if, after seeing them, you could be in company with Mr Martin again without perceiving him to be a very inferior creature – and rather wondering at yourself for having ever thought him at all agreeable before. Do not you begin to feel that now? Were not you struck? I am sure you must have been struck by his awkward look and abrupt manner – and the uncouthness of voice, which I heard to be wholly unmodulated as I stood here.'

'Certainly, he is not like Mr Knightley. He has not such a fine air and way of walking as Mr Knightley. I see the difference plain enough. But Mr Knightley is so very fine a man!'

'Mr Knightley's air is so remarkably good, that it is not fair to compare Mr Martin with *him*. You might not see one in a hundred, with *gentleman* so plainly written as in Mr Knightley. But he is not the only gentleman you have been lately used to. What say you to Mr Weston and Mr Elton? Compare Mr Martin with either of *them*. Compare their manner of carrying themselves; of walking; speaking; of being silent. You must see the difference.'

'Oh, yes! – there is a great difference. But Mr Weston is almost an old man. Mr Weston must be between forty and fifty.'

'Which makes his good manners the more valuable. The older a person grows, Harriet, the more important it is that their manners should not be bad – the more glaring and disgusting any loudness, or coarseness, or awkwardness becomes. What is passable in youth, is detestable in later age. Mr Martin is now awkward and abrupt; what will he be at Mr Weston's time of life?'

'There is no saying, indeed!' replied Harriet, rather solemnly.

'But there may be pretty good guessing. He will be a completely gross, vulgar farmer – totally inattentive to appearances, and thinking of nothing but profit and loss.'

'Will he, indeed, that will be very bad.'

'How much his business engrosses him already, is very plain from the circumstances of his forgetting to enquire for the book you recommended. He was a great deal too full of the market to think of any thing else – which is just as it should be, for a thriving man. What has he to do with books? And I have no doubt that he *will* thrive and be a very rich man in time – and his being illiterate and coarse need not disturb *us*.'

'I wonder he did not remember the book' – was all Harriet's answer, and spoken with a degree of grave displeasure which Emma thought might be safely left to itself. She, therefore, said no more for some time. Her next beginning was,

'In one respect, perhaps, Mr Elton's manners are superior to Mr Knightley's or Mr Weston's. They have more gentleness. They might be more safely held up as a pattern. There is an openness, quickness, almost a bluntness in Mr Weston, which every body likes in *him* because there is so much good humour with it – but that would not do to be copied. Neither would Mr Knightley's downright, decided, commanding sort of manner – though it suits *him* very well; his figure and look, and situation in life seem to allow it; but if any young man were to set about copying him, he would not be sufferable. On the contrary, I think a young man might be very safely recommended to take Mr Elton as a model. Mr Elton is good humoured, cheerful, obliging, and gentle. He seems to me, to be grown particularly gentle of late. I do not know whether he has any design of ingratiating himself with either of us, Harriet, by additional softness, but it strikes me that his manners are softer than they used to be. If he means anything, it must be to please you. Did not I tell you what he said of you the other day?'

She then repeated some warm personal praise which she had drawn from Mr Elton, and now did full justice to; and Harriet blushed and smiled, and said she had always thought Mr Elton very agreeable.

Mr Elton was the very person fixed on by Emma for driving the young farmer out of Harriet's head. She thought it would be an excellent match; and only too palpably desirable, natural, and probable, for her to have much merit in planning it. She feared it was what every body else must think of and predict. It was not likely, however, that any body should have equalled her in the date of the plan, as it had entered her brain during the very first evening of Harriet's coming to Hartfield. The longer she considered it, the greater was her sense of its expediency. Mr Elton's situation was most suitable, quite the gentleman himself, and without low connections; at the same time not of any family that could fairly object to the doubtful birth of Harriet. He had a comfortable home for her, and Emma imagined a very sufficient income; for though the vicarage of Highbury was not large, he was known to have some independent property; and she thought very highly of him as a good-humoured, well-meaning, respectable young man, without any deficiency of useful understanding or knowledge of the world.

She had already satisfied herself that he thought Harriet a beautiful girl, which she trusted, with such frequent meetings at Hartfield, was foundation enough on his side; and on Harriet's, there could be little doubt that the idea of being preferred by him would have all the usual weight and efficacy. And he was really a very pleasing young man, a young man whom any woman not fastidious might like. He was reckoned very handsome; his person much admired in general, though not by her, there being a want of elegance of feature which she could not dispense with: – but the girl who could be gratified by a Robert Martin's riding about the country to get walnuts for her, might very well be conquered by Mr Elton's admiration.

CHAPTER FIVE

'I DO NOT KNOW WHAT your opinion may be, Mrs Weston,' said Mr Knightley, 'of this great intimacy between Emma and Harriet Smith, but I think it a bad thing.'

'A bad thing! Do you really think it a bad thing? – why so?'

'I think they will neither of them do the other any good.'

'You surprize me! Emma must do Harriet good: and by supplying her with a new object of interest, Harriet may be said to do Emma good. I have been seeing their intimacy with the greatest pleasure. How very differently we feel! – Not think they will do each other any good! This will certainly be the beginning of one of our quarrels about Emma, Mr Knightley.'

'Perhaps you think I am come on purpose to quarrel with you, knowing Weston to be out, and that you must still fight your own battle.'

'Mr Weston would undoubtedly support me, if he were here, for he thinks exactly as I do on the subject. We were speaking of it only yesterday, and agreeing how fortunate it was for Emma, that there should be such a girl in Highbury for her to associate with. Mr Knightley, I shall not allow you to be a fair judge in this case. You are so much used to live alone, that you do not know the value of a companion; and perhaps no man can be a good judge of the comfort a woman feels in the society of one of her own sex, after being used to it all her life. I can imagine your objection to Harriet Smith. She is not the superior young woman which Emma's friend ought to be. But on the other hand, as Emma wants to see her better informed, it will be an inducement to her to read more herself. They will read together. She means it, I know.'

'Emma has been meaning to read more ever since she was twelve years old. I have seen a great many lists of her drawing up at various times of books that she meant to read regularly through – and very good lists they were – very well chosen, and very neatly arranged – sometimes alphabetically, and sometimes by some other rule. The list she drew up when only fourteen – I remember thinking it did her judgment so much credit, that I preserved it some time; and I dare say she may have made out a very good list now. But I have done with expecting any course of steady reading from Emma. She will never submit to any thing requiring industry and patience, and a subjection of the fancy to the understanding. Where Miss Taylor failed to stimulate, I may safely affirm that Harriet Smith will do nothing. – You could never persuade her to read half so much as you wished. – You know you could not.'

'I dare say,' replied Mrs Weston, smiling, 'that I thought so *then*; – but since we have parted, I can never remember Emma's omitting to do any thing I wished.'

'There is hardly any desiring to refresh such a memory as *that*' – said Mr Knightley, feelingly; and for a moment or two he had done. 'But I,' he soon added, 'who have had no such charm thrown over my senses, must still see, hear, and remember. Emma is spoiled by being the cleverest of her family. At ten years old, she had the misfortune of being able to answer questions which puzzled her sister at seventeen. She was always quick and assured, Isabella slow and diffident. And ever since she was twelve, Emma has been mistress of the house and of you all. In her mother she lost the only person able to cope with her. She inherits her mother's talents, and must have been under subjection to her.'

'I should have been sorry, Mr Knightley, to be dependent on *your* recommendation, had I quitted Mr Woodhouse's family and wanted another situation; I do not think you would have spoken a good word for me to any body. I am sure you always thought me unfit for the office I held.'

'Yes,' he said, smiling. 'You are better placed *here*; very fit for a wife, but not at all for a governess. But you were preparing yourself to be an excellent wife all the time you were at Hartfield. You might not give Emma such a complete education as your powers would seem to promise; but you were receiving a very good education from *her*, on the very material matrimonial point of submitting your own will, and doing as you were bid; and if Weston had asked me to recommend him a wife, I should certainly have named Miss Taylor.'

'Thank you. There will be very little merit in making a good wife to such a man as Mr Weston.'

'Why, to own the truth, I am afraid you are rather thrown away, and that with every disposition to bear, there will be nothing to be borne. We will not despair, however. Weston may grow cross from the wantonness of comfort, or his son may plague him.'

'I hope not *that*. – It is not likely. No, Mr Knightley, do not foretell vexation from that quarter.'

'Not I, indeed. I only name possibilities. I do not pretend to Emma's genius for foretelling and guessing. I hope, with all my heart, the young man may be a Weston in merit, and a Churchill in fortune. – But Harriet Smith – I have not half done about Harriet Smith. I think her the very worst sort of companion that Emma could possibly have. She knows nothing herself, and looks upon Emma as knowing every thing. She is a flatterer in all her ways; and so much the worse, because undesigned. Her ignorance is hourly flattery. How can Emma imagine she has anything to learn herself, while Harriet is presenting such a delightful inferiority? And as for Harriet, I will venture to say that *she* cannot gain by the acquaintance. Hartfield will only put her out of conceit with all the other places she belongs to. She will grow just refined enough to be uncomfortable with those among whom birth and circumstances have placed her home.. I am much mistaken if Emma's doctrines give any strength of mind, or tend at all to make a girl adapt herself rationally to the varieties of her situation in life. – They only give a little polish.'

'I either depend more upon Emma's good sense than you do, or am more anxious for her present comfort; for I cannot lament the acquaintance. How well she looked last night!'

'Oh! you would rather talk of her person than her mind, would you? Very well; I shall not attempt to deny Emma's being pretty.'

'Pretty! say beautiful rather. Can you imagine any thing nearer perfect beauty than Emma altogether – face and figure?'

'I do not know what I could imagine, but I confess that I have seldom seen a face or figure more pleasing to me than her's. But I am a partial old friend.'

'Such an eye! – the true hazle eye – and so brilliant! regular features, open countenance, with a complexion! oh! what a bloom of full health, and such a pretty height and size; such a firm and upright figure. There is health, not merely in her bloom, but in her air, her head, her glance. One hears sometimes of a child being 'the picture of health;' now Emma always gives me the idea of being the complete picture of grown-up health. She is loveliness itself. Mr Knightley, is not she?'

'I have not a fault to find with her person,' he replied. 'I think her all you describe. I love to look at her; and I will add this praise, that I do not think her personally vain. Considering how very handsome she is, she appears to be little occupied with it; her vanity lies another way. Mrs Weston, I am not to be talked out of my dislike of her intimacy with Harriet Smith, or my dread of its doing them both harm.'

'And I, Mr Knightley, am equally stout in my confidence of its not doing them any harm. With all dear Emma's little faults, she is an excellent creature. Where shall we see a better daughter, or a kinder sister, or a truer friend? No, no; she has qualities which may be trusted; she will never lead any one really wrong; she will make no lasting blunder; where Emma errs once, she is in the right a hundred times.'

'Very well; I will not plague you any more. Emma shall be an angel, and I will keep my spleen to myself till Christmas brings John and Isabella. John loves Emma with a reasonable and therefore not a blind affection, and Isabella always thinks as he does; except when he is not quite frightened enough about the children. I am sure of having their opinions with me.'

'I know that you all love her really too well to be unjust or unkind; but excuse me, Mr Knightley, if I take the liberty (I consider myself, you know, as having somewhat of the privilege of speech that Emma's mother might have had) the liberty of hinting that I do not think any possible good can arise from Harriet Smith's intimacy being made a matter of much discussion among you. Pray excuse me; but supposing any little inconvenience may be apprehended from the intimacy, it cannot be expected that Emma, accountable to nobody but her father, who perfectly approves the acquaintance, should put an end to it, so long as it is a source of pleasure to herself. It has been so many years my province to give advice, that you cannot be surprized, Mr Knightley, at this little remains of office.'

'Not at all,' cried he; 'I am much obliged to you for it. It is very good advice, and it shall have a better fate than your advice has often found; for it shall be attended to.'

'Mrs John Knightley is easily alarmed, and might be made unhappy about her sister.'

'Be satisfied,' said he, 'I will not raise any outcry. I will keep my ill-humour to myself. I have a very sincere interest in Emma. Isabella does not seem more my sister; has never excited a greater interest; perhaps hardly so great. There is an anxiety, a curiosity in what one feels for Emma. I wonder what will become of her!'

'So do I,' said Mrs Weston gently; 'very much.'

'She always declares she will never marry, which, of course, means just nothing at all. But I have no idea that she has yet ever seen a man she cared for. It would not be a bad thing for her to be very much in love with a proper object. I should like to see Emma in love, and in some doubt of a return; it would do her good. But there is nobody hereabouts to attach her; and she goes so seldom from home.'

'There does, indeed, seem as little to tempt her to break her resolution, at present,' said Mrs Weston, 'as can well be; and while she is so happy at Hartfield, I cannot wish her to be forming any attachment which would be creating such difficulties, on poor Mr Woodhouse's account. I do not recommend matrimony at present to Emma, though I mean no slight to the state I assure you.'

Part of her meaning was to conceal some favourite thoughts of her own and Mr Weston's on the subject, as much as possible. There were wishes at Randalls respecting Emma's destiny, but it was not desirable to have them suspected; and the quiet transition which Mr Knightley soon afterwards made to 'What does Weston think of the weather; shall we have rain?' convinced her that he had nothing more to say or surmise about Hartfield.

CHAPTER SIX

EMMA COULD NOT FEEL a doubt of having given Harriet's fancy a proper direction and raised the gratitude of her young vanity to a very good purpose, for she found her decidedly more sensible than before of Mr Elton's being a remarkably handsome young man, with most agreeable manners; and as she had no hesitation in following up the assurance of his admiration, by agreeable hints, she was soon pretty confident of creating as much liking on Harriet's side, as there could be any occasion for. She was quite convinced of Mr Elton's being in the fairest way of falling in love, if not in love already. She had no scruple with regard to him. He talked of Harriet, and praised her so warmly, that she could not suppose any thing wanting which a little time would not add. His perception of the striking improvement of Harriet's manner, since her introduction at Hartfield, was not one of the least agreeable proofs of his growing attachment.

'You have given Miss Smith all that she required,' said he; 'you have made her graceful and easy. She was a beautiful creature when she came to you, but, in my opinion, the attractions you have added are infinitely superior to what she received from nature.'

'I am glad you think I have been useful to her; but Harriet only wanted drawing out, and receiving a few, very few hints. She had all the natural grace of sweetness of temper and artlessness in herself. I have done very little.'

'If it were admissible to contradict a lady,' said the gallant Mr Elton –

'I have perhaps given her a little more decision of character, have taught her to think on points which had not fallen in her way before.'

'Exactly so; that is what principally strikes me. So much superadded decision of character! Skilful has been the hand.'

'Great has been the pleasure, I am sure. I never met with a disposition more truly amiable.'

'I have no doubt of it.' And it was spoken with a sort of sighing animation, which had a vast deal of the lover. She was not less pleased another day with the manner in which he seconded a sudden wish of her's, to have Harriet's picture.

'Did you ever have your likeness taken, Harriet?' said she: 'Did you ever sit for your picture?'

Harriet was on the point of leaving the room, and only stopt to say, with a very interesting naïveté,

'Oh! dear, no, never.'

No sooner was she out of sight, than Emma exclaimed,

'What an exquisite possession a good picture of her would be! I would give any money for it. I almost long to attempt her likeness myself. You do not know it I dare say, but two or three years ago I had a great passion for taking likenesses, and attempted several of my friends and was thought to have a tolerable eye in general. But from one cause or another, I gave it up in disgust. But really, I could almost venture, if Harriet would sit to me. It would be a delight to have her picture!'

'Let me entreat you,' cried Mr Elton; 'it would indeed be a delight! Let me entreat you, Miss Woodhouse, to exercise so charming a talent in favour of your friend. I know what your drawings are. How could you suppose me ignorant? Is not this room rich in specimens of your landscapes and flowers; and has not Mrs Weston some inimitable figure-pieces in her drawing-room, at Randalls?'

Yes, good man! – thought Emma – but what has all that to do with taking likenesses? You know nothing of drawing. Don't pretend to be in raptures about mine. Keep your raptures for Harriet's face. 'Well, if you give me such kind encouragement, Mr. Elton, I believe I shall try what I can do. Harriet's features are very delicate, which makes a likeness difficult; and yet there is a peculiarity in the shape of the eye and the lines about the mouth which one ought to catch.'

'Exactly so – The shape of the eye and the lines about the mouth – I have not a doubt of your success. Pray, pray attempt it. As you will do, it will indeed, to use your own words, be an exquisite possession.'

'But I am afraid, Mr Elton, Harriet will not like to sit. She thinks so little of her own beauty. Did not you observe her manner of answering me? How completely it meant, "why should my picture be drawn?"'

'Oh! yes, I observed it, I assure you. It was not lost on me. But still I cannot imagine she would not be persuaded.'

Harriet was soon back again, and the proposal almost immediately made; and she had no scruples which could stand many minutes against the earnest pressing of both the others. Emma wished to go to work directly, and therefore produced the portfolio containing her various attempts at portraits, for not one of them had ever been finished, that they might decide together on the best size for Harriet. Her many beginnings were displayed. Minatures, half-lengths, whole lengths, pencil, crayon, and water-colours had been all tried in turn. She had always wanted to do everything, and had made more progress both in drawing and music than many might have done with so little labour as she would ever submit to. She played and sang; – and drew in almost every style; but steadiness had always been wanting; and in nothing had she approached the degree of excellence which she would have been glad to command, and ought not to have failed of. She was not much deceived as to her own skill, either as an artist or a musician, but she was not unwilling to have others deceived, or sorry to know her reputation for accomplishment often higher than it deserved.

There was merit in every drawing – in the least finished, perhaps the most; her style was spirited; but had there been much less, or had there been ten times more, the delight and admiration of her two companions would have been the same. They were both in extasies. A likeness pleases every body, and Miss Woodhouse's performances must be capital.

'No great variety of faces for you,' said Emma. 'I had only my own family to study from. There is my father – another of my father – but the idea of sitting for his picture made him so nervous, that I could only take him by stealth; neither of them very like therefore. Mrs Weston again, and again, and again, you see. Dear Mrs Weston! always my kindest friend on every occasion. She would sit whenever I asked her. There is my sister; and really quite her own little elegant figure! – and the face not unlike. I should have made a good likeness of her, if she would have sat longer, but she was in such a hurry to have me draw her four children that she would not be quiet. Then, here come all my attempts at three of those four children; – there they are, Henry and John and Bella, from one end of the sheet to the other; and any one of them might do for any of the rest. She was so eager to have them drawn that I could not refuse; but there is no making children of three or four years old stand still you know; nor can it be very easy to take any likeness of them, beyond the air and complexion, unless they are coarser featured than any mama's children ever were. Here is my sketch of the fourth, who was a baby. I took him, as he was sleeping on the sofa, and it is as strong a likeness of his cockade as you would wish to see. He had nestled down his head most conveniently. That's very like. I am rather proud of little George. The corner of the sofa is very good. Then here is my last' – unclosing a pretty sketch of a gentleman in small size, whole-length – 'my last and my best – my brother, Mr John Knightley. – This did not want much of being finished, when I put it away in a pet, and vowed I would never take another likeness. I could not help being provoked; for after all my pains, and when I had really made a very good likeness of it – (Mrs Weston and I were quite agreed in thinking if *very* like) – only too handsome – too flattering – but that was a fault on the right side – after all this, came poor dear Isabella's cold approbation of – 'Yes, it was a little like – but to be sure it did not do him justice.' We had had a great deal of trouble in persuading him to sit at all. It was made a great favour of; and altogether it was more than I could bear; and so I never would finish it, to have it apologized over as an unfavourable likeness, to every morning visitor in Brunswick-square; – and, as I said, I did then forswear ever drawing anybody again. But for Harriet's sake, or rather for my own, and as there are no husbands and wives in the case at present, I will break my resolution now.'

Mr Elton seemed very properly struck and delighted by the idea, and was repeating, 'No husbands and wives in the case *at present* indeed, as you observe. Exactly so. No husbands and wives,' with so interesting a consciousness, that Emma began to consider whether she had not better leave them together at once. But as she wanted to be drawing, the declaration must wait a little longer.

She had soon fixed on the size and sort of portrait. It was to be a whole-length in water-colours, like Mr John Knightley's, and was destined, if she could please herself, to hold a very honourable station over the mantlepiece.

The sitting began; and Harriet, smiling and blushing, and afraid of not keeping her attitude and countenance, presented a very sweet mixture of youthful expression to the steady eyes of the artist. But there was no doing anything, with Mr Elton fidgeting behind her and watching every touch. She gave him credit for stationing himself where he might gaze and gaze again without offence; but was really obliged to put an end to it, and request him to place himself elsewhere. It then occurred to her to employ him in reading.

'If he would be so good as to read to them, it would be a kindness indeed! It would amuse away the difficulties of her part, and lessen the irksomeness of Miss Smith's.'

Mr Elton was only too happy. Harriet listened, and Emma drew in peace. She must allow him to be still frequently coming to look; anything less would certainly have been too little in a lover; and he was ready at the smallest intermission of the pencil, to jump up and see the progress, and be charmed. – There was no being displeased with such an encourager, for his admiration made him discern a likeness almost before it was possible. She could not respect his eye, but his love and his complaisance were unexceptionable.

The sitting was altogether very satisfactory; she was quite enough pleased with the first day's sketch to wish to go on. There was no want of likeness, she had been fortunate in the attitude, and as she meant to throw in a little improvement to the figure, to give a little more height, and considerably more elegance, she had great confidence of its being in every way a pretty drawing at last, and of its filling its destined place with credit to them both – a standing memorial of the beauty of one, the skill of the other, and the friendship of both; with as many other agreeable associations as Mr Elton's very promising attachment was likely to add.

Ready to jump up and see the progress.

Harriet was to sit again the next day; and Mr Elton, just as he ought, entreated for the permission of attending and reading to them again.

'By all means. We shall be most happy to consider you as one of the party.'

The same civilities and courtesies, the same success and satisfaction, took place on the morrow, and accompanied the whole progress of the picture, which was rapid and happy. Every body who saw it was pleased, but Mr Elton was in continual raptures, and defended it through every criticism.

'Miss Woodhouse has given her friend the only beauty she wanted,' – observed Mrs Weston to him – not in the least suspecting that she was addressing a lover. – 'The expression of the eye is most correct, but Miss Smith has not those eye-brows and eye-lashes. It is the fault of her face that she has them not.'

'Do you think so?' replied he. 'I cannot agree with you. It appears to me a most perfect resemblance in every feature. I never saw such a likeness in my life. We must allow for the effect of shade, you know.'

'You have made her too tall, Emma,' said Mr Knightley.

Emma knew that she had, but would not own it, and Mr Elton warmly added,

'Oh, no! certainly not too tall; not in the least too tall. Consider, she is sitting down – which naturally presents a different – which in short gives exactly the idea – and the proportions must be preserved, you know. Proportions, fore-shortening. Oh, no! it gives one exactly the idea of such a height as Miss Smith's. Exactly so indeed!'

'It is very pretty,' said Mr Woodhouse. 'So prettily done! Just as your drawings always are, my dear. I do not know anybody who draws as well as you do. The only thing I do not thoroughly like is, that she seems to be sitting out of doors, with only a little shawl over her shoulders – and it makes one think she must catch cold.'

'But, my dear papa, it is supposed to be summer; a warm day in Summer. Look at the tree.'

'But it is never safe to sit out of doors, my dear.'

'You, sir, may say any thing,' cried Mr Elton; 'but I must confess that I regard it as a most happy thought, the placing of Miss Smith out of doors; and the tree is touched with such inimitable spirit! Any other situation would have been much less in character. The naïveté of Miss Smith's manners – and altogether – Oh, it is most admirable – I cannot keep my eyes from it. I never saw such a likeness.'

The next thing wanted was to get the picture framed; and here were a few difficulties. It must be done directly; it must be done in London; the order must go through the hands of some intelligent person whose taste could be depended on; and Isabella, the usual doer of all commissions, must not be applied to, because it was December, and Mr Woodhouse could not bear the idea of her stirring out of her house in the fogs of December. But no sooner was the distress known to Mr Elton, than it was removed. His gallantry was always on the alert. 'Might he be trusted with the commission, what infinite pleasure should he have in executing it! he could ride to London at any time. It was impossible to say how much he should be gratified by being employed on such an errand.'

'He was too good! – she could not endure the thought! – she would not give him such a troublesome office for the world' – brought on the desired repetition of entreaties and assurances, – and a very few minutes settled the business.

Mr Elton was to take the drawing to London, chuse the frame, and give the directions; and Emma thought she could so pack it as to ensure its safety without much incommoding him, while he seemed mostly fearful of not being incommoded enough.

'What a precious deposit!' said he with a tender sigh, as he received it.

'This man is almost too gallant to be in love,' thought Emma. 'I should say so, but that I suppose there may be a hundred different ways of being in love. He is an excellent young man, and will suit Harriet exactly; it will be an "Exactly so," as he says himself; but he does sigh and languish, and study for compliments rather more than I could endure as a principal. I come in for a pretty good share as a second. But it is his gratitude on Harriet's account.'

CHAPTER SEVEN

THE VERY DAY OF MR ELTON's going to London produced a fresh occasion for Emma's services towards her friend. Harriet had been at Hartfield, as usual, soon after breakfast; and after a time, had gone home to return again to dinner: she returned, and sooner than had been talked of, and with an agitated, hurried look, announcing something extraordinary to have happened which she was longing to tell. Half a minute brought it all out. She had heard, as soon as she got back to Mrs Goddard's, that Mr Martin had been there an hour before, and finding she was not at home, nor particularly expected, had left a little parcel for her from one of his sisters, and gone away; and on opening this parcel, she had actually found, besides the two songs which she had lent Elizabeth to copy, a letter to herself; and this letter was from him, from Mr Martin, and contained a direct proposal of marriage. 'Who could have thought it! She was so surprized she did not know what to do. Yes, quite a proposal of marriage; and a very good letter, at least she thought so. And he wrote as if he really loved her very much – but she did not know – and so, she was come as fast as she could to ask Miss Woodhouse what she should do.' – Emma was half ashamed of her friend for seeming so pleased and so doubtful.

'Upon my word,' she cried, 'the young man is determined not to lose any thing for want of asking. He will connect himself well if he can.'

'Will you read the letter?' cried Harriet. 'Pray do. I'd rather you would.'

Emma was not sorry to be pressed. She read, and was surprized. The style of the letter was much above her expectation. There were not merely no grammatical errors, but as a composition it would not have disgraced a gentleman; the language, though plain was strong and unaffected, and the sentiments it conveyed very much to the credit of the writer. It was short, but expressed good sense, warm attachment, liberality, propriety, even delicacy of feeling. She paused over it, while Harriet stood anxiously watching for her opinion, with a 'Well, well,' and was at last forced to add, 'Is it a good letter? or is it too short?'

'Yes, indeed, a very good letter,' replied Emma rather slowly – 'so good a letter, Harriet, that every thing considered, I think one of his sisters must have helped him. I can hardly imagine the young man whom I saw talking with you the other day could express himself so well, if left quite to his own powers, and yet it is not the style of a woman; no, certainly, it is too strong and concise; not diffuse enough for a woman. No doubt he is a sensible man, and I suppose may have a natural talent for – thinks strongly and clearly – and when he takes a pen in hand, his thoughts naturally find proper words. It is so with some men. Yes, I understand the sort of mind. Vigorous, decided, with sentiments to a certain point, not coarse. A better written letter, Harriet, (returning it,) than I had expected.'

'Well,' said the still waiting Harriet; – 'well – and – and what shall I do?'

'What shall you do! In what respect? Do you mean with regard to this letter?'

'Yes.'

'But what are you in doubt of? You must answer it of course – and speedily.'

'Yes. But what shall I say? Dear Miss Woodhouse, do advise me.'

'Oh, no, no! the letter had much better be all your own. You will express yourself very properly, I am sure. There is no danger of your not being intelligible, which is the first thing. Your meaning must be unequivocal; no doubts or demurs: and such expressions of gratitude and concern for the pain you are inflicting as propriety requires, will present themselves unbidden to *your* mind, I am persuaded. *You* need not be prompted to write with the appearance of sorrow for his disappointment.'

'You think I ought to refuse him then,' said Harriet, looking down.

'Ought to refuse him! My dear Harriet, what do you mean? Are you in any doubt as to that? I thought – but I beg your pardon, perhaps I have been under a mistake. I certainly have been misunderstanding you, if you feel in doubt as to the *purport* of your answer. I had imagined you were consulting me only as to the wording of it.'

Harriet was silent. With a little reserve of manner, Emma continued:

'You mean to return a favourable answer, I collect.'

'No, I do not; that is, I do not mean – What shall I do? What would you advise me to do? Pray, dear Miss Woodhouse, tell me what I ought to do?'

'I shall not give you any advice, Harriet, I will have nothing to do with it. This is a point which you must settle with your own feelings.'

'I had no notion that he liked me so very much,' said Harriet, contemplating the letter. For a little while Emma persevered in her silence; but beginning to apprehend the bewitching flattery of that letter might be too powerful, she thought it best to say.

'I lay it down as a general rule, Harriet, that if a woman *doubts* as to whether she should accept a man or not, she certainly ought to refuse him. If she can hesitate as to "Yes," she ought to say "No" directly. It is not a state to be safely entered into with doubtful feelings, with half a heart. I thought it my duty as a friend, and older than yourself, to say thus much to you. But do not imagine that I want to influence you.'

'Oh! no, I am sure you are a great deal too kind to – but if you would just advise me what I had best do – No, no, I do not mean that – As you say, one's mind ought to be quite made up – One should not be hesitating – It is a very serious thing, It will be safer to say "No", perhaps. – Do you think I had better say "No?" '

'Not for the world,' said Emma, smiling graciously, 'would I advise you either way. You must be the best judge of your own happiness. If you prefer Mr Martin to every other person; if you think him the most agreeable man you have ever been in company with, why should you hesitate? You blush, Harriet. – Does any body else occur to you at this moment under such a definition? Harriet, Harriet, do not deceive yourself; do not be run away with by gratitude and compassion. At this moment whom are you thinking of?'

The symptoms were favourable. – Instead of answering, Harriet turned away confused, and stood thoughtfully by the fire; and though the letter was still in her hand, it was now mechanically twisted about without regard. Emma waited the result with impatience, but not without strong hopes. At last, with some hesitation, Harriet said –

'Miss Woodhouse, as you will not give me your opinion, I must do as well as I can by myself; and I have now quite determined, and really almost made up my mind – to refuse Mr Martin. Do you think I am right?'

'Perfectly, perfectly right, my dearest Harriet; you are doing just what you ought. While you were at all in suspense I kept my feelings to myself, but now that you are so completely decided I have no hesitation in approving. Dear Harriet, I give myself joy of this. It would have grieved me to lose your acquaintance, which must have been the consequence of your marrying Mr Martin. While you were in the smallest degree wavering, I said nothing about it, because I would not influence; but it would have been the loss of a friend to me. I could not have visited Mrs Robert Martin, of Abbey-Mill Farm. Now I am secure of you for ever.'

Harriet had not surmised her own danger, but the idea of it struck her forcibly.

'You could not have visited me!' she cried, looking aghast. 'No, to be sure you could not; but I never thought of that before. That would have been too dreadful! – What an escape! – Dear Miss Woodhouse, I would not give up the pleasure and honour of being intimate with you for any thing in the world.'

'Indeed, Harriet, it would have been a severe pang to lose you; but it must have been. You would have thrown yourself out of all good society. I must have given you up.'

'Dear me! – How should I ever have borne it! It would have killed me never to come to Hartfield any more!'

'Dear affectionate creature! – *You* banished to Abbey-Mill Farm! – *You* confined to the society of the illiterate and vulgar all your life! I wonder how the young man could have the assurance to ask it. He must have a pretty good opinion of himself.'

'I do not think he is conceited either, in general,' said Harriet, her conscience opposing such censure; 'at least he is very good natured, and I shall always feel much obliged to him, and have a great regard for – but that is quite a different thing from – and you know, though he may like me, it does not follow that I should – and certainly I must confess that since my visiting here I have seen people – and if one comes to compare them, person and manners, there is no comparison at all, *one* is so very handsome and agreeable. However, I do really think Mr Martin a very amiable young man, and have a great opinion of him; and his being so much attached to me – and his writing such a letter – but as to leaving you, it is what I would not do upon any consideration.'

'Thank you, thank you, my own sweet little friend. We will not be parted. A woman is not to marry a man merely because she is asked, or because he is attached to her, and can write a tolerable letter.'

'Oh! no; – and it is but a short letter too.'

Emma felt the bad taste of her friend, but let it pass with a 'very true; and it would be a small consolation to her, for the clownish manner which might be offending her every hour of the day, to know that her husband could write a good letter.'

'Oh! yes, very. Nobody cares for a letter; the thing is, to be always happy with pleasant companions. I am quite determined to refuse him. But how shall I do? What shall I say?'

Emma assured her there would be no difficulty in the answer, and advised its being written directly, which was agreed to, in the hope of her assistance; and though Emma continued to protest against any assistance being wanted, it was in fact given in the formation of every sentence. The looking over his letter again, in replying to it, had such a softening tendency, that it was particularly necessary to brace her up with a few decisive expressions; and she was so very much concerned at the idea of making him unhappy, and thought so much of what his mother and sisters would think and say, and was so anxious that they should not fancy her ungrateful that Emma believed if the young man had come in her way at that moment, he would have been accepted after all.

This letter, however, was written, and sealed, and sent. The business was finished, and Harriet safe. She was rather low all the evening, but Emma could allow for her amiable regrets, and sometimes relieved them by speaking of her own affection, sometimes by bringing forward the idea of Mr Elton.

'I shall never be invited to Abbey-Mill again,' was said in rather a sorrowful tone.

'Nor if you were, could I ever bear to part with you, my Harriet. You are a great deal too necessary at Hartfield, to be spared to Abbey-Mill.'

'And I am sure I should never want to go there; for I am never happy but at Hartfield.'

Some time afterwards it was, 'I think Mrs Goddard would be very much surprized if she knew what had happened. I am sure Miss Nash would – for Miss Nash thinks her own sister very well married, and it is only a linen-draper.'

'One should be sorry to see greater pride or refinement in the teacher of a school, Harriet. I dare say Miss Nash would envy you such an opportunity as this of being married. Even this conquest would appear valuable in her eyes. As to anything superior for you, I suppose she is quite in the dark. The attentions of a certain person can hardly be among the tittle-tattle of Highbury yet. Hitherto I fancy you and I are the only people to whom his looks and manners have explained themselves.'

Harriet blushed and smiled, and said something about wondering that people should like her so much. The idea of Mr Elton was certainly cheering; but still, after a time, she was tender-hearted again towards the rejected Mr Martin.

'Now he has got my letter,' said she softly. 'I wonder what they are all doing – whether his sisters know – if he's unhappy, they will be unhappy too. I hope he will not mind it so very much.'

'Let us think of those among our absent friends who are more cheerfully employed,' cried Emma. 'At this moment, perhaps, Mr Elton is shewing your picture to his mother and sisters, telling how much more beautiful is the original, and after being asked for it five or six times, allowing them to hear your name, your own dear name.'

'My picture! – But he has left my picture in Bond-street.'

'Has he so! – Then I know nothing of Mr Elton. No, my dear little modest Harriet, depend upon it the picture will not be in Bond-street till just before he mounts his horse to-morrow. It is his companion all this evening, his solace, his delight. It opens his designs to his family, it introduces you among them, it diffuses through the party those pleasantest feelings of our nature, eager

Shewing your picture to his mother and sisters.

curiosity and warm prepossession. How cheerful, how animated, how suspicious, how busy their imaginations all are!'

Harriet smiled again, and her smiles grew stronger.

CHAPTER EIGHT

HARRIET SLEPT AT Hartfield that night. For some weeks past she had been spending more than half her time there, and gradually getting to have a bed-room appropriated to herself; and Emma judged it best in every respect, safest and kindest, to keep her with them as much as possible just at present. She was obliged to go the next morning for an hour or two to Mrs Goddard's, but it was then to be settled that she should return to Hartfield, to make a regular visit of some days.

While she was gone, Mr Knightley called, and sat some time with Mr Woodhouse and Emma, till Mr Woodhouse, who had previously made up his mind to walk out, was persuaded by his daughter not to defer it, and was induced by the entreaties of both, though against the scruples of his own civility, to leave Mr Knightley for that purpose. Mr Knightley, who had nothing of ceremony about him, was offering by his short, decided answers, an amusing contrast to the protracted apologies and civil hesitations of the other.

'Well, I believe, if you will excuse me, Mr Knightley, if you will not consider me as doing a very rude thing, I shall take Emma's advice and go out for a quarter of an hour. As the sun is out, I believe I had better take my three turns while I can. I treat you without ceremony, Mr Knightley. We invalids think we are privileged people.'

'My dear sir, do not make a stranger of me.'

'I leave an excellent substitute in my daughter. Emma will be happy to entertain you. And therefore I think I will beg your excuse and take my three turns – my winter walk.'

'You cannot do better, sir.'

'I would ask for the pleasure of your company, Mr Knightley, but I am a very slow walker, and my pace would be tedious to you; and besides, you have another long walk before you, to Donwell Abbey.'

'Thank you, sir, thank you; I am going this moment myself; and I think the sooner *you* go the better. I will fetch your great coat and open the garden door for you.'

Mr Woodhouse at last was off; but Mr Knightley, instead of being immediately off likewise, sat down again, seemingly inclined for more chat. He began speaking of Harriet, and speaking of her with more voluntary priase than Emma had ever heard before.

'I cannot rate her beauty as you do,' said he; 'but she is a pretty little creature, and I am inclined to think very well of her disposition. Her character depends upon those she is with; but in good hands she will turn out a valuable woman.'

'I am glad you think so; and the good hands, I hope, may not be wanting.'

'Come,' said he, 'you are anxious for a compliment, so I will tell you that you have improved her. You have cured her of her schoolgirl's giggle; she really does you credit.'

'Thank you. I should be mortified indeed if I did not believe I had been of some use; but it is not every body who will bestow praise where they may. *You* do not often overpower me with it.'

'You are expecting her again, you say, this morning?'

'Almost every moment. She has been gone longer already than she intended.'

'Something has happened to delay her; some visitors perhaps.'

'Highbury gossips! – Tiresome wretches!'

'Harriet may not consider every body tiresome that you would.'

Emma knew this was too true for contradiction, and therefore said nothing. He presently added, with a smile,

'I do not pretend to fix on times or places, but I must tell you that I have good reason to believe your little friend will soon hear of something to her advantage.'

'Indeed! how so? of what sort?'

'A very serious sort, I assure you,' still smiling.

'Very serious! I can think of but one thing – Who is in love with her? Who makes you their confidant?'

Emma was more than half in hopes of Mr Elton's having dropt a hint. Mr Knightley was a sort of general friend and adviser, and she knew Mr Elton looked up to him.

'I have reason to think,' he replied, 'that Harriet Smith will soon have an offer of marriage, and from a most unexceptionable quarter: – Robert Martin is the man. Her visit to Abbey-Mill, this summer, seems to have done his business. He is desperately in love and means to marry her.'

'He is very obliging,' said Emma; 'but is he sure that Harriet means to marry him?!'

'Well, well, means to make her an offer then. Will that do? He came to the Abbey two evenings ago, on purpose to consult me about it. He knows I have a thorough regard for him and all his family, and, I believe, considers me as one of his best friends. He came to ask me whether I thought it would be imprudent in him to settle so early; whether I thought her too young: in short, whether I approved his choice altogether; having some apprehension perhaps of her being considered (especially since *your* making so much of her) as in a line of society above him. I was very much pleased with all that he said. I never hear better sense from anyone than Robert Martin. He always speaks to the purpose; open, straight forward, and very well judging. He told me every thing; his circumstances and plans, and what they all proposed doing in the event of his marriage. He is an excellent young man, both as son and brother. I had no hesitation in advising him to marry. He proved to me that he could afford it; and that being the case, I was convinced he could not do better. I praised the fair lady too, and altogether sent him away very happy. If he had never esteemed my opinion before, he would have thought highly of me then; and, I dare say, left the house thinking me the best friend and counsellor man ever had. This happened the night before last. Now, as we may fairly suppose, he would not allow much time to pass before he spoke to the lady, and as he does not appear to have spoken yesterday, it is not unlikely that he should be at Mrs Goddard's today; and she may be detained by a visitor, without thinking him at all a tiresome wretch.'

'Pray, Mr Knightley,' said Emma, who had been smiling to herself through a great part of this speech, 'how do you know that Mr Martin did not speak yesterday?'

'Certainly,' replied he, surprized, 'I do not absolutely know it; but it may be inferred. Was not she the whole day with you?'

'Come,' said she, 'I will tell you something, in return for what you have told me. He did speak yesterday – that is, he wrote, and was refused.'

This was obliged to be repeated before it could be believed; and Mr Knightley actually looked red with surprize and displeasure, as he stood up, in tall indignation, and said,

'Then she is a greater simpleton than I ever believed her. What is the foolish girl about?'

'Oh! to be sure,' cried Emma, 'it is always incomprehensible to a man that a woman should ever refuse an offer of marriage. A man always imagines a woman to be ready for anybody who asks her.'

'Nonsense! a man does not imagine any such thing. But what is the meaning of this? Harriet Smith refuse Robert Martin? madness, if it is so; but I hope you are mistaken.'

'I saw her answer, nothing could be clearer.'

'You saw her answer! you wrote her answer too. Emma, this is your doing. You persuaded her to refuse him.'

'And if I did, (which, however, I am far from allowing,) I should not feel that I had done wrong. Mr Martin is a very respectable young man, but I cannot admit him to be Harriet's equal; and am rather surprized indeed that he should have ventured to address her. By your account, he does seem to have had some scruples. It is a pity that they were ever got over.'

'Not Harriet's equal!' exclaimed Mr Knightley loudly and warmly; and with calmer asperity, added, a few moments afterwards, 'No, he is not her equal indeed, for he is as much her superior in sense as in situation. Emma, your infatuation about that girl blinds you. What are Harriet Smith's claims, either of birth, nature or education, to any connection higher than Robert Martin? She is the natural daughter of nobody knows whom, with probably no settled provision at all, and certainly no respectable relations. She is known only as parlour-boarder at a common school. She is not a sensible girl, nor a girl of any information. She has been taught nothing useful, and is too young and too simple to have acquired any thing herself. At her age she can have no experience, and with her little wit, is not very likely ever to have any that can avail her. She is pretty, and she is good tempered, and that is all. My only scruple in advising the match was on his account, as being beneath his deserts, and a bad connexion for him. I felt, that as to fortune, in all probability he might do much better; and that as to a rational companion or useful helpmate, he could not do worse. But I could not reason so to a man in love, and was willing to trust to there being no harm in her, to her having that sort of disposition, which, in good hands, like his, might be easily led aright and turn out very well. The advantage of the match I felt to be all on her side; and had not the smallest doubt (nor have I now) that there would be a general cry-out upon her extreme good luck. Even *your* satisfaction I made sure of. It crossed my mind immediately that you would not regret your friend's leaving Highbury, for the sake of her being settled so well. I remember saying to myself, "Even Emma, with all her partiality for Harriet will think this a good match." '

'I cannot help wondering at your knowing so little of Harriet as to say any such thing. What! think a farmer, (and with all his sense and all his merit Mr Martin is nothing more,) a good match for my intimate friend! Not regret her leaving Highbury for the sake of marrying a man whom I could never admit as an acquaintance of my own! I wonder you should think it possible for me to have such feelings. I assure you mine are very different. I must think your statement by no means fair. You are not just to Harriet's claims. They would be estimated very differently by others as well as myself; Mr Martin may be the richest of the two, but he is undoubtedly her inferior as to rank in society. – The sphere in which she moves is much above his. – It would be a degradation.'

'A degradation to illegitimacy and ignorance, to be married to a respectable, intelligent gentleman-farmer!'

'As to the circumstances of her birth, though in a legal sense she may be called Nobody, it will not hold in common sense. She is not to pay for the offence of others, by being held below the level of those with whom she is brought up. – There can scarcely be a doubt that her father is a gentleman – and a gentleman of fortune. – Her allowance is very liberal; nothing has ever been grudged for her improvement or comfort. – That she is a gentleman's daughter, is indubitable to me; that she associates with gentlemen's daughters, no one, I apprehend, will deny. – She is superior to Mr Robert Martin.'

'Whoever might be her parents,' said Mr Knightley, 'whoever may have had the charge of her, it does not appear to have been any part of their plan to introduce her into what you would call good society. After receiving a very indifferent education she is left in Mrs Goddard's hands to shift as she can; – to move, in short, in Mrs Goddard's line, to have Mrs Goddard's acquaintance. Her friends evidently thought this good enough for her; and it *was* good enough. She desired nothing better herself. Till you chose to turn her into a friend, her mind had no distaste for her own set, nor any ambition beyond it. She was as happy as possible with the Martins in the summer. She had no sense of superiority then. If she has it now, you have given it. You have been no friend to Harriet Smith, Emma. Robert Martin would never have proceeded so far if he had not felt persuaded of her not being disinclined to him. I know him well. He has too much real feeling to address any woman on the hap-hazard of selfish passion. And as to conceit, he is the farthest from it of any man I know. Depend upon it he had encouragement.'

It was most convenient to Emma not to make a direct reply to this assertion; she chose rather to take up her own line of the subject again.

'You are a very warm friend to Mr Martin; but, as I said before, are unjust to Harriet. Harriet's claims to marry well are not so contemptible as you represent them. She is not a clever girl, but she has better sense than you are aware of, and does not deserve to have her understanding spoken of so slightingly. Waving that point, however, and supposing her to be, as you describe her, only pretty and good-natured, let me tell you, that in the degree she possesses them, they are not trivial recommendations to the world in general, for she is, in fact, a beautiful girl, and must be thought so by ninety-nine people out of an hundred; and till it appears that men are much more philosophic on the subject of beauty than they are generally supposed; till they do fall in love with well-informed minds instead of handsome faces, a girl, with such loveliness as Harriet, has a certainty of being admired and sought after, of having the power of choosing from among many, consequently a claim to be nice. Her good-nature, too, is not so very slight a claim, comprehending, as it does, real, thorough sweetness of temper and manner, a very humble opinion of herself, and a great readiness to be pleased with other people. I am very much mistaken if your sex in general would not think such beauty, and such temper, the highest claims a woman could possess.'

'Upon my word, Emma, to hear you abusing the reason you have, is almost enough to make me think so too. Better be without sense, than misapply it as you do.'

'To be sure!' cried she playfully. 'I know *that* is the feeling of you all. I know that such a girl as Harriet is exactly what every man delights in – what at once bewitches his senses and satisfies his judgment. Oh! Harriet may pick and choose. Were you, yourself, ever to marry, she is the very woman for you. And is she, at seventeen, just entering into life, just beginning to be known, to be wondered at because she does not accept the first offer she receives? no – pray let her have time to look about her.'

'I have always thought it a very foolish intimacy,' said Mr Knightley presently, 'though I have kept my thoughts to myself; but I now perceive that it will be a very unfortunate one for Harriet. You will puff her up with such ideas of her own beauty, and of what she has a claim to, that, in a little while, nobody within her reach will be good enough for her. Vanity working on a weak head, produces every sort of mischief. Nothing so easy as for a young lady to raise her expectations too high. Miss Harriet Smith may not find offers of marriage flow in so fast, though she is a very pretty girl. Men of sense, whatever you may chuse to say, do not want silly wives. Men of family would not be very fond of connecting themselves with a girl of such obscurity – and most prudent men would be afraid of the inconvenience and disgrace they might be involved in, when the mystery of her parentage came to be revealed. Let her marry Robert Martin, and she is safe, respectable, and happy for ever; but if you encourage her to expect to marry greatly, and teach her to be satisfied with nothing less than a man of consequence and large fortune, she may be a parlour-boarder at Mrs Goddard's all the rest of her life – or, at least, (for Harriet Smith is a girl who will marry somebody or other,) till she grows desperate, and is glad to catch at the old writing master's son.'

'We think so very differently on this point, Mr Knightley, that there can be no use in canvassing it. We shall only be making each other more angry. But as to my *letting* her marry Robert Martin, it is impossible; she has refused him, and so decidedly, I think, as must prevent any second application. She must abide by the evil of having refused him, whatever it may be; and as to the refusal itself, I will not pretend to say that I might not influence her a little; but I assure you there was very little for me or for anybody to do. His appearance is so much against him, and his manner so bad, that if she ever were disposed to favour him, she is not now. I can imagine, that before she had seen anybody superior, she might tolerate him. He was the brother of her friends, and he took pains to please her; and altogether, having seen nobody better (that must have been his great assistant) she might not, while she was at Abbey-Mill, find him disagreeable. But the case is altered now. She knows now what gentlemen are; and nothing but a gentleman in eduation and manner has any chance with Harriet.'

'Nonsense, errant nonsense, as ever was talked!' cried Mr Knightley. – 'Robert Martin's manners have sense, sincerity, and good-humour to recommend them; and his mind has more true gentility than Harriet Smith could understand.'

Emma made no answer, and tried to look cheerfully unconcerned, but was really feeling uncomfortable and wanting him very much to be gone. She did not repent what she had done; she still thought herself a better judge of such a point of female right and refinement than he could be; but yet she had a sort of habitual respect for his judgment in general, which made her dislike having it so loudly against her; and to have him sitting just opposite to her in angry state, was very disagreeable. Some minutes passed in this unpleasant silence, with only one attempt on Emma's side to talk of the weather, but he made no answer. He was thinking. The result of his thoughts appeared at last in these words.

'Robert Martin has no great loss – if he can but think so; and I hope it will not be long before he does. Your views for Harriet are best known to yourself; but as you make no secret of your love of match-making, it is fair to suppose that views, and plans, and projects you have; – and as a friend I shall just hint to you that if Elton is the man, I think it will be all labour in vain.'

Emma laughed and disclaimed. He continued,

'Depend upon it, Elton will not do. Elton is a very good sort of man, and a very respectable vicar of Highbury, but not at all likely to make an imprudent match. He knows the value of a good income as well as anybody. Elton may talk sentimentally, but he will act rationally. He is as well acquainted with his own claims, as you can be with Harriet's. He knows that he is a very handsome young man, and a great favourite wherever he goes; and from his general way of talking in unreserved moments, when there are only men present, I am convinced that he does not mean to throw himself away. I have heard him speak with great animation of a large family of young ladies that his sisters are intimate with, who have all twenty thousand pounds apiece.'

'I am very much obliged to you,' said Emma, laughing again. 'If

I had set my heart on Mr Elton's marrying Harriet, it would have been very kind to open my eyes, but at present I only want to keep Harriet to myself. I have done with match-making indeed. I could never hope to equal my own doings at Randalls. I shall leave off while I am well.'

'Good morning to you,' – said he, rising and walking off abruptly. He was very much vexed. He felt the disappointment of the young man, and was mortified to have been the means of promoting it, by the sanction he had given; and the part which he was persuaded Emma had taken in the affair, was provoking him exceedingly.

Emma remained in a state of vexation too; but there was more indistinctness in the causes of her's, than in his. She did not always feel so absolutely satisfied with herself, so entirely convinced that her opinions were right and her adversary's wrong, as Mr Knightley. He walked off in more complete self-approbation than he left for her. She was not so materially cast down, however, but that a little time and the return of Harriet were very adequate restoratives. Harriet's staying away so long was beginning to make her uneasy. The possibility of the young man's coming to Mrs Goddard's that morning, and meeting with Harriet and pleading his own cause, gave alarming idea. The dread of such a failure after all became the prominent uneasiness; and when Harriet appeared, and in very good spirits, and without having any such reason to give for her long absence, she felt a satisfaction which settled her with her own mind, and convinced her, that let Mr Knightley think or say what he would, she had done nothing which woman's friendship and woman's feelings would not justify.

He had frightened her a little about Mr Elton; but when she considered that Mr Knightley could not have observed him as she had done, neither with the interest, nor (she must be allowed to tell herself, in spite of Mr Knightley's pretensions) with the skill of such an observer on such a question as herself, that he had spoken it hastily and in anger, she was able to believe, that he had rather said what he wished resentfully to be true, than what he knew anything about. He certainly might have heard Mr Elton speak with more unreserve than she had ever done, and Mr Elton might not be of an imprudent, inconsiderate disposition as to money-matters; he might naturally be rather attentive than otherwise to them; but then, Mr Knightley did not make due allowance for the influence of a strong passion at war with all interested motives. Mr Knightley saw no such passion, and of course thought nothing of its effects; but she saw too much of it, to feel a doubt of its overcoming any hesitations that a reasonable prudence might originally suggest; and more than a reasonable, becoming degree of prudence, she was very sure did not belong to Mr Elton.

Harriet's cheerful look and manner established her's: she came back, not to think of Mr Martin, but to talk of Mr Elton. Miss Nash had been telling her something, which she repeated immediately with great delight. Mr Perry had been to Mrs Goddard's to attend a sick child, and Miss Nash had seen him, and he had told

Rode off in great spirits.

Miss Nash, that as he was coming back yesterday from Clayton Park, he had met Mr Elton, and found to his great surprize that Mr Elton was actually on his road to London, and not meaning to return till the morrow, though it was the whist-club night, which he had been never known to miss before; and Mr Perry had remonstrated with him about it, and told him how shabby it was in him, their best player, to absent himself, and tried very much to persuade him to put off his journey only one day; but it would not do; Mr Elton had been determined to go on, and had said in a *very particular* way indeed, that he was going on business which he would not put off for any inducement in the world; and something about a very enviable commission, and being the bearer of something exceedingly precious. Mr Perry could not quite understand him, but he was very sure there must be a *lady* in the case, and he told him so; and Mr Elton only looked very conscious and smiling, and rode off in great spirits. Miss Nash had told her all this, and had talked a great deal more about Mr Elton; and said, looking so very significantly at her, 'that she did not pretend to understand what his business might be, but she only knew that any woman whom Mr Elton could prefer, she should think the luckiest woman in the world; for, beyond a doubt, Mr Elton had not his equal for beauty or agreeableness.'

CHAPTER NINE

MR KNIGHTLEY MIGHT quarrel with her, but Emma could not quarrel with herself. He was so much displeased, that it was longer than usual before he came to Hartfield again; and when they did meet, his grave looks shewed that she was not forgiven. She was sorry, but could not repent. On the contrary, her plans and proceedings were more and more justified, and endeared to her by the general appearances of the next few days.

The Picture, elegantly framed, came safely to hand soon after Mr Elton's return, and being hung over the mantle-piece of the common sitting-room, he got up to look at it, and sighed out his half sentences of admiration just as he ought; and as for Harriet's feelings, they were visibly forming themselves into as strong and steady an attachment as her youth and sort of mind admitted. Emma was soon perfectly satisfied of Mr Martin's being no otherwise remembered, than as he furnished a contrast with Mr Elton, of the utmost advantage to the latter.

Her views of improving her little friend's mind, by a great deal of useful reading and conversation, had never yet led to more than a few first chapters, and the intention of going on tomorrow. It was much easier to chat than to study; much pleasanter to let her imagination range and work at Harriet's fortune, than to be labouring to enlarge her comprehension or exercise it on sober facts; and the only literary pursuit which engaged Harriet at present, the only mental provision she was making for the evening of her life, was the collecting and transcribing all the riddles of every sort that she could meet with, into a thin quarto of hot-pressed paper, made up by her friend, and ornamented with cyphers and trophies.

In this age of literature, such collections on a very grand scale are not uncommon. Miss Nash, head-teacher at Mrs Goddard's, had written out at least three hundred; and Harriet, who had taken the first hint of it from her, hoped, with Miss Woodhouse's help, to get a great many more. Emma assisted with her invention, memory and taste; and as Harriet wrote a very pretty hand, it was likely to be an arrangement of the first order, in form as well as quantity.

Mr Woodhouse was almost as much interested in the business as the girls, and tried very often to recollect something worth their putting in. 'So many clever riddles as there used to be when he was young – he wondered he could not remember them! but he hoped he should in time.' And it always ended in 'Kitty, a fair but frozen maid.'

His good friend Perry too, whom he had spoken to on the subject, did not at present recollect any thing of the riddle kind; but he had desired Perry to be upon the watch, and as he went about so much, something, he thought, might come from that quarter.

It was by no means his daughter's wish that the intellects of Highbury in general should be put under requisition. Mr Elton was the only one whose assistance she asked. He was invited to contribute any really good enigmas, charades, or conundrums that he might recollect; and she had the pleasure of seeing him most intently at work with his recollections; and at the same time, as she could perceive, most earnestly careful that nothing ungallant, nothing that did not breathe a compliment to the sex should pass his lips. They owed to him their two or three politest puzzles; and the joy and exultation with which at last he recalled, and rather sentimentally recited, that well-known charade,

My first doth affliction denote,
Which my second is destin'd to feel
And my whole is the best antidote
That affliction to soften and heal. –

made her quite sorry to acknowledge that they had transcribed it some pages ago already.

'Why will not you write one yourself for us, Mr Elton?' said she; 'that is the only security for its freshness; and nothing could be easier to you.'

'Oh, no! he had never written, hardly ever, any thing of the kind in his life. The stupidest fellow! He was afraid not even Miss Woodhouse' – he stopt a moment – 'or Miss Smith could inspire him.'

The very next day however produced some proof of inspiration. He called for a few moments, just to leave a piece of paper on the table containing, as he said, a charade, which a friend of his had addressed to a young lady, the object of his admiration, but which, from his manner, Emma was immediately convinced must be his own.

'I do not offer it for Miss Smith's collection,' said he. 'Being my friend's, I have no right to expose it in any degree to the public eye, but perhaps you may not dislike looking at it.'

The speech was more to Emma than to Harriet, which Emma could understand. There was deep consciousness about him, and he found it easier to meet her eye than her friend's. He was gone the next moment: – after another moment's pause.

'Take it,' said Emma, smiling, and pushing the paper towards Harriet – 'it is for you. Take your own.'

But Harriet was in a tremor, and could not touch it; and Emma, never loth to be first, was obliged to examine it herself.

To Miss –.
CHARADE.

My first displays the wealth and pomp of kings,
Lords of the earth! their luxury and ease.
Another view of man, my second brings,
Behold him there, the monarch of the seas!

But, ah! united, what reverse we have!
Man's boasted power and freedom, all are flown;
Lord of the earth and sea, he bends a slave,
And woman, lovely woman, reigns alone.

Thy ready wit the word will soon supply,
May its approval beam in that soft eye!

She cast her eye over it, pondered, caught the meaning, read it through again to be quite certain, and quite mistress of the lines, and then passing it to Harriet, sat happily smiling, and saying to herself, while Harriet was puzzling over the paper in all the confusion of hope and dulness, 'Very well, Mr Elton, very well, indeed. I have read worse charades. *Courtship* – a very good hint. I give you credit for it. This is feeling your way. This is saying very plainly – "Pray, Miss Smith, give me leave to pay my addresses to you. Approve my charade and my intentions in the same glance.'

May its approval beam in that soft eye!

Harriet exactly. Soft, is the very word for her eye – of all epithets, the justest that could be given.

Thy ready wit the word will soon supply

Humph – Harriet's ready wit! All the better. A man must be very much in love indeed to describe her so. Ah! Mr Knightley, I wish you had the benefit of this; I think this would convince you. For once in your life you would be obliged to own yourself mistaken. An excellent charade indeed! and very much to the purpose. Things must come to a crisis soon now.'

She was obliged to break off from these very pleasant observations, which were otherwise of a sort to run into great length, by the eagerness of Harriet's wondering questions.

'What can it be, Miss Woodhouse? – what can it be? I have not an idea – I cannot guess it in the least. What can it possibly be? Do try to find it out, Miss Woodhouse. Do help me. I never saw any thing so hard. Is it kingdom? I wonder who the friend was – and who could be the young lady! Do you think it is a good one? Can it be woman?

And woman, lovely woman, reigns alone.

Can it be Neptune?

Behold him there, the monarch of the seas!

Or a trident? or a mermaid? or a shark? Oh, no! shark is only one syllable. It must be very clever, or he would not have brought it. Oh! Miss Woodhouse, do you think we shall ever find out?'

'Mermaids and sharks! Nonsense! My dear Harriet, what are you thinking of? Where would be the use of his bringing us a charade made by a friend upon a mermaid or a shark? Give me the paper and listen.

'For Miss –, read Miss Smith.

My first displays the wealth and pomp of kings,
Lords of the earth! their luxury and ease.

That is *court*.

Another view of man, my second brings;
Behold him there, the monarch of the seas!

That is *ship*; – plain as can be. – Now for the cream.

But ah! united, (courtship, *you know,) what reverse we have!*
Man's boasted power and freedom, all are flown.
Lord of the earth and sea, he bends a slave,
And woman, lovely woman, reigns alone.

A very proper compliment! – and then follows the application, which I think, my dear Harriet, you cannot find much difficulty in comprehending. Read it in comfort to yourself. There can be no doubt of its being written for you and to you.'

Harriet could not long resist so delightful a persuasion. She read the concluding lines, and was all flutter and happiness. She could not speak. But she was not wanted to speak. It was enough for her to feel. Emma spoke for her.

'There is so pointed, and so particular a meaning in this compliment,' said she, 'that I cannot have a moment's doubt as to Mr Elton's intentions. You are his object – and you will soon receive the completest proof of it. I thought it must be so. I thought I could not be so deceived; but now, it is clear; the state of his mind is as clear and decided, as my wishes on the subject have been ever since I knew you. Yes, Harriet, just so long have I been wanting the very circumstance to happen which has happened. I could never tell whether an attachment between you and Mr Elton were most desirable or most natural. Its probability and its eligibility have really so equalled each other! I am very happy. I congratulate you, my dear Harriet, with all my heart. This is an attachment which a woman may well feel pride in creating. This is a connection which offers nothing but good. It will give you every thing that you want – consideration, independence, a proper home – it will fix you in the centre of all your real friends, close to Hartfield and to me, and confirm our intimacy for ever. This, Harriet, is an alliance which can never raise a blush in either of us.'

'Dear Miss Woodhouse' – and 'Dear Miss Woodhouse,' was all that Harriet, with many tender embraces could articulate at first; but when they did arrive at something more like conversation, it was sufficiently clear to her friend that she saw, felt, anticipated, and remembered just as she ought. Mr Elton's superiority had very ample acknowledgment.

'Whatever you say is always right,' cried Harriet, 'and therefore I suppose, and believe, and hope it must be so; but otherwise I could not have imagined it. It is so much beyond any thing I deserve. Mr Elton, who might marry any body! There cannot be two opinions about *him*. He is so very superior. Only think of those sweet verses – "To Miss –." Dear me, how clever! – Could it really be meant for me?'

'I cannot make a question, or listen to a question about that. It is a certainty. Receive it on my judgment. It is a sort of prologue to the play, a motto to the chapter; and will be soon followed by matter-of-fact prose.'

'It is a sort of thing which nobody could have expected. I am sure, a month ago, I had no more idea myself! – The strangest things do take place!'

'When Miss Smiths and Mr Eltons get acquainted – they do indeed – and really it is strange; it is out of the common course that what is so evidently, so palpably desirable – what courts the pre-arrangement of other people, should so immediately shape itself into the proper form. You and Mr Elton are by situation called together; you belong to one another by every circumstance of your respective homes. Your marrying will be equal to the match at Randalls. There does seem to be a something in the air of Hartfield which gives love exactly the right direction, and sends it into the very channel where it ought to flow.

The course of true love never did run smooth –

A Hartfield edition of Shakespeare would have a long note on that passage.'

'That Mr Elton should really be in love with me, – me, of all people, who did not know him, to speak to him, at Michaelmas!

And he, the very handsomest man that ever was, and a man that every body looks up to, quite like Mr Knightley! His company so sought after, that every body says he need not eat a single meal by himself if he does not chuse it; that he has more invitations than there are days in the week. And so excellent in the Church! Miss Nash has put down all the texts he has ever preached from since he came to Highbury. Dear me! When I look back to the first time I saw him! How little did I think! – The two Abbotts and I ran into the front room and peeped through the blind when we heard he was going by, and Miss Nash came and scolded us away, and staid to look through herself; however, she called me back presently, and let me look too, which was very good-natured. And how beautiful we thought he looked! He was arm in arm with Mr Cole.'

'This is an alliance which, whoever – whatever your friends may be, must be agreeable to them, provided at least they have common sense; and we are not to be addressing our conduct to fools. If they are anxious to see you *happily* married, here is a man whose amiable character gives every assurance of it; – if they wish to have you settled in the same country and circle which they have chosen to place you in, here it will be accomplished; and if their only object is that you should, in the common phrase, be *well* married, here is the comfortable fortune, the respectable establishment, the rise in the world which must satisfy them.'

'Yes, very true. How nicely you talk; I love to hear you. You understand every thing. You and Mr Elton are one as clever as the other. This charade! – If I had studied a twelvemonth, I could never have made any thing like it.'

'I thought he meant to try his skill, by his manner of declining it yesterday.'

'I do think it is, without exception, the best charade I ever read.'

'I never read one more to the purpose, certainly.'

'It is as long again as almost all we have had before.'

'I do not consider its length as particularly in its favour. Such things in general cannot be too short.'

Harriet was too intent on the lines to hear. The most satisfactory comparisons were rising in her mind.

'It is one thing,' said she, presently – her cheeks in a glow – 'to have very good sense in a common way, like every body else, and if there is any thing to say, to sit down and write a letter, and say just what you must, in a short way; and another, to write verses and charades like this.'

Emma could not have desired a more spirited rejection of Mr Martin's prose.

'Such sweet lines!' continued Harriet – 'these two last! – But how shall I ever be able to return the paper, or say I have found it out? – Oh! Miss Woodhouse, what can we do about that?'

'Leave it to me. You do nothing. He will be here this evening, I dare say, and then I will give it him back, and some nonsense or other will pass between us, and you shall not be committed. – Your soft eyes shall chuse their own time for beaming. Trust to me.'

'Oh! Miss Woodhouse, what a pity that I must not write this beautiful charade into my book! I am sure I have not got one half so good.'

'Leave out the two last lines, and there is no reason why you should not write it into your book.'

'Oh! but those two lines are' –

'– The best of all. Granted; – for private enjoyment; and for private enjoyment keep them. They are not at all the less written you know, because you divide them. The couplet does not cease to be, nor does its meaning change. But take it away, and all *appropriation* ceases, and a very pretty gallant charade remains, fit for any collection. Depend upon it, he would not like to have his charade slighted, much better than his passion. A poet in love must be encouraged in both capacities, or neither. Give me the book, I will write it down, and then there can be no possible reflection on you.'

Harriet submitted, though her mind could hardly separate the parts, so as to feel quite sure that her friend were not writing down a declaration of love. It seemed too precious an offering for any degree of publicity.

'I shall never let that book go out of my hands,' said she.

'Very well,' replied Emma; 'a most natural feeling; and the longer it lasts, the better I shall be pleased. But there is my father coming: you will not object to my reading the charade to him. It will be giving him so much pleasure! He loves any thing of the sort, and especially any thing that pays woman a compliment. He has the tenderest spirit of gallantry towards us all! – You must let me read it to him.'

Harriet looked grave.

'My dear Harriet, you must not refine too much upon this charade. – You will betray your feelings improperly, if you are too conscious and too quick, and appear to affix more meaning, or even quite all the meaning which may be affixed to it. Do not be overpowered by such a little tribute of admiration. If he had been anxious for secrecy, he would not have left the paper while I was by; but he rather pushed it towards me than towards you. Do not let us be too solemn on the business. He has encouragement enough to proceed, without our sighing out our souls over this charade.'

'Oh! no – I hope I shall not be ridiculous about it. Do as you please.'

Mr Woodhouse came in, and very soon led to the subject again, by the recurrence of his very frequent inquiry of 'Well, my dears, how does your book go on? – Have you got any thing fresh?'

'Yes, papa, we have something to read you, something quite fresh. A piece of paper was found on the table this morning – (dropt, we suppose, by a fairy) – containing a very pretty charade, and we have just copied it in.'

She read it to him, just as he liked to have any thing read, slowly and distinctly, and two or three times over, with explanations of every part as she proceeded – and he was very much pleased, and, as she had foreseen, especially struck with the complimentary conclusion.

'Aye, that's very just, indeed, that's very properly said. Very true. "Woman, lovely woman." It is such a pretty charade, my dear, that I can easily guess what fairy brought it. – Nobody could have written so prettily, but you, Emma.'

Emma only nodded, and smiled. – After a little thinking, and a very tender sigh, he added,

'Ah! it is no difficulty to see who you take after! Your dear mother was so clever at all those things! If I had but her memory! But I can remember nothing; – not even that particular riddle which you have heard me mention; I can only recollect the first stanza; and there are several.

Kitty, a fair but frozen maid,
Kindled a flame I yet deplore,
The hood-wink'd boy I called to aid,
Though of his near approach afraid,
So fatal to my suit before.

And that is all that I can recollect of it – but it is very clever all the way through. But I think, my dear, you said you had got it.'

'Yes, papa, it is written out in our second page. We copied it from the Elegant Extracts. It was Garrick's, you know.'

'Aye, very true. – I wish I could recollect more of it.

Kitty, a fair but frozen maid.

The name makes me think of poor Isabella; for she was very near being christened Catherine after her grandmama. I hope we shall have her here next week. Have you thought, my dear, where you shall put her – and what room there will be for the children?'

'Oh! yes – she will have her own room, of course; the room she always has; – and there is the nursery for the children, – just as usual, you know. – Why should there be any change?'

'I do not know, my dear – but it is so long since she was here! – not since last Easter, and then only for a few days. – Mr John Knightley's being a lawyer is very inconvenient. – Poor Isabella! – she is sadly taken away from us all! – and how sorry she will be when she comes, not to see Miss Taylor here!'

'She will not be surprized, papa, at least.'

'I do not know, my dear. I am sure I was very much surprized when I first heard she was going to be married.'

'We must ask Mr and Mrs Weston to dine with us, while Isabella is here.'

'Yes, my dear, if there is time. – But – (in a very depressed tone) – she is coming for only one week. There will not be time for any thing.'

'It is unfortunate that they cannot stay longer – but it seems a case of necessity. Mr John Knightley must be in town again on the 28th, and we ought to be thankful, papa, that we are to have the whole of the time they can give to the country, that two or three days are not to be taken out for the Abbey. Mr Knightley promises to give up his claim this Christmas – though you know it is longer since they were with him, than with us.'

'It would be very hard indeed, my dear, if poor Isabella were to be anywhere but at Hartfield.'

Mr Woodhouse could never allow for Mr Knightley's claims on his brother, or any body's claims on Isabella, except his own. He sat musing a little while, and then said,

'But I do not see why poor Isabella should be obliged to go back so soon, though he does. I think, Emma, I shall try and persuade her to stay longer with us. She and the children might stay very well.'

'Ah! papa – that is what you never have been able to accomplish, and I do not think you ever will. Isabella cannot bear to stay behind her husband.'

This was too true for contradiction. Unwelcome as it was, Mr Woodhouse could only give a submissive sigh; and as Emma saw his spirits affected by the idea of his daughter's attachment to her husband, she immediately led to such a branch of the subject as must raise them.

'Tosses them up to the ceiling.'

'Harriet must give us as much of her company as she can while my brother and sister are here. I am sure she will be pleased with the children. We are very proud of the children, are not we, papa? I wonder which she will think the handsomest, Henry or John?'

'Aye, I wonder which she will. Poor little dears, how glad they will be to come. They are very fond of being at Hartfield, Harriet.'

'I dare say they are, sir. I am sure I do not know who is not.'

'Henry is a fine boy, but John is very like his mamma. Henry is the eldest, he was named after me, not after his father. John, the second, is named after his father. Some people are surprized, I believe, that the eldest was not, but Isabella would have him called Henry, which I thought very pretty of her. And he is a very clever boy, indeed. They are all remarkably clever; and they have so many pretty ways. They will come and stand by my chair, and say, "Grandpapa, can you give me a bit of string?" and once Henry asked me for a knife, but I told him knives were only made for grandpapas. I think their father is too rough with them very often.'

'He appears rough to you,' said Emma, 'because you are so very gentle yourself; but if you could compare him with other papas, you would not think him rough. He wishes his boys to be active and handy; and if they misbehave, can give them a sharp word now and then; but he is an affectionate father – certainly Mr John Knightley is an affectionate father. The children are all fond of him.'

'And then their uncle comes in, and tosses them up to the ceiling in a very frightful way!'

'But they like it, papa; there is nothing they like so much. It is such enjoyment to them, that if their uncle did not lay down the rule of their taking turns, which ever began would never give way to the other.'

'Well, I cannot understand it.'

'That is the case with us all, papa. One half of the world cannot understand the pleasures of the other.'

Later in the morning, and just as the girls were going to separate in preparation for the regular four o'clock dinner, the hero of this inimitable charade walked in again. Harriet turned away; but Emma could receive him with the usual smile, and her quick eye soon discerned in his the consciousness of having made a push – of having thrown a die; and she imagined he was come to see how it might turn up. His ostensible reason, however, was to ask whether Mr Woodhouse's party could be made up in the evening without him, or whether he should be in the smallest degree necessary at Hartfield. If he were, every thing else must give way; but otherwise his friend Cole had been saying so much about his dining with him – had made such a point of it, that he had promised him conditionally to come.

Emma thanked him, but could not allow of his disappointing his friend on their account; her father was sure of his rubber. He re-urged – she re-declined; and he seemed then about to make his bow, when taking the paper from the table, she returned it –

'Oh! here's the charade you were so obliging as to leave with us;

thank you for the sight of it. We admired it so much, that I have ventured to write it into Miss Smith's collection. Your friend will not take it amiss I hope. Of course I have not transcribed beyond the eight first lines.'

Mr Elton certainly did not very well know what to say. He looked rather doubtingly – rather confused; said something about 'honour;' – glanced at Emma and at Harriet, and then seeing the book open on the table, took it up, and examined it very attentively. With the view of passing off an awkward moment, Emma smilingly said,

'You must make my apologies to your friend; but so good a charade must not be confined to one or two. He may be sure of every woman's approbation while he writes with such gallantry.'

'I have no hesitation in saying,' replied Mr Elton, though hesitating a good deal while he spoke, 'I have no hesitation in saying – at least if my friend feels at all as I do – I have not the smallest doubt that, could he see his little effusion honoured as I see it, (looking at the book again, and replacing it on the table,) he would consider it as the proudest moment of his life.'

After this speech he was gone as soon as possible, Emma could not think it too soon; for with all his good and agreeable qualities, there was a sort of parade in his speeches which was very apt to incline her to laugh. She ran away to indulge the inclination, leaving the tender and the sublime of pleasure to Harriet's share.

CHAPTER TEN

THOUGH NOW THE MIDDLE of December, there had yet been no weather to prevent the young ladies from tolerably regular exercise; and on the morrow, Emma had a charitable visit to pay to a poor sick family, who lived a little way out of Highbury.

Their road to this detached cottage was down Vicarage-lane, a lane leading at right-angles from the broad, though irregular, main street of the place; and, as may be inferred, containing the blessed abode of Mr Elton. A few inferior dwellings were first to be passed, and then, about a quarter of mile down the lane rose the Vicarage; an old and not very good house, almost as close to the road as it could be. It had no advantage of situation; but had been very much smartened up by the present proprietor; and, such as it was, there could be no possibility of the two friends passing it without a slackened pace and observing eyes. – Emma's remark was –

'There it is. There go you and your riddle-book one of these days.' – Harriet's was –

'Oh! what a sweet house! – How very beautiful! – There are the yellow curtains that Miss Nash admires so much.'

'I do not often walk this way *now*,' said Emma, as they proceeded, 'but *then* there will be an inducement, and I shall gradually get intimately acquainted with all the hedges, gates, pools, and pollards of this part of Highbury.'

Harriet, she found, had never in her life been within side the Vicarage, and her curiosity to see it was so extreme, that, considering exteriors and probabilities, Emma could only class it, as a proof of love, with Mr Elton's seeing ready wit in her.

'I wish we could contrive it,' said she: 'but I cannot think of any tolerable pretence for going in; – no servant that I want to inquire about of his housekeeper – no message from my father.'

She pondered, but could think of nothing. After a mutual silence of some minutes, Harriet thus began again –

'I do so wonder, Miss Woodhouse, that you should not be married, or going to be married! so charming as you are!' –

Emma laughed, and replied.

'My being charming, Harriet, is not quite enough to induce me to marry; I must find other people charming – one other person at least. And I am not only, not going to be married, at present, but have very little intention of ever marrying at all.'

'Ah! – so you say; but I cannot believe it.'

'I must see somebody very superior to any one I have seen yet, to be tempted; Mr Elton, you know, (recollecting herself,) is out of the question: and I do *not* wish to see any such person. I would rather not be tempted. I cannot really change for the better. If I were to marry, I must expect to repent it.'

'Dear me! – it is so odd to hear a woman talk so!' –

'I have none of the usual inducements of women to marry. Were I to fall in love, indeed, it would be a different thing! but I never have been in love; it is not my way, or my nature; and I do not think I ever shall. And, without love, I am sure I should be a fool to change such a situation as mine. Fortune I do not want; employment I do not want; consequence I do not want: I believe few married women are half as much mistress of their husband's house, as I am of Hartfield; and never, never could I expect to be so truly beloved and important; so always first and always right in any man's eyes as I am in my father's.'

'But then, to be an old maid at last, like Miss Bates!'

'That is as formidable an image as you could present, Harriet; and if I thought I should ever be like Miss Bates! so silly – so satisfied – so smiling – so prosing – so undistinguishing and unfastidious – and so apt to tell every thing relative to every body about me, I would marry to-morrow. But between *us*, I am convinced there never can be any likeness, except in being unmarried.'

'But still, you will be an old maid! and that's so dreadful!'

'Never mind, Harriet, I shall not be a poor old maid; and it is poverty only which makes celibacy contemptible to a generous public! A single woman, with a very narrow income, must be a ridiculous, disagreeable, old maid! the proper sport of boys and girls; but a single woman, of good fortune, is always respectable, and may be as sensible and pleasant as anybody else. And the distinction is not quite so much against the candour and common sense of the world as appears at first; for a very narrow income has a tendency to contract the mind, and sour the temper. Those who can barely live, and who live perforce in a very small, and generally very inferior, society, may well be illiberal and cross. This does not apply, however, to Miss Bates; she is only too good natured and too silly to suit me; but, in general, she is very much to the taste of every body, though single and though poor. Poverty certainly has not contracted her mind: I really believe, if she had only a shilling in the world, she would be very likely to give away sixpence of it; and nobody is afraid of her: that is a great charm.'

'Dear me! but what shall you do? how shall you employ yourself when you grow old?'

'If I know myself, Harriet, mine is an active, busy mind, with a great many independent resources; and I do not perceive why I should be more in want of employment at forty or fifty than one-and-twenty. Woman's usual occupations of eye and hand and mind will be as open to me then, as they are now; or with no important variation. If I draw less, I shall read more; if I give up music, I shall take to carpet-work. And as for objects of interest, objects for the affections, which is in truth the great point of inferiority, the want of which is really the great evil to be avoided in *not* marrying, I shall be very well off, with all the children of a sister I love so much, to care about. There will be enough of them, in all probability, to supply every sort of sensation that declining life can need. There will be enough for every hope and every fear; and though my attachment to none can equal that of a parent, it suits my ideas of comfort better than what is warmer and blinder. My nephews and nieces! – I shall often have a niece with me.'

'Do you know Miss Bates's niece? That is, I know you must have seen her a hundred times – but are you acquainted?'

'Oh! yes; we are always forced to be acquainted whenever she comes to Highbury. By the bye, *that* is almost enough to put one out of conceit with a niece. Heaven forbid! at least, that I should ever bore people half so much about all the Knightleys together, as she does about Jane Fairfax. One is sick of the very name of Jane Fairfax. Every letter from her is read forty times over; her compliments to all friends go round and round again; and if she does but send her aunt the pattern of a stomacher, or knit a pair of garters for her grandmother, one hears of nothing else for a month. I wish Jane Fairfax very well; but she tires me to death.'

They were now approaching the cottage, and all idle topics were superseded. Emma was very compassionate; and the distresses of the poor were as sure of relief from her personal attention and kindness, her counsel and her patience, as from her purse. She understood their ways, could allow for their ignorance and their temptations, had no romantic expectations of extraordinary virtue from those, for whom education had done so little; entered into their troubles with ready sympathy, and always gave her assistance with as much intelligence as good-will. In the present instance, it was sickness and poverty together which she came to visit; and after remaining there as long as she could give comfort or advice, she quitted the cottage with such an impression of the scene as made her say to Harriet, as they walked away,

'These are the sights, Harriet, to do one good. How trifling they make every thing else appear! – I feel now as if I could think of nothing but these poor creatures all the rest of the day; and yet, who can say how soon it may all vanish from my mind?'

'Very true,' said Harriet. 'Poor creatures! one can think of nothing else.'

'And really, I do not think the impression will soon be over,' said Emma, as she crossed the low hedge, and tottering footstep which ended the narrow, slippery path through the cottage garden, and brought them into the lane again. 'I do not think it will,' stopping to look once more at all the outward wretchedness of the place, and recall the still greater within.

'Oh! dear, no,' said her companion.

They walked on. The lane made a slight bend; and when that bend was passed, Mr Elton was immediately in sight; and so near as to give Emma time only to say farther,

'Ah! Harriet, here comes a very sudden trial of our stability in good thoughts. Well, (smiling,) I hope it may be allowed that if compassion has produced exertion and relief to the sufferers, it has done all that is truly important. If we feel for the wretched, enough to do all we can for them, the rest is empty sympathy, only distressing to ourselves.'

Harriet could just answer, 'Oh! dear, yes,' before the gentleman joined them. The wants and sufferings of the poor family, however, were the first subject on meeting. He had been going to call on them. His visit he would now defer; but they had a very interesting parley about what could be done and should be done. Mr Elton then turned back to accompany them.

'To fall in with each other on such an errand as this,' thought Emma; 'to meet in a charitable scheme; this will bring a great increase of love on each side. I should not wonder if it were to bring on the declaration. It must, if I were not here. I wish I were anywhere else.'

Anxious to separate herself from them as far as she could, she soon afterwards took possession of a narrow footpath, a little raised on one side of the lane, leaving them together in the main road. But she had not been there two minutes when she found that Harriet's habits of dependence and imitation were bringing her up too, and that, in short, they would both be soon after her. This would not do; she immediately stopped, under pretence of having some alteration to make in the lacing of her half-boot, and stooping down in complete occupation of the footpath, begged them to have the goodness to walk on, and she would follow in half a minute. They did as they were desired; and by the time she judged it reasonable to have done with her boot, she had the comfort of further delay in her power, being overtaken by a child from the cottage, setting out, according to orders, with her pitcher, to fetch broth from Hartfield. To walk by the side of this child, and talk to and question her, was the most natural thing in the world, or would have been the most natural, had she been acting just then without design; and by this means the others were still able to keep ahead, without any obligation of waiting for her. She gained on them, however, involuntarily; the child's pace was quick, and theirs rather slow; and she was the more concerned at it, from their being evidently in a conversation which interested them. Mr Elton was speaking with animation, Harriet listening with a very pleased attention; and Emma having sent the child on, was beginning to think how she might draw back a little more, when they both looked around, and she was obliged to join them.

Mr Elton was still talking, still engaged in some interesting detail; and Emma experienced some disappointment when she found that he was only giving his fair companion an account of the yesterday's party at his friend Cole's, and that she was comc in herself for the Stilton cheese, the north Wiltshire, the butter, the cellery, the beet-root and all the dessert.

'This would soon have led to something better of course,' was her consoling reflection; 'any thing interests between those who love; and any thing will serve as introduction to what is near the heart. If I could but have kept longer away!'

They now walked on together quietly, till within view of the vicarage pales, when a sudden resolution, of at least getting Harriet into the house, made her again find something very much amiss about her boot, and fall behind to arrange it once more. She then broke the lace off short, and dexterously throwing it into a ditch, was presently obliged to entreat them to stop, and acknowledge her inability to put herself to rights so as to be able to walk home in tolerable comfort.

'Part of my lace is gone,' said she, 'and I do not know how I am to contrive. I really am a most troublesome companion to you both, but I hope I am not often so ill-equipped. Mr Elton, I must beg leave to stop at your house, and ask your housekeeper for a bit of ribband or string, or any thing just to keep my boot on.'

Mr Elton looked all happiness at this proposition; and nothing could exceed his alertness and attention in conducting them into his house and endeavouring to make every thing appear to advantage. The room they were taken into was the one he chiefly occupied, and looking forwards; behind it was another with which it immediately communicated; the door between them was open, and Emma passed into it with the housekeeper to receive her assistance in the most comfortable manner. She was obliged to leave the door ajar as she found it; but she fully intended that Mr Elton should close it. It was not closed however, it still remained ajar; but by engaging the housekeeper in incessant conversation, she hoped to make it practicable for him to chuse his own subject in the adjoining room. For ten minutes she could hear nothing but herself. It could be protracted no longer. She was then obliged to be finished and make her appearance.

The lovers were standing together at one of the windows. It had a most favourable aspect; and, for half a minute, Emma felt the glory of having schemed successfully. But it would not do; he had not come to the point. He had been most agreeable, most delightful; he had told Harriet that he had seen them go by, and had purposely followed them; other little gallantries and allusions had been dropt, but nothing serious.

'Cautious, very cautious,' thought Emma; 'he advances inch by inch, and will hazard nothing till he believes himself secure.'

Still, however, though every thing had not been accomplished by her ingenious device, she could not but flatter herself that it had been the occasion of much present enjoyment to both, and must be leading them forward to the great event.

CHAPTER ELEVEN

Mr Elton must now be left to himself. It was no longer in Emma's power to superintend his happiness or quicken his measures. The coming of her sister's family was so very near at hand, that first in anticipation and then in reality, it became henceforth her prime object of interest; and during the ten days of their stay at Hartfield it was not to be expected – she did not herself expect – that any thing beyond occasional, fortuitous assistance could be afforded by her to the lovers. They might advance rapidly if they would, however; they must advance somehow or other whether they would or no. She hardly wished to have more leisure for them. There are people, who the more you do for them, the less they will do for themselves.

Mr and Mrs John Knightley, from having been longer than usual absent from Surrey, were exciting of course rather more than the usual interst. Till this year, every long vacation since their marriage had been divided between Hartfield and Donwell Abbey; but all the holidays of this autumn had been given to sea-bathing for the children, and it was therefore many months since they had been seen in a regular way by their Surrey connections, or seen at all by Mr Woodhouse, who could not be induced to get so far as London, even for poor Isabella's sake; and who consequently was now most nervously and apprehensively happy in forestalling this too short visit.

He thought much of the evils of the journey for her, and not a little of the fatigues of his own horses and coachman who were to bring some of the party the last half of the way; but his alarms were needless; the sixteen miles being happily accomplished, and Mr and Mrs John Knightley, their five children, and a competent number of nursery-maids, all reaching Hartfield in safety. The bustle and joy of such an arrival, the many to be talked to, welcomed, encouraged, and variously dispersed and disposed of, produced a noise and confusion which his nerves could not have born under any other cause, nor have endured much longer even for this; but the ways of Hartfield and the feelings of her father were so respected by Mrs John Knightley, that in spite of maternal solicitude for the immediate enjoyment of her little ones, and for their having instantly all the liberty and attendance, all the eating and drinking, and sleeping and playing, which they could possibly wish for, without the smallest delay, the children were never allowed to be long a disturbance to him, either in themselves or in any restless attendance on them.

Mrs John Knightley was a pretty, elegant little woman, of gentle, quiet manners, and a disposition remarkably amiable and affectionate; wrapt up in her family; a devoted wife, a doating mother, and so tenderly attached to her father and sister that, but for these higher ties, a warmer love might have seemed impossible. She could never see a fault in any of them. She was not a woman of strong understanding or any quickness; and with this resemblance of her father, she inherited also much of his constitution; was delicate in her own health, over-careful of that of her children, had many fears and many nerves, and was as fond of her own Mr Wingfield in town as her father could be of Mr Perry. They were alike too, in general benevolence of temper, and a strong habit of regard for every old acquaintance.

Mr John Knightley was a tall, gentleman-like, and very clever man; rising in his profession, domestic, and respectable in his private character; but with reserved manners which prevented his being generally pleasing; and capable of being sometimes out of humour. He was not an ill-tempered man, not so often unreasonably cross as to deserve such a reproach; but his temper was not his great perfection; and, indeed, with such a worshipping wife, it was hardly possible that any natural defects in it should not be increased. The extreme sweetness of her temper must hurt his. He had all the clearness and quickness of mind which she wanted, and he could sometimes act an ungracious, or say a severe thing. He was not a great favourite with his fair sister-in-law. Nothing wrong in him escaped her. She was quick in feeling the little injuries to Isabella, which Isabella never felt herself. Perhaps she might have passed over more had his manners been flattering to Isabella's sister, but they were only those of a calmly kind brother and friend, without praise and without blindness; but hardly any degree of personal compliment could have made her regardless of that greatest fault of all in her eyes which he sometimes fell into, the want of respectful forbearance towards her father. There he had not always the patience that could have been wished. Mr Woodhouse's peculiarities and fidgettiness were sometimes provoking him to a rational remonstrance or sharp retort equally ill bestowed. It did not often happen; for Mr John Knightley had really a great regard for his father-in-law, and generally a strong sense of what was due to him; but it was too often for Emma's charity, especially as there was all the pain of apprehension frequently to be endured, though the offence came not. The beginning, however, of every visit displayed none but the properest feelings, and this being of necessity so short might be hoped to pass away in unsullied cordiality. They had not been long seated and composed when Mr Woodhouse, with a melancholy shake of the head and a sigh, called his daughter's attention to the sad change at Hartfield since she had been there last.

'Ah! my dear,' said he, 'poor Miss Taylor – It is a grievous business!'

'Oh! yes, sir,' cried she with ready sympathy, 'how you must miss her! And dear Emma too! – what a dreadful loss to you both! – I have been so grieved for you. – I could not imagine how you could possibly do without her. – It is a sad change indeed. – But I hope she is pretty well, sir.'

'Pretty well, my dear – I hope – pretty well. – I do not know but that the place agrees with her tolerably.'

Mr John Knightley here asked Emma quietly whether there were any doubts of the air of Randalls.

'Oh! no – none in the least. I never saw Mrs Weston better in my life – never looking so well. Papa is only speaking his own regret.'

'Very much to the honour of both,' was the handsome reply.

'And do you see her, sir, tolerably often?' asked Isabella in the plaintive tone which just suited her father.

Mr Woodhouse hesitated. – 'Not near so often, my dear, as I could wish.'

'Oh! papa, we have missed seeing them but one entire day since they married. Either in the morning or evening of every day, excepting one, have we seen either Mr Weston or Mrs Weston, and generally both, either at Randalls or here – and as you may suppose, Isabella, most frequently here. They are very, very kind in their visits. Mr Weston is really as kind as herself. Papa, if you speak in that melancholy way, you will be giving Isabella a false idea of us all. Every body must be aware that Miss Taylor must be missed, but every body ought also to be assured that Mr and Mrs Weston do really prevent our missing her by any means to the extent we ourselves anticipated – which is the exact truth.'

'Just as it should be,' said Mr John Knightley, 'and just as I hoped it was from your letters. Her wish of shewing you attention could not be doubted, and his being a disengaged and social man makes it all easy. I have been always telling you, my love, that I had no idea of the change being so very material to Hartfield as you apprehended; and now you have Emma's account, I hope you will be satisfied.'

'Why to be sure,' said Mr Woodhouse – 'yes, certainly – I cannot deny that Mrs Weston, poor Mrs Weston, does come and see us pretty often – but then – she is always obliged to go away again.'

'It would be very hard upon Mr Weston if she did not, papa. – You quite forget poor Mr Weston.'

Flying Henry's kite for him.

'I think, indeed,' said John Knightley pleasantly, 'that Mr Weston has some little claim. You and I, Emma, will venture to take the part of the poor husband. I, being a husband, and you not being a wife, the claims of the man may very likely strike us with equal force. As for Isabella, she has been married long enough to see the convenience of putting all the Mr Westons aside as much as she can.'

'Me, my love,' cried his wife, hearing and understanding only in part. – 'Are you talking about me? – I am sure nobody ought to be, or can be, a greater advocate for matrimony that I am; and if it had not been for the misery of her leaving Hartfield, I should never have thought of Miss Taylor but as the most fortunate woman in the world; and as to slighting Mr Weston, that excellent Mr Weston, I think there is nothing he does not deserve. I believe he is one of the very best tempered men that ever existed. Excepting yourself and your brother, I do not know his equal for temper. I shall never forget his flying Henry's kite for him that very windy day last Easter – and ever since his particular kindness last September twelvemonth in writing that note, at twelve o'clock at night, on purpose to assure me that there was no scarlet fever at Cobham, I have been convinced there could not be a more feeling heart nor a better man in existence. – If any body can deserve him, it must be Miss Taylor.'

'Where is the young man?' said John Knightley, 'Has he been here on this occasion – or has he not?'

'He has not been here yet,' replied Emma. 'There was a strong expectation of his coming soon after the marriage, but it ended in nothing; and I have not heard him mentioned lately.'

'But you should tell them of the letter, my dear,' said her father. 'He wrote a letter to poor Mrs Weston, to congratulate her, and a very proper, handsome letter it was. She shewed it to me. I thought it very well done of him indeed. Whether it was his own idea you know, one cannot tell. He is but young, and his uncle perhaps – '

'My dear papa, he is three-and-twenty. – You forget how time passes.'

'Three-and-twenty! – is he indeed? – Well, I could not have thought it – and he was but two years old when he lost his poor mother! Well, time does fly indeed! – and my memory is very bad. However, it was an exceeding good, pretty letter, and gave Mr and Mrs Weston a great deal of pleasure. I remember it was written from Weymouth, and dated Sept. 28th – and began, "My dear Madam," but I forget how it went on; and it was signed "F. C. Weston Churchill." – I remember that perfectly.'

'How very pleasing and proper of him!' cried the good-hearted

Mrs John Knightley. 'I have no doubt of his being a most amiable young man. But how sad it is that he should not live at home with his father! There is something so shocking in a child's being taken away from his parents and natural home! I never can comprehend how Mr Weston could part with him. To give up one's child! I really never could think well of any body who proposed such a thing to any body else.'

'Nobody ever did think well of the Churchills, I fancy,' observed Mr John Knightley coolly. 'But you need not imagine Mr Weston to have felt what you would feel in giving up Henry or John. Mr Weston is rather an easy, cheerful tempered man, than a man of strong feelings; he takes things as he finds them, and makes enjoyment of them somehow or other, depending, I suspect, much more upon what is called *society* for his comforts, that is, upon the power of eating and drinking, and playing whist with his neighbours five times a-week, than upon family affection, or any thing that home affords.'

Emma could not like what bordered on a reflection on Mr Weston, and had half a mind to take it up; but she struggled, and let it pass. She would keep the peace if possible; and there was something honourable and valuable in the strong domestic habits, the all-sufficiency of home to himself, whence resulted her brother's disposition to look down on the common rate of social intercourse, and those to whom it was important. – It had a high claim to forbearance.

CHAPTER TWELVE

Mr Knightley was to dine with them – rather against the inclination of Mr Woodhouse, who did not like that any one should share with him in Isabella's first day. Emma's sense of right however had decided it; and besides the consideration of what was due to each brother, she had particular pleasure, from the circumstance of the late disagreement between Mr Knightley and herself, in procuring him the proper invitation.

She hoped they might now become friends again. She thought it was time to make up. Making-up indeed would not do. *She* certainly had not been in the wrong, and *he* would never own that he had. Concession must be out of the question; but it was time to appear to forget that they had ever quarrelled; and she hoped it might rather assist the restoration of friendship, that when he came into the room she had one of the children with her! the youngest, a nice little girl about eight months old, who was now making her first visit to Hartfield, and very happy to be danced about in her aunt's arms. It did assist; for though he began with grave looks and short questions, he was soon led on to talk of them all in the usual way, and to take the child out of her arms with all the unceremoniousness of perfect amity. Emma felt they were friends again; and the conviction giving her at first great satisfaction, and then a little sauciness, she could not help saying, as he was admiring the baby,

'What a comfort it is, that we think alike about our nephews and nieces. As to men and women, our opinions are sometimes very different; but with regard to these children, I observe we never disagree.'

'If you were as much guided by nature in your estimate of men and women, and as little under the power of fancy and whim in your dealings with them, as you are where these children are concerned, we might always think alike.'

'To be sure – our discordancies must always arise from my being in the wrong.'

'Yes,' said he, smiling – 'and reason good. I was sixteen years old when you were born.'

'A material difference then,' she replied – 'and no doubt you were much my superior in judgment at that period of our lives; but does not the lapse of one-and-twenty years bring our understandings a good deal nearer?'

'Yes – a good deal *nearer.*'

'But still, not near enough to give me a chance of being right, if we think differently.'

'I have still the advantage of you by sixteen years' experience, and by not being a pretty young woman and a spoiled child. Come, my dear Emma, let us be friends and say no more about it. Tell your aunt, little Emma, that she ought to set you a better example than to be renewing old grievances, and that if she were not wrong before, she is now.'

'That's true,' she cried – 'very true. Little Emma, grow up a better woman than your aunt. Be infinitely cleverer and not half so conceited. Now, Mr Knightley, a word or two more, and I have done. As far as good intentions went, we were *both* right, and I must say that no effects on my side of the argument have yet proved wrong. I only want to know that Mr Martin is not very, very bitterly disappointed.'

'A man cannot be more so,' was his short, full answer.

'Ah! – Indeed I am very sorry. – Come, shake hands with me.'

This had just taken place and with great cordiality, when John Knightley made his appearance, and 'How d'ye do, George?' and 'John, how are you?' succeeded in the true English style, burying under a calmness that seemed all but indifference, the real attachment which would have led either of them, if requisite, to do every thing for the good of the other.

The evening was quiet and conversible, as Mr Woodhouse declined cards entirely for the sake of comfortable talk with his dear Isabella, and the little party made two natural divisions; on one side he and his daughter; on the other the two Mr Knightleys; their subjects totally distinct, or very rarely mixing – and Emma only occasionally joining in one or the other.

The brothers talked of their own concerns and pursuits, but principally of those of the elder, whose temper was by much the most communicative, and who was always the greater talker. As a magistrate, he had generally some point of law to consult John about, or, at least, some curious anecdote to give; and as a farmer, as keeping in hand the home-farm at Donwell, he had to tell what every field was to bear next year, and to give all such local information as could not fail of being interesting to a brother whose home it had equally been the longest part of his life, and whose attachments were strong. The plan of a drain, the change of a fence, the felling of a tree, and the destination of every acre for wheat, turnips, or spring corn, was entered into with as much equality of interest by John, as his cooler manners rendered possible; and if his willing brother ever left him any thing to enquire about, his enquiries even approached a tone of eagerness.

While they were thus comfortably occupied, Mr Woodhouse was enjoying a full flow of happy regrets and fearful affection with his daughter.

'My poor dear Isabella,' said he, fondly taking her hand, and interrupting, for a few moments, her busy labours for some one of her five children – 'How long it is, how terribly long since you were here! And how tired you must be after your journey! You must go to bed early, my dear – and I recommend a little gruel to you before you go. – You and I will have a nice basin of gruel together. My dear Emma, suppose we all have a little gruel.'

Emma could not suppose any such thing, knowing, as she did, that both the Mr Knightleys were as unpersuadable on that article as herself; – and two basins only were ordered. After a little more discourse in praise of gruel, with some wondering at its not being taken every evening by every body, he proceeded to say, with an air of grave reflection.

'It was an awkward business, my dear, your spending the autumn at South End instead of coming here. I never had much opinion of the sea air.'

'Mr Wingfield most strenuously recommended it, sir – or we should not have gone. He recommended it for all the children, but particularly for the weakness in little Bella's throat, – both sea air and bathing.'

'Ah! my dear, but Perry had many doubts about the sea doing her any good; and as to myself, I have been long perfectly convinced, though perhaps I never told you so before, that the sea is very rarely of use to any body. I am sure it almost killed me once.'

'Come, come,' cried Emma, feeling this to be an unsafe subject, 'I must beg you not to talk of the sea. It makes me envious and miserable; – I who have never seen it! South End is prohibited, if you please. My dear Isabella, I have not heard you make one enquiry after Mr Perry yet; and he never forgets you.'

'Oh! good Mr Perry – how is he, sir?'

'Why, pretty well; but not quite well. Poor Perry is bilious, and he has not time to take care of himself – he tells me he has not time to take care of himself – which is very sad – but he is always wanted all round the country. I suppose there is not a man in such practice any where. But then, there is not so clever a man any where.'

'And Mrs Perry and the children, how are they? do the children grow? – I have a great regard for Mr Perry. I hope he will be calling soon. He will be so pleased to see my little ones.'

'I hope he will be here to-morrow, for I have a question or two to ask him about myself of some consequence. And, my dear, whenever he comes, you had better let him look at little Bella's throat.'

'Oh! my dear sir, her throat is so much better that I have hardly any uneasiness about it. Either bathing has been of the greatest service to her, or else it is to be attributed to an excellent embrocation of Mr Wingfield's, which we have been applying at times ever since August.'

'It is not very likely, my dear, that bathing should have been of use to her – and if I had known you were wanting an embrocation, I would have spoken to – '

'You seem to me to have forgotten Mrs and Miss Bates,' said Emma, 'I have not heard one enquiry after them.'

'Oh! the good Bateses – I am quite ashamed of myself – but you mention them in most of your letters. I hope they are quite well.

Good old Mrs Bates – I will call upon her to-morrow, and take my children. – They are always so pleased to see my children. – And that excellent Miss Bates! – such thorough worthy people! – How are they, sir?'

'Why, pretty well, my dear, upon the whole. But poor Mrs Bates had a bad cold about a month ago.'

'How sorry I am! But colds were never so prevalent as they have been this autumn. Mr Wingfield told me that he had never known them more general or heavy – except when it has been quite an influenza.'

'That has been a good deal the case, my dear; but not to the degree you mention. Perry says that colds have been very general, but not so heavy as he has very often known them in November. Perry does not call it altogether a sickly season.'

'No, I do not know that Mr Wingfield considers it *very* sickly except – '

'Ah! my poor dear child, the truth is, that in London it is always a sickly season. Nobody is healthy in London, nobody can be. It is a dreadful thing to have you forced to live there! – so far off! – and the air so bad!'

'No, indeed – *we* are not at all in a bad air. Our part of London is so very superior to most others! – You must not confound us with London in general, my dear Sir. The neighbourhood of Brunswick Square is very different from almost all the rest. We are so very airy! I should be unwilling, I own, to live in any other part of the town; – there is hardly any other that I could be satisfied to have my children in: – but *we* are so remarkably airy! – Mr Wingfield thinks the vicinity of Brunswick Square decidedly the most favourable as to air.'

'Ah! my dear, it is not like Hartfield. You make the best of it – but after you have been a week at Hartfield, you are all of you different creatures; you do not look like the same. Now I cannot say, that I think you are any of you looking well at present.'

'I am sorry to hear you say so, sir; but I assure you, excepting those little nervous head-aches and palpitations which I am never entirely free from any where, I am quite well myself; and if the children were rather pale before they went to bed, it was only because they were a little more tired than usual, from their journey and the happiness of coming. I hope you will think better of their looks to-morrow; for I assure you Mr Wingfield told me, that he did not believe he had ever sent us off altogether, in such good case. I trust, at least, that you do not think Mr Knightley looking ill,' – turning her eyes with affectionate anxiety towards her husband.

'Middling, my dear; I cannot compliment you. I think Mr John Knightley very far from looking well.'

'What is the matter, sir?! Did you speak to me?' cried Mr John Knightley, hearing his own name.

'I am sorry to find, my love, that my father does not think you looking well – but I hope it is only from being a little fatigued. I could have wished, however, as you know, that you had seen Mr Wingfield before you left home.'

'My dear Isabella,' – exclaimed he hastily – 'pray do not concern yourself about my looks. Be satisfied with doctoring and coddling yourself and the children, and let me look as I chuse.'

'I did not thoroughly understand what you were telling your brother,' cried Emma, 'about your friend Mr Graham's intending to have a bailiff from Scotland, to look after his new estate. But will it answer? Will not the old prejudice be too strong?'

And she talked in this way so long and successfully that, when forced to give her attention again to her father and sister, she had nothing worse to hear than Isabella's kind inquiry after Jane Fairfax; – and Jane Fairfax, though no great favourite with her in general, she was at that moment very happy to assist in praising.

'That sweet, amiable Jane Fairfax!' said Mrs John Knightley – 'It is so long since I have seen her, except now and then for a moment accidentally in town! What happiness it must be to her good old grandmother and excellent aunt, when she comes to visit them! I always regret excessively on dear Emma's account that she cannot be more at Highbury; but now their daughter is married, I suppose Colonel and Mrs Campbell will not be able to part with her at all. She would be such a delightful companion for Emma.'

Mr Woodhouse agreed to it all, but added,

'Our little friend Harriet Smith, however, is just such another pretty kind of young person. You will like Harriet. Emma could not have a better companion than Harriet.'

'I am most happy to hear it – but only Jane Fairfax one knows to be so very accomplished and superior! – and exactly Emma's age.'

This topic was discussed very happily, and others succeeded of similar moment, and passed away with similar harmony; but the evening did not close without a little return of agitation. The gruel came and supplied a great deal to be said – much praise and many comments – undoubting decision of its wholesomeness for every constitution, and pretty severe Philippics upon the many houses where it was never met with tolerable; – but, unfortunately, among the failures which the daughter had to instance, the most recent, and therefore most prominent, was in her own cook at South End,

She had never been able to get anything tolerable.

a young woman hired for the time, who never had been able to understand what she meant by a basin of nice smooth gruel thin, but not too thin. Often as she had wished for and ordered it, she had never been able to get any thing tolerable. Here was a dangerous opening.

'Ah!' said Mr Woodhouse, shaking his head and fixing his eyes on her with tender concern. – The ejaculation in Emma's ear expressed, 'Ah! there is no end of the sad consequences of your going to South End. It does not bear talking of.' And for a little while she hoped he would not talk of it, and that a silent rumination might suffice to restore him to the relish of his own smooth gruel. After an interval of some minutes, however, he began with,

'I shall always be very sorry that you went to the sea this autumn, instead of coming here.'

'But why should you be sorry, sir? – I assure you, it did the children a great deal of good.'

'And, moreover, if you must go to the sea, it had better not have been to South End. South End is an unhealthy place. Perry was surprized to hear you had fixed upon South End.'

'I know there is such an idea with many people, but indeed it is quite a mistake, sir. – We all had our health perfectly well there, never found the least inconvenience from the mud; and Mr Wingfield says it is entirely a mistake to suppose the place unhealthy; and I am sure he may be depended on, for he thoroughly understands the nature of the air, and his own brother and family have been there repeatedly.'

'You should have gone to Cromer, my dear, if you went any where. – Perry was a week at Cromer once, and he holds it to be the best of all the sea-bathing places. A fine open sea, he says, and very pure air. And, by what I understand, you might have had lodgings there quite away from the sea – a quarter of a mile off – very comfortable. You should have consulted Perry.'

'But, my dear sir, the difference of the journey; – only consider how great it would have been. – A hundred miles, perhaps, instead of forty.'

'Ah! my dear,' as Perry says, 'where health is at stake, nothing else should be considered; and if one is to travel, there is not much to chuse between forty miles and an hundred. – Better not move at all, better stay in London altogether than travel forty miles to get into a worse air. This is just what Perry said. It seemed to him a very ill-judged measure.'

Emma's attempts to stop her father had been vain; and when he had reached such a point as this, she could not wonder at her brother-in-law's breaking out.

'Mr Perry,' said he, in a voice of very strong displeasure, 'would do as well to keep his opinion till it is asked for. Why does he make it any business of his, to wonder at what I do? – at my taking my family to one part of the coast or another? – I may be allowed, I hope, the use of my judgment as well as Mr Perry. – I want his directions no more than his drugs.' He paused – and growing cooler in a moment, added, with only sarcastic dryness, 'If Mr Perry can tell me how to convey a wife and five children a distance of an hundred and thirty miles with no greater expense of inconvenience than a distance of forty, I should be as willing to prefer Cromer to South End as he could himself.'

'True, true,' cried Mr Knightley, with most ready interposition – 'very true. That's a consideration indeed. – But John, as to what I was telling you of my idea of moving the path to Langham, of turning it more to the right that it may not cut through the home meadows, I cannot conceive any difficulty. I should not attempt it, if it were to be the means of inconvenience to the Highbury people, but if you call to mind exactly the present line of the path. . . . The only way of proving it, however, will be to turn to our maps. I shall see you at the Abbey to-morrow morning I hope, and then we will look them over, and you shall give me your opinion.'

Mr Woodhouse was rather agitated by such harsh reflections on his friend Perry, to whom he had, in fact, though unconsciously, been attributing many of his own feelings and expressions; – but the soothing attentions of his daughters gradually removed the present evil, and the immediate alertness of one brother, and better recollections of the other, prevented any renewal of it.

CHAPTER THIRTEEN

THERE COULD HARDLY be an happier creature in the world, than Mrs John Knightley, in this short visit to Hartfield, going about every morning among her old acquaintance with her five children, and talking over what she had done every evening with her father and sister. She had nothing to wish otherwise, but that the days did not pass so swiftly. It was a delightful visit; – perfect, in being much too short.

In general their evenings were less engaged with friends than their mornings: but one complete dinner engagement, and out of the house too, there was no avoiding, though at Christmas. Mr Weston would take no denial; they must all dine at Randalls one day; – even Mr Woodhouse was persuaded to think it a possible thing in preference to a division of the party.

How they were all to be conveyed, he would have made a difficulty if he could, but as his son and daughter's carriage and horses were actually at Hartfield, he was not able to make more than a simple question on that head; it hardly amounted to a doubt; nor did it occupy Emma long to convince him that they might in one of the carriages find room for Harriet also.

Harriet, Mr Elton, and Mr Knightley, their own especial set, were the only persons invited to meet them; – the hours were to be early, as well as the numbers few, Mr Woodhouse's habits and inclinations being consulted in every thing.

The evening before this great event (for it was a very great event that Mr Woodhouse should dine out, on the 24th of December) had been spent by Harriet at Hartfield, and she had gone home so much indisposed with a cold, that, but for her own earnest wish of being nursed by Mrs Goddard, Emma could not have allowed her to leave the house. Emma called on her the next day, and found her doom already signed with regard to Randalls. She was very feverish and had a bad sore-throat: Mrs Goddard was full of care and affection, Mr Perry was talked of, and Harriet herself was too ill and low to resist the authority which excluded her from this delightful engagement, though she could not speak of her loss without many tears.

Emma sat with her as long as she could, to attend her in Mrs Goddard's unavoidable absences, and raise her spirits by representing how much Mr Elton's would be depressed when he knew her state; and left her at last tolerably comfortable, in the sweet dependence of his having a most comfortless visit, and of their all missing her very much. She had not advanced many yards from Mrs Goddard's door, when she was met by Mr Elton himself, evidently coming towards it, and as they walked on slowly together in conversation about the invalid – of whom he, on the rumour of considerable illness, had been going to inquire, that he might carry some report of her to Hartfield – they were overtaken by Mr John Knightley returning from the daily visit to Donwell, with his two eldest boys, whose healthy, glowing faces shewed all the benefit of a country run, and seemed to ensure a quick dispatch of the roast mutton and rice pudding they were hastening home for. They joined company and proceeded together. Emma was just describing the nature of her friend's complaint; – 'a throat very much inflamed, with a great deal of heat about her, a quick low pulse, &c. and she was sorry to find from Mrs Goddard that Harriet was liable to very bad sore-throats, and had often alarmed her with them.' Mr Elton looked all alarm on the occasion, as he exclaimed,

'A sore-throat! – I hope not infectious. I hope not of a putrid infectious sort. Has Perry seen her? Indeed you should take care of yourself as well as of your friend. Let me entreat you to run no risks. Why does not Perry see her?'

Emma, who was not really at all frightened herself, tranquillized this excess of apprehension by assurances of Mrs Goddard's experience and care; but as there must still remain a degree of uneasiness which she could not wish to reason away, which she would rather feed and assist than not, she added soon afterwards – as if quite another subject,

'It is so cold, so very cold – and looks and feels so very much like snow, that if it were to any other place or with any other party, I should really try not to go out to-day – and dissuade my father from venturing; but as he has made up his mind, and does not seem to feel the cold himself, I do not like to interfere, as I know it would be so great a disappointment to Mr and Mrs Weston. But, upon my word, Mr Elton, in your case, I should certainly excuse myself. You appear to me a little hoarse already, and when you consider what demand of voice and what fatigues to-morrow will bring, I think it would be no more than common prudence to stay at home and take care of yourself tonight.'

Mr Elton looked as if he did not very well know what answer to make; which was exactly the case; for though very much gratified by the kind care of such a fair lady, and not liking to resist any advice of her's, he had not really the least inclination to give up the visit; – but Emma, too eager and busy in her own previous conceptions and views to hear him impartially, or see him with clear vision, was very well satisfied with his muttering acknowledgment of its being 'very cold, certainly very cold,' and walked on, rejoicing in having extricated himself from Randalls, and secured him the power of sending to enquire after Harriet every hour of the evening.

'You do quite right,' said she; – 'We will make your apologies to Mr and Mrs Weston.'

But hardly had she so spoken, when she found her brother was civilly offering a seat in his carriage, if the weather were Mr Elton's only objection, and Mr Elton actually accepting the offer with much prompt satisfaction. It was a done thing; Mr Elton was to go, and never had his broad handsome face expressed more pleasure than at this moment; never had his smile been stronger, nor his eyes more exulting than when he next looked at her.

'Well,' she said to herself, 'this is most strange! – After I had got him off so well, to chuse to go into company, and leave Harriet ill behind! – Most strange indeed! – But there is, I believe, in many men, especially single men, such an inclination – such a passion for dining out – a dinner engagement is so high in the class of their pleasures, their employments, their dignities, almost their duties, that any thing gives way to it – and this must be the case with Mr Elton; a most valuable, amiable, pleasing young man undoubtedly, and very much in love with Harriet; but still, he cannot refuse an invitation, he must dine out wherever he is asked. What a strange thing love is! he can see ready wit in Harriet, but will not dine alone for her.'

Soon afterwards Mr Elton quitted them, and she could not but do him the justice of feeling that there was a great deal of sentiment in his manner of naming Harriet at parting; in the tone of his voice while assuring her that he should call at Mrs Goddard's for news of her fair friend, the last thing before he prepared for the happiness of meeting her again, when he hoped to be able to give a better report; and he sighed and smiled himself off in a way that left the balance of approbation much in his favour.

After a few minutes of entire silence between them, John Knightley began with –

'I never in my life saw a man more intent on being agreeable than Mr Elton. It is downright labour to him where ladies are concerned. With men he can be rational and unaffected, but when he has ladies to please every feature works.'

'Mr Elton's manners are not perfect,' replied Emma; 'but where there is a wish to please, one ought to overlook, and one does overlook a great deal. Where a man does his best with only moderate powers, he will have the advantage over negligent superiority. There is such perfect good temper and good will in Mr Elton as one cannot but value.'

'Yes,' said Mr John Knightley presently, with some slyness, 'he seems to have a great deal of good-will towards *you*.'

'Me!' she replied with a smile of astonishment, 'are you imagining me to be Mr Elton's object?'

'Such an imagination has crossed me, I own, Emma; and if it never occurred to you before, you may as well take it into consideration now.'

'Mr Elton in love with me! – What an idea!'

'I do not say it is so; but you will do well to consider whether it is so or not, and to regulate your behaviour accordingly. I think your manners to him encouraging. I speak as a friend, Emma. You had better look about you, and ascertain what you do, and what you mean to do.'

'I thank you; but I assure you you are quite mistaken. Mr Elton and I are very good friends, and nothing more;' and she walked on, amusing herself in the consideration of the blunders which often arise from a partial knowledge of circumstance, of the mistakes which people of high pretensions to judgment are for ever falling into; and not very well pleased with her brother for imagining her blind and ignorant, and in want of counsel. He said no more.

Mr Woodhouse had so completely made up his mind to the visit, that in spite of the increasing coldness, he seemed to have no idea of shrinking from it, and set forward at last most punctually with his eldest daughter in his own carriage, with less apparent consciousness of the weather than either of the others; too full of the wonder of his own going, and the pleasure it was to afford at Randalls to see that it was cold, and too well wrapt up to feel it. The cold, however, was severe; and by the time the second carriage was in motion, a few flakes of snow were finding their way down, and the sky had the appearance of being so overcharged as to want only a milder air to produce a very white world in a very short time.

Emma soon saw that her companion was not in the happiest humour. The preparing and the going abroad in such weather, with the sacrifice of his children after dinner, were evils, were disagreeables at least, which Mr John Knightley did not by any means like; he anticipated nothing in the visit that could be at all worth the purchase; and the whole of their drive to the Vicarage was spent by him in expressing his discontent.

'A man,' said he, 'must have a very good opinion of himself when he asks people to leave their own fireside, and encounter such a day as this, for the sake of coming to see him. He must think himself a most agreeable fellow; I could not do such a thing. It is the greatest absurdity – Actually snowing at this moment! – The folly of not allowing people to be comfortable at him – and the folly of people's not staying comfortably at home when they can! If we were obliged to go out such an evening as this, by any call of duty or business, what a hardship we should deem it; – and here are we, probably with rather thinner clothing than usual, setting forward voluntarily, without excuse, in defiance of the voice of nature, which tells man, in every thing given to his view or his feelings, to stay at home himself, and keep all under shelter that he can; – here are we setting forward to spend five dull hours in another man's house, with nothing to say or to hear that was not said and heard yesterday, and may not be said and heard again tomorrow. Going in dismal weather, to return probably in worse; – four horses and four servants taken out for nothing but to convey five idle, shivering creatures into colder rooms and worse company than they might have had at home.'

Emma did not find herself equal to give the pleased assent, which no doubt he was in the habit of receiving, to emulate the 'Very true, my love,' which must have been usually administered by his travelling companion; but she had resolution enough to refrain from making any answer at all. She could not be complying, she dreaded being quarrelsome; her heroism reached only to silence. She allowed him to talk, and arranged the glasses, and wrapped herself up, without opening her lips.

They arrived, the carriage turned, the step was let down, and Mr Elton, spruce, black, and smiling, was with them instantly. Emma thought with pleasure of some change of subject. Mr Elton was all obligation and cheerfulness; he was so very cheerful in his civilities indeed, that she began to think he must have received a different account of Harriet from what had reached her. She had sent while dressing, and the answer had been, 'Much the same – not better.'

'*My* report from Mrs Goddard's,' said she presently, 'was not so pleasant as I had hoped – "Not better," was *my* answer.'

His face lengthened immediately; and his voice was the voice of sentiment as he answered.

'Oh! no – I am grieved to find – I was on the point of telling you that when I called at Mrs Goddard's door, which I did the very last thing before I returned to dress, I was told that Miss Smith was not better, by no means better, rather worse. Very much grieved and concerned – I had flattered myself that she must be better after such a cordial as I knew had been given in the morning.'

Emma smiled and answered – 'My visit was of use to the nervous part of her complaint, I hope; but not even I can charm away a sore throat; it is a most severe cold indeed. Mr Perry has been with her, as you probably heard.'

'Yes – I imagined – that is – I did not – '

'He has been used to her in these complaints, and I hope tomorrow morning will bring us both a more comfortable report. But it is impossible not to feel uneasiness. Such a sad loss to our party to-day!'

'Dreadful! – Exactly so, indeed. – She will be missed every moment.'

This was very proper; the sigh which accompanied it was really estimable, but it should have lasted longer. Emma was rather in dismay when only half a minute afterwards he began to speak of other things, and in a voice of the greatest alacrity and enjoyment.

'What an excellent device,' said he, 'the use of a sheep-skin for carriages. How very comfortable they make it; – impossible to feel cold with such precautions. The contrivances of modern days indeed have rendered a gentleman's carriage perfectly complete. One is so fenced and guarded from the weather, that not a breath of air can find its way unpermitted. Weather becomes absolutely of no consequence. It is a very cold afternoon – but in this carriage we know nothing of the matter. – Ha! snows a little I see.'

'Yes,' said John Knightley, 'and I think we shall have a good deal of it.'

'Christmas weather,' observed Mr Elton. 'Quite seasonable; and extremely fortunate we may think ourselves that it did not begin yesterday, and prevent this day's party, which it might very possibly have done, for Mr Woodhouse would hardly have ventured had there been much snow on the ground; but now it is of no consequence. This is quite the season indeed for friendly meetings. At Christmas every body invites their friends about them, and people think little of even the worst weather. I was snowed up at a friend's house once for a week. Nothing could be pleasanter. I went for only one night, and could not get away till that very day se'nnight.'

Mr John Knightly looked as if he did not comprehend the pleasure, but said only, coolly,

'I cannot wish to be snowed up a week at Randalls.'

At another time Emma might have been amused, but she was too much astonished now at Mr Elton's spirits for other feelings. Harriet seemed quite forgotten in the expectation of a pleasant party.

'We are sure of excellent fires,' continued he, 'and every thing in the greatest comfort. Charming people, Mr and Mrs Weston; – Mrs Weston indeed is much beyond praise, and he is exactly what one values, so hospitable, and so fond of society; – it will be a small party, but where small parties are select, they are perhaps the most agreeable of any. Mr Weston's dining-room does not accommodate more than ten comfortably; and for my part, I would rather, under such circumstances, fall short by two than exceed by two I think you will agree with me, (turning with a soft air to Emma,) I think I shall certainly have your approbation, though Mr Knightley perhaps, from being used to the large parties of London, may not quite enter into our feelings.'

'I know nothing of the large parties of London, sir – I never dine with any body.'

'Indeed! (in a tone of wonder and pity,) I had no idea that the law had been so great a slavery. Well, sir, the time must come when you will be paid for all this, when you will have little labour and great enjoyment.'

'My first enjoyment,' replied John Knightley, as they passed through the sweep-gate, 'will be to find myself safe at Hartfield again.'

CHAPTER FOURTEEN

Some change of countenance was necessary for each gentleman as they walked into Mrs Weston's drawing-room; – Mr Elton must compose his joyous looks, and Mr John Knightley disperse his ill-humour. Mr Elton must smile less, and Mr John Knightley more,

As they walked into Mrs Weston's drawing-room.

to fit them for the place. – Emma only might be as nature prompted, and shew herself just as happy as she was. To her, it was real enjoyment to be with the Westons. Mr Weston was a great favourite, and there was not a creature in the world to whom she spoke with such unreserve, as to his wife; not any one, to whom she related with such conviction of being listened to and understood, of being always interesting and always intelligible, the little affairs, arrangements, perplexities and pleasures of her father and herself. She could tell nothing of Hartfield, in which Mrs Weston had not a lively concern; and half an hour's uninterrupted communication of all those little matters on which the daily happiness of private life depends, was one of the first gratifications of each.

This was a pleasure which perhaps the whole day's visit might not afford, which certainly did not belong to the present half hour; but the very sight of Mrs Weston, her smile, her touch, her voice was grateful to Emma, and she determined to think as little as possible of Mr Elton's oddities, or of any thing else unpleasant, and enjoy all that was enjoyable to the utmost.

The misfortune of Harriet's cold had been pretty well gone through before her arrival. Mr Woodhouse had been safely seated long enough to give the history of it, besides all the history of his own and Isabella's coming, and of Emma's being to follow, and had indeed just got to the end of his satisfaction that James should come and see his daughter, when the others appeared, and Mrs Weston, who had been almost wholly engrossed by her attentions to him, was able to turn away and welcome her dear Emma.

Emma's project of forgetting Mr Elton for a while, made her rather sorry to find, when they had all taken their places, that he was close to her. The difficulty was great of driving this strange insensibility towards Harriet, from her mind, while he not only sat at her elbow, but was continually obtruding his happy countenance on her notice, and solicitously addressing her upon every occasion. Instead of forgetting him, his behaviour was such that she could not avoid the internal suggestion of 'Can it really be as my brother imagined? Can it be possible for this man to be beginning to transfer his affections from Harriet to me? – Absurd and insufferable? – Yet he would be so anxious for her being perfectly warm, would be so interested about her father, and so delighted with Mrs Weston; and at last would begin admiring her drawings with so much zeal and so little knowledge as seemed terribly like a would-be lover, and made it some effort with her to preserve her good manners. For her own sake she could not be rude; and for Harriet's, in the hope that all would yet turn out right, she was even positively civil; but it was an effort; especially as something was going on amongst the others, in the most overpowering period of Mr Elton's nonsense, which she particularly wished to listen to. She heard enough to know that Mr Weston was giving some information about his son; she heard the words 'my son', and 'Frank,' and 'my son,' repeated several times over; and from a few other half-syllables very much suspected that he was announcing an early visit from his son; but before she could quiet Mr Elton, the subject was so completely past that any reviving question from her would have been awkward.

Now, it so happened that in spite of Emma's resolution of never marrying, there was something in the name, in the idea of Mr Frank Churchill, which always interested her. She had frequently thought – especially since his father's marriage with Miss Taylor – that if she *were* to marry, he was the very person to suit her in age, character and condition. He seemed by this connection between the families, quite to belong to her. She could not but suppose it to be a match that every body who knew them must think of. That Mr and Mrs Weston did think of it, she was very strongly persuaded, and though not meaning to be induced by him, or by any body else, to give up a situation which she believed more replete with good than any she could change it for, she had a great curiosity to see him, a decided intention of finding him pleasant, of being liked by him to a certain degree, and a sort of pleasure in the idea of their being coupled in their friends' imaginations.

With such sensations, Mr Elton's civilities were dreadfully ill-timed; but she had the comfort of appearing very polite, while feeling very cross – and of thinking that the rest of the visit could not possibly pass without bringing forward the same information again, or the substance of it, from the open-hearted Mr Weston. – So it proved; – for when happily released from Mr Elton, and seated by Mr Weston, at dinner, he made use of the very first interval in the cares of hospitality, the very first leisure from the saddle of mutton, to say to her,

'We want only two more to be just the right number. I should like to see two more here, – your pretty little friend Miss Smith, and my son – and then I should say we were quite complete. I believe you did not hear me telling the others in the drawing-room that we are expecting Frank? I had a letter from him this morning, and he will be with us within a fortnight.'

Emma spoke with a very proper degree of pleasure; and fully assented to his proposition of Mr Frank Churchill and Miss Smith making their party quite complete.

'He has been wanting to come to us,' continued Mr Weston, 'ever since September: every letter has been full of it; but he cannot command his own time. He has those to please who must be pleased, and who (between ourselves) are sometimes to be pleased only by a good many sacrifices. But now I have no doubt of seeing him here about the second week in January.'

'What a very great pleasure it will be to you! and Mrs Weston is so anxious to be acquainted with him, that she must be almost as happy as yourself.'

'Yes, she would be, but that she thinks there will be another put-off. She does not depend upon his coming so much as I do: but she does not know the parties so well as I do. The case, you see, is – (but this is quite between ourselves: I did not mention a syllable of it in the other room. There are secrets in all families, you know? – The case is, that a party of friends are invited to pay a visit at Enscombe in January; and that Frank's coming depends upon their being put off. If they are not put off, he cannot stir. But I know they will, because it is a family that a certain lady, of some consequence, at Enscombe, has a particular dislike to: and though it is thought necessary to invite them once in two or three years, they always are put off when it comes to the point. I have not the smallest doubt of the issue. I am as confident of seeing Frank here before the middle of January, as I am of being here myself: but your good friend there (nodding towards the upper end of the table) has so few vagaries herself, and has been so little used to them at Hartfield, that she cannot calculate on their effects, as I have been long in the practice of doing.'

'I am sorry there should be any thing like doubt in the case,' replied Emma; 'but am disposed to side with you, Mr Weston. If you think he will come, I shall think so too; for you know Enscombe.'

'Yes – I have some right to that knowledge; though I have never been at the place in my life. – She is an odd woman! – But I never allow myself to speak ill of her, on Frank's account; for I do believe her to be very fond of him. I used to think she was not capable of being fond of any body, except herself: but she has always been kind to him (in her way – allowing for little whims and caprices, and expecting every thing to be as she likes). And it is no small credit, in my opinion, to him, that he should excite such an affection; for, though I would not say it to any body else, she has no more heart than a stone to people in general; and the devil of a temper.'

Emma liked the subject so well, that she began upon it, to Mrs Weston, very soon after their moving into the drawing-room: wishing her joy – yet observing, that she knew the first meeting must be rather alarming. – Mrs Weston agreed to it; but added, that she should be very glad to be secure of undergoing the anxiety of a first meeting at the time talked of: 'for I cannot depend upon his coming. I cannot be so sanguine as Mr Weston. I am very much afraid that it will all end in nothing. Mr Weston, I dare say, has been telling you exactly how the matter stands.'

'Yes – it seems to depend upon nothing but the ill-humour of Mrs Churchill, which I imagine to be the most certain thing in the world.'

'My Emma,' replied Mrs Weston, smiling, 'what is the certainty of caprice?' Then turning to Isabella, who had not been attending before – 'You must know, my dear Mrs Knightley, that we are by no means so sure of seeing Mr Frank Churchill, in my opinion, as his father thinks. It depends entirely upon his aunt's spirits and pleasure; in short, upon her temper. To you – to my two daughters, I may venture on the truth. Mrs Churchill rules at Enscombe, and is a very odd-tempered woman; and his coming now, depends upon her being willing to spare him.'

'Oh, Mrs Churchill; every body knows Mrs Churchill,' replied Isabella: 'and I am sure I never think of that poor young man without the greatest compassion. To be constantly living with an ill-tempered person, must be dreadful. It is what we happily have never known any thing of; but it must be a life of misery. What a blessing that she never had any children! Poor little creatures, how unhappy she would have made them!'

Emma wished she had been alone with Mrs Weston. She should then have heard more: Mrs Weston would speak to her, with a degree of unreserve which she would not hazard with Isabella; and she really believed, would scarcely try to conceal any thing relative to the Churchills from her, excepting those views on the young man, of which her own imagination had already given her such instinctive knowledge. But at present there was nothing more to be said. Mr Woodhouse very soon followed them into the drawing-room. To be sitting long after dinner, was a confinement that he could not endure. Neither wine nor conversation was any thing to him; and gladly did he move to those with whom he was always comfortable.

While he talked to Isabella, however, Emma found an opportunity of saying.

'And so you do not consider this visit from your son as by any means certain. I am sorry for it. The introduction must be unpleasant, whenever it takes place, and the sooner it could be over, the better.'

'Yes; and every delay makes one more apprehensive of other delays. Even if this family, the Braithwaites, are put off, I am still afraid that some excuse may be found for disappointing us. I cannot bear to imagine any reluctance on his side, but I am sure there is a great wish on the Churchill's to keep him to themselves. There is jealousy. They are jealous even of his regard for his father. In short, I can feel no dependence on his coming, and I wish Mr Weston were less sanguine.'

'He ought to come,' said Emma. 'If he could stay only a couple of days, he ought to come; and one can hardly conceive a young man's not having it in his power to do as much as that. A young *woman*, if she fall into bad hands, may be teazed, and kept at a distance from those she wants to be with; but one cannot comprehend a young *man's* being under such restraint, as not to be able to spend a week with his father, if he likes it.'

'One ought to be at Enscombe, and know the ways of the family, before one decides upon what he can do,' replied Mrs Weston. 'One ought to use the same caution, perhaps, in judging of the conduct of any one individual of any one family; but Enscombe, I believe, certainly must not be judged by general rules: *she* is so very unreasonable; and every thing gives way to her.'

'But she is so fond of the nephew: he is so very great a favourite. Now, according to my idea of Mrs Churchill, it would be most natural, that while she makes no sacrifice for the comfort of the husband, to whom she owes every thing, while she exercises incessant caprice towards *him*, she should frequently be governed by the nephew, to whom she owes nothing at all.'

'My dearest Emma, do not pretend, with your sweet temper, to understand a bad one, or to lay down rules for it: you must let it go its own way. I have no doubt of his having at times, considerable influence; but it may be perfectly impossible for him to know beforehand *when* it will be.'

Emma listened, and then coolly said, 'I shall not be satisfied, unless he comes.'

'He may have a great deal of influence on some points,' continued Mrs Weston, 'and on others, very little: and among those, on which she is beyond his reach, it is but too likely, may be this very circumstance of his coming away from them to visit us.'

CHAPTER FIFTEEN

Mr Woodhouse was soon ready for his tea; and when he had drank his tea he was quite ready to go home; and it was as much as his three companions could do, to entertain away his notice of the lateness of the hour, before the other gentlemen appeared. Mr Weston was chatty and convivial, and no friend to early separations of any sort; but at last the drawing-room party did receive an augmentation. Mr Elton, in very good spirits, was one of the first to walk in. Mrs Weston and Emma were sitting together on a sopha. He joined them immediately, and with scarcely an invitation, seated himself between them.

Emma, in good spirits too, from the amusement afforded her mind by the expectation of Mr Frank Churchill, was willing to forget his late improprieties, and be as well satisfied with him as before, and on making Harriet his very first subject, was ready to listen with most friendly smiles.

He professed himself extremely anxious about her fair friend – her fair, lovely, amiable friend. 'Did she know? – had she heard any thing about her, since their being at Randalls? – he felt anxiety – he must confess that the nature of her complaint alarmed him considerably.' And in this style he talked on for some time very properly, not much attending to any answer, but altogether sufficiently awake to the terror of a bad sore throat; and Emma was quite in charity with him.

But at last there seemed a perverse turn; it seemed all at once as if he were more afraid of its being a bad sore throat on her account, than on Harriet's – more anxious that she should escape the infection, than that there should be no infection in the complaint. He began with great earnestness to entreat her to refrain from visiting the sick chamber again, for the present – to entreat her to *promise him* not to venture into such hazard till he had seen Mr Perry and learnt his opinion; and though she tried to laugh it off and bring the subject back into its proper course, there was no putting an end to his extreme solicitude about her. She was vexed. It did appear – there was no concealing it – exactly like the pretence of being in love with her, instead of Harriet; an inconstancy, if real, the most contemptible and abominable! and she had difficulty in behaving with temper. He turned to Mrs Weston to implore her assistance,

'Is this fair, Mrs Weston?'

'Would not she give him her support? - would not she add her persuasions to his, to induce Miss Woodhouse not to go to Mrs Goddard's till it were certain that Miss Smith's disorder had no infection? He could not be satisfied without a promise – would not she give him her influence in procuring it?'

'So scrupulous for others,' he continued, 'and yet so careless for herself! She wanted me to nurse my cold by staying at home to-day, and yet will not promise to avoid the danger of catching an ulcerated sore throat herself! Is this fair, Mrs Weston? – Judge between us. Have not I some right to complain? I am sure of your kind support and aid.'

Emma saw Mrs Weston's surprize, and felt that it must be great, at an address which, in words and manner, was assuming to himself the right of first interest in her; and as for herself, she was too much provoked and offended to have the power of directly saying any thing to the purpose. She could only give him a look; but it was such a look as she thought must restore him to his senses; and then left the sopha, removing to a seat by her sister, and giving her all her attention.

She had not time to know how Mr Elton took the reproof, so rapidly did another subject succeed, for Mr John Knightley now came into the room from examining the weather, and opened on them all with the information of the ground being covered with snow, and of its still snowing fast, with a strong drifting wind; concluding with these words to Mr Woodhouse:

'This will prove a spirited beginning of your winter engagements, sir. Something new for your coachman and horses to be making their way through a storm of snow.'

Poor Mr Woodhouse was silent from consternation; but every body else had something to say; every body was either surprized or not surprized, and had some question to ask, or some comfort to offer. Mrs Weston and Emma tried earnestly to cheer him and turn his attention from his son-in-law, who was pursuing his triumph rather unfeelingly.

'I admired your resolution very much, sir,' said he, 'in venturing out in such weather, for of course you saw there would be snow very soon. Every body must have seen the snow coming on. I admired your spirit; and I dare say we shall get home very well. Another hour or two's snow can hardly make the road impassable; and we are two carriages; if *one* is blown over in the bleak part of the common field there will be the other at hand. I dare say we shall be all safe at Hartfield before midnight.'

Mr Weston, with triumph of a different sort, was confessing that he had known it to be snowing some time, but had not said a word, lest it should make Mr Woodhouse uncomfortable, and be an excuse for his hurrying away. As to there being any quantity of snow fallen or likely to fall to impede their return, that was a mere joke; he was afraid they would find no difficulty. He wished the road might be impassable, that he might be able to keep them all at Randalls; and with the utmost good-will was sure that accommodation might be found for every body, calling on his wife to agree with him, that, with a little contrivance, every body might be lodged, which she hardly knew how to do, from the consciousness of there being but two spare rooms in the house.

'What is to be done, my dear Emma? – what is to be done?' was Mr Woodhouse's first exclamation, and all that he could say for some time. To her he looked for comfort; and her assurances of safety, her representation of the excellence of the horses, and of

James, and of their having so many friends about them, revived him a little.

His eldest daughter's alarm was equal to his own. The horror of being blocked up at Randalls, while her children were at Hartfield, was full in her imagination; and fancying the road to be now just passable for adventurous people, but in a state that admitted no delay, she was eager to have it settled, that her father and Emma should remain at Randalls, while she and her husband set forward instantly through all the possible accumulations of drifted snow that might impede them.

'You had better order the carriage directly, my love,' said she: 'I dare say we shall be able to get along, if we set off directly, and if we do come to any thing very bad, I can get out and walk. I am not at all afraid. I should not mind walking half the way. I could change my shoes, you know, the moment I got home, and it is not the sort of thing that gives me cold.'

'Indeed!' replied he. 'Then, my dear Isabella, it is the most extraordinary sort ot thing in the world, for in general every thing does give you cold. Walk home! – you are prettily shod for walking home, I dare say. It will be bad enough for the horses.'

Isabella turned to Mrs Weston for her approbation of the plan. Mrs Weston could only approve. Isabella then went to Emma; but Emma could not so entirely give up the hope of their being all able to get away; and they were still discussing the point, when Mr Knightley, who had left the room immediately after his brother's first report of the snow, came back again, and told them that he had been out of doors to examine, and could answer for there not being the smallest difficulty in their getting home, whenever they liked it, either now or an hour hence. He had gone beyond the sweep – some way along the Highbury road – the snow was no where above half an inch deep – in many places hardly enough to whiten the ground; a very few flakes were falling at present, but the clouds were parting, and there was every appearance of its being soon over. He had seen the coachmen, and they both agreed with him in there being nothing to apprehend.

To Isabella, the relief of such tidings was very great, and they were scarcely less acceptable to Emma on her father's account, who was immediately set as much at ease on the subject as his nervous constitution allowed; but the alarm that had been raised could not be appeased so as to admit of any comfort for him while he continued at Randalls. He was satisfied of there being no present danger in returning home, but no assurances could convince him that it was safe to stay; and while the others were variously urging and recommending, Mr Knightley and Emma settled it in a few brief sentences: thus –

'Your father will not be easy; why do not you go?'

'I am ready, if the others are.'

'Shall I ring the bell?'

'Yes, do.'

And the bell was rung, and the carriages spoken for. A few minutes more, and Emma hoped to see one troublesome companion deposited in his own house, to get sober and cool, and the other recover his temper and happiness when this visit of hardship were over.

The carriages came: and Mr Woodhouse, always the first object on such occasions, was carefully attended to his own by Mr Knightley and Mr Weston; but not all that either could say could prevent some renewal of alarm at the sight of the snow which had actually fallen, and the discovery of a much darker night than he had been prepared for. 'He was afraid they should have a very bad drive. He was afraid poor Isabella would not like it. And there would be poor Emma in the carriage behind. He did not know what they had best do. They must keep as much together as they could;' and James was talked to, and given a charge to go very slow and wait for the other carriage.

Isabella stept in after her father; John Knightley, forgetting that he did not belong to their party, stept in after his wife very naturally; so that Emma found on being escorted and followed into the second carriage by Mr Elton, that the door was to be lawfully shut on them, and that they were to have a tête-à-tête drive. It would not have been the awkwardness of a moment, it would have been rather a pleasure, previous to the suspicions of this very day; she could have talked to him of Harriet, and the three-quarters of a mile would have seemed but one. But now, she would rather it had not happened. She believed he had been drinking too much of Mr Weston's good wine, and felt sure that he would want to be talking nonsense.

To restrain him as much as might be, by her own manners, she was immediately preparing to speak with exquisite calmness and gravity of the weather and the night; but scarcely had she begun, scarcely had they passed the sweep-gate and joined the other carriage, than she found her subject cut up – her hand seized – her attention demanded, and Mr Elton actually making violent love to her: availing himself of the precious opportunity, declaring sentiments which must be already well known, hoping – fearing – adoring – ready to die if she refused him; but flattering himself that his ardent attachment and unequalled love and unexampled passion could not fail of having some effect, and in short, very much resolved on being seriously accepted as soon as possible. It really was so. Without scruple – without apology – without much apparent diffidence, Mr Elton, the lover of Harriet, was professing himself *her* lover. She tried to stop him; but vainly; he would go on, and say it all. Angry as she was, the thought of the moment made her resolve to restrain herself when she did speak. She felt that half this folly must be drunkenness, and therefore could hope that it might belong only to the passing hour. Accordingly, with a mixture of the serious and the playful, which she hoped would best suit his half and half state, she replied,

'I am very much astonished, Mr Elton. This to *me!* you forget yourself – you take me for your friend – any message to Miss Smith I shall be happy to deliver; but no more of this to *me*, if you please,'

'Miss Smith! – Message to Miss Smith! – What could she possibly mean!' – And he repeated her words with such assurance of accent, such boastful pretence of amazement, that she could not help replying with quickness,

'Mr Elton, this is the most extraordinary conduct! and I can account for it only in one way; you are not yourself, or you could not speak either to me, or of Harriet, in such a manner. Command yourself enough to say no more, and I will endeavour to forget it.'

But Mr Elton had only drunk wine enough to elevate his spirits, not at all to confuse his intellects. He perfectly knew his own meaning; and having warmly protested against her suspicion as most injurious, and slightly touched upon his respect for Miss Smith as her friend – but acknowledging his wonder that Miss Smith should be mentioned at all, – he resumed the subject of his own passion, and was very urgent for a favourable answer.

As she thought less of his inebriety, she thought more of his inconstancy and presumption; and with fewer struggles for politeness, replied,

'It is impossible for me to doubt any longer. You have made yourself too clear. Mr Elton, my astonishment is much beyond any thing I can express. After such behaviour, as I have witnessed during the last month, to Miss Smith – such attentions as I have been in the daily habit of observing – to be addressing me in this manner – this is an unsteadiness of character, indeed, which I had not supposed possible! Believe me, sir, I am far, very far, from gratified in being the object of such professions.'

'Good heaven!' cried Mr Elton, 'what can be the meaning of this? – Miss Smith! any attentions, but as your friend: never cared whether she were dead or alive, but as your friend. If she was fancied otherwise, her own wishes have misled her, and I am very sorry – extremely sorry – But, Miss Smith, indeed! – Oh! Miss Woodhouse! who can think of Miss Smith, when Miss Woodhouse is near! No, upon my honour, there is no unsteadiness of character. I have thought only of you. I protest against having paid the smallest attention to any one else. Every thing that I have said or done, for many weeks past, has been with the sole view of marking my adoration of yourself. You cannot really, seriously, doubt it. No! – (in an accent meant to be insinuating) – I am sure you have seen and understood me.

It would be impossible to say what Emma felt, on hearing this – which of all her unpleasant sensations was uppermost. She was too completely overpowered to be immediately able to reply: and two moments of silence being ample encouragement for Mr Elton's sanguine state of mind, he tried to take her hand again, as he joyously exclaimed –

'Charming Miss Woodhouse! allow me to interpret this interesting silence. It confesses that you have long understood me.'

'No, sir,' cried Emma, 'it confesses no such thing. So far from having long understood you, I have been in a most complete error with respect to your views, till this moment. As to myself, I am very sorry that you should have been giving way to any feelings – Nothing could be farther from my wishes – your attachment to my friend Harriet – your pursuit of her, (pursuit, it appeared,) gave me great pleasure, and I have been very earnestly wishing you success: but had I supposed that she were not your attraction to Hartfield, I should certainly have thought you judged ill in making your visits so frequent. Am I to believe that you have never sought to recommend yourself particularly to Miss Smith? – that you have never thought seriously of her?'

'Never, madam,' cried he, affronted, in his turn: 'never, I assure you. I think seriously of Miss Smith! – Miss Smith is a very good sort of girl; and I should be happy to see her respectably settled. I wish her extremely well: and, no doubt, there are men who might not object to – Every body has their level: but as for myself, I am not, I think, quite so much at a loss. I need not so totally despair of an equal alliance, as to be addressing myself to Miss Smith! – No, madam, my visits to Hartfield have been for yourself only; and the encouragement I received – '

'Encouragement! – I give you encouragement! – sir, you have been entirely mistaken in supposing it. I have seen you only as the admirer of my friend. In no other light could you have been more to me than a common acquaintance. I am exceedingly sorry: but it is as well that the mistake ends where it does. Had the same behaviour continued, Miss Smith might have been led into a misconception of your views; not being aware, probably, any more than myself, of the very great inequality which you are so sensible of. But, as it is, the disappointment is single, and, I trust, will not be lasting. I have no thoughts of matrimony at present.'

He was too angry to say another word; her manner too decided to invite supplication; and in this state of swelling resentment, and mutually deep mortification, they had to continue together a few minutes longer, for the fears of Mr Woodhouse had confined them to a foot pace. If there had not been so much anger, there would have been desperate awkwardness; but their straightforward emotions left no room for the little zigzags of embarrassment. Without knowing when the carriage turned into Vicarage-lane, or when it stopped, they found themselves, all at once, at the door of his house; and he was out before another syllable passed. – Emma then felt it indispensable to wish him a good night. The compliment was just returned, coldly and proudly; and, under indescribable irritation of spirits, she was then conveyed to Hartfield.

There she was welcomed, with the utmost delight, by her father, who had been trembling for the dangers of a solitary drive from Vicarage-lane – turning a corner which he could never bear to think of – and in strange hands – a mere common coachman – no James; and there it seemed as if her return only were wanted to make every thing go well: for Mr John Knightley, ashamed of his ill-humour, was now all kindness and attention; and so particularly solicitous for the comfort of her father, as to seem – if not quite ready to join him in a basin of gruel – perfectly sensible of its being exceedingly wholesome; and the day was concluding in peace and comfort to all their little party, except herself. – But her mind had never been in such perturbation, and it needed a very strong effort to appear attentive and cheerful till the usual hour of separating allowed her the relief of quiet reflection.

CHAPTER SIXTEEN

THE HAIR WAS CURLED, and the maid sent away, and Emma sat down to think and be miserable. – It was a wretched business, indeed! – Such an overthrow of every thing she had been wishing for! – Such a development of every thing most unwelcome! – Such a blow for Harriet! – That was the worst of all. Every part of it brought pain and humiliation, of some sort or other; but, compared with the evil to Harriet, all was light; and she would gladly have submitted to feel yet more mistaken – more in error – more disgraced by mis-judgment, than she actually was, could the effects of her blunders have been confined to herself.

'If I had not persuaded Harriet into liking the man, I could have born any thing. He might have doubled his presumption to me – But poor Harriet!'

How she could have been so deceived! – He protested that he had never thought seriously of Harriet – never! She looked back as well as she could; but it was all confusion. She had taken up the idea, she supposed, and made every thing bend to it. His manners, however, must have been unmarked, wavering, dubious, or she could not have been so misled.

The picture! – How eager he had been about the picture! – and the charade! – and an hundred other circumstances; – how clearly they had seemed to point at Harriet. To be sure, the charade, with its 'ready wit' – but then, 'the soft eyes' – in fact it suited neither; it was just a jumble without taste or truth. Who could have seen through such thick-headed nonsense?

Certainly she had often, especially of late, thought his manners to herself unnecessarily gallant; but it had passed as his way, as a mere error of judgment, of knowledge, of taste, as one proof among others that he had not always lived in the best society, that with all the gentleness of his address, true elegance was sometimes wanting; but, till this very day, she had never, for an instant, suspected it to mean any thing but grateful respect to her as Harriet's friend.

To Mr John Knightley she was indebted for her first idea on the subject, for the first start of its possibility. There was no denying that those brothers had penetration. She remembered what Mr Knightley had once said to her about Mr Elton, the caution he had given, the conviction he had professed that Mr Elton would never marry indiscreetly; and blushed to think how much truer a knowledge of his character had been there shewn than any she had reached herself. It was dreadfully mortifying; but Mr Elton was proving himself, in many respects the very reverse of what she had meant and believed him; proud, assuming, conceited; very full of his own claims, and little concerned about the feelings of others.

Contrary to the usual course of things, Mr Elton's wanting to pay his addresses to her had sunk him in her opinion. His professions and his proposals did him no service. She thought nothing of his attachment, and was insulted by his hopes. He wanted to marry well, and having the arrogance to raise his eyes to her, pretended to be in love; but she was perfectly easy as to his not suffering any disappointment that need be cared for. There had been no real affection either in his language or manners. Sighs and fine words had been given in abundance; but she could hardly devise any set of expression, or fancy any tone of voice, less allied with real love. She need not trouble herself to pity him. He only wanted to aggrandize and enrich himself; and if Miss Woodhouse of Hartfield, the heiress of thirty thousand pounds, were not quite so easily obtained as he had fancied, he would soon try for Miss Somebody else with twenty, or with ten.

But – that he should talk of encouragement, should consider her as aware of his views, accepting his attentions, meaning (in short), to marry him! – should suppose himself her equal in connection or mind! – look down upon her friend, so well understanding the gradations of rank below him, and be so blind to what rose above, as to fancy himself shewing no presumption in addressing her! – It was most provoking.

Perhaps it was not fair to expect him to feel how very much he was her inferior in talent, and all the elegancies of mind. The very want of such equality might prevent his perception of it; but he must know that in fortune and consequence she was greatly his superior. He must know that the Woodhouses had been settled for several generations at Hartfield, the younger branch of a very ancient family – and that the Eltons were nobody. The landed property of Hartfield certainly was inconsiderable, being but a sort of notch in the Donwell Abbey estate, to which all the rest of Highbury belonged, but their fortune, from other sources, was such as to make them scarcely secondary to Donwell Abbey itself, in every other kind of consequence; and the Woodhouses had long held a high place in the consideration of the neighbourhood which Mr Elton had first entered not two years ago, to make his way as he could, without any alliances but in trade, or any thing to recommend him to notice but his situation and his civility. – But he had fancied her in love with him, that evidently must have been his dependence; and after raving a little about the seeming incongruity of gentle manners and a conceited head, Emma was obliged on common honesty to stop and admit that her own behaviour to him had been so complaisant and obliging, so full of courtesy and attention, as (supposing her real motive unperceived) might warrant a man of ordinary observation and delicacy, like Mr Elton, in fancying himself a very decided favourite. If *she* had so misinterpreted his feelings, she had little right to wonder that *he*, with self-interest to blind him, should have mistaken her's.

The first error and the worst lay at her door. It was foolish, it was wrong, to take so active a part in bringing any two people together. It was adventuring too far, assuming too much, making light of what ought to be serious, a trick of what ought to be simple. She was quite concerned and ashamed, and resolved to do such things no more.

'Here have I,' said she, 'actually talked poor Harriet into being

A pert young lawyer.

very much attached to this man. She might never have thought of him but for me, and certainly never would have thought of him with hope, if I had not assured her of his attachment, for she is as modest and humble as I used to think him. Oh! that I had been satisfied with persuading her not to accept young Martin. There I was quite right. That was well done for me; but there I should have stopped, and left the rest to time and chance. I was introducing her into good company, and giving her the opportunity of pleasing some one worth having; I ought not to have attempted more. But now, poor girl, her peace is cut up for some time. I have been but half a friend to her; and if she was *not* to feel this disappointment so very much, I am sure I have not an idea of any body else who would be at all desirable for her; – William Coxe – Oh! no, I could not endure William Coxe – a pert young lawyer.'

She stopt to blush and laugh at her own relapse, and then resumed a more serious, more dispiriting cogitation upon what had been, and might be, and must be. The distressing explanation she had to make to Harriet, and all that poor Harriet would be suffering, with the awkwardness of future meetings, the difficulties of continuing or discontinuing the acquaintance, of subduing feelings, concealing resentment, and avoiding éclat, were enough to occupy her in most unmirthful reflections some time longer, and she went to bed at last with nothing settled but the conviction of her having blundered most dreadfully.

To youth and natural cheerfulness like Emma's, though under temporary gloom at night, the return of day will hardly fall to bring return of spirits. The youth and cheerfulness of morning are in happy analogy, and of powerful operation; and if the distress be not poignant enough to keep the eyes unclosed, they will be sure to open to sensations of softened pain and brighter hope.

Emma got up on the morrow more disposed for comfort than she had gone to bed, more ready to see alleviations of the evil before her, and to depend on getting tolerably out of it.

It was a great consolation that Mr Elton should not be really in love with her, or so particularly amiable as to make it shocking to disappoint him – that Harriet's nature should not be of that superior sort in which the feelings are most acute and retentive – and that there could be no necessity for any body's knowing what had passed except the three principals, and especially for her father's being given a moment's uneasiness about it.

These were very cheering thoughts; and the sight of a great deal of snow on the ground did her further service, for any thing was welcome that might justify their all three being quite asunder at present.

The weather was most favourable for her; though Christmas-day, she could not go to church. Mr Woodhouse would have been miserable had his daughter attempted it, and she was therefore safe from either exciting or receiving unpleasant and most unsuitable ideas. The ground covered with snow, and the atmosphere in that unsettled state between frost and thaw, which is of all others the most unfriendly for exercise, every morning beginning in rain or snow, and every evening setting in to freeze, she was for many days a most honourable prisoner. No intercourse with Harriet possible but by note; no church for her on Sunday any more than on Christmas-day; and no need to find excuses for Mr Elton's absenting himself.

It was weather which might fairly confine every body at home; and though she hoped and believed him to be really taking comfort in some society or other, it was very pleasant to have her father so well satisfied with his being all alone in his own house, too wise to stir out; and to hear him say to Mr Knightley, whom no weather could keep entirely from them, –

'Ah! Mr Knightley, why do not you stay at home like poor Mr Elton?'

These days of confinement would have been, but for her private perplexities, remarkably comfortable, as such seclusion exactly suited her brother, whose feelings must always be of great importance to his companions; and he had, besides, so thoroughly cleared of his ill-humour at Randalls, that his amiableness never failed him during the rest of his stay at Hartfield. He was always agreeable and obliging, and speaking pleasantly of every body. But with all the hopes of cheerfulness, and all the present comfort of delay, there was still such an evil hanging over her in the hour of explanation with Harriet, as made it impossible for Emma to be ever perfectly at ease.

CHAPTER SEVENTEEN

Mr and Mrs John Knightley were not detained long at Hartfield. The weather soon improved enough for those to move who must move; and Mr Woodhouse having, as usual, tried to persuade his daughter to stay behind with all her children, was obliged to see the whole party set off, and return to his lamentations over the destiny of poor Isabella; – which poor Isabella, passing her life with those she doated on, full of their merits, blind to their faults, and always innocently busy, might have been a model of right feminine happiness.

The evening of the very day on which they went, brought a note from Mr Elton to Mr Woodhouse, a long civil, ceremonious note, to say, with Mr Elton's best compliments, 'that he was proposing to leave Highbury the following morning in his way to Bath, where, in compliance with the pressing entreaties of some friends, he had engaged to spend a few weeks, and very much regretted the impossibility he was under, from various circumstances of weather and business, of taking a personal leave of Mr Woodhouse, of whose friendly civilities he should ever retain a grateful sense – and had Mr Woodhouse any commands, should be happy to attend to them.'

Emma was most agreeably surprized. – Mr Elton's absence just at this time was the very thing to be desired. She admired him for contriving it, though not able to give him much credit for the manner in which it was announced. Resentment could not have been more plainly spoken than in a civility to her father, from which she was so pointedly excluded. She had not even a share in his opening compliments. – Her name was not mentioned; – and there was so striking a change in all this, and such an ill-judged solemnity of leave-taking in his grateful acknowledgments, as she thought, at first, could not escape her father's suspicion.

It did however. – Her father was quite taken up with the surprize of so sudden a journey, and his fears that Mr Elton might never get safely to the end of it, and saw nothing extraordinary in his language. It was a very useful note, for it supplied them with fresh matter for thought and conversation during the rest of their lonely evening. Mr Woodhouse talked over his alarms, and Emma was in spirits to persuade them away with all her usual promptitude.

She now resolved to keep Harriet no longer in the dark. She had reason to believe her nearly recovered from her cold, and it was desirable that she should have as much time as possible for getting the better of her other complaint before the gentleman's return. She went to Mrs Goddard's accordingly the very next day, to undergo the necessary penance of communication; and a severe one it was. – She had to destroy all the hopes which she had been so industriously feeding – to appear in the ungracious character of the one preferred – and acknowlegde herself grossly mistaken and misjudging in all her ideas on one subject, all her observations, all her convictions, all her prophesies for the last six weeks.

The confession completely renewed her first shame – and the sight of Harriet's tears made her think that she should never be in charity with herself again.

Harriet bore the intelligence very well – blaming nobody – and in every thing testifying such an ingenuousness of disposition and lowly opinion of herself, as must appear with particular advantage at that moment to her friend.

Emma was in the humour to value simplicity and modesty to the utmost; and all that was amiable, all that ought to be attaching, seemed on Harriet's side, not her own. Harriet did not consider herself as having any thing to complain of. The affection of such a man as Mr Elton would have been too great a distinction. – She never could have deserved him – and nobody but so partial and kind a friend as Miss Woodhouse would have thought it possible.

Her tears fell abundantly – but her grief was so truly artless, that no dignity could have made it more respectable in Emma's eyes – and she listened to her and tried to console her with all her heart and understanding – really for the time convinced that Harriet was the superior creature of the two – and that to resemble her would be more for her own welfare and happiness than all that genius or intelligence could do.

It was rather too late in the day to set about being simple-minded and ignorant; but she left her with every previous resolution confirmed of being humble and discreet, and repressing imagination all the rest of her life. Her second duty now, inferior only to her father's claims, was to promote Harriet's comfort, and endeavour to prove her own affection in some better method than by match-making. She got her to Hartfield, and shewed her the most unvarying kindness, striving to occupy and amuse her, and by books and conversation, to drive Mr Elton from her thoughts.

Time, she knew, must be allowed for this being thoroughly done; and she could suppose herself but an indifferent judge of such matters in general, and very inadequate to sympathize in an attachment to Mr Elton in particular; but it seemed to her reasonable that at Harriet's age, and with the entire extinction of all hope, such a progress might be made towards a state of composure by the time of Mr Elton's return, as to allow them all to meet again in the common routine of acquaintance, without any danger of betraying sentiments or increasing them.

Harriet did think him all perfection, and maintain the non-existence of any body equal to him in person or goodness – and did, in truth, prove herself more resolutely in love than Emma had forseen; but yet it appeared to her so natural, so inevitable to strive against an inclination of that sort *unrequited*, that she could not comprehend its continuing very long in equal force.

If Mr Elton, on his return, made his own indifference as evident and indubitable as she could not doubt he would anxiously do, she could not imagine Harriet's persisting to place her happiness in the sight or the recollection of him.

Their being fixed, so absolutely fixed, in the same place, was bad for each, for all three. Not one of them had the power of removal, or of effecting any material change of society. They must encounter each other, and make the best of it.

Harriet was further unfortunate in the tone of her companions at Mrs Goddard's; Mr Elton being the adoration of all the teachers and great girls in the school; and it must be at Hartfield only that she could have any chance of hearing him spoken of with cooling moderation or repellent truth. Where the wound had been given, there must the cure be found if anywhere; and Emma felt that, till she saw her in the way of cure, there could be no true peace for herself.

CHAPTER EIGHTEEN

MR FRANK CHURCHILL did not come. When the time proposed drew near, Mrs Weston's fears were justified in the arrival of a letter of excuse. For the present, he could not be spared, to his 'very great mortification and regret, but still he looked forward with the hope of coming to Randalls at no distant period.'

Mrs Weston was exceedingly disappointed – much more disappointed, in fact, than her husband, though her dependence on seeing the young man had been so much more sober: but a sanguine temper, though for ever expecting more good than occurs, does not always pay for its hopes by any proportionate depression. It soon flies over the present failure, and begins to hope again. For half an hour Mr Weston was surprized and sorry; but then he began to perceive that Frank's coming two or three months later would be a much better plan, better time of year; better weather; and that he would be able, without any doubt, to stay considerably longer with them than if he had come sooner.

These feelings rapidly restored his comfort, while Mrs Weston, of a more apprehensive disposition, foresaw nothing but a repetition of excuses and delays; and after all her concern for what her husband was to suffer, suffered a great deal more herself.

Emma was not at this time in a state of spirits to care really about Mr Frank Churchill's not coming except as a disappointment at Randalls. The acquaintance at present had no charm for her. She wanted, rather, to be quiet, and out of temptation; but still, as it was desirable that she should appear, in general, like her usual self, she took care to express as much interest in the circumstance, and enter as warmly into Mr and Mrs Weston's disappointment, as might naturally belong to their friendship.

She was the first to announce it to Mr Knightley; and exclaimed quite as much as was necessary, (or, being acting a part, perhaps rather more,) at the conduct of the Churchills, in keeping him away. She then proceeded to say a good deal more than she felt, of the advantage of such an addition to their confined society in Surrey; the pleasure of looking at some body new; the gala-day to Highbury entire, which the sight of him would have made; and ending with reflections on the Churchills again, found herself directly involved in a disagreement with Mr Knightley; and, to her great amusement, perceived that she was taking the other side of the question from her real opinion, and making use of Mrs Weston's arguments against herself.

'The Churchills are very likely in fault,' said Mr Knightley, coolly; 'but I dare say he might come if he would.'

'I do not know why you should say so. He wishes exceedingly to come; but his uncle and aunt will not spare him.'

'I cannot believe that he has not the power of coming, if he made a point of it. It is too unlikely, for me to believe it without proof.'

'How odd you are! What has Mr Frank Churchill done, to make you suppose him such an unnatural creature?'

'I am not supposing him at all an unnatural creature, in suspecting that he may have learnt to be above his connections, and to care very little for any thing but his own pleasure, from living with those who have always set him the example of it. It is a great deal more natural than one could wish, that a young man, brought up by those who are proud, luxurious, and selfish, should be proud, luxurious, and selfish too. If Frank Churchill had wanted to see his father, he would have contrived it between September and January. A man at his age – what is he? – three or four-and-twenty – cannot be without the means of doing as much as that. It is impossible.'

'That's easily said, and easily felt by you, who have always been your own master. You are the worst judge in the world, Mr

Knightley, of the difficulties of dependence. You do not know what it is to have tempers to manage.'

'It is not to be conceived that a man of three or four-and-twenty should not have liberty of mind or limb to that amount. He cannot want money – he cannot want leisure. We know, on the contrary, that he has so much of both, that he is glad to get rid of them at the idlest haunts in the kingdom. We hear of him for ever at some watering-place or other. A little while ago, he was at Weymouth. This proves that he can leave the Churchills.'

'Yes, sometimes he can.'

'And those times are, whenever he thinks it worth his while; whenever there is any temptation of pleasure.'

'It is very unfair to judge of any body's conduct, without an intimate knowledge of their situation. Nobody, who has not been in the interior of a family, can say what the difficulties of any individual of that family may be. We ought to be acquainted with Enscombe, and with Mrs Churchill's temper, before we pretend to decide upon what her nephew can do. He may, at times, be able to do a great deal more than he can at others.'

'There is one thing, Emma, which a man can always do, if he chuses, and that is, his duty; not by manoeuvring and finessing, but by vigour and resolution. It is Frank Churchill's duty to pay this attention to his father. He knows it to be so, by his promises and messages; but if he wished to do it, it might be done. A man who felt rightly would say at once, simply and resolutely, to Mrs Churchill – "Every sacrifice of mere pleasure you will always find me ready to make to your convenience; but I must go and see my father immediately. I know he would be hurt by my failing in such a remark of respect to him on the present occasion. I shall, therefore set off tomorrow." – If he would say so to her at once, in the tone of decision becoming a man, there would be no opposition made to his going.'

'No,' said Emma laughing; 'but perhaps there might be some made to his coming back again. Such language for a young man entirely dependent, to use! – Nobody but you, Mr Knightley, would imagine it possible. But you have not an idea of what is requisite in situations directly opposite to your own. Mr Frank Churchill to be making such a speech as that to the uncle and aunt, who have brought him up, and are to provide for him! – Standing up in the middle of the room, I suppose, and speaking as loud as he could! – How can you imagine such conduct practicable?'

'Depend upon it, Emma, a sensible man would find no difficulty in it. He would feel himself in the right; and the declaration, – made, of course, as a man of sense would make it, in a proper manner – would do him more good, raise him higher, fix his interest stronger with the people he depended on, than all that a line of shifts and expedients can ever do. Respect would be added to affection. They would feel that they could trust him; that the nephew, who had done rightly by his father, would do rightly by them; for they know, as well as he does, as well as all the world must know, that he ought to pay this visit to his father; and while exerting their power to delay it, are in their hearts not thinking the better of him for submitting to their whims. Respect for right conduct is felt by every body. If he would act in this sort of manner, on principle, consistently, regularly, their little minds would bend to his.'

'I rather doubt that. You are very fond of bending little minds; but where little minds belong to rich people in authority, I think they have a knack of swelling out, till they are quite as unmanageable as great ones. I can imagine that if you, as you are, Mr Knightley, were to be transported and placed all at once in Mr Frank Churchill's situation, you would be able to say and do just what you have been recommending for him; and it might have a very good effect. The Churchills might not have a word to say in return; but then, you would have no habits of early obedience and long observance to break through. To him who has, it might not be so easy to burst forth at once into perfect independence, and set all their claims on his gratitude and regard at nought. He may have as strong a sense of what would be right, as you can have, without being so equal under particular circumstances to act up to it.'

'Then, it would not be so strong a sense. If it failed to produce equal exertion, it could not be an equal conviction.'

'Oh! the difference of situation and habit! I wish you would try to understand what an amiable young man may be likely to feel in directly opposing those, whom as child and boy he has been looking up to all his life.'

'Your amiable young man is a very weak young man, if this be the first occasion of his carrying through a resolution to do right against the will of others. It ought to have been an habit with him by this time, of following his duty, instead of consulting expediency. I can allow for the fears of the child, but not of the man. As he became rational, he ought to have roused himself and shaken off all that was unworthy in their authority. He ought to have opposed the first attempt on their side to make him slight his father. Had he begun as he ought, there would have been no difficulty now.'

'We shall never agree about him,' cried Emma; 'but that is nothing extraordinary. I have not the least idea of his being a weak young man: I feel sure that he is not. Mr Weston would not be blind to folly, though in his own son; but he is very likely to have a more yielding, complying, mild disposition than would suit your notions of man's perfection. I dare say he has; and though it may cut him off from some advantages, it will secure him many others.'

'Yes; all the advantages of sitting still when he ought to move, and of leading a life of mere idle pleasure, and fancying himself extremely expert in finding excuses for it. He can sit down and write a fine flourishing letter, full of professions and falsehoods, and persude himself that he has hit upon the very best method in the world of preserving peace at home and preventing his father's having any right to complain. His letters disgust me.'

'Your feelings are singular. They seem to satisfy every body else.'

'I suspect they do not satisfy Mrs Weston. They hardly can satisfy a woman of her good sense and quick feelings: standing in a mother's place, but without a mother's affection to blind her. It is on her account that attention to Randalls is doubly due, and she must doubly feel the omission. Had she been a person of consequence herself, he would have come I dare say; and it would not have signified whether he did or no. Can you think your friend behind-hand in these sort of considerations? Do you suppose she does not often say all this to herself? No, Emma, your amiable young man can be amiable only in French, not in English. He may be very "amiable", have very good-manners, and be very agreeable; but he can have no English delicacy towards the feelings of other people: nothing really amiable about him.'

'You seem determined to think ill of him.'

'Me! – not at all,' replied Mr Knightley, rather displeased; 'I do not want to think ill of him. I should be as ready to acknowledge his merits as any other man; but I hear of none, except what are merely personal; that he is well grown and good-looking, with smooth, plausible manners.'

'Well, if he have nothing else to recommend him, he will be a treasure at Highbury. We do not often look upon fine young men, well-bred and agreeable. We must not be nice and ask for all the virtues into the bargain. Cannot you imagine, Mr Knightley, what a *sensation* his coming will produce? There will be but one subject throughout the Parishes of Donwell and Highbury; but one interest – one object of curiosity; it will be all Mr Frank Churchill; we shall think and speak of nobody else.'

'You will excuse my being so much overpowered. If I find him conversible, I shall be glad of his acquaintance; but if he is only a chattering coxcomb, he will not occupy much of my time or thoughts.'

'My idea of him is, that he can adapt his conversation to the taste of every body, and has the power as well as the wish of being universally agreeable. To you, he will talk of farming; to me, of drawing or music; and so on to everybody, having that general information on all subjects which will enable him to follow the lead, or take the lead, just as propriety may require, and to speak extremely well on each; that is my idea of him.'

'And mine,' said Mr Knightley warmly, 'is, that if he turn out any thing like it, he will be the most insufferable fellow breathing! What! at three-and-twenty to be the king of his company – the great man – the practised politician, who is to read every body's character, and make every body's talents conduce to the display of his own superiority; to be dispensing his flatteries around, that he may make all appear like fools compared with himself! My dear Emma, your own good sense could not endure such a puppy when it came to the point.'

'I will say no more about him,' cried Emma, 'you turn every thing to evil. We are both prejudiced, you against, I for him, and we have no chance of agreeing till he is really here.'

'Prejudiced! I am not prejudiced.'

'But I am very much, and without being at all ashamed of it. My love for Mr and Mrs Weston gives me a decided prejudice in his favour.'

'He is a person I never think of from one month's end to another,' said Mr Knightley, with a degree of vexation, which made Emma immediately talk of something else, though she could not comprehend why he should be angry.

To take a dislike to a young man, only because he appeared to be of a different disposition from himself, was unworth the real liberality of mind which she was always used to acknowledge in him; for with all the high opinion of himself, which she had often laid to his charge, she had never before for a moment supposed it could make him unjust to the merit of another.

CHAPTER NINETEEN

EMMA AND HARRIET HAD been walking together one morning, and, in Emma's opinion, been talking enough of Mr Elton for that day. She could not think that Harriet's solace or her own sins required more; and she was therefore industriously getting rid of the subject as they returned; – but it burst out again when she thought she had succeeded, and after speaking some time of what the poor must suffer in winter, and receiving no other answer than a very plaintive – 'Mr Elton is so good to the poor!' – she found something else must be done.

They were just approaching the house where lived Mrs and Miss Bates. She determined to call upon them and seek safety in numbers. There was always sufficient reason for such an attention; Mrs and Miss Bates loved to be called on, and she knew she was considered by the very few who presumed ever to see imperfection in her, as rather negligent in that respect, and as not contributing what she ought to the stock of their scanty comforts.

She had had many a hint from Mr Knightley and some from her own heart, as to her deficiency – but none were equal to counteract the persuasion of its being very disagreeable, – a waste of time – tiresome women – and all the horror of being in danger of falling in with the second rate and third rate of Highbury, who were calling on them for ever, and therefore she seldom went near them. But now she made the sudden resolution of not passing their door without going in – observing, as she proposed it to Harriet, that, as well as she could calculate, they were just now quite safe from any letter from Jane Fairfax.

The house belonged to people in business. Mrs and Miss Bates occupied the drawing-room floor; and there, in the very moderate sized apartment, which was every thing to them, the visitors were most cordially and even gratefully welcomed: the quiet neat old lady, who with her knitting was seated in the warmest corner, wanting even to give up her place to Miss Woodhouse, and her more active, talking daughter, almost ready to overpower them with care and kindness, thanks for their visit, solicitude for their shoes, anxious enquiries after Mr Woodhouse's health, cheerful communications about her mother's, and sweetcake from the beaufet – 'Mrs Cole had just been there, just called in for ten minutes, and had been so good as to sit an hour with them, and *she* had taken a piece of cake and been so kind as to say she liked it very much; and therefore she hoped Miss Woodhouse and Miss Smith would do them the favour to eat a piece too.'

The mention of the Coles was sure to be followed by that of Mr Elton. There was intimacy between them, and Mr Cole had heard from Mr Elton since his going away. Emma knew what was coming; they must have the letter over again, and settle how long he had been gone, and how much he was engaged in company, and what a favourite he was wherever he went, and how full the Master of the Ceremonies' ball had been; and she went through it very well, and with all the interest and all the commendation that could be requisite, and always putting forward to prevent Harriet's being obliged to say a word.

This she had been prepared for when she entered the house; but meant, having once talked him handsomely over, to be no farther incommoded by any troublesome topic, and to wander at large amongst all the Mistresses and Misses of Highbury and their card-parties. She had not been prepared to have Jane Fairfax succeed Mr Elton; but he was actually hurried off by Miss Bates, she jumped away from him at last abruptly to the Coles, to usher in a letter from her niece.

'Oh! yes – Mr Elton, I understood – certainly as to dancing – Mrs Cole was telling me that dancing at the rooms at Bath was – Mrs Cole was so kind as to sit some time with us, talking of Jane; for as soon as she came in, she began enquiring after her, Jane is so very great a favourite there. Whenever she is with us, Mrs Cole does not know how to shew her kindness enough; and I must say that Jane deserves it as much as anybody can. And so she began enquiring after her directly, saying, "I know you cannot have heard from Jane lately, because it is not her time for writing;" and when I immediately said, "But indeed we have, we had a letter this very morning," I do not know that I ever saw anybody more surprized. "Have you, upon your honour!" said she; "well, that is quite unexpected. Do let me hear what she says." '

Emma's politeness was at hand directly, to say, with smiling interest –

'Have you heard from Miss Fairfax so lately? I am extremely happy. I hope she is well?'

'Thank you. You are so kind!' replied the happily deceived aunt, while eagerly hunting for the letter. – 'Oh! here it is. I was sure it could not be far off: but I had put my huswife upon it, you see, without being aware, and so it was quite hid, but I had it in my hand so very lately that I was almost sure it must be on the table. I was reading it to Mrs Cole, and since she went away, I was reading it again to my mother, for it is such a pleasure to her – a letter from Jane – that she can never hear it often enough; so I knew it could not be far off, and here it is, only just under my huswife – and since you are so kind as to wish to hear what she says; – but, first of all, I really must, in justice to Jane, apologise for her writing so short a letter – only two pages you see – hardly two – and in general she fills the whole paper and crosses half. My mother often wonders that I can make it out so well. She often says, when the letter is

'Oh, here it is.'

first opened, "Well, Hetty, now I think you will be put to it to make out all that chequer-work" – don't you, ma'am? – and then I tell her, I am sure she would contrive to make it out herself, if she had nobody to do it for her – every word of it – I am sure she would pore over it till she had made out every word. And, indeed, though my mother's eyes are not so good as they were, she can see amazingly well still, thank God! with the help of spectacles. It is such a blessing! My mother's are really very good indeed. Jane often says, when she is here, "I am sure, grandmama, you must have had very strong eyes to see as you do – and so much fine work as you have done too! – I only wish my eyes may last as well." '

All this spoken extremely fast obliged Miss Bates to stop for breath; and Emma said something very civil about the excellence of Miss Fairfax's handwriting.

'You are extremely kind,' replied Miss Bates, highly gratified;

'you who are such a judge, and write so beautifully yourself. I am sure there is nobody's praise that could give us so much pleasure at Miss Woodhouse's. My mother does not hear; she is a little deaf you know. Ma'am,' addressing her, 'do you hear what Miss Woodhouse is so obliging to say about Jane's handwriting?'

And Emma had the advantage of hearing her own silly compliment repeated twice over before the good old lady could comprehend it. She was pondering, in the mean while, upon the possibility, without seeming very rude, of making her escape from Jane Fairfax's letter, and had almost resolved on hurrying away directly under some slight excuse, when Miss Bates turned to her again and seized her attention.

'My mother's deafness is very trifling you see – just nothing at all. By only raising my voice, and saying anything two or three times over, she is sure to hear; but then she is used to my voice. But it is very remarkable that she should always hear Jane better than she does me. Jane speaks so distinct! However, she will not find her grandmama at all deafer than she was two years ago; which is saying a great deal at my mother's time of life – and it really is full two years, you know, since she was here. We never were so long without seeing her before, and as I was telling Mrs Cole, we shall hardly know how to make enough of her now.'

'Are you expecting Miss Fairfax here soon?'

'Oh, yes; next week.'

'Indeed! – That must be a very great pleasure.'

'Thank you. You are very kind. Yes, next week. Every body is so surprized; and every body says the same obliging things. I am sure she will be as happy to see her friends at Highbury, as they can be to see her. Yes, Friday, or Saturday; she cannot say which because Colonel Campbell will be wanting the carriage himself one of those days. So very good of them to send her the whole way! But they always do, you know. Oh, yes, Friday or Saturday next. That is what she writes about. That is the reason of her writing out of rule, as we call it; for, in the common course, we should not have heard from her before next Tuesday or Wednesday.'

'Yes, so I imagined. I was afraid there could be little chance of my hearing any thing of Miss Fairfax today.'

'So obliging of you! No, we should not have heard, if it had not been for this particular circumstance, of her being to come here so soon. My mother is so delighted! – for she is to be three months with us at least. Three months, she says so, positively, as I am going to have the pleasure of reading to you. The case is, you see, that the Campbells are going to Ireland. Mrs Dixon has persuaded her father and mother to come over and see her directly. They had not intended to go over till the summer, but she is so impatient to see them again – for till she married, last October, she was never away from them so much as a week, which must make it very strange to be in different kingdoms, I was going to say, but however, different countries, and so she wrote a very urgent letter to her mother – or her father, I declare I do not know which it was, but we shall see presently in Jane's letter – wrote in Mr Dixon's name as well as her own, to press their coming over directly, and they would give them the meeting in Dublin, and take them back to their country-seat, Baly-craig, a beautiful place, I fancy. Jane has heard a great deal of its beauty; from Mr Dixon I mean – I do not know that she ever heard about it from any body else; but it was very natural, you know, that he should like to speak of his own place while he was paying his addresses – and as Jane used to be very often walking out with them – for Colonel and Mrs Campbell were very particular about their daughter's not walking out often with only Mr Dixon, for which I do not at all blame them; of course she heard everything he might be telling Miss Campbell about his own home in Ireland. And I think she wrote us word that he had shewn them some drawings of the place, views that he had taken himself. He is a most amiable, charming young man, I believe. Jane was quite longing to go to Ireland, from his account of things.'

At this moment, an ingenious and animating suspicion entering Emma's brain with regard to Jane Fairfax, this charming Mr Dixon, and the not going to Ireland, she said, with the insidious design of further discovery.

'You must feel it very fortunate that Miss Fairfax should be allowed to come to you at such a time. Considering the very particular friendship between her and Mrs Dixon, you could hardly have expected her to be excused from accompanying Colonel and Mrs Campbell.'

'Very true, very true, indeed. The very thing we have always been rather afraid of; for we should not have liked to have her at such a distance from us, for months together – not able to come if anything was to happen. But you see, every thing turns out for the best. They want her (Mr and Mrs Dixon) excessively to come over with Colonel and Mrs Campbell; quite depend upon it; nothing can be more kind or pressing than their *joint* invitation, Jane says, as you will hear presently; Mr Dixon does not seem in the least backward in any attention. He is a most charming young man. Ever since the service he rendered Jane at Weymouth, when they were out in that party on the water, and she, by the sudden whirling round of something or other among the sails, would have been dashed into the sea at once, and actually was all but gone, if he had not, with the greatest presence of mind, caught hold of her habit – (I can never think of it without trembling!) – But ever since we had the history of that day, I have been so fond of Mr Dixon!'

'But, in spite of all her friend's urgency, and her own wish of seeing Ireland, Miss Fairfax prefers devoting the time to you and Mrs Bates?'

'Yes – entirely her own doing, entirely her own choice; and Colonel and Mrs Campbell think she does quite right, just what they should recommend; and indeed they particularly *wish* her to try her native air, as she has not been quite so well as usual lately.'

'I am concerned to hear of it. I think they judge wisely. But Mrs Dixon must be very much disappointed. Mrs Dixon, I understand, has no remarkable degree of personal beauty; is not, by any means to be compared with Miss Fairfax.'

'Oh! no. You are very obliging to say such things – but certainly not. There is no comparison between them. Miss Campbell always was absolutely plain – but extremely elegant and amiable.'

'Yes, that of course.'

'Jane caught a bad cold, poor thing! so long ago as the 7th of November, (as I am going to read to you,) and has never been well since. A long time, is not it, for a cold to hang upon her? She never mentioned it before, because she would not alarm us. Just like her! so considerate! – But however, she is so far from well, that her kind friends the Campbells think she had better come home, and try an air that always agrees with her; and they have no doubt that three or four months at Highbury will entirely cure her – and it is certainly a great deal better that she should come here, than go to Ireland, if she is unwell. Nobody could nurse her, as we should do.'

'It appears to me the most desirable arrangement in the world.'

'And so she is to come to us next Friday or Saturday, and the Campbells leave town in their way to Holyhead the Monday following – as you will find from Jane's letter. So sudden! – You may guess, dear Miss Woodhouse, what a flurry it has thrown me in! If it was not for the drawback of her illness – but I am afraid we must expect to see her grown thin, and looking very poorly. I must tell you what an unlucky thing happened to me, as to that, I always make a point of reading Jane's letters through to myself first, before I read them aloud to my mother, you know, for fear of there being any thing in them to distress her. Jane desired me to do it, so I always do; and so I began to-day with my usual caution; but no sooner did I come to the mention of her being unwell, than I burst out quite frightened with, "Bless me! poor Jane is ill!" – which my mother, being on the watch, heard distinctly, and was sadly alarmed at. However, when I read on, I found it was not near so bad as I fancied at first; and I make so light of it now to her, that she does not think much about it. But I cannot imagine how I could be so off my guard! If Jane does not get well soon, we will call in Mr Perry. The expence shall not be thought of; and though he is so liberal, and so fond of Jane that I dare say he would not mean to charge anything for attendance, we could not suffer it to be so, you know. He has a wife and family to maintain, and is not to be giving away his time. Well, now I have just given you a hint of what Jane writes about, we will turn to her letter, and I am sure she tells her own story a great deal better than I can tell it for her.'

'I am afraid we must be running away,' said Emma, glancing at Harriet, and beginning to rise – 'My father will be expecting us. I had no intention, I thought I had no power of staying more than five minutes, when I first entered the house. I merely called, because I would not pass the door without enquiring after Mrs Bates; but I have been so pleasantly detained! Now, however, we must wish you and Mrs Bates good morning.'

And not all that could be urged to detain her succeeded. She regained the street – happy in this, that though much had been forced on her against her will, though she had in fact heard the whole substance of Jane Fairfax's letter, she had been able to escape the letter itself.

CHAPTER TWENTY

JANE FAIRFAX WAS AN orphan, the only child of Mrs Bates's youngest daughter.

The marriage of Lieut. Fairfax, of the – regiment of infantry, and Miss Jane Bates, had had its day of fame and pleasure, hope and interest, but nothing now remained of it, save the melancholy remembrance of him dying in action abroad – of his widow sinking under consumption and grief soon afterwards – and this girl.

By birth she belonged to Highbury: and when at three years old, on losing her mother, she became the property, the charge, the consolation, the fondling of her grandmother and aunt, there had seemed every probability of her being permanently fixed there; for her being taught only what very limited means could command,

and growing up with no advantages of connection or improvements to be engrafted on what nature had given her in a pleasing person, good understanding, and warm-hearted, well meaning relations.

But the compassionate feelings of a friend of her father gave a change to her destiny. This was Colonel Campbell, who had very highly regarded Fairfax, as an excellent officer and most deserving young man; and farther, had been indebted to him for such attentions, during a severe camp-fever, as he believed had saved his life. These were claims which he did not learn to overlook, though some years passed away from the death of poor Fairfax, before his own return to England put any thing in his power. When he did return, he sought out the child and took notice of her. He was a married man, with only one living child, a girl, about Jane's age: and Jane became their guest, paying them long visits and growing a favourite with all; and, before she was nine years old, his daughter's great fondness for her, and his own wish of being a real friend, united to produce an offer from Colonel Campbell of undertaking the whole charge of her education. It was accepted; and from that period Jane had belonged to Colonel Campbell's family, and had lived with them entirely, only visiting her grandmother from time to time.

The plan was that she should be brought up for educating others; the very few hundred pounds which she inherited from her father making independence impossible. To provide for her otherwise was out of Colonel Campbell's power; for though his income by pay and appointments, was handsome, his fortune was moderate and must be all his daughter's; but, by giving her an education, he hoped to be supplying the means of respectable subsistance hereafter.

Such was Jane Fairfax's history. She had fallen into good hands, known nothing but kindness from the Campbell's, and been given an excellent education. Living constantly with right-minded and well-informed people, her heart and understanding had received every advantage of discipline and culture; and Col. Campbell's residence being in London, every lighter talent had been done full justice to, by the attendance of first-rate masters. Her disposition and abilities were equally worthy of all that friendship could do; and at eighteen or nineteen she was, as far as such an early age can be qualified for the care of children, fully competent to the office of instruction herself; but she was too much beloved to be parted with. Neither father nor mother could promote, and the daughter could not endure it. The evil day was put off. It was easy to decide that she was still too young; and Jane remained with them, sharing as another daughter, in all the rational pleasures of an elegant society, and a judicious mixture of home and amusement, with only the drawback of the future, the sobering suggestions of her own good understanding to remind her that all this might soon be over.

The affection of the whole family, the warm attachment of Miss Campbell in particular, was the more honourable to each party from the circumstance of Jane's decided superiority both in beauty and acquirements. That nature had given it in feature could not be unseen by the young woman, nor could her higher powers of mind be unfelt by the parents. They continued together with unabated regard however, till the marriage of Miss Campbell, who by that chance, that luck which so often defies anticipation in matrimonial affairs, giving attraction to what is moderate rather than to what is superior, engaged the affections of Mr Dixon, a young man, rich and agreeable, almost as soon as they were acquainted; and was eligibly and happily settled, while Jane Fairfax had yet her bread to earn.

This event had very lately taken place; too lately for any thing to be yet attempted by her less fortunate friend towards entering on her path of duty; though she had now reached the age which her own judgment had fixed on for beginning. She had long resolved that one-and-twenty should be the period. With the fortitude of a devoted noviciate, she had resolved at one-and-twenty to complete the sacrifice, and retire from all the pleasures of life, of rational intercourse, equal society, peace and hope, to penance and mortification for ever.

The good sense of Colonel and Mrs Campbell could not oppose such a resolution, though their feelings did. As long as they lived, no exertions would be necessary, their home might be her's for ever; and for their own comfort they would have retained her wholly; but this would be selfishness: – what must be at last, had better be soon. Perhaps they began to feel it might have been kinder and wiser to have resisted the temptation of any delay, and spared her from a taste of such enjoyments of ease and leisure as must now be relinquished. Still, however, affection was glad to catch at any reasonable excuse for not hurrying on the wretched moment. She had never been quite well since the time of their daughter's marriage; and till she should have completely recovered her usual strength, they must forbid her engaging in duties, which, so far from being compatible with a weakened frame and varying spirits, seemed, under the most favourable circumstances, to require something more than human perfection of body and mind to be discharged with tolerable comfort.

With regard to her not accompanying them to Ireland, her account to her aunt contained nothing but truth, though there might be some truths not told. It was her own choice to give the time of their absence to Highbury; to spend, perhaps, her last months of perfect liberty with those kind relations to whom she was so very dear; and the Campbells, whatever might be their motive or motives, whether single, or double, or treble, gave the arrangement their ready sanction, and said, that they depended more on a few months spent in her native air, for the recovery of her health, than on anything else. Certain it was that she was to come; and that Highbury, instead of welcoming that perfect novelty which had been so long promised it – Mr Frank Churchill – must put up for the present with Jane Fairfax, who could bring only the freshness of two years absence.

Emma was sorry; – to have to pay civilities to a person she did not like through three long months! – to be always doing more than she wished, and less than she ought! Why she did not like Jane Fairfax might be a difficult question to answer; Mr Knightley had once told her it was because she saw in her the really accomplished young woman, which she wanted to be thought herself; and though the accusation had been eagerly refuted at the time, there were moments of self-examination in which her conscience could not quite acquit her. But 'she could never get acquainted with her; she did not know how it was, but there was such coldness and reserve – such apparent indifference whether she pleased or not – and then, her aunt was such an eternal talker! – and she was made such a fuss by every body! – and it had been always imagined that they were to be so intimate – because their ages were the same, every body had supposed they must be so fond of each other.' These were her reasons – she had no better.

It was a dislike so little just – every imputed fault was so magnified by fancy, that she never saw Jane Fairfax the first time after any considerable absence, without feeling that she had injured her; and now, when the due visit was paid, on her arrival, after a two years' interval, she was particularly struck with the very appearance and manners, which for those two whole years she had been depreciating. Jane Fairfax was very elegant, remarkably elegant; and she had herself the highest value for elegance. Her height was pretty, just such as almost everybody would think tall, and nobody could think very tall; her figure particularly graceful; her size a most becoming medium, between fat and thin, though a slight appearance of ill-health seemed to point out the likeliest evil of the two. Emma could not but feel all this; and then, her face – her features – there was more beauty in them all together than she had remembered; it was not regular, but it was very pleasing beauty. Her eyes, a deep grey, with dark eye-lashes and eye-brows, had never been denied their praise; but the skin, which she had been used to cavil at, as wanting colour, had a clearness and delicacy, of which elegance was the reigning character, and, as such, she must, in honour, by all her principles, admire it: – elegance, which, whether of person or of mind, she saw so little in Highbury. There, not to be vulgar, was distinction, and merit.

In short, she sat, during the first visit, looking at Jane Fairfax with twofold complacency; the sense of pleasure and the sense of rendering justice, and was determining that she would dislike her no longer. When she took in her history, indeed, her situation, as well as her beauty; when she considered what all this elegance was destined to, what she was going to sink from, how she was going to live, it seemed impossible to feel any thing but compassion and respect; especially, if to every well-known particular entitling her to interest, were added the highly probable circumstance of an attachment to Mr Dixon, which she had so naturally started to herself. In that case, nothing could be more pitiable or more honourable than the sacrifices she had resolved on. Emma was very willing now to acquit her of having seduced Mr Dixon's affections from his wife, or of any thing mischievous which her imagination had suggested at first. If it were love, it might be simple, single, successless love on her side alone. She might have been unconsciously sucking in the sad poison, while a sharer of his conversation with her friend; and from the best, the purest motives, might now be denyihg herself this visit to Ireland, and resolving to divide herself effectually from him and his connections by soon beginning her career of laborious duty.

Upon the whole, Emma left her with such softened, charitable feelings, as made her look around in walking home, and lament that Highbury afforded no young man worthy of giving her independence; nobody that she could wish to scheme about for her.

These were charming feelings – but not lasting. Before she had committed herself by any public profession of eternal friendship for Jane Fairfax, or done more towards a recantation of past prejudices and errors, than saying to Mr Knightley, 'She certainly is handsome; she is better than handsome!' Jane had spent an evening at Hartfield with her grandmother and aunt, and every thing was relapsing much into its usual state. Former provocations re-appeared. The aunt was as tiresome as ever; more tiresome, because anxiety for her health was now added to admiration of her powers; and they had to listen to the description of exactly how little bread and butter she ate for breakfast, and how small a slice of mutton for dinner, as well as to see exhibitions of new caps and new work-bags for her mother and herself; and Jane's offences rose again. They had music; Emma was obliged to play; and the thanks and praise which necessarily followed appeared to her an affectation of candour, and air of greatness, meaning only to shew off in higher style her own very superior performance. She was, besides, which was the worst of all, so cold, so cautious! There was no getting at her real opinion. Wrapt up in a cloak of politeness, she seemed determined to hazard nothing. She was disgustingly, was suspiciously reserved.

If any thing could be more, where all was most, she was more reserved on the subject of Weymouth and the Dixons than any thing. She seemed bent on giving no real insight into Mr Dixon's character, or her own value for his company, or opinion of the suitableness of the match. It was all general approbation and smoothness; nothing delineated or distinguished. It did her no service however. Her caution was thrown away. Emma saw its artifice, and returned to her first surmises. There probably *was* something more to conceal than her own preference; Mr Dixon, perhaps, had been very near changing one friend for the other, or been fixed only to Miss Campbell, for the sake of the future twelve thousand pounds.

The like reserve prevailed on other topics. She and Mr Frank Churchill had been at Weymouth at the same time. It was known that they were a little acquainted; but not a syllable of real information could Emma procure as to what he truly was. 'Was he handsome?' – 'She believed he was reckoned a very fine young man.' 'Was he agreeable?' – 'He was generally thought so.' 'Did he appear a sensible young man; a young man of information?' – 'At a watering-place, or in a common London acquaintance, it was difficult to decide on such points. Manners were all that could be safely judged of, under a much longer knowledge than they had yet had of Mr Churchill. She believed every body found his manners pleasing.' Emma could not forgive her.

CHAPTER TWENTY-ONE

EMMA COULD NOT FORGIVE her; – but as neither provocation nor resentment were discerned by Mr Knightley, who had been of the party, and had seen only proper attention and pleasing behaviour on each side, he was expressing the next morning, being at Hartfield again on business with Mr Woodhouse, his approbation of the whole; not so openly as he might have done had her father been out of the room, but speaking plain enough to be very intelligible to Emma. He had been used to think her unjust to Jane, and had now great pleasure in marking an improvement.

'A very pleasant evening,' he began, as soon as Mr Woodhouse had been talked into what was necessary, told that he understood, and the papers swept away; – 'particularly pleasant. You and Miss Fairfax gave us some very good music. I do not know a more luxurious state, sir, than sitting at one's ease to be entertained a whole evening by two such young women; sometimes with music and sometimes with conversation. I am sure Miss Fairfax must have found the evening pleasant, Emma. You left nothing undone. I was glad you made her play so much, for having no instrument at her grandmother's, it must have been a real indulgence.'

'I am happy you approved,' said Emma, smiling; 'but I hope I am not often deficient in what is due to guests at Hartfield.'

'No, my dear,' said her father instantly; '*that* I am sure you are not. There is nobody half so attentive and civil as you are. If any thing, you are too attentive. The muffin last night – if it had been handed round once, I think it would have been enough.'

'No,' said Mr Knightley, nearly at the same time; 'you are not often deficient; not often deficient either in manner or comprehension. I think you understand me, therefore.'

An arch look expressed – 'I understand you well enough;' but she said only, 'Miss Fairfax is reserved.'

'I always told you she was – a little; but you will soon overcome all that part of her reserve which ought to be overcome, all that has its foundation in diffidence. What arises from discretion must be honoured.'

'You think her diffident. I do not see it.

'My dear Emma,' said he, moving from his chair into one close by her, 'you are not going to tell me, I hope, that you had not a pleasant evening.'

'Oh! no; I was pleased with my own perseverance in asking questions; and amused to think how little information I obtained.'

'I am disappointed,' was his only answer.

'I hope every body had a pleasant evening,' said Mr Woodhouse, in his quiet way. 'I had. Once, I felt the fire rather too much; but then I moved back my chair a little, a very little, and it did not disturb me. Miss Bates was very chatty and good-humoured, as she always is; though she speaks rather too quick. However, she is very agreeable, and Mrs Bates too, in a different way. I like old friends; and Miss Jane Fairfax is a very pretty sort of young lady, a very pretty and a very well-behaved young lady indeed. She must have found the evening agreeable, Mr Knightley, because she had Emma.'

'True, sir; and Emma, because she had Miss Fairfax.'

Emma saw his anxiety, and wishing to appease it, at least for the present, said, and with a sincerity which no one could question –

'She is a sort of elegant creature that one cannot keep one's eyes from. I am always watching her to admire; and I do pity her from my heart.'

Mr Knightley looked as if he were more gratified than he cared to express; and before he could make any reply, Mr Woodhouse, whose thoughts were on the Bates's, said –

'It is a great pity that their circumstances should be so confined!

'Miss Bates was very chatty and good-humoured.'

a great pity indeed! and I have often wished – but it is so little one can venture to do – small, trifling presents, of any thing uncommon – Now we have killed a porker, and Emma thinks of sending them a loin or a leg; it is very small and delicate – Hartfield pork is not like any other pork – but still it is pork – and, my dear Emma, unless one could be sure of their making it into steaks, nicely fried, as our's are fried, without the smallest grease, and not roast it, for no stomach can bear roast pork, – I think we had better send the leg – do not you think so, my dear?'

'My dear papa, I sent the whole hind-quarter. I knew you would wish it. There will be the leg to be salted, you know, which is so very nice, and the loin to be dressed directly in any manner they like.'

'That's right, my dear, very right. I had not thought of it before, but that was the best way. They must not over-salt the leg; and then, if it is not over-salted, and if it is very thoroughly boiled, just as Serle boils our's, and eaten very moderately of, with a boiled turnip, and a little carrot or parsnip, I do not consider it unwholesome.'

'Emma,' said Mr Knightley presently, 'I have a piece of news for you. You like news – and I heard an article in my way hither that I think will interest you.'

'News! Oh! yes, I always like news. What is it? – why do you smile so? – where did you hear it? – at Randalls?'

He had time only to say,

'No, not at Randalls; I have not been near Randalls,' when the door was thrown open, and Miss Bates and Miss Fairfax walked into the room. Full of thanks, and full of news, Miss Bates knew not which to give quickest. Mr Knightley soon saw that he had lost his moment, and that not another syllable of communication could rest with him.

'Oh! my dear sir, how are you this morning? My dear Miss Woodhouse – I come quite overpowered. Such a beautiful hind-quarter of pork! You are too bountiful! Have you heard the news? Mr Elton is going to be married.'

Emma had not had time even to think of Mr Elton, and she was so completely surprized that she could not avoid a little start, and a blush, at the sound.

'There is my news; – I thought it would interest you,' said Mr Knightley, with a smile which implied a conviction of some part of what had passed between them.

'But where could *you* hear it?' cried Miss Bates. 'Where could you possibly hear it, Mr Knightley? For it is not five minutes since I received Mrs Cole's note – no, it cannot be more than five – or at least ten – for I had got my bonnet and spencer on, just ready to come out – I was only gone down to speak to Patty again about the pork – Jane was standing in the passage – were not you, Jane? – for my mother was so afraid that we had not any salting-pan large enough. So I said I would go down and see, and Jane said, "Shall I go down instead? for I think you have a little cold, and Patty has been washing the kitchen." 'Oh! my dear, said I – well, and just then came the note. A Miss Hawkins – that's all I know. A Miss Hawkins of Bath. But, Mr Knightley, how could you possibly have heard it? for the very moment Mr Cole told Mrs Cole of it, she sat down and wrote to me. A Miss Hawkins' –

'I was with Mr Cole on business an hour and half ago. He had just read Elton's letter as I was shewn in, and handed it to me directly.'

'Well! that is quite – I suppose there never was a piece of news more generally interesting. My dear sir, you really are too bountiful. My mother desires her very best compliments and regards, and a thousand thanks, and says you really quite oppress her.'

'We consider our Hartfield pork,' replied Mr Woodhouse – 'indeed it certainly is, so very superior to all other pork, that Emma and I cannot have a greater pleasure than' –

'Oh! my dear sir, as my mother says, our friends are only too good to us. If ever there were people who, without having great wealth themselves, had every thing they could wish for, I am sure it is us. We may well say that "our lot is cast in a goodly heritage." Well, Mr Knightley, and so you actually saw the letter; well' –

'It was short, merely to announce – but cheerful, exulting, of course.' – Here was a sly glance at Emma. 'He had been so fortunate as to – I forget the precise words – one had no business to remember them. The information was, as you state, that he was going to be married to a Miss Hawkins. By his style, I should imagine it just settled.'

'Mr Elton going to be married!' said Emma, as soon as she could speak. 'He will have everybody's wishes for his happiness.'

'He is very young to settle,' was Mr Woodhouse's observation. 'He had better not be in a hurry. He seemed to me very well off as he was. We were always glad to see him at Hartfield.'

'A new neighbour for us all, Miss Woodhouse!' said Miss Bates, joyfully; 'my mother is so pleased! – she says she cannot bear to have the poor old Vicarage without a mistress. This is great news, indeed. Jane, you have never seen Mr Elton! – no wonder that you have such a curiosity to see him.'

Jane's curiosity did not appear of that absorbing nature as wholly to occupy her.

'No – I have never seen Mr Elton,' she replied, starting on this appeal; 'is he – is he a tall man?'

'Who shall answer that question?' cried Emma. 'My father would say "yes," Mr Knightley, "no;" and Miss Bates and I that he is just the happy medium. When you have been here a little longer, Miss Fairfax, you will understand that Mr Elton is the standard of perfection in Highbury, both in person and mind.'

'Very true, Miss Woodhouse, so she will. He is the very best young man – But, my dear Jane, if you remember, I told you yesterday he was precisely the height of Mr Perry. Miss Hawkins, – I dare say, an excellent young woman. His extreme attention to my mother – wanting her to sit in the vicarage-pew, that she might hear the better, for my mother is a little deaf, you know – it is not much, but she does not hear quite quick. Jane says that Colonel Campbell is a little deaf. He fancied bathing might be good for it – the warm bath – but she says it did him no lasting benefit. Colonel Campbell, you know, is quite our angel. And Mr Dixon seems a very charming young man, quite worthy of him. It is such a happiness when good people get together – and they always do. Now, here will be Mr Elton and Miss Hawkins; and there are the Coles, such very good people; and the Perrys – I suppose there never was a happier or a better couple than Mr and Mrs Perry. I say, sir,' turning to Mr Woodhouse, 'I think there are few places with such society as Highbury. I always say, we are quite blessed in our neighbours. – My dear sir, if there is one thing my mother loves better than another, it is pork – a roast loin of pork' –

'As to who, or what Miss Hawkins is, or how long he has been acquainted with her,' said Emma, 'nothing I suppose can be known. One feels that it cannot be a very long acquaintance. He has been gone only four weeks.'

Nobody had any information to give; and, after a few more wonderings, Emma said,

'You are silent, Miss Fairfax – but I hope you mean to take an interest in this news. You, who have been hearing and seeing so much of late on these subjects, who must have been so deep in the business on Miss Campbell's account – we shall not excuse your being indifferent about Mr Elton and Miss Hawkins.'

'When I have seen Mr Elton,' replied Jane, 'I dare say I shall be interested – but I believe it requires *that* with me. And as it is some months since Miss Campbell married, the impression may be a little worn off.'

'Yes, he has been gone just four weeks, as you observe, Miss Woodhouse,' said Miss Bates, 'four weeks yesterday. – A Miss Hawkins. – Well, I had always rather fancied it would be some young lady hereabouts; not that I ever – Mrs Cole once whispered to me – but I immediately said, "No, Mr Elton is a most worthy young man – but" – In short, I do not think I am particularly quick at those sort of discoveries. I do not pretend to it. What is before me, I see. At the same time, nobody could wonder if Mr Elton should have aspired – Miss Woodhouse lets me chatter on, so good-humouredly. She knows I would not offend for the world. How does Miss Smith do? She seems quite recovered now. Have you heard from Mrs John Knightley lately? Oh! those dear little children. Jane, do you know I always fancy Mr Dixon like Mr John Knightley? I mean in person – tall, and with that sort of look – and not very talkative.'

'Quite wrong, my dear aunt; there is no likeness at all.'

'Very odd! but one never does form a just idea of any body beforehand. One takes up a notion, and runs away with it. Mr Dixon, you say, is not, strictly speaking, handsome.'

'Handsome; Oh! no – far from it – certainly plain. I told you he was plain.'

'My dear, you said that Miss Campbell would not allow him to be plain, and that you yourself – '

'Oh! as for me, my judgment is worth nothing. Where I have a regard, I always think a person well-looking. But I gave what I believed the general opinion, when I called him plain.'

'Well, my dear Jane, I believe we must be running away. The weather does not look well, and grandmamma will be uneasy. You are too obliging, my dear Miss Woodhouse; but we really must take leave. This has been a most agreeable piece of news indeed. I shall just go round by Mrs Cole's; but I shall not stop three minutes: and, Jane, you had better go home directly – I would not have you out in a shower! – We think she is the better for Highbury already. Thank you, we do indeed. I shall not attempt calling on Mrs Goddard, for I really do not think she cares for any thing but *boiled* pork: when we dress the leg it will be another thing. Good morning to you, my dear sir. Oh! Mr Knightley is coming too. Well, that is so very! – I am sure if Jane is tired, you will be so kind as to give her your arm. – Mr Elton, and Miss Hawkins. – Good morning to you.'

Emma, alone with her father, had half her attention wanted by him, while he lamented that young people would be in such a hurry to marry – and to marry strangers too – and the other half she could

'Who should come in but Elizabeth and her brother!'

give to her own view of the subject. It was to herself an amusing and a very welcome piece of news, as proving that Mr Elton could not have suffered long; but she was sorry for Harriet; Harriet must feel it – and all that she could hope was, by giving the first information herself, to save her from hearing it abruptly from others. It was now about the time that she was likely to call. If she were to meet Miss Bates in her way! – and upon its beginning to rain, Emma was obliged to expect that the weather would be detaining her at Mrs Goddard's, and that the intelligence would undoubtedly rush upon her without preparation.

The shower was heavy, but short; and it had not been over five minutes, when in came Harriet, with just the heated, agitated look which hurrying thither with a full heart was likely to give; and the 'Oh! Miss Woodhouse, what do you think has happened!' which instantly burst forth, had all the evidence of corresponding perturbation. As the blow was given, Emma felt that she could not now shew greater kindness than in listening; and Harriet, unchecked, ran eagerly through what she had to tell. 'She had set out from Mrs Goddard's half an hour ago – she had been afraid it would rain – she had been afraid it would pour down every moment – but she thought she might get to Hartfield first – she had hurried on as fast as possible; but then, as she was passing by the house where a young woman was making up a gown for her, she thought she would just step in and see how it went on; and though she did not seem to stay half a moment there, soon after she came out it began to rain, and she did not know what to do; so she ran on directly, as fast as she could, and took shelter at Ford's.' – Ford's was the principal woollen-draper, linen-draper, and haberdasher's shop united; the shop first in size and fashion in the place. – 'And so, there she had set, without an idea of any thing in the world, full ten minutes, perhaps – when, all of a sudden, who should come in – to be sure it was so very odd! – but they always dealt at Ford's – who should come in, but Elizabeth Martin and her brother! – Dear Miss Woodhouse! only think. I thought I should have fainted. I did not know what to do. I was sitting near the door – Elizabeth saw me directly; but he did not; he was busy with the umbrella. I am sure she saw me, but she looked away directly, and took no notice; and they both went to quite the farther end of the shop; and I am kept sitting near the door! – Oh! dear; I was so miserable! I am sure I must have been as white as my gown. I could not go away you know, because of the rain; but I did so wish myself any where in the world but there. – Oh! dear, Miss Woodhouse – well, at last, I fancy, he looked round and saw me; for instead of going on with their buyings, they began whispering to one another. I am sure they were talking of me; and I could not help thinking that he was persuading her to speak to me – (do you think he was, Miss Woodhouse?) – for presently she came forward – came quite up to me, and asked me how I did, and seemed ready to shake hands, if I would. She did not do any of it in the same way that she used; I could see she was altered; but, however, she seemed to try to be very friendly, and we shook hands, and stood talking some time, but I know no more what I said – I was in such a tremble! – I remember she said she was sorry we never met now; which I thought almost too kind! Dear, Miss Woodhouse, I was absolutely miserable! By that time, it was beginning to hold up, and I was determined that nothing should stop me from getting away – and then – only think! – I found he was coming up towards me too – slowly you know, and as if he did not quite know what to do; and so he came and spoke, and I answered – and I stood for a minute, feeling dreadfully, you know, one can't tell how; and then I took courage, and said it did not rain, and I must go: and so off I set; and I had not got three yards from the door, when he came after me, only to say, if I was going to Hartfield, he thought I had much better go round by Mr Cole's stables, for I should find the near way quite floated by this rain. Oh! dear, I thought it would have been the death of me! So I said, I was very much obliged to him: you know I could not do less; and then he went back to Elizabeth, and I came round by the stables – I believe I did – but I hardly knew where I was, any thing than have had it happen: and yet, you know, there was a sort of satisfaction in seeing him behave so pleasantly and so kindly. And Elizabeth, too, Oh! Miss Woodhouse, do talk to me and make me comfortable again.'

Very sincerely did Emma wish to do so; but it was not immediately in her power. She was obliged to stop and think. She was not thoroughly comfortable herself. The young man's conduct, and his sister's, seemed the result of real feeling, and she could not but pity them. As Harriet described it, there had been an interesting mixture of wounded affection and genuine delicacy in their behaviour. But she had believed them to be well meaning, worthy people before; and what difference did this make in the evils of the connection? It was folly to be disturbed by it. Of course, he must be sorry to lose her – they must be all sorry. Ambition, as well as love, had probably been mortified. They might all have hoped to rise by Harriet's acquaintance; and besides, what was the value of Harriet's description? – so easily pleased – so little discerning; – what signified her praise?

She exerted herself; and did try to make her comfortable, by considering all that had passed as a mere trifle, and quite unworthy of being dwelt on.

'It might be distressing, for the moment,' said she; 'but you seem to have behaved extremely well; and it is over – and may never – can never, as a first meeting, occur again, and therefore you need not think about it.'

Harriet said, 'very true;' and she 'would not think about it;' but still she talked of it – still she could talk of nothing else; and Emma, at last, in order to put the Martins out of her head, was obliged to hurry on the news, which she had meant to give with so much tender caution; hardly knowing herself whether to rejoice or be angry, ashamed or only amused, at such a state of mind in poor Harriet – such a conclusion of Mr Elton's importance with her!

Mr Elton's rights, however, gradually revived. Though she did not feel the first intelligence as she might have done the day before, or an hour before, its interest soon increased; and before their first conversation was over, she had talked herself into all the sensations of curiosity, wonder and regret, pain and pleasure, as to this fortunate Miss Hawkins, which could conduce to place the Martins under proper subordination in her fancy.

Emma learned to be rather glad that there had been such a meeting. It had been serviceable in deadening the first shock, without retaining any influence to alarm. As Harriet now lived, the Martins could not get at her, without seeking her, where hitherto they had wanted either the courage or the condescension to seek her; for since her refusal of the brother, the sisters had never been at Mrs Goddard's; and a twelvemonth might pass without their being thrown together again, with any necessity, or even any power of speech.

CHAPTER TWENTY-TWO

HUMAN NATURE IS SO well disposed towards those who are in interesting situations, that a young person, who either marries or dies, is sure of being kindly spoken of.

A week had not passed since Miss Hawkins's name was first mentioned in Highbury, before she was, by some means or other, discovered to have every recommendation of person and mind; to be handsome, elegant, highly accomplished, and perfectly amiable; and when Mr Elton himself arrived to triumph in his happy prospects, and circulate the fame of her merits, there was very little more for him to do, than to tell her Christian name, and say whose music she principally played.

Mr Elton returned, a very happy man. He had gone away rejected and mortified – disappointed in a very sanguine hope, after a series of what had appeared to him strong encouragement; and not only losing the right lady, but finding himself debased to the level of a very wrong one. He had gone away deeply offended – he came back engaged to another – and to another as superior, of course, to the first, as under such circumstances what is gained always is to what is lost. He came back gay and self-satisfied, eager and busy, caring nothing for Miss Woodhouse, and defying Miss Smith.

The charming Augusta Hawkins, in addition to all the usual advantages of perfect beauty and merit, was in possession of an independent fortune, of so many thousands as would always be called ten; a point of some dignity, as well as some convenience: the story told well; he had not thrown himself away – he had gained a woman of 10,000*l.* or thereabouts; and he had gained her with such delightful rapidity – the first hour of introduction had been so very soon followed by distinguishing notice; the history which he had to give Mrs Cole of the rise and progress of the affair was so glorious – the steps so quick, from the accidental rencontre, to the dinner at Mr Green's, and the party at Mrs Brown's – smiles and blushes rising in importance – with consciousness and agitation richly scattered – the lady had been so easily impressed – so sweetly disposed – had in short, to use a most intelligible phrase, been so very ready to have him, that vanity and prudence were equally contented.

He had caught both substance and shadow – both fortune and affection, and was just the happy man he ought to be; talking only of himself and his own concerns – expecting to be congratulated – ready to be laughed at – and, with cordial, fearless smiles, now addressing all the young ladies of the place, to whom, a few weeks ago, he would have been more cautiously gallant.

The wedding was no distant event, as the parties had only themselves to please, and nothing but the necessary preparations to wait for; and when he set out for Bath again, there was a general expectation, which a certain glance of Mrs Cole's did not seem to contradict, that when he next entered Highbury he would bring his bride.

During his present short stay, Emma had barely seen him; but just enough to feel that the first meeting was over, and to give her the impression of his not being improved by the mixture of pique and pretension, now spread over his air. She was, in fact, beginning very much to wonder that she had ever thought him pleasing at all; and his sight was so inseparably connected with some very disagreeable feelings, that except in a moral light, as a penance, a lesson, a source of profitable humiliation to her own mind, she would have been thankful to be assured of never seeing him again. She wished him very well; but he gave her pain, and his welfare twenty miles off would administer most satisfaction.

The pain of his continued residence in Highbury, however, must certainly be lessened by his marriage. Many vain solicitudes would be prevented – many awkwardnesses smoothed by it. A *Mrs Elton* would be an excuse for any change of intercourse; former intimacy might sink without remark. It would be almost beginning their life of civility again.

Of the lady, individually, Emma thought very little. She was good enough for Mr Elton, no doubt; accomplished enough for Highbury – handsome enough – to look plain, probably, by Harriet's side. As to connection, there Emma was perfectly easy; persuaded, that after all his own vaunted claims and disdain of Harriet, he had done nothing. On that article, truth seemed attainable. *What* she was, must be uncertain; but *who* she was, might be found out; and setting aside the 10,000*l.* it did not appear that she was at all Harriet's superior. She brought no name, no blood, no alliance. Miss Hawkins was all youngest of the two daughters of a Bristol – merchant, of course, he must be called; but, as the whole of the profits of his mercantile life appeared so very moderate, it was not unfair to guess the dignity of his line of trade had been very moderate also. Part of every winter she had been used to spend in Bath; but Bristol was her home, the very heart of Bristol; for though the father and mother had died some years ago, an uncle remained – in the law line – nothing more distinctly honourable was hazarded of him, than that he was in the law line; and with him the daughter had lived. Emma guessed him to be the drudge of some attorney, and too stupid to rise. And all the grandeur of the connection, seemed dependent on the elder sister, who was *very well married*, to a gentleman in a *great way*, near Bristol, who kept two carriages! That was the wind-up of the history; that was the glory of Miss Hawkins.

Could she but have given Harriet her feelings about it all! She had talked her into love; but alas! she was not so easily to be talked out of it. The charm of an object to occupy the many vacancies of Harriet's mind was not to be talked away. He might be superseded by another; he certainly would indeed; nothing could be clearer; even a Robert Martin would have been sufficient; but nothing else, she feared, would cure her. Harriet was one of those, who, having once begun, would be always in love. And now, poor girl! she was considerably worse from this re-appearance of Mr Elton. She was always having a glimpse of him somewhere or other. Emma saw him only once; but two or three times every day Harriet was sure *just* to meet with him, or *just* to miss him, *just* to hear his voice, or see his shoulder, *just* to have something occur to preserve him in her fancy, in all the favouring warmth of surprize and conjecture. She was, moreover, perpetually hearing about him; for, excepting when at Hartfield, she was always among those who saw no fault in Mr Elton, and found nothing so interesting as the discussion of his concerns; and every report, therefore, every guess – all that had already occurred, all that might occur in the arrangement of his affairs, comprehending income, servants, and furniture, was continually in agitation around her. Her regard was receiving strength by invariable praise of him, and her regrets kept alive, and feelings irritated by ceaseless repetitions of Miss Hawkins's happiness, and continual observation of, how much he seemed attached! – his air as he walked by the house – the very sitting of his hat, being all in proof of how much he was in love!

Had it been allowable entertainment, had there been no pain to her friend, or reproach to herself, in the waverings of Harriet's mind, Emma would have been amused by its variations. Sometimes Mr Elton predominated, sometimes the Martins; and each was occasionally useful as a check to the other. Mr Elton's engagement had been the cure of the agitation of meeting Mr Martin. The unhappiness produced by the knowledge of that engagement had been a little put aside by Elizabeth Martin's calling at Mrs Goddard's a few days afterwards. Harriet had not been at home; but a note had been prepared and left for her, written in the very style to touch; a small mixture of reproach, with a great deal of kindness; and till Mr Elton himself appeared, she had been much occupied by it, continually pondering over what could be done in return, and wishing to do more than she dared to confess. But Mr Elton, in person, had driven away all such cares. While he staid, the Martins were forgotten; and on the very morning of his setting off for Bath again, Emma, to dissipate some of the distress it occasioned, judged it best for her to return Elizabeth Martin's visit.

How that visit was to be acknowledged – what would be necessary – and what might be safest, had been a point of some doubtful consideration. Absolute neglect of the mother and sisters, when invited to come, would be ingratitude. It must not be: and yet the danger of a renewal of the acquaintance! –

After much thinking, she could determine on nothing better, than Harriet's returning the visit; but in a way that, if they had understanding, should convince them that it was to be only a formal acquaintance. She meant to take her in the carriage, leave her at the Abbey Mill, while she drove a little farther, and call for her again so soon, as to allow no time for insidious applications or dangerous recurrences to the past, and give the most decided proof of what degree of intimacy was chosen for the future.

She could think of nothing better; and though there was something in it which her own heart could not approve – something of ingratitude, merely glossed over – it must be done, or what would become of Harriet?

CHAPTER TWENTY-THREE

SMALL HEART HAD HARRIET for visiting. Only half an hour before her friend called for her at Mrs Goddard's, her evil stars had led her to the very spot where, at that moment, a trunk, directed to *The Rev. Philip Elton, White-Hart, Bath*, was to be seen under the operation of being lifted into the butcher's cart, which was to convey it to where the coaches past; and every thing in this world, excepting that trunk and the direction, was consequently a blank.

She went, however; and when they reached the farm, and she was to be put down, at the end of the broad, neat gravel-walk, which led between espalier apple-trees to the front door, the sight of every thing which had given her so much pleasure the autumn before, was beginning to revive a little agitation; and when they parted, Emma observed her to be looking around with a sort of fearful curiosity, which determined her not to allow the visit to exceed the proposed quarter of an hour. She went on herself, to give that portion of time to an old servant who was married, and settled in Donwell.

The quarter of an hour brought her punctually to the white gate again; and Miss Smith receiving her summons, was with her without delay, and unattended by any alarming young man. She came solitarily down the gravel walk – a Miss Martin just appearing at the door, and parting with her seemingly with ceremonious civility.

Harriet could not very soon give an intelligible account. She was feeling too much; but at last Emma collected from her enough to understand the sort of meeting, and the sort of pain it was creating. She had seen only Mrs Martin and the two girls. They had received her doubtingly, if not coolly; and nothing beyond the merest common-place had been talked almost all the time – till just at last, when Mrs Martin's saying, all of a sudden, that she thought Miss Smith was grown, had brought on a more interesting subject, and a warmer manner. In that very room she had been measured last September, with her two friends. There were the pencilled marks and memorandums on the wainscot by the window. *He* had done it. They all seemed to remember the day, the hour, the party, the occasion – to feel the same consciousness, the same regrets – to be ready to return to the same good understanding; and they were just growing again like themselves, (Harriet, as Emma must suspect, as ready as the best of them to be cordial and happy,) when the carriage re-appeared, and all was over. The style of the visit, and the shortness of it, were then felt to be decisive. Fourteen minutes to be given to those with whom she had thankfully passed six weeks not six months ago! – Emma could not but picture it all, and feel how justly they might resent, how naturally Harriet must suffer. It was a bad business. She would have given a great deal, or endured a great deal, to have had the Martins in a higher rank of life. They

In that very room she had been measured.

were so deserving, that a *little* higher should have been enough: but as it was, how could she have done otherwise? – Impossible! – She could not repent. They must be separated; but there was a great deal of pain in the process – so much to herself at this time, that she soon felt the necessity of a little consolation, and resolved on going home by way of Randalls to procure it. Her mind was quite sick of Mr Elton and the Martins. The refreshment of Randalls was absolutely necessary.

It was a good scheme; but on driving to the door they heard that neither 'master nor mistress was at home;' they had both been out some time; the man believed they were gone to Hartfield.

'This is too bad,' cried Emma, as they turned away. 'And now we shall just miss them; too provoking! – I do not know when I have been so disappointed.' And she leaned back in the corner, to indulge her murmurs, or to reason them away; probably a little of both – such being the commonest process of a not ill-disposed mind. Presently the carriage stopt; she looked up; it was stopt by Mr and Mrs Weston, who were standing to speak to her. There was instant pleasure in the sight of them, and still greater pleasure was conveyed in sound – for Mr Weston immediately accosted her with,

'How d'ye do? – how d'ye do? – We have been sitting with your father – glad to see him so well. Frank comes to-morrow – I had a letter this morning – we see him to-morrow by dinner time to a certainty – he is at Oxford today, and he comes for a whole fortnight; I knew it would be so. If he had come at Christmas he could not have staid three days; I was always glad he did not come at Christmas; now we are going to have just the right weather for him, fine, dry, settled weather. We shall enjoy him completely: every thing has turned out exactly as we could wish.'

There was no resisting such news, no possibility of avoiding the influence of such a happy face as Mr Weston's, confirmed as it all was by the words and the countenance of his wife, fewer and quieter, but not less to the purpose. To know that *she* thought his coming certain was enough to make Emma consider it so, and sincerely did she rejoice in their joy. It was a most delightful re-animation of exhausted spirits. The worn-out past was sunk in the freshness of what was coming; and in the rapidity of half a moment's thought, she hoped Mr Elton would now be talked of no more.

Mr Weston gave her the history of the engagement at Enscombe, which allowed his son to answer for having an entire fortnight at his command, as well as the route and the method of his journey; and she listened, and smiled, and congratulated.

'I shall soon bring him over to Hartfield,' said he, at the conclusion.

Emma could imagine she saw a touch of the arm at this speech, from his wife.

'We had better move on, Mr Weston,' said she, 'we are detaining the girls.'

'Well, well, I am ready;' – and turning again to Emma, 'but you must not be expecting such a *very* fine young man; you have only had *my* account you know; I dare say he is really nothing extraordinary:' – though his own sparkling eyes at the moment were speaking a very different conviction.

Emma could look perfectly unconscious and innocent, and answer in a manner that appropriated nothing.

'Think of me to-morrow, my dear Emma, about four o'clock,' was Mrs Weston's parting injunction; spoken with some anxiety, and meant only for her.

'Four o'clock! – depend upon it he will be here by three,' was Mr Weston's quick amendment; and so ended a most satisfactory meeting. Emma's spirits were mounted quite up to happiness; every thing wore a different air; James and his horses seemed not half so sluggish as before. When she looked at the hedges, she thought the elder at least must soon be coming out; and when she turned round to Harriet, she saw something like a look of spring, a tender smile even there.

'Will Mr Frank Churchill pass through Bath as well as Oxford?' – was a question, however, which did not augur much.

But neither geography nor tranquillity could come all at once, and Emma was now in a humour to resolve that they should both come in time.

The morning of the interesting day arrived, and Mrs Weston's faithful pupil did not forget either at ten, or eleven, or twelve o'clock, that she was to think of her at four.

'My dear, dear, anxious friend,' – said she, in mental soliloquy, while walking down stairs from her own room, 'always over-careful for everybody's comfort but your own; I see you now in all your little fidgets, going again and again into his room, to be sure that all is right.' The clock struck twelve as she passed through the hall. ''Tis twelve. I shall not forget to think of you four hours hence; and by this time to-morrow, perhaps, or a little later, I may be thinking of the possibility of their all calling here. I am sure they will bring him soon.'

She opened the parlour door, and saw two gentlemen sitting with her father – Mr Weston and his son. They had been arrived only a few minutes, and Mr Weston had scarcely finished his explanation of Frank's being a day before his time, and her father was yet in the midst of his very civil welcome and congratulations, when she appeared, to have her share of surprize, introduction, and pleasure.

The Frank Churchill so long talked of, so high in interest, was actually before her – he was presented to her, and she did not think too much had been said in his praise; he was a *very* good looking young man; height, air, addresss, all were unexceptionable, and his countenance had a great deal of the spirit and liveliness of his father's; he looked quick and sensible. She felt immediately that she should like him; and there was a wellbred ease of manner, and a readiness to talk, which convinced her that he came intending to be acquainted with her, and that acquainted they soon must be.

He had reached Randalls the evening before. She was pleased with the eagerness to arrive which had made him alter his plan, and travel earlier, later, and quicker, that he might gain half a day.

'I told you yesterday,' cried Mr Weston with exultation, 'I told you all that he would be here before the time named. I remembered what I used to do myself. One cannot creep upon a journey; one cannot help getting on faster than one had planned; and the pleasure of coming in upon one's friends before the look-out begins, is worth a great deal more than any little exertion it needs.'

'It is a great pleasure where one can indulge in it,' said the young man, 'though there are not many houses that I should presume on so far; but in coming *home* I felt I might do any thing.'

The word *home* made his father look on him with fresh complacency. Emma was directly sure that he knew how to make himself agreeable; the conviction was strengthened by what followed. He was very much pleased with Randalls, thought it a most admirably arranged house, would hardly allow it even to be very small, admired the situation, the walk to Highbury, Highbury itself, Hartfield still more, and professed himself to have always felt the sort of interest in the country which none but one's *own* country gives, and the greatest curiosity to visit it. That he should never have been able to indulge so amiable a feeling before, passed suspiciously through Emma's brain; but still if it were a falsehood, it was a pleasant one, and pleasantly handled. His manner had no air of study or exaggeration. He did really look and speak as if in a state of no common enjoyment.

Their subjects in general were such as belongs to an opening acquaintance. On his side were the enquiries, – 'Was she a horse-woman? – Pleasant rides? – Pleasant walks? – Had they a large neighbourhood? – Highbury, perhaps, afforded society enough? –

There were several very pretty houses in and about it. – Balls – had they balls? – Was it a musical society?'

But when satisfied on all these points, and their acquaintance proportionably advanced, he contrived to find an opportunity, while their two fathers were engaged with each other, of introducing his mother-in-law, and speaking of her with so much handsome praise, so much warm admiration, so much gratitude for the happiness she secured to his father, and her very kind reception of himself, as was an additional proof of his knowing how to please – and of his certainly thinking it worth while to try to please her. He did not advance a word of praise beyond what she knew to be thoroughly deserved by Mrs Weston; but undoubtedly he could know very little of the matter. He understood what would be welcome; he could be sure of little else. 'His father's marriage,' he said, 'had been the wisest measure, every friend must rejoice in it; and the family from whom he had received such a blessing must be ever considered as having conferred the highest obligation on him.'

He got as near as he could to thanking her for Miss Taylor's merits, without seeming quite to forget that in the common course of things it was to be rather supposed that Miss Taylor had formed Miss Woodhouse's character, than Miss Woodhouse Miss Taylor's. And at last, as if resolved to qualify his opinion completely for travelling round to its object, he wound it all up with astonishment at the youth and beauty of her person.

'Elegant, agreeable manners, I was prepared for,' said he; 'but I confess that, considering every thing, I had not expected more than a very tolerably well-looking woman of a certain age; I did not know that I was to find a pretty young woman in Mrs Weston.'

'You cannot see too much perfection in Mrs Weston for my feelings,' said Emma; 'were you to guess her to be *eighteen*, I should listen with pleasure; but *she* would be ready to quarrel with you for using such words. Don't let her imagine that you have spoken of her as a pretty young woman.'

'I hope I should know better,' he replied; 'no depend upon it, (with a gallant bow,) that in addressing Mrs Weston I should understand whom I might praise without any danger of being thought extravagant in my terms.'

Emma wondered whether the same suspicion of what might be expected from their knowing each other, which had taken strong possession of her mind, had ever crossed his; and whether his compliments were to be considered as marks of acquiescence, or proofs of defiance. She must see more of him to understand his ways; at present she only felt they were agreeable.

She had no doubt of what Mr Weston was often thinking about. His quick eye she detected again and again glancing towards them with a happy expression; and even, when he might have determined not to look, she was confident that he was often listening.

Her own father's perfect exemption from any thought of the kind, the entire deficiency in him of all such sort of penetration or suspicion, was a most comfortable circumstance. Happily he was not farther from approving matrimony than from foreseeing it. – Though always objecting to every marriage that was arranged, he never suffered beforehand from the apprehension of any; it seemed as if he could not think so ill of any two persons' understanding as to suppose they meant to marry till it were proved against them. She blessed the favouring blindness. He could now, without the drawback of a single unpleasant surmise, without a glance forward at any possible treachery in his guest, give way to all his natural kind-hearted civility in solicitous enquiries after Mr Frank Churchill's accommodation on his journey, through the sad evils of sleeping two nights on the road, and express very genuine unmixed anxiety to know that he had certainly escaped catching cold – which, however, he could not allow him to feel quite assured of himself till after another night.

A reasonable visit paid, Mr Weston began to move. – 'He must be going. He had business at the Crown about his hay, and a great many errands for Mrs Weston at Ford's; but he need not hurry anybody else.' His son, too well bred to hear the hint, rose immediately also, saying,

'As you are going farther on business, sir, I will take the opportunity of paying a visit, which must be paid some day or other, and therefore may as well be paid now. I have the honour of being acquainted with a neighbour of yours, (turning to Emma,) a lady residing in or near Highbury, a family of the name of Fairfax. I shall have no difficulty, I suppose, in finding the house; though Fairfax, I believe, is not the proper name – I should rather say Barnes, or Bates. Do you know any family of that name?'

'To be sure we do,' cried his father; 'Mrs Bates – we passed her house – I saw Miss Bates at the window. True, true, you are acquainted with Miss Fairfax; I remember you knew her at Weymouth, and a fine girl she is. Call upon her, by all means.'

'There is no necessity for my calling this morning,' said the young man; 'another day would do as well; but there was that degree of acquaintance at Weymouth which' –

'Oh! go today, go today. Do not defer it. What is right to be done cannot be done too soon. And, besides, I must give you a hint, Frank; any want of attention to her *here* should be carefully avoided. You saw her with the Campbells when she was the equal of every body she mixed with, but here she is with a poor old grandmother, who has barely enough to live on. If you do not call early it will be a slight.'

The son looked convinced.

'I have heard her speak of the acquaintance,' said Emma, 'she is a very elegant young woman.'

He agreed to it, but with so quiet a 'Yes,' as inclined her almost to doubt his real concurrence; and yet there must be a very distinct sort of elegance for the fashionable world, if Jane Fairfax could be thought only ordinarily gifted with it.

'If you were never particularly struck by her manners before,' said she, 'I think you will today. You will see her to advantage; see her and hear her – no, I am afraid you will not hear her at all, for she has an aunt who never holds her tongue.'

'You are acquainted with Miss Jane Fairfax, sir, are you?' said Mr Woodhouse, always the last to make his way in conversation; 'then give me leave to assure you that you will find her a very agreeable young lady. She is staying here on a visit to her grandmamma and aunt, very worthy people; I have known them all my life. They will be extremely glad to see you, I am sure, and one of my servants shall go with you to shew you the way.'

'My dear sir, upon no account in the world; my father can direct me.'

'But your father is not going so far; he is only going to the Crown, quite on the other side of the street, and there are a great many houses; you might be very much at a loss, and it is a very dirty walk, unless you keep on the foot-path; but my coachman can tell you where you had best cross the street.'

Mr Frank Churchill still declined it, looking as serious as he could, and his father gave his hearty support by calling out, 'My good friend, this is quite unnecessary; Frank knows a puddle of water when he sees it, and as to Mrs Bates's, he may get there from the Crown in a hop, step, and jump.'

They were permitted to go alone; and with a cordial nod from one, and a grateful bow from the other, the two gentlemen took leave. Emma remained very well pleased with this beginning of the acquaintance, and could now engage to think of them all at Randalls any hour of the day, with full confidence in their comfort.

CHAPTER TWENTY-FOUR

The next morning brought Mr Frank Churchill again. He came with Mrs Weston, to whom and to Highbury he seemed to take very cordially. He had been sitting with her, it appeared, most companionably at home, till her usual hour of exercise; and on being desired to chuse their walk, immediately fixed on Highbury. – 'He did not doubt there being very pleasant walks in every direction, but if left to him, he should always chuse the same. Highbury, that airy, cheerful, happy-looking Highbury, would be his constant attraction.' – Highbury, with Mrs Weston, stood for Hartfield; and she trusted to its bearing the same construction with him. They walked thither directly.

Emma had hardly expected them: for Mr Weston, who had called in for half a minute, in order to hear that his son was very handsome, knew nothing of their plans; and it was an agreeable surprize to her, therefore, to perceive them walking up to the house together, arm in arm. She was wanting to see him again, and especially to see him in company with Mrs Weston, upon his behaviour to whom her opinion of him was to depend. If he were deficient there, nothing should make amends for it. But on seeing them together, she became perfectly satisfied. It was not merely in fine words or hyperbolical compliment that he paid his duty; nothing could be more proper or pleasing than his whole manner to her – nothing could more agreeably denote his wish of considering her as a friend and securing her affection. And there was time enough for Emma to form a reasonable judgment, as their visit included all the rest of the morning. They were all three walking about together for an hour or two – first round the shrubberies of Hartfield, and afterwards in Highbury. He was delighted with every thing; admired Hartfield sufficiently for Mr Woodhouse's ear; and when their going farther was resolved on, confessed his wish to be made acquainted with the whole village, and found matter of commendation and interest much oftener than Emma could have supposed.

Some of the objects of his curiosity spoke very amiable feelings. He begged to be shewn the house which his father had lived in so long, and which had been the home of his father's father; and on recollecting that an old woman who had nursed him was still living, walked in quest of her cottage from one end of the street to the

He stopt to look in.

other; and though in some points of pursuit or observation there was no positive merit, they shewed, altogether, a good-will towards Highbury in general, which must be very like a merit to those he was with.

Emma watched and decided, that with such feelings as were now shewn, it could not be fairly supposed that he had been ever voluntarily absenting himself; that he had not been acting a part, or making a parade of insincere professions; and that Mr Knightley certainly had not done him justice.

Their first pause was at the Crown Inn, an inconsiderable house, though the principal one of the sort, where a couple of pair of post-horses were kept, more for the convenience of the neighbourhood than from any run on the road; and his companions had not expected to be detained by any interest excited there; but in passing it they gave the history of the large room visibly added; it had been built many years ago for a ballroom, and while the neighbourhood had been in a particularly populous, dancing state, had been occasionally used as such; – but such brilliant days had long since passed away, and now the highest purpose for which it was ever wanted was to accommodate a whist club established among the gentlemen and half-gentlemen of the place. He was immediately interested. Its character as a ball-room caught him; and instead of passing on, he stopt for several minutes at the two superior sashed windows which were open, to look in and contemplate its capabilities, and lament that its original purpose should have ceased. He saw no fault in the room, he would acknowledge none which they suggested. No, it was long enough, broad enough, handsome enough. It would hold the very number for comfort. They ought to have balls there at least every fortnight, through the winter. Why had not Miss Woodhouse revived the former good old days of the room? – She who could do any thing in Highbury! The want of proper families in the place, and the conviction that none beyond the place and its immediate environs could be tempted to attend, were mentioned; but he was not satisfied. He could not be persuaded that so many good-looking houses as he saw around him, could not furnish numbers enough for such a meeting; and even when particulars were given and families described, he was still unwilling to admit that the inconvenience of such a mixture would be any thing, or that there would be the smallest difficulty in every body's returning into their proper place the next morning. He argued like a young man very much bent on dancing; and Emma was rather surprized to see the constitution of the Weston prevail so decidedly against the habits of the Churchills. He seemed to have all the life and spirit, cheerful feelings, and social inclinations of his father, and nothing of the pride or reserve of Enscombe. Of pride, indeed, there was, perhaps scarcely enough; his indifference to a confusion of rank, bordered too much on inelegance of mind. He could be no judge, however, of the evil he was holding cheap. It was but an effusion of lively spirits.

At last he was persuaded to move on from the front of the Crown; and being now almost facing the house where the Bateses lodged, Emma recollected his intended visit the day before, and asked him if he had paid it.

'Yes, oh! yes' – he replied; 'I was just going to mention it. A very successful visit: – I saw all the three ladies; and felt very much obliged to you for your preparatory hint. If the talking aunt had taken me quite by surprize, it must have been the death of me. As it was, I was only betrayed into paying a most unreasonable visit. Ten minutes would have been all that was necessary, perhaps all that was proper; and I had told my father I should certainly be at home before him – but there was no getting away, no pause; and, to my utter astonishment, I found, when he (finding me no where else) joined me there at last, that I had been actually sitting with them very nearly three quarters of an hour. The good lady had not given me the possibility of escape before.'

'And how do you think Miss Fairfax looking?'

'Ill, very ill – that is, if a young lady can ever be allowed to look ill. But the expression is hardly admissible, Mrs Weston, is it? Ladies can never look ill. And, seriously, Miss Fairfax is naturally so pale, as almost always to give the appearance of ill health. – A most deplorable want of complexion.'

Emma would not agree to this, and began a warm defence of Miss Fairfax's complexion. 'It was certainly never brilliant, but she would not allow it to have a sickly hue, in general; and there was a softness and delicacy in her skin which gave peculiar elegance to the character of her face.' He listened with all due deference; acknowledged that he had heard many people say the same – but yet he must confess, that to him nothing could make amends for the want of the fine glow of health. Where features were indifferent, a fine complexion gave beauty to them all; and where they were good, the effect was – fortunately he need not attempt to describe what the effect was.

'Well,' said Emma, 'there is no disputing about taste. – At least you admire her except her complexion.'

He shook his head and laughed. – 'I cannot separate Miss Fairfax and her complexion.'

'Did you see her often at Weymouth? Were you often in the same society?'

At this moment they were approaching Ford's, and he hastily exclaimed, 'Ha! this must be the very shop that every body attends every day of their lives, as my father informs me. He comes to Highbury himself, he says, six days out of the seven, and has always business at Ford's. If it be not inconvenient to you, pray let us go in, that I may prove myself to belong to the place, to be a true citizen of Highbury. I must buy something at Ford's. It will be taking out my freedom. – I dare say they sell gloves.'

'Oh! yes, gloves and every thing. I do admire your patriotism. You will be adored in Highbury. You were very popular before you came, because you were Mr Weston's son – but lay out half-a-guinea at Ford's, and your popularity will stand upon your own virtues.'

They went in; and while the sleek, well-tied parcels of 'Men's Beavers' and 'York Tan' were bringing down and displaying on the counter, he said – 'But I beg your pardon, Miss Woodhouse, you were speaking to me, you were saying something at the very moment of this burst of my *amor patriae*. Do not let me lose it. I assure you the utmost stretch of public fame would not make me amends for the loss of any happiness in private life.'

'I merely asked, whether you had known much of Miss Fairfax and her party at Weymouth.'

'And now that I understand your question, I must pronounce it to be a very unfair one. It is always the lady's right to decide on the degree of acquaintance. Miss Fairfax must already have given her account. – I shall not commit myself by claiming more than she may chuse to allow.'

'Upon my word! you answer as discreetly as she could do herself. But her account of every thing leaves so much to be guessed, she is so very reserved, so very unwilling to give the least information about anybody, that I really think you may say what you like of your acquaintance with her.'

'May I indeed? – Then I will speak the truth, and nothing suits me so well. I met her frequently at Weymouth. I had known the Campbells a little in town; and at Weymouth we were very much in the same set. Col. Campbell is a very agreeable man, and Mrs Campbell a friendly, warm-hearted woman. I like them all.'

'You know Miss Fairfax's situation in life, I conclude; what she is destined to be.'

'Yes – (rather hesitatingly) – I believe I do.'

'You get upon delicate subjects, Emma,' said Mrs Weston smiling, 'remember that I am here. – Mr Frank Churchill hardly knows what to say when you speak of Miss Fairfax's situation in life. I will move a little farther off.'

'I certainly do forget to think of *her*,' said Emma, 'as having ever been any thing but my friend and my dearest friend.'

He looked as if he fully understood and honoured such a sentiment.

When the gloves were brought and they had quitted the shop again, 'Did you ever hear the young lady we were speaking of, play?' said Frank Churchill.

'Ever hear her!' repeated Emma. 'You forget how much she

belongs to Highbury. I have heard her every year of our lives since we both began. She plays charmingly.'

'You think so, do you? – I wanted the opinion of someone who could really judge. She appeared to me to play well, that is, with considerable taste, but I know nothing of the matter myself. – I am excessively fond of music, but without the smallest skill or right of judging of any body's performance. – I have been used to hear her's admired; and I remember one proof of her being thought to play well: – a man, a very musical man, and in love with another woman – engaged to her – on the point of marriage – would yet never ask that other woman to sit down to the instrument, if the lady in question could sit down instead – never seemed to like to hear one if he could hear the other. That I thought, in a man of known musical talent, was some proof.'

'Proof, indeed!' said Emma, highly amused. – 'Mr Dixon is very musical, is he? We shall know more about them all, in half an hour, from you, than Miss Fairfax would have vouchsafed in half a year.'

'Yes, Mr Dixon and Miss Campbell were the persons; and I thought it a very strong proof.'

'Certainly – very strong it was; to own the truth, a great deal stronger than, if *I* had been Miss Campbell, would have been at all agreeable to me. I could not excuse a man's acute sensibility to fine sounds than to my feelings. How did Miss Campbell appear to like it?'

'It was her very particular friend, you know.'

'Poor comfort!' said Emma, laughing. 'One would rather have a stranger preferred than one's very particular friend – with a stranger it might not recur again – but the misery of having a very particular friend always at hand, to do every thing better than one does oneself! – Poor Mrs Dixon! Well, I am glad she is gone to settle in Ireland.'

'You are right. It was not very flattering to Miss Campbell; but she really did not seem to feel it.'

'So much the better – or so much the worse: – I do not know which. But, be it sweetness or be it stupidity in her – quickness of friendship, or dulness of feeling – there was one person, I think, who must have felt it: Miss Fairfax herself. *She* must have felt the improper and dangerous distinction.'

'As to that – I do not – '

'Oh! do not imagine that I expect an account of Miss Fairfax's sensations from you, or from any body else. They are known to no human being, I guess, but herself. But if she continued to play whenever she was asked by Mr Dixon, one may guess what one chuses.'

'There appeared such a perfectly good understanding among them all – ' he began rather quickly, but checking himself, added, 'however, it is impossible for me to say on what terms they really were – how it might all be behind the scenes. I can only say that there was smoothness outwardly. But you, who have known Miss Fairfax from a child, must be a better judge of her character, and of how she is likely to conduct herself in critical situations, than I can be.'

'I have known her from a child, undoubtedly; we have been children and women together; and it is natural to suppose that we should be intimate, – that we should have taken to each other whenever she visited her friends. But we never did. I hardly know how it has happened; a little perhaps, from that wickedness on my side which was prone to take disgust towards a girl so idolized and so cried up as she always was, by her aunt and grandmother, and all their set. And then, her reserve – I never could attach myself to anyone so completely reserved.'

'It is a most repulsive quality, indeed,' said he. 'Oftentimes very convenient, no doubt, but never pleasing. There is safety in reserve, but no attraction. One cannot love a reserved person.'

'Not till the reserve ceases towards oneself; and then the attraction may be the greater. But I must be more in want of a friend, or an agreeable companion, than I have yet been, to take the trouble of conquering any body's reserve to procure one. Intimacy between Miss Fairfax and me is quite out of the question. I have no reason to think ill of her – not at least – except that such extreme and perpetual cautiousness of word and manner, such a dread of giving a distinct idea about any body, is apt to suggest suspicions of there being something to conceal.'

He perfectly agreed with her: and after walking together so long, and thinking so much alike, Emma felt herself so well acquainted with him, that she could hardly believe it to be only their second meeting. He was not exactly what she had expected; less of the man of the world in some of his notions, less of the spoiled child of fortune, therefore better than she had expected. His ideas seemed more moderate – his feelings warmer. She was particularly struck by his manner of considering Mr Elton's house, which, as well as the church, he would go and look at, and would not join them in finding much fault with. No, he could not believe it a bad house; not such a house as a man was to be pitied for having. If it were to be shared with the woman he loved, he could not think any man to be pitied for having that house. There must be ample room in it for every real comfort. The man must be a blockhead who wanted more.

Mrs Weston laughed, and said he did not know what he was talking about. Used only to a large house himself, and without ever thinking how many advantages and accommodations were attached to its size, he could be no judge of the privations inevitably belonging to a small one. But Emma, in her own mind, determined that he *did* know what he was talking about, and that he shewed a very amiable inclination to settle early in life, and to marry, from worthy motives. He might not be aware of the inroads on domestic peace to be occasioned by no housekeeper's room, or a bad butler's pantry, but no doubt he did perfectly feel that Enscombe could not make him happy, and that whenever he were attached, he would willingly give up much of wealth to be allowed an early establishment.

CHAPTER TWENTY-FIVE

EMMA'S VERY GOOD opinion of Frank Churchill was a little shaken the following day, by hearing that he was gone off to London, merely to have his hair cut. A sudden freak seemed to have seized him at breakfast, and he had sent for a chaise and set off, intending to return to dinner, but with no more important view that appeared than having his hair cut. There was certainly no harm in his travelling sixteen miles twice over on such an errand; but there was an air of foppery and nonsense in it which she could not approve. It did not accord with the rationality of plan, the moderation in expense, or even the unselfish warmth of heart which she had believed herself to discern in him yesterday. Vanity, extravagance, love of change, restlessness of temper, which must be doing something, good or bad; heedlessness as to the pleasure of his father and Mrs Weston, indifference as to how his conduct might appear in general; he became liable to all these charges. His father only called him a coxcomb, and thought it a very good story; but that Mrs Weston did not like it, was clear enough, by her passing it over as quickly as possible, and making no other comment than that 'all young people would have their little whims.'

With the exception of this little blot, Emma found that his visit hitherto had given her friend only good ideas of him. Mrs Weston was very ready to say how attentive and pleasant a companion he made himself – how much she saw to like in his disposition altogether. He appeared to have a very open temper – certainly a very cheerful and lively one; she could observe nothing wrong in his notions, a great deal decidedly right; he spoke of his uncle with warm regard, was fond of talking to him – said he would be the best man in the world if he were left to himself; and though there was no being attached to the aunt, he acknowledged her kindness with gratitude, and seemed to mean always to speak of her with respect. This was all very promising; and, but for such an unfortunate fancy for having his hair cut, there was nothing to denote him unworthy of the distinguished honour which her imagination had given him; the honour, if not of being really in love with her, of being at least very near it, and saved only by her own indifference

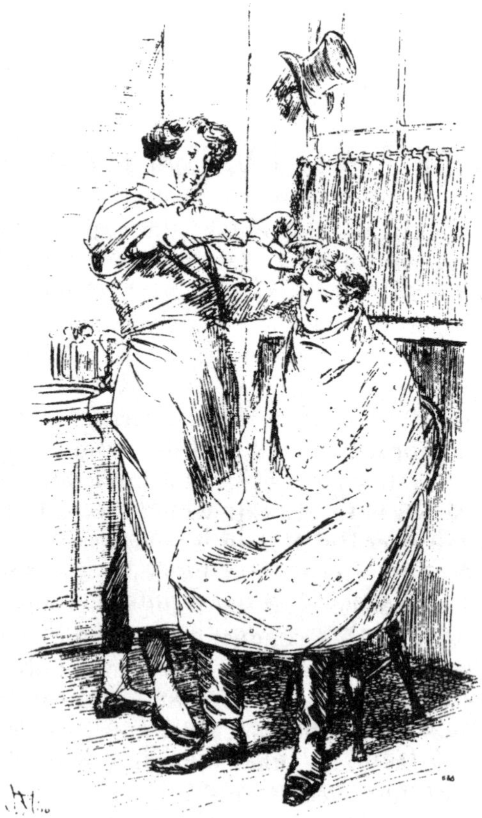

Having his hair cut.

– (for still her resolution held of never marrying) – the honour, in short, of being marked out for her by all their joint acquaintance.

Mr Weston, on his side, added a virtue to the account which must have some weight. He gave her to understand that Frank admired her extremely – thought her very beautiful and very charming; and with so much to be said to him altogether, she found she must not judge him harshly. As Mrs Weston observed, 'all young people would have their little whims.'

There was one person among his new acquaintance in Surrey, not so leniently disposed. In general he was judged, throughout the parishes of Donwell and Highbury, with great candour; liberal allowances were made for the little excess of such a handsome young man – one who smiled so often and bowed so well; but there was one spirit among them not to be softened from its power of censure, by bows or smiles – Mr Knightley. The circumstance was told him at Hartfield; for the moment he was silent; but Emma heard him almost immediately afterwards say to himself, over a newspaper he held in his hand, 'Hum! just the trifling, silly fellow I took him for.' She had half a mind to resent; but an instant's observation convinced her that it was really said only to relieve his own feelings, and not meant to provoke; and therefore she let it pass.

Although in one instance the bearers of not good tidings, Mr and Mrs Weston's visit this morning was in another respect particularly opportune. Something occurred while they were at Hartfield, to make Emma want their advice; and, which was still more lucky, she wanted exactly the advice they gave.

This was the occurrence: – The Coles had been settled some years in Highbury, and were very good sort of people – friendly, liberal, and unpretending; but, on the other hand, they were of low origin, in trade, and only moderately genteel. On their first coming into the country, they had lived in proportion to their income, quietly, keeping little company, and that little unexpensively; but the last year or two had brought them a considerable increase of means – the house in town had yielded greater profits, and fortune in general had smiled on them. With their wealth, their views increased; their want of a larger house, their inclination for more company. They added to their house, to their number of servants, to their expenses of every sort; and by this time were, in fortune and style of living, second only to the family at Hartfield. Their love of society, and their new dining-room, prepared every body for their keeping dinner-company; and a few parties, chiefly among the single men, had already taken place. The regular and best families Emma could hardly suppose they would presume to invite – neither Donwell, nor Hartfield, nor Randalls. Nothing should tempt *her* to go, if they did; and she regretted that her father's known habits would be giving her refusal less meaning than she could wish. The Coles were very respectable in their way, but they ought to be taught that it was not for them to arrange the terms on which the superior families would visit them. This lesson, she very much feared, they would receive only from herself; she had little hope of Mr Knightley, none of Mr Weston.

But she had made up her mind how to meet this presumption so many weeks before it appeared, that when the insult came at last, it found her very differently affected. Donwell and Randalls had received their invitation, and none had come for her father and herself; and Mrs Weston's accounting for it with 'I suppose they will not take the liberty with you; they know you do not dine out,' was not quite sufficient. She felt that she should like to have the power of refusal; and afterwards, as the idea of the party to be assembled there, consisting precisely of those whose society was dearest to her, occurred again and again, she did not know that she might not have been tempted to accept. Harriet was to be there in the evening, and the Bateses. They had been speaking of it as they walked about Highbury the day before, and Frank Churchill had most earnestly lamented her absence. Might not the evening end in a dance? had been a question of his. The bare possibility of it acted as a further irritation on her spirits; and her being left in solitary grandeur, even supposing the omission to be intended as a compliment, was but poor comfort.

It was the arrival of this very invitation while the Westons were at Hartfield, which made their presence so acceptable; for though her first remark, on reading it, was that 'of course it must be declined,' she so very soon proceeded to ask them what they advised her to do, that their advice for her going was most prompt and successful.

She owned that, considering every thing, she was not absolutely without inclination for the party. The Coles expressed themselves so properly – there was so much real attention in the manner of it – so much consideration for her father. 'They would have solicited the honour earlier, but had been waiting the arrival of a folding-screen from London, which they hoped might keep Mr Woodhouse from any draught of air, and therefore induce him the more readily to give them the honour of his company.' Upon the whole, she was very persuadable; and it being briefly settled among themselves how it might be done without neglecting his comfort – how certainly Mrs Goddard, if not Mrs Bates, might be depended on for bearing him company – Mr Woodhouse was to be talked into an acquiescence of his daughter's going out to dinner on a day now near at hand, and spending the whole evening away from him. As for *his* going, Emma did not wish him to think it possible; the hours would be too late, and the party too numerous. He was soon pretty well resigned.

'I am not fond of dinner-visiting,' said he – 'I never was. No more is Emma. Late hours do not agree with us. I am sorry Mr and Mrs Cole should have done it. I think it would be much better if they would come in one afternoon next summer, and take their tea with us – take us in their afternoon walk; which they might do, as our hours are so reasonable, and yet get home without being out in the damp of the evening. The dews of a summer evening are what I would not expose any body to. However, as they are so very desirous to have dear Emma dine with them, and as you will both be there, and Mr Knightley too, to take care of her, I cannot wish to prevent it, provided the weather be what it ought, neither damp, nor cold, nor windy.' Then turning to Mrs Weston, with a look of gentle reproach – 'Ah! Miss Taylor, if you had not married, you would have staid at home with me.'

'Well, sir,' cried Mr Weston, 'as I took Miss Taylor away, it is incumbent on me to supply her place, if I can; and I will step to Mrs Goddard in a moment, if you wish it.'

But the idea of any thing to be done in a *moment*, was increasing, not lessening Mr Woodhouse's agitation. The ladies knew better how to allay it. Mr Weston must be quiet, and every thing deliberately arranged.

With this treatment, Mr Woodhouse was soon composed enough for talking as usual. 'He should be happy to see Mrs Goddard. He had a great regard for Mrs Goddard; and Emma should write a line, and invite her. James could take the note. But first of all, there must be an answer written to Mrs Cole.'

'You will make my excuses, my dear, as civilly as possible. You will say that I am quite an invalid, and go no where, and therefore must decline their obliging invitation; beginning with my *compliments*, of course. But you will do every thing right. I need not tell you what is to be done. We must remember to let James know that the carriage will be wanted on Tuesday. I shall have no fears for you with him. We have never been there above once since the new approach was made; but still I have no doubt that James will take you very safely. And when you get there, you must tell him at what time you would have him come for you again; and you had better name an early hour. You will not like staying late. You will get very tired when tea is over.'

'But you would not wish me to come away before I am tired, papa?'

'Oh! no, my love; but you will soon be tired. There will be a great many people talking at once. You will not like the noise.'

'But, my dear sir,' cried Mr Weston, 'if Emma comes away early, it will be breaking up the party.'

'And no great harm if it does,' said Mr Woodhouse. 'The sooner every party breaks up, the better.'

'But you do not consider how it may appear to the Coles. Emma's going away directly after tea might be giving offence. They are good-natured people, and think little of their own claims; but still they must feel that any body's hurrying away is no great compliment; and Miss Woodhouse's doing it would be more thought of than any other person's in the room. You would not wish to disappoint and mortify the Coles, I am sure, sir; friendly, good sort of people as ever lived, and who have been your neighbours these *ten* years.'

'No, upon no account in the world. Mr Weston, I am much obliged to you for reminding me. I should be extremely sorry to be giving them any pain. I know what worthy people they are. Perry tells me that Mr Cole never touches malt liquor. You would not think it to look at him, but he is bilious – Mr Cole is very bilious. No, I would not be the means of giving them any pain. My dear Emma, we must consider this. I am sure, rather than run the risk of hurting Mr and Mrs Cole, you would stay a little longer than you might wish. You will not regard being tired. You will be perfectly safe, you know, among your friends.'

'Oh, yes, papa. I have no fears at all for myself; and I should have no scruples of staying as late as Mrs Weston, but on your account. I am only afraid of your sitting up for me. I am not afraid of your not being exceedingly comfortable with Mrs Goddard. She loves piquet, you know; but when she is gone home, I am afraid you will be sitting up by yourself, instead of going to bed at your usual time – and the idea of that would entirely destroy my comfort. You must promise me not to sit up.'

He did, on the condition of some promises on her side: such as that, if she came home cold, she would be sure to warm herself thoroughly; if hungry, that she would take something to eat; that her own maid should sit up for her; and that Serle and the butler should see that every thing were safe in the house, as usual.

CHAPTER TWENTY-SIX

FRANK CHURCHILL CAME back again; and if he kept his father's dinner waiting, it was not known at Hartfield; for Mrs Weston was too anxious for his being a favourite with Mr Woodhouse, to betray any imperfection which could be concealed.

He came back, had had his hair cut, and laughed at himself with a very good grace, but without seeming really at all ashamed of what he had done. He had no reason to wish his hair longer, to conceal any confusion of face; no reason to wish the money unspent, to improve his spirits. He was quite as undaunted and as lively as ever; and after seeing him, Emma thus moralized to herself: –

'I do not know whether it ought to be so, but certainly silly things do cease to be silly if they are done by sensible people in an impudent way. Wickedness is always wickedness, but folly is not always folly. – It depends upon the character of those who handle it. Mr Knightley, he is *not* a trifling, silly young man. If he were, he would have done this differently. He would either have gloried in the achievement, or been ashamed of it. There would have been either the ostentation of a coxcomb, or the evasions of a mind too weak to defend its own vanities. – No, I am perfectly sure that he is not trifling or silly.'

With Tuesday came the agreeable prospect of seeing him again, and for a longer time than hitherto; of judging of his general manners, and by influence, of the meaning of his manners towards herself; of guessing how soon it might be necessary for her to throw coldness into her air; and of fancying what the observations of all those might be, who were now seeing them together for the first time.

She meant to be very happy, in spite of the scene being laid at Mr Cole's; and without being able to forget that among the failings of Mr Elton, even in the days of his favour, none had disturbed her more than his propensity to dine with Mr Cole.

Her father's comfort was amply secured, Mrs Bates as well as Mrs Goddard being able to come; and her last pleasing duty, before she left the house, was to pay her respects to them as they sat together after dinner; and while her father was fondly noticing the beauty of her dress, to make the two ladies all the amends in her power, by helping them to large slices of cake and full glasses of wine, for whatever unwilling self-denial his care of their constitution might have obliged them to practise during the meal. – She had provided a plentiful dinner for them; she wished she could know that they had been allowed to eat it.

She followed another carriage to Mr Cole's door; and was pleased to see that it was Mr Knightley's; for Mr Knightley keeping no horses, having little spare money and a great deal of health, activity, and independence, was too apt, in Emma's opinion, to get about as he could, and not use his carriage so often as became the owner of Donwell Abbey. She had an opportunity now of speaking her approbation while warm from her heart, for he stopped to hand her out.

'This is coming as you should do,' said she, 'like a gentleman. – I am quite glad to see you.'

He thanked her, observing, 'How lucky that we should arrive at the same moment; for, if we had met first in the drawing-room, I doubt whether you would have discerned me to be more of a gentleman than usual. – You might not have distinguished how I came, by my look or manner.'

'Yes I should, I am sure I should. There is always a look of consciousness or bustle when people come in a way which they know to be beneath them. You think you carry it off very well, I dare say, but with you it is a sort of bravado, an air of affected unconcern; I always observe it whenever I meet you under those circumstances. *Now* you have nothing to try for. You are not afraid of being supposed ashamed. You are not striving to look taller than any body else. *Now* I shall really be very happy to walk into the same room with you.'

'Nonsensical girl!' was his reply, but not at all in anger.

Emma had as much reason to be satisfied with the rest of the party as with Mr Knightley. She was received with a cordial respect which could not but please, and given all the consequence she could wish for. When the Westons arrived, the kindest looks of love, the strongest of admiration were for her, from both husband and wife; the son approached her with a cheerful eagerness which marked her as his peculiar object, and at dinner she found him seated by her – and, as she firmly believed, not without some dexterity on his side.

The party was rather large, as it included one other family, a proper unobjectionable country family, whom the Coles had the advantage of naming among their acquaintance, and the male part of Mr Cox's family, the lawyer of Highbury. The less worthy females were to come in the evening, with Miss Bates, Miss Fairfax, and Miss Smith; but already, at dinner, they were too numerous for any subject of conversation to be general; and while politics and Mr Elton were talked over, Emma could fairly surrender all her attention to the pleasantness of her neighbour. The first remote sound to which she felt herself obliged to attend, was the name of Jane Fairfax. Mrs Cole seemed to be relating something of her that was expected to be very interesting. She listened, and found it well worth listening to. That very dear part of Emma, her fancy, received an amusing supply. Mrs Cole was telling that she had been calling on Miss Bates, and as soon as she entered the room had been struck by the sight of a pianoforté – a very elegant looking instrument – not a grand, but a large-sized square pianoforté; and the substance of the story, the end of all the dialogue which ensued of surprize, and enquiry, and congratulations on her side, and explanations on Miss Bates's, was, that this pianoforté had arrived from Broadwood's the day before, to the great astonishment of both aunt and niece – entirely unexpected; that at first, by Miss Bates's account, Jane herself was quite at a loss, quite bewildered to think who could possibly have ordered it – but now, they were both perfectly satisfied that it could be only one quarter; – of course it must be from Col. Campbell.

'One can suppose nothing else,' added Mrs Cole, 'and I was only surprized that there could ever have been a doubt. But Jane, it seems, had a letter from them very lately, and not a word was said about it. She knows their ways best; but I should not consider their silence as any reason for their not meaning to make the present. They might chuse to surprize her.'

Mrs Cole had many to agree with her; every body who spoke on the subject was equally convinced that it must come from Col. Campbell, and equally rejoiced that such a present had been made; and there were enough ready to speak to allow Emma to think her own way, and still listen to Mrs Cole.

'I declare, I do not know when I have heard any thing that has given me more satisfaction! – It always has quite hurt me that Jane Fairfax, who plays so delightfully, should not have an instrument. It seemed quite a shame, especially considering how many houses there are where fine instruments are absolutely thrown away. This is like giving ourselves a slap, to be sure! and it was but yesterday I was telling Mr Cole, I really was ashamed to look at our new grand pianoforté in the drawing-room, while I do not know one note from another, and our little girls, who are but just beginning, perhaps may never make any thing of it; and there is poor Jane Fairfax, who is mistress of music, has not any thing of the nature of an instrument, not even the pitifullest old spinnet in the world, to amuse herself with. – I was saying this to Mr Cole but yesterday, and he quite agreed with me; only he is so particularly fond of music that he could not help indulging himself in the purchase, hoping that some of our good neighbours might be so obliging occasionally to put it to a better use than we can; and that really is the reason why the instrument was bought – or else I am sure we ought to be ashamed of it. – We are in great hopes that Miss Woodhouse may be prevailed with to try it this evening.'

Miss Woodhouse made the proper acquiescence; and finding that nothing more was to be entrapped from any communication of Mrs Cole's, turned to Frank Churchill.

'Why do you smile?' said she.

'Nay, why do you?'

'Me! – I suppose I smile for pleasure at Col. Campbell's being so rich and so liberal. – It is a handsome present.'

'Very.'

'I rather wonder that it was never made before.'

'Perhaps Miss Fairfax has never been staying here so long before.'

'Or that he did not give her the use of their own instrument – which must now be shut up in London, untouched by any body.'

'That is a grand pianoforté, and he might think it too large for Mrs Bates's house.'

'You may *say* what you chuse – but your countenance testifies that your *thoughts* on this subject are very much like mine.'

'I do not know. I rather believe you are giving me more credit for acuteness than I deserve. I smile because you smile, and shall probably suspect whatever I find you suspect; but at present I do not see what there is to question. If Col. Campbell is not the person, who can be?'

'What do you say to Mrs Dixon?'

'Mrs Dixon! very true indeed. I had not thought of Mrs Dixon. She must know as well as her father, how acceptable an instrument would be; and perhaps the mode of it, the mystery, the surprize, is more like a young woman's scheme than an elderly man's. It is Mrs Dixon I dare say. I told you that your suspicions would guide mine.'

'If so, you must extend your suspicions and comprehend Mr Dixon in them.'

'Mr Dixon. – Very well. Yes, I immediately perceive that it must be the joint present of Mr and Mrs Dixon. We were speaking the other day, you know, of his being so warm an admirer of her performance.'

'Yes, and what you told me on that head, confirmed an idea which I had entertained before. – I do not mean to reflect upon the good intentions of either Mr Dixon or Miss Fairfax, but I cannot help suspecting either that, after making his proposals to her friend, he had the misfortune to fall in love with *her*, or that he became conscious of a little attachment on her side. One might guess twenty things without guessing exactly the right; but I am sure there must be a particular cause for her chusing to come to Highbury instead of going with the Campbells to Ireland. Here, she must be leading a life of privation and penance; there it would have been all enjoyment. As to the pretence of trying her native air, I look upon that as a mere excuse. – In the summer it might have passed; but what can any body's native air do for them in the months of January, February, and March; Good fires and carriages would be much more to the purpose in most cases of delicate health, and I dare say in her's. I do not require you to adopt all my suspicions, though you make so noble a profession of doing it, but I honestly tell you what they are.'

'And, upon my word, they have an air of great probability. Mr Dixon's preference of her music to her friend's, I can answer for being very decided.'

'And then, he saved her life. Did you ever hear of that? – A water-party; and by some accident she was falling overboard. He caught her.'

'He did. I was there – one of the party.'

'Were you really? – Well! – But you observed nothing of course, for it seems to be a new idea to you. – If I had been there, I think I should have made some discoveries.'

'I dare say you would; but I, simple I, saw nothing but the fact, that Miss Fairfax was nearly dashed from the vessel and that Mr Dixon caught her. – It was the work of a moment. And though the consequent shock and alarm was very great and much more durable – indeed I believe it was half an hour before any of us were comfortable again – yet that was too general a sensation for any thing of peculiar anxiety to be observable. I do not mean to say, however, that you might not have made discoveries.'

The conversation was here interrupted. They were called on to share in the awkwardness of a rather long interval between courses, and obliged to be as formal and as orderly as the others; but when the table was again safely covered, when every corner dish was placed exactly right, and occupation and ease were generally restored, Emma said,

'The arrival of this pianoforté is decisive with me. I wanted to know a little more, and this tells me quite enough. Depend upon it, we shall soon hear that it is a present from Mr and Mrs Dixon.'

'And if the Dixons should absolutely deny all knowledge of it we must conclude it to come from the Campbells.'

'No, I am sure it is not from the Campbells. Miss Fairfax knows it is not from the Campbells, or they would have been guessed at first. She would not have been puzzled, had she dared fix on them. I may not have convinced you perhaps, but I am perfectly convinced myself that Mr Dixon is a principal in the business.'

'Indeed you injure me if you suppose me unconvinced. Your reasonings carry my judgment along with them entirely. At first, while I supposed you satisfied that Col. Campbell was the giver, I saw it only as paternal kindness, and thought it the most natural thing in the world. But when you mentioned Mrs Dixon, I felt how much more probable that it should be the tribute of warm female friendship. And now I can see it in no other light than as an offering of love.'

There was no occasion to press the matter farther. The conviction seemed real; he looked as if he felt it. She said no more, other subjects took their turn; and the rest of the dinner passed away; the dessert succeeded, the children came in, and were talked to and admired amid the usual rate of conversation; a few clever things said, a few downright silly, but by much the larger proportion neither the one nor the other – nothing worse than every day remarks, dull repetitions, old news, and heavy jokes.

The ladies had not been long in the drawing-room, before the other ladies, in their different divisions, arrived. Emma watched the entrée of her own particular little friend; and if she could not exult in her dignity and grace, she could not only love the blooming sweetness and the artless manner, but could most heartily rejoice in that light, cheerful, unsentimental disposition which allowed her so many alleviations of pleasure, in the midst of the pangs of disappointed affection. There she sat – and who would have guessed how many tears she had been lately shedding? To be in company, nicely dressed herself and seeing others nicely dressed, to sit and smile and look pretty, and say nothing, was enough for the happiness of the present hour. Jane Fairfax did look and move superior; but Emma suspected she might have been glad to change feelings with Harriet, very glad to have purchased the mortification of having loved – yes, of having loved even Mr Elton in vain – by the surrender of all the dangerous pleasure of knowing herself beloved by the husband of her friend.

In so large a party it was not necessary that Emma should approach her. She did not wish to speak of the pianoforté, she felt too much in the secret herself, to think the appearance of curiosity or interest fair, and therefore purposely kept at a distance; but by the others, the subject was almost immediately introduced, and she saw the blush of consciousness with which congratulations were received, the blush of guilt which accompanied the name of 'my excellent friend Col. Campbell.'

Mrs Weston, kind-hearted and musical, was particularly interested by the circumstance, and Emma could not help being amused at her perseverance in dwelling on the subject; and having so much to ask and to say as to tone, touch, and pedal, totally unsuspicious of that wish of saying as little about it as possible, which she plainly read in the fair heroine's countenance.

They were soon joined by some of the gentlemen; and the very first of the early was Frank Churchill. In he walked, the first and the handsomest; and after paying his compliments en passant to Miss Bates and her niece, made his way directly to the opposite side of the circle, where sat Miss Woodhouse; and till he could find a seat by her, would not sit at all. Emma divined what every body present must be thinking. She was his object, and every body must perceive it. She introduced him to her friend, Miss Smith, and, at convenient moments afterwards, heard what each thought of the other. 'He had never seen so lovely a face, and was delighted with her naïveté,' And she, – 'Only to be sure it was paying him too great a compliment, but she did think there were some looks a little like Mr Elton.' Emma restrained her indignation, and only turned from her in silence.

Smiles of intelligence passed between her and the gentleman on first glancing towards Miss Fairfax; but it was most prudent to avoid speech. He told her that he had been impatient to leave the dining room – hated sitting long – was always the first to move when he could – that his father, Mr Knightley, Mr Cox, and Mr Cole, were left very busy over parish business – that as long as he had staid, however, it had been pleasant enough, as he found them in general a set of gentlemen-like, sensible men; and spoke so handsomely of Highbury altogether – thought it so abundant in agreeable families – that Emma began to feel she had been used to despise the place rather too much. She questioned him as to the society in Yorkshire – the extent of the neighbourhood about Enscombe, and the sort; and could make out from his answers that, as far as Enscombe was concerned, there was very little going on; that their visitings were among a range of great families, none very near; and that even when days were fixed, and invitations accepted, it was an even chance that Mrs Churchill were not in health or spirits for going; that they made a point of visiting no fresh person; and that, though he had his separate engagements, it was not without difficulty, without considerable address *at times*, that he could get away, or introduce an acquaintance for a night.

She saw that Enscombe could not satisfy, and that Highbury, taken in its best, might reasonably please a young man who had more retirement at home than he liked. His importance at Enscombe was very evident. He did not boast, but it naturally betrayed itself, that he had persuaded his aunt where his uncle could do nothing, and on her laughing and noticing it, he owned that he believed (excepting one or two points) he could *with time* persuade her to any thing. One of those points on which his influence failed, he then mentioned. He had wanted very much to go abroad – had been very eager indeed to be allowed to travel – but she would not hear of it. This had happened the year before. *Now*, he said, he was beginning to have no longer the same wish.

The unpersuadable point, which he did not mention, Emma guessed to be good behaviour to his father.

'I have made a most wretched discovery,' said he, after a short pause. – 'I have been here a week to-morrow! – And I have hardly begun to enjoy myself. But just got acquainted with Mrs Weston, and others! – I hate the recollection.'

'Perhaps you may now begin to regret that you spent one whole day, out of so few, in having your hair cut.'

'No,' said he, smiling, 'that is no subject of regret at all. I have no pleasure in seeing my friends, unless I can believe myself fit to be seen.'

The rest of the gentlemen being now in the room, Emma found herself obliged to turn from him for a few minutes, and listen to Mr Cole. When Mr Cole had moved away, and her attention could be restored as before, she saw Frank Churchill looking intently across the room at Miss Fairfax, who was sitting exactly opposite.

'What is the matter?' said she.

He started. 'Thank you for rousing me,' he replied. 'I believe I have been very rude; but really Miss Fairfax has done her hair in so odd a way – so very odd a way – that I cannot keep my eyes from her. I never saw any thing so outrée! – Those curls! – This must be a fancy of her own. I see nobody else looking like her! – I must go and ask her whether it is an Irish fashion. Shall I? – Yes, I will – I declare I will – and you shall see how she takes it; – whether she colours.'

He was gone immediately; and Emma soon saw him standing before Miss Fairfax, and talking to her; but as to its effect on the young lady, as he had improvidently placed himself exactly between them, exactly in front of Miss Fairfax, she could absolutely distinguish nothing.

Before he could return to his chair, it was taken by Mrs Weston.

'This is the luxury of a large party,' said she: – 'one can get near everybody, and say every thing. My dear Emma, I am longing to talk to you. I have been making discoveries and forming plans, just like yourself, and I must tell them while the idea is fresh. Do you know how Miss Bates and her niece came here?'

'How! – They were invited, were not they?'

'Oh! yes – but how they were conveyed hither? – the manner of their coming?'

'They walked, I concluded. How else could they come?'

'Very true. – Well, a little while ago it occurred to me how very sad it would be to have Jane Fairfax walking home again, late at night, and cold as the nights are now. And as I looked at her, though I never saw her appear to more advantage, it struck me that she was heated, and would therefore be particularly liable to take cold. Poor girl! I could not bear the idea of it; so, as soon as Mr Weston came into the room, and I could get at him, I spoke to him about the carriage. You may guess how readily he came into my wishes; and having his approbation, I made my way directly to Miss Bates, to assure her that the carriage would be at her service before it took us home; for I thought it would be making her comfortable at once. Good soul! she was as grateful as possible, you may be sure. "Nobody was ever so fortunate as herself!" – but with many, many thanks, – "there was no occasion to trouble us, for Mr Knightley's carriage had brought, and was to take them home again." I was quite surprized; – very glad, I am sure; but really quite surprized. Such a very kind attention – and so thoughtful an attention! – the sort of thing that so few men would think of. And, in short, from knowing his usual ways, I am very much inclined to think that it was for their accommodation the carriage was used at all. I do suspect he would not have had a pair of horses for himself, and that it was only as an excuse for assisting them.'

'Very likely,' said Emma – 'nothing more likely. I know no man more likely than Mr Knightley to do the sort of thing – to do any thing really good-natured, useful, considerate, or benevolent. He is not a gallant man, but he is a very humane one; and this, considering Jane Fairfax's ill health, would appear a case of humanity to him; – and for an act of un-ostentatious kindness, there is nobody whom I would fix on more than on Mr Knightley. I know he had horses to-day – for we arrived together; and I laughed at him about it, but he said not a word that could betray.'

'Well,' said Mrs Weston, smiling, 'you give him credit for more simple, disinterested benevolence in this instance than I do; for while Miss Bates was speaking, a suspicion darted into my head, and I have never been able to get it out again. The more I think of it, the more probable it appears. In short, I have made a match between Mr Knightley and Jane Fairfax. See the consequence of keeping you company! – What do you say to it?'

'Mr Knightley and Jane Fairfax!' exclaimed Emma. 'Dear Mrs Weston, how could you think of such a thing? – Mr Knightley! – Mr Knightley must not marry! – You would not have little Henry cut out from Donwell? – Oh! no, no, Henry must have Donwell. I cannot at all consent to Mr Knightley's marrying; and I am sure it is not at all likely. I am amazed that you should think of such a thing.'

'My dear Emma, I have told you what led me to think of it. I do not want the match – I do not want to injure dear little Henry – but the idea has been given me by circumstances; and if Mr Knightley really wished to marry, you would not have him refrain on Henry's account, a boy of six years old, who knows nothing of the matter?'

'Yes, I would. I could not bear to have Henry supplanted. – Mr Knightley marry! – No, I have never had such an idea, and I cannot adopt it now. And Jane Fairfax, too, of all women!'

'Nay, she has always been a first favourite with him, as you very well know.'

'But the imprudence of such a match!'

'I am not speaking of its prudence; merely its probability.'

'I see no probability in it, unless you have better foundation than what you mention. His good-nature, his humanity, as I tell you, would be quite enough to account for the horses. He has a great regard for the Bateses, you know, independent of Jane Fairfax – and is always glad to shew them attention. My dear Mrs Weston, do not take to match-making. You do it very ill. Jane Fairfax mistress of the Abbey! – Oh! no, no; – every feeling revolts. For his own sake, I would not have him do so mad a thing.'

'Imprudent, if you please – but not mad. Excepting inequality of fortune, and perhaps a little disparity of age, I can see nothing unsuitable.'

'But Mr Knightley does not want to marry. I am sure he has not the least idea of it. Do not put it into his head. Why should he marry? – He is as happy as possible by himself; with his farm, and his sheep, and his library, and all the parish to manage; and he is extremely fond of his brother's children. He has no occasion to marry, either to fill up his time or his heart.'

'My dear Emma, as long as he thinks so, it is so; but if he really loves Jane Fairfax – '

'Nonsense! He does not care about Jane Fairfax. In the way of love, I am sure he does not. He would do any good to her, or her family; but – '

'Well,' said Mrs Weston laughing, 'perhaps the greatest good he could do them, would be to give Jane such a respectable home.'

'If it would be good to her, I am sure it would be evil to himself; a very shameful and degrading connection. How would he bear to have Miss Bates belonging to him? – To have her haunting the Abbey, and thanking him all day long for his great kindness in marrying Jane? – "So very kind and obliging! – But he always had been such a very kind neighbour!" And then fly off, through half a sentence, to her mother's old petticoat. "Not that it was such a very old petticoat either – for still it would last a great while – and, indeed, she must thankfully say that their petticoats were all very strong." '

'For shame, Emma! Do not mimic her. You divert me against my conscience. And, upon my word, I do not think Mr Knightley would be much disturbed by Miss Bates. Little things do not irritate him. She might talk on; and if he wanted to say any thing himself, he would only talk louder, and drown her voice. But the question is not, whether it would be bad connexion for him, but whether he wishes it; and I think he does. I have heard him speak, and so must you, so very highly of Jane Fairfax! The interest he takes in her – his anxiety about her health – his concern that she should have no happier prospect! I have heard him express himself so warmly on those points! – Such an admirer of her performance on the piano-forté, and of her voice! I have heard him say that he could listen to her for ever. Oh! and I had almost forgotten one idea that occurred to me – this pianoforté that had been sent by somebody – though we have all been so well satisfied to consider it a present from the Campbells, may it not be from Mr Knightley? I cannot help suspecting him. I think he is just the person to do it, even without being in love.'

'Then it can be no argument to prove that he is in love. But I do not think it is at all a likely thing for him to do. Mr Knightley does nothing mysteriously.'

'I have heard him lamenting her having no instrument repeatedly; oftener than I should suppose such a circumstance would, in the common course of things, occur to him.'

'Very well; and if he had intended to give her one, he would have told her so.'

'There might be scruples of delicacy, my dear Emma. I have a very strong notion that it comes from him. I am sure he was particularly silent when Mrs Cole told us of it at dinner.'

'You take up an idea, Mrs Weston, and run away with it; as you have many a time reproached me with doing. I see no sign of attachment – I believe nothing of the pianoforté – and proof only shall convince me that Mr Knightley has any thought of marrying Jane Fairfax.'

They combated the point some time longer in the same way; Emma rather gaining ground over the mind of her friend; for Mrs Weston was the most used of the two to yield; till a little bustle in the room shewed them that tea was over, and the instrument in preparation; – and at the same moment Mr Cole approaching to entreat Miss Woodhouse would do them the honour of trying it. Frank Churchill, of whom, in the eagerness of her conversation with Mrs Weston, she had been seeing nothing, except that he had found a seat by Miss Fairfax, followed Mr Cole, to add his very pressing entreaties; and as, in every respect, it suited Emma best to lead, she gave a very proper compliance.

She knew the limitations of her own powers too well to attempt more than she could perform with credit; she wanted neither taste nor spirit in the little things which are generally acceptable, and could accompany her own voice well. One accompaniment to her song took her agreeably by surprize – a second, slightly but correctly taken by Frank Churchill. Her pardon was duly begged at the close of the song, and every thing usual followed. He was accused of having a delightful voice, and a perfect knowledge of music; which was properly denied: and that he knew nothing of the matter, and had no voice at all, roundly asserted. They sang together once more; and Emma would then resign her place to Miss Fairfax, whose performance, both vocal and instrumental, she never could attempt to conceal from herself, was infinitely superior to her own.

With mixed feelings, she seated herself at a little distance from the numbers round the instrument, to listen. Frank Churchill sang again. They had sung together once or twice, it appeared, at Weymouth. But the sight of Mr Knightley among the most attentive, soon drew away half Emma's mind; and she fell into a train of thinking on the subject of Mrs Weston's suspicions, to which the sweet sounds of the united voices gave only momentary interruptions. Her objections to Mr Knightley's marrying did not in the least subside. She could see nothing but evil in it. It would be a great disappointment to Mr John Knightley; consequently to Isabella. A real injury to the children – a most mortifying change, and material loss to them all; – a very great deduction from her father's daily comfort – and, as to herself, she could not at all endure the idea of Jane Fairfax at Donwell Abbey. A Mrs Knightley for them all to give way to! – No – Mr Knightley must never marry. Little Henry must remain the heir of Donwell.

Presently Mr Knightley looked back, and came and sat down by her. They talked at first only of the performance. His admiration was certainly very warm; yet she thought, but for Mrs Weston, it would not have struck her. As a sort of touchstone, however she began to speak of his kindness in conveying the aunt and niece; and though his answer was in the spirit of cutting the matter short, she believed it to indicate only his disinclination to dwell on any kindness of his own.

'I often feel concerned,' said she, 'that I dare not make *our* carriage more useful on such occasions. It is not that I am without the wish; but you know how impossible my father would deem it that James should put-to for such a purpose.'

'Quite out of the question, quite out of the question.' he replied; – 'but you must often wish it, I am sure.' And he smiled with such seeming pleasure at the conviction, that she must proceed another step.

'This present from the Campbells,' said she – 'This pianoforté is very kindly given.'

'Yes,' he replied, and without the smallest apparent embarrassment. – 'But they would have done better had they given her notice of it. Surprizes are foolish things. The pleasure is not enhanced, and the inconvenience is often considerable. I should have expected better judgment in Colonel Campbell.'

From that moment, Emma could have taken her oath that Mr Knightley had had no concern in giving the instrument. But whether he were entirely free from peculiar attachment – whether there were no actual preference – remained a little longer doubtful. Towards the end of Jane's second song, her voice grew thick.

'That will do,' said he, when it was finished, thinking aloud – 'You have sung quite enough for one evening – now, be quiet.'

Another song, however, was soon begged for. 'One more; – they would not fatigue Miss Fairfax on any account, and would only ask for one more.' And Frank Churchill was heard to say, 'I think you could manage this without effort; the first part is so very trifling. The strength of the song falls on the second.'

Mr Knightley grew angry.

Had secured her hand.

'That fellow,' said he, indignantly, 'thinks of nothing but shewing off his own voice. This must not be.' And touching Miss Bates, who at that moment passed near – 'Miss Bates, are you mad, to let your niece sing herself hoarse in this manner? Go, and interfere. They have no mercy on her.'

Miss Bates in her real anxiety for Jane, could hardly stay even to be grateful, before she stept forward and put an end to all further singing. Here ceased the concert part of the evening, for Miss Woodhouse and Miss Fairfax were the only young-lady-performers; but soon (within five minutes) the proposal of dancing – originating nobody exactly knew where – was so effectually promoted by Mr and Mrs Cole, that every thing was rapidly clearing away, to give proper space. Mrs Weston, capital in her country-dances, was seated, and beginning an irresistible waltz; and Frank Churchill, coming up with most becoming gallantry to Emma, had secured her hand, and led her up to the top.

While waiting till the other young people could pair them selves off, Emma found time, in spite of the compliments she was receiving on her voice and her taste, to look about, and see what became of Mr Knightley. This would be a trial. He was no dancer in general. If he were to be very alert in engaging Jane Fairfax now, it might augur something. There was no immediate appearance. No; he was talking to Mrs Cole – he was looking on unconcerned; Jane was asked by somebody else, and he was still talking to Mrs Cole.

Emma had no longer an alarm for Henry; his interest was yet safe; and she led off the dance with genuine spirit and enjoyment. Not more than five couple could be mustered; but the rarity and the suddenness of it made it very delightful, and she found herself well matched in a partner. They were a couple worth looking at.

Two dances, unfortunately, were all that could be allowed. It was growing late, and Miss Bates became anxious to get home, on her mother's account. After some attempts, therefore, to be permitted to begin again, they were obliged to thank Mrs Weston, look sorrowful, and have done.

'Perhaps it is as well,' said Frank Churchill, as he attended Emma to her carriage. 'I must have asked Miss Fairfax, and her languid dancing would not have agreed with me, after your's.'

CHAPTER TWENTY-SEVEN

EMMA DID NOT REPENT her condescension in going to the Coles. The visit afforded her many pleasant recollections the next day; and all that she might be supposed to have lost on the side of dignified seclusion, must be amply repaid in the splendour of popularity. She must have delighted the Coles – worthy people, who deserved to be made happy! – And left a name behind her that would not soon die away.

Perfect happiness, even in memory, is not common; and there were two points on which she was not quite easy. She doubted whether she had not transgressed the duty of woman by woman, in betraying her suspicions of Jane Fairfax's feelings to Frank Churchill. It was hardly right; but it had been so strong an idea, that it would escape her, and his submission to all that she told, was a compliment to her penetration which made it difficult for her to be quite certain that she ought to have held her tongue.

The other circumstance of regret related also to Jane Fairfax; and there she had no doubt. She did unfeignedly and unequivocally regret the inferiority of her own playing and singing. She did most heartily grieve over the idleness of her childhood – and sat down and practised vigorously an hour and a half.

She was then interrupted by Harriet's coming in; and if Harriet's praise could have satisfied her, she might soon have been comforted.

'Oh! if I could but play as well as you and Miss Fairfax!'

'Don't class us together, Harriet. My playing is no more like her's than a lamp is like sunshine.'

'Oh! dear – I think you play the best of the two. I think you play quite as well as she does. I am sure I had much rather hear you. Every body last night said how well you played.'

'Those who knew any thing about it, must have felt the difference. The truth is, Harriet, that my playing is just good enough to be praised, but Jane Fairfax's is much beyond it.'

'Well, I always shall think that you play quite as well as she does, or that if there is any difference nobody would ever find it out. Mr Cole said how much taste you had; and Mr Frank Churchill talked a great deal about your taste, and that he valued taste much more than execution.'

'Ah! but Jane Fairfax has them both, Harriet.'

'Are you sure? I saw she had execution, but I did not know she had any taste. Nobody talked about it. And I hate Italian singing. – There is no understanding a word of it. Besides, if she does play so very well, you know, it is no more than she is obliged to do, because she will have to teach. The Coxes were wondering last night whether she would get into any great family. How did you think the Coxes looked?'

'Just as they always do – very vulgar.'

'They told me something,' said Harriet rather hesitatingly, 'but it is nothing of any consequence.'

Emma was obliged to ask what they had told her, though fearful of its producing Mr Elton.

'They told me – that Mr Martin dined with them last Saturday.'

'Oh!'

'He came to their father upon some business, and he asked him to stay to dinner.'

'Oh!'

'They talked a great deal about him, especially Anne Cox. I do not know what she meant, but she asked me if I thought I should go and stay there again next summer.'

'She meant to be impertinently curious, just as such as Anne Cox should be.'

'She said he was very agreeable the day he dined there. He sat by her at dinner. Miss Nash thinks either of the Coxes would be very glad to marry him.'

'Very likely. – I think they are, without exception, the most vulgar girls in Highbury.'

Harriet had business at Ford's. – Emma thought it most prudent to go with her. Another accidental meeting with the Martins was possible, and, in her present state, would be dangerous.

Harriet, tempted by every thing and swayed by half a word, was always very long at a purchase; and while she was still hanging over muslins and changing her mind, Emma went to the door for amusement. – Much could not be hoped from the traffic of even the busiest part of Highbury; – Mr Perry walking hastily by, Mr William Cox letting himself in at the office door, Mr Cole's carriage horses returning from exercise, or a stray letter-boy on an obstinate mule, were the liveliest objects she could presume to expect; and when her eyes fell only on the butcher with his tray, a tidy old woman travelling homewards from shop with her full basket, two curs quarrelling over a dirty bone, and a string of dawdling children round the baker's little bow-window eyeing the gingerbread, she knew she had not reason to complain, and was amused enough; quite enough still to stand at the door. A mind lively and at ease, can do with seeing nothing, and can see nothing that does not answer.

She looked down the Randalls road. The scene enlarged; two persons appeared; Mrs Weston and her son-in-law; they were walking into Highbury; – to Hartfield of course. They were stopping, however, in the first place at Mrs Bates's; whose house was a little nearer Randalls than Ford's; and had all but knocked, when Emma caught their eye. – Immediately they crossed the road and came forward to her; and the agreeableness of yesterday's engagement seemed to give fresh pleasure to the present meeting. Mrs Weston informed her that she was going to call on the Bateses in order to hear the new instrument.

'For my companion tells me,' said she, 'that I absolutely promised Miss Bates last night, that I would come this morning. I was not aware of it myself. I did not know that I had fixed a day, but as he says I did, I am going now.'

'And while Mrs Weston pays her visit, I may be allowed, I hope,' said Frank Churchill, 'to join your party and wait for her at Hartfield – if you are going home.'

Mrs Weston was disappointed.

'I thought you meant to go with me. They would be very much pleased.'

'Me! I should be quite in the way. But, perhaps – I may be equally in the way here. Miss Woodhouse looks as if she did not want me. My aunt sends me off when she is shopping. She says I fidget her to death; and Miss Woodhouse looks as if she could almost say the same. What am I to do?'

'I am here on no business of my own,' said Emma. 'I am only waiting for my friend. She will probably have soon done, and then we shall go home. But you had better go with Mrs Weston and hear the instrument.'

'Well – if you advise it. – But (with a smile) if Col. Campbell should have employed a careless friend, and if it should prove to have an indifferent tone – what shall I say? I shall be no support to Mrs Weston. She might do very well by herself. A disagreeable truth would be palatable through her lips, but I am the wretchedest being in the world at a civil falsehood.'

'I do not believe any such thing,' replied Emma. – 'I am persuaded that you can be as insincere as your neighbours, when it is necessary; but there is no reason to suppose the instrument is indifferent. Quite otherwise indeed, if I understood Miss Fairfax's opinion last night.'

'Do come with me,' said Mrs Weston, 'if it be not very disagreeable to you. It need not detain us long. We will go to Hartfield afterwards. We will follow them to Hartfield. I really wish you to call with me. It will be felt so great an attention! and I always thought you meant it.'

He could say no more; and with the hope of Hartfield to reward him, returned with Mrs Weston to Mrs Bates's door. Emma watched them in, and then joined Harriet at the interesting counter, – trying, with all the force of her own mind, to convince her that if she wanted plain muslin it was of no use to look at figured; and that a blue ribbon, be it ever so beautiful, would still never match her yellow pattern. At last it was all settled, even to the destination of the parcel.

'Should I send it to Mrs Goddard's, ma'am?' asked Mrs Ford. 'Yes – no – yes, to Mrs Goddard's. Only my pattern gown is at Hartfield. No, you shall send it to Hartfield, if you please. But then, Mrs Goddard will want to see it. – And I could take the pattern gown home any day. But I shall want the ribbon directly – so it had better go to Hartfield – at least the ribbon. You could make it into two parcels, Mrs Ford, could not you?'

'It is not worth while, Harriet, to give Mrs Ford the trouble of two parcels.'

'No more it is.'

'No trouble in the world, ma'am,' said the obliging Mrs Ford.

'Oh! but indeed I would much rather have it only in one. Then, if you please, you shall send it all to Mrs Goddard's – I do not know – No, I think, Miss Woodhouse, I may just as well have it sent to Hartfield, and take it home with me at night. What do you advise?'

'That you do not give another half-second to the subject. To Hartfield, if you please, Mrs Ford.'

'Aye, that will be much best,' said Harriet, quite satisfied, 'I should not at all like to have it sent to Mrs Goddard's.'

Voices approached the shop – or rather one voice and two ladies; Mrs Weston and Miss Bates met them at the door.

'My dear Miss Woodhouse,' said the latter, 'I am just run across to entreat the favour of you to come and sit down with us a little while, and give us your opinion of our new instrument; you and Miss Smith. How do you do, Miss Smith? – Very well I thank you. – And I begged Mrs Weston to come with me, that I might be sure of succeeding.'

'I hope Mrs Bates and Miss Fairfax are' –

'Very well, I am much obliged to you. My mother is delightfully well; and Jane caught no cold last night. How is Mr Woodhouse? – I am so glad to hear such a good account. Mrs Weston told me you were here. – Oh! then, said I, I must run across, I am sure Miss Woodhouse will allow me just to run across and entreat her to come in; my mother will be so very happy to see her – and now we are such a nice party, she cannot refuse. "Aye, pray do," said Mr Frank Churchill, "Miss Woodhouse's opinion of the instrument will be worth having." – But, said I, I shall be more sure of succeeding if one of you will go with me. – "Oh!" said he, "wait half-a-minute till I have finished my job." – For, would you believe it, Miss Woodhouse, there he is, in the most obliging manner in the world, fastening in the rivet of my mother's spectacles. – The rivet came out, you know, this morning. – So very obliging! For my mother had no use of her spectacles – could not put them on. And, by the bye, every body ought to have two pair of spectacles; they should indeed. Jane said so. I meant to take them over to John Saunders the first thing I did, but something or other hindered me all the morning; first one thing, then another, there is no saying what, you know. At one time Patty came to say she thought the kitchen chimney wanted sweeping. Oh! said I, Patty do not come with your bad news to me. Here is the rivet of your mistress's spectacles out. Then the baked apples came home, Mrs Wallis sent them by her boy; they are extremely civil and obliging to us, the Wallises, always – I have heard some people say that Mrs Wallis can be uncivil and give a very rude answer, but we have never known any thing but the greatest attention from them. And it cannot be for the value of our custom now, for what is our consumption of bread, you know? Only three of us – besides dear Jane at prsent – and she really eats nothing – makes such a shocking breakfast, you would be quite frightened if you saw it. I dare not let my mother know how little she eats – so I say one thing and then I say another, and it passes off. But about the middle of the day she gets hungry, and there is nothing she likes so well as these baked apples, and they are extremely wholesome, for I took the opportunity the other day of asking Mr Perry; I happened to meet him in the street. Not that I had any doubt before – I have so often heard Mr Woodhouse recommend a baked apple. I believe it is the only way that Mr Woodhouse thinks the fruit thoroughly wholesome. We have apple dumplings, however, very often. Patty makes an excellent apple-dumpling. Well, Mrs Weston, you have prevailed, I hope, and these ladies will oblige us.'

Emma would be 'very happy to wait on Mrs Bates, &c.' and they did at last move out of the shop, with no further delay from Miss Bates than,

'How do you do, Mrs Ford? I beg your pardon. I did not see you before. I hear you have a charming collection of new ribbons from town. Jane came back delighted yesterday. Thank ye, the gloves do very well – only a little too large about the wrist; but Jane is taking them in.'

'What was I talking of?' said she, beginning again when they were all in the street.

Emma wondered on what, of all the medley, she would fix.

'I declare I cannot recollect what I was talking of. – Oh! my mother's spectacles. So very obliging of Mr Frank Churchill! "Oh!" said he, "I do think I can fasten the rivet; I like a job of this kind excessively." – Which you know shewed him to be so very. . . . Indeed I must say that, much as I had heard of him before and much as I had expected, he very far exceeds any thing. . . . I do congratulate you, Mrs Weston, most warmly. He seems every thing the fondest parent could. . . . "Oh!" said he, "I can fasten the rivet. I like a job of that sort excessively." I never shall forget his manner. And when I brought out the baked apples from the closet, and hoped our friends would be so very obliging as to take some, "Oh!" said he directly, "there is nothing in the way of fruit half so good, and these are the finest looking home-baked apples I ever saw in my life." That, you know, was so very . . . And I am sure, by his manner, it was no compliment. Indeed they are very delightful apples, and Mrs Wallis does them full justice – only we do not have them baked more than twice, and Mr Woodhouse made us promise to have them done three times – but Miss Woodhouse will be so good as not to mention it. The apples themselves are the very finest sort for baking, beyond a doubt; all from Donwell – some of Mr Knightley's most liberal supply. He sends us a sack every year; and certainly there never was such a keeping apple any where as one of his trees – I believe there is two of them. My mother says the orchard was always famous in her younger days. But I was really quite shocked the other day – for Mr Knightley called one morning, and Jane was eating these apples, and we talked about them and said how much she enjoyed them, and he asked whether we were not got to the end of our stock. "I am sure you must be," said he, "and I will send you another supply; for I have a great many more than I can ever use. William Larkins let me keep a larger quantity than usual this year. I will send you some more, before they get good for nothing." So I begged he would not – for really as to ours being gone, I could not absolutely say that we had a great many left – it was but half a dozen indeed; but they should be all kept for Jane; and I could not at all bear that he should be sending us more, so liberal as he had been already; and Jane said the same. And when he was gone, she almost quarrelled with me – No, I should not say quarrelled, for we never had a quarrel in our lives; but she was quite distressed that I had owned the apples were so nearly gone; she wished I had made him believe we had a great many left. Oh! said I, my dear, I did say as much as I could. However, the very same evening Williams Larkins came over with a large basket of apples, the same sort of apples, a bushel at least and I was very much obliged, and went down and spoke to William Larkins and said every thing, as you may suppose. William Larkins is such an old acquaintance! I am always glad to see him. But, however, I found afterwards from Patty, that William said it was all the apples of *that* sort his master had; he had brought them all – and now his master had not one left to bake or boil. William did not seem to mind it himself, he was so pleased to think his master had sold so many; for William, you know, thinks more of his master's profit than any thing; but Mrs Hodges, he said, was quite displeased at their being all sent away. She could not bear that her master should not be able to have another apple-tart this spring. He told Patty this, but bid her not mind it, and be sure not to say any thing to us about it for Mrs Hodges *would* be cross sometimes, and as long as so many sacks were sold, it did not signify who ate the remainder. And so Patty told me, and I was excessively shocked indeed! I would not have Mr Knightley know any thing about it for the world! He would be so very . . . I wanted to keep it from Jane's knowledge; but unluckily, I had mentioned it before I was aware.'

Miss Bates had just done as Patty opened the door; and her visitors walked up stairs without having any regular narration to attend to, pursued only by the sounds of her desultory good-will.

'Pray take care, Mrs Weston, there is a step at the turning. Pray take care, Miss Woodhouse, ours is rather a dark staircase – rather darker and narrower than one could wish. Miss Smith, pray take care. Miss Woodhouse, I am quite concerned, I am sure you hit your foot. Miss Smith, the step at the turning.'

CHAPTER TWENTY-EIGHT

THE APPEARANCE OF the little sitting-room as they entered, was tranquillity itself; Mrs Bates, deprived of her usual employment, slumbering on one side of the fire, Frank Churchill, at a table near her, most deeply occupied about her spectacles, and Jane Fairfax, standing with her back to them, intent on her pianoforté.

Busy as he was, however, the young man was yet able to shew a most happy countenance on seeing Emma again.

'This is a pleasure,' said he, in rather a low voice, 'coming at least ten minutes earlier than I had calculated. You find me trying to be useful; tell me if you think I shall succeed.'

'What!' said Mrs Weston, 'have you not finished it yet? you would not earn a very good livelihood as a working-silversmith at this rate.'

'I have not been working uninterruptedly,' he replied, 'I have been assisting Miss Fairfax in trying to make her instrument stand steadily, it was not quite firm; an unevenness in the floor, I believe. You see we have been wedging one leg with paper. This was very kind of you to be persuaded to come. I was almost afraid you would be hurrying home.'

He contrived that she should be seated by him; and was sufficiently employed in looking out the best baked apple for her, and trying to make her help or advise him in his work, till Jane Fairfax was quite ready to sit down to the pianoforté again. That she was not immediately ready, Emma did suspect to arise from the state of her nerves; she had not yet possessed the instrument long enough to touch it without emotion; she must reason herself into the power of performance; and Emma could not but pity such feelings, whatever their origin, and could not but resolve never to expose them to her neighbour again.

Deeply occupied about her spectacles.

At last Jane began, and though the first bars were feebly given, the powers of the instrument were gradually done full justice to. Mrs Weston had been delighted before, and was delighted again; Emma joined her in all her praise; and the pianoforté, with every proper discrimination, was pronounced to be altogether of the highest promise.

'Whoever Col. Campbell might employ,' said Frank Churchill, with a smile at Emma, 'the person has not chosen ill. I heard a good deal of Col. Campbell's taste at Weymouth; and the softness of the upper notes I am sure is exactly what he and *all that party* would particularly prize. I dare say, Miss Fairfax, that he either gave his friend very minute directions, or wrote to Broadwood himself. Do you not think so?'

Jane did not look round. She was not obliged to hear. Mrs Weston had been speaking to her at the same moment.

'It is not fair,' said Emma in a whisper, 'mine was a random guess. Do not distress her.'

He shook his head with a smile, and looked as if he had very little doubt and very little mercy. Soon afterwards he began again.

'How much your friends in Ireland must be enjoying your pleasure on this occasion, Miss Fairfax. I dare say they often think of you, and wonder which will be the day, the precise day of the instrument's coming to hand. Do you imagine Col. Campbell knows the business to be going forward just at this time? – Do you imagine it to be the consequence of an immediate commission from him, or that he may have sent only a general direction, an order indefinite as to time, to depend upon contingencies and conveniences?'

He paused. She could not but hear; she could not avoid answering.

'Till I have a letter from Col. Campbell,' said she, in a voice of forced calmness, 'I can imagine nothing with any confidence. It must all be conjecture.'

'Conjecture – aye, sometimes one conjectures right, and sometimes one conjectures wrong. I wish I could conjecture how soon I shall make this rivet quite firm. What nonsense one talks, Miss Woodhouse, when hard at work, if one talks at all; – your real workmen, I suppose, hold their tongues; but we gentlemen labourers if we get hold of a word – Miss Fairfax said something about conjecturing. There, it is done. I have the pleasure, madam, (to Mrs Bates,) of restoring your spectacles, healed for the present.'

He was very warmly thanked both by mother and daughter; to escape a little from the latter, he went to the pianoforté, and begged Miss Fairfax, who was still sitting at it, to play something more.

'If you are very kind,' said he, 'it will be one of the waltzes we danced last night; – let me live them over again. You did not enjoy them as I did, you appeared tired the whole time. I believe you were glad we danced no longer; but I would have given worlds – all the worlds one ever has to give – for another half hour.'

She played.

'What felicity it is to hear a tune again which *has* made one happy! – If I mistake not that was danced at Weymouth.'

She looked up at him for a moment, coloured deeply, and played something else. He took some music from a chair near the piano-forté, and turning to Emma, said,

'Here is something quite new to me. Do you know it? – Cramer. – And here are a new set of Irish melodies. That, from such a quarter, one might expect. This was all sent with the instrument. Very thoughtful of Col. Campbell, was not it? – He knew Miss Fairfax could have no music here. I honour that part of the attention particularly; it shews it to have been so thoroughly from the heart. Nothing hastily done; nothing incomplete. True affection only could have prompted it.'

Emma wished he would be less pointed, yet could not help being amused; and when on glancing her eye towards Jane Fairfax she caught the remains of a smile, when she saw that with all the deep blush of consciousness, there had been a smile of secret delight, she had less scruple in the amusement, and much less compunction with respect to her. – This amiable, upright, perfect Jane Fairfax was apparently cherishing very reprehensible feelings.

He brought all the music to her, and they looked it over together. – Emma took the opportunity of whispering.

'You speak too plain. She must understand you.'

'I hope she does. I would have her understand me. I am not in the least ashamed of my meaning.'

'But really, I am half ashamed, and wish I had never taken up the idea.'

'I am very glad you did, and that you communicated it to me. I have now a key to all her odd looks and ways. Leave shame to her. If she does wrong, she ought to feel it.'

'She is not entirely without it, I think.'

'I do not see much sign of it. She is playing *Robin Adair* at this moment – *his* favourite.'

Shortly afterwards Miss Bates, passing near the window, descried Mr Knightley on horseback not far off.

'Mr Knightley I declare! – I must speak to him if possible, just to thank him. I will not open the window here; it would give you all cold; but I can go into my mother's room you know. I dare say he will come in when he knows who is here. Quite delightful to have you all meet so! – Our little room so honoured!'

She was in the adjoining chamber while she still spoke, and opening the casement there, immediately called Mr Knightley's attention, and every syllable of their conversation was as distinctly heard by the others, as if it had passed within the same apartment.

'How d'ye do? – How d'ye do? – Very well, I thank you. So obliged to you for the carriage last night. We were just in time; my mother just ready for us. Pray come in; do come in. You will find some friends here.'

So began Miss Bates; and Mr Knightley seemed determined to be heard in his turn, for most resolutely and commandingly did he say,

'How is your niece, Miss Bates? – I want to enquire after you all, but particularly your niece. How is Miss Fairfax? – I hope she caught no cold last night. How is she today? Tell me how Miss Fairfax is.'

And Miss Bates was obliged to give a direct answer before he would hear her in any thing else. The listeners were amused; and Mrs Weston gave Emma a look of particular meaning. But Emma still shook her head in steady scepticism.

'So obliged to you! – so very much obliged to you for the carriage,' resumed Miss Bates.

He cut her short with,

'I am going to Kingston. Can I do any thing for you?'

'Oh! dear, Kingston – are you? – Mrs Cole was saying the other day she wanted something from Kingston.'

'Mrs Cole has servants to send. Can I do any thing for *you*?'

'No, I thank you. But do come in. Who do you think is here? – Miss Woodhouse and Miss Smith; so kind as to call to hear the new pianoforté. Do put up your horse at The Crown, and come in.'

'Well,' said he in a deliberating manner, 'for five minutes, perhaps.'

'And here is Mrs Weston and Mr Frank Churchill too! – Quite delightful; so many friends!'

'No, not now, I thank you. I could not stay two minutes. I must get on to Kingston as fast as I can.'

'Oh! do come in. They will be so very happy to see you.'

'No, no, your room is full enough. I will call another day, and hear the pianoforté.'

'Well, I am so sorry! – Oh! Mr Knightley, what a delightful party last night; how extremely pleasant. – Did you ever see such dancing? – Was not it delightful? – Miss Woodhouse and Mr Frank Churchill; I never saw any thing equal to it.'

'Oh, Mr Knightley, one moment more.'

'Oh! very delightful indeed; I can say nothing less, for I suppose Miss Woodhouse and Mr Frank Churchill are hearing every thing that passes. And (raising his voice still more) I do not see why Miss Fairfax should not be mentioned too. I think Miss Fairfax dances very well; and Mrs Weston is the very best country-dance player, without exception, in England. Now, if your friends have any gratitude, they will say something pretty loud about you and me in return; but I cannot stay to hear it.'

'Oh! Mr Knightley, one moment more; something of consequence – so shocked! – Jane and I both so shocked about the apples!'

'What is the matter now?'

'To think of your sending us all your store apples. You said you had a great many, and now you have not one left. We really are so shocked! Mrs Hodges may well be angry. William Larkins mentioned it here. You should not have done it, indeed you should not. Ah! he is off. He never can bear to be thanked. But I thought he would have staid now, and it would have been a pity not to have mentioned . . . Well, (returning into the room,) I have not been able to succeed. Mr Knightley cannot stop. He is going to Kingston. He asked me if he could do any thing'. . . .

'Yes,' said Jane, 'we heard his kind offers, we heard every thing.'

'Oh! yes, my dear, I dare say you might, because you know the door was open, and the window was open, and Mr Knightley spoke loud. You must have heard every thing to be sure. "Can I do any thing for you at Kingston?" said he; so I just mentioned. . . . Oh! Miss Woodhouse, must you be going? – You seem but just come – so very obliging of you.'

Emma found it really time to be at home; the visit had already lasted long; and on examining watches, so much of the morning was perceived to be done, that Mrs Weston and her companion taking leave also, could allow themselves only to walk with the two young ladies to Hartfield gates, before they set off for Randalls.

CHAPTER TWENTY-NINE

It may be possible to do without dancing entirely. Instances have been known of young people passing many, many months successively, without being at any ball of any description, and no material injury accrue either to body or mind; – but when a beginning is made – when the felicities of rapid motion have once been, though slightly, felt – it must be a very heavy set that does not ask for more.

Frank Churchill had danced once at Highbury, and longed to dance again; and the last half hour of an evening which Mr Woodhouse was persuaded to spend with his daughter at Randalls, was passed by the two young people in schemes on the subject. Frank's was the first idea; and his the greatest zeal in pursuing it; for the lady was the best judge of the difficulties, and the most solicitous for accommodation and appearance. But still she had inclination enough for shewing people again how delightfully Mr Frank Churchill and Miss Woodhouse danced – for doing that in which she need not blush to compare herself with Jane Fairfax – and even for simple dancing itself, without any of the wicked aids of vanity – to assist him first in pacing out the room they were in to see what it could be made to hold – and then in taking the dimensions of the other parlour, in the hope of discovering, in spite of all that Mr Weston could say of their exactly equal size, that it was a little the largest.

His first proposition and request, that the dance begun at Mr Cole's should be finished there – that the same party should be collected, and the same musician engaged, met with the readiest acquiescence. Mr Weston entered into the idea with thorough enjoyment, and Mrs Weston most willingly undertook to play as long as they could wish to dance; and the interesting employment had followed, of reckoning up exactly who there would be, and portioning out the indispensable division of space to every couple.

'You and Miss Smith, and Miss Fairfax, will be three, and the two Miss Coxes five,' had been repeated many times over. 'And there will be the two Gilberts, young Cox, my father, and myself, besides Mr Knightley. Yes, that will be quite enough for pleasure. You and Miss Smith, and Miss Fairfax, will be three, and the two Miss Coxes five; and for five couple there will be plenty of room.'

But soon it came to be on one side,

'But will there be good room for five couple? – I really do not think there will.'

On another,

'And after all, five couple are not enough to make it worth while to stand up. Five couple are nothing, when one thinks seriously about it. It will not do to *invite* five couple. It can be allowable only as the thought of the moment.'

Somebody said that *Miss* Gilbert was expected at her brother's, and must be invited with the rest. Somebody else believed *Mrs* Gilbert would have danced the other evening, if she had been asked. A word was put in for a second young Cox; and at last, Mr Weston naming one family of cousins who must be included, and another of very old acquaintance who could not be left out, it became a certainty that the five couple would be at least ten, and a very interesting speculation in what possible manner they could be disposed of.

The doors of the two rooms were just opposite each other. 'Might not they use both rooms, and dance across the passage?' It seemed the best scheme; and yet it was not so good but that many of them wanted a better. Emma said it would be awkward; Mrs Weston was in distress about the supper; and Mr Woodhouse opposed it earnestly, on the score of health. It made him so very unhappy, indeed, that it could not be persevered in.

'Oh! no,' said he, 'it would be the extreme of imprudence. I could not bear it for Emma! – Emma is not strong. She would catch a dreadful cold. So would poor little Harriet. So you would all. Mrs Weston, you would be quite laid up; do not let them talk of such a wild thing. Pray do not let them talk of it. That young man (speaking lower) is very thoughtless. Do not tell his father, but that young man is not quite the thing. He has been opening the doors very often this evening, and keeping them open very inconsiderately. He does not think of the draught. I do not mean to set you against him, but indeed he is not quite the thing!'

Mrs Weston was sorry for such a charge. She knew the importance of it, and said every thing in her power to do it away. Every door was now closed, the passage plan given up, and the first scheme of dancing only in the room they were in resorted to again; and with such good-will on Frank Churchill's part, that the space which a quarter of an hour before had been deemed barely sufficient for five couple, was now endeavoured to be made out quite enough for ten.

'We were too magnificent,' said he. 'We allowed unnecessary room. Ten couple may stand here very well.'

Emma demurred. 'It would be a crowd – a sad crowd; and what could be worse than dancing without space to turn in?'

'Very true,' he gravely replied; 'it was very bad.' But still he went on measuring, and still he ended with,

'I think there will be very tolerable room for ten couple.'

'No, no' said she, 'you are quite unreasonable. It would be dreadful to be standing so close! Nothing can be farther from pleasure than to be dancing in a crowd – and a crowd in a little room!'

'There is no denying it,' he replied. 'I agree with you exactly. A crowd in a little room – Miss Woodhouse, you have the art of giving pictures in a few words. Exquisite, quite exquisite! – Still, however, having proceeded so far, one is unwilling to give the matter up. It would be a disappointment to my father – and altogether – I do not know that – I am rather of opinion that ten couple might stand here very well.'

Emma perceived that the nature of his gallantry was a little self-willed, and that he would rather oppose than lose the pleasure of dancing with her; but she took the compliment, and forgave the rest. Had she intended ever to *marry* him, it might have been worth while to pause and consider, and try to understand the value of his preference, and the character of his temper, but for all the purposes of their acquaintance, he was quite amiable enough.

Before the middle of the next day, he was at Hartfield; and he entered the room with such an agreeable smile as certified the continuance of the scheme. It soon appeared that he came to announce an improvement.

'Well, Miss Woodhouse,' he almost immediately began, 'your inclination for dancing has not been quite frightened away, I hope, by the terrors of my father's little rooms. I bring a new proposal on the subject: – a thought of my father's, which waits only your approbation to be acted upon. May I hope for the honour of your hand for the two first dances of this little projected ball, to be given, not at Randalls, but at the Crown Inn?'

'The Crown!'

'Yes; if you and Mr Woodhouse see no objection, and I trust you cannot, my father hopes his friends will be so kind as to visit him there. Better accommodations, he can promise them, and not a less grateful welcome than at Randalls. It is his own idea. Mrs Weston sees no objection to it, provided you are satisfied. This is what we all feel. Oh! you were perefectly right! Ten couple, in either of the Randalls rooms, would have been insufferable! – Dreadful! – I felt how right you were the whole time, but was too anxious for securing *any thing* to like to yield. Is not it a good exchange? – You consent – I hope you consent?'

'It appears to me a plan that nobody can object to, if Mr and Mrs Weston do not. I think it admirable; and, as far as I can answer for myself, shall be most happy – It seems the only improvement that could be. Papa, do you not think it an excellent improvement?'

She was obliged to repeat and explain it, before it was fully comprehended; and then, being quite new, further representations were necessary to make it acceptable.

'No; he thought it very far from an improvement – a very bad plan – much worse than the other. A room at an inn was always damp and dangerous; never properly aired, or fit to be inhabited. If they must dance, they had better dance at Randalls. He had never been in the room at the Crown in his life – did not know the people who kept it by sight. – Oh! no – a very bad plan. They would catch worse colds at the Crown than any where.'

'I was going to observe, sir,' said Frank Churchill, 'that one of the great recommendations of this change would be the very little danger of any body's catching cold – so much less danger at the Crown than at Randalls! Mr Perry might have reason to regret the alteration, but nobody else could.'

'Sir,' said Mr Woodhouse, rather warmly, 'you are very much mistaken if you suppose Mr Perry to be that sort of character. Mr Perry is extremely concerned when any of us are ill. But I do not understand how the room at the Crown can be safer for you than your father's house.'

'From the very circumstance of its being larger, sir. We shall have no occasion to open the windows at all – not once the whole evening; and it is that dreadful habit of opening the windows, letting in cold air upon heated bodies, which (as you well know, sir) does the mischief.'

'Open the windows! – but surely, Mr Churchill, nobody would think of opening the windows at Randalls. Nobody could be so imprudent! I never heard of such a thing. Dancing with open windows! – I am sure, neither your father nor Mrs Weston (poor Miss Taylor that was) would suffer it.'

'Ah! sir – but a thoughtless young person will sometimes step behind a window-curtain and throw up a sash, without its being suspected. I have often known it done myself.'

'Have you indeed, sir? – Bless me! I never could have supposed it. But I live out of the world, and am often astonished at what I hear. However, this does make a difference; and, perhaps, when we come to talk it over – but these sort of things require a good deal of consideration. One cannot resolve upon them in a hurry. If Mr and Mrs Weston will be so obliging as to call here one morning, we may talk it over, and see what can be done.'

'But, unfortunately, sir, my time is so limited – '

'Oh!' interrupted Emma, 'there will be plenty of time for talking every thing over. There is no hurry at all. If it can be contrived to be at the Crown, papa, it will be very convenient for the horses. They will be so near their own stable.'

'So they will, my dear. That is a great thing. Not that James ever complains; but it is right to spare our horses when we can. If I could be sure of the rooms being thoroughly aired – but is Mrs Stokes to be trusted? I doubt it. I do not know her, even by sight.'

'I can answer for every thing of that nature, sir, because it will be under Mrs Weston's care. Mrs Weston undertakes to direct the whole.'

'There, papa! – Now you must be satisfied – Our own dear Mrs Weston, who is carefulness itself. Do not you remember what Mr

Perry said, so many years ago, when I had the measles? "If *Miss Taylor* undertakes to wrap Miss Emma up, you need not have any fears, sir." How often have I heard you speak of it as such a compliment to her!'

'Aye, very true. Mr Perry did say so. I shall never forget it. Poor little Emma! You were very bad with the measles; that is, you would have been very bad, but for Perry's great attention. He came four times a day for a week. He said, from the first, it was a very good sort – which was our great comfort; but the measles are a dreadful complaint. I hope whenever poor Isabella's little ones have the measles, she will send for Perry.'

'My father and Mrs Weston are at the Crown at this moment,' said Frank Churchill, 'examining the capabilities of the house. I left them there and came on to Hartfield, impatient for your opinion, and hoping you might be persuaded to join them and give your advice on the spot. I was desired to say so from both. It would be the greatest pleasure to them, if you could allow me to attend you there. They can do nothing satisfactorily without you.'

Emma was most happy to be called to such a council, and her father, engaging to think it all over while she was gone, the two young people set off together without delay for the Crown. There were Mr and Mrs Weston; delighted to see her and receive her approbation, very busy and very happy in their different way; she, in some little distress; and he, finding every thing perfect.

'Emma,' said she, 'this paper is worse than I expected. Look! in places you see it is dreadfully dirty; and the wainscot is more yellow and forlorn than any thing I could have imagined.'

'My dear, you are too particular,' said her husband. 'What does all that signify? You will see nothing of it by candle-light. It was be as clean as Randalls by candle-light. We never see any thing of it on our club-nights.'

The ladies here probably exchanged looks which meant, 'Men never know when things are dirty or not;' and the gentlemen perhaps thought each to himself. 'Women will have their little nonsenses and needless cares.'

One perplexity, however, arose, which the gentlemen did not disdain. It regarded a supper-room. At the time of the hall-room's being built, suppers had not been in question; and a small card-room adjoining, was the only addition. What was to be done? This card-room would be wanted as a card-room now; or, if cards were conveniently voted unnecessary by their four selves, still was not it too small for any comfortable supper? Another room of much better size might be secured for the purpose; but it was at the other end of the house, and a long awkward passage must be gone through to get at it. This made a difficulty. Mrs Weston was afraid of draughts for the young people in that passage; and neither Emma nor the gentlemen could tolerate the prospect of being miserably crowded at supper.

Mrs Weston proposed having no regular supper; merely sandwiches, &c. set out in the little room; but that was scouted as a wretched suggestion. A private dance, without sitting down to supper, was pronounced an infamous fraud upon the rights of men and women; and Mrs Weston must not speak of it again. She then took another line of expediency, and looking into the doubtful room observed,

'I do not think it *is* so very small. We shall not be many, you know.'

And Mr Weston at the same time, walking briskly with long steps through the passage, was calling out,

'You talk a great deal of the length of this passage, my dear. It is a mere nothing after all; and not the least draught from the stairs.'

'I wish,' said Mrs Weston, 'one could know which arrangement our guests in general would like best. To do what would be most generally pleasing must be our object – if one could but tell what that would be.'

'Yes, very true,' cried Frank, 'very true. You want your neighbours' opinions. I do not wonder at you. If one could ascertain what the chief of them – the Coles, for instance. They are not far off. Shall I call upon them? Or Miss Bates? She is still nearer; – And I do not know whether Miss Bates is not as likely to understand the inclinations of the rest of the people as any body. I think we do want a larger council. Suppose I go and invite Miss Bates to join us?'

'Well – if you please,' said Mrs Weston rather hesitating, 'if you think she will be of any use.'

'You will get nothing to the purpose from Miss Bates,' said Emma. 'She will be all delight and gratitude, but she will tell you nothing. She will not even listen to your questions. I see no advantage in consulting Miss Bates.'

'But she is so amusing, so extremely amusing! I am very fond of hearing Miss Bates talk. And I need not bring the whole family, you know.'

Here Mr Weston joined them, and on hearing what was proposed, gave it his decided approbation.

'Aye, do Frank. – Go and fetch Miss Bates, and let us end the matter at once. She will enjoy the scheme, I am sure; and I do not know a properer person for shewing us how to do away difficulties. Fetch Miss Bates. We are growing a little too nice. She is a standing lesson of how to be happy. But fetch them both. Invite them both.'

'Both sir! Can the old lady?' . . .

'The old lady! No, the young lady, to be sure. I shall think you a great blockhead, Frank, if you bring the aunt without the niece.'

'Oh! I beg your pardon, sir. I did not immediately recollect. Undoubtedly if you wish it, I will endeavour to persuade them both.' And away he ran.

'He has asked her, my dear.'

Long before he re-appeared, attending the short, neat, brisk-moving aunt, and her elegant niece, – Mrs Weston, like a sweet-tempered woman and a good wife, had examined the passage again, and found the evils of it much less than she had supposed before – indeed very trifling; and here ended the difficulties of decision. All the rest, in speculation at least, was perfectly smooth. All the minor arrangements of table and chair, lights and music, tea and supper, made themselves; or were left as mere trifles to be settled at any time between Mrs Weston and Mrs Stokes. – Every body invited, was certainly to come; Frank had already written to Enscombe to propose staying a few days beyond his fortnight, which could not possibly be refused. And a delightful dance it was to be.

Most cordially, when Miss Bates arrived, did she agree that it must. As a counsellor she was not wanted; but as an approver, (a much safer character,) she was truly welcome. Her approbation, at once general and minute, warm and incessant, could not but please; and for another half-hour they were all walking to and fro, between the different rooms, some suggesting, some attending, and all in happy enjoyment of the future. The party did not break up without Emma's being positively secured for the two first dances by the hero of the evening, nor without her overhearing Mr Weston whisper to his wife. 'He has asked her, my dear. That's right. I knew he would!'

CHAPTER THIRTY

One thing only was wanting to make the prospect of the ball completely satisfactory to Emma – its being fixed for a day within the granted term of Frank Churchill's stay in Surrey; for, in spite of Mr Weston's confidence, she could not think it so very impossible that the Churchills might not allow their nephew to remain a day beyond his fortnight. But this was not judged feasible. The preparations must take their time, nothing could be properly ready till the third week were entered on, and for a few days they must be planning, proceeding and hoping in uncertainty – at the risk – in her opinion, the great risk, of its being all in vain.

Enscombe however was gracious, gracious in fact, if not in word. His wish of staying longer evidently did not please; but it was not opposed. All was safe and prosperous; and as the removal of one solicitude generally makes way for another, Emma, being now certain of her ball, began to adopt as the next vexation Mr Knightley's provoking indifference about it. Either because he did not dance himself, or because the plan had been formed without his being consulted, he seemed resolved that it should not interest him, determined against its exciting any present curiosity, or affording him any future amusement. To her voluntary communications Emma could get no more approving reply, than,

'Very well. If the Westons think it worth while to be at all this trouble for a few hours of noisy entertainment, I have nothing to say against it, but that they shall not choose pleasures for me. – Oh! yes, I must be there; I could not refuse; and I will keep as much awake as I can; but I would rather be at home, looking over William Larkins's week's account; much rather, I confess. – Pleasure in seeing dancing! – not I, indeed – I never look at it – I do not know who does. – Fine dancing, I believe, like virtue, must be its own reward. Those who are standing by are usually thinking of something very different.'

This Emma felt was aimed at her; and it made her quite angry. It was not in compliment to Jane Fairfax however that he was so indifferent, or so indignant; he was not guided by *her* feelings in reprobating the ball, for *she* enjoyed the thought of it to an extraordinary degree. It made her animated – open hearted – she voluntarily said; –

'Oh! Miss Woodhouse, I hope nothing may happen to prevent the ball. What a disappointment it would be! I do look forward to it, I own, with *very* great pleasure.'

It was not to oblige Jane Fairfax therefore that he would have preferred the society of William Larkins. No! – she was more and more convinced that Mrs Weston was quite mistaken in that surmise. There was a great deal of friendly and of compassionate attachment on his side – but no love.

Alas! there was soon no leisure for quarrelling with Mr Knightley. Two days of joyful security were immediately followed by the overthrow of every thing. A letter arrived from Mr Churchill to urge his nephew's instant return. Mrs Churchill was unwell – far too unwell to do without him; she had been in a very suffering state (so said her husband) when writing to her nephew two days before, though from her usual unwillingness to give pain, and constant habit of never thinking of herself, she had not mentioned it; but now she was too ill to trifle, and must entreat him to set off for Enscombe without delay.

The substance of this letter was forwarded to Emma, in a note from Mrs Weston, instantly. As to his going, it was inevitable. He must be gone within a few hours, though without feeling any real alarm for his aunt, to lessen his repugnance. He knew her illnesses; they never occurred but for her own convenience.

Mrs Weston added, 'that he could only allow himself time to hurry to Highbury, after breakfast, and take leave of the few friends there whom he could suppose to feel any interest in him; and that he might be expected at Hartfield very soon.'

This wretched note was the finalé of Emma's breakfast. When once it had been read, there was no doing any thing, but lament and exclaim. The loss of the ball – the loss of the young man – and all that the young man might be feeling! – It was too wretched! – Such a delightful evening as it would have been! – Every body so happy! and she and her partner the happiest! – 'I said it would be so,' was the only consolation.

Her father's feelings were quite distinct. He thought principally of Mrs Churchill's illness, and wanted to know how she was treated; and as for the ball, it was shocking to have dear Emma disappointed; but they would all be safer at home.

Emma was ready for her visitor some time before he appeared; but if this reflected at all upon his impatience, his sorrowful look and total want of spirits when he did come might redeem him. He felt the going away almost too much to speak of it. His dejection was most evident. He sat really lost in thought for the first few minutes, and when rousing himself, it was only to say,

'Of all horrid things, leave-taking is the worst.'

'But you will come again,' said Emma. 'This will not be your only visit to Randalls.'

'Ah! – (shaking his head) – the uncertainty of when I may be able to return! – I shall try for it with a zeal! – It will be the object of all my thoughts and cares! – and if my uncle and aunt go to town this spring – but I am afraid – they did not stir last spring – I am afraid it is a custom gone for ever.'

'Our poor ball must be quite given up.'

'Ah! that ball! – why did we wait for any thing? – why not seize the pleasure at once? – How often is happiness destroyed by preparation, foolish preparation! – You told us it would be so. – Oh! Miss Woodhouse, why are you always so right?'

'Indeed, I am very sorry to be right in this instance. I would much rather have been merry than wise.'

'If I can come again, we are still to have our ball. My father depends on it. Do not forget your engagement.'

Emma looked graciously.

'Such a fortnight as it has been!' he continued; 'every day more precious and more delightful than the day before! – every day making me less fit to bear any other place. Happy those, who can remain at Highbury!'

'As you do us such ample justice now,' said Emma, laughing. 'I will venture to ask, whether you did not come a little doubtingly at first? Do not we rather surpass your expectations? I am sure we do. I am sure you did not much expect to like us. You would not have been so long in coming, if you had had a pleasant idea of Highbury.'

He laughed rather consciously, and though denying the sentiment, Emma was convinced that it had been so.

'And you must be off this very morning?'

'Yes; my father is to join me there: we shall walk back together, and I must be off immediately. I am almost afraid that every moment will bring him.'

'Not five minutes to spare even for your friends Miss Fairfax and Miss Bates? how unlucky! Miss Bates's powerful, argumentative mind might have strengthened yours.'

'Yes – I *have* called there; passing the door, I though it better. It was a right thing to do. I went in for three minutes, and was detained by Miss Bates's being absent. She was out; and I felt it impossible not to wait till she came in. She is a woman that one may, that one *must* laugh at; but that one would not wish to slight. It was better to pay my visit, then' –

He hesitated, got up, walked to a window.

'In short,' said he, 'perhaps, Miss Woodhouse – I think you can hardly be quite without suspicion' –

He looked at her, as if wanting to read her thoughts. She hardly knew what to say. It seemed like the forerunner of something absolutely serious, which she did not wish. Forcing herself to speak, therefore, in the hope of putting it by, she calmly said,

'You were quite in the right; it was most natural to pay your visit, then' –

He was silent. She believed he was looking at her; probably reflecting on what she had said, and trying to understand the manner. She heard him sigh. It was natural for him to feel that he had *cause* to sigh. He could not believe her to be encouraging him. A few awkward moments passed, and he sat down again; and in a more determined manner said,

'It was something to feel that all the rest of my time might be given to Hartfield. My regard for Hartfield is most warm' –

He stopt again, rose again, and seemed quite embarrassed. – He was more in love with her than Emma had supposed; and who can say how it might have ended, if his father had not made his appearance? Mr Woodhouse soon followed; and the necessity of exertion made him composed.

A very few minutes more, however, completed the present trial. Mr Weston, always alert when business was to be done, and as incapable of procrastinating any evil that was inevitable, as of foreseeing any that was doubtful, said, 'It was time to go;' and the young man, though he might and did sigh, could not but agree, and rise to take leave.

'I shall hear about you all,' said he; 'that is my chief consolation. I shall hear of everything that's going on among you. I have engaged Mrs Weston to correspond with me. She has been so kind as to promise it. Oh! the blessing of a female correspondent, when one is really interested in the absent! – she will tell me every thing. In her letters I shall be at dear Highbury again.'

A very friendly shake of the hand, a very earnest 'Good bye,' closed the speech, and the door had soon shut out Frank Churchill. Short had been the notice – short their meeting; he was gone; and Emma felt so sorry to part, and foresaw so great a loss to their little society from his absence as to begin to be afraid of being too sorry, and feeling it too much.

It was a sad change. They had been meeting almost every day since his arrival. Certainly his being at Randalls had given great spirit to the last two weeks – indescribable spirit; the idea, the expectation of seeing him which every morning had brought, the assurance of his attentions, his liveliness, his manners! It had been a very happy fortnight, and forlorn must be the sinking from it into the common course of Hartfield days. To complete every other recommendation, he had *almost* told her that he loved her. What strength, or what constancy of affection he might be subject to, was another point; but at present she could not doubt his having a decidedly warm admiration, a conscious preference of herself; and this persuasion, joined to all the rest, made her think that she *must* be a little in love with him, in spite of every previous determination against it.

'I certainly must,' said she. 'This sensation of listlessness, weariness, stupidity, this disinclination to sit down and employ myself, this feeling of every thing's being dull and insipid about the house! – I must be in love; I should be the oddest creature in the world if I were not – for a few weeks at least. Well! evil to some is always good to others. I shall have many fellow-mourners for the ball, if not for Frank Churchill; but Mr Knightley will be happy. He may spend the evening with his dear William Larkins now if he likes.'

Mr Knightley, however, shewed no triumphant happiness. He

could not say that he was sorry on his own account; his very cheerful look would have contradicted him if he had; but he said, and very steadily, that he was sorry for the disappointment of the others, and with considerable kindness added.

'You, Emma, who have so few opportunities of dancing, you are really out of luck; you are very much out of luck!'

It was some days before she saw Jane Fairfax, to judge of her honest regret in this woeful change; but when they did meet, her composure was odious. She had been particularly unwell, however, suffering from headache to a degree, which made her aunt declare, that had the ball taken place, she did not think Jane could have attended it; and it was charity to impute some of her unbecoming indifference to the languor of ill-health.

CHAPTER THIRTY-ONE

EMMA CONTINUED TO entertain no doubt of her being in love. Her ideas only varied as to the how much. At first, she thought it was a good deal; and afterwards, but little. She had great pleasure in hearing Frank Churchill talked of; and, for his sake, greater pleasure than ever seeing Mr and Mrs Weston; she was very often thinking of him, and quite impatient for a letter, that she might know how he was, how were his spirits, how was his aunt, and what was the chance of his coming to Randalls again this Spring. But, on the other hand, she could not admit herself to be unhappy, nor, after the first morning, to be less disposed for employment than usual; she was still busy and cheerful; and, pleasing as he was, she could yet imagine him to have faults; and farther, though thinking of him so much, and, as she sat drawing or working, forming a thousand amusing schemes for the progress and close of their attachment, fancying interesting dialogues, and inventing elegant letters; the conclusion of every imaginary declaration on his side was that she *refused* him. Their affection was always to subside into friendship. Every thing tender and charming was to mark their parting; but still they were to part. When she became sensible of this, it struck her that she could not be very much in love; for in spite of her previous and fixed determination never to quit her father, never to marry, a strong attachment certainly must produce more of a struggle than she could foresee in her own feelings.

'I do not find myself making any use of the word *sacrifice*,' said she. – 'In not one of all my clever replies, my delicate negatives, is there any allusion to making a sacrifice. I do suspect that he is not really necessary to my happiness. So much the better. I certainly will not persuade myself to feel more than I do. I am quite enough in love. I should be sorry to be more.'

Upon the whole, she was equally contented with her view of his feelings.

'*He* is undoubtedly very much in love – every thing denotes it – very much in love indeed! – and when he comes again, if his affection continue, I must be on my guard not to encourage it. – It would be most inexcusable to do otherwise, as my own mind is quite made up. Not that I imagine he can think I have been encouraging him hitherto. No, if he had believed me at all to share his feelings, he would not have been so wretched. Could he have thought himself encouraged, his looks and language at parting would have been different. – Still however, I must be on my guard. This is in the supposition of his attachment continuing what it now is; but I do not know that I expect it will; I do not look upon him to be quite the sort of man – I do not altogether build upon his steadiness or constancy. – His feelings are warm, but I can imagine them rather changeable. – Every consideration of the subject, in short, makes me thankful that my happiness is not more deeply involved. – I shall do very well again after a little while – and then, it will be a good thing over; for they say every body is in love once in their lives, and I shall have been let off easily.'

When his letter to Mrs Weston arrived, Emma had the perusal of it; and she read it with a degree of pleasure and admiration which made her at first shake her head over her own sensations, and think she had undervalued their strength. It was a long, well-written letter, giving the particulars of his journey and of his feelings, expressing all the affection, gratitude, and respect which was natural and honourable, and describing every thing exterior and local that could be supposed attractive, with spirit and precision. No suspicious flourishes now of apology or concern; it was the language of real feeling towards Mrs Weston; and the transition from Highbury to Enscombe, the contrast between the places in some of the first blessings of social life was just enough touched on to shew how keenly it was felt, and how much more might have been said but for the restraints of propriety. – The charm of her own name was not wanting. *Miss Woodhouse* appeared more than once, and never without something of pleasing connection, either a compliment to her taste, or a remembrance of what she had said; and in the very last time of its meeting her eyes, unadorned as it was by any such broad wreath of gallantry, she yet could discern the effect of her influence and acknowledge the greatest compliment perhaps of all conveyed. Compressed into the very lowest vacant corner were these words – 'I had not a spare moment on Tuesday, as you know, for Miss Woodhouse's beautiful little friend. Pray make my excuses and adieus to her.' This, Emma could not doubt, was all for herself. Harriet was remembered only from being *her* friend. His information and prospects as to Enscombe were neither worse nor better than had been anticipated; Mrs Churchill was recovering, and he dared not yet, even in his own imagination, fix a time for coming to Randalls again.

Gratifying, however, and stimulative as was the letter in the material part, its sentiments, she yet found, when it was folded up and returned to Mrs Weston, that it had not added any lasting warmth, that she could still do without the writer, and that he must learn to do without her. Her intentions were unchanged. Her resolution of refusal only grew more interesting by the addition of a scheme for his subsequent consolation and happiness. His recollection of Harriet, and the words which clothed it, the 'beautiful little friend,' suggested to her the idea of Harriet's succeeding her in his affections. Was it impossible? – No. – Harriet undoubtedly was greatly his inferior in understanding; but he had been very much struck with the loveliness of her face and the warm simplicity of her manner; and all the probabilities of circumstance and connection were in her favour. – For Harriet, it would be advantageous and delightful indeed.

'I must not dwell upon it,' said she. – 'I must not think of it. I know the danger of indulging such speculations. But stranger things have happened; and when we cease to care for each other as we do now, it will be the means of confirming us in that sort of true disinterested friendship which I can already look forward to with pleasure.'

It was well to have a comfort in store on Harriet's behalf, though it might be wise to let the fancy touch it seldom; for evil in that quarter was at hand. As Frank Churchill's arrival had succeeded Mr Elton's engagement in the conversation of Highbury, as the latest interest had entirely born down the first, so now upon Frank Churchill's disappearance, Mr Elton's concerns were assuming the most irresistible form. – His wedding-day was named. He would soon be among them again; Mr Elton and his bride. There was hardly time to talk over the first letter from Enscombe before 'Mr Elton and his bride' was in every body's mouth, and Frank Churchill was forgotten. Emma grew sick at the sound. She had had three weeks of happy exemption from Mr Elton; and Harriet's mind, she had been willing to hope, had been lately gaining strength. With Mr Weston's ball in view at least, there had been a great deal of insensibility to other things; but it was now too evident that she had not attained such a state of composure as could stand against the actual approach – new carriage, bell ringing and all.

Poor Harriet was in a flutter of spirits which required all the reasonings and soothings and attentions of every kind that Emma could give. Emma felt that she could not do too much for her, that Harriet had a right to all her ingenuity and all her patience; but it was heavy work to be for ever convincing without producing any effect, for ever agreed to, without being able to make their opinions the same. Harriet listened submissively, and said 'it was very true – it was just as Miss Woodhouse described – it was not worth while to think about them – and she would not think about them any longer' – but no change of subject could avail, and the next half hour saw her as anxious and restless about the Eltons as before. – At last Emma attacked her on another ground.

'Your allowing yourself to be so occupied and so unhappy about Mr Elton's marrying, Harriet, is the strongest reproach you can make *me*. You could not give me a greater reproof for the mistake I fell into. It was all my doing, I know. I have not forgotten it, I assure you. – Deceived myself, I did very miserably deceive you – and it will be a painful recollection to me for ever. Do not imagine me in danger of forgetting it.'

Harriet felt this too much to utter more than a few words of eager exclamation. Emma continued.

'I have not said, exert yourself Harriet for my sake; think less, talk less of Mr Elton for my sake; because for your own sake rather. I would wish it to be done, for the sake of what is more important than my comfort, a habit of self-command in you, a consideration of what is your duty, an attention to propriety, an endeavour to avoid the suspicions of others, to save your health and credit, and restore your tranquillity. These are the motives which I have been pressing on you. They are very important – and sorry I am that you cannot feel them sufficiently to act upon them. My being saved from pain is a very secondary consideration. I want you to save yourself from greater pain. Perhaps I may sometimes have felt that Harriet would not forget what was due – or rather what would be kind by me.'

This appeal to her affections did more than all the rest. The idea of wanting gratitude and consideration for Miss Woodhouse, whom she really loved extremely, made her wretched for a while, and when the violence of grief was comforted away, still remained powerful enough to prompt to what was right and support her in it very tolerably.

'You, who have been the best friend I ever had in my life – Want gratitude to you! – Nobody is equal to you! – I care for nobody as I do for you! – Oh! Miss Woodhouse, how ungrateful I have been!'

Such expressions, assisted as they were by every thing that look and manner could do, made Emma feel that she had never loved Harriet so well, nor valued her affection so highly before.

'There is no charm equal to tenderness of heart,' said she afterwards to herself. 'There is nothing to be compared to it. Warmth and tenderness of heart, with an affectionate, open manner, will beat all the clearness of head in the world, for attraction. I am sure it will. It is tenderness of heart which makes my dear father so generally beloved – which gives Isabella all her popularity. – I have it not – but I know how to prize and respect it. – Harriet is my superior in all the charm and all the felicity it gives. Dear Harriet! – I would not change you for the clearest-headed, longest-sighted, best-judging female breathing. Oh! the coldness of a Jane Fairfax! – Harriet is worth a hundred such. – And for a wife – a sensible man's wife – it is invaluable. I mention no names; but happy the man who changes Emma for Harriet!'

CHAPTER THIRTY-TWO

Mrs Elton was first seen at church; but though devotion might be interrupted, curiosity could not be satisfied by a bride in a pew, and it must be left for the visits in form which were then to be paid, to settle whether she were very pretty indeed, or only rather pretty, or not pretty at all.

Emma had feelings, less of curiosity than of pride or propriety, to make her resolve on not being the last to pay her respects; and she made a point of Harriet's going with her, that the worst of the business might be gone through as soon as possible.

She could not enter the house again, could not be in the same room to which she had with such vain artifice retreated three months ago, to lace up her boot, without *recollecting*. A thousand vexatious thoughts would recur. Compliments, charades, and horrible blunders; and it was not to be supposed that poor Harriet should not be recollecting too; but she behaved very well, and was only rather

Mrs Elton was first seen at church.

pale and silent. The visit was of course short; and there was so much embarrassment and occupation of mind to shorten it, that Emma would not allow herself entirely to form an opinion of the lady, and on no account to give one, beyond the nothing-meaning terms of being 'elegantly dressed, and very pleasing.'

She did not really like her. She would not be in a hurry to find fault, but she suspected that there was no elegance; ease, but not elegance. – She was almost sure that for a young woman, a stranger, a bride, there was too much ease. Her person was rather good; her face not unpretty; but neither feature, nor air, nor voice, nor manner, were elegant. Emma thought at least it would turn out so.

As for Mr Elton, his manners did not appear – but no, she would not permit a hasty or a witty word from herself about his manners. It was an awkward ceremony at any time to be receiving wedding-visits, and a man had need be all grace to acquit himself well through it. The woman was better off; she might have the assistance of fine clothes, and the privilege of bashfulness, but the man had only his own good sense to depend on; and when she considered how peculiarly unlucky poor Mr Elton was in being in the same room at once with the woman he had just married, the woman he had wanted to marry, and the woman whom he had been expected to marry, she must allow him to have the right to look as little wise, and to be as much affectedly, and as little really easy as could be.

'Well Miss Woodhouse,' said Harriet, when they had quitted the house, and after waiting in vain for her friend to begin; 'Well Miss Woodhouse, (with a gentle sigh,) what do you think of her? – Is not she very charming?'

There was a little hesitation in Emma's answer.

'Oh! yes – very – a very pleasing young woman.'

'I think her beautiful, quite beautiful.'

'Very nicely dressed, indeed; a remarkably elegant gown.'

'I am not at all surprized that he should have fallen in love.'

'Oh! no – there is nothing to surprize one at all. – A pretty fortune; and she came in his way.'

'I dare say,' returned Harriet, sighing again, 'I dare say she was very much attached to him.'

'Perhaps she might; but it is not every man's fate to marry the woman who loves him best. Miss Hawkins perhaps wanted a home, and thought this the best offer she was likely to have.'

'Yes,' said Harriet earnestly, 'and well she might, nobody could ever have a better. Well, I wish them happy with all my heart. And now, Miss Woodhouse, I do not think I shall mind seeing them again. He is just as superior as ever; – but still married, you know, it is quite a different thing. No, indeed, Miss Woodhouse, you need not be afraid; I can sit and admire him now without any great misery. To know that he has not thrown himself away, is such a comfort! – She does seem a charming young woman, just what he deserves. Happy creature! He called her "Augusta." How delightful!'

When the visit was returned, Emma made up her mind. She could then see more and judge better. From Harriet's happening not to be at Hartfield, and her father's being present to engage Mr Elton, she had a quarter of an hour of the lady's conversation to herself, and could composedly attend to her; and the quarter of an hour quite convinced her that Mrs Elton was a vain woman, extremely well satisfied with herself, and thinking much of her own importance; that she meant to shine and be very superior, but with manners which had been formed in a bad school, pert and familiar; that all her notions were drawn from one set of people, and one style of living, that if not foolish she was ignorant, and that her society would certainly do Mr Elton no good.

Harriet would have been a better match. If not wise or refined herself, she would have connected him with those who were; but Miss Hawkins, it might be fairly supposed from her easy conceit, had been the best of her own set. The rich brother-in-law near Bristol was the pride of the alliance, and his place and his carriages were the pride of him.

The very first subject after being seated was Maple Grove, 'My brother Mr Suckling's seat' – a comparison of Hartfield to Maple Grove. The grounds of Hartfield were small, but neat and pretty; and the house was modern and well-built. Mrs Elton seemed most favourably impressed by the size of the room, the entrance, and all that she could see or imagine. 'Very like Maple Grove indeed! – She was quite struck by the likeness! – That room was the very shape and size of the morning-room at Maple Grove; her sister's favourite room.' – Mr Elton was appealed to. – 'Was not it astonishingly like? – She could really almost fancy herself at Maple Grove.'

'And the staircase – You know, as I came in, I observed how very like the staircase was; placed exactly in the same part of the house. I really could not help exclaiming! I assure you, Miss Woodhouse, it is very delightful to me, to be reminded of a place I am so extremely partial to as Maple Grove. I have spent so many happy months there! (with a little sigh of sentiment). A charming place, undoubtedly. Every body who sees it is struck by its beauty; but to me, it has been quite a home. Whenever you are transplanted, like me, Miss Woodhouse, you will understand how very delightful it is to meet with any thing at all like what one has left behind. I always say this is quite one of the evils of matrimony.'

Emma made as slight a reply as she could; but it was fully sufficient for Mrs Elton, who only wanted to be talking herself.

'So extremely like Maple Grove! And it is not merely the house – the grounds, I assure you, as far as I could observe, are strikingly like. The laurels at Maple Grove are in the same profusion as here, and stand very much in the same way – just across the lawn; and I had a glimpse of a fine large tree, with a bench round it, which put me so exactly in mind! My brother and sister will be enchanted with this place. People who have extensive grounds themselves are always pleased with any thing in the same style.'

Emma doubted the truth of this sentiment. She had a great idea that people who had extensive grounds themselves cared very little for the extensive grounds of any body else; but it was not worth while to attack an error so double-dyed, and therefore only said in reply,

'When you have seen more of this country, I am afraid you will think you have over-rated Hartfield. Surrey is full of beauties.'

'Oh! yes, I am quite aware of that. It is the garden of England, you know. Surrey is the garden of England.'

'Yes; but we must not rest our claims on that distinction. Many counties, I believe, are called the garden of England, as well as Surrey.'

'No, I fancy not,' replied Mrs Elton, with a most satisfied smile. 'I never heard any county but Surrey called so.'

Emma was silenced.

'My brother and sister have promised us a visit in the spring, or summer at farthest,' continued Mrs Elton; 'and that will be our time for exploring. While they are with us, we shall explore a great deal, I dare say. They will have their barouche-landau, of course, which holds four perfectly; and therefore, without saying any thing of *our* carriage, we should be able to explore the different beauties extremely well. They would hardly come in their chaise, I think, at that season of the year. Indeed, when the time draws on, I shall decidedly recommend their bringing the barouche-landau; it will be so very much preferable. When people come into a beautiful country of this sort, you know, Miss Woodhouse, one naturally wishes them to see as much as possible; and Mr Suckling is extremely fond of exploring. We explored to King's-Weston twice last summer, in that way, most delightfully, just after their first having the barouche-landau. You have many parties of that kind here, I suppose, Miss Woodhouse, every summer?'

'No; not immediately here. We are rather out of distance of the very striking beauties which attract the sort of parties you speak of; and we are a very quiet set of people, I believe; more disposed to stay at home than engage in schemes of pleasure.'

'Ah! there is nothing like staying at home, for real comfort. Nobody can be more devoted to home than I am. I was quite a proverb for it at Maple Grove. Many a time has Selina said, when she has been going to Bristol. "I really cannot get this girl to move from the house. I absolutely must go in by myself, though I hate being stuck up in the barouche-landau without a companion; but Augusta, I believe, with her own good will, would never stir beyond the park paling." Many a time has she said so; and yet I am no advocate for entire seclusion. I think, on the contrary, when people shut themselves up entirely from society, it is a very bad thing; and that it is much more advisable to mix in the world in a proper degree, without living in it either too much or too little. I perfectly understand your situation, however, Miss Woodhouse – (looking towards Mr Woodhouse) – Your father's state of health must be a great drawback. Why does not he try Bath? – Indeed he should. Let me recommend Bath to you. I assure you I have no doubt of its doing Mr Woodhouse good.'

'My father tried it more than once, formerly; but without receiving any benefit; and Mr Perry, whose name, I dare say, is not unknown to you, does not conceive it would be at all more likely to be useful now.'

'Ah! that's a great pity; for I assure you, Miss Woodhouse, where the waters do agree, it is quite wonderful the relief they give. In my Bath life, I have seen such instances of it! And it is so cheerful a place, that it could not fail of being of use to Mr Woodhouse's spirits, which, I understand, are sometimes much depressed. And as to its recommendations to *you*, I fancy I need not take much pains to dwell on them. The advantages of Bath to the young are pretty generally understood. It would be a charming introduction for you, who have lived so secluded a life; and I could immediately secure you some of the best society in the place. A line from me would bring you a little host of acquaintance; and my particular friend, Mrs Partridge, the lady I have always resided with when in Bath, would be most happy to shew you any attentions, and would be the very person for you to go into public with.'

It was as much as Emma could bear, without being impolite. The idea of her being indebted to Mrs Elton for what was called an *introduction* – or her going into public under the auspices of a friend of Mrs Elton's, probably some vulgar, dashing widow, who, with the help of a boarder, just made a shift to live! – The dignity of Miss Woodhouse, of Hartfield, was sunk indeed!

She restrained herself, however, from any of the reproofs she could have given, and only thanked Mrs Elton coolly; 'but their going to Bath was quite out of the question; and she was not perfectly convinced that the place might suit her better than her father.' And then, to prevent further outrage and indignation, changed the subject directly:

'I do not ask whether you are musical, Mrs Elton. Upon these occasions, a lady's character generally precedes her; and Highbury has long known that you are a superior performer.'

'Oh! no, indeed; I must protest against any such idea. A superior performer! – very far from it, I assure you. Consider from how partial a quarter your information came. I am doatingly fond of music – passionately fond; – and my friends say I am not entirely devoid of taste; but as to any thing else, upon my honour my performance is *mediocre* to the last degree. You, Miss Woodhouse, I well know, play delightfully. I assure you it has been the greatest satisfaction, comfort, and delight to me, to hear what a musical

Some vulgar, dashing widow.

society I am got into. I absolutely cannot do without music. It is a necessary of life to me; and having always been used to a very musical society, both at Maple Grove and in Bath, it would have been a most serious sacrifice. I honestly said as much to Mr E. when he was speaking of my future home, and expressing his fears lest the retirement of it should be disagreeable; and the inferiority of the house too – knowing what I had been accustomed to – of course he was not wholly without apprehension. When he was speaking of it in that way, I honestly said that *the world* I could give up – parties, balls, plays – for I had no fear of retirement. Blessed with so many resources within myself, the world was not necessary to *me*. I could do very well, without it. To those who had no resources it was a different thing; but my resources made me quite independent. And as to smaller-sized rooms than I had been used to, I really could not give it a thought. I hoped I was perfectly equal to any sacrifice of that description. Certainly I had been accustomed to every luxury at Maple Grove; but I did assure him that two carriages were not necessary to my happiness, nor were spacious apartments. "But" said I, "to be quite honest, I do not think I can live without something of a musical society. I condition for nothing else; but without music, life would be a blank to me." '

'We cannot suppose,' said Emma, smiling, 'that Mr Elton would hesitate to assure you of there being a *very* musical society in Highbury; and I hope you will not find he has outstepped the truth more than may be pardoned, in consideration of the motive.'

'No, indeed, I have no doubts at all on that head. I am delighted to find myself in such a circle. I hope we shall have many sweet little concerts together. I think, Miss Woodhouse, you and I must establish a musical club, and have regular weekly meetings at your house, or ours. Will not it be a good plan? If *we* exert ourselves, I think we shall not be long in want of allies. Something of that nature would be particularly desirable for *me*, as an inducement to keep me in practice; for married women, you know – there is a sad story against them, in general. They are but too apt to give up music.'

'But you, who are so extremely fond of it – there can be no danger, surely.'

'I should hope not; but really when I look round among my acquaintance, I tremble. Selina has entirely given up music – never touches the instrument – though she played sweetly. And the same may be said of Mrs Jeffereys – Clara Partridge, that was – and of the two Milmans, now Mrs Bird and Mrs James Cooper; and of more than I can enumerate. Upon my word it is enough to put one in a fright. I used to be quite angry with Selina; but really I begin now to comprehend that a married woman has many things to call her attention. I believe I was half an hour this morning shut up with my housekeeper.'

'But every thing of that kind,' said Emma, 'will soon be in so regular a train – '

'Well,' said Mrs Elton, laughing, 'we shall see.'

Emma, finding her so determined upon neglecting her music, had nothing more to say; and, after a moment's pause, Mrs Elton chose another subject.

'We have been calling at Randalls,' said she, 'and found them both at home; and very pleasant people they seem to be. I like them extremely. Mr Weston seems an excellent creature – quite a first-rate favourite with me already, I assure you. And *she* appears so truly good – there is something so motherly and kindhearted about her, that it wins upon one directly. She was your governess, I think?'

Emma was almost too much astonished to answer; but Mrs Elton hardly waited for the affirmative before she went on.

'Having understood as much, I was rather astonished to find her so very lady-like! But she is really quite the gentlewoman.'

'Mrs Weston's manners,' said Emma, 'were always particularly good. Their propriety, simplicity, and elegance, would make them the safest model for any young woman.'

'And who do you think came in while we were there?'

Emma was quite at a loss. The tone implied some old acquaintance and how could she possibly guess?

'Knightley!' continued Mrs Elton; – 'Knightley himself! – Was not it lucky? – for, not being within when he called the other day, I had never seen him before; and of course, as so particular a friend of Mr E.'s, I had a great curiosity. "My friend Knightley" had been so often mentioned, that I was really impatient to see him; and I must do my caro sposo the justice to say that he need not be ashamed of his friend. Knightley is quite the gentleman. I like him very much. Decidedly, I think, a very gentleman-like man.'

Happily it was now time to be gone. They were off; and Emma could breathe.

'Insufferable woman!' was her immediate exclamation. 'Worse than I had supposed. Absolutely insufferable! Knightley! – I could not have believed it. Knightley! – never seen him in her life before, and call him Knightley! – and discover that he is a gentleman! A little upstart, vulgar being, with her Mr E., and her *caro sposo*, and her resources, and all her airs of pert pretension and under-bred finery. Actually to discover that Mr Knightley is a gentleman! I doubt whether he will return the compliment, and discover her to be a lady. I could not have believed it! And to propose that she and I should unite to form a musical club! One would fancy we were bosom friends! And Mrs Weston! – Astonished that the person who had brought me up should be a gentlewoman! Worse and worse. I never met with her equal. Much beyond my hopes. Harriet is disgraced by any comparison. Oh! what would Frank Churchill say to her, if he were here? How angry and how diverted he would be! Ah! there I am – thinking of him directly. Always the first person to be thought of! How I catch myself out! Frank Churchill comes as regularly into my mind!' –

All this ran so glibly through her thoughts, that by the time her father had arranged himself, after the bustle of the Eltons' departure, and was ready to speak, she was very tolerably capable of attending.

'Well, my dear,' he deliberately began, 'considering we never saw her before, she seems a very pretty sort of young lady; and I dare say she was very much pleased with you. She speaks a little too quick. A little quickness of voice there is which rather hurts the ear. But I believe I am nice; I do not like strange voices; and nobody speaks like you and poor Miss Taylor. However, she seems a very obliging, pretty-behaved young lady, and no doubt will make him a very good wife. Though I think he had better not have married. I made the best excuses I could for not having been able to wait on him and Mrs Elton on this happy occasion; I said that I hoped I *should* in the course of the Summer. But I ought to have gone before. Not to wait upon a bride is very remiss. Ah! it shews what a sad invalid I am! But I do not like the corner into Vicarage-lane.'

'I dare say your apologies were accepted, sir. Mr Elton knows you.'

'Yes: but a young lady – a bride – I ought to have paid my respects to her if possible. It was being very deficient.'

'But, my dear papa, you are no friend to matrimony; and therefore why should you be so anxious to pay your respects to a *bride*? It ought to be no recommendation to *you*. It is encouraging people to marry if you make so much of them.'

'No, my dear, I never encouraged any body to marry, but I would always wish to pay every proper attention to a lady – and a bride, especially, is never to be neglected. More is avowedly due to *her*. A bride you know, my dear, is always the first in company, let the others be who they may.'

'Well, papa, if this is not encouragement to marry, I do not know what is. And I should never have expected you to be lending your sanction to such vanity-baits for poor young ladies.'

'My dear, you do not understand me. This is a matter of mere common politeness and good-breeding, and has nothing to do with any encouragement to people to marry.'

Emma had done. Her father was growing nervous, and could not understand *her*. Her mind returned to Mrs Elton's offences, and long, very long, did they occupy her.

CHAPTER THIRTY-THREE

EMMA WAS NOT REQUIRED, by any subsequent discovery, to retract her ill opinion of Mrs Elton. Her observation had been pretty correct. Such as Mrs Elton appeared to her on this second interview, such she appeared whenever they met again, – self-important, presuming, familiar, ignorant, and ill-bred. She had a little beauty and a little accomplishment, but so little judgment that she thought herself coming with superior knowledge of the world, to enliven and improve a country neighbourhood; and conceived Miss Hawkins to have held such a place in society as Mrs Elton's consequence only could surpass.

There was no reason to suppose Mr Elton thought at all differently from his wife. He seemed not merely happy with her, but proud. He had the air of congratulating himself on having brought such a woman to Highbury, as not even Miss Woodhouse could equal; and the greater part of her new acquaintance, disposed to commend, or not in the habit of judging, following the lead of Miss Bates's good-will or taking it for granted that the bride must be as clever and as agreeable as she professed herself, were very well satisfied; so that Mrs Elton's praise passed from one mouth to another as it ought to do, unimpeded by Miss Woodhouse, who readily continued her first contribution and talked with a good grace of her being 'very pleasant and very elegantly dressed.'

In one respect Mrs Elton grew even worse than she had appeared at first. Her feelings altered towards Emma. – Offended, probably, by the little encouragement which her proposals of intimacy met with, she drew back in her turn and gradually became much more cold and distant; and though the effect was agreeable, the ill-will which produced it was necessarily increasing Emma's dislike. Her manners too – and Mr Elton's, were unpleasant towards Harriet. They were sneering and negligent. Emma hoped it must rapidly work Harriet's cure; but the sensations which could prompt such behaviour sunk them both very much. – It was not to be doubted that poor Harriet's attachment had been an offering to conjugal unreserve, and her own share in the story, under a colouring the least favourable to her and the most soothing to him, had in all likelihood been given also. She was, of course, the object of their joint dislike. – When they had nothing else to say, it must be always easy to begin abusing Miss Woodhouse; and the enmity which they dared not shew in open disrespect to her, found a broader vent in contemptuous treatment of Harriet.

Mrs Elton took a great fancy to Jane Fairfax; and from the first. Not merely when a state of warfare with one young lady might be supposed to recommend the other, but from the very first; and she was not satisfied with expressing a natural and reasonable admiration – but without solicitation, or plea, or privilege, she must be wanting to assist and befriend her. – Before Emma had forfeited her confidence, and about the third time of their meeting, she heard all Mrs Elton's knight-errantry on the subject. –

'Jane Fairfax is absolutely charming, Miss Woodhouse. – I quite rave about Jane Fairfax. – A sweet, interesting creature. So mild and ladylike – and with such talents! – I assure you I think she has very extraordinary talents. I do not scruple to say that she plays extremely well. I know enough of music to speak decidedly on that point. Oh! she is absolutely charming! You will laugh at my warmth – but upon my word, I talk of nothing but Jane Fairfax. – And her situation is so calculated to affect one! – Miss Woodhouse, we must exert ourselves and endeavour to do something for her. We must bring her forward. Such talents as her's must not be suffered to remain unknown. – I dare say you have heard those charming lines of the poet,

> *"Full many a flower is born to blush unseen,*
> *'And waste its fragrance on the desert air."*

We must not allow them to be verified in sweet Jane Fairfax.'

'I cannot think there is any danger of it,' was Emma's calm answer – 'and when you are better acquainted with Miss Fairfax's situation and understand what her home has been, with Col. and Mrs Campbell, I have no idea that you will suppose her talents can be unknown.'

'Oh! but dear Miss Woodhouse, she is now in such retirement, such obscurity, so thrown away. – Whatever advantages she may have enjoyed with the Campbells are so palpably at an end! And I think she feels it. I am sure she does. She is very timid and silent.

'You have heard those charming lines of the poet.'

One can see that she feels the want of encouragement. I like her the better for it. I must confess it is a recommendation to me. I am a great advocate for timidity – and I am sure one does not often meet with it. – But in those who are at all inferior, it is extremely prepossessing. Oh! I assure you, Jane Fairfax is a very delightful character, and interests me more than I can express.'

'You appear to feel a great deal – but I am not aware how you or any of Miss Fairfax's acquaintance here, any of those who have known her longer than yourself, can shew her any other attention than' –

'My dear Miss Woodhouse, a vast deal may be done by those who dare to act. You and I need not be afraid. If *we* set the example, many will follow it as far as they can; though all have not our situations. *We* have carriages to fetch and convey her home, and *we* live in a style which could not make the addition of Jane Fairfax, at any time, the least inconvenient. – I should be extremely displeased if Wright were to send us up such a dinner, as could make me regret having asked *more* than Jane Fairfax to partake of it. I have no idea of that sort of thing. It is not likely that I *should*, considering what I have been used to. My greatest danger, perhaps, in housekeeping, may be quite the other way, in doing too much, and being too careless of expense. Maple Grove will probably be my model more than it ought to be – for we do not at all affect to equal my brother, Mr Suckling, in income. – However, my resolution is taken as to noticing Jane Fairfax. – I shall certainly have her very often at my house, shall introduce her wherever I can, shall have musical parties to draw out her talents, and shall be constantly on the watch for an eligible situation. My acquaintance is so very extensive, that I have little doubt of hearing of something to suit her shortly. – I shall introduce her, of course, very particularly to my brother and sister when they come to us. I am sure they will like her extremely; and when she gets a little acquainted with them, her fears will completely wear off, for there really is nothing in the manners of either but what is highly conciliating. – I shall have her very often indeed while they are with me, and I dare say we shall sometimes find a seat for her in the barouche-landau in some of our exploring parties.'

'Poor Jane Fairfax!' – thought Emma. – 'You have not deserved this. You may have done wrong with regard to Mr Dixon, but this is a punishment beyond what you can have merited! – The kindness and protection of Mrs Elton! – "Jane Fairfax and Jane Fairfax." Heavens! Let me not suppose that she dares go about, Emma Woodhouse-ing me! – But upon my honour, there seem no limits to the licentiousness of that woman's tongue!'

Emma had not to listen to such paradings again – to any so exclusively addressed to herself – so disgustingly decorated with a 'dear Miss Woodhouse.' The change on Mrs Elton's side soon afterwards appeared, and she was left in peace – neither forced to be the very particular friend of Mrs Elton, nor, under Mrs Elton's guidance, the very active patroness of Jane Fairfax, and only sharing with others in a general way, in knowing what was felt, what was meditated, what was done.

She looked on with some amusement. – Miss Bates's gratitude for Mrs Elton's attentions to Jane was in the first style of guileless simplicity and warmth. She was quite one of her worthies – the most amiable, affable, delightful woman – just as accomplished and condescending as Mrs Elton meant to be considered. Emma's only surprize was that Jane Fairfax should accept those attentions and tolerate Mrs Elton as she seemed to do. She heard of her walking with the Eltons, sitting with the Eltons, spending a day with the Eltons! This was astonishing! – She could not have believed it possible that the taste or the pride of Miss Fairfax could endure such society and friendship as the Vicarage had to offer.

'She is a riddle, quite a riddle!' said she. – 'To chuse to remain here month after month, under privations of every sort! And now to chuse the mortifications of Mrs Elton's notice and the penury of her conversation, rather than return to the superior companions who have always loved her with such real, generous affection.'

Jane had come to Highbury professedly for three months; the Campbells were gone to Ireland for three months; but now the Campbells had promised their daughter to stay at least till Mid-Summer, and fresh invitations had arrived for her to join them there. According to Miss Bates – it all came from her – Mrs Dixon had written most pressingly. Would Jane but go, means were to be found, servants sent, friends contrived – no travelling difficulty allowed to exist; but still she had declined it!

'She must have some motive, more powerful than appears, for refusing this invitation,' was Emma's conclusion. 'She must be under some sort of penance, inflicted either by the Campbells or herself. There is great fear, great caution, great resolution somewhere. – She is *not* to be with the *Dixons.* The decree is issued by somebody. But why must she consent to be with the Eltons? – Here is quite a separate puzzle.'

Upon her speaking her wonder aloud on that part of the subject, before the few who knew her opinion of Mrs Elton, Mrs Weston ventured this apology for Jane.

'We cannot suppose that she has any great enjoyment at the Vicarage, my dear Emma – but it is better than being always at home. Her aunt is a good creature, but, as a constant companion, must be very tiresome. We must consider what Miss Fairfax quits, before we condemn her taste for what she goes to.'

'You are right, Mrs Weston,' said Mr Knightley warmly, 'Miss Fairfax is as capable as any of us of forming a just opinion of Mrs Elton. Could she have chosen with whom to associate, she would not have chosen her. But (with a reproachful smile at Emma) she receives attentions from Mrs Elton, which nobody else pays her.'

Emma felt that Mrs Weston was giving her a momentary glance; and she was herself struck by his warmth. With a faint blush, she presently replied,

'Such attentions as Mrs Elton's, I should have imagined, would rather disgust than gratify Miss Fairfax. Mrs Elton's invitations I should have imagined any thing but inviting.'

'I should not wonder,' said Mrs Weston, 'if Miss Fairfax were to have been drawn on beyond her own inclination, by her aunt's eagerness in accepting Mrs Elton's civilities for her. Poor Miss Bates may very likely have committed her niece and hurried her into a greater appearance of intimacy than her own good sense would have dictated, in spite of the very natural wish of a little change.'

Both felt rather anxious to hear him speak again; and after a few minutes silence, he said,

'Another thing must be taken into consideration too – Mrs Elton does not talk *to* Miss Fairfax as she speaks *of* her. We all know the difference between the pronouns he or she and thou, the plainest-spoken amongst us; we all feel the influence of a something beyond common civility in our personal intercourse with each other – a something more early implanted. We cannot give any body the disagreeable hints that we may have been very full of the hour before. We feel things differently. And besides the operation of this, as a general principle, you may be sure that Miss Fairfax awes Mrs Elton by her superiority both of mind and manner; and that face to face Mrs Elton treats her with all the respect which she has a claim to. Such a woman as Jane Fairfax probably never fell in Mrs Elton's way before – and no degree of vanity can prevent her acknowledging her own comparative littleness in action, if not in consciousness.'

'I know how highly you think of Jane Fairfax,' said Emma. Little Henry was in her thoughts, and a mixture of alarm and delicacy made her irresolute what else to say.

'Yes,' he replied, 'any body may know how highly I think of her.'

'And yet,' said Emma, beginning hastily and with an arch look, but soon stopping – it was better, however, to know the worst at once – she hurried on – 'And yet, perhaps, you may hardly be aware yourself how highly it is. The extent of your admiration may take you by surprize some day or other.'

Mr Knightley was hard at work upon the lower buttons of his thick leather gaiters, and either the exertion of getting them together, or some other cause, brought the colour into his face, as he answered,

'Oh! are you there? – But you are miserably behind-hand. Mr Cole gave me a hint of it six weeks ago.'

He stopped. – Emma felt her foot pressed by Mrs Weston, and did not herself know what to think. In a moment he went on –

'That will never be, however, I can assure you. Miss Fairfax, I dare say, would not have me if I were to ask her – and I am very sure I shall never ask her.'

Emma returned her friend's pressure with interest; and was pleased enough to exclaim,

'You are not vain, Mr Knightley. I will say that for you.'

He seemed hardly to hear her; he was thoughtful – and in a manner which shewed him not pleased, soon afterwards said,

'So you have been settling that I should marry Jane Fairfax.'

'No indeed I have not. You have scolded me too much for match-making, for me to presume to take such a liberty with you. What I said just now, meant nothing. One says those sort of things, of course, without any idea of a serious meaning. Oh! no, upon my word I have not the smallest wish for your marrying Jane Fairfax or Jane any body. You would not come in and sit with us in this comfortable way, if you were married.'

Mr Knightley was thoughtful again. The result of his reverie was, 'No, Emma, I do not think the extent of my admiration for her will ever take me by surprize. – I never had a thought of her in that way, I assure you.' And soon afterwards, 'Jane Fairfax is a very charming young woman – but not even Jane Fairfax is perfect. She has a fault. She has not the open temper which a man would wish for in a wife.'

Emma could not but rejoice to hear that she had a fault. 'Well,' said she, 'and you soon silenced Mr Cole, I suppose?'

'Yes, very soon. He gave me a quiet hint; I told him he was mistaken; he asked my pardon and said no more. Cole does not want to be wiser or wittier than his neighbours.'

'In that respect how unlike dear Mrs Elton, who wants to be wiser and wittier than all the world! I wonder how she speaks of the Coles – what she calls them! How can she find any appellation for them, deep enough in familiar vulgarity? She calls you, Knightley – what can she do for Mr Cole? And so I am not to be surprized that Jane Fairfax accepts her civilities and consents to be with her. Mrs Weston, your argument weighs most with me. I can much more readily enter into the temptation of getting away from Miss Bates, than I can believe in the triumph of Miss Fairfax's mind over Mrs

Elton. I have no faith in Mrs Elton's acknowledging herself the inferior in thought, word, or deed; or in her being under any restraint beyond her own scanty rule of good-breeding. I cannot imagine that she will not be continually insulting her visitor with praise, encouragement, and offers of service; that she will not be continually detailing her magnificent intentions, from the procuring her a permanent situation to the including her in those delightful exploring parties which are to take place in the barouche-landau.'

'Jane Fairfax has feeling,' said Mr Knightley – 'I do not accuse her of want of feeling. Her sensibilities, I suspect, are strong – and her temper excellent in its power of forbearance, patience, self-control; but it wants openness. She is reserved, more reserved, I think, than she used to be. – And I love an open temper. No – till Cole alluded to my supposed attachment, it had never entered my head. I saw Jane Fairfax and conversed with her, with admiration and pleasure always – but with no thought beyond.'

'Well, Mrs Weston,' said Emma triumphantly when he left them, 'what do you say now to Mr Knightley's marrying Jane Fairfax?'

'Why really, dear Emma, I say that he is so very much occupied by the idea of *not* being in love with her, that I should not wonder if it were to end in his being so at last. Do not beat me.'

CHAPTER THIRTY-FOUR

EVERY BODY IN AND about Highbury who had ever visited Mr Elton, was disposed to pay him attention on his marriage. Dinner-parties and evening-parties were made for him and his lady; and invitations flowed in so fast that she had soon the pleasure of apprehending they were never to have a disengaged day.

'I see how it is,' said she. 'I see what a life I am to lead among you. Upon my word we shall be abolutely dissipated. We really seem quite the fashion. If this is living in the country, it is nothing very formidable. From Monday next to Saturday, I assure you we have not a disengaged day! – A woman with fewer resources than I have, need not have been at a loss.'

No invitation came amiss to her. Her Bath habits made evening-parties perfectly natural to her, and Maple Grove had given her a taste for dinners. She was a little shocked at the want of two drawing rooms, at the poor attempt at rout-cakes, and there being no ice in the Highbury card parties. Mrs Bates, Mrs Perry, Mrs Goddard and others, were a good deal behind hand in knowledge of the world, but *she* would soon shew them how every thing ought to be arranged. In the course of the Spring she must return their civilities by one very superior party – in which her card tables should be set out with their separate candles and unbroken packs in the true style – and more waiters engaged for the evening than their own establishment could furnish, to carry round the refreshments at exactly the proper hour, and in the proper order.

Emma, in the meanwhile, could not be satisfied without a dinner at Hartfield for the Eltons. They must not do less than others, or she should be exposed to odious suspicions, and imagined capable of pitiful resentment. A dinner there must be. After Emma had talked about it for ten minutes, Mr Woodhouse felt no unwillingness, and only made the usual stipulation of not sitting at the bottom of the table himself, with the usual regular difficulty of deciding who should do it for him.

The persons to be invited, required little thought. Besides the Eltons, it must be the Westons and Mr Knightley; so far it was all of course – and it was hardly less inevitable that poor little Harriet must be asked to make the eighth: – but this invitation was not given with equal satisfaction, and on many accounts Emma was particularly pleased by Harriet's begging to be allowed to decline it. 'She would rather not be in *his* company more than she could help. She was not yet quite able to see him and his charming happy wife together, without feeling uncomfortable. If Miss Woodhouse would not be displeased, she would rather stay at home.' It was precisely what Emma would have wished, had she deemed it possible enough for wishing. She was delighted with the fortitude of her little friend – for fortitude she knew it was in her to give up being in company and stay at home; and she could now invite the very person whom she really wanted to make the eighth, Jane Fairfax. – Since her last conversation with Mrs Weston and Mr Knightley, she was more conscience-stricken about Jane Fairfax than she had often been. – Mr Knightley's words dwelt with her. He had said that Jane Fairfax received attentions from Mrs Elton which nobody else paid her.

'This is very true,' said she, 'at least as far as relates to me, which was all that was meant – and it is very shameful. – Of the same age – and always knowing her – I ought to have been more her friend. – She will never like me now. I have neglected her too long. But I will shew her greater attention than I have done.'

Every invitation was successful. They were all disengaged and all happy. – The preparatory interest of this dinner, however, was not yet over. A circumstance rather unlucky occurred. The two eldest little Knightleys were engaged to pay their grandpapa and aunt a visit of some weeks in the Spring, and their papa now proposed bringing them, and staying one whole day at Hartfield – which one day would be the very day of this party. – His professional engagements did not allow of his being put off, but both father and daughter were disturbed by its happening so. Mr Woodhouse considered eight persons at dinner together as the utmost that his nerves could bear – and here would be a ninth – and Emma apprehended that it would be a ninth very much out of humour at not being able to come even to Hartfield for forty-eight hours without falling in with a dinner-party.

She comforted her father better than she could comfort herself, by representing that though he certainly would make them nine, yet he always said so little, that the increase of noise would be very immaterial. She thought it in reality a sad exchange for herself, to have him with his grave looks and reluctant conversation opposed to her instead of his brother.

The event was more favourable to Mr Woodhouse than to Emma. John Knightley came; but Mr Weston was unexpectedly summoned to town and must be absent on the very day. He might be able to join them in the evening, but certainly not to dinner. Mr Woodhouse was quite at ease; and the seeing him so, with the arrival of the little boys and the philosophic composure of her brother on hearing his fate, removed the chief of even Emma's vexation.

The day came, the party were punctually assembled, and Mr John Knightley seemed early to devote himself to the business of being agreeable. Instead of drawing his brother off to a window while they waited for dinner, he was talking to Miss Fairfax. Mrs Elton, as elegant as lace and pearls could make her, he looked at in silence – wanting only to observe enough for Isabella's information – but Miss Fairfax was an old acquaintance and a quiet girl, and he could talk to her. He had met her before breakfast as he was returning from a walk with his little boys, when it had been just beginning to rain. It was natural to have some civil hopes on the subject, and he said,

'I hope you did not venture far, Miss Fairfax, this morning, or I am sure you must have been wet. – *We* scarcely got home in time. I hope you turned directly.'

'I went only to the post-office,' said she, 'and reached home before the rain was much. It is my daily errand. I always fetch the letters when I am here. It saves trouble, and is a something to get me out. A walk before breakfast does me good.'

'Not a walk in the rain, I should imagine.'

'No, but it did not absolutely rain when I set out.'

Mr John Knightley smiled, and replied,

'That is to say, you chose to have your walk, for you were not six yards from your own door when I had the pleasure of meeting you; and Henry and John had seen more drops than they could count long before. The post-office has a great charm at one period of our lives. When you have lived to my age, you will begin to think letters are never worth going through the rain for.'

There was a little blush, and then this answer,

'I must not hope to be ever situated as you are, in the midst of every dearest connection, and therefore I cannot expect that simply growing older should make me indifferent about letters.'

'Indifferent! Oh! no – I never conceived you could become indifferent. Letters are no matter of indifference; they are generally a very positive curse.'

'You are speaking of letters of business; mine are letters of friendship.'

'I have often thought them the worst of the two,' replied he coolly. 'Business, you know, may bring money, but friendship hardly ever does.'

'Ah! you are not serious now. I know Mr John Knightley too well – I am very sure he understands the value of friendship as well as any body. I can easily believe that letters are very little to you, much less than to me, but it is not your being ten years older than myself which makes the difference, it is not age, but situation. You have every body dearest to you always at hand, I, probably, never shall again; and therefore till I have outlived all my affections, a post-office, I think, must always have power to draw me out, in worse weather than to-day.'

'When I talked of your being altered by time, by the progress of years,' said John Knightley, 'I meant to imply the change of situation which time usually brings. I consider one as including the other. Time will generally lessen the interest of every attachment not within the daily circle – but that is not the change I had in view for you. As an old friend, you will allow me to hope, Miss Fairfax, that ten years hence you may have as many concentrated objects as I have.'

It was kindly said, and very far from giving offence. A pleasant 'thank you' seemed meant to laugh it off, but a blush, a quivering lip, a tear in the eye, shewed that it was felt beyond a laugh. Her attention was now claimed by Mr Woodhouse, who being, according to his custom on such occasions, making the circle of his guests, and paying his particular compliments to the ladies, was ending with her – and with all his mildest urbanity, said,

'I am very sorry to hear, Miss Fairfax, of your being out this morning in the rain. Young ladies should take care of themselves. – Young ladies are delicate plants. They should take care of their health and their complexion. My dear, did you change your stockings?'

'Yes, sir, I did indeed; and I am very much obliged by your kind solicitude about me.'

'My dear Miss Fairfax, young ladies are very sure to be cared for. – I hope your good grandmamma and aunt are well. They are some

'I am very sorry to hear, Miss Fairfax, of your being out this morning in the rain.'

of my very old friends. I wish my health allowed me to be a better neighbour. You do us a great deal of honour today, I am sure. My daughter and I are both highly sensible of your goodness, and have the greatest satisfaction in seeing you at Hartfield.'

The kind-hearted, polite old man might then sit down and feel that he had done his duty, and made every fair lady welcome and easy.

By this time, the walk in the rain had reached Mrs Elton, and her remonstrances now opened upon Jane.

'My dear Jane, what is this I hear? – Going to the post-office in the rain! – This must not be, I assure you. – You sad girl, how could you do such a thing? – It is a sign I was not there to take care of you.'

Jane very patiently assured her that she had not caught any cold.

'Oh! do not tell *me*. You really are a very sad girl, and do not know how to take care of yourself. – To the post-office indeed! Mrs Weston, did you ever hear the like? You and I must positively exert our authority.'

'My advice,' said Mrs Weston kindly and persuasively, 'I certainly do feel tempted to give. Miss Fairfax, you must not run such risks. – Liable as you have been to severe colds, indeed you ought to be particularly careful, especially at this time of year. The Spring I always think requires more than common care. Better wait an hour or two, or even half a day for your letters, than run the risk of bringing on your cough again. Now do not you feel that you had? Yes, I am sure you are much too reasonable. You look as if you would not do such a thing again.'

'Oh! she *shall not* do such a thing again,' eagerly rejoined Mrs Elton. 'We will not allow her to do such a thing again:' – and nodding significantly – 'there must be some arrangement made, there must indeed. I shall speak to Mr E. The man who fetches our letters every morning (one of our men, I forget his name) shall enquire for your's too and bring them to you. That will obviate all difficulties you know; and from *us* I really think, my dear Jane, you can have no scruple to accept such an accommodation.'

'You are extremely kind,' said Jane; 'but I cannot give up my early walk. I am advised to be out of doors as much as I can, I must walk somewhere, and the post-office is an object; and upon my word, I have scarcely ever had a bad morning before.'

'My dear Jane, say no more about it. The thing is determined, that is (laughing affectedly) as far as I can presume to determine any thing without the concurrence of my lord and master. You know, Mrs Weston, you and I must be cautious how we express ourselves.

But I do flatter myself, my dear Jane, that my influence is not entirely worn out. If I meet with no insuperable difficulties therefore, consider that point as settled.'

'Excuse me,' said Jane earnestly, 'I cannot by any means consent to such an arrangement, so needlessly troublesome to your servant. If the errand were not a pleasure to me, it could be done, as it always is when I am not here, by my grandmamma's.'

'Oh! my dear; but so much as Patty has to do! – And it is a kindness to employ our men.'

Jane looked as if she did not mean to be conquered; but instead of answering, she began speaking again to Mr John Knightley.

'The post-office is a wonderful establishment!' said she. – 'The regularity and despatch of it! If one thinks of all that it has to do, and all that it does so well, it is really astonishing!'

'It is certainly very well regulated.'

'So seldom that any negligence or blunder appears! So seldom that a letter, among the thousands that are constantly passing about the kingdom is even carried wrong – and not one in a million, I suppose, actually lost! And when one considers the variety of hands, and of bad hands too, that are to be deciphered, it increases the wonder!'

'The clerks grow expert from habit. – They must begin with some quickness of sight and hand, and exercise improves them. If you want any further explanation,' continued he, smiling, 'they are paid for it. That is the key to a great deal of capacity. The public pays and must be served well.'

The varieties of hand-writing were farther talked of, and the usual observations made.

'I have heard it asserted,' said John Knightley, 'that the same sort of hand-writing often prevails in a family; and where the same master teaches, it is natural enough. But for that reason, I should imagine the likeness must be chiefly confined to the females, for boys have very little teaching after an early age, and scramble into any hand they can get. Isabella and Emma, I think, do write very much alike. I have not always known their writing apart.'

'Yes,' said his brother hesitatingly, 'there is a likeness. I know what you mean – but Emma's hand is the strongest.'

'Isabella and Emma both write beautifully,' said Mr Woodhouse; 'and always did. And so does poor Mrs Weston' – with half a sigh and half a smile at her.

'I never saw any gentleman's handwriting' – Emma began, looking also at Mrs Weston; but stopped, on perceiving that Mrs Weston was attending to someone else – and the pause gave her time to reflect, 'Now, how am I going to introduce him? – Am I unequal to speaking his name at once before all these people? Is it necessary for me to use any roundabout phrase? – Your Yorkshire friend – your correspondent in Yorkshire; – that would be the way, I suppose, if I were very bad. – No, I can pronounce his name without the smallest distress. I certainly get better and better. – Now for it.'

Mrs Weston was disengaged and Emma began again – 'Mr Frank Churchill writes one of the best gentlemen's hands I ever saw.'

'I do not admire it,' said Mr Knightley. 'It is too small – wants strength. It is like a woman's writing.'

This was not submitted to by either lady. They vindicated him against the base aspersion. 'No, it by no means wanted strength – it was not a large hand, but very clear and certainly strong. Had not Mrs Weston any letter about her to produce?' No, she had heard from him very lately, but having answered the letter, had put it away.

'If we were in the other room,' said Emma, 'if I had my writing-desk, I am sure I could produce a specimen. I have a note of his. – Do not you remember, Mrs Weston, employing him to write for you one day?'

'He chose to say he was employed' –

'Well, well, I have that note; and can shew it after dinner to convince Mr Knightley.'

'Oh! when a gallant young man, like Mr Frank Churchill,' said Mr Knightley drily, 'writes to a fair lady like Miss Woodhouse, he will, of course, put forth his best.'

Dinner was on table. – Mrs Elton, before she could be spoken to, was ready; and before Mr Woodhouse had reached her with his request to be allowed to hand her into the dining-parlour, was saying –

'Must I go first? I really am ashamed of always leading the way.'

Jane's solicitude about fetching her own letters had not escaped Emma. She had heard and seen it all; and felt some curiosity to know whether the wet walk of this morning had produced any. She suspected that it *had*; that it would not have been so resolutely encountered but in full expectation of hearing from someone very dear, and that it had not been in vain. She thought there was an air of greater happiness than usual – a glow both of complexion and spirits.

She could have made an enquiry or two, as to the expedition and the expense of the Irish mails; – it was at her tongue's end – but she abstained. She was quite determined not to utter a word that should hurt Jane Fairfax's feelings; and they followed the other ladies out of the room, arm in arm, with an appearance of good-will highly becoming to the beauty and grace of each.

CHAPTER THIRTY-FIVE

When the ladies returned to the drawing-room after dinner, Emma found it hardly possible to prevent their making two distinct parties: – with so much perseverance in judging and behaving ill did Mrs Elton engross Jane Fairfax and slight herself. She and Mrs Weston were obliged to be almost always either talking together or silent together. Mrs Elton left them no choice. If Jane repressed her for a little time, she soon began again; and though much that passed between them was in a half-whisper, especially on Mrs Elton's side, there was no avoiding a knowledge of their principal subjects: – The post-office – catching cold – fetching letters – and friendship, were long under discussion; and to them succeeded one, which must be at least equally unpleasant to Jane – enquiries whether she had yet heard of any situation likely to suit her, and professions of Mrs Elton's meditated activity.

'Here is April come!' said she, 'I get quite anxious about you. June will soon be here.'

'But I have never fixed on June or any other month – merely looked forward to the summer in general.'

'But have you really heard of nothing?'

'I have not even made any enquiry; I do not wish to make any yet.'

'Oh! my dear, we cannot begin too early; you are not aware of the difficulty of procuring exactly the desirable thing.'

'I not aware!' said Jane, shaking her head; 'dear Mrs Elton, who can have thought of it as I have done?'

'But you have not seen so much of the world as I have. You do not know how many candidates there always are for the *first* situations. I saw a vast deal of that in the neighbourhood round Maple Grove. A cousin of Mr Suckling, Mrs Bragge, had such an infinity of applications; every body was anxious to be in her family, for she moves in the first circle. Wax-candles in the schoolroom! You may imagine how desirable! Of all houses in the kingdom Mrs Bragge's is the one I would most wish to see you in.'

'Col. and Mrs Campbell are to be in town again by mid-summer,' said Jane. 'I must spend some time with them; I am sure they will want it; – afterwards I may probably be glad to dispose of myself. But I would not wish you to take the trouble of making any enquiries at present.'

'Trouble! aye, I know your scruples. You are afraid of giving me trouble; but I assure you, my dear Jane, the Campbells can hardly be more interested about you than I am. I shall write to Mrs Partridge in a day or two, and shall give her a strict charge to be on the look-out for any thing eligible.'

'Thank you, but I would rather you did not mention the subject to her; till the time draws nearer, I do not wish to be giving any body trouble.'

'But, my dear child, the time *is* drawing near; here is April, and June, or say even July, is very near, with such business to accomplish before us. Your inexperience really amuses me! A situation such as you deserve, and your friends would require for you, is no every day occurrence, is not obtained at a moment's notice; indeed, indeed, we must begin enquiring directly.'

'Excuse me, ma'am, but this is by no means my intention; I make no enquiry myself, and should be sorry to have any made by my friends. When I am quite determined as to the time, I am not at all afraid of being long unemployed. There are places in town, offices, where enquiry would soon produce something – Offices for the sale – not quite of human flesh – but of human intellect.'

'Oh! my dear, human flesh! You quite shock me; if you mean a fling at the slave-trade, I assure you Mr Suckling was always rather a friend to the abolition.'

'I did not mean, I was not thinking of the slave-trade,' replied Jane; 'governess-trade, I assure you, was all that I had in view; widely different certainly as to the guilt of those who carry it on; but as to the greater misery of the victims, I do not know where it lies. But I only mean to say that there are advertising offices, and that by applying to them I should have no doubt of very soon meeting with something that would do.'

'Something that would do!' repeated Mrs Elton. 'Aye, *that* may suit your humble ideas of yourself; – I know what a modest creature you are; but it will not satisfy your friends to have you taking up with any thing that may offer, any inferior, commonplace situation, in a family not moving in a certain circle, or able to command the elegancies of life.'

'You are very obliging; but as to all that, I am very indifferent; it would be no object to me to be with the rich; my mortifications,

I think, would only be the greater; I should suffer more from comparison. A gentleman's family is all that I should condition for.'

'I know you, I know you; you would take up with any thing; but I shall be a little more nice, and I am sure the good Campbells will be quite on my side; with your superior talents, you have a right to move in the first circle. Your musical knowledge alone would entitle you to name your own terms, have as many rooms as you like, and mix in the family as much as you chose; – that is – I do not know – if you knew the harp, you might do all that, I am very sure; but you sing as well as play; – yes, I really believe you might, even without the harp, stipulate for what you chose; – and you must and shall be delightfully, honourably and comfortably settled before the Campbells or I have any rest.'

'You may well class the delight, the honour, and the comfort of such a situation together,' said Jane, 'they are pretty sure to be equal; however, I am very serious in not wishing any thing to be attempted at present for me. I am exceedingly obliged to you, Mrs Elton, I am obliged to any body who feels for me, but I am quite serious in wishing nothing to be done till the summer. For two or three months longer I shall remain where I am, and as I am.'

'And I am quite serious too, I assure you,' replied Mrs Elton gaily, 'in resolving to be always on the watch, and employing my friends to watch also, that nothing really unexceptionable may pass us.'

In this style she ran on; never thoroughly stopped by any thing till Mr Woodhouse came into the room; her vanity had then a change of object, and Emma heard her saying in the same halfwhisper to Jane,

'Here comes this dear old beau of mine, I protest! – Only think of his gallantry in coming away before the other men! – what a dear creature he is; – I assure you I like him excessively. I admire all that quaint, old-fashioned politeness; it is much more to my taste than modern ease; modern ease often disgusts me. But this good old Mr Woodhouse, I wish you had heard his gallant speeches to me at dinner. Oh! I assure you I began to think my caro sposo would be absolutely jealous. I fancy I am rather a favourite; he took notice of my gown. How do you like it? – Selina's choice – handsome, I think, but I do not know whether it is not overtrimmed; I have the greatest dislike to the idea of being overtrimmed – quite a horror of finery. I must put on a few ornaments *now*, because it is expected of me. A bride, you know, must appear like a bride, but my natural taste is all for simplicity; a simple style of dress is so infinitely preferable to finery. But I am quite in the minority, I believe; few people seem to value simplicity of dress, – shew and finery are every thing. I have some notion of putting such a trimming as this to my white and silver poplin. Do you think it will look well?'

The whole party were but just reassembled in the drawing-room when Mr Weston made his appearance among them. He had returned to a late dinner, and walked to Hartfield as soon as it was over. He had been too much expected by the best judges, for surprize – but there was great joy. Mr Woodhouse was almost as glad to see him now, as he would have been sorry to see him before. John Knightley only was in mute astonishment. – That a man who might have spent his evening quietly at home after a day of business in London, should set off again, and walk half-a-mile to another man's house, for the sake of being in mixed company till bed-time, of finishing his day in the efforts of civility and the noise of numbers, was a circumstance to strike him deeply. A man who had been in motion since eight o'clock in the morning, and might now have been still, who had been long talking; and might have been silent, who had been in more than one crowd, and might have been alone! – Such a man, to quit the tranquillity and independence of his own fire-side, and on the evening of a cold sleety April day rush out again into the world! – Could he by a touch of his finger have instantly taken back his wife, there would have been a motive; but his coming would probably prolong rather than break up the party. John Knightley looked at him with amazement, then shrugged his shoulders, and said, 'I could not have believed it even of *him*.'

Mr Weston, meanwhile, perfectly unsuspicious of the indignation he was exciting, happy and cheerful as usual, and with all the right of being principal talker, which a day spent any where from home confers, was making himself agreeable among the rest; and having satisfied the inquiries of his wife as to his dinner, convincing her that none of all her careful directions to the servants had been forgotten, and spread abroad what public news he had heard, was proceeding to a family communication, which, though principally addressed to Mrs Weston, he had not the smallest doubt of being highly interesting to every body in the room. He gave her a letter, it was from Frank, and to herself; he had met with it in his way, and had taken the liberty of opening it.

'Read it, read it,' said he, 'it will give you pleasure; only a few lines – will not take you long; read it to Emma.'

The two ladies looked over it together; and he sat smiling and talking to them the whole time, in a voice a little subdued, but very audible to every body.

'Well, he is coming, you see; good news, I think. Well, what do you say to it? – I always told you he would be here again soon, did not I? – Anne, my dear, did not I always tell you so, and you would not believe me? – In town next week, you see – at the latest, I dare say; for *she* is as impatient as the black gentleman when any thing is to be done; most likely they will be there to-morrow or Saturday. As to her illness, all nothing of course. But it is an excellent thing to have Frank among us again, so near as town. They will stay a good while when they do come, and he will be half his time with us. This is precisely what I wanted. Well, pretty good news, is not it? Have you finished it? Has Emma read it all? Put it up, put it up; we will have a good talk about it some other time, but it will not do now. I shall only just mention the circumstance to the others in a common way.'

Mrs Weston was most comfortably pleased on the occasion. Her looks and words had nothing to restrain them. She was happy, she knew she was happy, and knew she ought to be happy. Her congratulations were warm and open; but Emma could not speak so fluently. *She* was a little occupied in weighing her own feelings, and trying to understand the degree of her agitation, which she rather thought was considerable.

Mr Weston, however, too eager to be very observant, too communicative to want others to talk, was very well satisfied with what she did say, and soon moved away to make the rest of his friends happy by a partial communication of what the whole room must have overheard already.

It was well that he took every body's joy for granted, or he might not have thought either Mr Woodhouse or Mr Knightley particularly delighted. They were the first entitled, after Mrs Weston and Emma, to be made happy; – from them he would have proceeded to Miss Fairfax, but she was so deep in conversation with John Knightley, that it would have been too positive an interruption; and finding himself close to Mrs Elton, and her attention disengaged, he necessarily began on the subject with her.

CHAPTER THIRTY-SIX

'I HOPE I SHALL SOON have the pleasure of introducing my son to you,' said Mr Weston.

Mrs Elton, very willing to suppose a particular compliment intended her by such a hope, smiled most graciously.

'You have heard of a certain Frank Churchill, I presume,' he continued – 'and know him to be my son, though he does not bear my name.'

'Oh! yes, and I shall be very happy in his acquaintance. I am sure Mr Elton will lose no time in calling on him; and we shall both have great pleasure in seeing him at the Vicarage.'

'You are very obliging. – Frank will be extremely happy, I am sure. – He is to be in town next week, if not sooner. We have notice of it in a letter to-day. I met the letters in my way this morning, and seeing my son's hand, presumed to open it – though it was not directed to me – it was to Mrs Weston. She is his principal correspondent, I assure you. I hardly ever get a letter.'

'And so you absolutely opened what was directed to her! oh! Mr Weston – (laughing affectedly) I must protest against that. – A most dangerous precedent indeed! – I beg you will not let your neighbours follow your example. – Upon my word, if this is what I am to expect, we married women must begin to exert ourselves! – Oh! Mr Weston, I could not have believed it of you!'

'Aye, we men are sad fellows. You must take care of yourself, Mrs Elton. – This letter tells us – it is a short letter – written in a hurry, merely to give us notice – it tells us that they are all coming up to town directly, on Mrs Churchill's account – she has not been well the whole winter, and thinks Enscombe too cold for her – so they are all to move southward without loss of time.'

'Indeed! – from Yorkshire, I think. Enscombe is in Yorkshire?'

'Yes, they are about 190 miles from London. A considerable journey.'

'Yes, upon my word, very considerable. Sixty-five miles farther than from Maple Grove to London. But what is distance, Mr Weston, to people of large fortune? – You would be amazed to hear how my brother, Mr Suckling, sometimes flies about. You will hardly believe me – but twice in one week he and Mr Bragge went to London and back again with four horses.'

'The evil of the distance from Enscombe,' said Mr Weston, 'is, that Mrs Churchill, *as we understand*, has not been able to leave the sopha for a week together. In Frank's last letter she complained, he said, of being too weak to get into her conservatory without having both his arm and his uncle's! This, you know, speaks a great degree of weakness – but now she is so impatient to be in town, that she means to sleep only two nights on the road. – So Frank writes word. Certainly, delicate ladies have very extraordinary constitutions, Mrs Elton. You must grant me that.'

'No, indeed, I shall grant you nothing. I always take the part of

'How my brother, Mr Suckling, sometimes flies about.'

my own sex. I do indeed. I give you notice – You will find me a formidable antagonist on that point. I always stand up for women – and I assure you, if you knew how Selina feels with respect to sleeping at an inn, you would not wonder at Mrs Churchill's making incredible exertions to avoid it. Selina says it is quite horror to her – and I believe I have caught a little of her nicety. She always travels with her own sheets; an excellent precaution. Does Mrs Churchill do the same?'

'Depend upon it, Mrs Churchill does every thing that any other fine lady ever did. Mrs Churchill will not be second to any lady in the land for' –

Mrs Elton eagerly interposed with,

'Oh! Mr Weston, do not mistake me. Selina is no fine lady, I assure you. Do not run away with such an idea.'

'Is not she? Then she is no rule for Mrs Churchill, who is as thorough a fine lady as any body ever beheld.'

Mrs Elton began to think she had been wrong in disclaiming so warmly. It was by no means her object to have it believed that her sister was *not* a fine lady; perhaps there was want of spirit in the pretence of it; – and she was considering in what way she had best retract, when Mr Weston went on.

'Mrs Churchill is not much in my good graces, as you may suspect – but this is quite between ourselves. She is very fond of Frank, and therefore I would not speak ill of her. Besides, she is out of health now; but *that* indeed, by her own account, she has always been. I would not say so to every body, Mrs Elton, but I have not much faith in Mrs Churchill's illness.'

'If she is really ill, why not go to Bath, Mr Weston? – To Bath, or to Clifton?'

'She has taken it into her head that Enscombe is too cold for her. The fact is, I suppose, that she is tired of Enscombe. She has now been a longer time stationary there, than she ever was before, and she begins to want change. It is a retired place. A fine place, but very retired.'

'Aye – like Maple Grove, I dare say. Nothing can stand more retired from the road than Maple Grove. Such an immense plantation all round it! You seem shut out from every thing – in the most complete retirement. – And Mrs Churchill probably has not health or spirits like Selina to enjoy that sort of seclusion. Or, perhaps she may not have resources enough in herself to be qualified for a country life. I always say a woman cannot have too many resources – and I feel very thankful that I have so many myself as to be quite independent of society.'

'Frank was here in February for a fortnight.'

'So I remember to have heard. He will find an *addition* to the society of Highbury when he comes again; that is, if I may presume to call myself an addition. But perhaps he may never have heard of there being such a creature in the world.'

This was too loud a call for a compliment to be passed by, and Mr Weston, with a very good grace, immediately exclaimed,

'My dear madam! Nobody but yourself could imagine such a thing possible. Not heard of you! – I believe Mrs Weston's letters lately have been full of very little else than Mrs Elton.'

He had done his duty and could return to his son.

'When Frank left us,' continued he, 'it was quite uncertain when we might see him again, which makes this day's news doubly welcome. It has been completely unexpected. That is, I always had a strong persuasion he would be here again soon, I was sure something favourable would turn up – but nobody believed me. He and Mrs Weston were both dreadfully desponding. 'How could he contrive to come? And how could it be supposed that his uncle and aunt would spare him again?' and so forth – I always felt that something would happen in our favour; and so it has, you see. I have observed, Mrs Elton, in the course of my life, that if things are going untowardly one month, they are sure to mend the next.'

'Very true, Mr Weston, perfectly true. It is just what I used to say to a certain gentleman in company in the days of courtship, when, because things did not go quite right, did not proceed with all the rapidity which suited his feelings, he was apt to be in despair, and exclaim that he was sure at this rate it would be *May* before Hymen's saffron robe would be put on for us! Oh! the pains I have been at to dispel those gloomy ideas and give him cheerfuller views! The carriage – we had disappointments about the carriage; – one morning, I remember, he came to me quite in despair.'

She was stopped by a slight fit of coughing, and Mr Weston instantly seized the opportunity of going on.

'You were mentioning May. May is the very month which Mrs Churchill is ordered, or has ordered herself, to spend in some warmer place than Enscombe – in short, to spend in London; so that we have the agreeable prospect of frequent visits from Frank the whole spring – precisely the season of the year which one should have chosen for it: days almost at the longest; weather genial and pleasant, always inviting one out, and never too hot for exercise. When he was here before, we made the best of it; but there was a good deal of wet, damp, cheerless weather; there always is in February, you know, and we could not do half that we intended. Now will be the time. This will be complete enjoyment; and I do not know, Mrs Elton, whether the uncertainty of our meetings, the sort of constant expectation there will be of his coming in to-day or to-morrow, and at any hour, may not be more friendly to happiness than having him actually in the house. I think it is so. I think it is the state of mind which gives most spirit and delight. I hope you will be pleased with my son; but you must not expect a prodigy. He is generally thought a fine young man, but do not expect a prodigy. Mrs Weston's partiality for him is very great, and, as you may suppose, most gratifying to me. She thinks nobody equal to him.'

'And I assure you, Mr Weston, I have very little doubt that my opinion will be decidedly in his favour. I have heard so much in praise of Mr Frank Churchill. – At the same time it is fair to observe, that I am one of those who always judge for themselves, and are by no means implicitly guided by others. I give you notice that as I find your son, so I shall judge of him. – I am no flatterer.'

Mr Weston was musing.

'I hope,' said he presently, 'I have not been severe upon poor Mrs Churchill. If she is ill I should be sorry to do her injustice; but there are some traits in her character which make it difficult for me to speak of her with the forbearance I could wish. You cannot be ignorant, Mrs Elton, of my connection with the family, nor of the treatment I have met with; and, between ourselves, the whole blame of it is to be laid to her. She was the instigator. Frank's mother would never have been slighted as she was but for her. Mr Churchill has pride; but his pride is nothing to his wife's: his is a quiet, indolent, gentleman-like sort of pride that would harm nobody, and only make himself a little helpless and tiresome; but her pride is arrogance and insolence! And what inclines one less to bear, she has no fair pretence of family or blood. She was nobody when he married her, barely the daughter of a gentleman; but ever since her being turned into a Churchill she has out-Churchill'd them all in high and mighty claims: but in herself, I assure you, she is an upstart.'

'Only think! well, that must be infinitely provoking! I have quite a horror of upstarts. Maple Grove has given me a thorough disgust to people of that sort; for there is a family in that neighbourhood who are such an annoyance to my brother and sister from the airs they give themselves! Your description of Mrs Churchill made me think of them directly. People of the name of Tupman, very lately settled there, and encumbered with many low connections, but giving themselves immense airs, and expecting to be on a footing with the old established families. A year and a half is the very utmost that they can have lived at West Hall; and how they got their fortune nobody knows. They came from Birmingham, which is not a place to promise much, you know, Mr Weston. One has not great hopes from Birmingham. I always say there is something direful in the sound: but nothing more is positively known of the Tupmans, though a good many things I assure you are suspected; and yet by their manners they evidently think themselves equal even to my brother, Mr Suckling, who happens to be one of their nearest neighbours. It is infinitely too bad. Mr Suckling, who has been eleven years a resident at Maple Grove, and whose father had it before him – I believe, at least – I am almost sure that old Mr Suckling had completed the purchase before his death.'

They were interrupted. Tea was carrying round, and Mr Weston, having said all that he wanted, soon took the opportunity of walking away.

After tea, Mr and Mrs Weston, and Mr Elton sat down with Mr Woodhouse to cards. The remaining five were left to their own powers, and Emma doubted their getting on very well; for Mr Knightley seemed little disposed for conversation; Mrs Elton was wanting notice, which nobody had inclination to pay, and she was herself in a worry of spirits which would have made her prefer being silent.

Mr John Knightley proved more talkative than his brother. He was to leave them early the next day; and he soon began with –

'Well, Emma, I do not believe I have any thing more to say about the boys; but you have your sister's letter, and every thing is down at full length there we may be sure. My charge would be much more concise than her's, and probably not much in the same spirit; all that I have to recommend being comprised in, do not spoil them, and do not physic them.'

'I rather hope to satisfy you both,' said Emma, 'for I shall do all in my power to make them happy, which will be enough for Isabella; and happiness must preclude false indulgence and physic.'

'And if you find them troublesome, you must send them home again.'

'That is very likely. You think so, do not you?'

'I hope I am aware that they may be too noisy for your father – or even may be some incumbrance to you, if your visiting-engagements continue to increase as much as they have done lately.'

'Increase!'

'Certainly; you must be sensible that the last half year has made a great difference in your way of life.'

'Difference! No indeed I am not.'

'There can be no doubt of your being much more engaged with company than you used to be. Witness this very time. Here am I come down for only one day, and you are engaged with a dinner-party! – When did it happen before, or any thing like it? Your neighbourhood is increasing, and you mix more with it. A little while ago, every letter to Isabella brought an account of fresh gaieties; dinners at Mr Cole's or balls at the Crown. The difference which Randalls, Randalls alone makes in your goings-on, is very great.'

'Yes,' said his brother quickly, 'it is Randalls that does it all.'

'Very well – and as Randalls, I suppose, is not likely to have less influence than heretofore, it strikes me as a possible thing, Emma, that Henry and John may be sometimes in the way. And if they are, I only beg you to send them home.'

'No,' cried Mr Knightley, 'that need not be the consequence. Let them be sent to Donwell. I shall certainly be at leisure.'

'Upon my word,' exclaimed Emma, 'you amuse me! I should like to know how many of all my numerous engagements take place without your being of the party; and why I am to be supposed in danger of wanting leisure to attend to the little boys. These amazing engagements of mine – what have they been? Dining once with the Coles – and having a ball talked of, which never took place. I can understand you – (nodding at Mr John Knightley) – your good fortune in meeting with so many of your friends at once here, delights you too much to pass unnoticed. But you, (turning to Mr Knightley,) who know how very, very seldom I am ever two hours from Hartfield, why you should foresee such a series of dissipation for me, I cannot imagine. And as to my dear little boys, I must say, that if aunt Emma has not time for them, I do not think they would fare much better with uncle Knightley, who is absent from home about five hours where she is absent one – and who, when he is at home, is either reading to himself or settling his accounts.'

Mr Knightley seemed to be trying not to smile; and succeeded without difficulty, upon Mrs Elton's beginning to talk to him.

CHAPTER THIRTY-SEVEN

A VERY LITTLE QUIET reflection was enough to satisfy Emma as to the nature of her agitation on hearing this news of Frank Churchill. She was soon convinced that it was not for herself she was feeling at all apprehensive or embarrassed; it was for him. Her own attachment had really subsided into a mere nothing; it was not worth thinking of; – but if he, who had undoubtedly been always so much the most in love of the two, were to be returning with the same warmth of sentiment which he had taken away, it would be very distressing. If a separation of two months should not have cooled him, there were dangers and evils before her: – caution for him and for herself would be necessary. She did not mean to have her own affections entangled again, and it would be incumbent on her to avoid any encouragement of his.

She wished she might be able to keep him from an absolute declaration. That would be so very painful a conclusion of their present acquaintance! – and yet, she could not help rather anticipating something decisive. She felt as if the spring would not pass without bringing a crisis, an event, a something to alter her present composed and tranquil state.

It was not very long, though rather longer than Mr Weston had foreseen, before she had the power of forming some opinion of Frank Churchill's feelings. The Enscombe family were not in town quite so soon as had been imagined, but he was at Highbury very soon afterwards. He rode down for a couple of hours; he could not yet do more; but as he came from Randalls immediately to Hartfield, she could then exercise all her quick observation, and speedily determine how he was influenced, and how she must act. They met with the utmost friendliness. There could be no doubt of his great pleasure in seeing her. But she had an almost instant doubt of his caring for her as he had done, of his feeling the same tenderness in the same degree. She watched him well. It was a clear thing he was less in love than he had been. Absence, with the conviction probably of her indifference, had produced this very natural and very desirable effect.

He was in high spirits; as ready to talk and laugh as ever, and seemed delighted to speak of his former visit, and recur to old stories: and he was not without agitation. It was not in his calmness that she read his comparative indifference. He was not calm; his spirits were evidently fluttered; there was restlessness about him. Lively as he was, it seemed a liveliness that did not satisfy himself; but what decided her belief on the subject, was his staying only a quarter of an hour, and hurrying away to make other calls in Highbury. 'He had seen a group of old acquaintance in the street as he passed – he had not stopped, he would not stop for more than a word – but he had the vanity to think they would be disappointed if he did not call, and much as he wished to stay longer at Hartfield, he must hurry off.'

She had no doubt as to his being less in love – but neither his agitated spirits, nor his hurrying away, seemed like a perfect cure; and she was rather inclined to think it implied a dread of her returning power, and a discreet resolution of not trusting himself with her long.

This was the only visit from Frank Churchill in the course of ten days. He was often hoping, intending to come – but was always prevented. His aunt could not bear to have him leave her. Such was his own account at Randalls. If he were quite sincere, if he really tried to come, it was to be inferred that Mrs Churchill's removal to London had been of no service to the wilful or nervous part of her disorder. That she was really ill was very certain; he had declared himself convinced of it, at Randalls. Though much might be fancy, he could not doubt, when he looked back, that she was in a weaker state of health than she had been half a year ago. He did not believe it to proceed from any thing that care and medicine might not remove, or at least that she might not have many years of existence before her; but he could not be prevailed on by all his father's doubts, to say that her complaints were merely imaginary, or that she was as strong as ever.

It soon appeared that London was not the place for her. She could not endure its noise. Her nerves were under continual irritation and suffering; and by the ten days' end, her nephew's letter to Randalls communicated a change of plan. They were going to remove immediately to Richmond. Mrs Churchill had been recommended to the medical skill of an eminent person there, and had otherwise a fancy for the place. A ready-furnished house in a favourite spot was engaged, and much benefit expected from the change.

Emma heard that Frank wrote in the highest spirits of this arrangement, and seemed most fully to appreciate the blessing of having two months before him of such near neighbourhood to many dear friends – for the house was taken for May and June. She was told that now he wrote with the greatest confidence of being often with them, almost as often as he could wish.

Emma saw how Mr Weston understood these joyous prospects. He was considering her as the source of all the happiness they offered. She hoped it was not so. Two months must bring it to the proof.

Mr Weston's own happiness was indisputable. He was quite delighted. It was the very circumstance he could have wished for. Now, it would be really having Frank in their neighbourhood. What were nine miles to a young man? – An hour's ride. He would be always coming over. The difference in that respect of Richmond and London was enough to make the whole difference of seeing him always and seeing him never. Sixteen miles – nay, eighteen – it must be full eighteen to Manchester-street – was a serious obstacle. Were he ever able to get away, the day would be spent in coming and returning. There was no comfort in having him in London; he might as well be at Enscombe; but Richmond was the very distance for easy intercourse. Better than nearer!

One good thing was immediately brought to a certainty by this removal, – the ball at the Crown. It had not been forgotten before, but it had been soon acknowledged vain to attempt to fix a day. Now, however, it was absolutely to be; every preparation was resumed, and, very soon after the Churchills had removed to Richmond, a few lines from Frank, to say that his aunt felt already much better for the change, and that he had no doubt of being able to join them for twenty-four hours at any given time, induced them to name as early a day as possible.

Mr Weston's ball was to be a real thing. A very few to-morrows stood between the young people of Highbury and happiness.

Mr Woodhouse was resigned. The time of year lightened the evil to him. May was better for every thing than February. Mrs Bates was engaged to spend the evening at Hartfield, James had due notice, and he sanguinely hoped that neither dear little Henry nor dear little John would have any thing the matter with them, while dear Emma were gone.

CHAPTER THIRTY-EIGHT

NO MISFORTUNE OCCURRED, again to prevent the ball. The day approached, the day arrived; and, after a morning of some anxious watching, Frank Churchill, in all the certainty of his own self, reached Randalls before dinner, and every thing was safe.

No second meeting had there yet been between him and Emma. The room at the Crown was to witness it; – but it would be better than a common meeting in a crowd. Mr Weston had been so very earnest in his entreaties for her early attendance, for her arriving there as soon as possible after themselves, for the purpose of taking her opinion as to the propriety and comfort of the rooms before any other persons came, that she could not refuse him, and must therefore spend some quiet interval in the young man's company. She was to convey Harriet, and they drove to the Crown in good time, the Randalls party just sufficiently before them.

Frank Churchill seemed to have been on the watch; and though he did not say much, his eyes declared that he meant to have a delightful evening. They all walked about together, to see that every thing was as it should be; and within a few minutes were joined by the contents of another carriage, which Emma could not hear the sound of at first, without great surprise. 'So unreasonably early!' she was going to exclaim; but she presently found that it was a family of old friends, who were coming, like herself, by particular desire, to help Mr Weston's judgment; and they were so very closely followed by another carriage of cousins, who had been entreated to come early with the same distinguishing earnestness, on the same errand, that it seemed as if half the company might soon be collected together for the purpose of preparatory inspection.

Emma perceived that her taste was not the only taste on which Mr Weston depended, and felt, that to be the favourite and intimate of a man who had so many intimates and confidantes, was not the very first distinction in the scale of vanity. She liked his open manners, but a little less of open-heartedness would have made him a higher character. – General benevolence, but not general friendship, made a man what he ought to be. – She could fancy such a man.

The whole party walked about, and looked, and praised again; and then, having nothing else to do, formed a sort of half circle round the fire, to observe in their various modes, till other subjects were started, that, though *May*, a fire in the evening was still very pleasant.

Emma found that it was not Mr Weston's fault that the number of privy counsellors was not yet larger. They had stopped at Mrs Bates's door to offer the use of their carriage, but the aunt and niece were to be brought by the Eltons.

Frank was standing by her, but not steadily; there was a restlessness, which showed a mind not at ease. He was looking about, he was going to the door, he was watching for the sound of other carriages, – impatient to begin, or afraid of being always near her.

Mrs Elton was spoken of. 'I think she must be here soon,' said he. 'I have a great curiosity to see Mrs Elton, I have heard so much of her. It cannot be long, I think, before she comes.'

A carriage was heard. He was on the move immediately; but coming back, said,

'I am forgetting that I am not acquainted with her. I have never seen either Mr or Mrs Elton. I have no business to put myself forward.'

Mr and Mrs Elton appeared; and all the smiles and the proprieties passed.

'But Miss Bates and Miss Fairfax!' said Mr Weston, looking about. 'We thought you were to bring them.'

The mistake had been slight. The carriage was sent for them now. Emma longed to know what Frank's first opinion of Mrs Elton might be; how he was affected by the studied elegance of her dress, and her smiles of graciousness. He was immediately qualifying himself to form an opinion, by giving her very proper attention, after the introduction had passed.

In a few minutes the carriage returned. – Somebody talked of rain. – 'I will see that there are umbrellas, sir,' said Frank to his father: 'Miss Bates must not be forgotten:' and away he went. Mr Weston was following; but Mrs Elton detained him, to gratify him by her opinion of his son; and so briskly did she begin, that the young man himself, though by no means moving slowly, could hardly be out of hearing.

'A very fine young man indeed, Mr Weston. You know I candidly told you I should form my own opinion; and I am happy to say that I am extremely pleased with him. – You may believe me. I never compliment. I think him a very handsome young man, and his manners are precisely what I like and approve – so truly the gentleman, without the least conceit or puppyism. You must know I have a vast dislike to puppies – quite a horror of them. They were never tolerated at Maple Grove. Neither Mr Suckling nor me had ever any patience with them; and we used sometimes to say very cutting things! Selina, who is mild almost to a fault, bore with them much better.'

While she talked of his son, Mr Weston's attention was chained; but when she got to Maple Grove, he could recollect that there were ladies just arriving to be attended to, and with happy smiles must hurry away.

Mrs Elton turned to Mrs Weston. 'I have no doubt of its being our carriage with Miss Bates and Jane. Our coachman and horses are so extremely expeditious! – I believe we drive faster than anybody. – What a pleasure it is to send one's carriage for a friend! – I understand you were so kind as to offer, but another time it will be quite unnecessary. You may be very sure I shall always take care of *them*.'

Miss Bates and Miss Fairfax, escorted by the two gentlemen, walked into the room; and Mrs Elton seemed to think it as much her duty as Mrs Weston's to receive them. Her gestures and movements might be understood by any one who looked on like Emma, but her words, every body's words, were soon lost under the incessant flow of Miss Bates, who came in, talking, and had not finished her speech under many minutes after her being admitted into the circle at the fire. As the door opened she was heard,

So very obliging of you! – No rain at all. Nothing to signify. I do not care for myself. Quite thick shoes. And Jane declares – Well! – (as soon as she was within the door) Well! This is brilliant indeed! – This is admirable! – Excellently contrived, upon my word. Nothing wanting. Could not have imagined it. – So well lighted up. – Jane, Jane, look – did you ever see any thing? Oh! Mr Weston, you must really have had Aladdin's lamp. Good Mrs Stokes would not know her own room again. I saw her as I came in; she was standing in the entrance. "Oh! Mrs Stokes," said I – but I had not time for more.' – She was now met by Mrs Weston. – 'Very well, I thank you, ma'am. I hope you are quite well. Very happy to hear it. So afraid you might have a headache! – seeing you pass by so often, and knowing how much trouble you must have. Delighted to hear it indeed. Ah! dear Mrs Elton, so obliged to you for the carriage! – excellent time. – Jane and I quite ready. Did not keep the horses a moment. Most comfortable carriage. – Oh! and I am sure our thanks

'Well! This is brilliant indeed!'

are due to you, Mrs Weston, on that score. Mrs Elton had most kindly sent Jane a note, or we should have been. – But two such offers in one day! – Never were such neighbours. I said to my mother, "Upon my word, ma'am –." Thank you, my mother is remarkably well. Gone to Mr Woodhouse's. I made her take her shawl – for the evenings are not warm – her large new shawl – Mrs Dixon's wedding present. – So kind of her to think of my mother! Bought at Weymouth, you know – Mr Dixon's choice. There were three others, Jane says, which they hesitated about some time. Colonel Campbell rather preferred an olive. My dear Jane, are you sure you did not wet your feet? – It was but a drop or two, but I am so afraid: – but Mr Frank Churchill was so extremely – and there was a mat to step upon – I shall never forget his extreme politeness. – Oh! Mr Frank Churchill, I must tell you my mother's spectacles have never been in fault since; the rivet never came out again. My mother often talks of your goodnature. Does not she, Jane? – Do not we often talk of Mr Frank Churchill? – Ah! here's Miss Woodhouse. – Dear Miss Woodhouse, how do you do? – Very well I thank you, quite well. This is meeting quite in fairy-land! – Such a transformation! – Must not compliment, I know – (eyeing Emma most complacently) – that would be rude – but upon my word, Miss Woodhouse, you do look – how do you like Jane's hair? – You are a judge. – She did it all herself. Quite wonderful how she does her hair! – No hairdresser from London I think could. – Ah! Dr Hughes I declare – and Mrs Hughes. Must go and speak to Dr and Mrs Hughes for a moment. – How do you do? How do you do? – Very well, I thank you. This is delightful, is not it? – Where's dear Mr Richard? – Oh! there he is. Don't disturb him. Much better employed talking to the young ladies. How do you do, Mr Richard? – I saw you the other day as you rode through the town – Mrs Otway, I protest! – and good Mr Otway, and Miss Otway and Miss Caroline. – Such a host of friends! – and Mr George and Mr Arthur! – How do you do? How do you all do? – Quite well, I am much obliged to you. Never better. – Don't I hear another carriage? – Who can this be? – very likely the worthy Coles. – Upon my word, this is charming to be standing about among such friends! And such a noble fire! – I am quite roasted. No coffee, I thank you, for me – never take coffee. – A little tea if you please sir, by and bye, – no hurry – Oh! here it comes. Everything so good!'

Frank Churchill returned to his station by Emma; and as soon as Miss Bates was quiet, she found herself necessarily overhearing the discourse of Mrs Elton and Miss Fairfax, who were standing a little way behind her. – He was thoughtful. Whether he were overhearing too, she could not determine. After a good many compliments to Jane on her dress and look, compliments very quietly and properly taken, Mrs Elton was evidently wanting to be complimented herself – and it was, 'How do you like my gown? – How do you like my trimming? – How has Wright done my hair?' – with many other relative questions, all answered with patient politeness. Mrs Elton then said,

'Nobody can think less of dress in general than I do – but upon such an occasion as this, when everybody's eyes are so much upon me, and in compliment to the Westons – who I have no doubt are giving this ball chiefly to do me honour – I would not wish to be inferior to others. And I see very few pearls in the room except mine. – So Frank Churchill is a capital dancer, I understand. – We shall see if our styles suit. – A fine young man certainly is Frank Churchill. I like him very well.'

At this moment Frank began talking so vigorously, that Emma could not but imagine he had overheard his own praises, and did not want to hear more; – and the voices of the ladies were drowned for awhile, till another suspension brought Mrs Elton's tones again distinctly forward. – Mr Elton had just joined them, and his wife was exclaiming,

'Oh! you have found us out at last, have you, in our seclusion? – I was this moment telling Jane, I thought you would begin to be impatient for tidings of us.'

'Jane!' – repeated Frank Churchill, with a look of surprise and displeasure. – 'That is easy – but Miss Fairfax does not disapprove it, I suppose.'

'How do you like Mrs Elton?' said Emma in a whisper.

'Not at all.'

'You are ungrateful.'

'Ungrateful! – What do you mean?' Then changing from a frown to a smile – 'No, do not tell me – I do not want to know what you mean. – Where is my father? – When are we to begin dancing?'

Emma could hardly understand him; he seemed in an odd humour. He walked off to find his father, but was quickly back again with both Mr and Mrs Weston. He had met with them in a little perplexity, which must be laid before Emma. It had just occurred to Mrs Weston that Mrs Elton must be asked to begin the ball; that she would expect it; which interfered with all their wishes of giving Emma that distinction. – Emma heard the sad truth with fortitude.

'And what are we to do for a proper partner for her?' said Mr Weston. 'She will think Frank ought to ask her.'

Frank turned instantly to Emma, to claim her former promise; and boasted himself an engaged man, which his father looked his most perfect approbation of – and it then appeared that Mrs Weston was wanting *him* to dance with Mrs Elton himself, and that their business was to help to persuade him into it, which was done pretty soon. – Mr Weston and Mrs Elton led the way, Mr Frank Churchill and Miss Woodhouse followed. Emma must submit to stand second to Mrs Elton, though she had always considered the ball as peculiarly for her. It was almost enough to make her think of marrying.

Mrs Elton had undoubtedly the advantage, at this time, in vanity completely gratified; for though she had intended to begin with Frank Churchill, she could not lose by the change. Mr Weston might be his son's superior. – In spite of this little rub, however, Emma was smiling with enjoyment, delighted to see the respectable length of the set as it was forming, and to feel that she had so many hours of unusual festivity before her. – She was more disturbed by Mr Knightley's not dancing, than by any thing else. – There he was, among the standers-by, where he ought not to be; he ought to be dancing, – not classing himself with the husbands, and fathers, and whist-players, who were pretending to feel an interest in the dance till their rubbers were made up, – so young as he looked! – He could not have appeared to greater advantage perhaps any where, than where he had placed himself. His tall, firm, upright figure, among the bulky forms and stooping shoulders of the elderly men, was such as Emma felt must draw every body's eyes; and, excepting her own partner, there was not one among the whole row of young men who could be compared with him. – He moved a few steps nearer, and those few steps were enough to prove in how gentleman-like a manner, with what natural grace, he must have danced, would he but take the trouble. – Whenever she caught his eye, she forced him to smile; but in general he was looking grave. She wished he could love a ballroom better, and could like Frank Churchill better. – He seemed often observing her. She must not flatter herself that he thought of her dancing, but if he were criticising her behaviour, she did not feel afraid. There was nothing like flirtation between her and her partner. They seemed more like cheerful, easy friends, than lovers. That Frank Churchill thought less of her than he had done, was indubitable.

The ball proceeded pleasantly. The anxious cares, the incessant attentions of Mrs Weston, were not thrown away. Every body seemed happy; and the praise of being a delightful ball, which is

Among the bulky forms and stooping shoulders.

seldom bestowed till after a ball has ceased to be, was repeatedly given in the very beginning of the existence of this. Of very important, very recordable events, it was not more productive than such meetings usually are. There was one, however, which Emma thought something of. – The two last dances before supper were begun, and Harriet had no partner; – the only young lady sitting down; – and so equal had been hitherto the number of dancers, that how there could be any one disengaged was the wonder! – But Emma's wonder lessened soon afterwards, on seeing Mr Elton sauntering about. He would not ask Harriet to dance if it were possible to be avoided: she was sure he would not – and she was expecting him every moment to escape into the card-room.

Escape, however, was not his plan. He came to the part of the room where the sitter-by were collected, spoke to some, and walked about in front of them, as if to show his liberty, and his resolution of maintaining it. He did not omit being sometimes directly before Miss Smith, or speaking to those who were close to her. – Emma saw it. She was not yet dancing; she was working her way up from the bottom, and had therefore leisure to look around, and by only turning her head a little she saw it all. When she was half way up the set, the whole group were exactly behind her, and she would no longer allow her eyes to watch; but Mr Elton was so near, that she heard every syllable of a dialogue which just then took place between him and Mrs Weston; and she perceived that his wife, who was standing immediately above her, was not only listening also, but even encouraging him by significant glances. – The kind-hearted, gentle Mrs Weston had left her seat to join him and say, 'Do not you dance, Mr Elton?' to which his prompt reply was, 'Most readily, Mrs Weston, if you will dance with me?'

'Me! – oh! no – I would get you a better partner than myself. I am no dancer.'

'If Mrs Gilbert wishes to dance,' said he, 'I shall have great pleasure, I am sure – for, though beginning to feel myself rather an old married man, and that my dancing days are over, it would give me very great pleasure at any time to stand up with an old friend like Mrs Gilbert.'

'Mrs Gilbert does not mean to dance, but there is a young lady disengaged whom I should be very glad to see dancing – Miss Smith.' 'Miss Smith! – oh! – I had not observed. – You are extremely obliging – and if I were not an old married man. – But my dancing days are over, Mrs Weston. You will excuse me. Any thing else I should be most happy to do, at your command – but my dancing days are over.'

Mrs Weston said no more; and Emma could imagine with what surprise and mortification she must be returning to her seat. This was Mr Elton! the amiable, obliging gentle Mr Elton. – She looked round for a moment; he had joined Mr Knightley at a little distance, and was arranging himself for settled conversation, while smiles of high glee passed between him and his wife.

She would not look again. Her heart was in a glow, and she feared her face might be as hot.

In another moment a happier sight caught her; – Mr Knightley leading Harriet to the set! – Never had she been more surprised, seldom more delighted, than at that instant. She was all pleasure and gratitude, both for Harriet and herself, and longed to be thanking him; and though too distant for speech, her countenance said much, as soon as she could catch his eye again.

His dancing proved to be just what she had believed it, extremely good; and Harriet would have seemed almost too lucky, if it had not been for the cruel state of things before, and for the very complete enjoyment and very high sense of the distinction which her happy features announced. It was not thrown away on her, she bounded higher than ever, flew farther down the middle, and was in a continual course of smiles.

Mr Elton had retreated into the cardroom, looking (Emma trusted) very foolish. She did not think he was quite so hardened as his wife, though growing very like her; – *she* spoke some of her feelings, by observing audibly to her partner,

'Knightley had taken pity on poor little Miss Smith! – Very goodnatured, I declare.'

Supper was announced. The move began; and Miss Bates might be heard from that moment, without interruption, till her being seated at table and taking up her spoon.

'Jane, Jane, my dear Jane, where are you? – Here is your tippet. Mrs Weston begs you to put on your tippet. She says she is afraid there will be draughts in the passage, though every thing has been done – One door nailed up – Quantities of matting – My dear Jane, indeed you must. Mr Churchill, oh! you are too obliging! How well you put it on! – so gratified! Excellent dancing indeed! – Yes, my dear, I ran home, as I said I should, to help grandmamma to bed, and got back again, and nobody missed me. – I set off without a word, just as I told you. Grandmamma was quite well, had a charming evening with Mr Woodhouse, a vast deal of chat, and backgammon. – Tea was made down stairs, biscuits and baked apples and wine before she came away: amazing luck in some of her throws: and she enquired a great deal about you, how you were amused, and who were your partners. "Oh!" said I, "I shall not forestall Jane; I left her dancing with Mr George Otway; she will love to tell you all about it herself to-morrow: her first partner was Mr Elton, I do not know who will ask her next, perhaps Mr William Cox." My dear sir, you are too obliging. – Is there nobody you would not rather? – I am not helpless. Sir, you are most kind. Upon my word, Jane on one arm and me on the other! – Stop, stop, let us stand a little back, Mrs Elton is going; dear Mrs Elton, how elegant she looks! – Beautiful lace! – Now we all follow in her train. Quite the queen of the evening! – Well, here we are at the passage. Two steps, Jane, take care of the two steps. Oh! no, there is but one. Well, I was persuaded there were two. How very odd! I was convinced there were two, and there is but one. I never saw any thing equal to the comfort and style – Candles every where. – I was telling you of your grandmamma, Jane. – There was a little disappointment. – The baked apples and biscuits, excellent in their way, you know; but there was a delicate fricassee of sweetbread and some asparagus brought in at first, and good Mr Woodhouse, not thinking the asparagus quite boiled enough, sent it all out again. Now there is nothing grandmamma loves better than sweetbread and asparagus – so she was rather disappointed, but we agreed we would not speak of it to any body, for fear of its getting round to dear Miss Woodhouse, who would be so very much concerned! – Well, this is brilliant! I am all amazement! could not have supposed any thing! – Such elegance and profusion! – I have seen nothing like it since – Well, where shall we sit? where shall we sit? Any where so that Jane is not in a draught. Where *I* sit is of no consequence. Oh! do you recommend this side? – Well, I am sure, Mr Churchill – only it seems too good – but just as you please. What you direct in this house cannot be wrong. Dear Jane, how shall we ever recollect half the dishes for grandmamma? Soup too! Bless me! I should not be helped so soon, but it smells most excellent, and I cannot help beginning.'

Emma had no opportunity of speaking to Mr Knightley till after supper; but, when they were all in the ball-room again, her eyes invited him irresistibly to come to her and be thanked. He was warm in his reprobation of Mr Elton's conduct; it had been unpardonable rudeness; and Mrs Elton's looks also received the due share of censure.

'They aimed at wounding more than Harriet,' said he. 'Emma, why is it that they are your enemies?'

He looked with smiling penetration; and, on receiving no answer, added, '*She* ought not to be angry with you, I suspect, whatever he may be. – To that surmise, you say nothing, of course; but confess, Emma, that you did want him to marry Harriet.'

'I did,' replied Emma, 'and they cannot forgive me.'

He shook his head; but there was a smile of indulgence with it, and he only said,

'I shall not scold you. I leave you to your own reflections.'

'Can you trust me with such flatterers? – Does my vain spirit ever tell me I am wrong?'

'Not your vain spirit, but your serious spirit. – If one leads you wrong, I am sure the other tells you of it.'

'I do own myself to have been completely mistaken in Mr Elton. There is a littleness about him which you discovered, and which I did not: and I was fully convinced of his being in love with Harriet. It was through a series of strange blunders!'

'And, in return for your acknowledging so much, I will do you the justice to say, that you would have chosen for him better than he has chosen for himself. – Harriet Smith has some first-rate qualities, which Mrs Elton is totally without. An unpretending, single-minded, artless girl – infinitely to be preferred by any man of sense and taste to such a woman as Mrs Elton. I found Harriet more conversable than I expected.'

Emma was extremely gratified. – They were interrupted by the bustle of Mr Weston calling on every body to begin dancing again.

'Come Miss Woodhouse, Miss Otway, Miss Fairfax, what are you all doing? – Come Emma, set your companions the example. Every body is lazy. Every body is asleep!'

'I am ready,' said Emma, 'whenever I am wanted.'

'Whom are you going to dance with?' asked Mr Knightley.

She hesitated a moment, and then replied, 'With you, if you will ask me.'

'Will you?' said he, offering his hand.

'Indeed I will. You have shown that you can dance, and you know we are not really so much brother and sister as to make it at all improper.'

'Brother and sister! no, indeed.'

CHAPTER THIRTY-NINE

THIS LITTLE EXPLANATION with Mr Knightley gave Emma considerable pleasure. It was one of the agreeable recollections of the ball, which she walked about the lawn the next morning to enjoy. – She was extremely glad that they had come to so good an understanding respecting the Eltons, and that their opinions of both husband and wife were so much alike; and his praise of Harriet, his concession in her favour, was peculiarly gratifying. The impertinence of the Eltons, which for a few minutes had threatened to ruin the rest of her evening, had been the occasion of some of its highest satisfactions; and she looked forward to another happy result – the cure of Harriet's infatuation. – From Harriet's manner of speaking of the circumstance before they quitted the ball-room, she had strong hopes. It seemed as if her eyes were suddenly opened, and she were enabled to see that Mr Elton was not the superior creature she had believed him. The fever was over, and Emma could harbour little fear of the pulse being quickened again by injurious courtesy. She depended on the evil feelings of the Eltons for supplying all the discipline of pointed neglect that could be further requisite. – Harriet rational, Frank Churchill not too much in love, and Mr Knightley not wanting to quarrel with her, how very happy a summer must be before her!

She was not to see Frank Churchill this morning. He had told her that he could not allow himself the pleasure of stopping at Hartfield, as he was to be at home by the middle of the day. She did not regret it.

Having arranged all these matters, looked them through, and put them all to rights, she was just turning to the house with spirits freshened up for the demands of the two little boys, as well as of their grandpapa, when the great iron sweepgate opened, and two persons entered who she had never less expected to see together – Frank Churchill, with Harriet leaning on his arm – actually Harriet! – A moment sufficed to convince her that something extraordinary had happened. Harriet looked white and frightened, and he was trying to cheer her. – The iron gates and the front door were not twenty yards asunder; – they were all three soon in the hall, and Harriet immediately sinking into a chair fainted away.

A young lady who faints, must be recovered; questions must be answered, and surprises be explained. Such events are very interesting, but the suspense of them cannot last long. A few minutes made Emma acquainted with the whole.

Miss Smith, and Miss Bickerton, another parlour boarder at Mrs Goddard's who had been also at the ball, had walked out together, and taken a road, the Richmond road, which, though apparently public enough for safety, had led them into alarm. – About half a mile beyond Highbury, making a sudden turn, and deeply shaded by elms on each side, it became for a considerable stretch very retired; and when the young ladies had advanced some way into it, they had suddenly perceived at a small distance before them, on a broader patch of greensward by the side, a party of gipsies. A child on the watch, came towards them to beg; and Miss Bickerton, excessively frightened, gave a great scream, and calling on Harriet to follow her, ran up a steep bank, cleared a slight hedge at the top, and made the best of her way by a short cut back to Highbury. But poor Harriet could not follow. She had suffered very much from cramp after dancing, and her first attempt to mount the bank brought on such a return of it as made her absolutely powerless –

and in this state, and exceedingly terrified, she had been obliged to remain.

How the trampers might have behaved, had the young ladies been more courageous, must be doubtful; but such an invitation for attack could not be resisted; and Harriet was soon assailed by half a dozen children, headed by a stout woman and a great boy, all clamorous, and impertinent in look, though not absolutely in word. – More and more frightened, she immediately promised them money, and

Harriet was soon assailed.

taking out her purse, gave them a shilling, and begged them not to want more, or to use her ill. – She was then able to walk, though but slowly, and was moving away – but her terror and her purse were too tempting, and she was followed, or rather surrounded, by the whole gang, demanding more.

In this state Frank Churchill had found her, she trembling and conditioning, they loud and insolent. By a most fortunate chance his leaving Highbury had been delayed so as to bring him to her assistance at this critical moment. The pleasantness of the morning had induced him to walk forward, and leave his horses to meet him by another road, a mile or two beyond Highbury – and happening to have borrowed a pair of scissars the night before of Miss Bates, and to have forgotten to restore them, he had been obliged to stop at her door, and go in for a few minutes: he was therefore later than he had intended; and being on foot, was unseen by the whole party till almost close to them. The terror which the woman and boy had been creating in Harriet was then their own portion. He had left them completely frightened; and Harriet eagerly clinging to him, and hardly able to speak, had just strength enough to reach Hartfield, before her spirits were quite overcome. It was his idea to bring her to Hartfield: he had thought of no other place.

This was the amount of the whole story, – of his communication and of Harriet's as soon as she had recovered her senses and speech. – He dared not stay longer than to see her well; these several delays left him not another minute to lose; and Emma engaging to give assurance of her safety to Mrs Goddard, and notice of there being such a set of people in the neighbourhood to Mr Knightley, he set off, with all the grateful blessings that she could utter for her friend and herself.

Such an adventure as this, – a fine young man and a lovely young woman thrown together in such a way, could hardly fail of suggesting certain ideas to the coldest heart and the steadiest brain. So Emma thought, at least. Could a linguist, could a grammarian, could even a mathematician have seen what she did, have witnessed their appearance together, and heard their history of it, without feeling that circumstances had been at work to make them peculiarly interesting to each other? – How much more must an imaginist, like herself, be on fire with speculation and foresight! – especially with such a ground-work of anticipation as her mind had already made.

It was a very extraordinary thing! Nothing of the sort had ever occurred before to any young ladies in the place, within her memory; no rencontre, no alarm of the kind; – and now it had happened to the very person, and at the very hour, when the other very person was chancing to pass by to rescue her! – It certainly was very extraordinary! – And knowing, as she did, the favourable state of mind of each at this period, it struck her the more. He was wishing to get the better of his attachment to herself, she just recovering from her mania for Mr Elton. It seemed as if every thing united to promise the most interesting consequences. It was not possible that the occurrence should not be strongly recommending each to the other.

In the few minutes' conversation which she had yet had with him, while Harriet had been partially insensible, he had spoken of her terror, her naïveté, her fervor as she seized and clung to his arm, with a sensibility amused and delighted; and just at last, after Harriet's own account had been given, he had expressed his indignation at the abominable folly of Miss Bickerton in the warmest terms. Every thing was to take its natural course, however, neither impelled nor assisted. She would not stir a step, nor drop a hint. No, she had had enough of interference. There could be no harm in a scheme, a mere passive scheme. It was no more than a wish. Beyond it she would on no account proceed.

Emma's first resolution was to keep her father from the knowledge of what had passed, – aware of the anxiety and alarm it would occasion; but she soon felt that concealment must be impossible. Within half an hour it was known all over Highbury. It was the very event to engage those who talk most, the young and the low; and all the youth and servants in the place were soon in the happiness of frightful news. The last night's ball seemed lost in the gipsies. Poor Mr Woodhouse trembled as he sat, and, as Emma had foreseen, would scarcely be satisfied without their promising never to go beyond the shrubbery again. It was some comfort to him that many enquiries after himself and Miss Woodhouse (for his neighbours knew that he loved to be enquired after), as well as Miss Smith, were coming in during the rest of the day; and he had the pleasure of returning for answer, that they were all very indifferent – which, though not exactly true, for she was perfectly well, and Harriet not much otherwise, Emma would not interfere with. She had an unhappy state of health in general for the child of such a man, for she hardly know what indisposition was; and if he did not invent illnesses for her, she could make no figure in a message.

The gipsies did not wait for the operations of justice; they took themselves off in a hurry. The young ladies of Highbury might have walked again in safety before their panic began, and the whole history dwindled soon into a matter of little importance but to

Emma and her nephews; – in her imagination it maintained its ground, and Henry and John were still asking every day for the story of Harriet and the gipsies, and still tenaciously setting her right if she varied in the slightest particular from the original recital.

CHAPTER FORTY

A VERY FEW DAYS HAD passed after this adventure, when Harriet came one morning to Emma with a small parcel in her hand, and after sitting down and hesitating, thus began:

'Miss Woodhouse – if you are at leisure – I have something that I should like to tell you – a sort of confession to make – and then, you know, it will be over.'

Emma was a good deal surprized; but begged her to speak. There was a seriousness in Harriet's manner which prepared her, quite as much as her words, for something more than ordinary.

'It is my duty, and I am sure it is my wish,' she continued, 'to have no reserves with you on this subject. As I am happily quite an altered creature in *one respect*, it is very fit that you should have the satisfaction of knowing it. I do not want to say more than is necessary – I am too much ashamed of having given way as I have done, and I dare say you understand me.'

'Yes,' said Emma, 'I hope I do.'

'How I could so long a time be fancying myself! . . .' cried Harriet, warmly, 'It seems like madness! I can see nothing at all extraordinary in him now. – I do not care whether I meet him or not – except that of the two I had rather not see him – and indeed I would go any distance round to avoid him – but I do not envy his wife in the least; I neither admire her nor envy her, as I have done: she is very charming, I dare say, and all that, but I think her very ill-tempered and disagreeable – I shall never forget her look the other night! – However, I assure you, Miss Woodhouse, I wish her no evil. – No, let them be ever so happy together, it will not give me another moment's pang: and to convince you that I have been speaking truth, I am now going to destroy – what I ought to have destroyed long ago – what I ought never to have kept – I know that very well (blushing as she spoke), – However, now I will destroy it all – and it is my particular wish to do it in your presence, that you may see how rational I am grown. Cannot you guess what this parcel holds?' said she, with a conscious look.

'Not the least in the world. – Did he every give you any thing?'

'No – I cannot call them gifts; but they are things that I have valued very much.'

She held the parcel towards her, and Emma read the words *Most precious treasures* on the top. Her curiosity was greatly excited. Harriet unfolded the parcel, and she looked on with impatience. Within abundance of silver paper was a pretty little Tunbridge-ware box, which Harriet opened: it was well lined with the softest cotton: but, excepting the cotton, Emma saw only a small piece of court plaister.

'Now,' said Harriet, 'you *must* recollect.'

'No, indeed I do not.'

'Dear me! I should not have thought it possible you could forget what passed in this very room about court plaister, one of the very last times we ever met in it! – It was but a very few days before I had my sore throat – just before Mr and Mrs John Knightley came – I think the very evening. – Do not you remember his cutting his finger with your new penknife, and your recommending court plaister? – But as you had none about you, and knew I had, you desired me to supply him; and so I took mine out and cut him a piece; but it was a great deal too large, and he cut it smaller and kept playing some time with what was left, before he gave it back to me. And so then, in my nonsense, I could not help making a treasure of it – so I put it by never to be used, and looked at it now and then as a great treat.'

'My dearest Harriet!' cried Emma, putting her hand before her face, and jumping up, 'you make me more ashamed of myself than I can bear. Remember it? Ay, I remember it all now; all except your saving this relick – I knew nothing of that till this moment – but the cutting the finger, and my recommending court plaister, and saying I had none about me! – Oh! my sins, my sins! – And I had plenty all the while in my pocket! – One of my senseless tricks! – I deserve to be under a continual blush all the rest of my life. – Well – (sitting down again) go on – what else?'

'And had you really some at hand yourself? – I am sure I never suspected it, you did it so naturally.'

'And so you actually put this piece of court plaister by for his sake!' said Emma, recovering from her state of shame and feeling divided wonder and amusement. And secretly she added to herself, 'Lord bless me! when should I ever have thought of putting by in cotton a piece of court plaister that Frank Churchill had been pulling about! – I never was equal to this.'

'Here,' resumed Harriet, turning to her box again, 'here is something still more valuable. I mean that *has been* more valuable, because this is what did really once belong to him, which the court plaister never did.'

Emma was quite eager to see this superior treasure. It was the end of an old pencil, – the part without any lead.

'This was really his,' said Harriet. – 'Do not you remember one morning? – no, I dare say you do not. But one morning – I forget exactly the day – but perhaps it was the Tuesday or Wednesday before *that evening*, he wanted to make a memorandum in his pocket-book; it was about spruce beer. Mr Knightly had been telling him something about brewing spruce beer, and he wanted to put it down; but when he took out his pencil, there was so little lead that he soon cut it all away, and it would not do, so you lent him another, and this was left upon the table as good for nothing. But I kept my eye on it; and, as soon as I dared, caught it up, and never parted with it again from that moment.'

'I do remember it,' cried Emma; 'I perfectly remember it. – Talking about spruce beer. – Oh! yes – Mr Knightly and I both saying we liked it, and Mr Elton's seeming resolved to learn to like it too. I perfectly remember it. – Stop; Mr Knightley was standing just here, was not he? – I have an idea he was standing just here.'

'Ah! I do not know, I cannot recollect. – It is very odd, but I cannot recollect. – Mr Elton was sitting here, I remember, much about where I am now.' –

'Well, go on.'

'Oh! that's all. I have nothing more to show you, or to say – except that I am now going to throw them both behind the fire, and I wish you to see me do it.'

'My poor dear Harriet! and have you actually found happiness in treasuring up these things?'

'Yes, simpleton as I was! – but I am quite ashamed of it now, and wish I could forget as easily as I can burn them. It was very wrong of me, you know, to keep any remembrances, after he was married. I knew it was – but had not resolution enough to part with them.'

'But, Harriet, is it necessary to burn the court plaister? – I have not a word to say for the bit of old pencil, but the court plaister might be useful.'

'I shall be happier to burn it,' replied Harriet. 'It has a disagreeable look to me. I must get rid of every thing. – There it goes, and there is an end, thank Heaven! of Mr Elton.'

'And when,' thought Emma, 'will there be a beginning of Mr Churchill?'

She had soon afterwards reason to believe that the beginning was already made, and could not but hope that the gipsy, though she had *told* no fortune, might be proved to have made Harriet's. – About a fortnight after the alarm, they came to a sufficient explanation, and quite undesignedly. Emma was not thinking of it at the moment, which made the information she received more valuable. She merely said, in the course of some trivial chat. 'Well, Harriet, whenever you marry I would advise you to do so and so' – and thought no more of it, till after a minute's silence she heard Harriet say in a very serious tone, 'I shall never marry.'

Emma then looked up, and imemdiately saw how it was; and after a moment's debate, as to whether it should pass unnoticed or not, replied,

'Never marry! – This is a new resolution.'

'It is one that I shall never change, however.'

After another short hesitation, 'I hope it does not proceed from – I hope it is not in compliment to Mr Elton?'

'Mr Elton, indeed!' cried Harriet indignantly. – 'Oh! no' – and Emma could just catch the words, 'so superior to Mr Elton!'

She then took a longer time for consideration. Should she proceed no farther? – should she let it pass, and seem to suspect nothing? – Perhaps Harriet might think her cold or angry if she did; or perhaps if she were totally silent, it might only drive Harriet into asking her to hear too much; and against any thing like such an unreserve as had been, such an open and frequent discussion of hopes and changes, she was perfectly resolved. – She believed it would be wiser for her to say and know at once, all that she meant to say and know. Plain dealing was always best. She had previously determined how far she would proceed, on any application of the sort; and it would be safer for both, to have the judicious law of her own brain laid down with speed. – She was decided, and thus spoke –

'Harriet, I will not affect to be in doubt of your meaning. Your resolution, or rather your expectation of never marrying, results from an idea that the person whom you might prefer, would be too greatly your superior in situation to think of you. Is not it so?'

'Oh! Miss Woodhouse, believe me I have not the presumption to suppose – Indeed I am not so mad. – But it is a pleasure to me to admire him at a distance – and to think of his infinite superiority to all the rest of the world, with the gratitude, wonder and veneration, which are so proper, in me especially.'

'I am not at all surprised at you, Harriet. The service he rendered you was enough to warm your heart.'

'Service! oh! it was such an inexpressible obligation! – The very recollection of it, and all that I felt at the time – when I saw him coming – his noble look – and my wretchedness before. Such a change! In one moment such a change! From perfect misery to perfect happiness.'

'It is very natural. It is natural, and it is honourable. – Yes, honourable, I think, to choose so well and so gracefully. – But that it will be a fortunate preference is more than I can promise. I do not advise you to give way to it, Harriet. I do not by any means engage for its being returned. Consider what you are about. Perhaps it will be wisest in you to check your feelings while you can; at any rate do not let them carry you far, unless you are persuaded of his liking you. Be observant of him. Let his behaviour be the guide of your sensations. I give you this caution now, because I shall never speak of you again on the subject. I am determined against all interference. Henceforward I know nothing of the matter. Let no name ever pass our lips. We were very wrong before; we will be cautious now. – He is your superior, no doubt, and there do seem objections and obstacles of a very serious nature; but yet, Harriet, more wonderful things have taken place, there have been matches of greater disparity. But take care of yourself. I would not have you too sanguine; though, however it may end, be assured that your raising your thought to *him*, is a mark of good taste which I shall always know how to value.'

Harriet kissed her hand in silent and submissive gratitude. Emma was very decided in thinking such an attachment no bad thing for her friend. Its tendency would be to raise and refine her mind – and it must be saving her from the danger of degradation.

CHAPTER FORTY-ONE

IN THIS STATE OF SCHEMES, and hopes, and connivance, June opened upon Hartfield. To Highbury in general it brought no material change. The Eltons were still talking of a visit from the Sucklings, and of the use to be made of their barouche-landau; and Jane Fairfax was still at her grandmother's; and as the return of the Campbells from Ireland was again delayed, and August, instead of Midsummer, fixed for it, she was likely to remain there full two months longer, provided at least she were able to defeat Mrs Elton's activity in her service, and save herself from being hurried into a delightful situation against her will.

Mr Knightley, who, for some reason best known to himself, had certainly taken an early dislike to Frank Churchill, was only growing to dislike him more. He began to suspect him of some double dealing in his pursuit of Emma. That Emma was his object appeared undisputable. Every thing declared it; his own attentions, his father's hints, his mother-in-law's guarded silence; it was all in unison; words, conduct, discretion, and indiscretion, told the same story. But while so many were devoting him to Emma, and Emma herself making him over to Harriet, Mr Knightley began to suspect him of some inclination to trifle with Jane Fairfax. He could not understand it; but there were symptoms of intelligence between them – he thought so at least – symptoms of admiration on his side, which, having once observed, he could not persuade himself to think entirely void of meaning, however he might wish to escape any of Emma's errors of imagination. *She* was not present when the suspicion first arose. He was dining with the Randalls' family, and Jane, at the Eltons'; and he had seen a look, more than a single look, at Miss Fairfax, which, from the admirer of Miss Woodhouse, seemed somewhat out of place. When he was again in their company, he could not help remembering what he had seen; nor could he avoid observations which, unless it were like Cowper and his fire at twilight,

'Myself creating what I saw,'

brought him yet stronger suspicion of there being a something of private liking, of private understanding even, between Frank Churchill and Jane.

He had walked up one day after dinner, as he very often did, to spend his evening at Hartfield. Emma and Harriet were going to walk; he joined them; and, on returning, they fell in with a larger party, who, like themselves, judged it wisest to take their exercise early, as the weather threatened rain; Mr and Mrs Weston and their son, Miss Bates and her niece, who had accidentally met. They all united; and, on reaching Hartfield gates, Emma, who knew it was exactly the sort of visiting that would be welcome to her father, pressed them all to go in and drink tea with him. The Randalls party agreed to it immediately; and after a pretty long speech from Miss Bates, which few persons listened to, she also found it possible to accept dear Miss Woodhouse's most obliging invitation.

As they were turning into the grounds, Mr Perry passed by on horseback. The gentlemen spoke of his horse.

Mr Perry passed by on horseback.

'By the bye,' said Frank Churchill to Mrs Weston presently, 'what became of Mr Perry's plan of setting up his carriage?'

Mrs Weston looked surprised, and said, 'I did not know that he ever had any such plan.'

'Nay, I had it from you. You wrote me word of it three months ago.'

'Me! impossible!'

'Indeed you did. I remember it perfectly. You mentioned it as what was certainly to be very soon. Mrs Perry had told somebody, and was extremely happy about it. It was owing to *her* persuasion, as she thought his being out in bad weather did him a great deal of harm. You must remember it now?'

'Upon my word I never heard of it till this moment.'

'Never! really, never! – Bless me! how could it be? – Then I must have dreamt it – but I was completely persuaded – Miss Smith, you walk as if you were tired. You will not be sorry to find yourself at home.'

'What is this? – What is this?' cried Mr Weston, 'about Perry and a carriage? Is Perry going to set up his carriage, Frank? I am glad he can afford it. You had it from himself, had you?'

'No, sir', replied his son laughing, 'I seem to have had it from nobody. – Very odd! – I really was persuaded of Mrs Weston's having mentioned it in one of her letters to Enscombe, many weeks ago, with all these particulars – but as she declares she never heard a syllable of it before, of course it must have been a dream. I am a great dreamer. I dream of every body at Highbury when I am away – and when I have gone through my particular friends, then I begin dreaming of Mr and Mrs Perry.'

'It is odd though,' observed his father, 'that you should have had such a regular connected dream about people whom it was not very likely you should be thinking of at Enscombe. Perry's setting up his carriage! and his wife's persuading him to it, out of care for his health – just what will happen, I have no doubt, some time or other; only a little premature. What an air of probability sometimes runs through a dream! and at others, what a heap of absurdities it is! Well, Frank, your dream certainly shows that Highbury is in your thoughts when you are absent. Emma, you are a great dreamer, I think?'

Emma was out of hearing. She had hurried on before her guests to prepare her father for their appearance, and was beyond the reach of Mr Weston's hint.

'Why, to own the truth,' cried Miss Bates, who had been trying in vain to be heard the last two minutes, 'if I must speak on this subject, there is no denying that Mr Frank Churchill might have – I do not mean to say that he did not dream it – I am sure I have sometimes the oddest dreams in the world – but if I am questioned about it, I must acknowledge that there was such an idea last spring; for Mrs Perry herself mentioned it to my mother, and the Coles knew of it as well as ourselves – but it was quite a secret, known to nobody else, and only thought of about three days. Mrs Perry was very anxious that he should have a carriage, and came to my mother in great spirits one morning because she thought she had prevailed. Jane, don't you remember grandmamma's telling us of it when we got home? – I forget where we had been walking to – very likely to Randalls; yes, I think it was to Randalls. Mrs Perry was always particularly fond of my mother – indeed I do not know who is not – and she had mentioned it to her in confidence; she had no objection to her telling us, of course, but it was not to go beyond: and, from that day to this, I never mentioned it to a soul that I know of. At the same time, I will not positively answer for my having never dropt a hint, because I know I do sometimes pop out a thing before I am aware. I am a talker, you know; I am rather a talker; and now and then I have let a thing escape me which I should not. I am not like Jane; I wish I were. I will answer for it *she* never betrayed the least thing in the world. Where is she? – Oh! just behind. Perfectly remember Mrs Perry's coming. – Extraordinary dream indeed!'

They were entering the hall. Mr Knightly's eyes had preceded Miss Bates's in a glance at Jane. From Frank Churchill's face, where he thought he saw confusion suppressed or laughed away, he had involuntarily turned to her's; but she was indeed behind, and too busy with her shawl. Mr Weston had walked in. The two other gentlemen waited at the door to let her pass. Mr Knightley suspected in Frank Churchill the determination of catching her eye – he seemed watching her intently – in vain, however, if it were so – Jane passed between them into the hall, and looked at neither.

There was no time for further remark or explanation. The dream must be borne with, and Mr Knightley must take his seat with the rest round the large modern circular table which Emma had introduced at Hartfield, and which none but Emma could have had power to place there and persuade her father to use, instead of the small-sized Pembroke, on which two of his daily meals had, for forty years, been crowded. Tea passed pleasantly, and nobody seemed in a hurry to move.

'Miss Woodhouse,' said Frank Churchill, after examining a table behind him, which he could reach as he sat, 'have your nephews taken away their alphabets – their box of letters? It used to stand here. Where is it? This is a sort of dull-looking evening, that ought to be treated rather as winter than summer. We had great amusement with those letters one morning. I want to puzzle you again.'

Emma was pleased with the thought; and producing the box, the table was quickly scattered over with alphabets, which no one seemed so much disposed to employ as their two selves. They were rapidly forming words for each other, or for any body else who would be puzzled. The quietness of the game made it particularly eligible for Mr Woodhouse, who had often been distressed by the more animated sort, which Mr Weston had occasionally introduced, and who now sat happily occupied in lamenting, with tender melancholy, over the departure of the 'poor little boys,' or in fondly pointing out, as he took up any stray letter near him, how beautifully Emma had written it.

Frank Churchill placed a word before Miss Fairfax. She gave a slight glance round the table, and applied herself to it. Frank was next to Emma. Jane opposite to them – and Mr Knightly so placed as to see them all; and it was his object to see as much as he could, with as little apparent observation. The word was discovered, and with a faint smile pushed away. If meant to be immediately mixed with the others, and buried from sight, she should have looked on the table instead of looking just across, for it was not mixed; and Harriet, eager after every fresh word, and finding out none, directly took it up, and fell to work. She was sitting by Mr Knightley, and turned to him for help. The word was *blunder*; and as Harriet exultingly proclaimed it, there was a blush on Jane's cheek which gave it a meaning not otherwise ostensible. Mr Knightley connected it with the dream; but how it could all be, was beyond his comprehension. How the delicacy, the discretion of his favourite could have been so lain asleep! He feared there must be some decided involvement. Disingenuousness and double-dealing seemed to meet him at every turn. These letters were but the vehicle for gallantry and trick. It was a child's play, chosen to conceal a deeper game on Frank Churchill's part.

With great indignation did he continue to observe him; with great alarm and distrust, to observe also his two blinded companions. He saw a short word prepared for Emma, and given to her with a look sly and demure. He saw that Emma had soon made it out, and found it highly entertaining, though it was something which she judged it proper to appear to censure; for she said, 'Nonsense! for shame!' He heard Frank Churchill next say, with a glance towards Jane, 'I will give it to her – shall I?' – and as clearly heard Emma, opposing it with eager laughing warmth. 'No, no, you must not; you shall not, indeed.'

It was done however. This gallant young man, who seemed to love without feeling, and to recommend himself without complaisance, directly handed over the word to Miss Fairfax, and with a particular degree of sedate civility entreated her to study it. Mr Knightley's excessive curiosity to know what this word might be, made him seize every possible moment for darting his eye towards it, and it was not long before he saw it to be *Dixon*. Jane Fairfax's perception seemed to accompany his; her comprehension was certainly more equal to the covert meaning, the superior intelligence of those five letters so arranged. She was evidently displeased; looked up, and seeing herself watched, blushed more deeply than he had ever perceived her, and saying only, 'I did not know that proper names were allowed,' pushed away the letters with even an angry spirit, and looked resolved to be engaged by no other word that could be offered. Her face was averted from those who had made the attack, and turned towards her aunt.

'Ay, very true, my dear,' cried the latter, though Jane had not spoken a word – 'I was just going to say the same thing. It is time for us to be going indeed. The evening is closing in, and grandmamma will be looking for us. My dear sir, you are too obliging. We really must wish you good night.'

Jane's alertness in moving, proved her as ready as her aunt had preconceived. She was immediately up, and wanting to quit the table; but so many were also moving, that she could not get away; and Mr Knightley thought he saw another collection of letters anxiously pushed towards her, and resolutely swept away by her unexamined. She was afterwards looking for her shawl – Frank Churchill was looking also – it was growing dusk, and the room was in confusion; and how they parted, Mr Knightley could not tell.

He remained in Hartfield after all the rest, his thoughts full of what he had seen; so full, that when the candles came to assist his observations, he must – yes, he certainly must, as a friend – an anxious friend – give Emma some hint, ask her some question. He could not see her in a situation of such danger, without trying to preserve her. It was his duty.

'Pray, Emma,' said he, 'may I ask in what lay the great amusement, the poignant sting of the last word given to you and Miss Fairfax? I saw the word, and am curious to know how it could be so very entertaining to the one, and so very distressing to the other.'

Emma was extremely confused. She could not endure to give him the true explanation; for though her suspicions were by no means removed, she was really ashamed of having ever imparted them.

'Oh!' she cried in evident embarrassment, 'it all meant nothing; a mere joke among ourselves.'

'The joke,' he replied gravely, 'seemed confined to you and Mr Churchill.'

He had hoped she would speak again, but she did not. She would rather busy herself about any thing than speak. He sat a little while in doubt. A variety of evils crossed his mind. Interference – fruitless interference. Emma's confusion, and the acknowledged intimacy, seemed to declare her affection engaged. Yet he would speak. He owed it to her, to risk any thing that might be involved in an unwelcome interference, rather than her welfare; to encounter any thing, rather than the remembrance of neglect in such a cause.

'My dear Emma,' said he at last, with earnest kindness, 'do you think you perfectly understand the degree of acquaintance between the gentleman and lady we have been speaking of?'

'Between Mr Frank Churchill and Miss Fairfax. Oh – yes, perfectly. – Why do you make a doubt of it?'

'Have you never at any time had reason to think that he admired her, or that she admired him?'

'Never, never!' – she cried with a most open eagerness – 'Never, for the twentieth part of a moment, did such an idea occur to me. And how could it possibly come into your head?'

'I have lately imagined that I saw symptoms of attachment between them – certain expressive looks, which I did not believe meant to be public.'

'Oh! you amuse me excessively. I am delighted to find that you can vouchsafe to let your imagination wander – but it will not do – very sorry to check you in your first essay – but indeed it will not do. There is no admiration between them, I do assure you, and the appearances which have caught you, have arisen from some peculiar circumstances – feelings rather of a totally different nature: – it is impossible exactly to explain: – there is a good deal of nonsense in it – but the part which is capable of being communicated, which is sense, is, that they are as far from any attachment or admiration for one another, as any two beings in the world can be. That is, I *presume* it to be so on her side, and I can *answer* for its being so on his. I will answer for the gentleman's indifference.'

She spoke with a confidence which staggered, with a satisfaction which silenced, Mr Knightley. She was in gay spirits, and would have prolonged the conversation, wanting to hear the particulars of his suspicions, every look described, and all the wheres and hows of a circumstance which highly entertained her; but his gaity did not meet her's. He found he could not be useful, and his feelings were too much irritated for talking. That he might not be irritated into an absolute fever, by the fire which Mr Woodhouse's tender habits required almost every evening throughout the year, he soon afterwards took a hasty leave, and walked home to the coolness and solitude of Donwell Abbey.

CHAPTER FORTY-TWO

After being long fed with hopes of a speedy visit from Mr and Mrs Suckling, the Highbury world were obliged to endure the mortification of hearing that they could not possibly come till the autumn. No such importation of novelties could enrich their intellectual stores at present. In the daily interchange of news, they must be again restricted to the other topics with which for a while the Sucklings' coming had been united, such as the last accounts of Mrs Churchill, whose health seemed every day to supply a different report, and the situation of Mrs Weston, whose happiness it was to be hoped might eventually be as much increased by the arrival of a child, as that of all her neighbours was by the approach of it.

Mrs Elton was very much disappointed. It was the delay of a great deal of pleasure and parade. Her introductions and recommendations must all wait, and every projected party be still only talked of. So she thought at first: – but a little consideration convinced her that every thing need not be put off. Why should not they explore to Box Hill though the Sucklings did not come? They could go there again with them in the autumn. It was settled that they should go to Box Hill. That there was to be such a party had been long generally known: it had even given the idea of another. Emma had never been to Box Hill; she wished to see what every body found so well worth seeing, and she and Mr Weston had agreed to choose some fine morning and drive thither. Two or three more of the chosen only were to be admitted to join them, and it was to be done in a quiet, unpretending, elegant way, infinitely superior to the bustle and preparation, the regular eating and drinking, and picnic parade of the Eltons and the Sucklings.

This was so very well understood between them, that Emma could not but feel some surprize, and a little displeasure, on hearing from Mr Weston that he had been proposing to Mrs Elton, as her brother and sister had failed her, that the two parties should unite, and go together; and that as Mrs Elton had very readily acceded to it, so it was to be, if she had no objection. Now, as her objection was nothing but her very great dislike of Mrs Elton, of which Mr Weston must already be perfectly aware, it was not worth bringing forward again: – it could not be done without reproof to him, which would be giving pain to his wife; and she found herself therefore obliged to consent to an arrangement which she would have done a great deal to avoid; an arrangement which would probably expose her even to the degradation of being said to be of Mrs Elton's party! Every feeling was offended; and the forbearance of her outward submission left a heavy arrear due of secret severity in her reflections on the unmanageable good-will of Mr Weston's temper.

'I am glad you approve of what I have done,' said he very comfortably. 'But I thought you would. Such schemes as these are nothing without numbers. One cannot have too large a party. A large party secures its own amusement. And she is a good-natured woman after all. One could not leave her out.'

Emma denied none of it aloud, and agreed to none of it in private.

It was now the middle of June, and the weather fine; and Mrs Elton was growing impatient to name the day, and settle with Mr Weston as to pigeon-pies and cold lamb, when a lame carriage-horse threw every thing into sad uncertainty. It might be weeks, it might be only a few days, before the horse were useable, but no preparations could be ventured on, and it was all melancholy stagnation. Mrs Elton's resources were inadequate to such an attack.

'Is not this most vexatious, Knightly?' she cried. – 'And such weather for exploring! – These delays and disappointments are quite odious. What are we to do? – The year will wear away at this rate, and nothing done. Before this time last year I assure you we had had a delightful exploring party from Maple Grove to Kings Weston.'

'You had better explore to Donwell,' replied Mr Knightley. 'That may be done without horses. Come, and eat my strawberries. They are ripening fast.'

If Mr Knightley did not begin seriously, he was obliged to proceed so, for his proposal was caught at with delight; and 'Oh! I should like it of all things,' was not plainer in words than manner. Donwell was famous for its strawberry-beds, which seemed a plea for the invitation: but no plea was necessary; cabbage-beds would have been enough to tempt the lady, who only wanted to be going somewhere. She promised him again and again to come – much oftener than he doubted – and was extremely gratified by such a proof of intimacy, such a distinguishing compliment as she chose to consider it.

'You may depend upon me,' said she. 'I certainly will come. Name your day, and I will come. You will allow me to bring Jane Fairfax?'

'I cannot name a day,' said he, 'till I have spoken to some others whom I would wish to meet you.'

'Oh! leave all that to me. Only give me a carte-blanche. – I am

Lady Patroness, you know. It is my party. I will bring friends with me.'

'I hope you will bring Elton,' said he: – 'but I will not trouble you to give any other invitations.'

'Oh! now you are looking very sly. But consider; – you need not be afraid of delegating power to *me*. I am no young lady on her preferment. Married women, you know, may be safely authorized. It is my party. Leave it all to me. I will invite your guests.'

'No,' – he calmly replied, – 'there is but one married woman in the world whom I can allow to invite what guests she pleases to Donwell, and that one is – '

'Oh, now you are looking very sly.'

'– Mrs Weston, I suppose,' interrupted Mrs Elton, rather mortified.

'No – Mrs Knightley; – and, till she is in being, I will manage such matters myself.'

'Ah! you are an odd creature!' she cried, satisfied to have no one preferred to herself. – 'You are a humorist, and may say what you like. Quite a humorist. Well, I shall bring Jane with me – Jane and her aunt. – The rest I leave to you. I have no objections at all to meeting the Hartfield family. Don't scruple. I know you are attached to them.'

'You certainly will meet them if I can prevail; and I shall call on Miss Bates on my way home.'

'That's quite unnecessary; I see Jane every day. – but as you like. It is to be a morning scheme, you know, Knightley; quite a simple thing. I shall wear a large bonnet, and bring one of my little baskets hanging on my arm. Here, – probably this basket with pink ribbon. Nothing can be more simple, you see. And Jane will have such another. There is to be no form or parade – a sort of gipsy party. – We are to walk about your gardens, and gather the strawberries ourselves, and sit under trees; – and whatever else you may like to provide, it is to be all out of doors – a table spread in the shade, you know. Every thing as natural and simple as possible. Is not that your idea?'

'Not quite. My idea of the simple and the natural will be to have the table spread in the dining-room. The nature and the simplicity of gentlemen and ladies, with their servants and furniture, I think is best observed by meals within doors. When you are tired of eating strawberries in the garden, there shall be cold meat in the house.'

'Well – as you please; only don't have a great set out. And, by the bye, can I or my housekeeper be of any use to you with our opinion? – Pray be sincere, Knightley. If you wish me to talk to Mrs Hodges, or to inspect anything – .'

'I have not the least wish for it, I thank you.'

'Well – but if any difficulties should arise, my housekeeper is extremely clever.'

'I will answer for it, that mine thinks herself full as clever, and would spurn anybody's assistance.'

'I wish we had a donkey. The thing would be for us all to come on donkies, Jane, Miss Bates, and me – and my caro sposo walking by. I really must talk to him about purchasing a donkey. In a country life I conceive it to be a sort of necessary; for, let a woman have ever so many resources, it is not possible for her to be always shut up at home; – and very long walks, you know – in summer there is dust, and in winter there is dirt.'

'You will not find either, between Donwell and Highbury. Donwell-lane is never dusty, and now it is perfectly dry. Come on a donkey, however, if you prefer it. You can borrow Mrs Cole's. I would wish every thing to be as much to your taste as possible.'

'That I am sure you would. Indeed I do you justice, my good friend. Under that peculiar sort of dry, blunt manner, I know you have the warmest heart. As I tell Mr E., you are a thorough humourist. – Yes, believe me, Knightley, I am fully sensible of your attention to me in the whole of this scheme. You have hit upon the very thing to please me.'

Mr Knightley had another reason for avoiding a table in the shade. He wished to persuade Mr Woodhouse, as well as Emma, to join the party; and he knew that to have any of them sitting down out of doors to eat would inevitably make him ill. Mr Woodhouse must not, under the specious pretence of a morning drive, and an hour or two spent at Donwell, be tempted away to his misery.

He was invited on good faith. No lurking horrors were to upbraid him for his easy credulity. He did consent. He had not been at Donwell for two years. 'Some very fine morning, he, and Emma, and Harriet, could go very well; and he could sit still with Mrs Weston, while the dear girls walked about the gardens. He did not suppose they could be damp now, in the middle of the day. He should like to see the old house again exceedingly, and should be very happy to meet Mr and Mrs Elton, and any other of his neighbours. – He could not see any objection at all to his, and Emma's, and Harriet's, going there some very fine morning. He thought it very well done of Mr Knightley to invite them – very kind and sensible – much cleverer than dining out. – He was not fond of dining out.'

Mr Knightley was fortunate in every body's most ready concurrence. The invitation was every where so well received, that it seemed as if, like Mrs Elton, they were all taking the scheme as a particular compliment to themselves. – Emma and Harriet professed very high expectations of pleasure from it; and Mr Weston, unasked, promised to get Frank over to join them, if possible, a proof of approbation and gratitude which could have been dispensed with. – Mr Knightley was then obliged to say that he should be glad to see him; and Mr Weston engaged to lose no time in writing, and spare no arguments to induce him to come.

In the meanwhile the lame horse recovered so fast, that the party to Box Hill was again under happy consideration; and at last

Donwell was settled for one day, and Box Hill for the next, – the weather appearing exactly right.

Under a bright mid-day sun, at almost Midsummer, Mr Woodhouse was safely conveyed in his carriage, with one window down, to partake of this al-fresco party; and in one of the most comfortable rooms in the Abbey, especially prepared for him by a fire all the morning, he was happily placed, quite at his ease, ready to talk with pleasure of what had been achieved, and advise every body to come and sit down, and not to heat themselves. – Mrs Weston, who seemed to have walked there on purpose to be tired, and sit all the time with him, remained, when all the others were invited or persuaded out, his patient listener and sypathizer.

It was so long since Emma had been at the Abbey, that as soon as she was satisfied to her father's comfort, she was glad to leave him, and look around her; eager to refresh and correct her memory with more particular observation, more exact understanding of a house and grounds which must ever be so interesting to her and all her family.

She felt all the honest pride and complacency which her alliance with the present and future proprietor could fairly warrant, as she viewed the respectable size and style of the building, its suitable, becoming, characteristic situation, low and sheltered – its ample gardens stretching down to meadows washed by a stream, of which the Abbey, with all the old neglect of prospect, had scarcely a sight – and its abundance of timber in rows and avenues, which neither fashion nor extravagance had rooted up. – The house was larger than Hartfield, and totally unlike it, covering a good deal of ground, rambling and irregular, with many comfortable and one or two handsome rooms. – It was just what it ought to be, and it looked what it was – and Emma felt an increasing respect for it, as the residence of a family of such true gentility, untainted in blood and understanding. – Some faults of temper John Knightley had; but Isabella had connected herself unexceptionably. She had given them neither men, nor names, nor places, that could raise a blush. There were pleasant feelings, and she walked about and indulged them till it was necessary to do as the others did, and collect round the strawberry beds. – The whole party were assembled, excepting Frank Churchill, who was expected every moment from Richmond; and Mrs Elton, in all her apparatus of happiness, her large bonnet and her basket, was very ready to lead the way in gathering, accepting, or talking – strawberries, and only strawberries, could now be thought or spoken of. – 'The best fruit in England – every body's favourite – always wholesome. – These the finest beds and finest sorts. – Delightful to gather for one's self – the only way of really enjoying them. – Morning decidedly the best time – never tired – every sort good – hautboy infinitely superior – no comparison – the others hardly eatable – hautboys very scarce – Chili preferred – white wood finest flavour of all – price of strawberris in London – abundance about Bristol – Maple Grove – cultivation – beds when to be renewed – gardeners thinking exactly different – no general rule – gardeners never to be put out of their way – delicious fruit – only too rich to be eaten much of – inferior to cherries – currants more refreshing – only objection to gathering strawberries the stooping – glaring sun – tired to death – could bear it no longer – must go and sit in the shade.'

Such, for half an hour, was the conversation – interrupted only once by Mrs Weston, who came out, in her solicitude after her son-in-law, to inquire if he were come – and she was a little uneasy. – She had some fears of his horse.

Seats tolerably in the shade were found; and now Emma was obliged to overhear what Mrs Elton and Jane Fairfax were talking of. – A situation, a most desirable situation, was in question. Mrs Elton had received notice of it that morning, and was in raptures. It was not with Mrs Suckling, it was not with Mrs Bragge, but in felicity and splendour it fell short only of them: it was with a cousin of Mrs Bragge, and acquaintance of Mrs Suckling, a lady known at Maple Grove. Delightful, charming, superior, first circles, spheres, lines, ranks, every thing – Mrs Elton was wild to have the offer closed with immediately. – On her side, all was warmth, energy and triumph – and she positively refused to take her friend's negative, though Miss Fairfax continued to assure her that she would not at present engage in any thing, repeating the same motives which she had been heard to urge before.

– Still Mrs Elton insisted on being authorized to write an acquiescence by the morrow's post. – How Jane could bear it all, was astonishing to Emma. – She did look vexed, she did speak pointedly – and at last, with a decision of action unusual to her, proposed a removal. – 'Should not they walk? – Would not Mr Knightley show them the gardens – all the gardens? – She wished to see the whole extent.' – The pertinacity of her friend seemed more than she could bear.

It was hot; and after walking some time over the gardens in a scattered, dispersed way, scarcely any three together, they insensibly followed one another to the delicious shade of a broad short avenue of limes, which stretching beyond the garden at an equal distance from the river, seemed the finish of the pleasure grounds. – It led to nothing; nothing but a view at the end of a low stone wall with high pillars, which seemed intended, in their erection, to give the appearance of an approach to the house, which never had been there. Disputable, however, as might be the taste of such a termination, it was in itself a charming walk, and the view which closed it extremely pretty. – The considerable slope, at nearly the foot of which the Abbey stood, gradually acquired a steeper form beyond its grounds; and at half a mile distant was a bank of considerable abruptness and grandeur, well clothed with wood; – and at the bottom of this bank, favourably placed and sheltered, rose the Abbey-Mill Farm, with meadows in front, and the river making a close and handsome curve around it.

It was a sweet view – sweet to the eye and the mind. English verdure, English culture, English comfort, seen under a sun bright, without being oppressive.

In this walk Emma and Mr Weston found all the others assembled; and towards this view she immediately perceived Mr Knightley and Harriet distinct from the rest, quietly leading the way. Mr Knightley and Harriet! – It was an odd tête-à-tête, but she was glad to see it. – There had been a time when he would have scorned her as a companion, and turned from her with little ceremony. Now they seemed in pleasant conversation. There had been a time also when Emma would have been sorry to see Harriet in a spot so favourable for the Abbey-Mill Farm; but now she feared it not. It might be safely viewed with all its appendages of prosperity and beauty, its rich pastures, spreading flocks, orchard in blossom, and light column of smoke ascending. – She joined them at the wall, and found them more engaged in talking than in looking around. He was giving Harriet information as to modes of agriculture, &c. and Emma received a smile which seemed to say. 'These are my own concerns. I have a right to talk on such subjects, without being suspected of introducing Robert Martin.' – She did not suspect him. It was too old a story. – Robert Martin had probably ceased to think of Harriet. – They took a few turns together along the walk. – The shade was most refreshing, and Emma found it the pleasantest part of the day.

The next remove was to the house; they must all go in and eat; – and they were all seated and busy, and still Frank Churchill did not come. Mrs Weston looked, and looked in vain. His father would not own himself uneasy, and laughed at her fears; but she could not be cured of wishing that he would part with his black mare. He had expressed himself as to coming, with more than common certainty. 'His aunt was so much better, that he had not a doubt of getting over to them.' – Mrs Churchill's state, however, as many were ready to remind her, was liable to such sudden variation as might disappoint her nephew in the most reasonable dependence – and Mrs Weston was at last persuaded to believe, or to say, that it must be some attack of Mrs Churchill that he was prevented coming. – Emma looked at Harriet while the point was under consideration; she behaved very well and betrayed no emotion.

The cold repast was over, and the party were to go out once more to see what had not yet been seen, the old Abbey fish-ponds; perhaps get as far as the clover, which was to be begun cutting on the morrow, or, at any rate, have the pleasure of being hot, and growing cool again. – Mr Woodhouse, who had already taken his little round in the highest part of the gardens, where no damps from the river were imagined even by him, stirred no more; and his daughter resolved to remain with him, that Mrs Weston might be persuaded away by her husband to the exercise and variety her spirits seemed to need.

Mr Knightley had done all in his power for Mr Woodhouse's entertainment. Books of engravings, drawers of medals, cameos, corals, shells, and every other family collection within his cabinets, had been prepared for his old friend, to while away the morning; and the kindness had perfectly answered. Mr Woodhouse had been exceedingly well amused. Mrs Weston had been showing them all to him, and now he would show them all to Emma: – fortunate in having no other resemblance to a child, than in a total want of taste for what he saw, for he was slow, constant, and methodical. – Before this second looking over was begun, however, Emma walked into the hall for the sake of a few moments' free observations of the entrance and ground-plot of the house – and was hardly there, when Jane Fairfax appeared, coming quickly in from the garden, and with a look of escape. – Little expecting to meet Miss Woodhouse so soon, there was a start at first; but Miss Woodhouse was the very person she was in quest of.

'Will you be so kind,' said she, 'When I am missed, as to say that I am gone home? – I am going this moment. – My aunt is not aware how late it is, nor how long we have been absent – but I am sure we shall be wanted, and I am determined to go directly. – I have said nothing about it to any body. It would only be giving trouble and distress. Some are gone to the ponds, and some to the lime walk. Till the all come in I shall not be missed; and when they do, will you have the goodness to say that I am gone?'

'Certainly, if you wish it; – but you are not going to walk to Highbury alone?'

'Yes – what should hurt me? – I walk fast. I shall be at home in twenty minutes.'

'But it is too far, indeed it is, to be walking quite alone. Let my father's servant go with you. – Let me order the carriage. It can be round in five minutes.'

'Thank you, thank you – but on no account – I would rather walk. – And for *me* to be afraid of walking alone! – I, who may so soon have to guard others!'

She spoke with great agitation; and Emma very feelingly replied, 'That can be no reason for your being exposed to danger now. I must order the carriage. The heat even would be danger. – You are fatigued already.'

'I am' – she answered – 'I am fatigued; but it is not the sort of fatigue – quick walking will refresh me. – Miss Woodhouse, we all know at times what it is to be wearied in spirits. Mine, I confess, are exhausted. The greatest kindness you can show me, will be to let me have my own way, and only say that I am gone when it is necessary.'

Emma had not another word to oppose. She saw it all; and entering into her feelings, promoted her quitting the house immediately, and watched her safely off with the zeal of a friend. Her parting look was grateful – and her parting words, 'Oh! Miss Woodhouse, the comfort of being sometimes alone!' – seemed to burst from an overcharged heart, and to describe somewhat of the continual endurance to be practised by her even towards some of those who loved her best.

'Such a home, indeed! such an aunt!' said Emma, as she turned back into the hall again. 'I do pity you. And the more sensibility you betray of their just horrors, the more I shall like you.'

Jane had not been gone a quarter of an hour, and they had only accomplished some views of St Mark's Place, Venice, when Frank Churchill entered the room. Emma had not been thinking of him, she had forgotten to think of him – but she was very glad to see him. Mrs Weston would be at ease. The black mare was blameless; *they* were right who had named Mrs Churchill as the cause. He had been detained by a temporary increase of illness in her, a nervous seizure, which had lasted some hours – and he had quite given up every thought of coming, till very late; – and had he known how hot a ride he should have, and now late, with all his hurry, he must be, he believed he should not have come at all. The heat was excessive; he had never suffered any thing like it – almost wished he had staid at home – nothing killed him like heat – he could bear any degree of cold, &c. but heat was intolerable – and he sat down, at the greatest possible distance from the slight remains of Mr Woodhouse's fire, looking very deplorable.

'You will soon be cooler, if you sit still,' said Emma.

'As soon as I am cooler I shall go back again. I could very ill be spared – but such a point had been made of my coming! You will all be going soon I suppose; the whole party breaking up. I met *one* as I came – Madness in such weather! – – absolute madness!'

Emma listened, and looked, and soon perceived that Frank Churchill's state might be best defined by the expressive phrase of being out of humour. Some people were always cross when they were hot. Such might be his constitution; and as she knew that eating and drinking were often the cure of such incidental complaints, she recommended his taking some refreshment; he would find abundance of every thing in the dining-room – and she humanely pointed out the door.

'No – he should not eat. He was not hungry; it would only make him hotter.' In two minutes, however, he relented in his own favour; and muttering something about spruce beer, walked off. Emma returned all her attention to her father, saying in secret –

'I am glad I have done being in love with him. I should not like a man who is so soon discomposed by a hot morning. Harriet's sweet easy temper will not mind it.'

He was gone long enough to have had a very comfortable meal, and came back all the better – grown quite cool – and, with good manners, like himself – able to draw a chair close to them, take an interest in their employment; and regret, in a reasonable way, that he should be so late. He was not in his best spirits, but seemed trying to improve them; and, at last, made himself talk nonsense very agreeably. They were looking over views in Swisserland.

'As soon as my aunt gets well, I shall go abroad,' said he. 'I shall never be easy till I have seen some of these places. You will have my sketches, some time or other, to look at – or my tour to read – or my poem. I shall do something to expose myself.'

'That may be – but not by sketches in Swisserland. You will never go to Swisserland. Your uncle and aunt will never allow you to leave England.'

'They may be induced to go too. A warm climate may be prescribed for her. I have more than half an expectation of our all going abroad. I assure you I have. I feel a strong persuasion, this morning, that I shall soon be abroad. I ought to travel. I am tired of doing nothing. I want a change. I am serious, Miss Woodhouse, whatever your penetrating eyes may fancy – I am sick of England – and would leave it to-morrow, if I could.'

Able to take an interest in their employment.

'You are sick of prosperity and indulgence. Cannot you invent a few hardships for yourself, and be contented to stay?'

'*I* sick of prosperity and indulgence! – You are quite mistaken. I do not look upon myself as either prosperous or indulged. I am thwarted in every thing material. I do not consider myself at all a fortunate person.'

'You are not quite so miserable, though, as when you first came. Go and eat and drink a little more, and you will do very well. Another slice of cold meat, another draught of Madeira and water, will make you nearly on a par with the rest of us.'

'No – I shall not stir. I shall sit by you. You are my best cure.'

'We are going to Box Hill to-morrow; – you will join us. It is not Swisserland, but it will be something for a young man so much in want of a change. You will stay, and go with us?'

'No, certainly not; I shall go home in the cool of the evening.'

'But you may come again in the cool of to-morrow morning.'

'No – it will not be worth while. If I come, I shall be cross.'

'Then pray stay at Richmond.'

'But if I do, I shall be crosser still. I can never bear to think of you all there without me.'

'These are difficulties which you must settle for yourself. Choose your own degree of crossness. I shall press you no more.'

The rest of the party were now returning, and all were soon collected. With some there was great joy at the sight of Frank Churchill; others took it very composedly; but there was a very general distress and disturbance of Miss Fairfax's disappearance being explained. That it was time for every body to go, concluded the subject; and with a short final arrangement for the next day's scheme, they parted. Frank Churchill's little inclination to exclude himself increased so much, that his last words to Emma were,

'Well; – if *you* wish me to stay, and join the party, I will.'

She smiled her acceptance; and nothing less than a summons from Richmond was to take him back before the following evening.

CHAPTER FORTY-THREE

THEY HAD A VERY FINE day for Box Hill; and all the other outward circumstances of arrangement, accommodation, and punctuality, were in favour of a pleasant party. Mr Weston directed the whole, officiating safely between Hartfield and the vicarage, and every body was in good time. Emma and Harriet went together, Miss Bates and her niece, with the Eltons; the gentlemen on horseback. Mrs Weston remained with Mr Woodhouse. Nothing was wanting but to be happy when they got there. Seven miles were travelled in expectation of enjoyment, and every body had a burst of admiration on first arriving; but in the general amount of the day there was deficiency. There was a languor, a want of spirits, a want of union, which could not be got over. They separated too much into parties. The Eltons walked together; Mr Knightley took charge of Miss Bates and Jane; and Emma and Harriet belonged to Frank Churchill. And Mr Weston tried, in vain, to make them harmonize better. It seemed at first an accidental division, but it never materially varied. Mr and Mrs Elton, indeed, showed no unwillingness to mix, and be as agreeable as they could; but during the two whole hours that were spent on the hill, there seemed a principle of separation, between the other parties, too strong for any fine prospects, or any cold collation, or any cheerful Mr Weston, to remove.

At first it was downright dulness to Emma. She had never seen Frank Churchill so silent and stupid. He said nothing worth hearing – looked without seeing – admired without intelligence – listened without knowing what she said. While he was so dull, it was no wonder that Harriet should be dull likewise, and they were both insufferable.

When they all sat down it was better; to her taste a great deal better, for Frank Churchill grew talkative and gay, making her his first object. Every distinguishing attention that could be paid, was paid to her. To amuse her, and be agreeable in her eyes, seemed all that he cared for – and Emma, glad to be enlivened, not sorry to be flattered, was gay and easy too, and gave him all the friendly encouragement, the admission to be gallant, which she had ever given in the first and most animating period of their acquaintance; but which now, in her own estimation, meant nothing, though in the judgment of most people looking on it must have had such an appearance as no English word but flirtation could very well describe. 'Mr Frank Churchill and Miss Woodhouse flirted together excessively.' They were laying themselves open to that very phrase – and to having it sent off in a letter to Maple Grove by one lady, to Ireland by another. Not that Emma was gay and thoughtless from any real felicity; it was rather because she felt less happy than she had expected. She laughed because she was disappointed; and though she liked him for his attentions, and thought them all, whether in friendship, admiration, or playfulness, extremely judicious, they were not winning back her heart. She still intended him for her friend.

'How much I am obliged to you,' said he, 'for telling me to come to-day! – If it had not been for you, I should certainly have lost all the happiness of this party. I had quite determined to go away again.'

'Yes, you were very cross; and I do not know what about, except that you were too late for the best strawberries. I was a kinder friend than you deserved. But you were humble. You begged hard to be commanded to come.'

'Don't say I was cross. I was fatigued. The heat overcame me.'

'It is hotter to-day.'

'Not to my feelings. I am perfectly comfortable to-day.'

'You are comfortable because you are under command.'

'Your command? – Yes.'

'Perhaps I intend you to say so, but I meant self-command. You had, somehow or other, broken bounds yesterday, and run away from your own management; but to-day you are got back again – and as I cannot be always with you, it is best to believe your temper under your own command rather than mine.'

'It comes to the same thing. I can have no self-command without a motive. You order me, whether you speak or not. And you can be always with me. You are always with me.'

'Dating from three o'clock yesterday. My perpetual influence could not begin earlier, or you would not have been so much out of humour before.'

'Three o'clock yesterday! That is your date. I thought I had seen your first in February.'

'Your gallantry is really unanswerable. But (lowering her voice) – nobody speaks except ourselves, and it is rather too much to be talking nonsense for the entertainment of seven silent people.'

'I say nothing of which I am ashamed,' replied he, with lively impudence. 'I saw you first in February. Let every body on the Hill hear me if they can. Let my accents swell to Mickleham on one side, and Dorking on the other. I saw you first in February.' And then whispering – 'Our companions are excessively stupid. What shall we do to rouse them? Any nonsense will serve. They *shall* talk. Ladies and gentlemen, I am ordered by Miss Woodhouse (who, wherever she is, presides,) to say, that she desires to know what you are all thinking of.'

Some laughed, and answered good-humouredly. Miss Bates said a great deal; Mrs Elton swelled at the idea of Miss Woodhouse's presiding; Mr Knightley's answer was the most distinct.

'Is Miss Woodhouse sure that she would like to hear what we are all thinking of?'

'Oh! no, no' – cried Emma, laughing as carelessly as she could – 'Upon no account in the world. It is the very last thing I would stand the brunt of just now. Let me hear any thing rather than what you are all thinking of. I will not say quite all. There are one or two, perhaps, (glancing at Mr Weston and Harriet), whose thoughts I might not be afraid of knowing.'

'It is a sort of thing,' cried Mrs Elton emphatically, 'which *I* should not have thought myself privileged to enquire into. Though, perhaps, as the *Chaperon* of the party – *I* never was in any circle – exploring parties – young ladies – married women – '

Her mutterings were chiefly to her husband; and he murmured, in reply.

'Very true, my love, very true. Exactly so, indeed – quite unheard of – but some ladies say any thing. Better pass it off as a joke. Every body knows what is due to *you.*'

'It will not do,' whispered Frank to Emma, 'they are most of them affronted. I will attack them with more address. Ladies and gentlemen – I am ordered by Miss Woodhouse to say, that she waves her right of knowing exactly what you may all be thinking of, and only requires something very entertaining from each of you, in a general way. Here are seven of you, besides myself, (who, she is pleased to say, am very entertaining already,) and she only demands from each of you either one thing very clever, be it prose or verse, original or repeated – or two things moderately clever – or three things very dull indeed, and she engages to laugh heartily at them all.'

'Oh! very well,' exclaimed Miss Bates, 'then I need not be uneasy. "Three things very dull indeed." That will just do for me, you know. I shall be sure to say three dull things as soon as ever I open my mouth, shan't I? – (looking round with most good-humoured dependence on every body's assent) – Do not you all think I shall?'

Emma could not resist.

'Ah! ma'am, but there may be a difficulty. Pardon me – but you will be limited as to number – only three at once.'

Miss Bates, deceived by the mock ceremony of her manner, did not immediately catch her meaning; but, when it burst upon her, it could not anger, though a slight blush showed that it could pain her.

'Ah! – well – to be sure. Yes, I see what she means, (turning to Mr Knightley,) and I will try to hold my tongue. I must make myself very disagreeable, or she would not have said such a thing to an old friend.'

'I like your plan,' cried Mr Weston. 'Agreed, agreed. I will do my best. I am making a conundrum. How will a conundrum reckon?'

'Low, I am afraid, sir, very low,' answered his son; – 'but we shall be indulgent – especially to any one who leads the way.'

'No, no,' said Emma, 'it will not reckon low. A conundrum of Mr Weston's shall clear him and his next neighbour. Come, sir, pray let me hear it.'

'I doubt it's being clever myself,' said Mr Weston. 'It is too much a matter of fact, but here it is. – What two letters of the alphabet are there, that express perfection?'

'What two letters! – express perfection! I am sure I do not know.'

'Ah! you will never guess. You, (to Emma), I am certain, will never guess. – I will tell you. – M. and A. – Em – ma. – Do you understand?'

Understanding and gratification came together. It might be a very indifferent piece of wit; but Emma found a great deal to laugh at and enjoy in it – and so did Frank and Harriet. – It did not seem to touch the rest of the party equally; some looked very stupid about it, and Mr Knightley gravely said,

'This explains the sort of clever thing that is wanted, and Mr Weston has done very well for himself; but he must have knocked up every body else. *Perfection* should not have come quite so soon.'

'Oh! for myself, I protest I must be excused,' said Mrs Elton; 'I really cannot attempt – I am not at all fond of the sort of thing. I had an acrostic once sent to me upon my own name, which I was not at all pleased with. I knew who it came from. An abominable puppy! – You know who I mean – (nodding to her husband). These kind of things are very well at Christmas, when one is sitting round the fire; but quite out of place, in my opinion, when one is exploring about the country in summer. Miss Woodhouse must excuse me. I am not one of those who have witty things at every body's service. I do not pretend to be a wit. I have a great deal of vivacity in my own way, but I really must be allowed to judge when to speak and when to hold my tongue. Pass us, if you please, Mr Churchill. Pass Mr E., Knightley, Jane and myself. We have nothing clever to say – not one of us.'

'Yes, yes, pray pass *me*,' added her husband, with a sort of sneering consciousness; '*I* have nothing to say that can entertain Miss Woodhouse, or any other young lady. An old married man – quite good for nothing. Shall we walk, Augusta?'

'With all my heart. I am really tired of exploring so long on one spot. Come, Jane, take my other arm.'

Jane declined it, however, and the husband and wife walked off. 'Happy couple!' said Frank Churchill, as soon as they were out of hearing; – 'How well they suit one another! – Very lucky – marrying as they did, upon an acquaintance formed only in a public place! – They only knew each other, I think, a few weeks in Bath! Peculiarly lucky! – for as to any real knowledge of a person's disposition that Bath, or any public place, can give – it is all nothing; there can be no knowledge. It is only by seeing women in their own homes, among their own set, just as they always are, that you can form any just judgment. Short of that, it is all guess and luck – and will generally be ill-luck. How many a man has committed himself on a short acquaintance, and rued it all the rest of his life!'

Miss Fairfax, who had seldom spoken before, except among her own confederates, spoke now.

'Such things do occur, undoubtedly.' – She was stopped by a cough. Frank Churchill turned towards her to listen.

'You were speaking,' said he, gravely. She recovered her voice.

'I was only going to observe, that though such unfortunate circumstances do sometimes occur both to men and women, I cannot imagine them to be very frequent. A hasty and imprudent attachment may arise – but there is generally time to recover from it afterwards. I would be understood to mean, that it can be only weak, irresolute characters, (whose happiness must be always at the mercy of chance,) who will suffer an unfortunate acquaintance to be an inconvenience, an oppression for ever.'

He made no answer; merely looked, and bowed in submission; and soon afterwards said, in a lively tone,

'Well, I have so little confidence in my own judgment, that whenever I marry, I hope somebody will choose my wife for me. Will you? (turning to Emma.) Will you choose a wife for me? – I am sure I should like any body fixed on by you. You provide for the family, you know, (with a smile at his father). Find somebody for me. I am in no hurry. Adopt her, educate her.'

'And make her like myself.'

'By all means, if you can.'

'Very well, I undertake the commission. You shall have a charming wife.'

'She must be very lively, and have hazel eyes. I care for nothing else. I shall go abroad for a couple of years – and when I return, I shall come to you for my wife. Remember.'

Emma was in no danger of forgetting. It was a commission to touch every favourite feeling. Would not Harriet be the very creature described? – Hazel eyes excepted, two years more might make her all that he wished. He might even have Harriet in his thoughts at the moment; who could say? Referring the education to her seemed to imply it.

'Now, ma'am,' said Jane to her aunt, 'shall we join Mrs Elton?'

'If you please, my dear. With all my heart. I am quite ready. I was ready to have gone with her, but this will do just as well. We shall soon overtake her. There she is – no, that's somebody else. That's one of the ladies in the Irish car party, not at all like her. – Well, I declare – '

They walked off, followed in half a minute by Mr Knightley. Mr Weston, his son, Emma, and Harriet, only remained; and the young man's spirits now rose to a pitch almost unpleasant. Even Emma grew tired at last of flattery and merriment, and wished herself rather walking quietly about with any of the others, or sitting almost alone, and quite unattended to, in tranquil observation of the beautiful views beneath her. The appearance of the servants looking out for them to give notice of the carriages was a joyful sight; and even the bustle of collecting and preparing to depart, and the solicitude of Mrs Elton to have *her* carriage first, were gladly endured, in the prospect of the quiet drive home which was to close the very questionable enjoyments of this day of pleasure. Such another scheme, composed of so many ill-assorted people, she hoped never to be betrayed into again.

While waiting for the carriage, she found Mr Knightley by her side. He looked around, as if to see that no one were near, and then said,

'Emma, I must once more speak to you as I have been used to do: a privilege rather endured than allowed, perhaps, but I must still use it. I cannot see you acting wrong, without a remonstrance. How could you be so unfeeling to Miss Bates? How could you be so insolent in your wit to a woman of her character, age, and situation? – Emma, I had not thought it possible.'

Emma recollected, blushed, was sorry, but tried to laugh it off.

'Nay, how could I help saying what I did? – Nobody could have helped it. It was not so very bad. I dare say she did not understand me.'

'I assure you she did. She felt your full meaning. She has talked of it since. I wish you could have heard how she talked of it – with what candour and generosity. I wish you could have heard her honouring your forbearance, in being able to pay her such attentions, as she was for ever receiving from yourself and your father, when her society must be so irksome.'

'Oh!' cried Emma. 'I know there is not a better creature in the world; but you must allow, that what is good and what is ridiculous are most unfortunately blended in her.'

'They are blended,' said he, 'I acknowledge; and, were she prosperous, I could allow much for the occasional prevalence of the ridiculous over the good. Were she a woman of fortune, I would leave every harmless absurdity to take its chance, I would not quarrel with you for any liberties of manner. Were she your equal in situation – but, Emma, consider how far this is from being the case. She is poor, she has sunk from the comforts she was born to; and, if she live to old age, must probably sink more. Her situation should secure your compassion. It was badly done, indeed! – You, whom she had known from an infant, whom she had seen grow up from a period when her notice was an honour, to have you now, in thoughtless spirits, and the pride of the moment, laugh at her, humble her – and before her niece, too – and before others, many of whom (certainly *some*,) would be entirely guided by *your* treatment of her. – This is not pleasant to you, Emma – and it is very far from pleasant to me; but I must, I will, – I will tell you truths while I can, satisfied with proving myself your friend by very faithful counsel, and trusting that you will some time or other do me greater justice than you can do now.'

While they talked, they were advancing towards the carriage; it was ready; and, before she could speak again, he had handed her in. He had misinterpreted the feelings which had kept her face averted, and her tongue motionless. They were combined only of anger against herself, mortification, and deep concern. She had not been able to speak; and, on entering the carriage, sunk back for a moment overcome – then reproaching herself for having taken no leave, making no acknowledgement, parting in apparent sullenness, she looked out with voice and hand eager to show a difference; but it was just too late. He had turned away, and the horses were in motion. She continued to look back, but in vain; and soon, with what appeared unusual speed, they were half way down the hill, and every thing left far behind. She was vexed beyond what could have been expressed – almost beyond what she could conceal. Never had she felt so agitated, mortified, grieved, at any circumstance in her life. She was most forcibly struck. The truth of his representation there was no denying. She felt it at her heart. How could she have been so brutal, so cruel to Miss Bates! – How could she have exposed herself to such ill opinion in any one she valued! And how suffer him to leave her without saying one word of gratitude, of concurrence, of common kindness!

Time did not compose her. As she reflected more, she seemed but to feel it more. She never had been so depressed. Happily it was not necessary to speak. There was only Harriet, who seemed not in spirits herself, fagged, and very willing to be silent; and Emma felt the tears running down her cheeks almost all the way home, without being at any trouble to check them, extraordinary as they were.

CHAPTER FORTY-FOUR

THE WRETCHEDNESS OF a scheme to Box Hill was in Emma's thoughts all the evening. How it might be considered by the rest of the party, she could not tell. They, in their different homes, and their different ways, might be looking back on it with pleasure; but in her view it was a morning more completely misspent, more totally bare of rational satisfaction at the time, and more to be abhorred in recollection, than any she had ever passed. A whole evening of backgammon with her father, was felicity to it. *There*, indeed, lay real pleasure, for there she was giving up the sweetest hours of the twenty-four to his comfort; and feeling that, unmerited as might be the degree of his fond affection and confiding esteem, she could not, in her general conduct, be open to any severe reproach. As a daughter, she hoped she was not without a heart. She hoped no one could have said to her. 'How could you be so unfeeling to your father? – I must, I will tell truths while I can.' Miss Bates should never again – no never! If attention, in future, could do away the past, she might hope to be forgiven. She had been often remiss, her conscience told her so; remiss, perhaps, more in thought than fact; scornful, ungracious. But it should be so no more. In the warmth of true contrition, she would call upon her the very next morning, and it should be the beginning, on her side, of a regular, equal, kindly intercourse.

She was just as determined when the morrow came, and went early, that nothing might prevent her. It was not unlikely, she thought, that she might see Mr Knightley in her way; or, perhaps, he might come in while she were paying her visit. She had no objection. She would not be ashamed of the appearance of the penitence, so justly and truly hers. Her eyes were towards Donwell as she walked, but she saw him not.

'The ladies were all at home.' She had never rejoiced at the sound before, nor ever before entered the passage, nor walked up the stairs, with any wish of giving pleasure, but in conferring obligation, or of deriving it, except in subsequent ridicule.

There was a bustle on her approach; a good deal of moving and talking. She heard Miss Bates's voice, something was to be done in a hurry; the maid looked frightened and awkward; hoped she would be pleased to wait a moment, and then ushered her in too soon.

The aunt and niece seemed both escaping into the adjoining room. Jane she had a distinct glimpse of, looking extremely ill; and, before the door had shut them out, she heard Miss Bates saying, 'Well, my dear, I shall *say* you are laid down upon the bed, and I am sure you are ill enough.'

Poor old Mrs Bates, civil and humble as usual, looked as if she did not quite understand what was going on.

'I am afraid Jane is not very well,' said she, 'but I do not know; they *tell* me she is well. I dare say my daughter will be here presently, Miss Woodhouse. I hope you find a chair. I wish Hetty had not gone. I am very little able – Have you a chair, ma'am? Do you sit where you like? I am sure she will be here presently.'

Emma seriously hoped she would. She had a moment's fear of Miss Bates keeping away from her. But Miss Bates soon came – 'Very happy and obliged' – but Emma's conscience told her that there was not the same cheerful volubility as before – less ease of look and manner. A very friendly inquiry after Miss Fairfax, she hoped, might lead the way to a return of old feelings. The touch seemed immediate.

'Ah! Miss Woodhouse, how kind you are! – I suppose you have heard – and are come to give us joy. This does not seem much like joy, indeed, in me – (twinkling away a tear or two) – but it will be very trying for us to part with her, after having had her so long, and she has a dreadful headache just now, writing all the morning: – such long letters, you know, to be written to Colonel Campbell, and Mrs Dixon. "My dear," said I, "you will blind yourself" – for tears were in her eyes perpetually. One cannot wonder, one cannot wonder. It is a great change; and though she is amazingly fortunate – such a situation, I suppose, as no young woman before ever met with on first going out – do not think us ungrateful, Miss Woodhouse, for such surprising good fortune – (again dispersing her tears) – but, poor dear soul! if you were to see what a headache she has. When one is in great pain, you know one cannot feel any blessing quite as it may deserve. She is as low as possible. To look at her, nobody would think how delighted and happy she is to have secured such a situation. You will excuse her not coming to you – she is not able – she is gone into her own room – I want her to lie down upon the bed. "My dear," said I, "I shall say you are laid down upon the bed:" but, however, she is not; she is walking about the room. But, now that she has written her letters, she says she shall soon be well. She will be extremely sorry to miss seeing you, Miss Woodhouse, but your kindness will excuse her. You were kept waiting at the door – I was quite ashamed – but somehow there was a little bustle – for it so happened that we had not heard the knock, and till you were on the stairs, we did not know any body was coming. "It is only Mrs Cole," said I, "depend upon it. Nobody else would come so early." "Well," said she, "it must be borne some time or other, and it may as well be now." But then Patty came in, and said it was you. "Oh!" said I, "it is Miss Woodhouse: I am sure you will like to see her." – "I can see nobody," said she; and up she got, and would go away; and that was what made us keep you waiting – and extremely sorry and ashamed we were. "If you must go, my dear," said I, "you must, and I will say you are laid down upon the bed." '

Emma was most sincerely interested. Her heart had been long growing kinder towards Jane; and this picture of her present sufferings acted as a cure of every former ungenerous suspicion, and left her nothing but pity; and the remembrance of the less just and less gentle sensations of the past, obliged her to admit that Jane might very naturally resolve on seeing Mrs Cole or any other steady friend, when she might not bear to see herself. She spoke as she felt, with earnest regret and solicitude – sincerely wishing that the circumstances which she collected from Miss Bates to be now actually determined on, might be as much for Miss Fairfax's advantage and comfort as possible. 'It must be a severe trial to them all. She had understood it was to be delayed till Colonel Campbell's return.'

'So very kind!' replied Miss Bates. 'But you are always kind.'

There was no bearing such an 'always;' and to break through her dreadful gratitude, Emma made the direct inquiry of –

'Where – may I ask? – is Miss Fairfax going?'

'To a Mrs Smallridge – charming woman – most superior – to have the charge of her three little girls – delightful children. Impossible that any situation could be more replete with comfort; if we except, perhaps, Mrs Suckling's own family, and Mrs Bragge's; but Mrs Smallridge is intimate with both, and in the very same neighbourhood: – lives only four miles from Maple Grove. Jane will be only four miles from Maple Grove.'

'Mrs Elton, I suppose, has been the person to whom Miss Fairfax owes –

'Yes, our good Mrs Elton. The most indefatigable, true friend. She would not take a denial. She would not let Jane say "No;" for when Jane first heard of it, (it was the day before yesterday, the very morning we were at Donwell,) when Jane first heard of it, she was quite decided against accepting the offer, and for the reasons you mention; exactly as you say, she had made up her mind to close with nothing till Colonel Campbell's return, and nothing should induce her to enter into any engagement at present – and so she told Mrs Elton over and over again – and I am sure I had no more idea that she would change her mind! – but that good Mrs Elton, whose judgment never fails her, saw farther than I did. It is not every body that would have stood out in such a kind way as she did, and refuse to take Jane's answer; but she positively declared she would *not* write any such denial yesterday, as Jane wished her; she would wait – and, sure enough, yesterday evening it was all settled that Jane should go. Quite a surprise to me! I had not the least idea! – Jane took Mrs Elton aside, and told her at once, that upon thinking over the advantages of Mrs Suckling's situation, she had come to the resolution of accepting it. – I did not know a word of it till it was all settled.'

'You spent the evening with Mrs Elton?'

'Yes, all of us; Mrs Elton would have us come. It was settled so, upon the hill, while we were walking about with Mr Knightley. "You *must all* spend your evening with us," said she – "I positively must have you *all* come." '

'Mr Knightley was there too, was he?'

'No, not Mr Knightley; he declined it from the first; and though I thought he would come, because Mrs Elton declared she would not let him off, he did not; – but my mother, and Jane, and I, were all there, and a very agreeable evening we had. Such kind friends, you know, Miss Woodhouse, one must always find agreeable, though every body seemed rather fagged after the morning's party. Even pleasure, you know, is fatiguing – and I cannot say that any of them seemed very much to have enjoyed it. However, I shall always think it a very pleasant party, and feel extremely obliged to the kind friends who included me in it.'

'Miss Fairfax, I suppose, though you were not aware of it, had been making up her mind the whole day.'

'I dare say she had.'

'Whenever the time may come, it must be unwelcome to her and all her friends – but I hope her engagement will have every alleviation that is possible – I mean, as to the character and manners of the family.'

'Thank you, dear Miss Woodhouse. Yes, indeed, there is every thing in the world that can make her happy in it. Except the Sucklings and Bragges, there is not such another nursery establishment, so liberal and elegant, in all Mrs Elton's acquaintance. Mrs Smallridge, a most delightful woman! – A style of living almost equal to Maple Grove – and as to the children, except the little Sucklings and little Bragges, there are not such elegant sweet children any where. Jane will be treated with such regard and kindness! – It will be nothing but pleasure, a life of pleasure. – And her salary! – I really cannot venture to name her salary to you, Miss Woodhouse. Even you, used as you are to great sums, would hardly believe that so much could be given to a young person like Jane.'

'Ah! madam,' cried Emma, 'if other children are at all like what I remember to have been myself, I should think five times the amount of what I have ever yet heard named as a salary on such occasions, dearly earned.'

'You are so noble in your ideas!'

'And when is Miss Fairfax to leave you?'

'Very soon, very soon indeed; that's the worst of it. Within a fortnight. Mrs Smallridge is in a great hurry. My poor mother does not know how to bear it. So then, I try to put it out of her thoughts, and say, Come ma'am, do not let us think about it any more.'

'Her friends must all be sorry to lose her; and will not Colonel and Mrs Campbell be sorry to find that she has engaged herself before their return?'

'Yes; Jane says she is sure they will; but yet, this is such a situation as she cannot feel herself justified in declining. I was so astonished when she first told me what she had been saying to Mrs Elton, and when Mrs Elton at the same moment came congratulating me upon it! I was before tea – stay – no, it could not be before tea, because we were just going to cards – and yet it was before tea, because I remember thinking – Oh! no, now I recollect, now I have it; something happened before tea, but not that. Mr Elton was called out of the room before tea, old John Abdy's son wanted to speak with him. Poor old John, I have a great regard for him; he was clerk to my poor father twenty-seven years; and now, poor old man, he is bed-ridden, and very poorly with the rheumatic gout in his joints – I must go and see him to-day; and so will Jane, I am sure, if she gets out at all. And poor John's son came to talk to Mr Elton about relief from the parish: he is very well to do himself, you know, being head man at the Crown, ostler, and every thing of that sort, but still he cannot keep his father without some help; and so, when Mr Elton came back, he told us what John ostler had been telling him, and then it came out about the chaise having been sent to Randalls to take Mr Frank Churchill to Richmond. That was what happened before tea. It was after tea that Jane spoke to Mrs Elton.'

Miss Bates would hardly give Emma time to say how perfectly new this circumstance was to her; but as without supposing it possible that she could be ignorant of any of the particulars of Mr

Frank Churchill's going, she proceeded to give them all, it was of no consequence.

What Mr Elton had learnt from the ostler on the subject, being the accumulation of the ostler's own knowledge, and the knowledge of the servants at Randalls, was, that a messenger had come over from Richmond soon after the return of the party from Box Hill – which messenger, however, had been no more than was expected; and that Mr Churchill had sent his nephew a few lines, containing, upon the whole, a tolerable account of Mrs Churchill, and only wishing him not to delay coming back beyond the next morning early; but that Mr Frank Churchill having resolved to go home directly, without waiting at all, and his horse seeming to have got a cold, Tom had been sent off immediately for the Crown chaise,

Seen the Crown chaise pass by.

and the ostler had stood out and seen it pass by, the boy going a good pace, and driving very steady.

There was nothing in all this either to astonish or interest, and it caught Emma's attention only as it united with the subject which already engaged her mind. The contrast between Mrs Churchill's importance in the world, and Jane Fairfax's, struck her; one was every thing, the other nothing – and she sat musing on the difference of woman's destiny, and quite unconscious on what her eyes were fixed, till roused by Miss Bates's saying.

'Ay, I see what you are thinking of, the piano forté. What is to become of that? – Very true. Poor dear Jane was talking of it just now. – "You must go," said she. "You and I must part. You will have no business here. – Let it stay, however," said she; "give it house-room till Colonel Campbell comes back. I shall talk about it to him; he will settle for me; he will help me out of all my difficulties." – And to this day, I do believe, she knows not whether it was his present or his daughter's.'

Now Emma was obliged to think of the piano forté; and the remembrance of all her former fanciful and unfair conjectures was so little pleasing, that she soon allowed herself to believe her visit had been long enough; and, with a repetition of every thing that she could venture to say of the good wishes which she really felt, took leave.

CHAPTER FORTY-FIVE

EMMA'S PENSIVE MEDITATIONS, as she walked home, were not interrupted; but on entering the parlour, she found those who must rouse her. Mr Knightley and Harriet had arrived during her absence, and were sitting with her father. – Mr Knightley immediately got up, and in a manner decidedly graver than usual, said,

'I would not go away without seeing you, but I have no time to spare, and therefore must now be gone directly. I am going to London, to spend a few days with John and Isabella. Have you any thing to send or say, besides the "love," which nobody carries?'

'Nothing at all. But is not this a sudden scheme?'

'Yes – rather – I have been thinking of it some little time.'

Emma was sure he had not forgiven her; he looked unlike himself. Time, however, she thought, would tell him that they ought to be friends again. While he stood, as if meaning to go, but not going – her father began his inquiries.

'Well, my dear, and did you get there safely? – And how did you find my worthy old friend and her daughter? – I dare say they must have been very much obliged to you for coming. Dear Emma has been to call on Mrs and Miss Bates, Mr Knightley, as I told you before. She is always so attentive to them!'

Emma's colour was heightened by this unjust praise; and with a smile, and shake of the head, which spoke much, she looked at Mr Knightley. – It seemed as if there were an instantaneous impression in her favour, as if his eyes received the truth from her's, and all that had passed of good in her feelings were at once caught and honoured. – He looked at her with a glow of regard. She was warmly gratified – and in another moment still more so, by a little movement of more than common friendliness on his part. He took her hand; – whether she had not herself made the first motion, she could not say – she might, perhaps, have rather offered it – but he took her hand, pressed it, and certainly was on the point of carrying it to his lips – when, from some fancy or other, he suddenly let go. – Why he should feel such a scruple, why he should change his mind when it was all but done, she could not perceive. – He would have judged better, she thought, if he had not stopped. – The intention, however, was indubitable; and whether it was that his manners had in general so little gallantry, or however else it happened, but she thought nothing became him more. – It was with him, of so simple, yet so dignified a nature. – She could not but recall the attempt with great satisfaction. It spoke such perfect amity. – He left them immediately afterwards – gone in a moment. He always moved with the alertness of a mind which could neither be undecided nor dilatory, but now he seemed more sudden than usual in his disappearance.

Emma could not regret her having gone to Miss Bates, but she wished she had left her ten minutes earlier; – it would have been a great pleasure to talk over Jane Fairfax's situation with Mr Knightley. – Neither would she regret that he should be going to Brunswick Square, for she knew how much his visit would be enjoyed – but it might have happened at a better time – and to have had longer notice of it, would have been pleasanter. – They parted thorough friends, however; she could not be deceived as to the meaning of his countenance, and his unfinished gallantry; – it was all done to assure her that she had fully recovered his good opinion. – He had been sitting with them half an hour, she found. It was a pity that she had not come back earlier!

In the hope of diverting her father's thoughts from the disagreeableness of Mr Knightley's going to London; and going so suddenly; and going on horseback, which she knew would be all very bad; Emma communicated her news of Jane Fairfax, and her dependence on the effect was justified; it supplied a very useful check, – interested without disturbing him. He had long made up his mind to Jane Fairfax's going out as governess, and could talk of it cheerfully, but Mr Knightley's going to London had been an unexpected blow.

'I am very glad indeed, my dear, to hear she is to be so comfortably settled. Mrs Elton is very good-natured and agreeable, and I dare say her acquaintance are just what they ought to be. I hope it is a dry situation, and that her health will be taken good care of. It ought to be a first object, as I am sure poor Miss Taylor's always was with me. You know, my dear, she is going to be to this new lady what Miss Taylor was to us. And I hope she will be better off in one respect, and not be induced to go away after it has been her home so long.'

The following day brought news from Richmond to throw every thing else into the back-ground. An express arrived at Randalls to announce the death of Mrs Churchill! Though her nephew had had no particular reason to hasten back on her account, she had not lived above six-and-thirty hours after his return. A sudden seizure of a different nature from any thing foreboded by her general state, had carried her off after a short struggle. The great Mrs Churchill was no more.

It was felt as such things must be felt. Every body had a degree of gravity and sorrow; tenderness towards the departed, solicitude for the surviving friends; and, in a reasonable time, curiosity to know where she would be buried. Goldsmith tells us, that when lovely woman stoops to folly, she has nothing to do but to die; and when she stoops to be disagreeable, it is equally to be recommended as a clearer of ill-fame. Mrs Churchill, after being disliked at least twenty-five years, was now spoken of with compassionate allowances. In one point she was fully justified. She had never been admitted before to be seriously ill. The event acquitted her of all the fancifulness, and all the selfishness of imaginary complaints.

'Poor Mrs Churchill! no doubt she had been suffering a great deal: more than any body had ever supposed – and continual pain would try the temper. It was a sad event – a great shock – with all her faults, what would Mr Churchill do without her? Mr Churchill's loss would be dreadful indeed. Mr Churchill would never get over it'. – Even Mr Weston shook his head, and looked solemn, and said, 'Ah! poor woman, who would have thought it!' and resolved, that his mourning should be as handsome as possible; and his wife sat sighing and moralizing over her broad hems with a commiseration and good sense, true and steady. How it would affect Frank was among the earliest thought of both. It was also a very early speculation with Emma. The character of Mrs Churchill, the grief of her husband – her mind glanced over them both with awe and compassion – and then rested with lightened feelings on how Frank might be affected by the event, how benefited, how freed. She saw in a moment all the possible good. Now, an attachment to Harriet Smith would have nothing to encounter. Mr Churchill, independent of his wife, was feared by nobody; an easy, guidable man, to be persuaded into any thing by his nephew. All that remained to be wished was, that the nephew should form the attachment, as, with all her good will in the cause, Emma could feel no certainty of its being already formed.

Harriet behaved extremely well on the occasion, with great self-command. Whatever she might feel of brighter hope, she betrayed nothing. Emma was gratified, to observe such a proof in her of strengthened character, and refrained from any allusion that might endanger its maintenance. They spoke, therefore, of Mrs Churchill's death with mutual forbearance.

Short letters from Frank were received at Randalls, communicating all that was immediately important of their state and plans. Mr Churchill was better than could be expected; and their first removal, on the departure of the funeral for Yorkshire, was to be the house of a very old friend in Windsor, to whom Mr Churchill had been promising a visit the last ten years. At present, there was nothing to be done for Harriet; good wishes for the future were all that could yet be possible on Emma's side.

It was a more pressing concern to show attention to Jane Fairfax, whose prospects were closing, while Harriet's opened, and whose engagements now allowed of no delay in any one at Highbury, who wished to show her kindness – and with Emma it was grown into a first wish. She had scarcely a stronger regret than for her past coldness; and the person, whom she had been so many months neglecting, was now the very one on whom she would have lavished every distinction of regard or sympathy. She wanted to be of use to her; wanted to show a value for her society, and testify respect and consideration. She resolved to prevail on her to spend a day at Hartfield. A note was written to urge it. The invitation was refused, and by a verbal message. 'Miss Fairfax was not well enough to write;' and when Mr Perry called at Hartfield, the same morning it appeared that she was so much indisposed to have been visited, though against her own consent, by himself, and that she was suffering under severe headaches, and a nervous fever to a degree, which made him doubt the possibility of her going to Mrs Smallridge's at the time proposed. Her health seemed for the moment completely deranged – appetite quite gone – and though there were no absolutely alarming symptoms, nothing touching the pulmonary complaint, which was the standing apprehension of the family, Mr Perry was uneasy about her. He thought she had undertaken more than she was equal to, and that she felt it so herself, though she would not own it. Her spirits seemed overcome. Her present home, he could not but observe, was unfavourable to a nervous disorder: – confined always to one room; – he could have wished it otherwise – and her good aunt, though his very old friend, he must acknowledge to be not the best companion for an invalid of that description. Her care and attention could not be questioned; they were, in fact, only too great. He was very much feared that Miss Fairfax derived more evil than good from them. Emma listened with the warmest concern; grieved for her more and more, and looked around eager to discover some way of being useful. To take her – be it only an hour or two – from her aunt, to give her change of air and scene, and quiet rational conversation, even for an hour or two, might do her good; and the following morning she wrote again to say, in the most feeling language she could command, that she would call for her in the carriage at any hour that Jane would name – mentioning that she had Mr Perry's decided opinion, in favour of such exercise for his patient. The answer was only in this short note:

'Miss Fairfax's compliments and thanks, but is quite unequal to any exercise.'

Emma felt that her own note had deserved something better; but it was impossible to quarrel with words, whose tremulous inequality showed indisposition so plainly, and she thought only of how she might best counteract this unwillingness to be seen or assisted. In spite of the answer, therefore, she ordered the carriage, and drove to Mrs Bates's in the hope that Jane would be induced to join her – but it would not do; – Miss Bates came to the carriage door, all gratitude, and agreeing with her most earnestly in thinking an airing might be of the greatest service – and every thing that message could do was tried – but all in vain. Miss Bates was obliged to return without success; Jane, was quite unpersuadable; the mere proposal of going out seemed to make her worse. – Emma wished she could have seen her, and tried her own powers; but, almost before she could hint the wish, Miss Bates made it appear that she

Miss Bates came to the carriage door.

had promised her niece on no account to let Miss Woodhouse in. 'Indeed, the truth was, that poor dear Jane could not bear to see anybody – anybody at all – Mrs Elton, indeed, could not be denied – and Mrs Cole had made such a point – and Mrs Perry had said so much – but, except them, Jane would really see nobody.'

Emma did not want to be classed with the Mrs Eltons, the Mrs Perrys, and the Mrs Coles, who would force themselves anywhere; neither could she feel any right of preference herself – she submitted, therefore, and only questioned Miss Bates farther as to her niece's appetite and diet, which she longed to be able to assist. On that subject poor Miss Bates was very unhappy, and very communicative; Jane would hardly eat any thing: – Mr Perry recommended nourishing food; but every thing they could command (and never had anybody such good neighbours) was distasteful.

Emma, on reaching home, called the housekeeper directly, to an examination of her stores; and some arrow-root of very superior quality was speedily despatched to Miss Bates with a most friendly note. In half an hour the arrow-root was returned, with a thousand thanks from Miss Bates, but 'dear Jane would not be satisfied without its being sent back; it was a thing she could not take – and, moreover, she insisted on her saying, that she was not at all in want of any thing.'

When Emma afterwards heard that Jane Fairfax had been seen wandering about the meadows, at some distance from Highbury, on the afternoon of the very day on which she had, under the plea of being unequal to any exercise, so peremptorily refused to go out with her in the carriage, she could have no doubt – putting every thing together – that Jane was resolved to receive no kindness from *her*. She was sorry, very sorry. Her heart was grieved for a state which seemed but the more pitiable from this sort of irritation of spirits, inconsistency of action, and inequality of powers; and it mortified her that she was given so little credit for proper feeling, or esteemed so little worthy as a friend: but she had the consolation of knowing that her intentions were good, and of being able to say to herself, that could Mr Knightley have been privy to all her attempts of assisting Jane Fairfax, could he even have seen into her heart, he would not, on this occasion, have found any thing to reprove.

CHAPTER FORTY-SIX

ONE MORNING, ABOUT ten days after Mrs Churchill's decease, Emma was called down stairs to Mr Weston, who 'could not stay five minutes, and wanted particularly to speak with her.' – He met her at the parlour door, and hardly asking her how she did, in the natural key of his voice, sunk it immediately, to say, unheard by her father,

'Can you come to Randalls at any time this morning? – Do, if it be possible. Mrs Weston wants to see you. She must see you.'

'Is she unwell?'

'No, no, not at all – only a little agitated. She would have ordered the carriage, and come to you, but she must see you *alone*, and that you know – (nodding towards her father) – Humph! – Can you come?'

'Certainly. This moment, if you please. It is impossible to refuse what you ask in such a way. But what can be the matter? – Is she really not ill?'

'Depend upon me – but ask no more questions. You will know it all in time. The most unaccountable business! But hush, hush!'

To guess what all this meant, was impossible even for Emma. Something really important seemed announced by his looks; but, as her friend was well, she endeavoured not to be uneasy, and settling it with her father, that she would take her walk now, she and Mr Weston were soon out of the house together and on their way at a quick pace for Randalls.

'Now,' – said Emma, when they were fairly beyond the sweep gates, – 'now Mr Weston, do let me know what has happened.'

'No, no,' – he gravely replied. – 'Don't ask me. I promised my wife to leave it all to her. She will break it to you better than I can. Do not be impatient, Emma; it will all come out too soon.'

'Break it to me,' cried Emma, standing still with terror. – 'Good God! – Mr Weston, tell me at once. – Something has happened in Brunswick Square. I know it has. Tell me, I charge you tell me this moment what it is.'

'No, indeed you are mistaken.' –

'Mr Weston do not trifle with me. – Consider how many of my dearest friends are now in Brunswick Square. Which of them is it? – I charge you by all that is sacred, not to attempt concealment.'

'Upon my word, Emma.' –

'Your word! – why not your honour! – why not say upon your honour, that it has nothing to do with any of them? Good Heavens! – What can be to be *broke* to me, that does not relate to one of that family?'

'Upon my honour,' said he very seriously, 'it does not. It is not in the smallest degree connected with any human being of the name of Knightley.'

Emma's courage returned, and she walked on.

'I was wrong,' he continued, 'in talking of its being *broke* to you. I should not have used the expression. In fact, it does not concern you – it concerns only myself, – that is, we hope. – Humph! – In short, my dear Emma, there is no occasion to be so uneasy about it. I don't say that it is not a disagreeable business – but things might be much worse. – If we walk fast, we shall soon be at Randalls.'

Emma found that she must wait; and now it required little effort. She asked no more questions therefore, merely employed her own fancy, and that soon pointed out to her the probability of its being some money concern – something just come to light, of a disagreeable nature in the circumstances of the family, – something which the late event at Richmond had brought forward. Her fancy was very active. Half a dozen natural children, perhaps – and poor Frank cut off! – This, though very undesirable, would be no matter of agony to her. It inspired little more than an animating curiosity.

'Who is that gentleman on horseback?' said she, as they proceeded – speaking more to assist Mr Weston in keeping his secret, than with any other view.

'I do not know. – One of the Otways. – Not Frank; – it is not Frank, I assure you. You will not see him. He is half way to Windsor by this time.'

'Has your son been with you, then?'

'Oh! yes – did not you know? – Well, well, never mind.'

For a moment he was silent; and then added, in a tone much more guarded and demure,

'Yes, Frank came over this morning, just to ask us how we did.'

They hurried on, and were speedily at Randalls. – 'Well, my dear,' said he, as they entered the room – 'I have brought her, and now I hope you will soon be better. I shall leave you together. There is no use in delay. I shall not be far off, if you want me.' – And Emma distinctly heard him add, in a lower tone, before he quitted the room, – 'I have been as good as my word. She has not the least idea.'

Mrs Weston was looking so ill, and had an air of so much perturbation, that Emma's uneasiness increased; and the moment they were alone, she eagerly said,

'What is it my dear friend? Something of a very unpleasant nature, I find, has occurred; – do let me know directly what it is. I have been walking all this way in complete suspense. We both abhor suspense. Do not let mine continue longer. It will do you good to speak of your distress, whatever it may be.'

'Have you indeed no idea?' said Mrs Weston in a trembling voice. 'Cannot you, my dear Emma – cannot you form a guess as to what you are to hear?'

'So far as that it relates to Mr Frank Churchill, I do guess.'

'You are right. It does relate to him, and I will tell you directly;' (resuming her work, and seeming resolved against looking up.) 'He has been here this very morning, on a most extraordinary errand. It is impossible to express our surprize. He came to speak to his father on a subject, – to announce an attachment – '

She stopped to breathe. Emma thought first of herself, and then of Harriet.

'More than an attachment, indeed,' resumed Mrs Weston; 'an engagement – a positive engagement. – What will you say, Emma – what will anybody say, when it is known that Frank Churchill and Miss Fairfax are engaged; – nay, that they have been long engaged!'

Emma even jumped with surprize; – and, horror-struck, exclaimed,

'Jane Fairfax! – Good God! You are not serious? You do not mean it?'

'You may well be amazed,' returned Mrs Weston, still averting her eyes, and talking on with eagerness, that Emma might have time to recover – 'You may well be amazed. But it is even so. There has been a solemn engagement between them ever since October – formed at Weymouth, and kept a secret from everybody. Not a creature knowing it but themselves – neither the Campbells, nor her family, nor his. – It is so wonderful, that though perfectly convinced of the fact, it is yet almost incredible to myself. I can hardly believe it. – I thought I knew him'.

Emma scarcely heard what was said. – Her mind was divided between two ideas – her own former conversations with him about Miss Fairfax; and poor Harriet; – and for some time she could only exclaim, and require confirmation, repeated confirmation.

'Well,' said she at last, trying to recover herself; 'this is a circumstance which I must think of at least half a day, before I can at all comprehend it. What! – engaged to her all the winter – before either of them came to Highbury?'

'Engaged since October, – secretly engaged. – It has hurt me, Emma very much. It has hurt his father equally. *Some part* of his conduct we cannot excuse.'

Emma pondered a moment, and then replied, 'I will not pretend *not* to understand you; and to give you all the relief in my power, be assured that no such effect has followed his attentions to me, as you are apprehensive of.'

Mrs Weston looked up, afraid to believe; but Emma's countenance was as steady as her words.

'That you may have less difficulty in believing this boast, of my present perfect indifference,' she continued, 'I will farther tell you, that there was a period in the early part of our acquaintance, when I did like him, when I was very much disposed to be attached to him – nay, was attached – and how it came to cease, is perhaps the wonder. Fortunately, however, it did cease. I have really for some time past, for at least these three months, cared nothing about him. You may believe me, Mrs Weston. This is the simple truth.'

Mrs Weston kissed her with tears of joy; and when she could find utterance, assured her, that this protestation had done her more good than any thing else in the world could do.

'Mr Weston will be almost as much relieved as myself,' said she. 'On this point we have been wretched. It was our darling wish that you might be attached to each other – and we were persuaded that it was so. – Imagine what we have been feeling on your account.'

'I have escaped; and that I should escape, may be a matter of grateful wonder to you and myself. But this does not acquit *him*, Mrs Weston; and I must say, that I think him greatly to blame. What right had he to come among us with affection and faith engaged, and with manners so *very* disengaged? What right had he to endeavour to please, as he certainly did – to distinguish any one young woman with persevering attention, as he certainly did – while he really belonged to another? – How could he tell what mischief he might be doing? – How could he tell that he might not be making me in love with him? – very wrong, very wrong indeed.'

'From something that he said, my dear Emma, I rather imagine – '

'And how could *she* bear such behaviour! Composure with a witness! to look on, while repeated attentions were offering to another woman, before her face, and not resent it. – That is a degree of placidity, which I can neither comprehend nor respect.'

'There was misunderstandings between them, Emma; he said so expressly. He had not time to enter into much explanation. He was here only a quarter of an hour, and in a state of agitation which did not allow the full use even of the time he could stay – but that there had been misunderstandings he decidedly said. The present crisis, indeed, seemed to be brought on by them; and those misunderstandings might very possibly arise from the impropriety of his conduct.'

'Impropriety! Oh! Mrs Weston – it is too calm a censure. Much, much beyond impropriety! – It has sunk him, I cannot say how it has sunk him in my opinion. So unlike what a man should be! – None of that upright integrity, that strict adherence to truth and principle, that disdain of trick and littleness, which a man should display in every transaction of his life.'

'Nay, dear Emma, now I must take his part; for though he has been wrong in this instance, I have known him long enough to answer for his having many, very many, good qualities; and – '

'Good God!' cried Emma, not attending to her. – 'Mrs Smallridge, too! Jane actually on the point of going as governess! What could he mean by such horrible indelicacy? To suffer her to engage herself – to suffer her even to think of such a measure!'

'He knew nothing about it, Emma. On this article I can fully acquit him. It was a private resolution of her's, not communicated to him – or at least not communicated in a way to carry conviction. – Till yesterday, I know he said he was in the dark as to her plans. They burst on him, I do not know how, but by some letter or message – and it was the discovery of what she was doing, of this very project of her's, which determined him to come forward at once, own it all to his uncle, throw himself on his kindness, and, in short, put an end to the miserable state of concealment that had been carrying on so long.'

Emma began to listen better.

'I am to hear from him soon,' continued Mrs Weston. 'He told me at parting, that he should soon write; and he spoke in a manner which seemed to promise me many particulars that could not be given now. Let us wait, therefore, for his letter. It may bring many extenuations. It may make many things intelligible and excusable which now are not to be understood. Don't let us be severe, don't let us be in a hurry to condemn him. Let us have patience. I must love him; and now that I am satisfied on one point, the one material point, I am sincerely anxious for its all turning out well, and ready to hope that it may. They must both have suffered a great deal under such a system of secresy and concealment.'

'*His* sufferings,' replied Emma drily, 'do not appear to have done him much harm. Well, and how did Mr Churchill take it?'

'Most favourably for his nephew – gave his consent with scarcely a difficulty. Conceive what the events of a week have done in that family! While poor Mrs Churchill lived, I suppose there could not have been a hope, a chance, a possibility; – but scarcely are her remains at rest in the family vault, than her husband is persuaded to act exactly opposite to what she would have required. What a blessing it is, when undue influence does not survive the grave! – He gave his consent with very little persuasion.'

'Ah!' thought Emma, 'he would have done as much for Harriet.'

'This was settled last night, and Frank was off with the light this morning. He stopped at Highbury, at the Bates's, I fancy, some time – and then came on hither; but was in such a hurry to get back to his uncle, to whom he is just now more necessary than ever, that, as I tell you, he could stay with us but a quarter of an hour. – He was very much agitated – very much, indeed – to a degree that made him appear quite a different creature from any thing I had ever seen him before. – In addition to all the rest, there had been the shock of finding her so very unwell, which he had had no previous suspicion of – and there was every appearance of his having been feeling a great deal.'

'And do you really believe the affair to have been carrying on with such perfect secresy? – The Campbells, The Dixons, did none of them know of the engagement?'

Emma could not speak the name of Dixon without a little blush.

'None; not one. He positively said that it had been known to no being in the world but their two selves.'

'Well,' said Emma, 'I suppose we shall gradually grow reconciled to the idea, and I wish them very happy. But I shall always think it a very abominable sort of proceeding. What has it been but a system of hypocrisy and deceit, – espionage and treachery? – To come among us with professions of openness and simplicity; and such a league in secret to judge us all! – Here have we been, the whole winter and spring, completely duped, fancying ourselves all on an equal footing of truth and honour, with two people in the midst of us who may have been carrying round, comparing and sitting in judgment on sentiments and words that were never meant for both to hear. – They must take the consequence, if they have heard each other spoken of in a way not perfectly agreeable!'

'I am quite easy on that head,' replied Mrs Weston. 'I am very sure that I never said any thing of either to the other, which both might not have heard.'

'You are in luck. – Your only blunder was confined to my ear, when you imagined a certain friend of our's in love with the lady.'

'True. But as I have always had a thoroughly good opinion of Miss Fairfax, I never could, under any blunder, have spoken ill of her; and as to speaking ill of him, there I must have been safe.'

At this moment Mr Weston appeared at a little distance from the window, evidently on the watch. His wife gave him a look which invited him in; and, while he was coming round, added, 'Now, dearest Emma, let me intreat you to say and look every thing that may set his heart at ease, and incline him to be satisfied with the match. Let us make the best of it – and, indeed, almost every thing may be fairly said in her favour. It is not a connection to gratify; but if Mr Churchill does not feel that, why should we? and it may be a very fortunate circumstance for him, for Frank, I mean, that he should have attached himself to a girl of such steadiness of character and good judgment as I have always given her credit for – and still am disposed to give her credit for, in spite of this one great deviation from the strict rule of right. And how much may be said in her situation for even that error!'

'Much indeed!' cried Emma, feelingly. 'If a woman can ever be excused for thinking only of herself, it is in a situation like Jane Fairfax's. – Of such, one may almost say, that "the world is not their's, nor the world's law." '

She met Mr Weston on his entrance, with a smiling countenance, exclaiming,

'A very pretty trick you have been playing me, upon my word! This was a device, I suppose, to sport with my curiosity, and exercise my talent of guessing. But you really frightened me. I thought you had lost half your property, at least. And here, instead of its being a matter of condolence, it turns out to be one of congratulation. – I congratulate you, Mr Weston, with all my heart, on the prospect of having one of the most lovely and accomplished young women in England for your daughter.'

A glance or two between him and his wife, convinced him that all was as right as this speech proclaimed; and its happy effect on his spirits was immediate. His air and voice recovered their usual briskness: he shook her heartily and gratefully by the hand, and entered on the subject in a manner to prove, that he now only wanted time and persuasion to think the engagement no very bad thing. His companions suggested only what could palliate imprudence, or smooth objections; and by the time they had talked it all over together, and he had talked it all over again with Emma, in their walk back to Hartfield, he was becoming perfectly reconciled, and not far from thinking it the very best thing that Frank could possibly have done.

CHAPTER FORTY-SEVEN

'HARRIET, POOR HARRIET!' – Those were the words; in them lay the tormenting ideas which Emma could not get rid of, and which constituted the real misery of the business to her. Frank Churchill had behaved very ill by herself – very ill in many ways, – but it was not so much *his* behaviour as her *own*, which made her so angry with him. It was the scrape which he had drawn her into on Harriet's account, that gave the deepest hue to his offence. – Poor Harriet! to be a second time the dupe of her misconceptions and flattery. Mr Knightley had spoken prophetically, when he once said, 'Emma, you have been no friend to Harriet Smith.' – She was afraid she had done her nothing but disservice. – It was true that she had not to charge herself, in this instance as in the former, with being the sole and original author of the mischief; with having suggested such feelings as might otherwise never have entered Harriet's imagination; for Harriet had acknowledged her admiration and preference of Frank Churchill before she had ever given her a hint on the subject; but she felt completely guilty of having encouraged what she might have repressed. She might have prevented the indulgence and increase of such sentiments. Her influence would have been enough. And now she was very conscious that she ought to have prevented them. – She felt that she had been risking her friend's happiness on most insufficient grounds. Common sense would have directed her to tell Harriet, that she must not allow herself to think of him, and that there were five hundred chances to one against his ever caring for her. – 'But, with commonsense,' she added, 'I am afraid I have had little to do.'

She was extremely angry with herself. If she could not have been angry with Frank Churchill too, it would have been dreadful. – As for Jane Fairfax, she might at least relieve her feelings from any present solicitude on her account. Harriet would be anxiety enough; she need no longer be unhappy about Jane, whose troubles and whose ill health having, of course, the same origin, must be equally under cure. – Her days of insignificance and evil were over. – She would soon be well, and happy, and prosperous. – Emma could now imagine why her own attentions had been slighted. This discovery laid many smaller matters open. No doubt it had been from jealousy. – In Jane's eyes she had been a rival; and well might any thing she could offer of assistance or regard be repulsed. An airing in the Hartfield carriage would have been the rack, and arrow-root from the Hartfield storeroom must have been poison. She understood it all; and as far as her mind could disengage itself from the injustice and selfishness of angry feelings, she acknowledged that Jane Fairfax would have neither elevation nor happiness beyond her desert. But poor Harriet was such an engrossing charge! There was little sympathy to be spared for any body else. Emma was sadly fearful that this second disappointment would be more severe than the first. Considering the very superior claims of the object, it ought; and judging by its apparently stronger effect on Harriet's mind, producing reserve and self-command, it would. – She must communicate the painful truth, however, and as soon as possible. An injunction of secresy had been among Mr Weston's parting words. 'For the present, the whole affair was to be completely a secret. Mr Churchill had made a point of it, as a token of respect to the wife he had so very recently lost; and everybody admitted it to be no more than due decorum.' – Emma had promised; but still Harriet must be excepted. It was her superior duty.

In spite of her vexation, she could not help feeling it almost ridiculous, that she should have the very same distressing and delicate office to perform by Harriet, which Mrs Weston had just gone through by herself. The intelligence, which had been so anxiously announced to her, she was now to be anxiously announcing to another. Her heart beat quick on hearing Harriet's footstep and voice; so, she supposed, had poor Mrs Weston felt when *she* was approaching Randalls. Could the event of the disclosure bear an equal resemblance! – But of that, unfortunately, there could be no chance.

'Well, Miss Woodhouse!' cried Harriet, coming eagerly into the room – 'is not this the oddest news that ever was?'

'What news do you mean?' replied Emma, unable to guess, by look or voice, whether Harriet could indeed have received any hint.

'About Jane Fairfax. Did you ever hear any thing so strange? Oh! – you need not be afraid of owning it to me, for Mr Weston has told me himself. I met him just now. He told me it was to be a great secret; and, therefore, I should not think of mentioning it to any body but you, but he said you knew it.'

'What did Mr Weston tell you?' – said Emma, still perplexed.

'Oh! he told me all about it; that Jane Fairfax and Mr Frank Churchill are to be married, and that they have been privately engaged to one another this long while. How very odd!'

It was, indeed, so odd; Harriet's behaviour was so extremely odd, that Emma did not know how to understand it. Her character appeared absolutely changed. She seemed to propose showing no agitation, or disappointment, or peculiar concern in the discovery. Emma looked at her, quite unable to speak.

'Had you any idea,' cried Harriet, 'of his being in love with her? – You, perhaps, might. – You (blushing as she spoke) who can see into every body's heart; but nobody else – '

'Upon my word,' said Emma, 'I begin to doubt my having any such talent. Can you seriously ask me, Harriet, whether I imagined him attached to another woman at the very time that I was – tacitly, if not openly – encouraging you to give way to your own feelings? – I never had the slightest suspicion, till within the last hour, of Mr Frank Churchill's having the least regard for Jane Fairfax. You may be very sure that if I had, I should have cautioned you accordingly.'

'Me!' cried Harriet, colouring, and astonished. 'Why should you caution me? – You do not think I care about Mr Frank Churchill.'

'I am delighted to hear you speak so stoutly on the subject,' replied Emma, smiling; 'but you do not mean to deny that there was a time – and not very distant either – when you gave me reason to understand that you did care about him?'

'Him! – never, never. Dear Miss Woodhouse, how could you so mistake me?' turning away distressed.

'Harriet!' cried Emma, after a moment's pause – 'What do you mean? – Good Heaven! what do you mean? – Mistake you! – Am I to suppose then? – '

She could not speak another word – Her voice was lost; and she sat down, waiting in great terror till Harriet should answer.

Harriet, who was standing at some distance, and with face turned from her, did not immediately say any thing; and when she did speak, it was in a voice nearly as agitated as Emma's.

'I should not have thought it possible,' she began, 'that you could have misunderstood me! I know we agreed never to name him – but considering how infinitely superior he is to every body else, I should not have thought it possible that I could be supposed to mean any other person. Mr Frank Churchill, indeed! I do not know who would ever look at him in the company of the other. I hope I have a better taste than to think of Mr Frank Churchill, who is like nobody by his side. And that you should have been so mistaken, is amazing! – I am sure, but for believing that you entirely approved and meant to encourage me in my attachment, I should have considered it at first too great a presumption almost, to dare to think of him. At first, if you had not told me that more wonderful things had happened; that there had been matches of greater disparity (those were your very words); – I should not have dared to give way to – I should not have thought it possible – But if *you*, who had been always acquainted with him – '

'Harriet!' cried Emma, collecting herself resolutely – 'Let us understand each other now, without the possibility of farther mistake. Are you speaking of – Mr Knightley?'

'To be sure I am. I never could have an idea of any body else – and so I thought you knew. When we talked about him, it was clear as possible.'

'Not quite,' returned Emma, with forced calmness, 'for all that you then said, appeared to me to relate to a different person. I could almost assert that you had *named* Mr Frank Churchill. I am sure the service Mr Frank Churchill had rendered you, in protecting you from the gipsies, was spoken of.'

'Oh! Miss Woodhouse, how you do forget!'

'My dear Harriet, I perfectly remember the substance of what I said on the occasion. I told you that I did not wonder at your attachment; that considering the service he had rendered you, it was extremely natural: – and you agreed to it, expressing yourself very warmly as to your sense of that service, and mentioning even what your sensations had been in seeing him come forward to your rescue. – The impression of it is strong on my memory.'

'Oh, dear,' cried Harriet, 'now I recollect what you mean; but I was thinking of something very different at the time. It was not the gipsies – it was not Mr Frank Churchill that I meant. No! (with some elevation) I was thinking of a much more precious circumstance – of Mr Knightley's coming and asking me to dance, when Mr Elton would not stand up with me; and when there was no other partner in the room. That was the kind action; that was the noble benevolence and generosity; that was the service which made me begin to feel how superior he was to every other being upon earth.'

'Good God!' cried Emma, 'this has been a most unfortunate – most deplorable mistake! – What is to be done?'

'You would not have encouraged me, then, if you had understood me. At least, however, I cannot be worse off than I should have been, if the other had been the person; and now – it is possible –.'

She paused a few moments. Emma could not speak.

'I do not wonder, Miss Woodhouse,' she resumed, 'that you should feel a great difference between the two, as to me or as to anybody. You must think one five hundred million times more above me than the other. But I hope, Miss Woodhouse, that supposing – that if – strange as it may appear – . But you know they were your own words, that *more* wonderful things had happened, matches of *greater* disparity had taken place than between Mr Frank Churchill and me; and, therefore, it seems as if such a thing even as this, may have occurred before – and if I should be so fortunate, beyond expression, as to – if Mr Knightley should really – if *he* does not mind the disparity, I hope, dear Miss Woodhouse, you will not set yourself against it, and try to put difficulties in the way. But you are too good for that, I am sure.'

Harriet was standing at one of the windows. Emma turned round to look at her in consternation, and hastily said,

'Have you any idea of Mr Knightley's returning your affection?'

'Yes,' replied Harriet modestly, but not fearfully – 'I must say that I have.'

Emma's eyes were instantly withdrawn; and she sat silently meditating, in a fixed attitude, for a few minutes. A few minutes were sufficient for making her acquainted with her own heart. A mind like her's, once opening to suspicion, made rapid progress. She touched – she admitted – she acknowledged the whole truth. Why was it so much worse that Harriet should be in love with Mr Knightley, than with Frank Churchill? Why was the evil so dreadfully increased by Harriet's having some hope of a return? It darted through her, with the speed of an arrow, that Mr Knightley must marry no one but herself!

Her own conduct, as well as her own heart, was before her in the same few minutes. She saw it all with a clearness which had never blessed her before. How improperly had she been acting by Harriet! How inconsiderate, how indelicate, how irrational, how unfeeling had been her conduct! What blindness, what madness, had led her on! It struck her with dreadful force, and she was ready to give it every bad name in the world. Some portion of respect for herself, however, in spite of all these demerits – some concern for her own appearance, and a strong sense of justice by Harriet – (there would be no need of *compassion* to the girl who believed herself loved by Mr Knightley – but justice required that she should not be made unhappy by any coldness now,) gave Emma the resolution to sit and endure farther with calmness, with even apparent kindness. – For her own advantage indeed, it was fit that the utmost extent of Harriet's hopes should be enquired into; and Harriet had done nothing to forfeit the regard and interest which had been so voluntarily formed and maintained – or to deserve to be slighted by the person, whose counsels had never led her right. – Rousing from reflection, therefore, and subduing her emotion, she turned to Harriet again, and, in a more inviting accent, renewed the conversation; for as to the subject which had first introduced it, the wonderful story of Jane Fairfax, that was quite sunk and lost. – Neither of them thought but of Mr Knightley and themselves.

Harriet, who had been standing in no unhappy reverie, was yet very glad to be called from it, by the now encouraging manner of such a judge, and such a friend as Miss Woodhouse, and only wanted invitation, to give the history of her hopes with great, though trembling delight. – Emma's tremblings as she asked, and as she listened, were better concealed than Harriet's, but they were not less. Her voice was not unsteady; but her mind was in all the perturbation that such a development of self, such a burst of threatening evil, such a confusion of sudden and perplexing emotions, must create. – She listened with much inward suffering, but with great outward patience, to Harriet's detail. – Methodical, or well arranged, or very well delivered, it could not be expected to be; but it contained, when separated from all the feebleness and tautology of the narration, a substance to sink her spirit – especially with the corroborating circumstances, which her own memory brought in favour of Mr Knightley's most improved opinion of Harriet.

Harriet had been conscious of a difference in his behaviour ever since those two decisive dances. – Emma knew that he had, on that occasion, found her much superior to his expectation. From that evening, or at least from the time of Miss Woodhouse's encouraging her to think of him, Harriet had begun to be sensible of his talking to her much more than he had been used to do, and of his having indeed quite a different manner towards her; a manner of kindness and sweetness! – Latterly she had been more and more aware of it. When they had been all walking together, he had so often come and walked by her, and talked so very delightfully! – He seemed to want to be acquainted with her. Emma knew it to have been very much the case. She had often observed the change, to almost the same extent. – Harriet repeated expressions of approbation and praise from him – and Emma felt them to be in the closest agreement with what she had known of his opinion of Harriet. He praised her for being without art or affectation, for having simple, honest, generous, feelings. – She knew that he saw such recommendations in Harriet; he had dwelt on them to her more than once. – Much that lived in Harriet's memory, many little particulars of the notice she had received from him, a look, a speech, a removal from one chair to another, a compliment implied, a preference inferred, had been unnoticed, because unsuspected by Emma. Circumstances that might swell to half an hour's relation, and contained multiplied proofs to her who had seen them, had passed undiscerned by her who now heard them; but the two latest occurrences to be mentioned, the two of strongest promise to Harriet, were not without some degree of witness from Emma herself. – The first, was his walking with her apart from the others, in the lime walk at Donwell, where they had been walking some time before Emma came, and he had taken pains (as she was convinced) to draw her from the rest to himself – and at first, he had talked to her in a more particular way than he had ever done before, in a very particular way indeed! – (Harriet could not recall it without a blush.) He seemed to be almost asking her, whether her affections were engaged. – But as soon as she (Miss Woodhouse) appeared likely to join them, he changed the subject, and began talking about farming: – The second, was his having sat talking with her nearly half an hour before Emma came back from her visit, the very last morning of his being at Hartfield – though, when he first came in, he had said that he could not stay five minutes – and his having told her, during their conversation, that though he must go to London, it was very much against his inclination that he left home at all, which was much more (as Emma felt) than he had acknowledged to *her*. The superior degree of confidence towards Harriet, which this one article marked, gave her severe pain.

On the subject of the first of the two circumstances, she did, after a little reflection, venture the following question. 'Might he not? – Is not it possible, that when enquiring, as you thought, into the state of your affections, he might be alluding to Mr Martin – he might have Mr Martin's interest in view?' – But Harriet rejected the suspicion with spirit.

'Mr Martin! No indeed! – There was not a hint of Mr Martin. I hope I know better now, than to care for Mr Martin, or to be suspected of it.'

When Harriet had closed her evidence, she appealed to her dear Miss Woodhouse, to say whether she had not good ground for hope.

'I never should have presumed to think of it at first,' said she, 'but for you. You told me to observe him carefully, and let his behaviour be the rule of mine – and so I have. But now I seem to feel that I may deserve him; and that if he does choose me, it will not be any thing so very wonderful.'

The bitter feelings occasioned by this speech, the many bitter feelings, made the utmost exertion necessary on Emma's side, to enable her to say in reply.

'Harriet, I will only venture to declare, that Mr Knightley is the last man in the world, who would intentionally give any woman the idea of his feeling for her more than he really does.'

Harriet seemed ready to worship her friend for a sentence so satisfactory; and Emma was only saved from raptures and fondness, which at that moment would have been dreadful penance, by the sound of her father's footsteps. He was coming through the hall. Harriet was too much agitated to encounter him. 'She could not compose herself – Mr Woodhouse would be alarmed – she had better go;' – with most ready encouragement from her friend, therefore, she passed off through another door – and the moment she was gone, this was the spontaneous burst of Emma's feelings; 'Oh God! that I had never seen her!'

The rest of the day, the following night, were hardly enough for her thoughts. – She was bewildered amidst the confusion of all that had rushed on her within the last few hours. Every moment had brought a fresh surprise; and every surprize must be matter of humiliation to her. – How to understand it all! How to understand the deceptions she had been thus practising on herself, and living under! – The blunders, the blindness of her own head and heart! – she sat still, she walked about, she tried her own room, she tried the shrubbery – in every place, every posture, she perceived that she had acted most weakly; that she had been imposed on by others in a most mortifying degree; that she had been imposing on herself in a degree yet more mortifying; that she was wretched, and should probably find this day but the beginning of wretchedness.

To understand, thoroughly understand her own heart, was the first endeavour. To that point went every leisure moment which her father's claims on her allowed, and every moment of involuntary absence of mind.

How long had Mr Knightley been so dear to her, as every feeling declared him now to be? When had his influence, such influence begun? – When had he succeeded to that place in her affection, which Frank Churchill had once, for a short period, occupied? – She looked back, she compared the two – compared them, as they had always stood in her estimation, from the time of the latter's becoming known to her – and as they must at any time have been compared by her, had it – oh! had it, by any blessed felicity, occurred to her, to institute the comparison. – She saw that there never had been a time when she did not consider Mr Knightley as infinitely the superior, or when his regard for her had not been infinitely the most dear. She saw, that in persuading herself, in fancying, in acting to the contrary, she had been entirely under a delusion, totally ignorant of her own heart – and in short, that she had never really cared for Frank Churchill at all!

This was the conclusion of the first series of reflection. This was the knowledge of herself, on the first question of enquiry, which she reached; and without being long in reaching it. – She was most sorrowfully indignant; ashamed of every sensation but the one revealed to her – her affection for Mr Knightley. – Every other part of her mind was disgusting.

With insufferable vanity had she believed herself in the secret of everybody's feelings; with unpardonable arrogance proposed to arrange everybody's destiny. She was proved to have been universally mistaken; and she had not quite done nothing – for she had done mischief. She had brought evil on Harriet, on herself, and she too much feared, on Mr Knightley. – Were this most unequal of all connexions to take place, on her must rest all the reproach of having given it a beginning; for his attachment, she must believe to be produced only by a consciousness of Harriet's; – and even were this not the case, he would never have known Harriet at all but for her folly.

Mr Knightley and Harriet Smith! – It was an union to distance every wonder of the kind. – The attachment of Frank Churchill and Jane Fairfax became commonplace, threadbare, stale in the comparison, exciting no surprize, presenting no disparity, affording nothing to be said or thought. – Mr Knightley and Harriet Smith! – Such an elevation on her side! Such a debasement on his! – It was horrible to Emma to think how it must sink him in the general opinion, to foresee the smiles, the sneers, the merriment it would prompt at his expense; the mortification and disdain of his brother, the thousand inconveniences to himself. – Could it be? – No; it was impossible. And yet it was far, very far, from impossible. – Was it a new circumstance for a man of first-rate abilities to be captivated by very inferior powers? Was it new for one, perhaps too busy to seek, to be the prize of a girl who would seek him? – Was it new for any thing in this world to be unequal, inconsistent, incongruous – or for change and circumstance (as second causes) to direct the human fate?

Oh! had she never brought Harriet forward! Had she left her where she ought, and where he had told her she ought! – Had she not, with a folly which no tongue could express, prevented her marrying the unexceptionable young man who would have made her happy and respectable in the line of life to which she ought to belong – all would have been safe; none of this dreadful sequel would have been.

How Harriet could ever have had the presumption to raise her thoughts to Mr Knightley! – How she could dare to fancy herself the chosen of such a man till actually assured of it! – But Harriet was less humble, had fewer scruples than formerly. – Her inferiority, whether of mind or situation, seemed little felt. – She had seemed more sensible of Mr Elton's being to stoop in marrying her, than she now seemed of Mr Knightley's. – Alas! was not that her own doing too? Who had been at pains to give Harriet notions of self-consequence but herself? – Who but herself had taught her, that she was to elevate herself if possible, and that her claims were great to a high worldly establishment? – If Harriet, from being humble, were grown vain, it was her doing too.

CHAPTER FORTY-EIGHT

TILL NOW THAT SHE WAS threatened with its loss, Emma had never known how much of her happiness depended on being *first* with Mr Knightley, first in interest and affection. – Satisfied that it was so, and feeling it her due, she had enjoyed it without reflection; and only in the dread of being supplanted, found how inexpressibly important it had been. – Long, very long, she felt she had been first; for, having no female connexions of his own, there had been only Isabella whose claims could be compared with hers, and she had always known exactly how far he loved and esteemed Isabella. She had herself been first with him for many years past. She had not deserved it; she had often been negligent or perverse, slighting his advice, or even wilfully opposing him, insensible of half his merits, and quarrelling with him because he would not acknowledge her false and insolent estimate of her own – but still, from family attachment and habit, and thorough excellence of mind, he had loved her, and watched over her from a girl, with an endeavour to improve her, and an anxiety for her doing right, which no other creature had at all shared. In spite of all her faults, she knew she was dear to him; might she not say, very dear? – When the suggestions of hope, however, which must follow here, presented themselves, she could not presume to indulge them. Harriet Smith might think herself not unworthy of being peculiarly, exclusively, passionately loved by Mr Knightley. *She* could not. She could not flatter herself with any idea of blindness in his attachment to *her*. She had received a very recent proof of its impartiality. – How shocked had he been by her behaviour to Miss Bates! How directly, how strongly had he expressed himself to her on the subject! – Not too strongly for the offence – but far, far too strongly to issue from any feeling softer than upright justice and clear-sighted good will. – She had no hope, nothing to deserve the name of hope, that he could have that sort of affection for herself which was now in question; but there was a hope (at times a slight one, at times much stronger,) that Harriet might have deceived herself, and be overrating his regard for *her*. – Wish it she must, for his sake – be the consequence nothing to herself, but his remaining single all his life. Could she be secure of that, indeed, of his never marrying at all, she believed she should be perfectly satisfied. – Let him but continue the same

Mr Knightley to her and her father, the same Mr Knightley to all the world; let Donwell and Hartfield lose none of their precious intercourse of friendship and confidence, and her peace would be fully secured. – Marriage, in fact, would not do for her. It would be incompatible with what she owed to her father, and with what she felt for him. Nothing should separate her from her father. She would not marry, even if she were asked by Mr Knightley.

It must be her ardent wish that Harriet might be disappointed; and she hoped, that when able to see them together again, she might at least be able to ascertain what the chances for it were. – She should see them henceforward with the closest observance; and wretchedly as she had hitherto misunderstood even those she was watching, she did not know how to admit that she could be blinded here. – He was expected back every day. The power of observation would be soon given – frightfully soon it appeared when her thoughts were in one course. In the meanwhile, she resolved against seeing Harriet. – It would do neither of them good, it would do the subject no good, to be talking of it farther. – She was resolved not to be convinced, as long as she could doubt, and yet had no authority for opposing Harriet's confidence. To talk would be only to irritate. – She wrote to her, therefore, kindly, but decisively, to beg that she would not, at present, come to Hartfield; acknowledging it to be her conviction, that all farther confidential discussion on *one* topic had better be avoided; and hoping, that if a few days were allowed to pass before they met again, except in the company of others – she objected only to a tête-à-tête – they might be able to act as if they had forgotten the conversation of yesterday. – Harriet submitted, and approved, and was grateful.

This point was just arranged, when a visitor arrived to tear Emma's thoughts a little from the one subject which had engrossed them, sleeping or waking, the last twenty-four hours – Mrs Weston, who had been calling on her daughter-in-law elect, and took Hartfield in her way home, almost as much in duty to Emma as in pleasure to herself, to relate all the particulars of so interesting an interview.

Mr Weston had accompanied her to Mrs Bates's, and gone through his share of this essential attention most handsomely; but she having then induced Miss Fairfax to join her in an airing, was now returned with much more to say, and much more to say with satisfaction, than a quarter of an hour spent in Mrs Bates's parlour, with all the incumbrance of awkward feelings, could have afforded.

A little curiosity Emma had; and she made the most of it while her friend related. Mrs Weston had set off to pay the visit in a good deal of agitation herself; and in the first place had wished not to go at all at present, to be allowed merely to write to Miss Fairfax instead, and to defer this ceremonious call till a little time had passed, and Mr Churchill could be reconciled to the engagement's becoming known; as, considering every thing, she thought such a visit could not be paid without leading to reports: – but Mr Weston had thought differently; he was extremely anxious to shew his approbation to Miss Fairfax and her family, and did not conceive that any suspicion could be excited by it; or if it were, that it would be of any consequence; for 'such things,' he observed, 'always got about.' Emma smiled, and felt that Mr Weston had very good reason for saying so. They had gone, in short – and very great had been the evident distress and confusion of the lady. She had hardly been able to speak a word, and every look and action had shown how deeply she was suffering from consciousness. The quiet, heartfelt satisfaction of the old lady, and the rapturous delight of her daughter – who proved even too joyous to talk as usual, had been a gratifying, yet almost an affecting, scene. They were both so truly respectable in their happiness, so disinterested in every sensation; thought so much of Jane; so much of everybody, and so little of themselves, that every kindly feeling was at work for them. Miss Fairfax's recent illness had offered a fair plea for Mrs Weston to invite her to an airing; she had drawn back and declined at first, but on being pressed had yielded; and in the course of their drive, Mrs Weston had, by gentle encouragement, overcome so much of her embarrassment, as to bring her to converse on the important subject. Apologies for her seemingly ungracious silence in their first reception, and the warmest expressions of the gratitude she was always feeling towards herself and Mr Weston, must necessarily open the cause; but when these effusions were put by, they had talked a good deal of the present and of the future state of the engagement. Mrs Weston was convinced that such conversation must be the greatest relief to her companion, pent up within her own mind as every thing had so long been, and was very much pleased with all that she had said on the subject.

'On the misery of what she had suffered, during the concealment of so many months,' continued Mrs Weston, 'she was energetic. This was one of her expressions. I will not say, that since I entered into the engagement I have not had some happy moments; but I can say, that I have never known the blessing of one tranquil hour: – and the quivering lip, Emma, which uttered it, was an attestation that I felt at my heart.'

'Poor girl!' said Emma. 'She thinks herself wrong, then, for having consented to a private engagement?'

'Wrong! – No one, I believe, can blame her more than she is disposed to blame herself. "The consequence," said she, "has been a state of perpetual suffering to me; and so it ought. But after all the punishment that misconduct can bring, it is still not less misconduct. Pain is no expiation. I never can be blameless. I have been acting contrary to all my sense of right; and the fortunate turn that every thing has taken, and the kindness I am now receiving, is what my conscience tells me ought not to be. Do not imagine, madam," she continued, "that I was taught wrong. Do not let any reflection fall on the principles or the care of the friends who brought me up. The error has been all my own; and I do assure you that, with all the excuse that present circumstances may appear to give, I shall yet dread making the story known to Colonel Campbell." '

'Poor girl!' said Emma again. 'She loves him then excessively, I suppose. It must have been from attachment only, that she could be led to form the engagement. Her affection must have overpowered her judgment.'

'Yes, I have no doubt of her being extremely attached to him.'

'I am afraid,' returned Emma, sighing, 'that I must often have contributed to make her unhappy.'

'On your side, my love, it was very innocently done. But she probably had something of that in her thoughts, when alluding to the misunderstandings which he had given us hints of before. One natural consequence of the evil she had involved herself in, she said, was that of making her *unreasonable*. The consciousness of having done amiss, had exposed her to a thousand inquietudes, and made her captious and irritable to a degree that must have been – that had been – hard for him to bear. "I did not make the allowance," said she, "which I ought to have done, for his temper and spirits – his delightful spirits, and that gaiety, that playfulness of disposition, which, under any other circumstances, would, I am sure, have been as constantly bewitching to me, as they were at first." She then began to speak of you, and of the great kindness you had shown her during her illness; and with a blush which showed me how it was all connected, desired me, whenever I had an opportunity, to thank you – I could not thank you too much – for every wish and every endeavour to do her good. She was sensible that you had never received any proper acknowledgement from herself.'

'If I did not know her to be happy now,' said Emma, seriously, 'which, in spite of every little drawback from her scrupulous conscience, she must be, I could not bear these thanks; – for, oh!

Mrs Weston, if there were an account drawn up of the evil and the good I have done Miss Fairfax! – Well (checking herself, and trying to be more lively), this is all to be forgotten. You are very kind to bring me these interesting particulars. They show her to the greatest advantage. I am sure she is very good – I hope she will be very happy. It is fit that the fortune should be on his side, for I think the merit will be all on her's.'

Such a conclusion could not pass unanswered by Mrs Weston. She thought well of Frank in almost every respect; and, what was more, she loved him very much, and her defence was, therefore, earnest. She talked with a great deal of reason, and at least equal affection – but she had too much to urge for Emma's attention; it was soon gone to Brunswick Square or to Donwell; she forgot to attempt to listen; and when Mrs Weston ended with, 'We have not yet had the letter we are so anxious for, you know, but I hope it will soon come,' she was obliged to pause before she answered, and at last obliged to answer at random, before she could at all recollect what letter it was which they were so anxious for.

'Are you well, my Emma?' was Mrs Weston's parting question.

'Oh! perfectly. I am always well, you know. Be sure to give me intelligence of the letter as soon as possible.'

Mrs Weston's communications furnished Emma with more food for unpleasant reflection, by increasing her esteem and compassion, and her sense of past injustice towards Miss Fairfax. She bitterly regretted not having sought a closer acquaintance with her, and blushed for the envious feelings which had certainly been, in some measure, the cause. Had she followed Mr Knightley's known wishes, in paying that attention to Miss Fairfax, which was every way her due; had she tried to know her better; had she done her part towards intimacy; had she endeavoured to find a friend there instead of in Harriet Smith; she must, in all probability, have been spared from every pain which pressed on her now. – Birth, abilities, and education, had been equally marking one as an associate for her, to be received with gratitude; and the other – what was she? – Supposing even that they had never become intimate friends; that she had never been admitted into Miss Fairfax's confidence on this important matter – which was most probable – still, in knowing her as she ought, and as she might, she must have been preserved from the abominable suspicions of an improper attachment to Mr Dixon, which she had not only so foolishly fashioned and harboured herself, but had so unpardonably imparted; an idea which she greatly feared had been made a subject of material distress to the delicacy of Jane's feelings, by the levity or carelessness of Frank Churchill's.

Of all the sources of evil surrounding the former, since her coming to Highbury, she was persuaded that she must herself have been the worst. She must have been a perpetual enemy. They never could have been all three together, without her having stabbed Jane Fairfax's peace in a thousand instances; and on Box Hill, perhaps, it had been the agony of a mind that would bear no more.

The evening of this day was very long, and melancholy, at Hartfield. The weather added what it could of gloom. A cold stormy rain set in, and nothing of July appeared but in the trees and shrubs, which the wind was despoiling, and the length of the day, which only made such cruel sights the longer visible.

The weather affected Mr Woodhouse, and he could only be kept tolerably comfortable by almost ceaseless attention on his daughter's side, and by exertions which had never cost her half so much before. It reminded her of their first forlorn tête-à-tête, on the evening of Mrs Weston's wedding-day; but Mr Knightley had walked in then, soon after tea, and dissipated every melancholy fancy. Alas! such delightful proofs of Hartfield's attraction, as those sort of visits conveyed, might shortly be over. The picture which she had then drawn of the privations of the approaching winter, had proved erroneous; no friends had deserted them, no pleasures had been lost. – But her present forebodings she feared would experience no similar contradiction. The prospect before her now, was threatening to a degree that could not be entirely dispelled – that might not be even partially brightened. If all took place that might take place among the circle of her friends, Hartfield must be comparatively deserted; and she left to cheer her father with the spirits only of ruined happiness.

The child to be born at Randalls must be a tie there even dearer than herself; and Mrs Weston's heart and time would be occupied by it. They should lose her; and, probably, in great measure, her husband also. – Frank Churchill would return among them no more; and Miss Fairfax, it was reasonable to suppose, would soon cease to belong to Highbury. They would be married, and settled either at or near Enscombe. All that were good would be withdrawn; and if to these losses, the loss of Donwell were to be added, what would remain of cheerful or of rational society within their reach? Mr Knightley to be no longer coming there for his evening comfort! – No longer walking in at all hours, as if ever willing to change his own home for their's! – How was it to be endured? And if he were to be lost to them for Harriet's sake; if he were to be thought of hereafter, as finding in Harriet's society all that he wanted; if Harriet were to be the chosen, the first, the dearest, the friend, the wife to whom he looked for all the best blessings of existence; what could be increasing Emma's wretchedness but the reflection never far distant from her mind, that it had been all her own work?

When it came to such a pitch as this, she was not able to refrain from a start, or a heavy sigh, or even from walking about the room for a few seconds – and the only source whence any thing like consolation or composure could be drawn, was in the resolution of her own better conduct, and the hope that, however inferior in spirit and gaiety might be the following and every future winter of her life to the past, it would yet find her more rational, more acquainted with herself, and leave her less to regret when it were gone.

CHAPTER FORTY-NINE

THE WEATHER CONTINUED much the same all the following morning; and the same loneliness, and the same melancholy, seemed to reign at Hartfield – but in the afternoon it cleared; the wind changed into a softer quarter; the clouds were carried off; the sun appeared; it was summer again. With all the eagerness which such a transition gives, Emma resolved to be out of doors as soon as possible. Never had the exquisite sight, smell, sensation of nature, tranquil, warm, and brilliant after a storm, been more attractive to her. She longed for the serenity they might gradually introduce; and on Mr Perry's coming in soon after dinner, with a disengaged hour to give her father, she lost no time in hurrying into the shrubbery. – There, with spirits freshened, and thoughts a little relieved, she had taken a few turns, when she saw Mr Knightley passing through the garden door, and coming towards her. – It was the first intimation of his being returned from London. She had been thinking of him the moment before, as unquestionably sixteen miles distant. – There was time only for the quickest arrangement of mind. She must be collected and calm. In half a minute they were together. The 'How d'ye do's,' were quiet and constrained on each side. She asked after their mutual friends; they were all well. – When had he left them? – Only that morning. He must have had a wet ride. – Yes. – He meant to walk with her, she found. 'He had just looked into the dining-room, and as he was not wanted there, preferred being out of doors.' – She thought he neither looked nor spoke cheerfully; and the first possible cause for it, suggested by her fears, was, that he had perhaps been communicating his plans to his brother, and was pained by the manner in which they had been received.

They walked together. He was silent. She thought he was often looking at her, and trying for a fuller view of her face than it suited her to give. And this belief produced another dread. Perhaps he wanted to speak to her, of his attachment to Harriet; he might be watching for encouragement to begin. – She did not, could not, feel equal to lead the way to any such subject. He must do it all himself. Yet she could not bear this silence. With him it was most unnatural. She considered – resolved – and, trying to smile, began –

'You have some news to hear, now you are come back, that will rather surprize you.'

'Have I?' said he quietly, and looking at her; 'of what nature?'

'Oh! the best nature in the world – a wedding.'

After waiting a moment, as if to be sure she intended to say no more, he replied,

'If you mean Miss Fairfax and Frank Churchill, I have heard that already.'

'How is it possible?' cried Emma, turning her glowing cheeks towards him; for while she spoke, it occurred to her that he might have called at Mrs Goddard's in his way.

'I had a few lines on parish business from Mr Weston this morning, and at the end of them he gave me a brief account of what had happened.'

Emma was quite relieved, and could presently say, with a little more composure,

'*You* probably have been less surprized than any of us, for you have had your suspicions. – I have not forgotten that you once tried to give me a caution. – I wish I had attended to it – but – (with a sinking voice and a heavy sigh) I seem to have been doomed to blindness'.

For a moment or two nothing was said, and she was unsuspicious of having excited any particular interest, till she found her arm drawn within his, and pressed against his heart and heard him thus saying, in a tone of great sensibility, speaking low,

'Time, my dearest Emma, time will heal the wound. – Your own excellent sense – your exertions for your father's sake – I know you will not allow yourself – .' Her arm was pressed again, as he added, in a more broken and subdued accent, 'The feelings of the warmest friendship – Indignation – Abominable scoundrel!' – And in a louder, steadier tone, he concluded with, 'He will soon be gone. They will soon be in Yorkshire. I am sorry for *her*. She deserves a better fate.'

Emma understood him; and as soon as she could recover from the flutter of pleasure, excited by such tender consideration, replied,

'You are very kind – but you are mistaken – and I must set you right. – I am not in want of that sort of compassion. My blindness to what was going on, led me to act by them in a way that I must always be ashamed of, and I was very foolishly tempted to say and do many things which may well lay me open to unpleasant conjectures, but I have no other reason to regret that I was not in the secret earlier.'

'Emma!' cried he, looking eagerly at her, 'are you, indeed?' – but checking himself – 'No, no, I understand you – forgive me – I am pleased that you can say even so much. – He is no object of regret, indeed! and it will not be very long, I hope, before that becomes the acknowledgement of more than your reason. – Fortunate that your affections were not farther entangled! – I could never, I confess, from your manners, assure myself as to the degree of what you felt – I could only be certain that there was a preference – and a preference which I never believed him to deserve. – He is a disgrace to the name of man. – And is he to be rewarded with that sweet young woman? – Jane, Jane, you will be a miserable creature.'

'Mr Knightley,' said Emma, trying to be lively, but really confused – 'I am in a very extraordinary situation. I cannot let you continue in your error; and yet, perhaps, since my manners gave such an impression, I have as much reason to be ashamed of confessing that I never have been at all attached to the person we are speaking of, as it might be natural for a woman to feel in confessing exactly the reverse. – But I never have.'

He listened in perfect silence. She wished him to speak, but he would not. She supposed she must say more before she were entitled to his clemency; but it was a hard case to be obliged still to lower herself in his opinion. She went on, however.

'I have very little to say for my own conduct. – I was tempted by his attentions, and allowed myself to appear pleased. – An old story, probably – a common case – and no more than has happened to hundreds of my sex before; and yet it may not be the more excusable in one who sets up as I do for Understanding. Many circumstances assisted the temptation. He was the son of Mr Weston – he was continually here – I always found him very pleasant – and, in short, for (with a sigh) let me swell out the causes ever so ingeniously, they all centre in this at last – my vanity was flattered, and I allowed his attentions. Latterly, however – for some time, indeed – I have had no idea of their meaning any thing. – I thought them a habit, a trick, nothing that called for seriousness on my side.

He has imposed on me, but he has not injured me. I have never been attached to him. And now I can tolerably comprehend his behaviour. He never wished to attach me. It was merely a blind to conceal his real situation with another. – It was his object to blind all about him; and no one, I am sure, could be more effectually blinded than myself – except that I was *not* blinded – that it was my good fortune – that, in short, I was somehow or other safe from him.'

She had hoped for an answer here – for a few words to say that her conduct was at least intelligible; but he was silent; and, as far as she could judge, deep in thought. At last, and tolerably in his usual tone, he said,

'I have never had a high opinion of Frank Churchill. – I can suppose, however, that I may have under-rated him. My acquaintance with him has been but trifling. – And even if I have not underrated him hitherto, he may yet turn out well. – With such a woman he has a chance. – I have no motive for wishing him ill – and for her sake, whose happiness will be involved in his good character and conduct, I shall certainly wish him well.'

'I have no doubt of their being happy together,' said Emma; 'I believe them to be very mutually and very sincerely attached.'

'He is a most fortunate man!' returned Mr Knightley, with energy. 'So early in life – at three and twenty – a period when, if a man chooses a wife, he generally chooses ill. At three and twenty to have drawn such a prize! – What years of felicity that man, in all human calculation, has before him! – Assured of the love of such a woman – the disinterested love, for Jane Fairfax's character vouches for her disinterestedness; every thing in his favour, – equality of situation – I mean, as far as regards society, and all the habits and manners that are important; equality in every point but one – and that one, since the purity of her heart is not to be doubted, such as must increase his felicity, for it will be his to bestow the only advantages she wants. – A man would always wish to give a woman a better home than the one he takes her from; and he who can do it, where there is no doubt of *her* regard, must, I think, be the happiest of mortals. – Frank Churchill is, indeed, the favourite of fortune. Every thing turns out for his good. – He meets with a young woman at a watering-place, gains her affection, cannot even weary her by negligent treatment – and had he and all his family sought round the world for a perfect wife for him, they could not have found her superior. – His aunt is in the way. – His aunt dies. – He has only to speak. – His friends are eager to promote his happiness. – He has used every body ill – and they are all delighted to forgive him. – He is a fortunate man indeed!'

'You speak as if you envied him.'

'And I do envy him, Emma. In one respect he is the object of my envy.'

Emma could say no more. They seemed to be within half a sentence of Harriet, and her immediate feeling was to avert the subject, if possible. She made her plan; she would speak of something totally different – the children in Brunswick Square; and she only waited for breath to begin, when Mr Knightley startled her, by saying,

'You will not ask me what is the point of envy. – You are determined, I see, to have no curiosity. – You are wise – but *I* cannot be wise. Emma, I must tell what you will not ask, though I may wish it unsaid the next moment.'

'Oh! then, don't speak it, don't speak it,' she eagerly cried. 'Take a little time, consider, do not commit yourself.'

'Thank you,' said he, in an accent of deep mortification, and not another syllable followed.

Emma could not bear to give him pain. He was wishing to confide in her – perhaps to consult her; – cost her what it would, she would listen. She might assist his resolution, or reconcile him to it; she might give just praise to Harriet, or, by representing to him his own independence, relieve him from that state of indecision, which must be more intolerable than any alternative to such a mind as his. – They had reached the house.

'You are going in, I suppose,' said he.

'No' – replied Emma – quite confirmed by the depressed manner in which he still spoke – 'I should like to take another turn. Mr Perry is not gone.' And, after proceeding a few steps, she added – 'I stopped you ungraciously, just now, Mr Knightley, and, I am afraid, gave you pain. – But if you have any wish to speak openly to me as a friend, or to ask my opinion of any thing that you may have in contemplation – as a friend, indeed, you may command me. – I will hear whatever you like. I will tell you exactly what I think.'

'As a friend!' – repeated Mr Knightley. – 'Emma, that I fear is a word – No, I have no wish – Stay, yes, why should I hesitate? – I have gone too far already for concealment. – Emma, I accept your offer – Extraordinary as it may seem, I accept it, and refer myself to you as a friend. – Tell me, then, have I no chance of ever succeeding?'

He stopped in his earnestness to look the question, and the expression of his eyes overpowered her.

'My dearest Emma,' said he, 'for dearest you will always be, whatever the event of this hour's conversation, my dearest, most beloved Emma – tell me at once. Say "No", if it is to be said.' – She could really say nothing. – 'You are silent,' he cried, with great animation; 'absolutely silent! at present I ask no more.'

Emma was almost ready to sink under the agitation of this moment. The dread of being awakened from the happiest dream, was perhaps the most prominent feeling.

He stopped to look the question.

'I cannot make speeches, Emma:' – he soon resumed; and in a tone of such sincere, decided, intelligible tenderness as was tolerably convincing. – 'If I loved you less, I might be able to talk about it more. But you know what I am. – You hear nothing but truth from me. – I have blamed you, and lectured you, and you have borne it as no other women in England would have borne it. – Bear with the truths I would tell you now, dearest Emma, as well as you have borne with them. The manner, perhaps, may have as little to recommend them. God knows, I have been a very indifferent lover. – But you understand me. – Yes, you see, you understand my feelings – and will return them if you can. At present, I ask only to hear, once to hear your voice.'

While he spoke, Emma's mind was most busy, and, with all the wonderful velocity of thought, had been able – and yet without losing a word – to catch and comprehend the exact truth of the whole; to see that Harriet's hopes had been entirely groundless, a mistake, a delusion, as complete a delusion as any of her own – that Harriet was nothing; that she was every thing herself; that what she had been saying relative to Harriet had been all taken as the language of her own feelings; and that her agitation, her doubts, her reluctance, her discouragement, had been all received as discouragement from herself. – And not only was there time for these convictions, with all their glow of attendant happiness; there was time also to rejoice that Harriet's secret had not escaped her, and to resolve that it need not and should not. – It was all the service she could now render her poor friend; for as to any of that heroism of sentiment which might have prompted her to entreat him to transfer his affection from herself to Harriet, as infinitely the most worthy of the two – or even the more simple sublimity of resolving to refuse him at once and for ever, without vouchsafing any motive, because he could not marry them both, Emma had it not. She felt for Harriet, with pain and with contrition; but no flight of generosity run mad, opposing all that could be probable or reasonable, entered her brain. She had led her friend astray, and it would be a reproach to her for ever; but her judgment was as strong as her feelings, and as strong as it had ever been before, in reprobating any such alliance for him, as most unequal and degrading. Her way was clear, though not quite smooth. – She spoke then, on being so entreated. – What did she say? – Just what she ought, of course. A lady always does. – She said enough to show there need not be despair – and to invite him to say more himself. He *had* despaired at one period; he had received such an injunction to caution and silence, as for the time crushed every hope; – she had begun by refusing to hear him. – The change had perhaps been somewhat sudden; – her proposal of taking another turn, her renewing the conversation which she had just put an end to, might be a little extraordinary! – She felt its inconsistency; but Mr Knightley was so obliging as to put up with it, and seek no farther explanation.

Seldom, very seldom, does complete truth belong to any human disclosure; seldom can it happen that something is not a little disguised, or a little mistaken; but where, as in this case, though the conduct is mistaken, the feelings are not, it may not be very material. – Mr Knightley could not impute to Emma a more relenting heart than she possessed, or a heart more disposed to accept of his.

He had, in fact, been wholly unsuspicious of his own influence. He had followed her into the shrubbery with no idea of trying it. He had come, in his anxiety to see how she bore Frank Churchill's engagement, with no selfish view, no view at all, but of endeavouring, if she allowed him an opening, to soothe or counsel her. – The rest had been the work of the moment, the immediate effect of what he heard, on his feelings. The delightful assurance of her total indifference towards Frank Churchill, of her having a heart completely disengaged from him, had given birth to the hope, that, in time, he might gain her affection himself; – but it had been no present hope – he had only, in the momentary conquest of eagerness over judgment, aspired to be told that she did not forbid his attempt to attach her. – The superior hopes which gradually opened were so much the more enchanting. – The affection, which he had been asking to be allowed to create if he could, was already his! – Within half an hour, he had passed from a thoroughly distressed state of mind, to something so like perfect happiness, that it could bear no other name.

Her change was equal. – This one half hour had given to each the same precious certainty of being beloved, had cleared from each the same degree of ignorance, jealousy, or distrust. – On his side, there had been a long-standing jealousy, old as the arrival, of even the expectation, of Frank Churchill. – He had been in love with Emma, and jealous of Frank Churchill, from about the same period, one sentiment having probably enlightened him as to the other. It was his jealousy of Frank Churchill that had taken him from the country. – The Box-Hill party had decided him on going away. He would save himself from witnessing again such permitted, encouraged attentions. – He had gone to learn to be indifferent. – But he had gone to a wrong place. There was too much domestic happiness in his brother's house; woman wore too amiable a form in it; Isabella was too much like Emma – differing only in those striking inferiorities, which always brought the other in brilliancy before him, for much to have been done, even had his time been longer. – He had staid on, however, vigorously, day after day – till this very morning's post had conveyed the history of Jane Fairfax. – Then, with the gladness which must be felt, nay, which he did not scruple to feel, having never believed Frank Churchill to be at all deserving Emma, was there so much fond solicitude, so much keen anxiety for her, that he could stay no longer. He had ridden home through the rain; and had walked up directly after dinner, to see how this sweetest and best of all creatures, faultless in spite of all her faults, bore the discovery.

He had found her agitated and low. – Frank Churchill was a villain. – He heard her declare that she had never loved him. Frank Churchill's character was not desperate. – She was his own Emma, by hand and word, when they returned into the house; and if he could have thought of Frank Churchill then, he might have deemed him a very good sort of fellow.

CHAPTER FIFTY

WHAT TOTALLY DIFFERENT feelings did Emma take back into the house from what she had brought out! – she had then been only daring to hope for a little respite of suffering; – she was now in an exquisite flutter of happiness, and such happiness moreover as she believed must still be greater when the flutter should have passed away.

They sat down to tea – the same party round the same table – how often it had been collected! – and how often had her eyes fallen on the same shrubs in the lawn, and observed the same beautiful effect of the western sun! – But never in such a state of spirits, never in anything like it; and it was with difficulty that she could summon enough of her usual self to be the attentive lady of the house, or even the attentive daughter.

Poor Mr Woodhouse little suspected what was plotting against him in the breast of that man whom he was so cordially welcoming, and so anxiously hoping might not have taken cold from his ride. – Could he have seen the heart, he would have cared very little for the lungs; but without the most distant imagination of the impending evil, without the slightest perception of anything extraordinary in the looks or ways of either, he repeated to them very comfortably all the articles of news he had received from Mr Perry, and talked on with much self-contentment, totally unsuspicious of what they could have told him in return.

As long as Mr Knightley remained with them, Emma's fever continued; but when he was gone, she began to be a little tranquillized and subdued – and in the course of the sleepless night, which was the tax for such an evening, she found one or two such very serious points to consider, as made her feel, that even her happiness must have some alloy. Her father – and Harriet. She could not be alone without feeling the full weight of their separate claims; and how to guard the comfort of both to the utmost, was the question. With respect to her father, it was a question soon answered. She hardly knew yet what Mr Knightley would ask; but a very short parley with her own heart produced the most solemn resolution of never quitting her father. – She even wept over the idea of it, as a sin of thought. While he lived, it must be only an engagement; but she flattered herself, that if divested of the danger of drawing her away, it might become an increase of comfort to him. – How to do her best by Harriet, was of more difficult decision; – how to spare her from any unnecessary pain; how to make her any possible atonement; how to appear least her enemy? – On these subjects, her perplexity and distress were very great – and her mind had to pass again and again through every bitter reproach and sorrowful regret that had ever surrounded it. – She could only resolve at last, that she would still avoid a meeting with her, and communicate all that need be told by letter; that it would be inexpressibly desirable to have her removed just now for a time from Highbury, and – indulging in one scheme more – nearly resolve, that it might be practicable to get an invitation for her to Brunswick Square. – Isabella had been pleased with Harriet; and a few weeks spent in London must give her some amusement. – She did not think it in Harriet's nature to escape being benefited by novelty and variety, by the streets, the shops, and the children. – At any rate, it would be a proof of attention and kindness in herself, from whom every thing was due; a separation for the present; an averting of the evil day, when they must all be together again.

She rose early, and wrote her letter to Harriet; an employment which left her so very serious, so nearly sad, that Mr Knightley, in walking up to Hartfield to breakfast, did not arrive at all too soon; and half an hour stolen afterwards to go over the same ground again with him, literally and figuratively, was quite necessary to reinstate her in a proper share of the happiness of the evening before.

He had not left her long, by no means long enough for her to have the slightest inclination for thinking of anybody else, when a letter was brought her from Randalls – a very thick letter; – she guessed what it must contain, and deprecated the necessity of reading it. – She was now in perfect charity with Frank Churchill; she wanted no explanations, she wanted only to have her thoughts to herself – and as for understanding any thing he wrote, she was sure she was incapable of it. – It must be waded through, however. She opened the packet; it was too surely so; – a note from Mrs Weston to herself, ushered in the letter from Frank to Mrs Weston.

'I have the greatest pleasure, my dear Emma, in forwarding to you the enclosed. I know what thorough justice you will do it, and have scarcely a doubt of its happy effect. – I think we shall never materially disagree about the writer again; but I will not delay you by a long preface. – We are quite well. – This letter has been the cure of all the little nervousness I have been feeling lately. – I did not quite like your looks on Tuesday, but it was an ungenial morning; and though you will never own being affected by weather, I think every body feels a north-east wind. – I felt for your dear father very much in the storm of Tuesday afternoon and yesterday morning, but had the comfort of hearing last night, by Mr Perry, that it had not made him ill.

'Your's ever,

'A.W.'

[To Mrs Weston.]

Windsor – July.

My dear Madam,

'If I made myself intelligible yesterday, this letter will be expected; but expected or not, I know it will be read with candour and indulgence. – You are all goodness and I believe there will be need of even all your goodness to allow for some parts of my past conduct. – But I have been forgiven by one who had still more to resent. My courage rises while I write. It is very difficult for the prosperous to be humble. I have already met with such success in two applications for pardon, that I may be in danger of thinking myself too sure of your's and of those among your friends who have had any ground of offence. – You must all endeavour to comprehend the exact nature of my situation when I first arrived at Randalls; you must consider me as having a secret which was to be kept at all hazards. This was the fact. My right to place myself in a situation requiring such concealment, is another question. I shall not discuss it here. For my temptation to think it a right, I refer every caviller to a brick house, washed windows below and casements above, in Highbury. I dared not address her

openly; my difficulties in the then state of Enscombe must be too well known to require definition; and I was fortunate enough to prevail, before we parted at Weymouth, and to induce the most upright female mind in the creation to stoop in charity to a secret engagement. – Had she refused, I should have gone mad. – But you will be ready to say, what was your hope in doing this? – What did you look forward to? – To any thing, every thing – to time, chance, circumstance, slow effects, sudden bursts, perseverance and weariness, health and sickness. Every possibility of good was before me, and the first of blessings secured, in obtaining her promises of faith and correspondence. If you need farther explanation, I have the honour, my dear madam, of being your husband's son, and the advantage of inheriting a disposition to hope for good, which no inheritance of houses or lands can ever equal the value of. – See me, then, under these circumstances, arriving on my first visit to Randalls; – and here I am conscious of wrong, for that visit might have been sooner paid. You will look back and see that I did not come till Miss Fairfax was in Highbury; and as you *were the person slighted, you will forgive me instantly; but I must work on my father's compassion, by reminding him, that so long as I absented myself from his house, so long I lost the blessing of knowing you. My behaviour, during the very happy fortnight which I spent with you, did not, I hope, lay me open to reprehension, excepting on one point. And now I come to the principal, the only important part of my conduct while belonging to you, which excites my own anxiety, or requires very solicitous explanation. With the greatest respect, and the warmest friendship, do I mention Miss Woodhouse; my father perhaps will think I ought to add, with the deepest humiliation. – A few words which dropped from him yesterday spoke his opinion, and some censure I acknowledge myself liable to. – My behaviour to Miss Woodhouse indicated, I believe, more than it ought. – In order to assist a concealment so essential to me, I was led on to make more than an allowable use of the sort of intimacy into which we were immediately thrown. – I cannot deny that Miss Woodhouse was my ostensible object – but I am sure you will believe the declaration, that had I not been convinced of her indifference, I would not have been induced by any selfish views to go on. – Amiable and delightful as Miss Woodhouse is, she never gave me the idea of a young woman likely to be attached; and that she was perfectly free from any tendency to being attached to me, was as much my conviction as my wish. – She received my attentions with an easy, friendly, goodhumoured playfulness, which exactly suited me. We seemed to understand each other. From our relative situation, those attentions were her due, and were felt to be so. – Whether Miss Woodhouse began really to understand me before the expiration of that fortnight, I cannot say; – when I called to take leave of her, I remember that I was within a moment of confessing the truth, and I then fancied she was not without suspicion; but I have no doubt of her having since detected me, at least in some degree. – She may not have surmised the whole, but her quickness must have penetrated a part. I cannot doubt it. You will find, whenever the subject becomes freed from its present restraints, that it did not take her wholly by surprise. She frequently gave me hints of it. I remember her telling me at the ball, that I owed Mrs Elton gratitude for her attentions to Miss Fairfax. – I hope this history of my conduct towards her will be admitted by you and my father as great extenuation of what you saw amiss. While you considered me as having sinned against Emma Woodhouse, I could deserve nothing from either. Acquit me here, and procure for me, when it is allowable, the acquittal and good wishes of that said Emma Woodhouse, whom I regard with so much brotherly affection, as to long to have her as deeply and as happily in love as myself. – Whatever strange things I said or did during that fortnight, you have now a key to. My heart was in Highbury, and my business was to get my body thither as often as might be, and with the least suspicion. If you remember any queerness, set them all to the right account. – Of the pianoforté so much talked of, I feel it only necessary to say, that its being ordered was absolutely unknown to Miss F—, who would never have allowed me to send it, had any choice been given her. – The delicacy of her mind throughout the whole engagement, my dear madam, is much beyond my power of doing justice to. You will soon, I earnestly hope, know her thoroughly yourself. – No description can describe her. She must tell you herself what she is – yet not by word, for never was there a human creature who would so designedly suppress her own merit – Since I began this letter, which will be longer than I foresaw, I have heard from her. – She gives a good account of her own health, but as she never complains, I dare not depend. I want to have your opinion of her looks. I know you will soon call on her; she is living in dread of the visit. Perhaps it is paid already. Let me hear from you without delay; I am impatient for a thousand particulars. Remember how few minutes I was at Randalls, and in how bewildered, how mad a state: and I am not much better yet; still insane either from happiness or misery. When I think of the kindness and favour I have met with, of her excellence and patience, and my uncle's generosity, I am mad with joy; but when I recollect all the uneasiness I occasioned her, and how little I deserve to be forgiven, I am mad with anger. If*

I could but see her again! – But I must not propose it yet. My uncle has been too good for me to encroach. – I must still add to this long letter. You have not heard all that you ought to hear. I could not give any connected detail yesterday; but the suddenness, and, in one light, the unseasonableness, with which the affair burst out, needs explanation; for though the event of the 26th ult., as you will conclude, immediately opened to me the happiest prospects, I should not have presumed on such early measures, but from the very particular circumstances, which left me not an hour to lose. I should myself have shrunk from any thing so hasty, and she would have felt every scruple of mine with multiplied strength and refinement – But I had no choice. The hasty engagement she had entered into with that woman – Here, my dear madam, I was obliged to leave off abruptly, to recollect and compose myself. – I have been walking over the country, and am now, I hope, rational enough to make the rest of my letter what it ought to be. – It is, in fact, a most mortifying retrospect for me. I behaved shamefully. And here I can admit, that my manners to Miss W., in being unpleasant to Miss F., were highly blamable. She disapproved them, which ought to have been enough. – My plea of concealing the truth she did not think sufficient. – She was displeased; I thought unreasonably so: I thought her, on a thousand occasions, unnecessarily scrupulous and cautious: I thought her even cold. But she was always right. If I had followed her judgment, and subdued my spirits to the level of what she deemed proper, I should have escaped the greatest unhappiness I have ever known. – We quarrelled. – Do you remember the morning spent at Donwell? – There *every little dissatisfaction that had occurred before came to a crisis. I was late; I met her walking home by herself, and wanted to walk with her, but she would not suffer it. She absolutely refused to allow me, which I then thought most unreasonable. Now, however, I see nothing in it but a very natural and consistent degree of discretion. While I, to blind the world to our engagement, was behaving one hour with objectionable particularity to another woman, was she to be consenting the next to a proposal which might have made every previous caution useless? – Had we been met walking together between Donwell and Highbury, the truth must have been suspected. – I was mad enough, however, to resent. – I doubted her affection. I doubted it more the next day on Box-Hill; when, provoked by such conduct on my side, such shameful, insolent neglect of her, and such apparent devotion to Miss W., as it would have been impossible for any woman of sense to endure, she spoke her resentment in a form of words perfectly intelligible to me. – In short, my dear madam, it was a quarrel blameless on her side, abominable on mine; and I returned the same evening to Richmond, though I might have staid with you till the next morning, merely because I would be as angry with her as possible. Even then, I was not such a fool as not to mean to be reconciled in time; but I was the injured person, injured by her coldness, and I went away determined that she should make the first advances. – I shall always congratulate myself that you were not of the Box-Hill party. Had you witnessed my behaviour there, I can hardly suppose you would ever have thought well of me again. Its effect upon her appears in the immediate resolution it produced: as soon as she found I was really gone from Randalls, she closed with the offer of that officious Mrs Elton; the whole system of whose treatment of her, by the bye, has ever filled me with indignation and hatred. I must not quarrel with a spirit of forbearance which has been so richly extended towards myself; but, otherwise, I should loudly protest against the share of it which that woman has known. – 'Jane,' indeed! – You will observe that I have not yet indulged myself in calling her by that name, even to you. Think, then, what I must have endured in hearing it bandied between the Eltons with all the vulgarity of needless repetition, and all the insolence of imaginary superiority. Have patience with me, I shall soon have done. – She closed with this offer, resolving to break with me entirely, and wrote the next day to tell me that we never were to meet again. – She felt the engagement to be a source of repentance and misery to each: she dissolved it. – This letter reached me on the very morning of my poor aunt's death. I answered it within an hour; but from the confusion of my mind, and the multiplicity of business falling on me at once, my answer, instead of being sent with all the many other letters of that day, was locked up in my writing-desk; and I, trusting that I had written enough, though but a few lines, to satisfy her, remained without any uneasiness. – I was rather disappointed that I did not hear from her again speedily; but I made excuses for her, and was too busy, and – may I add? – too cheerful in my views to be captious. – We removed to Windsor; and two days afterwards I received a parcel from her, my own letters all returned! – and a few lines at the same time by the post, stating her extreme surprise at not having had the smallest reply to her last; and adding, that as silence on such a point could not be misconstrued, and as it must be equally desirable to both to have every subordinate arrangement concluded as soon as possible, she now sent me, by a safe conveyance, all my letters, and requested, that if I could not directly command her's, so as to send them to Highbury within a week, I would forward them after that period to her at –: in short, the full direction to Mr Smallridge's, near Bristol, stared me in the face. I knew the name, the place, I knew all about it, and instantly saw what she had been doing. It was perfectly accordant with that resolution of character which I knew her to possess; and the secrecy she had maintained, as to any such design in her former letter, was equally descriptive of its anxious delicacy. For the world would not she have seemed to threaten me. – Imagine the shock; imagine how, till I had actually detected my own blunder, I raved at the blunders of the post. – What was to be done? – One thing only. – I must speak to my uncle. Without his sanction I could not hope to be listened to again. – I spoke; circumstances were in my favour; the late event had softened away his pride, and he was, earlier than I could have anticipated, wholly reconciled and complying; and could say at last, poor man! with a deep sigh, that he wished I might find as much happiness in the marriage state as he had done. – I felt that it would be of a different sort. – Are you disposed to pity me for what I must have suffered in opening the cause to him, for my suspense while all was at stake? – No; do not pity me till I reached Highbury, and saw how ill I had made her. Do not pity me till I saw her wan, sick looks. – I reached Highbury at the time of day when, from my knowledge of their late breakfast hour, I was certain of a good chance of finding her alone. – I was not disappointed, and at last I was not disappointed either in the object of my journey. A great deal of very reasonable, very just displeasure I had to persuade away. But it is done; we are reconciled, dearer, much dearer, than ever, and no moment's uneasiness can ever occur between us again. Now, my dear madam, I will release you; but I could not conclude before. A thousand and a thousand thanks for all the kindness you have ever shown me, and ten thousand for the attentions your heart will dictate towards her. – If you think me in a way to be happier than I deserve, I am quite of your opinion. – Miss W. calls me the child of good fortune. I hope she is right. – In one respect, my good fortune is undoubted, that of being able to subscribe myself.*

Your obliged and affectionate Son,
F. C. Weston Churchill.

CHAPTER FIFTY-ONE

THIS LETTER MUST MAKE its way to Emma's feelings. She was obliged, in spite of her previous determination to the contrary, to do it all the justice that Mrs Weston foretold. As soon as she came to her own name, it was irresistible; every line relating to herself was interesting, and almost every line agreeable; and when this charm ceased, the subject could still maintain itself, by the natural return of her former regard for the writer, and the very strong attraction which any picture of love must have for her at that moment. She never stopt till she had gone through the whole; and though it was impossible not to feel that he had been wrong, yet he had been less wrong than she had supposed – and he had suffered, and was very sorry – and he was so grateful to Mrs Weston, and so much in love with Miss Fairfax, and she was so happy herself, that there was no being severe; and could he have entered the room, she must have shaken hands with him as heartily as ever.

She thought so well of the letter, that when Mr Knightley came again, she desired him to read it. She was sure of Mrs Weston's wishing it to be communicated; especially to one, who, like Mr Knightley, had seen so much to blame in his conduct.

'I shall be very glad to look it over,' said he, 'but it seems long. I will take it home with me at night.'

But that would not do. Mr Weston was to call in the evening, and she must return it by him.

'I would rather be talking to you,' he replied; 'but as it seems a matter of justice, it shall be done.'

He began – stopping, however, almost directly to say, 'Had I been offered the sight of one of this gentleman's letters to his mother-in-law a few months ago, Emma, it would not have been taken with such indifference.'

He proceeded a little farther, reading to himself; and then, with a smile, observed, 'Humph! – a fine complimentary opening: – But it is his way. One man's style must not be the rule of another's. We will not be severe.'

'It will be natural for me,' he added shortly afterwards, 'to speak my opinion aloud as I read. By doing it, I shall feel that I am near you. It will not be so great a loss of time: but if you dislike it – '

'Not at all. I should wish it.'

Mr Knightley returned to his reading with greater alacrity.

'He trifles here,' said he, 'as to the temptation. He knows he is wrong, and has nothing rational to urge. – Bad. – He ought not to have formed the engagement. – 'His father's disposition:' – he is unjust, however, to his father. Mr Weston's sanguine temper was a blessing on all his upright and honourable exertions; but Mr Weston earned every present comfort before he endeavoured to gain it. – Very true; he did not come till Miss Fairfax was here.'

'And I have not forgotten,' said Emma, 'how sure you were that he might have come sooner if he would. You pass it over very handsomely – but you were perfectly right.'

'I was not quite impartial in my judgment, Emma: – but yet, I think – had *you* not been in the case – I should still have distrusted him.'

When he came to Miss Woodhouse, he was obliged to read the whole of it aloud – all that related to her, with a smile; a look; a shake of the head; a word or two of assent, or disapprobation; or merely of love, as the subject required, concluding, however, seriously, and, after steady reflection, thus –

'Very bad – though it might have been worse. – Playing a most dangerous game. Too much indebted to the event for his acquittal. – No judge of his own manners by you. – Always deceived in fact by his own wishes, and regardless of little besides his own convenience. – Fancying you to have fathomed his secret. Natural enough! – his own mind full of intrigue, that he should suspect it in others. – Mystery; Finesse – how they pervert the understanding! My Emma, does not every thing serve to prove more and more the beauty of truth and sincerity in all our dealings with each other?'

Emma agreed to it, and with a blush of sensibility on Harriet's account, which she could not give any sincere explanation of.

'You had better go on,' said she.

He did so, but very soon stopt again to say, 'the pianoforté! Ah! That was the act of a very, very young man, one too young to consider whether the inconvenience of it might not very much exceed the pleasure. A boyish scheme, indeed! – I cannot comprehend a man's wishing to give a woman any proof of affection which he knows she would rather dispense with; and he did know that she would have prevented the instrument's coming if she could.'

After this, he made some progress without any pause. Frank Churchill's confession of having behaved shamefully was the first thing to call for more than a word in passing.

'I perfectly agree with you, sir,' – was then his remark. 'You did behave very shamefully. You never wrote a truer line.' And having gone through what immediately followed of the basis of their disagreement, and his persisting to act in direct opposition to Jane Fairfax's sense of right, he made a fuller pause to say, 'This is very bad. – He had induced her to place herself, for his sake, in a situation of extreme difficulty and uneasiness, and it should have been his first object to prevent her from suffering unnecessarily. – She must have had much more to contend with, in carrying on the correspondence, than he could. He should have respected even unreasonable scruples, had there been such; but her's were all reasonable. We must look to her one fault, and remember that she had done a wrong thing in consenting to the engagement, to bear that she should have been in such a state of punishment.'

Emma knew that he was now getting to the Box-Hill party, and grew uncomfortable. Her own behaviour had been so very improper! She was deeply ashamed, and a little afraid of his next look. It was all read, however, steadily, attentively, and without the smallest remark; and, excepting one momentary glance at her, instantly withdrawn, in the fear of giving pain – no remembrance of Box-Hill seemed to exist.

'There is no saying much for the delicacy of our good friends, the Eltons,' was his next observation. – 'His feelings are natural. – What! actually resolve to break with him entirely! – She felt the engagement to be a source of repentance and misery to each – she dissolved it. – What a view this gives of her sense of his behaviour! – Well, he must be a most extraordinary – '

'Nay, nay, read on. – You will find how very much he suffers.'

'I hope he does,' replied Mr Knightley coolly, and resuming the letter. – ' "Smallridge!" – What does this mean? What is all this?'

'She had engaged to go as governess to Mrs Smallridge's children – a dear friend of Mrs Elton's – a neighbour of Maple Grove; and, by the bye, I wonder how Mrs Elton bears the disappointment.'

'Say nothing, my dear Emma, while you oblige me to read – not even of Mrs Elton. Only one page more. I shall soon have done. What a letter the man writes!'

'I wish you would read it with a kinder spirit towards him.'

'Well, there *is* feeling here. – He does seem to have suffered in finding her ill. – Certainly, I can have no doubt of his being fond of her. "Dearer, much dearer than ever." I hope he may long continue to feel all the value of such a reconciliation. – He is a very liberal thanker, with his thousands and tens of thousands. – "Happier than I deserve." Come, he knows himself there. "Miss Woodhouse calls me the child of good fortune." – Those were Miss Woodhouse's words, were they? – And a fine ending – and there is the letter. The child of good fortune! That was your name for him, was it?'

'You do not appear so well satisfied with his letter as I am; but still you must, at least I hope you must, think the better of him for it. I hope it does him some service with you.'

'Yes, certainly it does. He has had great faults, faults of inconsideration and thoughtlessness; and I am very much of his opinion in thinking him likely to be happier than he deserves: but still as he is, beyond a doubt, really attached to Miss Fairfax, and will soon, it may be hoped, have the advantage of being constantly with her, I am very ready to believe his character will improve, and acquire from her's the steadiness and delicacy of principle that it wants. And now, let me talk to you of something else. I have another person's interest at present so much at heart, that I cannot think any longer about Frank Churchill. Ever since I left you this morning, Emma, my mind has been hard at work on one subject.'

The subject followed; it was in plain, unaffected, gentleman-like English, such as Mr Knightley used even to the woman he was in love with, how to be able to ask her to marry him, without attacking the happiness of her father. Emma's answer was ready at the first word. 'While her dear father lived, any change of condition must be impossible for her. She could never quit him.' Part only of this answer, however, was admitted. The impossibility of her quitting her father, Mr Knightley felt as strongly as herself; but the inadmissibility of any other change, he could not agree to. He had been thinking it over most deeply, most intently: he had at first hoped to induce Mr Woodhouse to remove with her to Donwell; he had wanted to believe it feasible, but his knowledge of Mr Woodhouse would not suffer him to deceive himself long; and now he confessed his persuasion, that such a transplantation would be a risk of her father's comfort, perhaps even of his life, which must not be hazarded. Mr Woodhouse taken from Hartfield! – No, he felt that it ought not to be attempted. But the plan which had arisen on the sacrifice of this, he trusted his dearest Emma would not find in any respect objectionable; it was, that he should be received at Hartfield; that so long as her father's happiness – in other words his life – required Hartfield to continue her home, it should be his likewise.

Of their all removing to Donwell, Emma had already had her own passing thoughts. Like him, she had tried the scheme and rejected it; but such an alternative as this had not occurred to her. She was sensible of all the affection it evinced. She felt that, in

Walking away from William Larkins.

quitting Donwell, he must be sacrificing a great deal of independence of hours and habits; that in living constantly with her father, and in no house of his own, there would be much, very much, to be borne with. She promised to think of it, and advised him to think of it more; but he was fully convinced, that no reflection could alter his wishes or his opinion on the subject. He had given it, he could assure you, very long and calm consideration; he had been walking away from William Larkins the whole morning, to have his thoughts to himself.

'Ah! There is one difficulty unprovided for,' cried Emma. 'I am sure William Larkins will not like it. You must get his consent before you ask mine.'

She promised, however, to think of it; and pretty nearly promised, moreover, to think of it, with the intention of finding it a very good scheme.

It is remarkable, that Emma, in the many, very many, points of view in which she was now beginning to consider Donwell Abbey, was never struck with any sense of injury to her nephew Henry, whose rights as heir expectant had formerly been so tenaciously regarded. Think she must of the possible difference to the poor little boy; and yet she only gave herself a saucy conscious smile about it, and found amusement in detecting the real cause of that violent dislike of Mr Knightley's marrying Jane Fairfax, or any body else, which at the time she had wholly imputed to the amiable solicitude of the sister and the aunt.

This proposal of his, this plan of marrying and continuing at Hartfield – the more she contemplated it, the more pleasing it became. His evils seemed to lessen, her own advantages to increase, their mutual good to outweigh every drawback. Such a companion for herself in the periods of anxiety and cheerlessness before her! – Such a partner in all those duties and cares to which time must be giving increase of melancholy!

She would have been too happy but for poor Harriet; but every blessing of her own seemed to involve and advance the suffering of her friend, who must now be even excluded from Hartfield. The delightful family-party which Emma was securing for herself, poor Harriet must, in mere charitable caution, be kept at a distance from. She would be a loser in every way. Emma could not deplore her future absence as any deduction from her own enjoyment. In such a party, Harriet would be rather a dead weight than otherwise; but for the poor girl herself, it seemed a peculiarly cruel necessity that was to be placing her in such a state of unmerited punishment.

In time, of course, Mr Knightley would be forgotten, that is, supplanted; but this could not be expected to happen very early. Mr Knightley himself would be doing nothing to assist the cure; – not like Mr Elton. Mr Knightley, always so kind, so feeling, so truly considerate for every body, would never deserve to be less worshipped than now; and it really was too much to hope even of Harriet, that she could be in love with more than *three* men in one year.

CHAPTER FIFTY-TWO

It was a very great relief to Emma to find Harriet as desirous as herself to avoid a meeting. Their intercourse was painful enough by letter. How much worse, had they been obliged to meet!

Harriet expressed herself very much as might be supposed, without reproaches, or apparent sense of ill usage; and yet Emma fancied there was a something of resentment, a something bordering on it in her style, which increased the desirableness of their being separate. – It might be only her own consciousness; but it seemed as if an angel only could have been quite without resentment under such a stroke.

She had no difficulty in procuring Isabella's invitation; and she was fortunate in having a sufficient reason for asking it, without resorting to invention. – There was a tooth amiss. Harriet really wished, and had wished some time, to consult a dentist. Mrs John Knightley was delighted to be of use; any thing of ill-health was a recommendation to her – and though not so fond of a dentist as of a Mr Wingfield, she was quite eager to have Harriet under her care. – When it was thus settled on her sister's side, Emma proposed it to her friend, and found her very persuadable. – Harriet was to go; she was invited for at least a fortnight; she was to be conveyed in Mr Woodhouse's carriage. – It was all arranged, it was all completed, and Harriet was safe in Brunswick Square.

Now Emma could, indeed, enjoy Mr Knightley's visits; now she could talk, and she could listen with true happiness, unchecked by that sense of injustice, of guilt, of something most painful, which had haunted her when remembering how disappointed a heart was near her, how much might at that moment, and at a little distance, be enduring by the feelings which she had led astray herself.

The difference of Harriet at Mrs Goddard's, or in London, made perhaps an unreasonable difference in Emma's sensations; but she could not think of her in London without objects of curiosity and employment, which must be averting the past, and carrying her out of herself.

She would not allow any other anxiety to succeed directly to the place in her mind which Harriet had occupied. There was a communication before her, one which *she* only could be competent to make – the confession of her engagement to her father; but she would have nothing to do with it at present. – She had resolved to defer the disclosure till Mrs Weston were safe and well. No additional agitation should be thrown at this period among those she loved – and the evil should not act on herself by anticipation before the appointed time. – A fortnight, at least, of leisure and peace of mind, to crown every warmer, but more agitating, delight, should be her's.

She soon resolved, equally as a duty and a pleasure, to employ half an hour of this holiday of spirits in calling on Miss Fairfax. – She ought to go – and she was longing to see her; the resemblance of their present situations increasing every other motive of good will. It would be a *secret* satisfaction; but the consciousness of a similarity of prospect would certainly add to the interest with which she should attend to any thing Jane might communicate.

She went – she had driven once unsuccessfully to the door, but had not been in to the house since the morning after Box-Hill, when poor Jane had been in such distress as had filled her with compassion, though all the worst of her sufferings had been unsuspected. – The fear of being still unwelcome, determined her, though assured of their being at home, to wait in the passage, and send up her name. – She heard Patty announcing it; but no such bustle succeeded as poor Miss Bates had before made so happily intelligible. – No; she heard nothing but the instant reply of, 'Beg her to walk up,' – and a moment afterwards she was met on the stairs by Jane herself, coming eagerly forwards, as if no other reception of her were felt sufficient. – Emma had never seen her look so well, so lovely, so engaging. There was consciousness, animation, and warmth; there was every thing which her countenance or manner could ever have wanted. – She came forward with an offered hand; and said, in a low, but very feeling tone,

'This is most kind, indeed! – Miss Woodhouse, it is impossible for me to express – I hope you will believe – Excuse me for being so entirely without words.'

Emma was gratified, and would soon have shown no want of words, if the sound of Mrs Elton's voice from the sitting-room had not checked her, and made it expedient to compress all her friendly and all her congratulatory sensations into a very, very earnest shake of the hand.

Mrs Bates and Mrs Elton were together. Miss Bates was out, which accounted for the previous tranquillity. Emma could have wished Mrs Elton elsewhere; but she was in a humour to have patience with every body; and as Mrs Elton met her with unusual graciousness, she hoped the recontre would do them no harm.

She soon believed herself to penetrate Mrs Elton's thoughts, and understood why she was, like herself, in happy spirits; it was being in Miss Fairfax's confidence, and fancying herself acquainted with what was still a secret to other people. Emma saw symptoms of it immediately in the expression of her face; and while paying her own compliments to Mrs Bates, and appearing to attend to the good old lady's replies, she saw her with a sort of anxious parade of mystery fold up a letter which she had apparently been reading aloud to Miss Fairfax, and return it into the purple and gold reticule by her side, saying, with significant nods,

'We can finish this some other time, you know. You and I shall not want opportunities. And, in fact, you have heard all the essential already. I only wanted to prove to you that Mrs S. admits our apology, and is not offended. You see how delightfully she writes. Oh! she is a sweet creature! You would have doated on her, had you gone. – But not a word more. Let us be discreet – quite on our good behaviour. – Hush! You remember those lines – I forgot the poem at this moment:

'For when a lady's in the case,
'You know all other things give place.'

Now I say, my dear, in *our* case, for *lady*, read – mum! a word to the wise. – I am in a fine flow of spirits, an't I? But I want to set your heart at ease as to Mrs S. – *My* representation, you see, has quite appeased her.'

And again, on Emma's merely turning her head to look at Mrs Bate's knitting, she added, in a half whisper,

'I mentioned no *names*, you will observe. – Oh! no; cautious as a minister of state. I managed it extremely well.'

Emma could not doubt. It was a palpable display, repeated on every possible occasion. When they had all talked a little while in harmony of the weather and Mrs Weston, she found herself abruptly addressed with,

'Do not you think, Miss Woodhouse, our saucy little friend here is charmingly recovered? – Do not you think her cure does Perry the highest credit? – (here was a side-glance of great meaning at Jane.) Upon my word, Perry has restored her in a wonderful short time! – Oh! if you had seen her, as I did, when she was at the worst!' – And when Mrs Bates was saying something to Emma, whispered farther, 'We do not say a word of any *assistance* that Perry might have; not a word of a certain young physician from Windsor. – Oh! no; Perry shall have all the credit.'

'I have scarce had the pleasure of seeing you, Miss Woodhouse,' she shortly afterwards began, 'since the party to Box-Hill. Very pleasant party. But yet I think there was something wanting. Things did not seem – that is, there seemed a little cloud upon the spirits of some. – So it appeared to me at least, but I might be mistaken. However, I think it answered so far as to tempt one to go again. What say you both to our collecting the same party, and exploring to Box-Hill again, while the fine weather lasts? – It must be the same party, you know, quite the same party, not *one* exception.'

Soon after this Miss Bates came in, and Emma could not help being diverted by the perplexity of her first answer to herself, resulting, she supposed, from doubt of what might be said, and impatience to say every thing.

'Thank you, dear Miss Woodhouse, you are all kindness. – It is impossible to say – Yes, indeed, I quite understand – dearest Jane's prospects – that is, I do not mean. – But she is charmingly recovered. – How is Mr Woodhouse? – I am so glad. – Quite out of my power. – Such a happy little circle as you find us here. – Yes, indeed. – Charming young man! – that is – so very friendly; I mean good Mr Perry! – such attention to Jane!' – And from her great, her more than commonly thankful delight towards Mrs Elton for being there, Emma guessed that there had been a little show of resentment towards Jane, from the vicarage quarter, which was now graciously overcome. – After a few whispers, indeed, which placed it beyond a guess, Mrs Elton, speaking louder, said,

'Yes, here I am, my good friend; and here I have been so long, that anywhere else I should think it necessary to apologize: but the truth is, that I am waiting for my lord and master. He promised to join me here, and pay his respects to you.'

'What! are we to have the pleasure of a call from Mr Elton? – That will be a favour indeed! for I know gentlemen do not like morning visits, and Mr Elton's time is so engaged.'

'Upon my word it is, Miss Bates. – He really is engaged from morning to night. – There is no end of people's coming to him, on some pretence or another. – The magistrates, and overseers, and churchwardens, are always wanting his opinion. They seem not able to do any thing without him. – "Upon my word, Mr E., I often say, rather you than I. – I do not know what would become of my crayons and my instrument, if I had half so many applicants." – Bad enough as it is, for I absolutely neglect them both to an unpardonable degree. – I believe I have not played a bar this fortnight. – However, he is coming, I assure you: yes, indeed on purpose to wait on you all.' – And putting up her hand to screen her words from Emma – 'A congratulatory visit, you know. – Oh! yes, quite indispensable.'

Miss Bates looked about her, so happily! –

'He promised to come to me as soon as he could disengage himself from Knightley; but he and Knightley are shut up together in deep consultation. – Mr E. is Knightley's right hand.'

Emma would not have smiled for the world, and only said, 'Is Mr Elton gone on foot to Donwell? – He will have a hot walk.'

'Oh! no, it is a meeting at the Crown, a regular meeting. Weston and Cole will be there too; but one is apt to speak only of those who lead. – I fancy Mr E. and Knightley have every thing their own way.'

'Have not you mistaken the day?' said Emma. 'I am almost certain that the meeting at the Crown is not till to-morrow. – Mr Knightley was at Hartfield yesterday, and spoke of it as for Saturday.'

'Oh! no; the meeting is certainly today,' was the abrupt answer, which denoted the impossibility of any blunder on Mrs Elton's side. – 'I do believe,' she continued, 'this is the most troublesome parish that ever was. We never heard of such things at Maple Grove.'

'Your parish there was small,' said Jane.

'Upon my word, my dear, I do not know, for I never heard the subject talked of.'

'But it is proved by the smallness of the school, which I have heard you speak of, as under the patronage of your sister and Mrs Bragge; the only school, and not more than five-and-twenty children.'

'Ah! you clever creature, that's very true. What a thinking brain you have! I say, Jane, what a perfect character you and I should make, if we could be shaken together. My liveliness and your solidity would produce perfection. – Not that I presume to insinuate, however, that *some* people may not think *you* perfection already. – But hush! – not a word, if you please.'

It seemed an unnecessary caution; Jane was wanting to give her words, not to Mrs Elton, but to Miss Woodhouse, as the latter plainly saw. The wish of distinguishing her, as far as civility permitted, was very evident, though it could not often proceed beyond a look.

Mr Elton made his appearance. His lady greeted him with some of her sparkling vivacity.

'Very pretty, sir, upon my word; to send me on here, to be an encumbrance to my friends, so long before you vouchsafe to come! – But you knew what a dutiful creature you had to deal with. You knew I should not stir till my lord and master appeared. – Here have I been sitting this hour, giving these young ladies a sample of true conjugal obedience – for who can say, you know, how soon it may be wanted?'

Mr Elton was so hot and tired, that all this wit seemed thrown away. His civilities to the other ladies must be paid; but his subsequent object was to lament over himself for the heat he was suffering, and the walk he had had for nothing.

'When I got to Donwell,' said he, 'Knightley could not be found.

'Such a dreadful broiling morning!'

Very odd! very unaccountable! after the note I sent him this morning, and the message he returned, that he should certainly be at home till one.'

'Donwell' cried his wife – 'My dear Mr E., you have not been to Donwell! – You mean the Crown; you come from the meeting at the Crown.'

'No, no, that's to-morrow; and I particularly wanted to see Knightley today on that very account. – Such a dreadful broiling morning! – I went over the fields too – (speaking in a tone of great ill usage,) which made it so much the worse. And then not to find him at home! I assure you I am not at all pleased. And no apology left, no message for me. The housekeeper declared she knew nothing of my being expected. – Very extraordinary! – And nobody knew at all which way he was gone. Perhaps to Hartfield, perhaps to the Abbey Mill, perhaps into his woods. – Miss Woodhouse, this is not like our friend Knightley. – Can you explain it?'

Emma amused herself by protesting that it was very extraordinary indeed, and that she had not a syllable to say for him.

'I cannot imagine,' cried Mrs Elton, (feeling the indignity as a wife ought to do,) 'I cannot imagine how he could do such a thing by you, of all people in the world! The very last person whom one should expect to be forgotten! – My dear Mr E., he must have left a message for you, I am sure he must. – Not even Knightley could be so very eccentric; – and his servants forgot it. Depend upon it, that was the case and very likely to happen with the Donwell servants, who are all, I have often observed, extremely awkward and remiss. – I am sure I would not have such a creature as his Harry stand at our sideboard for any consideration. And as for Mrs Hodges, Wright holds her very cheap indeed. – She promised Wright a receipt, and never sent it.'

'I met William Larkins,' continued Mr Elton, 'as I got near the house, and he told me I should not find his master at home, but I did not believe him. – William seemed rather out of humour. He did not know what was come to his master lately, he said, but he could hardly ever get the speech of him. I have nothing to do with William's wants, but it really is of very great importance that *I* should see Knightley today; and it becomes a matter, therefore, of very serious inconvenience that I should have had this hot walk to no purpose.'

Emma felt that she could not do better than go home directly. In all probability she was at this very time waited for there; and Mr Knightley might be preserved from sinking deeper in aggression towards Mr Elton, if not towards William Larkins.

She was pleased, on taking leave, to find Miss Fairfax determined to attend her out of the room, to go with her even down stairs; it gave her an opportunity which she immediately made use of, to say,

'It is as well, perhaps, that I have not had the possibility. Had you not been surrounded by other friends, I might have been tempted to introduce a subject, to ask questions, to speak more openly than might have been strictly correct. – I feel that I should certainly have been impertinent.'

'Oh!' cried Jane, with a blush and an hesitation which Emma thought infinitely more becoming to her than all the elegance of all her usual composure – 'there would have been no danger. The danger would have been of my wearying you. You could not have gratified me more than by expressing an interest. – Indeed, Miss Woodhouse, (speaking more collectedly,) with the consciousness which I have of misconduct, very great misconduct, it is particularly consoling to me to know that those of my friends, whose good opinion is most worth preserving, are not disgusted to such a degree as to – I have not time for half that I could wish to say. I long to make apologies, excuses, to urge something for myself. I feel it so very due. But, unfortunately – in short, if your compassion does not stand my friend – '

'Oh! you are too scrupulous, indeed you are,' cried Emma, warmly, and taking her hand. 'You owe me no apologies, and every body to whom you might be supposed to owe them, is so perfectly satisfied, so delighted even – '

'You are very kind, but I know what my manners were to you. – So cold and artificial! – I had always a part to act. – It was a life of deceit! I know that I must have disgusted you.'

'Pray say no more. I feel that all the apologies should be on my side. Let us forgive each other at once. We must do whatever is to be done quickest, and I think our feelings will lose no time there. I hope you have pleasant accounts from Windsor?'

'Very.'

'And the next news, I suppose, will be, that we are to lose you – just as I begin to know you.'

'Oh! as to all that, of course nothing can be thought of yet. I am here till claimed by Colonel and Mrs Campbell.'

'Nothing can be actually settled yet, perhaps,' replied Emma, smiling – 'but, excuse me, it must be thought of.'

The smile was returned as Jane answered,

'You are very right; it has been thought of. And I will own to you, (I am sure it will be safe), that so far as our living with Mr

Churchill at Enscombe, it is settled. There must be three months, at least, of deep mourning; but when they are over, I imagine there will be nothing more to wait for.'

'Thank you, thank you. – This is just what I wanted to be assured of. – Oh! if you knew how much I love every thing that is decided and open! – Goodbye, goodbye.'

CHAPTER FIFTY-THREE

MRS WESTON'S FRIENDS were all made happy by her safety; and if the satisfaction of her well-doing could be increased to Emma, it was by knowing her to be the mother of a little girl. She had been decided in wishing for a Miss Weston. She would not acknowledge that it was with any view of making a match for her, hereafter, with either of Isabella's sons; but she was convinced that a daughter would suit both father and mother best. It would be a great comfort to Mr Weston as he grew older – and even Mr Weston might be growing older ten years hence – to have his fireside enlivened by the sports and the nonsense, the freaks and the fancies of a child never banished from home; and Mrs Weston – no one could doubt that a daughter would be most to her, and it would be quite a pity that anyone who so well knew how to teach, should not have their powers in exercise again.

'She has had the advantage, you know, of practising on me,' she continued – 'like La Baronne d'Almane on La Comtesse d'Ostalis, in Madame de Genlis' Adelaide and Theodore, and we shall now see her own little Adelaide educated on a more perfect plan.'

'That is,' replied Mr Knightley, 'she will indulge her even more than she did you, and believe that she does not indulge her at all. It will be the only difference.'

'Poor child!' cried Emma; 'at that rate, what will become of her?'

'Nothing very bad – The fate of thousands. She will be disagreeable in infancy, and correct herself as she grows older. I am losing all my bitterness against spoilt children, my dearest Emma. I, who am owing all my happiness to *you*, would not it be horrible ingratitude in me to be severe on them?'

Emma laughed, and replied. 'But I had the assistance of all your endeavours to counteract the indulgence of other people. I doubt whether my own sense would have corrected me without it.'

'Do you? – I have no doubt. Nature gave you understanding: –

Miss Taylor gave you principles. You must have done well. My interference was quite as likely to do harm as good. It was very natural for you to say, what right has he to lecture me? – and I am afraid very natural for you to feel that it was done in a disagreeable manner. I do not believe I did you any good. The good was all to myself, by making you an object of the tenderest affection to me. I could not think about you so much without doating on you, faults and all, and by dint of fancying so many errors, have been in love with you ever since you were thirteen at least.'

'I am sure you were of use to me,' cried Emma. 'I was very often influenced rightly by you – oftener than I would own at the time. I am very sure you did me good. And if poor little Anna Weston is to be spoiled, it will be the greatest humanity in you to do as much for her as you have done for me, except falling in love with her when she is thirteen.'

'How often, when you were a girl, have you said to me, with one of your saucy looks – "Mr Knightley, I am going to do so and so; papa says I may, or, I have Miss Taylor's leave" – something which, you knew, I did not approve. In such cases my interference was giving you two bad feelings instead of one.'

'What an amiable creature I was! – No wonder you should hold my speeches in such affectionate remembrance.'

' "Mr Knightley." – You always called me, "Mr Knightley;" and, from habit, it has not so very formal a sound. – And yet it is formal. I want you to call me something else, but I do not know what.'

'I remember once calling you "George," in one of my amiable fits, about ten years ago. I did it because I thought it would offend you; but, as you made no objection, I never did it again.'

'And cannot you call me "George" now?'

'Impossible! – I never can call you any thing but "Mr Knightley." I will not promise even to equal the elegant terseness of Mrs Elton, by calling you Mr K. – But I will promise,' she added presently, laughing and blushing – 'I will promise to call you once by your Christian name. I do not say when, but perhaps you may guess where; – in the building in which N. takes M. for better, for worse.'

Emma grieved that she could not be more openly just to one important service which his better sense would have rendered her, in the advice which would have saved her from the worst of all her womanly follies – her wilful intimacy with Harriet Smith; but it was too tender a subject. – She could not enter on it. – Harriet was very seldom mentioned between them. This, on his side, might merely proceed from her not being thought of; but Emma was rather inclined to attribute it to delicacy, and a suspicion, from some appearances, that their friendship were declining. She was aware herself, that, parting under any other circumstances, they certainly should have corresponded more, and that her intelligence would not have rested, as it now almost wholly did, on Isabella's letters. He might observe that it was so. The pain of being obliged to practise concealment towards him, was very little inferior to the pain of having made Harriet unhappy.

Isabella sent quite as good an account of her visitor as could be expected; on her first arrival she had thought her out of spirits, which appeared perfectly natural, as there was a dentist to be consulted; but, since that business had been over, she did not appear to find Harriet different from what she had known her before. – Isabella, to be sure, was no very quick observer; yet if Harriet had not been equal to playing with the children, it would not have escaped her. Emma's comforts and hopes were most agreeably carried on, by Harriet's being to stay longer; her fortnight was likely to be a month at least. Mr and Mrs John Knightley were to come down in August, and she was invited to remain till they could bring her back.

'John does not even mention your friend,' said Mr Knightley. 'Here is his answer, if you like to see it.'

It was the answer to the communication of his intended marriage. Emma accepted it with a very eager hand, with an impatience all alive to know what he would say about it, and not at all checked by hearing that her friend was unmentioned.

'John enters like a brother into my happiness,' continued Mr Knightley, 'but he is no complimenter; and though I well know him to have, likewise, a most brotherly affection for you, he is so far from making flourishes, that any other young woman might think him rather cool in her praise. But I am not afraid of your seeing what he writes.'

'He writes like a sensible man,' replied Emma, when she had read the letter. 'I honour his sincerity. It is very plain that he considers the good fortune of the engagement as all on my side, but that he is not without hope of my growing, in time, as worthy of your affection, as you think me already. Had he said any thing to bear a different construction, I should not have believed him.'

'My Emma, he means no such thing. He only means – '

'He and I should differ very little in our estimation of the two,' – interrupted she, with a sort of serious smile – 'much less, perhaps, than he is aware of, if we could enter without ceremony or reserve on the subject.'

'Emma, my dear Emma – '

'Oh!' she cried with more thorough gaiety, 'if you fancy your brother does not do me justice, only wait till my dear father is in the secret, and hear his opinion. Depend upon it, he will be much farther from doing *you* justice. He will think all the happiness, all the advantage, on your side of the question; all the merit on mine. I wish I may not sink into "poor Emma" with him at once. – His tender compassion towards oppressed worth can go no farther.'

'Ah!' he cried, 'I wish your father might be half as easily convinced as John will be, of our having every right that equal worth can give, to be happy together. I am amused by one part of John's letter – did you notice it? – where he says, that my information did not take him wholly by surprise, that he was rather in expectation of hearing something of the kind.'

'If I understand your brother, he only means so far as your having some thoughts of marrying. He had no idea of me. He seems perfectly unprepared for that.'

'Yes, yes – but I am amused that he should have seen so far into my feelings. What has he been judging by? – I am not conscious of any difference in my spirits or conversation that could prepare him at this time for my marrying any more than at another. – But it was so, I suppose. I dare say there was a difference when I was staying with them the other day. I believe I did not play with the children quite so much as usual. I remember one evening the poor boys saying, "Uncle seems always tired now".'

The time was coming when the news must be spread farther, and other persons' reception of it tried. As soon as Mrs Weston was sufficiently recovered to admit Mr Woodhouse's visits, Emma having it in view that her gentle reasonings should be employed in the cause, resolved first to announce it at home, and then at Randalls. – But how to break it to her father at last! – She had bound herself to do it, in such an hour of Mr Knightley's absence, or when it came to the point her heart would have failed her, and she must have put it off; but Mr Knightley was to come at such a time, and follow up the beginning she was to make. – She was forced to speak, and to speak cheerfully too. She must not make it a more decided subject of misery to him, by a melancholy tone herself. She must not appear to think it a misfortune. – With all the spirits she could command, she prepared him first for something strange, and then, in few words, said, that if his consent and approbation could be obtained – which, she trusted, would be attended with no difficulty, since it was a plan to promote the happiness of all – she and Mr Knightley meant to marry: by which means Hartfield would receive the constant addition of that person's company whom she

Emma hung about him affectionately.

knew he loved, next to his daughters and Mrs Weston, best in the world.

Poor man! – it was at first a considerable shock to him, and he tried earnestly to dissuade her from it. She was reminded, more than once, of her having always said she would never marry, and assured that it would be a great deal better for her to remain single; and told of poor Isabella, and poor Miss Taylor. – But it would not do. Emma hung about him affectionately, and smiled, and said it must be so; and that he must not class her with Isabella and Mrs

Weston, whose marriages taking them from Hartfield, had, indeed, made a melancholy change: but she was not going from Hartfield, she should be always there; she was introducing no change in their numbers or their comforts but for the better; and she was very sure that he would be a great deal the happier for having Mr Knightley always at hand, when he were once got used to the idea. – Did not he love Mr Knightley very much? – He would not deny that he did, she was sure. – Whom did he ever want to consult on business but Mr Knightley? – Who was so useful to him, who so ready to write his letters, who so glad to assist him? – Who so cheerful, so attentive, so attached to him? – Would not he like to have him always on the spot? – Yes. That was all very true. Mr Knightley could not be there too often; he should be glad to see him every day; – but they did see him every day as it was. Why could not they go on as they had done?

Mr Woodhouse could not be soon reconciled; but the worst was overcome, the idea was given; time and continual repetition must do the rest. – To Emma's entreaties and assurances succeeded Mr Knightley's, whose fond praise of her gave the subject even a kind of welcome; and he was soon used to be talked to by each, on every fair occasion. – They had all the assistance which Isabella could give, by letters of the strongest approbation; and Mrs Weston was ready, on the first meeting, to consider the subject in the most serviceable light – first, as a settled, and secondly, as a good one – well aware of the nearly equal importance of the two recommendations to Mr Woodhouse's mind. – It was agreed upon, as what was to be; and every body by whom he was used to be guided assuring him that it would be for his happiness; and having some feelings himself which almost admitted it, he began to think that some time or other – in another year or two, perhaps – it might not be so very bad if the marriage did take place.

Mrs Weston was acting no part, feigning no feelings in all that she said to him in favour of the event. – She had been extremely surprized, never more so, than when Emma first opened the affair to her; but she saw in it only increase of happiness to all, and had no scruple in urging him to the utmost. – She had such a regard for Mr Knightley, as to think he deserved even her dearest Emma; and it was in every respect so proper, suitable, and unexceptionable a connexion, and in one respect, one point of the highest importance, so peculiarly eligible, so singularly fortunate, that now it seemed as if Emma could not safely have attached herself to any other creature, and that she had herself been the stupidest of beings in not having thought of it, and wished it long ago. – How very few of those men in a rank of life to address Emma would have renounced their own home for Hartfield! And who but Mr Knightley could know and bear with Mr Woodhouse, so as to make such an arrangement desirable! – The difficulty of disposing of poor Mr Woodhouse had been always felt in her husband's plans and her own, for a marriage between Frank and Emma. How to settle the claims of Enscombe and Hartfield had been a continual impediment – less acknowledged by Mr Weston than by herself – but even he had never been able to finish the subject better than by saying – 'Those matters will take care of themselves; the young people will find a way.' – But here there was nothing to be shifted off in a wild speculation on the future. It was all right, all open, all equal. No sacrifice on any side worth the name. It was a union of the highest promise of felicity in itself, and without one real, rational difficulty to oppose or delay it.

Mrs Weston, with her baby on her knee, indulging in such reflections as these, was one of the happiest women in the world. If any thing could increase her delight, it was perceiving that the baby would soon have outgrown its first set of caps.

The news was universally a surprize wherever it spread; and Mr Weston had his five minutes share of it; but five minutes were enough to familiarize the idea to his quickness of mind. – He saw the advantages of the match, and rejoiced in them with all the constancy of his wife; but the wonder of it was very soon nothing; and by the end of an hour he was not far from believing that he had always foreseen it.

'It is to be a secret, I conclude,' said he. 'These matters are always a secret, till it is found out that every body knows them. Only let me be told when I may speak out. – I wonder whether Jane has any suspicion.'

He went to Highbury the next morning, and satisfied himself on that point. He told her the news. Was not she like a daughter, his eldest daughter? – he must tell her; and Miss Bates being present, it passed, of course, to Mrs Cole, Mrs Perry, and Mrs Elton, immediately afterwards. It was no more than the principals were prepared for; they had calculated from the time of its being known at Randalls, how soon it would be over Highbury; and were thinking of themselves, as the evening wonder in many a family circle, with great sagacity.

In general, it was a very well approved match. Some might think him, and others might think her, the most in luck. One set might recommend their all removing to Donwell, and leaving Hartfield for the John Knightleys; and another might predict disagreements among their servants; but yet, upon the whole, there was no serious objection raised, except in one habitation, the vicarage. – There, the surprize was not softened by any satisfaction. Mr Elton cared little about it, compared with his wife; he only hoped 'the young lady's pride would now be contented;' and supposed 'she had always meant to catch Knightley if she could;' and, on the point of living at Hartfield, could daringly exclaim, 'Rather he than I!' – But Mrs Elton was very much discomposed indeed. – 'Poor Knightley! poor fellow! – sad business for him. – She was extremely concerned; for, though very eccentric, he had a thousand good qualities. – How could he be so taken in? – Did not think him at all in love – not in

It passed to Mrs Cole, Mrs Perry, and Mrs Elton.

the least. – Poor Knightley! – There would be an end of all pleasant intercourse with him. – How happy he had been to come and dine with them whenever they asked him! But that would be all over now. – Poor fellow! – No more exploring-parties to Donwell made for *her*. Oh; no; there would be a Mrs Knightley to throw cold water on every thing. – Extremely disagreeable! But she was not at all sorry that she had abused the housekeeper the other day. – Shocking plan, living together. It would never do. She knew a family near Maple Grove who had tried it, and been obliged to separate before the end of the first quarter.

CHAPTER FIFTY-FOUR

Time passed on. A few more to-morrows, and the party from London would be arriving. It was an alarming change; and Emma was thinking of it one morning as what must bring a great deal to agitate and grieve her, when Mr Knightley came in, and distressing thoughts were put by. After the first chat of pleasure he was silent; and then, in a graver tone, began with,

'I have something to tell you, Emma; some news.'

'Good or bad?' said she, quickly, looking up in his face.

'I do not know which it ought to be called.'

'Oh! good I am sure. – I see it in your countenance. You are trying not to smile.'

'I am afraid,' said he, composing his features, 'I am very much afraid, my dear Emma, that you will not smile when you hear it.'

'Indeed! but why so? – I can hardly imagine that any thing which pleases or amuses you, should not please and amuse me too.'

'There is one subject,' he replied, 'I hope but one, on which we do not think alike.' He paused a moment, again smiling, with his eyes fixed on her face. 'Does nothing occur to you? – Do not you recollect? – Harriet Smith.'

Her cheeks flushed at the name, and she felt afraid of something, though she knew not what.

'Have you heard from her yourself this morning?' cried he. 'You have, I believe, and know the whole.'

'No, I have not; I know nothing; pray tell me.'

'You are prepared for the worst, I see – and very bad it is. Harriet Smith marries Robert Martin.'

Emma gave a start, which did not seem like being prepared – and her eyes, in eager gaze, said, 'No, this is impossible!' but her lips were closed.

'It is so, indeed,' continued Mr Knightley; 'I have it from Robert Martin himself. He left me not half an hour ago.'

She was still looking at him with the most speaking amazement.

'You like it, my Emma, as little as I feared. – I wish our opinions were the same. But in time they will. Time, you may be very sure, will make one or the other of us think differently; and, in the meanwhile, we need not talk much on the subject.'

'You mistake me, you quite mistake me,' she replied, exerting herself. 'It is not that such a circumstance would now make me unhappy, but I cannot believe it. It seems an impossibility! – You cannot mean to say, that Harriet Smith has accepted Robert Martin. You cannot mean that he has even proposed to her again – yet. You only mean, that he intends it.'

'I mean that he has done it,' answered Mr Knightley, with smiling but determined decision, 'and been accepted.'

'Good God!' she cried. – 'Well!' – Then having recourse to her workbasket, in excuse for leaning down her face, and concealing all the exquisite feelings of delight and entertainment which she knew she must be expressing, she added, 'Well, now tell me every thing; make this intelligible to me. How, where, when? – Let me know it all. I never was more surprised – but it does not make me unhappy, I assure you. – How – how has it been possible?'

'It is a very simple story. He went to town on business three days ago, and I got him to take charge of some papers which I was wanting to send to John. – He delivered these papers to John, at his chambers, and was asked by him to join their party the same evening to Astley's. They were going to take the two eldest boys to Astley's. The party was to be our brother and sister, Henry, John – and Miss Smith. My friend Robert could not resist. They called for him in their way; were all extremely amused; and my brother asked him to dine with them the next day – which he did – and in the course of that visit (as I understand) he found an opportunity of speaking to Harriet; and certainly did not speak in vain. – She made him, by her acceptance, as happy even as he is deserving. He came down by yesterday's coach, and was with me this morning immediately after breakfast, to report his proceedings, first on my affairs, and then on his own. This is all that I can relate to the how, where, and when. Your friend Harriet will make a much longer history when you see her. – She will give you all the minute particulars, which only woman's language can make interesting. – In our communications we deal only in the great. – However, I must say that Robert

Martin's heart seemed for *him*, and to *me*, very overflowing; and that he did mention, without its being much to the purpose, that on quitting their box at Astley's, my brother took charge of Mrs John Knightley and little John, and he followed with Miss Smith and Henry; and that at one time they were in such a crowd, as to make Miss Smith rather uneasy.'

He stopped. – Emma dared not attempt any immediate reply. To speak, she was sure would be to betray a most unreasonable degree of happiness. She must wait a moment, or he would think her mad. Her silence disturbed him; and after observing her a little while, he added,

'Emma, my love, you said that this circumstance would not now make you unhappy; but I am afraid it gives you more pain than you expected. His situation is an evil – but you must consider it as what satisfies your friend; and I will answer for your thinking better and better of him as you know him more. His good sense and good principles would delight you. – As far as the man is concerned, you could not wish your friend in better hands. His rank in society I would alter if I could; which is saying a great deal I assure you, Emma. – You laugh at me about William Larkins; but I could quite as ill spare Robert Martin.'

He wanted her to look up and smile; and having now brought herself not to smile too broadly – she did – cheerfully answering,

'You need not be at any pains to reconcile me to the match. I think Harriet is doing extremely well. *Her* connections may be worse than *his*. In respectability of character, there can be no doubt that they are. I have been silent from surprize merely, excessive surprize. You cannot imagine how suddenly it has come on me! how peculiarly unprepared I was! – for I had reason to believe her very lately more determined against him, much more, than she was before.'

'You ought to know your friend best,' replied Mr Knightley; 'but I should say she was a good-tempered, soft-hearted girl, not likely to be very, very determined against any young man who told her he loved her.'

Emma could not help laughing as she answered, 'Upon my word, I believe you know her quite as well as I do. – But, Mr Knightley, are you perfectly sure that she has absolutely and downright *accepted* him. – I could suppose she might in time – but can she already? – Did not you misunderstand him? – You were both talking of other things; of business, shows of cattle, or new drills – and might not you, in the confusion of so many subjects, mistake him? – It was not Harriet's hand that he was certain of – it was the dimensions of some famous ox.'

The contrast between the countenance and air of Mr Knightley and Robert Martin was, at this moment, so strong to Emma's feelings, and so strong was the recollection of all that had so recently passed on Harriet's side, so fresh the sound of those words, spoken with such emphasis, 'No, I hope I know better than to think of Robert Martin,' that she was really expecting the intelligence to prove, in some measure, premature. It could not be otherwise.

'Do you dare say this?' cried Mr Knightley. 'Do you dare to suppose me so great a blockhead, as not to know what a man is talking of? – What do you deserve?'

'Oh! I always deserve the best treatment, because I never put up with any other; and, therefore, you must give me a plain, direct answer. Are you quite sure that you understand the terms on which Mr Martin and Harriet now are?'

'I am quite sure,' he replied, speaking very distinctly, 'that he told me she had accepted him; and that there was no obscurity, nothing doubtful, in the words he used; and I think I can give you a proof that it must be so. He asked my opinion as to what he was now to do. He knew of no one but Mrs Goddard to whom he could apply for information of her relations or friends. Could I mention any thing more fit to be done, than to go to Mrs Goddard? I assured him that I could not. Then, he said, he would endeavour to see her in the course of this day.'

'I am perfectly satisfied,' replied Emma, with the brightest smiles, 'and most sincerely wish them happy.'

'You are materially changed since we talked on this subject before.'

'I hope so – for at that time I was a fool.'

'And I am changed also; for I am now very willing to grant you all Harriet's good qualities. I have taken some pains for your sake, and for Robert Martin's sake, (whom I have always had reason to believe as much in love with her as ever,) to get acquainted with her. I have often talked to her a good deal. You must have seen that I did. Sometimes, indeed, I have thought you were half suspecting me of pleading poor Martin's cause, which was never the case: but, from all my observations, I am convinced of her being an artless, amiable girl, with very good notions, very seriously good principles, and placing her happiness in the affections and utility of domestic life. – Much of this, I have no doubt, she may thank you for.'

'Me!' cried Emma, shaking her head. – 'Ah! poor Harriet!'

She checked herself, however, and submitted quietly to a little more praise than she deserved.

Their conversation was soon afterwards closed by the entrance of her father. She was not sorry. She wanted to be alone. Her mind was in a state of flutter and wonder, which made it impossible for her to be collected. She was in dancing, singing, exclaiming spirits; and till she had moved about, and talked to herself, and laughed and reflected, she could be fit for nothing rational.

Her father's business was to announce James's being gone out to put the horses to, preparatory to their now daily drive to Randalls; and she had, therefore, an immediate excuse for disappearing.

The joy, the gratitude, the exquisite delight of her sensations may be imagined. The sole grievance and alloy thus removed in the prospect of Harriet's welfare, she was really in danger of becoming too happy for security. – What had she to wish for? Nothing, but to grow more worthy of him, whose intentions and judgment had been ever so superior to her own. Nothing, but that the lessons of her past folly might teach her humility and circumspection in future.

Serious she was, very serious in her thankfulness, and in her resolutions; and yet there was no preventing a laugh, sometimes in the very midst of them. She must laugh at such a close! Such an end of the doleful disappointment of five weeks back! Such a heart – such a Harriet!

Now there would be pleasure in her returning. – Every thing would be a pleasure. It would be a great pleasure to know Robert Martin.

High in the rank of her most serious and heartfelt felicities, was the reflection that all necessity of concealment from Mr Knightley would soon be over. The disguise, equivocation, mystery, so hateful to her to practise, might soon be over. She could now look forward to giving him that full and perfect confidence which her disposition was most ready to welcome as a duty.

In the gayest and happiest spirits she set forward with her father; not always listening, but always agreeing to what he said; and, whether in speech or silence, conniving at the comfortable persuasion of his being obliged to go to Randalls every day, or poor Mrs Weston would be disappointed.

They arrived. – Mrs Weston was alone in the drawing-room; – but hardly had they been told of the baby, and Mr Woodhouse received the thanks for coming, which he asked for, when a glimpse was caught through the blind, of two figures passing near the window.

'It is Frank and Miss Fairfax,' said Mrs Weston. 'I was just going to tell you of our agreeable surprize in seeing him arrive this morning. He stays till to-morrow, and Miss Fairfax has been persuaded to spend the day with us. – They are coming in, I hope.'

In half a minute they were in the room. Emma was extremely glad to see him – but there was a degree of confusion – a number of embarrassing recollections on each side. They met readily and smiling, but with a consciousness which at first allowed little to be said; and having all sat down again, there was for some time such a blank in the circle, that Emma began to doubt whether the wish now indulged, which she had long felt, of seeing Frank Churchill once more, and of seeing him with Jane, would yield its proportion of pleasure. When Mr Weston joined the party, however, and when the baby was fetched, there was no longer a want of subject or animation – or of courage and opportunity for Frank Churchill to draw near her and say,

'I have to thank you, Miss Woodhouse, for a very kind forgiving message in one of Mrs Weston's letters. I hope time has not made you less willing to pardon. I hope you do not retract what you then said.'

'No, indeed,' cried Emma, most happy to begin, 'not in the least. I am particularly glad to see and shake hands with you – and to give you joy in person.'

He thanked her with all his heart, and continued some time to speak with serious feeling of his gratitude and happiness.

'Is not she looking well?' said he, turning his eyes towards Jane. 'Better than she ever used to do? – You see how my father and Mrs Weston doat upon her.'

But his spirits were soon rising again, and with laughing eyes, after mentioning the expected return of the Campbells, he named the name of Dixon. – Emma blushed, and forbad its being pronounced in her hearing.

'I can never think of it,' she cried, 'without extreme shame.'

'The shame,' he answered, 'is all mine, or ought to be. But is it possible that you had no suspicion? – I mean of late. Early, I know you had none.'

'I never had the smallest, I assure you.'

'That appears quite wonderful. I was once very near – and I wish I had – it would have been better. But though I was always doing wrong things, they were very *bad* wrong things, and such as did me no service. – It would have been a much better transgression had I broken the bond of secrecy and told you every thing.'

'It is not worth a regret,' said Emma.

'I have some hope,' resumed he, 'of my uncle's being persuaded to pay a visit at Randalls; he wants to be introduced to her. When the Campbells are returned, we shall meet them in London, and continue there, I trust, till we may carry her northward. – But now, I am at such a distance from her – is not it hard, Miss Woodhouse? – Till this morning, we have not once met since the day of reconciliation. Do not you pity me?'

Emma spoke her pity so very kindly, that, with a sudden accession of gay thought, he cried,

'Ah! by the bye,' – then sinking his voice, and looking demure for the moment – 'I hope Mr Knightley is well?' He paused. – She coloured and laughed. – 'I know you saw my letter, and think you may remember my wish in your favour. Let me return your congratulations. – I assure you that I have heard the news with the warmest interest and satisfaction. – He is a man whom I cannot presume to praise.'

Emma was delighted, and only wanted him to go on in the same style; but his mind was the next moment in his own concerns and with his own Jane, and his next words were,

'Did you ever see such a skin? – such smoothness! such delicacy! – and yet without being actually fair. – One cannot call her fair. It is a most uncommon complexion, with her dark eye-lashes and hair – a most distinguishing complexion! – So peculiarly the lady in it. – Just colour enough for beauty.'

'I have always admired her complexion,' replied Emma, archly; 'but do not I remember the time when you found fault with her for being so pale? – When we first began to talk of her. – Have you quite forgotten?'

'Oh! no – what an impudent dog I was! – How could I dare – '

But he laughed so heartily at the recollection, that Emma could not help saying,

'I do suspect that in the midst of your perplexities at that time, you had very great amusement in tricking us all. – I am sure you had. – I am sure it was a consolation to you.'

'Oh! no, no, no – how can you suspect me of such a thing? – I was the most miserable wretch!'

'Not quite so miserable as to be insensible to mirth. I am sure it was a source of high entertainment to you, to feel that you were taking us all in. – Perhaps I am the readier to suspect, because to tell you the truth, I think it might have been some amusement to myself in the same situation. I think there is a little likeness between us.'

He bowed.

'If not in our dispositions,' she presently added, with a look of true sensibility, 'there is a likeness in our destiny; the destiny which bids fair to connect us with two characters so much superior to our own.'

'True, true,' he answered, warmly. 'No, not true on your side. You can have no superior, but most true on mine. – She is a complete angel. Look at her. Is not she an angel in every gesture? Observe the turn of her throat. Observe her eyes, as she is looking up at my father. – You will be glad to hear (inclining his head, and whispering seriously) that my uncle means to give her all my aunt's jewels. They are to be new set. I am resolved to have some in an ornament for the head. Will not it be beautiful in her dark hair?'

'Very beautiful, indeed,' replied Emma: and she spoke so kindly, that he gratefully burst out,

'How delighted I am to see you again! and to see you in such excellent looks! – I would not have missed this meeting for the world. I should certainly have called at Hartfield, had you failed to come.'

The others had been talking of the child, Mrs Weston giving an account of a little alarm she had been under, the evening before, from the infant's appearing not quite well. She believed she had been foolish, but it had alarmed her, and she had been within half a minute of sending for Mr Perry. Perhaps she ought to be ashamed, but Mr Weston had been almost as uneasy as herself. – In ten minutes, however, the child had been perfectly well again. This was her history; and particularly interesting it was to Mr Woodhouse, who commended her very much for thinking of sending for Perry, and only regretted that she had not done it. 'She should always send for Perry, if the child appeared in the slightest degree disordered, were it only for a moment. She could not be too soon alarmed, nor send for Perry too often. It was a pity, perhaps, that he had not come last night; for, though the child seemed well now, very well considering, it would probably have been better if Perry had seen it.'

Frank Churchill caught the name.

'Perry!' said he to Emma, and trying, as he spoke, to catch Miss Fairfax's eye. 'My friend Mr Perry! What are they saying about Mr Perry? – Has he been here this morning? – And how does he travel now? – Has he set up his carriage?'

Emma soon recollected, and understood him; and while she joined in the laugh, it was evident from Jane's countenance that she too was really hearing him, though trying to seem deaf.

'Such an extraordinary dream of mine!' he cried. 'I can never think of it without laughing. – She hears us, she hears us, Miss

Woodhouse. I see it in her cheek, her smile, her vain attempt to frown. Look at her. Do not you see that, at this instant, the very passage of her own letter, which sent me the report, is passing under her eye – that the whole blunder is spread before her – that she can attend to nothing else, though pretending to listen to the others?'

Jane was forced to smile completely, for a moment; and the smile partly remained as she turned towards him, and said in a conscious, low, yet steady voice,

'How you can bear such recollections, is astonishing to me! – They *will* sometimes obtrude – but how you can *court* them!'

He had a great deal to say in return, and very entertainingly; but Emma's feelings were chiefly with Jane, in the argument; and on leaving Randalls, and falling naturally into a comparison of the two men, she felt, that pleased as she had been to see Frank Churchill, and really regarding him as she did with friendship, she had never been more sensible for Mr Knightley's high superiority of character. The happiness of this most happy day, received its completion, in the animated contemplation of his worth which this comparison produced.

CHAPTER FIFTY-FIVE

IF EMMA HAD STILL, AT intervals, an anxious feeling for Harriet, a momentary doubt of its being possible for her to be really cured of her attachment to Mr Knightley, and really able to accept another man from unbiassed inclination, it was not long that she had to suffer from the recurrence of any such uncertainty. A very few days brought the party from London, and she had no sooner an opportunity of being one hour alone with Harriet, than she became perfectly satisfied – unaccountable as it was! – that Robert Martin had thoroughly supplanted Mr Knightley, and was now forming all her views of happiness.

Harriet was a little distressed – did look a little foolish at first; but having once owned that she had been presumptuous and silly, and self-deceived, before, her pain and confusion seemed to die away with the words, and leave her without a care for the past, and with the fullest exultation in the present and future; for, as to her friend's approbation, Emma had instantly removed every fear of that nature, by meeting her with the most unqualified congratulations. – Harriet was most happy to give every particular of the evening at

Astley's, and the dinner the next day; she could dwell on it all with the utmost delight. But what did such particulars explain? – The fact was, as Emma could now acknowledge, that Harriet had always liked Robert Martin; and that his continuing to love her had been irresistible. – Beyond this, it must ever be unintelligible to Emma.

The event, however, was most joyful, and every day was giving her fresh reason for thinking so. – Harriet's parentage became known. She proved to be the daughter of a tradesman, rich enough to afford her the comfortable maintenance which had ever been her's, and decent enough to have always wished for concealment. – Such was the blood of gentility which Emma had formerly been so ready to vouch for! – It was likely to be as untainted, perhaps, as the blood of many a gentleman: but what a connexion had she been preparing for Mr Knightley – or for the Churchills – or even for Mr Elton! – The stain of illegitimacy, unbleached by nobility or wealth, would have been a stain indeed.

No objection was raised on the father's side; the young man was treated liberally; it was all as it should be: and as Emma became acquainted with Robert Martin, who was now introduced at Hartfield, she fully acknowledged in him all the appearance of sense and worth which could bid fairest for her little friend. She had no doubt of Harriet's happiness with any good tempered man; but with him, and in the home he offered, there would be the hope of more, of security, stability, and improvement. She would be placed in the midst of those who loved her, and who had better sense than herself; retired enough for safety, and occupied enough for cheerfulness. She would be never led into temptation, nor left for it to find her out. She would be respectable and happy; and Emma admitted her to be the luckiest creature in the world, to have created so steady and persevering an affection in such a man; – or, if not quite the luckiest, to yield only to herself.

Harriet, necessarily drawn away by her engagements with the Martins, was less and less at Hartfield; which was not to be regretted. – The intimacy between her and Emma must sink; their friendship must change into a calmer sort of goodwill; and, fortunately, what ought to be, and must be, seemed already beginning, and in the most gradual, natural manner.

Before the end of September, Emma attended Harriet to church, and saw her hand bestowed on Robert Martin with so complete a satisfaction, as no remembrances, even connected with Mr Elton as he stood before them, could impair. – Perhaps, indeed, at that time she scarcely saw Mr Elton, but as the clergyman whose blessing at the altar might next fall on herself. – Robert Martin and Harriet

Smith, the latest couple engaged of the three, were the first to be married.

Jane Fairfax had already quitted Highbury, and was restored to the comforts of her beloved home with the Campbells. – The Mr Churchills were also in town; and they were only waiting for November.

The intermediate month was the one fixed on, as far as they dared, by Emma and Mr Knightley. – They had determined that their marriage ought to be concluded while John and Isabella were still at Hartfield, to allow them the fortnight's absence in a tour to the sea-side, which was the plan. – John and Isabella, and every other friend, were agreed in approving it. But Mr Woodhouse – how was Mr Woodhouse to be induced to consent? – he, who had never yet alluded to their marriage but as a distant event.

When first sounded on the subject, he was so miserable, that they were almost hopeless. – A second allusion, indeed, gave less pain. – He began to think it was to be, and that he could not prevent it – a very promising step of the mind on its way to resignation. Still, however, he was not happy. Nay, he appeared so much otherwise, that his daughter's courage failed. She could not bear to see him suffering, to know him fancying himself neglected; and though her understanding almost acquiesced in the assurance of both the Mr Knightleys, that when once the event were over, his distress would be soon over too, she hesitated – she could not proceed.

In this state of suspense they were befriended, not by any sudden illumination of Mr Woodhouse's mind, or any wonderful change of his nervous system, but by the operation of the same system in another way. – Mrs Weston's poultry-house was robbed one night of all her turkies – evidently by the ingenuity of man. Other poultry-yards in the neighbourhood also suffered. – Pilfering was *house-breaking* to Mr Woodhouse's fears. – He was very uneasy; and but for the sense of his son-in-law's protection, would have been under wretched alarm every night of his life. The strength, resolution, and presence of mind of the Mr Knightleys, commanded his fullest dependance. While either of them protected him and his, Hartfield was safe. – But Mr John Knightley must be in London again by the end of the first week in November.

The result of this distress was, that, with a much more voluntary, cheerful consent than his daughter had ever presumed to hope for at the moment, she was able to fix her wedding-day – and Mr Elton was called on, within a month from the marriage of Mr and Mrs Robert Martin, to join the hands of Mr Knightley and Miss Woodhouse.

The wedding was very much like other weddings, where the parties have no taste for finery or parade; and Mrs Elton, from the particulars detailed by her husband, thought it all extremely shabby, and very inferior to her own. – 'Very little white satin, very few lace veils; a most pitiful business! – Selina would stare when she heard of it.' – But, in spite of these deficiencies, the wishes, the hopes, the confidence, the predictions of the small band of true friends who witnessed the ceremony, were fully answered in the perfect happiness of the union.

Northanger Abbey

CHAPTER ONE

NO ONE WHO HAD EVER seen Catherine Morland in her infancy, would have supposed her born to be an heroine. Her situation in life, the character of her father and mother, her own person and disposition, were all equally against her. Her father was a clergyman, without being neglected, or poor, and a very respectable man, though his name was Richard – and he had never been handsome. He had a considerable independence, besides two good livings – and he was not in the least addicted to locking up his daughters. Her mother was a woman of useful plain sense, with a good temper, and, what is more remarkable, with a good constitution. She had three sons before Catherine was born; and instead of dying in bringing the latter into the world, as any body might expect, she still lived on – lived to have six children more – to see them growing up around her, and to enjoy excellent health herself. A family of ten children will be always called a fine family, where there are heads and arms and legs enough for the number; but the Morlands had little other right to the word, for they were in general very plain, and Catherine, for many years of her life, as plain as any. She had a thin awkward figure, a sallow skin without colour, dark lank hair, and strong features; – so much for her person; – and not less unpropitious for heroism seemed her mind. She was fond of all boys' plays, and greatly preferred cricket not merely to dolls, but to the more heroic enjoyments of infancy, nursing a dormouse, feeding a canary-bird, or watering a rose-bush. Indeed she had no taste for a garden; and if she gathered flowers at all, it was chiefly for the pleasure of mischief – at least so it was conjectured from her always preferring those which she was forbidden to take. – Such were her propensities – her abilities were quite as extraordinary. She never could learn or understand any thing before she was taught; and sometimes not even then, for she was often inattentive, and occasionally stupid. Her mother was three months in teaching her only to repeat the 'Beggar's Petition', and after all, her next sister, Sally, could say it better than she did. Not that Catherine was always stupid, – by no means; she learnt the fable of 'The Hare and many Friends', as quickly as any girl in England. Her mother wished her to learn music; and Catherine was sure she would like it, for she was very fond of tinkling the keys of the old forlorn spinnet; so, at eight years old she began. She learnt a year, and could not bear it; – and Mrs Morland, who did not insist on her daughters being accomplished in spite of incapacity or distaste, allowed her to leave off. The day which dismissed the music-master was one of the happiest of Catherine's life. Her taste for drawing was not superior; though whenever she could obtain the outside of a letter from her mother, or seize upon any other odd piece of paper, she did what she could in that way, by drawing houses and trees, hens and chickens, all very much like one another. – Writing and accounts she was taught by her father; French by her mother: her proficiency in either was not remarkable, and she shirked her lessons in both whenever she could. What a strange, unaccountable character! – for with all these symptons of profligacy at ten years old, she had neither a bad heart nor a bad temper; was seldom stubborn, scarcely ever quarrelsome, and very kind to the little ones, with few interruptions of tyranny; she was moreover noisy and wild, hated confinement and cleanliness, and loved nothing so well in the world as rolling down the green slope at the back of the house.

Such was Catherine Morland at ten. At fifteen, appearances were mending; she began to curl her hair and long for balls; her complexion improved; her features were softened by plumpness and colour, her eyes gained more animation, and her figure more consequence. Her love of dirt gave way to an inclination for finery, and she grew clean as she grew smart; she had now the pleasure of sometimes hearing her father and mother remark on her personal improvement. 'Catherine grows quite a good-looking girl, – she is almost pretty to day,' were words which caught her ears now and then; and how welcome were the sounds! To look *almost* pretty, is an acquisition of higher delight to a girl who has been looking plain the first fifteen years of her life, than a beauty from her cradle can ever receive.

Mrs Moorland was a very good woman, and wished to see her children every thing they ought to be; but her time was so much occupied in lying-in and teaching the little ones, that her elder daughters were inevitably left to shift for themselves; and it was not very wonderful that Catherine, who had by nature nothing heroic about her, should prefer cricket, base ball, riding on horseback, and running about the country at the age of fourteen, to books – or at least books of information – for, provided that nothing like useful knowledge could be gained from them, provided they were all story and no reflection, she had never any objection to books at all. But from fifteen to seventeen she was in training for a heroine; she read all such works as heroines must read to supply their memories with

'Catherine grows quite a good-looking girl.'

those quotations which are so serviceable and so soothing in the vicissitudes of their eventful lives.

From Pope, she learnt to censure those who

> *'bear about the mockery of woe.'*

From Gray, that

> *'Many a flower is born to blush unseen.*
> *'And waste its fragrance on the desert air.'*

From Thompson, that

——'It is a delightful task
'To teach the young idea how to shoot.'

And from Shakspeare she gained a great store of information – amongst the rest, that

——'Trifles light as air,
'Are, to the jealous, confirmation strong,
'As proofs of Holy Writ.'

That

'The poor beetle, which we tread upon,
'In corporal sufferance feels a pang as great
'As when a giant dies.'

And that a young woman in love always looks

——'like Patience on a monument
'Smiling at Grief.'

So far her improvement was sufficient – and in many other points she came on exceedingly well; for though she could not write sonnets, she brought herself to read them; and though there seemed no chance of her throwing a whole party into raptures by a prelude on the pianoforte, of her own composition, she could listen to other people's performance with very little fatigue. Her greatest deficiency was in the pencil – she had no notion of drawing – not enough even to attempt a sketch of her lover's profile, that she might be detected in the design. There she fell miserably short of the true heroic height. At present she did not know her own poverty, for she had no lover to pourtray. She had reached the age of seventeen, without having seen one amiable youth who could call forth her sensibility; without having inspired one real passion, and without having excited even any admiration but what was very moderate and very transient. This was strange indeed! But strange things may be generally accounted for if their cause be fairly searched out. There was not one lord in the neighbourhood; no – not even a baronet. There was not one family among their acquaintance who had reared and supported a boy accidentally found at their door – not one young man whose origin was unknown. Her father had no ward, and the squire of the parish no children.

But when a young lady is to be a heroine, the perverseness of forty surrounding families cannot prevent her. Something must and will happen to throw a hero in her way.

Mr Allen, who owned the chief of the property about Fullerton, the village in Wiltshire where the Morlands lived, was ordered to Bath for the benefit of a gouty constitution; – and his lady, a good-humoured woman, fond of Miss Morland, and probably aware that if adventures will not befall a young lady in her own village, she must seek them abroad, invited her to go with them. Mr and Mrs Morland were all compliance, and Catherine all happiness.

CHAPTER TWO

IN ADDITION TO WHAT has been already said of Catherine Morland's personal and mental endowments, when about to be launched into all the difficulties and dangers of a six weeks' residence in Bath, it may be stated, for the readers' more certain information, lest the following pages should otherwise fail of giving any idea of what her character is meant to be; that her heart was affectionate, her disposition cheerful and open, without conceit or affection of any kind – her manners just removed from the awkwardness and shyness of a girl; her person pleasing, and, when in good looks, pretty – and her mind about as ignorant and uninformed as the female mind at seventeen usually is.

When the hour of departure drew near, the maternal anxiety of Mrs Morland will be naturally supposed to be most severe. A thousand alarming presentiments of evil to her beloved Catherine from this terrific separation must oppress her heart with sadness, and drown her in tears for the last day or two of their being together; and advice of the most important and applicable nature must of course flow from her wise lips in their parting conference in her closet. Cautions against the violence of such noblemen and baronets as delight in forcing young ladies away to some remote farm-house, must, at such a moment, relieve the fulness of her heart. Who would not think so? But Mrs Morland knew so little of lords and baronets, that she entertained no notion of their general mischievousness, and was wholly unsuspicious of danger to her daughter from their machinations. Her cautions were confined to the following points. 'I beg Catherine, you will always wrap yourself up very warm about the throat when you come from the Rooms at night; and I wish you would try to keep some account of the money you spend; – I will give you this little book on purpose.'

Sally, or rather Sarah, (for what young lady of common gentility will reach the age of sixteen without altering her name as far as she can?) must from situation be at this time the intimate friend and confidante of her sister. It is remarkable, however, that she neither insisted on Catherine's writing by every post, nor exacted her promise of transmitting the character of every new acquaintance, nor a detail of every interesting conversation that Bath might produce. Every thing indeed relative to this important journey was done, on the part of the Morlands, with a degree of moderation and composure, which seemed rather consistent with the common feelings of common life, than with the refined susceptibilities, the tender emotions which the first separation of a heroine from her family ought always to excite. Her father, instead of giving her an unlimited order on his banker, or even putting an hundred pounds bank-bill into her hands, gave her only ten guineas, and promised her more when she wanted it.

Under these unpromising auspices, the parting took place, and the journey began. It was performed with suitable quietness and uneventful safety. Neither robbers nor tempests befriended them, nor one lucky overturn to introduce them to the hero. Nothing more alarming occurred than a fear on Mrs Allen's side, of having once left her clogs behind her at an inn, and that fortunately proved to be groundless.

They arrived at Bath. Catherine was all eager delight; – her eyes were here, there, every where, as they approached its fine and striking environs, and afterwards drove through those streets which conducted them to the hotel. She was come to be happy, and she felt happy already.

They were soon settled in comfortable lodgings in Pulteney-street.

It is now expedient to give some description of Mrs Allen, that the reader may be able to judge, in what manner her actions will hereafter tend to promote the general distress of the work, and how she will, probably, contribute to reduce poor Catherine to all the desperate wretchedness of which a last volume is capable – whether by her imprudence, vulgarity, or jealousy – whether by intercepting her letters, ruining her character, or turning her out of doors.

Mrs Allen was one of that numerous class of females, whose society can raise no other emotion than surprise at there being any men in the world who could like them well enough to marry them. She had neither beauty, genius, accomplishment, nor manner. The air of a gentlewoman, a great deal of quiet, inactive good temper, and a trifling turn of mind, were all that could account for her being the choice of a sensible, intelligent man, like Mr Allen. In one respect she was admirably fitted to introduce a young lady into public, being as fond of going every where and seeing every thing herself as any young lady could be. Dress was her passion. She had a most harmless delight in being fine; and our heroine's entrée into life could not take place till after three or four days had been spent in learning what was mostly worn, and her chaperon was provided with a dress of the newest fashion. Catherine too made some purchases herself, and when all these matters were arranged, the important evening came which was to usher her into the Upper Rooms. Her hair was cut and dressed by the best hand, her clothes put on with care, and both Mrs Allen and her maid declared she looked quite as she should do. With such encouragement, Catherine hoped at least to pass uncensured through the crowd. As for admiration, it was always very welcome when it came, but she did not depend on it.

Mrs Allen was so long in dressing, that they did not enter the ball-room till late. The season was full, the room crowded, and the two ladies squeezed in as well as they could. As for Mr Allen, he repaired directly to the card-room, and left them to enjoy a mob by themselves. With more care for the safety of her new gown than for the comfort of her protegée, Mrs Allen made her way through the throng of men by the door, as swiftly as the necessary caution would allow; Catherine, however, kept close at her side, and linked her arm too firmly within her friend's to be torn asunder by any common effort of a struggling assembly. But to her utter amazement she found that to proceed along the room was by no means the way to disengage themselves from the crowd; it seemed rather to increase as they went on, whereas she had imagined that when once fairly within the door, they should easily find seats and be able to watch the dances with perfect convenience. But this was far from being the case, and though by unwearied diligence they gained even the top of the room, their situation was just the same; they saw nothing of the dancers but the high feathers of some of the ladies. Still they moved on – something better was yet in view; and by a continued exertion of strength and ingenuity they found themselves at last in the passage behind the highest bench. Here there was something less of crowd than below; and hence Miss Morland had a comprehensive view of all the company beneath her, and of all the dangers of her late passage through them. It was a splendid sight, and she began, for the first time that evening, to feel herself at a ball; she longed to dance, but she had not an acquaintance in the room. Mrs Allen did all that she could do in such a case by saying very placidly, every now and then, 'I wish you could dance, my dear, – I wish you could get a partner.' For some time her young friend felt obliged to her for these wishes; but they were repeated so often, and proved so totally ineffectual, that Catherine grew tired at last, and would thank her no more.

They were not long able, however, to enjoy the repose of the eminence they had so laboriously gained. – Every body was shortly in motion for tea, and they must squeeze out like the rest. Catherine began to feel something of disappointment – she was tired of being continually pressed against by people, the generality of whose faces possessed nothing to interest, and with all of whom she was so wholly unacquainted, that she could not relieve the irksomeness of imprisonment by the exchange of a syllable with any of her fellow captives; and when at last arrived in the tea-room, she felt yet more the awkwardness of having no party to join, no acquaintance to claim, no gentleman to assist them. – They saw nothing of Mr Allen; and after looking about them in vain for a more eligible situation, were obliged to sit down at the end of a table, at which a large party were already placed, without having any thing to do there, or any body to speak to, except each other.

Mrs Allen congratulated herself, as soon as they were seated, on having preserved her gown from injury. 'It would have been very shocking to have it torn,' said she, 'would not it? – It is such a delicate muslin. – For my part I have not seen any thing I like so well in the whole room, I assure you.'

'How uncomfortable it is,' whispered Catherine, 'not to have a single acquaintance here!'

'Yes, my dear,' replied Mrs Allen, with perfect serenity, 'It is very uncomfortable indeed.'

'What shall we do? – The gentlemen and ladies at this table look as if they wondered why we came here – we seem forcing ourselves into their party.'

'Aye, so we do. – That is very disagreeable. I wish we had a large acquaintance here.'

'I wish we had *any*; – it would be somebody to go to.'

'Very true, my dear; and if we knew anybody we would join them directly. The Skinners were here last year – I wish they were here now.'

'Had not we better go away as it is? – Here are no tea things for us, you see.'

'No more there are, indeed. – How very provoking! But I think we had better sit still, for one gets so tumbled in such a crowd! How is my head, my dear? – Somebody gave me a push that has hurt it I am afraid.'

'No, indeed, it looks very nice. – But, dear Mrs Allen, are you sure there is nobody you know in all this multitude of people? I think you *must* know somebody.'

'I don't upon my word – I wish I did. I wish I had a large acquaintance here with all my heart, and then I should get you a partner. – I should be so glad to have you dance. There goes a

'What an odd gown she has got on.'

strange-looking woman! What an odd gown she has got on! – How old fashioned it is! Look at the back.'

After some time they received an offer of tea from one of their neighbours; it was thankfully accepted, and this introduced a light conversation with the gentleman who offered it, which was the only time that any body spoke to them during the evening, till they were discovered and joined by Mr Allen when the dance was over.

'Well, Miss Morland,' said he, directly, 'I hope you have had an agreeable ball.'

'Very agreeable indeed,' she replied, vainly endeavouring to hide a great yawn.

'I wish she had been able to dance,' said his wife, 'I wish we could have got a partner for her. – I have been saying how glad I should be if the Skinners were here this winter instead of last; or if the Parrys had come, as they talked of once, she might have danced with George Parry. I am so sorry she has not had a partner!'

'We shall do better another evening I hope,' was Mr Allen's consolation.

The company began to disperse when the dancing was over – enough to leave space for the remainder to walk about in some comfort; and now was the time for a heroine, who had not yet played a very distinguished part in the events of the evening, to be noticed and admired. Every five minutes, by removing some of the crowd, gave greater openings for her charms. She was now seen by many young men who had not been near her before. Not one, however, started with rapturous wonder on beholding her, no whisper of eager inquiry ran round the room, nor was she once called a divinity by any body. Yet Catherine was in very good looks, and had the company only seen her three years before, they would *now* have thought her exceedingly handsome.

She *was* looked at however, and with some admiration; for, in her own hearing, two gentlemen pronounced her to be a pretty girl. Such words had their due effect; she immediately thought the evening pleasanter than she had found it before – her humble vanity was contented – she felt more obliged to the two young men for this simple praise than a true quality heroine would have been for fifteen sonnets in celebration of her charms, and went to her chair in good humour with every body, and perfectly satisfied with her share of public attention.

CHAPTER THREE

EVERY MORNING NOW brought its regular duties; – shops were to be visited; some new part of the town to be looked at; and the Pump-room to be attended, where they paraded up and down for an hour, looking at every body and speaking to no one. The wish of a numerous acquaintance in Bath was still uppermost with Mrs Allen, and she repeated it after every fresh proof, which every morning brought, of her knowing nobody at all.

They made their appearance in the Lower Rooms; and here fortune was more favourable to our heroine. The master of the ceremonies introduced to her a very gentlemanlike young man as a partner; – his name was Tilney. He seemed to be about four or five and twenty, was rather tall, had a pleasing countenance, a very intelligent and lively eye, and, if not quite handsome, was very near it. His address was good, and Catherine felt herself in high luck. There was little leisure for speaking while they danced; but when they were seated at tea, she found him as agreeable as she had already given him credit for being. He talked with fluency and spirit – and there was an archness and pleasantry in his manner which interested, though it was hardly understood by her. After chatting for some time on such matters as naturally arose from the objects around them, he suddenly addressed her with – 'I have hitherto been very remiss, madam, in the proper attentions of a partner here; I have not yet asked you how long you have been in Bath; whether you were ever here before; whether you have been at the Upper Rooms, the theatre, and the concert; and how you like the place altogether. I have been very negligent – but are you now at leisure to satisfy me in these particulars? If you are I will begin directly.'

'You need not give yourself that trouble, sir.'

'No trouble I assure you, madam.' Then forming his features into a set smile, and affectedly softening his voice, he added, with a simpering air, 'Have you been long in Bath, madam?'

'About a week, sir,' replied Catherine, trying not to laugh.

'Really!' with affected astonishment.

'Why should you be surprized, sir?'

'Why, indeed!' said he, in his natural tone – 'but some emotion must appear to be raised by your reply, and surprize is more easily assumed, and not less reasonable than any other. – Now let us go on. Were you never here before, madam?'

'Never, sir.'

'Indeed! Have you yet honoured the Upper Rooms?'

'Yes, sir, I was there last Monday.'

'Have you been to the theatre?'

'Yes, sir, I was at the play on Tuesday.'

'To the concert?'

'Yes, sir, on Wednesday.'

'And are you altogether pleased with Bath?'

'Yes – I like it very well.'

'Now I must give one smirk, and then we may be rational again.'

Catherine turned away her head, not knowing whether she might venture to laugh.

'I see what you think of me,' said he gravely – 'I shall make but a poor figure in your journal to-morrow.'

'My journal!'

'Yes, I know exactly what you will say: Friday, went to the Lower Rooms; wore my sprigged muslin robe with blue trimmings – plain black shoes – appeared to much advantage; but was strangely harassed by a queer, half-witted man, who would make me dance with him, and distressed me by his nonsense.'

'Indeed I shall say no such thing.'

'Shall I tell you what you ought to say?'

'If you please.'

'I danced with a very agreeable young man, introduced by Mr King; had a great deal of conversation with him – seems a most extraordinary genius – hope I may know more of him. *That*, madam, is what I *wish* you to say.'

'But, perhaps, I keep no journal.'

'Perhaps you are not sitting in this room, and I am not sitting by you. These are points in which a doubt is equally possible. Not keep a journal! How are your absent cousins to understand the tenour of your life in Bath without one? How are the civilities and compliments of every day to be related as they ought to be, unless noted down every evening in a journal? How are your various dresses to be remembered, and the particular state of your complexion, and curl of your hair to be described in all their diversities, without having constant recourse to a journal? – My dear madam, I am not so ignorant of young ladies' ways as you wish to believe me; it is this delightful habit of journalizing which largely contributes to form the easy style of writing for which ladies are so generally celebrated. Every body allows that the talent of writing agreeable letters is peculiarly female. Nature may have done something, but I am sure it must be essentially assisted by the practice of keeping a journal.'

'I have sometimes thought,' said Catherine, doubtingly, 'whether ladies do write so much better letters than gentlemen! This is – I should not think the superiority was always on our side.'

'As far as I have had opportunity of judging, it appears to me that the usual style of letter-writing among women is faultless, except in three particulars.'

'And what are they?'

'A general deficiency of subject, a total inattention to stops, and a very frequent ignorance of grammar.'

'Upon my word! I need not have been afraid of disclaiming the compliment. You do not think too highly of us in that way.'

'I should no more lay it down as a general rule that women write better letters than men, than that they sing better duets, or draw better landscapes. In every power, of which taste is the foundation, excellence is pretty fairly divided between the sexes.'

They were interrupted by Mrs Allen: – 'My dear Catherine,' said she, 'do take this pin out of my sleeve; I am afraid it has torn a hole already; I shall be quite sorry if it has, for this is a favourite gown, though it cost but nine shillings a yard.'

'That is exactly what I should have guessed it, madam,' said Mr Tilney, looking at the muslin.

'Do you understand muslins, sir?'

'Particularly well; I always buy my own cravats, and am allowed to be an excellent judge; and my sister has often trusted me in the choice of a gown. I bought one for her the other day, and it was pronounced to be a prodigious bargain by every lady who saw it. I gave but five shillings a yard for it, and a true Indian muslin.'

Mrs Allen was quite struck by his genius. 'Men commonly take so little notice of those things,' said she: 'I can never get Mr Allen to know one of my gowns from another. You must be a great comfort to your sister, sir.'

'I hope I am, madam.'

'And pray, sir, what do you think of Miss Morland's gown?'

'It is very pretty, madam,' said he, gravely examining it; but I do not think it will wash well; I am afraid it will fray.'

'How can you,' said Catherine, laughing, 'be so – ' she had almost said, strange.

'I am quite of your opinion, sir,' replied Mrs Allen; 'and so I told Miss Morland when she bought it.'

'But then you know, madam, muslin always turns to some

account or other; Miss Morland will get enough out of it for a handkerchief, or a cap, or a cloak. – Muslin can never be said to be wasted. I have heard my sister say so forty times, when she has been extravagant in buying more than she wanted, or careless in cutting it to pieces.'

'Bath is a charming place, sir; there are so many good shops here. – We are sadly off in the country; not but what we have very good shops in Salisbury, but it is so far to go; – eight miles is a long way; Mr Allen says it is nine, measured nine; but I am sure it cannot be more than eight; and it is such a fag – I come back tired to death. Now here one can step out of doors and get a thing in five minutes.'

Mr Tilney was polite enough to seem interested in what she said; and she kept him on the subject of muslins till the dancing recommenced. Catherine feared, as she listened to their discourse, that he indulged himself a little too much with the foibles of others. – 'What are you thinking of so earnestly?' said he, as they walked back to the ball-room; – 'not of your partner, I hope, for, by that shake of the head, your meditations are not satisfactory.'

Catherine coloured, and said, 'I was not thinking of any thing.'

'That is artful and deep, to be sure; but I had rather be told at once that you will not tell me.'

'Well then, I will not.'

'Thank you; for now we shall soon be acquainted, as I am authorized to tease you on this subject whenever we meet, and nothing in the world advances intimacy so much.'

They danced again; and, when the assembly closed, parted, on the lady's side at least, with a strong inclination for continuing the acquaintance. Whether she thought of him so much, while she drank her warm wine and water, and prepared herself for bed, as to dream of him when there, cannot be ascertained; but I hope it was no more than in a slight slumber, or a morning doze at most; for if it be true, as a celebrated writer has maintained, that no young lady can be justified in falling in love before the gentleman's love is declared,* it must be very improper that a young lady should dream of a gentleman before the gentleman is first known to have dreamt of her. How proper Mr Tilney might be as a dreamer or a lover, had not yet perhaps entered Mr Allen's head, but that he was not objectionable as a common acquaintance for his young charge he was on inquiry satisfied; for he had early in the evening taken pains to know who her partner was, and had been assured of Mr Tilney's

* Vide a letter from Mr Richardson, No. 97, vol.ii. Rambler.

being a clergyman, and of a very respectable family in Gloucestershire.

CHAPTER FOUR

WITH MORE THAN USUAL eagerness did Catherine hasten to the Pump-room the next day, secure within herself of seeing Mr Tilney there before the morning were over, and ready to meet him with a smile: – but no smile was demanded – Mr Tilney did not appear. Every creature in Bath, except himself, was to be seen in the room at different periods of the fashionable hours; crowds of people were every moment passing in and out, up the steps and down; people whom nobody cared about, and nobody wanted to see; and he only was absent. 'What a delightful place Bath is,' said Mrs Allen, as they sat down near the great clock, after parading the room till they were tired; 'and how pleasant it would be if we had any acquaintance here.'

This sentiment had been uttered so often in vain, that Mrs Allen had no particular reason to hope it would be followed with more advantage now; but we are told to 'despair of nothing we would attain,' as 'unwearied diligence our point would gain;' and the unwearied diligence with which she had every day wished for the same thing was at length to have its just reward, for hardly had she been seated ten minutes before a lady of about her own age, who was sitting by her, and had been looking at her attentively for several minutes, addressed her with great complaisance in these words: – 'I think, madam, I cannot be mistaken; it is a long time since I had the pleasure of seeing you, but is not your name Allen?' This question answered, as it readily was, the stranger pronounced her's to be Thorpe; and Mrs Allen immediately recognized the features of a former schoolfellow and intimate, whom she had seen only once since their respective marriages, and that many years ago. Their joy on this meeting was very great, as well it might, since they had been contented to know nothing of each other for the last fifteen years. Compliments on good looks now passed; and, after observing how time had slipped away since they were last together, how little they had thought of meeting in Bath, and what a pleasure it was to see an old friend, they proceeded to make inquiries and give intelligence as to their families, sisters, and cousins, talking both together, far more ready to give than to receive information, and each hearing very little of what the other said. Mrs Thorpe, however, had one great advantage as a talker, over Mrs Allen, in a family of children; and when she expatiated on the talents of her sons, and the beauty of her daughters, – when she related their different situations and views, – that John was at Oxford, Edward at Merchant-Taylors', and William at sea, – and all of them more beloved and respected in their different station than any other three beings ever were, Mrs Allen had no similar information to give, no similar triumphs to press on the unwilling and unbelieving ear of her friend, and was forced to sit and appear to listen to all these maternal effusions, consoling herself, however, with the discovery, which her keen eye soom made, that the lace of Mrs Thorpe's pelisse was not half so handsome as that on her own.

'Here come my dear girls,' cried Mrs Thorpe, pointing at three smart looking females, who, arm in arm, were then moving towards her. 'My dear Mrs Allen, I long to introduce them; they will be so delighted to see you: the tallest is Isabella, my eldest; is not she a fine young woman? The others are very much admired too, but I believe Isabella is the handsomest.'

The Miss Thorpes were introduced; and Miss Morland, who had been for a short time forgotten, was introduced likewise. The name seemed to strike them all; and, after speaking to her with great civility, the eldest young lady observed aloud to the rest, 'How excessively like her brother Miss Morland is!'

'The very picture of him indeed!' cried the mother – and 'I should have known her any where for his sister!' was repeated by them all, two or three times over. For a moment Catherine was surprized; but Mrs Thorpe and her daughters had scarcely begun the history of their acquaintance with Mr James Morland, before she remembered that her eldest brother had lately formed an intimacy with a young man of his own college, of the name of Thorpe; and that he had spent the last week of the Christmas vacation with his family, near London.

The whole being explained, many obliging things were said by the Miss Thorpes of their wish of being better acquainted with her; of being considered as already friends, through the friendship of their brothers, &c. which Catherine heard with pleasure, and answered with all the pretty expressions she could command; and, as the first proof of amity, she was soon invited to accept an arm of the eldest Miss Thorpe, and take a turn with her about the room. Catherine was delighted with this extension of her Bath acquaintance, and almost forgot Mr Tilney while she talked to Miss Thorpe.

Friendship is certainly the finest balm for the pangs of disappointed love.

Their conversation turned upon those subjects, of which the free discussion has generally much to do in perfecting a sudden intimacy between two young ladies; such as dress, balls, flirtations, and quizzes. Miss Thorpe, however, being four years older than Miss Morland, and at least four years better informed, had a very decided advantage in discussing such points; she could compare the balls of Bath with those of Tunbridge; its fashions with the fashions of London; could rectify the opinions of her new friend in many articles of tasteful attire; could discover a flirtation between any gentleman and lady who only smiled on each other; and point out a quiz through the thickness of a crowd. These powers received due admiration from Catherine, to whom they were entirely new; and the respect which they naturally inspired might have been too great for familiarity, had not the easy gaiety of Miss Thorpe's manners, and her frequent expressions of delight on this acquaintance with her, softened down every feeling of awe, and left nothing but tender affection. Their increasing attachment was not to be satisfied with half a dozen turns in the Pump-room, but required, when they all quitted it together, that Miss Thorpe should accompany Miss Morland to the very door of Mr Allen's house; and that they should there part with a most affectionate and lengthened shake of hands, after learning, to their mutual relief, that they should see each other across the theatre at night, and say their prayers in the same chapel the next morning. Catherine then ran directly up stairs, and watched Miss Thorpe's progress down the street from the drawing-room window; admired the graceful spirit of her walk, the fashionable air of her figure and dress, and felt grateful, as well she might, for the chance which had procured her such a friend.

Mrs Thorpe was a widow, and not a very rich one; she was a good-humoured, well-meaning woman, and a very indulgent mother. Her eldest daughter had great personal beauty, and the younger ones, by pretending to be as handsome as their sister, imitating her air, and dressing in the same style, did very well.

This brief account of the family is intended to supersede the necessity of a long and minute detail from Mrs Thorpe herself, of her past adventures and sufferings, which might otherwise be expected to occupy the three or four following chapters; in which the worthlessness of lords and attornies might be set forth, and conversations, which had passed twenty years before, be minutely repeated.

CHAPTER FIVE

CATHERINE WAS NOT so much engaged at the theatre that evening, in returning the nods and smiles of Miss Thorpe, though they certainly claimed much of her leisure, as to forget to look with an inquiring eye for Mr Tilney in every box which her eye could reach; but she looked in vain. Mr Tilney was no fonder of the play than the Pump-room. She hoped to be more fortunate the next day; and when her wishes for fine weather were answered by seeing a beautiful morning, she hardly felt a doubt of it; for a fine Sunday in Bath empties every house of its inhabitants, and all the world appears on such an occasion to walk about and tell their acquaintance what a charming day it is.

As soon as divine service was over, the Thorpes and Allens eagerly joined each other; and after staying long enough in the Pump-room to discover that the crowd was insupportable, and that there was not a genteel face to be seen, which every body discovers every Sunday throughout the season, they hastened away to the Crescent, to breathe the fresh air of better company. Here Catherine and Isabella, arm in arm, again tasted the sweets of friendship in an unreserved conversation; – they talked much, and with much enjoyment; but again was Catherine disappointed in her hope of re-seeing her partner. He was no where to be met with; every search for him was equally unsuccessful in morning lounges or evening assemblies; neither at the upper nor lower rooms, at dressed or undressed balls, was he perceivable; nor among the walkers, the horsemen, or the curricle-drivers of the morning. His name was not in the Pump-room book, and curiosity could do no more. He must be gone from Bath. Yet he had not mentioned that his stay would be so short! This sort of mysteriousness, which is always so becoming in a hero, threw a fresh grace in Catherine's imagination around his person and manners, and increased her anxiety to know more of him. From the Thorpes she could learn nothing, for they had been only two days in Bath before they met with Mrs Allen. It was a subject, however, in which she often indulged with her friend, from whom she received every possible encouragement to continue to think of him; and his impression of her fancy was not suffered therefore to weaken. Isabella was very sure that he must be a charming young man; and was equally sure that he must have been delighted with her dear Catherine, and would therefore shortly return. She liked him the better for being a clergyman, 'for she must confess herself very partial to the profession;' and something like a sigh escaped her as she said it. Perhaps Catherine was wrong in not demanding the cause of that gentle emotion – but she was not experienced enough in the finesse of love, or the duties of friendship, to know when delicate raillery was properly called for, or when a confidence should be forced.

Mrs Allen was now quite happy – quite satisfied with Bath. She had found some acquaintance, had been so lucky too as to find in them the family of a most worthy old friend; and, as the completion of good fortune, had found these friends by no means so expensively dressed as herself. Her daily expressions were no longer, 'I wish we had some acquaintance in Bath!' They were changed into – 'How glad I am we have met with Mrs Thorpe!' – and she was as eager in promoting the intercourse of the two families, as her young charge and Isabella themselves could be; never satisfied with the day unless she spent the chief of it by the side of Mrs Thorpe, in what they called conversation, but in which there was scarcely ever any exchange of opinion, and not often any resemblance of subject, for Mrs Thorpe talked chiefly of her children, and Mrs Allen of her gowns.

The progress of the friendship between Catherine and Isabella was quick as its beginning had been warm, and they passed so rapidly through every gradation of increasing tenderness, that there was shortly no fresh proof of it to be given to their friends or themselves. They called each other by their Christian name, were always arm in arm when they walked, pinned up each other's train for the dance, and were not to be divided in the set; and if a rainy morning deprived them of other enjoyments, they were still resolute in meeting in defiance of wet and dirt, and shut themselves up, to read novels together. Yes, novels; – for I will not adopt that ungenerous and impolitic custom so common with novel writers, of degrading by their contemptuous censure the very performances, to the number of which they are themselves adding – joining with their greatest enemies in bestowing the harshest epithets on such works, and scarcely ever permitting them to be read by their own heroine, who, if she accidentally take up a novel, is sure to turn over its insipid pages with disgust. Alas! if the heroine of one novel be not patronized by the heroine of another, from whom can she expect protection and regard? I cannot approve of it. Let us leave it to the Reviewers to abuse such effusions of fancy at their leisure, and over every new novel to talk in threadbare strains of the trash with which the press

Pinned up each other's train for the dance.

now groans. Let us not desert one another; we are an injured body. Although our productions have afforded more extensive and unaffected pleasure than those of any other literary corporation in the world, no species of composition has been so much decried. From pride, ignorance, or fashion, our foes are almost as many as our readers. And while the abilities of the nine-hundredth abridger of the History of England, or of the man who collects and publishes in a volume some dozen lines of Milton, Pope, and Prior, with a paper from the Spectator, and a chapter from Sterne, are eulogized by a thousand pens, – there seems almost a general wish of decrying the capacity and undervaluing the labour of the novelist, and of slighting the performances which have only genius, wit, and taste to recommend them. 'I am no novel reader – I seldom look into novels – Do not imagine that *I* often read novels – It is really very well for a novel.' – Such is the common cant. – 'And what are you reading, Miss – ?' 'Oh! it is only a novel!' replies the young lady; while she lays down her book with affected indifference, or momentary shame. – 'It is only Cecilia, or Camilla, or Belinda;' or, in short, only some work in which the greatest powers of the mind are displayed, in which the most thorough knowledge of human nature, the happiest delineation of its varieties, the liveliest effusions of wit and humour are conveyed to the world in the best chosen language. Now, had the same young lady been engaged with a volume of the Spectator, instead of such a work, how proudly would she have produced the book, and told its name; though the chances must be against her being occupied by any part of that voluminous publication, of which either the matter or manner would not disgust a young person of taste: the substance of its papers so often consisting in the statement of improbable circumstances, unnatural characters, and topics of conversation, which no longer concern any one living; and their language, too, frequently so coarse as to give no very favourable idea of the age that could endure it.

CHAPTER SIX

THE FOLLOWING CONVERSATION, which took place between the two friends in the Pump-room one morning, after an acquaintance of eight or nine days, is given as a specimen of their very warm attachment, and of the delicacy, discretion, originality of thought, and literary taste which marked the reasonableness of that attachment.

They met by appointment; and as Isabella had arrived nearly five minutes before her friend, her first address naturally was – 'My dearest creature, what can have made you so late? I have been waiting for you at least this age!'

'Have you, indeed! – I am very sorry for it; but really I thought I was in very good time. It is but just one. I hope you have not been here long?'

'Oh! these ten ages at least. I am sure I have been here this half hour. But now, let us go and sit down at the other end of the room, and enjoy ourselves. I have an hundred things to say to you. In the first place, I was so afraid it would rain this morning, just as I wanted to set off; it looked very showery, and that would have thrown me into agonies! Do you know, I saw the prettiest hat you can imagine, in a shop window in Milsom-street just now – very like yours, only with coquelicot ribbons instead of green; I quite longed for it. But, my dearest Catherine, what have you been doing with yourself all this morning? – Have you gone on with Udolpho?'

'Yes, I have been reading it ever since I woke; and I am got to the black veil.'

'Are you, indeed? How delightful! Oh! I would not tell you what is behind the black veil for the world! Are not you wild to know?'

'Oh! yes, quite; what can it be? – But do not tell me – I would not be told upon any account. I know it must be a skeleton, I am sure it is Laurentina's skeleton. Oh! I am delighted with the book! I should like to spend my whole life in reading it. Assure you, if it had not been to meet you, I would not have come away from it for all the world.'

'Dear creature! how much I am obliged to you; and when you have finished Udolpho, we will read the Italian together; and I have made out a list of ten or twelve more of the same kind for you.'

'Have you, indeed! How glad I am! – What are they all?'

'I will read you their names directly; here they are, in my pocket-book. Castle of Wolfenbach, Clermont, Mysterious Warnings, Necromancer of the Black Forest, Midnight Bell, Orphan of the Rhine, and Horrid Mysteries. Those will last us some time.'

'Yes, pretty well; but are they all horrid, are you sure they are all horrid?'

'Yes, quite sure; for a particular friend of mine, a Miss Andrews, a sweet girl, one of the sweetest creatures in the world, has read every one of them. I wish you knew Miss Andrews, you would be delighted with her. She is netting herself the sweetest cloak you can conceive. I think her as beautiful as an angel, and I am so vexed with the men for not admiring her! – I scold them all amazingly about it.'

'Scold them! Do you scold them for not admiring her?'

'Yes, that I do. There is nothing I would not do for those who are really my friends. I have no notion of loving people by halves, it is not my nature. My attachments are always excessively strong. I told Capt. Hunt at one of our assemblies this winter, that if he was to tease me all night, I would not dance with him, unless he would allow Miss Andrews to be as beautiful as an angel The men think us incapable of real friendship you know, and I am determined to shew them the difference. Now, if I were to hear any body speak slightingly of you, I should fire up in a moment: – but that is not at all likely, for *you* are just the kind of girl to be a great favourite with the men.'

'Oh! dear,' cried Catherine, colouring, 'how can you say so?'

'I know you very well; you have so much animation, which is exactly what Miss Andrews wants, for I must confess there is something amazingly insipid about her. Oh! I must tell you, that just after we parted yesterday, I saw a young man looking at you so earnestly – I am sure he is in love with you.' Catherine coloured, and disclaimed again. Isabella laughed. 'It is very true, upon my honour, but I see how it is; you are indifferent to every body's admiration, except that of one gentleman, who shall be nameless. Nay, I cannot blame you – (speaking more seriously) – your feelings are easily understood. Where the heart is really attached, I know very well how little one can be pleased with the attention of any body else. Every thing is so insipid, so uninteresting, that does not relate to the beloved object! I can perfectly comprehend your feelings.'

'But you should not persuade me that I think so very much about Mr Tilney, for perhaps I may never see him again.'

'Not see him again! My dearest creature, do not talk of it. I am sure you would be miserable if you thought so.'

'No, indeed, I should not. I do not pretend to say that I was not very much pleased with him; but while I have Udolpho to read, I feel as if nobody could make me miserable. Oh! the dreadful black veil! My dear Isabella, I am sure there must be Laurentina's skeleton behind it.'

'It is so odd to me, that you should never have read Udolpho before; but I suppose Mrs Morland objects to novels.'

'No, she does not. She very often reads Sir Charles Grandison herself; but new books do not fall in our way.'

'Sir Charles Grandison! That is an amazing horrid book, is it not? – I remember Miss Andrews could not get through the first volume.'

'It is not like Udolpho at all; but yet I think it is very entertaining.'

'Do you indeed! – you surprize me; I thought it had not been readable. But, my dearest Catherine, have you settled what to wear on your head to-night? I am determined at all events to be dressed exactly like you. The men take notice of *that* sometimes you know.'

'But it does not dignify if they do;' said Catherine, very innocently.

'Signify! Oh, heavens! I make it a rule never to mind what they say. They are very often amazingly impertinent if you do not treat them with spirit, and make them keep their distance.'

'Are they? – Well, I never observed *that*. They always behave very well to me.'

'Oh! they give themselves such airs. They are the most conceited creatures in the world, and think themselves of so much importance! – By the bye, though I have thought of it a hundred times. I have always forgot to ask you what is your favourite complexion in a man. Do you like them best dark or fair?'

'I hardly know. I never much thought about it. Something between both, I think. Brown – not fair, and not very dark.'

'Very well, Catherine. That is exactly he. I have not forgot your description of Mr Tilney; – "a brown skin, with dark eyes, and rather dark hair." – Well, my taste is different. I prefer light eyes, and as to complexion – do you know – I like a sallow better than any other. You must not betray me, if you should ever meet with one of your acquaintance answering that description.'

'Betray you! – What do you mean?'

'Nay, do not distress me. I believe I have said too much. Let us drop the subject.'

Catherine, in some amazement, complied; and after remaining a few moments silent, was on the point of reverting to what interested her at that time rather more than any thing else in the world, Laurentina's skeleton; when her friend prevented her, by saying, – 'For Heaven's sake! let us move away from this end of the room. Do you know, there are two odious young men who have been staring at me this half hour. They really put me quite out of countenance. Let us go and look at the arrivals. They will hardly follow us there.'

Away they walked to the book; and while Isabella examined the names, it was Catherine's employment to watch the proceedings of these alarming young men.

'They are not coming this way, are they? I hope they are not so impertinent as to follow us. Pray let me know if they are coming. I am determined I will not look up.'

In a few moments Catherine, with unaffected pleasure, assured her that she need not be longer uneasy, as the gentlemen had just left the Pump-room.

'And which way are they gone?' said Isabella, turning hastily round. 'One was a very good-looking young man.'

'They went towards the churchyard.'

'Well, I am amazingly glad I have got rid of them! And now,

what say you to going to Edgar's Buildings with me, and looking at my new hat? You said you should like to see it.'

Catherine readily agreed, 'Only,' she added, 'perhaps we may overtake the two young men.'

'Oh! never mind that. If we make haste, we shall pass by them presently, and I am dying to shew you my hat.'

'But if we only wait a few minutes, there will be no danger of our seeing them at all.'

'I shall not pay them any such compliment, I assure you. I have no notion of treating men with such respect. *That* is the way to spoil them.'

Catherine had nothing to oppose against such reasoning; and therefore, to shew the independence of Miss Thorpe, and her resolution of humbling the sex, they set off immediately as fast as they could walk, in pursuit of the two young men.

CHAPTER SEVEN

HALF A MINUTE CONDUCTED them through the Pump-yard to the archway, opposite Union-passage; but here they were stopped. Every body acquainted with Bath may remember the difficulties of crossing Cheap-street at this point; it is indeed a street of so impertinent a nature, so unfortunately connected with the great London and Oxford roads, and the principal inn of the city, that a day never passes in which parties of ladies, however important their business, whether in quest of pastry, millinery, or even (as in the present case) of young men, are not detained on one side or other by carriages, horsemen, or carts. This evil had been felt and lamented, at least three times a day, by Isabella since her residence in Bath; and she was now fated to feel and lament it once more, for at the very moment of coming opposite to Union-passage, and within view of the two gentlemen who were proceeding through the crowds, and threading the gutters of that interesting alley, they were prevented crossing by the approach of a gig, drive along on bad pavement by a most knowing-looking coachman with all the vehemence that could most fitly endanger the lives of himself, his companion, and his horse.

'Oh, these odious gigs!' said Isabella, looking up, 'how I detest them.' But this detestation, though so just, was of short duration, for she looked again and exclaimed, 'Delightful! Mr Morland and my brother!'

'Good heaven! 'tis James!' was uttered at the same moment by Catherine; and, on catching the young men's eyes, the horse was immediately checked with a violence which almost threw him on his haunches, and the servant having now scampered up, the gentlemen jumped out, and the equipage was delivered to his care.

Catherine, by whom this meeting was wholly unexpected, received her brother with the liveliest pleasure; and he, being of a very amiable disposition, and sincerely attached to her, gave every proof on his side of equal satisfaction, which he could have leisure to do, while the bright eyes of Miss Thorpe were incessantly challenging his notice; and to her his devoirs were speedily paid, with a mixture of joy and embarrassment which might have informed Catherine, had she been more expert in the development of other people's feelings, and less simply engrossed by her own, that her brother thought her friend quite as pretty as she could do herself.

John Thorpe, who in the mean time had been giving orders about the horses, soon joined them, and from him she directly received the amends which were her due; for while he slightly and carelessly touched the hand of Isabella, on her he bestowed a whole scrape and half a short bow. He was a stout young man of middling height, who, with a plain face and ungraceful form, seemed fearful of being too handsome unless he wore the dress of a groom, and too much like a gentleman unless he were easy where he ought to be civil, and impudent where he might be allowed to be easy. He took out his watch: 'How long do you think we have been running it from Tetbury, Miss Morland?'

'I do not know the distance.' Her brother told her that it was twenty-three miles.

'*Three*-and twenty!' cried Thorpe; 'five-and-twenty if it is an inch.' Morland remonstrated, pleaded the authority of road-books, innkeepers, and milestones; but his friend disregarded them all; he had a surer test of distance. 'I know it must be five-and-twenty,' said he, 'by the time we have been doing it. It is now half after one; we drove out of the inn-yard at Tetbury as the town-clock struck eleven; and I defy any man in England to make my horse go less than ten miles an hour in harness; that makes it exactly twenty-five.'

'You have lost an hour,' said Morland; 'it was only ten o'clock when we came from Tetbury.'

'Ten o'clock! it was eleven, upon my soul! I counted every stroke. This brother of yours would persuade me out of my senses, Miss

Morland; do but look at my horse; did you ever see an animal so made for speed in your life?' (The servant had just mounted the carriage and was driving off.) 'Such true blood! Three hours and a half indeed coming only three-and-twenty miles! look at that creature, and suppose it possible if you can.'

'He *does* look very hot to be sure.'

'Hot! he had not turned a hair till we came to Walcot Church: but look at his forehand; look at his loins; only see how he moves; that horse *cannot* go less than ten miles an hour: tie his legs and he will get on. What do you think of my gig, Miss Morland? a neat one, is not it? Well hung; town built; I have not had it a month. It was built for a Christ-church man, a friend of mine, a very good sort of fellow; he ran it a few weeks, till, I believe, it was convenient to have done with it. I happened just then to be looking out for some light thing of the kind, though I had pretty well determined on a curricle too; but I chanced to meet him on Magdalen Bridge, as he was driving into Oxford, last term: "Ah! Thorpe," says he, "do you happen to want such a little thing as this? it is a capital one of the kind, but I am cursed tired of it." "Oh! d—," said I, "I am your man; what do you ask?" And how much do you think he did, Miss Morland?'

'I am sure I cannot guess at all.'

'Curricle-hung you see; seat, trunk, sword-case, splashing-board, lamps, silver moulding, all you see complete; the iron-work as good as new, or better. He asked fifty guineas; I closed with him directly, threw down the money, and the carriage was mine.'

'And I am sure,' said Catherine, 'I know so little of such things that I cannot judge whether it was cheap or dear.'

'Neither one nor t'other; I might have got it for less I dare say; but I hate haggling, and poor Freeman wanted cash.'

'That was very good-natured of you,' said Catherine, quite pleased.

'Oh! d— it, when one has the means of doing a kind thing by a friend, I hate to be pitiful.'

An inquiry now took place into the intended movements of the young ladies; and, on finding whither they were going, it was decided that the gentlemen should accompany them to Edgar's Buildings, and pay their respects to Mrs Thorpe. James and Isabella led the way; and so well satisfied was the latter with her lot, so contentedly was she endeavouring to ensure a pleasant walk to him who brought the double recommendation of being her brother's friend, and her friend's brother, so pure and uncoquettish were her feelings, that, though they overtook and passed the two offending young men in Milsom-street, she was so far from seeking to attract their notice, that she looked back at them only three times.

John Thorpe kept of course with Catherine, and, after a few minutes' silence, renewed the conversation about his gig – 'You will find, however, Miss Morland, it would be reckoned a cheap thing by some people, for I might have sold it for ten guineas more the next day; Jackson, of Oriel, bid me sixty at once; Morland was with me at the time.'

'Yes,' said Morland, who overheard this; 'but you forget that your horse was included.'

'My horse! oh, d— it! I would not sell my horse for a hundred. Are you fond of an open carriage, Miss Morland?'

'Yes, very; I have hardly ever had an opportunity of being in one; but I am particularly fond of it.'

'I am glad of it; I will drive you out in mine every day.'

'Thank you,' said Catherine, in some distress, from a doubt of the propriety of accepting such an offer.

'I will drive you up Lansdown Hill to-morrow.'

'Thank you; but will not your horse want rest?'

'Rest! he has only come three-and-twenty miles today; all nonsense; nothing ruins horses so much as rest; nothing knocks them up so soon. No, no; I shall exercise mine at the average of four hours every day while I am here.'

'Shall you indeed!' said Catherine very seriously, 'that will be forty miles a day.'

'Forty! aye fifty, for what I care. Well, I will drive you up Lansdown to-morrow; mind, I am engaged.'

'How delightful that will be!' cried Isabella, turning round; 'my dearest Catherine, I quite envy you; but I am afraid, brother, you will not have room for a third.'

'A third indeed! no, no; I did not come to Bath to drive my sisters about; that would be a good joke, faith! Morland must take care of you.'

This brought on a dialogue of civilities between the other two; but Catherine heard neither the particulars nor the result. Her companion's discourse now sunk from its hitherto animated pitch, to nothing more than a short decisive sentence of praise or condemnation on the face of every woman they met; and Catherine, after listening and agreeing as long as she could, with all the civility and deference of the youthful female mind, fearful of hazarding an opinion of its own in opposition to that of a self-assured man, especially where the beauty of her own sex is concerned, ventured at length to vary the subject by a question which had been long uppermost in her thoughts; it was, 'Have you ever read Udolpho, Mr Thorpe?'

'Udolpho! Oh, Lord! not I; I never read novels; I have something else to do.'

Catherine, humbled and ashamed, was going to apologize for her question, but he prevented her by saying, 'Novels are all so full of nonsense and stuff; there has not been a tolerably decent one come out since Tom Jones, except the Monk; I read that t'other day; but as for all the others, they are the stupidest things in creation.'

'I think you must like Udolpho, if you were to read it; it is so very interesting.'

'Not I, faith! No, if I read any, it shall be Mrs Radcliff's; her novels are amusing enough; they are worth reading; some fun and nature in *them*.'

'Udolpho was written by Mrs Radcliff,' said Catherine, with some hesitation, from the fear of mortifying him.

'No sure; was it? Aye, I remember, so it was; I was thinking of that other stupid book, written by that woman they make such a fuss about, she who married the French emigrant.'

'I suppose you mean Camilla?'

'Yes, that's the book; such unnatural stuff! – An old man playing at see-saw! I took up the first volume once and looked it over, but I soon found it would not do; indeed I guessed what sort of stuff it must be before I saw it: as soon as I heard she had married an emigrant, I was sure I should never be able to get through it.'

'I have never read it.'

'You had no loss I assure you; it is the horridest nonsense you can imagine; there is nothing in the world in it but an old man's playing at see-saw and learning Latin; upon my soul there is not.'

This critique, the justness of which was unfortunately lost on poor Catherine, brought them to the door of Mrs Thorpe's lodgings, and the feelings of the discerning and unprejudiced reader of Camilla gave way to the feelings of the dutiful and affectionate son, as they met Mrs Thorpe, who had described them from above, in the passage. 'Ah, mother! how do you do?' said he, giving her a hearty shake of the hand: 'where did you get that quiz of a hat, it makes you look like an old witch? Here is Morland and I come to stay a few days with you, so you must look out for a couple of good beds some where near.' And this address seemed to satisfy all the fondest wishes of the mother's heart, for she received him with the most delighted and exulting affection. On his two younger sisters he then bestowed an equal portion of his fraternal tenderness, for he asked each of them how they did, and observed that they both looked very ugly.

These manners did not please Catherine; but he was James's friend and Isabella's brother; and her judgment was further bought off by Isabella's assuring her, when they withdrew to see the new hat, that John thought her the most charming girl in the world, and by John's engaging her before they parted to dance with him that evening. Had she been older or vainer, such attacks might have done little; but, where youth and diffidence are united, it requires uncommon steadiness of reason to resist the attraction of being called the most charming girl in the world, and of being so very early engaged as a partner; and the consequence was, that, when the two Morlands, after sitting an hour with the Thorpes, set off to walk together to Mr Allen's, and James, as the door was closed on them, said, 'Well, Catherine, how do you like my friend Thorpe?' instead of answering, as she probably would have done, had there been no friendship and no flattery in the case. 'I do not like him at all;' she directly replied, 'I like him very much; he seems very agreeable.'

'He is as good-natured a fellow as ever lived; a little of a rattle; but that will recommend him to your sex I believe: and how do you like the rest of the family?'

'Very, very much indeed: Isabella particularly.'

'I am very glad to hear you say so; she is just the kind of young woman I could wish to see you attached to; she has so much good sense, and is so thoroughly unaffected and amiable; I always wanted you to know her; and she seems very fond of you. She said the highest things in your praise that could possibly be; and the praise of such a girl as Miss Thorpe even you, Catherine,' taking her hand with affection, 'may be proud of.'

'Indeed I am,' she replied; 'I love her exceedingly, and am delighted to find that you like her too. You hardly mentioned any thing of her, when you wrote to me after your visit there.'

'Because I thought I should soon see you myself. I hope you will be a great deal together while you are in Bath. She is a most amiable girl; such a superior understanding! How fond all the family are of her; she is evidently the general favourite; and how much she must be admired in such a place as this – is not she?'

'Yes, very much indeed, I fancy; Mr Allen thinks her the prettiest girl in Bath.'

'I dare say he does; and I do not know any man who is a better judge of beauty than Mr Allen. I need not ask you whether you are happy here, my dear Catherine; with such a companion and friend as Isabella Thorpe, it would be impossible for you to be otherwise; and the Allens I am sure are very kind to you?'

'Yes, very kind; I never was so happy before; and now you are come it will be more delightful than ever; how good it is of you to come so far on purpose to see *me*.'

James accepted this tribute of gratitude, and qualified his conscience for accepting it too, by saying with perfect sincerity, 'Indeed, Catherine, I love you dearly.'

Inquiries and communications concerning brothers and sisters, the situation of some, the growth of the rest, and other family matters, now passed between them, and continued, with only one small digression on James's part, in praise of Miss Thorpe, till they reached Pulteney-street, where he was welcomed with great kindness by Mr and Mrs Allen, invited by the former to dine with them, and summoned by the latter to guess the price and weigh the merits of a new muff and tippet. A pre-engagement in Edgar's Buildings prevented his accepting the invitation of one friend, and obliged him to hurry away as soon as he had satisfied the demands of the other. The time of the two parties uniting in the Octagon Room being correctly adjusted, Catherine was then left to the luxury of a raised, restless, and frightened imagination over the pages of Udolpho, lost from all worldly concerns of dressing and dinner, incapable of soothing Mrs Allen's fears on the delay of an expected dress-maker, and having only one minute in sixty to bestow even on the reflection of her own felicity, in being already engaged for the evening.

CHAPTER EIGHT

In spite of Udolpho and the dress-maker, however, the party from Pulteney-street reached the Upper-rooms in very good time. The Thorpes and James Morland were there only two minutes before them; and Isabella having gone through the usual ceremonial of meeting her friend with the most smiling and affectionate haste, of admiring the set of her gown, and envying the curl of her hair, they followed their chaperons, arm in arm into the ball-room, whispering to each other whenever a thought occurred, and supplying the place of many ideas by a squeeze of the hand or a smile of affection.

The dancing began within a few minutes after they were seated; and James, who had been engaged quite as long as his sister, was very importunate with Isabella to stand up; but John was gone into the card-room to speak to a friend, and nothing, she declared, should induce her to join the set before her dear Catherine could join it too: 'I assure you,' said she, 'I would not stand up without your dear sister for all the world; for if I did we should certainly be separated the whole evening.' Catherine accepted this kindness with gratitude, and they continued as they were for three minutes longer, when Isabella, who had been talking to James on the other side of her, turned again to his sister and whispered, 'My dear creature, I am afraid I must leave you, your brother is so amazingly impatient to begin; I know you will not mind my going away, and I dare say John will be back in a moment, and then you may easily find me out.' Catherine, though a little disappointed, had too much good-nature to make any opposition, and the others rising up, Isabella had only time to press her friend's hand and say, 'Good bye, my dear love,' before they hurried off. The younger Miss Thorpes being also dancing, Catherine was left to the mercy of Mrs Thorpe and Mrs Allen, between whom she now remained. She could not help being vexed at the non-appearance of Mr Thorpe, for she not only longed to be dancing, but was likewise aware that, as the real dignity of her situation could not be known, she was sharing with the scores of other young ladies still sitting down all the discredit of wanting a partner. To be disgraced in the eye of the world, to wear the appearance of infamy while her heart is all purity, her actions all innocence, and the misconduct of another the true source of her debasement, is one of those circumstances which peculiarly belong to the heroine's life, and her fortitude under it what particularly dignifies her character. Catherine had fortitude too; she suffered, but no murmur passed her lips.

From this state of humiliation, she was roused, at the end of ten minutes, to a pleasanter feeling, by seeing, not Mr Thorpe, but Mr Tilney, within three yards of the place where they sat; he seemed to be moving that way, but he did not see her, and therefore the smile and the blush, which his sudden reappearance raised in Catherine, passed away without sullying her heroic importance. He looked as handsome and as lively as ever, and was talking with interest to a fashionable and pleasing-looking young woman, who leant on his arm, and whom Catherine immediately guessed to be his sister; thus unthinkingly throwing away a fair opportunity of considering him lost to her for ever, by being married already. But guided only by what was simple and probable, it had never entered her head that Mr Tilney could be married; he had not behaved, he had not talked, like the married men to whom she had been used;

he had never mentioned a wife, and he had acknowledged a sister. From these circumstances sprang the instant conclusion of his sister's now being by his side; and therefore, instead of turning of a deathlike paleness, and falling in a fit on Mrs Allen's bosom, Catherine sat erect, in the perfect use of her senses, and with cheeks only a little redder than usual.

Mr Tilney and his companion, who continued, though slowly, to approach, were immediately preceded by a lady, an acquaintance of Mrs Thorpe; and this lady stopping to speak to her, they, as belonging to her, stopped likewise, and Catherine, catching Mr Tilney's eye, instantly received from him the smiling tribute of recognition. She returned it with pleasure, and then advancing still nearer, he spoke both to her and Mrs Allen, by whom he was very civilly acknowledged. 'I am very happy to see you again, sir indeed; I was afraid you had left Bath.' He thanked her for her fears, and said that he had quitted it for a week, on the very morning after his having had the pleasure of seeing her.

'Well, sir, and I dare say you are not sorry to be back again, for it is just the place for young people – and indeed for every body else too. I tell Mr Allen, when he talks of being sick of it, that I am sure he should not complain, for it is so very agreeable a place, that it is much better to be here than at home at this dull time of year. I tell him he is quite in luck to be sent here for his health.'

'And I hope, madam, that Mr Allen will be obliged to like the place, from finding it of service to him.'

'Thank you, sir. I have no doubt that he will. – A neighbour of ours, Dr Skinner, was here for his health last winter, and came away quite stout.'

'That circumstance must give great encouragement.'

'Yes, sir – and Dr Skinner and his family were here three months; so I tell Mr Allen he must not be in a hurry to get away.'

Here they were interrupted by a request from Mrs Thorpe to Mrs Allen, that she would move a little to accommodate Mrs Hughes and Miss Tilney with seats, as they had agreed to join their party. This was accordingly done, Mr Tilney still continuing standing before them; and after a few minutes consideration, he asked Catherine to dance with him. This compliment, delightful as it was, produced severe mortification to the lady; and in giving her denial, she expressed her sorrow on the occasion so very much as if she really felt it, that had Thorpe, who joined her just afterwards, been half a minute earlier, he might have thought her sufferings rather too acute. The very easy manner in which he then told her that he had kept her waiting, did not by any means reconcile her more to her lot; nor did the particulars which he entered into while they were standing up, of the horses and dogs of the friend whom he had just left, and of a proposed exchange of terriers between them, interest her so much as to prevent her looking very often towards that part of the room where she had left Mr Tilney. Of her dear Isabella, to whom she particularly longed to point out that gentleman, she could see nothing. They were in different sets. She was separated from all her party, and away from all her acquaintance;

'I beg your pardon, Miss Morland,'

– one mortification succeeded another, and from the whole she deduced this useful lesson, that to go previously engaged to a ball, does not necessarily increase either the dignity or enjoyment of a young lady. From such a moralizing strain as this, she was suddenly roused by a touch on the shoulder, and turning round, perceived Mrs Hughes directly behind her, attended by Miss Tilney and a gentleman. 'I beg your pardon, Miss Morland,' said she, 'for this liberty, – but I cannot any how get to Miss Thorpe, and Mrs Thorpe said she was sure you would not have the least objection to letting in this young lady by you.' Mrs Hughes could not have applied to any creature in the room more happy to oblige her than Catherine. The young ladies were introduced to each other, Miss Tilney expressing a proper sense of such goodness, Miss Morland with the real delicacy of a generous mind making light of the obligation; and Mrs Hughes, satisfied with having so respectably settled her young charge, returned to her party.

Miss Tilney had a good figure, a pretty face, and a very agreeable countenance; and her air, though it had not all the decided pretension, the resolute stilishness of Miss Thorpe's, had more real elegance. Her manners shewed good sense and good breeding; they were neither shy, nor affectedly open; and she seemed capable of being young, attractive, and at a ball, without wanting to fix the attention of every man near her, and without exaggerated feelings of extatic delight or inconceivable vexation on every little trifling occurrence. Catherine, interested at once by her appearance and her relationship to Mr Tilney, was desirous of being acquainted with her, and readily talked therefore whenever she could think of any thing to say, and had courage and leisure for saying it. but the hindrance thrown in the way of a very speedy intimacy, by the frequent want of one or more of these requisites, prevented their doing more than going through the first rudiments of an acquaintance, by informing themselves how well the other liked Bath, how much she admired its buildings and surrounding country, whether she drew, or played or sang, and whether she was fond of riding on horseback.

The two dances were scarcely concluded before Catherine found her arm gently seized by her faithful Isabella, who in great spirits exclaimed – 'At last I have got you. My dearest creature, I have been looking for you this hour. What could induce you to come into this set, when you knew I was in the other? I have been quite wretched without you.'

'My dear Isabella, how was it possible for me to get at you? I could not even see where you were.'

'So I told your brother all the time – but he would not believe me. Do you go and see for her, Mr Morland, said I – but all in vain – he would not stir an inch. Was not it so, Mr Morland? but you men are all so immoderately lazy! I have been scolding him to such a degree, my dear Catherine, you would be quite amazed. – You know I never stand upon ceremony with such people.'

'Look at that young lady with the white beads round her head,' whispered Catherine, detaching her friend from James – 'It is Mr Tilney's sister.'

'Oh! heavens! You don't say so! Let me look at her this moment. What a delightful girl! I never saw any thing half so beautiful! But where is her all-conquering brother? Is he in the room? Point him out to me this instant, if he is. I die to see him. Mr Morland, you are not to listen. We are not talking about you.'

'But what is all this whispering about? What is going on?'

'There now, I knew how it would be. You men have such restless curiosity! Talk of the curiosity of women, indeed! – 'tis nothing. But be satisfied, for you are not to know any thing at all of the matter.'

'And is that likely to satisfy me, do you think?'

'Well, I declare I never knew any thing like you. What can it signify to you, what we are talking of? Perhaps we are talking about you, therefore I would advise you not to listen, or you may happen to hear something not very agreeable.'

In this common-place chatter, which lasted some time, the original subject seemed entirely forgotten; and though Catherine was very well pleased to have it dropped for awhile, she could not avoid a little suspicion at the total suspension of all Isabella's impatient desire to see Mr Tilney. When the orchestra struck up a fresh dance, James would have led his fair partner away, but she resisted. 'I tell you, Mr Morland,' she cried, 'I would not do such a thing for all the world. How can you be so teasing; only conceive, my dear Catherine, what your brother wants me to do. He wants me to dance with him again, though I tell him that it is a most improper thing, and entirely against the rules. It would make us the talk of the place, if we were not to change partners.'

'Upon my honour,' said James, 'in these public assemblies, it is as often done as not.'

'Nonsense, how can you say so? But when you men have a point to carry, you never stick at any thing. My sweet Catherine, do support me, persuade your brother how impossible it is. Tell him, that it would quite shock you to see me do such a thing; now would not it?'

'No, not at all; but if you think it wrong, you had much better change.'

'There,' cried Isabella, 'you hear what your sister says, and yet you will not mind her. Well, remember that it is not my fault, if we set all the old ladies in Bath in a bustle. Come along, my dearest Catherine, for heaven's sake, and stand by me.' And off they went, to regain their former place. John Thorpe, in the meanwhile, had walked away; and Catherine, ever willing to give Mr Tilney an opportunity of repeating the agreeable request which had already flattered her once, made her way to Mrs Allen and Mrs Thorpe as fast as she could, in the hope of finding him still with them – a hope which, when it proved to be fruitless, she felt to have been highly unreasonable. 'Well, my dear,' said Mrs Thorpe, impatient for praise of her son, 'I hope you have had an agreeable partner.'

'Very agreeable, madam.'

'I am glad of it. John has charming spirits, has not he?'

'Did you meet Mr Tilney, my dear?' said Mrs Allen.

'No, where is he?'

'He was with us just now, and said he was so tired of lounging about, that he was resolved to go and dance; so I thought perhaps he would ask you, if he met with you.'

'Where can he be?' said Catherine, looking round; but she had not looked round long before she saw him leading a young lady to the dance.

'Ah! he has got a partner, I wish he had asked *you*,' said Mrs Allen; and after a short silence, she added, 'he is a very agreeable young man.'

'Indeed he is, Mrs Allen,' said Mrs Thorpe, smiling complacently; 'I must say it, though I *am* his mother, that there is not a more agreeable young man in the world.'

This inapplicable answer might have been too much for the comprehension of many; but it did not puzzle Mrs Allen, for after only a moment's consideration, she said, in a whisper to Catherine, 'I dare say she thought I was speaking of her son.'

Catherine was disappointed and vexed. She seemed to have missed by so little the very object she had had in view; and this persuasion did not incline her to a very gracious reply, when John Thorpe came up to her soon afterwards, and said, 'Well, Miss Morland, I suppose you and I are to stand up and jig it together again.'

'Oh, no; I am much obliged to you, our two dances are over; and, besides, I am tired, and do not mean to dance any more.'

'Do not you? – then let us walk about and quiz people. Come along with me, and I will shew you the four greatest quizzers in the room; my two younger sisters and their partners. I have been laughing at them this half hour.'

Again Catherine excused herself; and at last he walked off to quiz his sisters by himself. The rest of the evening she found very dull; Mr Tilney was drawn away from their party at tea, to attend that of his partner; Miss Tilney, though belonging to it, did not sit near her, and James and Isabella were so much engaged in conversing together, that the latter had no leisure to bestow more on her friend than one smile, one squeeze, and one 'dearest Catherine.'

CHAPTER NINE

THE PROGRESS OF CATHERINE'S unhappiness from the events of the evening, was as follows. It appeared first in a general dissatisfaction with every body about her, while she remained in the rooms, which speedily brought on considerable weariness and a violent desire to go home. This, on arriving in Pulteney-street, took the direction of extraordinary hunger, and when that was appeased, changed into an earnest longing to be in bed; such was the extreme point of her distress; for when there she immediately fell into a sound sleep which lasted nine hours, and from which she awoke perfectly revived, in excellent spirits, with fresh hopes and fresh schemes. The first wish of her heart was to improve her acquaintance with Miss Tilney, and almost her first resolution, to seek her for that purpose, in the Pump-room at noon. In the Pump-room, one so newly arrived in Bath must be met with, and that building she had already found so favourable for the discovery of female excellence, and the completions of female intimacy, so admirably adapted for secret discourses and unlimited conficence, that she was most reasonably encouraged to expect another friend from within its walls. Her plan for the morning thus settled, she sat quietly down to her book after breakfast, resolving to remain in the same place and the same employment till the clock struck one; and from habitude very little incommoded by the remarks and ejaculations of Mrs Allen, whose vacancy of mind and incapacity for thinking were such, that as she never talked a great deal, so she could never be entirely silent; and, therefore, while she sat at her work, if she lost her needle or broke her thread, if she heard a carriage in the street, or saw a speck upon her gown, she must observe it aloud, whether there were any one at leisure to answer her or not. At about half past twelve, a remarkably loud rap drew her in haste to the window, and scarcely had she time to inform Catherine of there being two open carriages at the door, in the first only a servant, her brother driving Miss Thorpe in the second, before John Thorpe came running up stairs, calling out, 'Well, Miss Morland, here I am. Have you been waiting long? We could not come before; the old devil of a coachmaker was such an eternity finding out a thing fit to be got into, and now it is ten thousand to one, but they break down before we are out of the street. How do you do, Mrs Allen? a famous ball last night, was not it? Come, Miss Morland, be quick, for the others are in a confounded hurry to be off. They want to get their tumble over.'

'What do you mean?' said Catherine, 'where are you all going to?'

'Going to? why, you have not forgot our engagement! Did not we agree together to take a drive this morning? What a head you have! We are going up Claverton Down.'

'Something was said about it, I remember,' said Catherine, looking at Mrs Allen for her opinion; 'but really I did not expect you.'

'Not expect me! that's a good one! And what a dust you would have made, if I had not come.'

Catherine's silent appeal to her friend, meanwhile, was entirely thrown away, for Mrs Allen, not being at all in the habit of conveying any expression herself by a look, was not aware of its being ever intended by any body else; and Catherine, whose desire of seeing Miss Tilney again could at that moment bear a short delay in favour of a drive, and who thought there could be no impropriety in her going with Mr Thorpe, as Isabella was going at the same time with James, was therefore obliged to speak plainer. 'Well, ma'am, what do you say to it? Can you spare me for an hour or two? shall I go?'

'Do just as you please, my dear,' replied Mrs Allen, with the most placid indifference. Catherine took the advice, and ran off to get ready. In a very few minutes she reappeared, having scarcely allowed the two others time enough to get through a few short sentences in her praise, after Thorpe had procured Mrs Allen's admiration of his gig; and then receiving her friend's parting good wishes, they both hurried down stairs. 'My dearest creature,' cried Isabella, to whom the duty of friendship immediately called her before she could get into the carriage, 'you have been at least three hours getting ready. I was afraid you were ill. What a delightful

Off they went, without a plunge or a caper.

ball we had last night. I have a thousand things to say to you; but make haste and get in, for I long to be off.'

Catherine followed her orders and turned away, but not too soon to hear her friend exclaim aloud to James, 'What a sweet girl she is! I quite doat on her.'

'You will not be frightened, Miss Morland,' said Thorpe, as he handed her in, 'if my horse should dance about a little at first setting off. He will, most likely, give a plunge or two, and perhaps take the rest for a minute; but he will soon know his master. He is full of spirits, playful as can be, but there is no vice in him.'

Catherine did not think the portrait a very inviting one, but it was too late to retreat, and she was too young to own herself frightened; so, resigning herself to her fate, and trusting to the animal's boasted knowledge of its owner, she sat peaceably down, and saw Thorpe sit down by her. Every thing being then arranged, the servant who stood at the horse's head was bid in an important voice 'to let him go,' and off they went in the quietest manner imaginable, without a plunge or a caper, or any thing like one. Catherine, delighted at so happy an escape, spoke her pleasure aloud with grateful surprize; and her companion immediately made the matter perfectly simple by assuring her that it was entirely owing to the peculiarly judicious manner in which he had then held the reins, and the singular discernment and dexterity with which he had directed his whip. Catherine, though she could not help wondering that with such perfect command of his horse, he should think it necessary to alarm her with a relation of its tricks, congratulated herself sincerely on being under the care of so excellent a coachman; and perceiving that the animal continued to go on in the same quiet manner, without shewing the smallest propensity towards any unpleasant vivacity, and (considering its inevitable pace was ten miles an hour) by no means alarmingly fast, gave herself up to all the enjoyment of air and exercise of the most invigorating kind, in a fine mild day of February, with the consciousness of safety. A silence of several minutes succeeded their first short dialogue; – it was broken by Thorpe's saying very abruptly, 'Old Allen is as rich as a Jew – is not he?' Catherine did not understand him – and he repeated his question, adding in explanation, 'Old Allen, the man you are with.'

'Oh! Mr Allen, you mean, Yes, I believe, he is very rich.'

'And no children at all?'

'No – not any.'

'A famous thing for his next heirs. He is *your* godfather, is not he?'

'My godfather! – no.'

'But you are always very much with them.'

'Yes, very much.'

'Aye, that is what I meant. He seems a good kind of old fellow enough, and has lived very well in his time, I dare say; he is not gouty for nothing. Does he drink his bottle a-day now?'

'His bottle a-day! – no. Why should you think of such a thing? He is a very temperate man, and you could not fancy him in liquor last night?'

'Lord help you! – You women are always thinking of men's being in liquor. Why you do not suppose a man is overset by a bottle? I am sure of *this* – that if every body was to drink their bottle a-day, there would not be half the disorders in the world there are now. It would be a famous good thing for us all.'

'I cannot believe it.'

'Oh! lord, it would be the saving of thousands. There is not the hundredth part of the wine consumed in this kingdom, that there ought to be. Our foggy climate wants help.'

'And yet I have heard that there is a great deal of wine drank in Oxford.'

'Oxford! There is no drinking at Oxford now, I assure you. Nobody drinks there. You hardly meet with a man who goes beyond his four pints at the utmost. Now, for instance, it was reckoned a remarkable thing at the last party in my rooms, that upon an average we cleared about five pints a head. It was looked upon as something out of the common way. *Mine* is famous good stuff to be sure. You would not often meet with any thing like it in Oxford – and that may account for it. But this will just give you a notion of the general rate of drinking there.'

'Yes, it does give a notion,' said Catherine, warmly, 'and that is, that you all drink a great deal more wine than I thought you did. However, I am sure James does not drink so much.'

This declaration brought on a loud and overpowering reply, of which no part was very distinct, except the frequent exclamations, amounting almost to oaths, which adorned it, and Catherine was left, when it ended, with rather a strengthened belief of there being a great deal of wine drank in Oxford, and the same happy conviction of her brother's comparative sobriety.

Thorpe's ideas then all reverted to the merits of his own equipage, and she was called on to admire the spirit and freedom with which his horse moved along, and the ease which his paces, as well as the excellence of the springs, gave the motion of the carriage. She followed him in all his admiration as well as she could. To go before, or beyond him was impossible. His knowledge and her ignorance of the subject, his rapidity of expression, and her diffidence of herself put that out of her power; she could strike out nothing new in commendation, but she readily echoed whatever he chose to assert, and it was finally settled between them without any difficulty, that his equipage was altogether the most complete of its kind in England, his carriage the neatest, his horse the best goer, and himself the best coachman. – 'You do not really think, Mr Thorpe,' said Catherine, venturing after some time to consider the matter as entirely decided, and to offer some little variation on the subject, 'that James's gig will break down?'

'Break down! Oh! lord! Did you ever see such a little tittuppy thing in your life? There is not a sound piece of iron about it. The wheels have been fairly worn out these ten years at least – and as for the body! Upon my soul, you might shake it to pieces yourself with a touch. It is the most devilish little ricketty business I ever beheld! – Thank God! we have got a better. I would not be bound to go two miles in it for fifty thousand pounds.'

'Good heavens!' cried Catherine, quite frightened, 'then pray let us turn back; they will certainly meet with an accident if we go on. Do let us turn back, Mr Thorpe; stop and speak to my brother, and tell him how very unsafe it is.'

'Unsafe! Oh, lord! what is there in that? they will only get a roll if it does break down; and there is plenty of dirt, it will be excellent falling. Oh, curse it! the carriage is safe enough, if a man knows how to drive it; a thing of that sort in good hands will last above twenty years after it is fairly worn out. Lord bless you! I would undertake for five pounds to drive it to York and back again, without losing a nail.'

Catherine listened with astonishment; she knew not how to reconcile two such different accounts of the same thing; for she had not been brought up to understand the propensities of a rattle, nor to know to how many idle assertions and impudent falsehoods the excess of vanity will lead. Her own family were plain matter-of-fact people, who seldom aimed at wit of any kind; her father, at the utmost, being contented with a pun, and her mother with a proverb; they were not in the habit therefore of telling lies to increase their importance, or of asserting at one moment what they would contradict the next. She reflected on the affair for some time in much perplexity, and was more than once on the point of requesting from Mr Thorpe a clearer insight into his real opinion on the subject; but she checked herself, because it appeared to her that he did not excel in giving those clearer insights, in making those things plain which he had before made ambiguous; and, joining to this, the consideration, that he would not really suffer his sister and his friend to be exposed to a danger from which he might easily preserve them, she concluded at last, that he must know the carriage to be in fact perfectly safe, and therefore would alarm herself no longer. By him the whole matter seemed entirely forgotten; and all the rest of his conversation, or rather talk, began and ended with himself and his own concerns. He told her of horses which he had bought for a trifle and sold for incredible sums; of racing matches, in which his judgment had infallibly foretold the winner; of shooting parties, in which he had killed more birds (though without having one good shot) than all his companions together; and described to her some famous day's sport, with the fox-hounds, in which his foresight and skill in directing the dogs had repaired the mistakes of the most experienced huntsman, and in which the boldness of his riding, though it had never endangered his own life for a moment, had been constantly leading others into difficulties, which he calmly concluded had broken the necks of many.

Little as Catherine was in the habit of judging for herself, and unfixed as were her general notions of what men ought to be, she could not entirely repress a doubt, while she bore with the effusions of his endless conceit, of his being altogether completely agreeable. It was a bold surmise, for he was Isabella's brother; and she had been assured by James, that his manners would recommend him to all her sex; but in spite of this, the extreme weariness of his company, which crept over her before they had been out an hour, and which continued unceasingly to increase till they stopped in Pulteney-street again, induced her, in some small degree, to resist high authority, and to distrust his powers of giving universal pleasure.

When they arrived at Mrs Allen's door, the astonishment of Isabella was hardly to be expressed, on finding that it was too late in the day for them to attend her friend into the house: – 'Past three o'clock!' it was inconceivable, incredible, impossible! and she would neither believe her own watch, nor her brother's, nor the servant's; she would believe no assurance of it founded on reason or reality, till Morland produced his watch, and ascertained the fact; to have doubted a moment longer *then*, would have been equally inconceivable, incredible, and impossible; and she could only protest, over and over again, that no two hours and a half had ever gone off so swiftly before, as Catherine was called on to confirm; Catherine could not tell a falsehood even to please Isabella; but the latter was spared the misery of her friend's dissenting voice, by not waiting for her answer. Her own feelings entirely engrossed her; her wretchedness was most acute on finding herself obliged to go directly home. – It was ages since she had had a moment's conversation with her dearest Catherine, and, though she had such thousands of things to say to her, it appeared as if they were never to be together again; so, with smiles of most exquisite misery, and the laughing eye of utter despondency, she bade her friend adieu and went on.

Catherine found Mrs Allen just returned from all the busy idleness of the morning, and was immediately greeted with, 'Well, my dear, here you are;' a truth which she had no greater inclination than power to dispute; 'and I hope you have had a pleasant airing?'

'Yes, ma'am, I thank you; we could not have had a nicer day.'

'So Mrs Thorpe said; she was vastly pleased at your all going.'

'You have seen Mrs Thorpe then?'

'Yes, I went to the Pump-room as soon as you were gone, and there I met her, and we had a great deal of talk together. She says there was hardly any veal to be got at market this morning, it is so uncommonly scarce.'

'Did you see any body else of our acquaintance?'

'Yes; we agreed to take in the Crescent, and there we met Mrs Hughes, and Mr and Miss Tilney walking with her.'

'Did you indeed? and did they speak to you?'

'Yes, we walked along the Crescent together for half an hour. They seem very agreeable people. Miss Tilney was in a very pretty spotted muslin, and I fancy, by what I can learn, that she always dresses very handsomely. Mrs Hughes talked to me a great deal about the family.'

'And what did she tell you of them?'

'Oh! a vast deal indeed; she hardly talked of any thing else.'

'Did she tell you what part of Gloucestershire they come from?'

'Yes, she did; but I cannot recollect now. But they are very good kind of people, and very rich. Mrs Tilney was a Miss Drummond, and she and Mrs Hughes were school fellows; and Miss Drummond had a very large fortune; and when she married, her father gave her twenty thousand pounds, and five hundred to buy wedding-clothes. Mrs Hughes saw all the clothes after they came from the warehouse.'

'And are Mr and Mrs Tilney in Bath?'

'Yes, I fancy they are, but I am not quite certain. Upon recollection, however, I have a notion they are both dead; at least the mother is; yes, I am sure Mrs Tilney is dead, because Mrs Hughes told me there was a very beautiful set of pearls that Mr Drummond gave his daughter on her wedding-day and that Miss Tilney has got now, for they were put by for her when her mother died.'

'And is Mr Tilney, my partner, the only son?'

'I cannot be quite positive about that, my dear; I have some idea he is; but, however, he is a very fine young man Mrs Hughes says, and likely to do well.'

Catherine enquired no further; she had heard enough to feel that Mrs Allen had no real intelligence to give, and that she was most particularly unfortunate herself in having missed such a meeting with both brother and sister. Could she have forseen such a circumstance, nothing should have persuaded her to go out with the others; and, as it was, she could only lament her ill-luck, and think over what she had lost, till it was clear to her, that the drive had by no means been very pleasant and that John Thorpe himself was quite disagreeable.

CHAPTER TEN

The Allens, Thorpes, and Morlands, all met in the evening at the theatre; and, as Catherine and Isabella sat together, there was then an opportunity for the latter to utter some few of the many thousand things which had been collecting within her for communication, in the immeasurable length of time which had divided them. – 'Oh, heavens! my beloved Catherine, have I got you at last?' was her address on Catherine's entering the box and sitting by her. 'Now, Mr Morland,' for he was close to her on the other side, 'I shall not speak another word to you all the rest of the evening; so I charge you not to expect it. My sweetest Catherine, how have you been this long age? but I need not ask you, for you look delightfully. You really have done your hair in a more heavenly style than ever: you mischievous creature, do you want to attract every body? I assure you, my brother is quite in love with you already; and as for Mr Tilney – but *that* is a settled thing – even *your* modesty cannot doubt his attachment now; his coming back to Bath makes it too plain. Oh! what would not I give to see him! I really am quite wild with impatience. My mother says he is the most delightful young man in the world, she saw him this morning you know: you must introduce him to me. Is he in the house now? – Look about for heaven's sake! I assure you, I can hardly exist till I see him.'

'No,' said Catherine, 'he is not here; I cannot see him any where.'

'Oh, horrid! am I never to be acquainted with him? How do you like my gown? I think it does not look amiss; the sleeves were entirely my own thought. Do you know I get so immoderately sick of Bath; your brother and I were agreeing this morning that, though it is vastly well to be here for a few weeks, we would not live here for millions. We soon found out that our tastes were exactly alike in preferring the country to every other place; really, our opinions were so exactly the same, it was quite ridiculous! There was not a single point in which we differed; I would not have had you by for the world; you are such a sly thing, I am sure you would have made some droll remark or other about it.'

'No, indeed I should not.'

'Oh, yes you would indeed; I know you better than you know

yourself. You would have told us that we seemed born for each other, or some nonsense of that kind, which would have distressed me beyond conception; my cheeks would have been as red as your roses; I would not have had you by for the world.'

'Indeed you do me injustice; I would not have made so improper a remark upon any account; and besides, I am sure it would never have entered my head.'

Isabella smiled incredulously, and talked the rest of the evening to James.

Catherine's resolution of endeavouring to meet Miss Tilney again continued in full force the next morning; and till the usual moment of going to the Pump-room, she felt some alarm from the dread of a second prevention. But nothing of that kind occurred, no visitors appeared to delay them, and they all three set off in good time for the Pump-room, where the ordinary course of events and conversation took place; Mr Allen, after drinking his glass of water, joined some gentlemen to talk over the politics of the day and compare the accounts of their newspapers; and the ladies walked about together, noticing every new face, and almost every new bonnet in the room. The female part of the Thorpe family, attended by James Morland, appeared among the crowd in less than a quarter of an hour, and Catherine immediately took her usual place by the side of her friend. James, who was now in constant attendance, maintained a similar position, and separating themselves from the rest of their party, they walked in that manner for some time, till Catherine began to doubt the happiness of a situation which confining her entirely to her friend and brother, gave her very little share in the notice of either. They were always engaged in some sentimental discussion or lively dispute, but their sentiment was conveyed in such whispering voices, and their vivacity attended with so much laughter, that though Catherine's supporting opinion was not unfrequently called for by one or the other, she was never able to give any, from not having heard a word of the subject. At length however she was empowered to disengage herself from her friend by the avowed necessity of speaking to Miss Tilney, whom she most joyfully saw just entering the room with Mrs Hughes, and whom she instantly joined, with a firmer determination to be acquainted, than she might have had courage to command, had she not been urged by the disappointment of the day before. Miss Tilney met her with great civility, returned her advances with equal good will, and they continued talking together as long as both parties remained in the room: and though in all probability not an observation was made, nor an expression used by either which had not been made and used some thousands of times before, under that roof, in every Bath season, yet the merit of their being spoken with simplicity and truth, and without personal conceit, might be something uncommon. –

'How well your brother dances!' was an artless exclamation of Catherine's towards the close of their conversation, which at once surprized and amused her companion.

'Henry!' she replied with a smile. 'Yes, he does dance very well.'

'He must have thought it very odd to hear me say I was engaged the other evening, when he saw me sitting down. But I really had been engaged the whole day to Mr Thorpe.' Miss Tilney could only

'Rid out this morning with my father.'

bow. 'You cannot think' added Catherine after a moment's silence, 'how surprized I was to see him again. I felt so sure of his being quite gone away.'

'When Henry had the pleasure of seeing you before, he was in Bath but for a couple of days. He came only to engage lodging for us.'

'*That* never occurred to me; and of course, not seeing him any where, I thought he must be gone. Was not the young lady he danced with on Monday a Miss Smith?'

'Yes, an acquaintance of Mrs Hughes.'

'I dare say she was very glad to dance. Do you think her pretty?'

'Not very.'

'He never comes to the Pump-room, I suppose?'

'Yes, sometimes; but he has rid out this morning with my father.'

Mrs Hughes now joined them, and asked Miss Tilney if she was ready to go. 'I hope I shall have the pleasure of seeing you again soon,' said Catherine. 'Shall you be at the cotillion ball to-morrow?'

'Perhaps we – yes, I think we certainly shall.'

'I am glad of it, for we shall all be there.' – This civility was duly returned; and they parted – on Miss Tilney's side with some knowledge of her new acquaintance's feelings, and on Catherine's, without the smallest consciousness of having explained them.

She went hor very happy. The morning had answered all her hopes, and the evening of the following day was now the object of expectation, the future good. What gown and what head-dress she should wear on the occasion became her chief concern. She cannot be justified in it. Dress is at all times a frivolous distinction, and excessive solicitude about it often destroys its own aim. Catherine knew all this very well; her great aunt had read her a lecture on the subject only the Christmas before; and yet she lay awake ten minutes on Wednesday night debating between her spotted and her tamboured muslin, and nothing but the shortness of the time prevented her buying a new one for the evening. This would have been an error in judgment, great though not uncommon, from which one of the other sex rather than her own, a brother rather than a great aunt might have warned her, for man only can be aware of the insensibility of man towards a new gown. It would be mortifying to the feelings of many ladies, could they be made to understand how little the heart of man is affected by what is costly or new in their attire; how little it is biassed by the texture of their muslin, and how unsusceptible of peculiar tenderness towards the spotted, the sprigged, the mull or the jackonet. Woman is fine for her own satisfaction alone. No man will admire her the more, no woman will like her the better for it. Neatness and fashion are enough for the former, and a something of shabbiness or impropriety will be most endearing to the latter. – But not one of these grave reflections troubled the tranquillity of Catherine.

She entered the rooms on Thursday evening with feelings very different from what had attended her thither the Monday before. She had then been exulting in her engagement to Thorpe, and was now chiefly anxious to avoid his sight, lest he should engage her again; for though she could not, dared not expect that Mr Tilney should ask her a third time to dance, her wishes, hopes and plans all centred in nothing less. Every young lady may feel for my heroine in this critical moment, for every young lady has at some time or other known the same agitation. All have been, or at least all have believed themselves to be, in danger from the pursuit of some one whom they wished to avoid; and all have been anxious for the attentions of some one whom they wished to please. As soon as they were joined by the Thorpes, Catherine's agony began; she fidgetted about if John Thorpe came towards her, and hid herself as much as possible from his view, and when he spoke to her pretended not to hear him. The cotillions were over, the country-dancing beginning, and she saw nothing of the Tilneys. 'Do not be frightened, my dear Catherine,' whispered Isabella, 'but I am really going to dance with your brother again. I declare positively it is quite shocking. I tell him he ought to be ashamed of himself, but you and John must keep us in countenance. Make haste, my dear creature, and come to us. John is just walked off, but he will be back in a moment.'

Catherine had neither time nor inclination to answer. The others walked away, John Thorpe was still in view, and she gave herself up for lost. That she might not appear, however, to observe or expect him, she kept her eyes intently fixed on her fan; and a self-condemnation for her folly, in supposing that among such a crowd they should even meet with the Tilneys in any reasonable time, had just passed through her mind, when she suddenly found herself addressed and again solicited to dance, by Mr Tilney himself. With what sparkling eyes and ready motion she granted his request, and with how pleasing a flutter of heart she went with him to the set, may be easily imagined. To escape, and, as she believed, so narrowly escape John Thorpe, and to be asked, so immediately on his joining her, asked by Mr Tilney, as if he had sought her on purpose! – it did not appear to her that life could supply any greater felicity.

Scarcely had they worked themselves into the quiet possession of a place, however, when her attention was claimed by John Thorpe, who stood behind her, 'Heyday, Miss Morland!' said he, 'what is the meaning of this? – I thought you and I were to dance together.'

'I wonder you should think so, for you never asked me.' 'That is a good one, by Jove! – I asked you as soon as I came into the room, and I was just going to ask you again, but when I turned round, you were gone! – this is a cursed shabby trick! I only came for the sake of dancing with *you*, and I firmly believe you were engaged to me ever since Monday. Yes; I remember, I asked you while you were waiting in the lobby for your cloak. And here have I been telling all my acquaintance that I was going to dance with the prettiest girl in the room; and when they see you standing up with somebody else, they will quiz me famously.'

'Oh, no; they will never think of *me*, after such a description as that.'

'By heavens, if they do not, I will kick them out of the room for blockheads. What chap have you there?' Catherine satisfied his curiosity. 'Tilney,' he repeated, 'Hum – I do not know him. A good figure of a man; well put together. – Does he want a horse? – Here is a friend of mine, Sam Fletcher, has got one to sell that would suit any body. A famous clever animal for the road – only forty guineas. I had fifty minds to buy it myself, for it is one of my maxims always to buy a good horse when I meet with one; but it would not answer my purpose, it would not do for the field. I would give any money for a real good hunter. I have three now, the best that ever were back'd. I would not take eight hundred guineas for them. Fletcher and I mean to get a house in Leicestershire, against the next season It is so d— uncomfortable, living at an inn.'

This was the last sentence by which he could weary Catherine's attention, for he was just then born off by the resistless pressure of a long string of passing ladies. Her partner now drew near, and said, 'That gentleman would have put me out of patience, had he staid with you half a minute longer. He has no business to withdraw the attention of my partner from me. We have entered into a contract of mutual agreeableness for the space of an evening, and all our agreeableness belongs solely to each other for that time. Nobody can fasten themselves on the notice of one, without injuring the rights of the other. I consider a country-dance as an emblem of marriage. Fidelity and complaisance are the principal duties of both; and those men who do not chuse to dance or marry themselves, have no business with the partners or wives of their neighbours.'

'But they are such very different things! – '

'– That you think they cannot be compared together.'

'To be sure not. People that marry can never part, but must go and keep house together. People that dance, only stand opposite each other in a long room for half an hour.'

'And such is your definition of matrimony and dancing. Taken in that light certainly, their resemblance is not striking; but I think I could place them in such a view. – You will allow, that in both, man has the advantage of choice, woman only the power of refusal; that in both, it is an engagement between man and woman, formed for the advantage of each; and that when once entered into, they belong exclusively to each other till the moment of its dissolution; that it is their duty, each to endeavour to give the other no cause for wishing that he or she had bestowed themselves elsewhere, and their best interest to keep their own imaginations from wandering towards the perfections of their neighbours, or fancying that they should have been better off with any one else. You will allow all this?'

'Yes, to be sure, as you state it, all this sounds very well; but still they are so very different. – I cannot look upon them at all in the same light, nor think the same duties belong to them.'

'In one respect, there certainly is a difference. In marriage, the man is supposed to provide for the support of the woman; the woman to make the home agreeable to the man; he is to purvey, and she is to smile. But in dancing, their duties are exactly changed; the agreeableness, the compliance are expected from him, while she furnishes the fan and the lavender water. *That*, I suppose, was the difference of duties which struck you, as rendering the conditions incapable of comparison.'

'No, indeed, I never thought of that.'

'Then I am quite at a loss. One thing, however, I must observe. This disposition on your side is rather alarming. You totally disallow any similarity in the obligations; and may I not thence infer, that your notions of the duties of the dancing state are not so strict as your partner might wish? Have I not reason to fear, that if the gentleman who spoke to you just now were to return, or if any other gentleman were to address you, there would be nothing to restrain you from conversing with him as long as you chose?'

'Mr Thorpe is such a very particular friend of my brother's, that if he talks to me, I must talk to him again, but there are hardly three young men in the room besides him, that I have any acquaintance with.'

'And is that to be my only security? alas, alas!'

'Nay, I am sure you cannot have a better; for if I do not know any body, it is impossible for me to talk to them; and, besides, I do not *want* to talk to any body.'

'Now you have given me a security worth having; and I shall proceed with courage. Do you find Bath as agreeable as when I had the honour of making the enquiry before?'

'Yes, quite – more so, indeed.'

'More so! – Take care, or you will forget to be tired of it at the proper time. – You ought to be tired at the end of six weeks.'

'I do not think I should be tired, if I were to stay here six months.'

'Bath, compared with London, has little variety, and so every body finds out every year. "For six weeks, I allow Bath is pleasant enough; but beyond *that*, it is the most tiresome place in the world." You would be told so by people of all descriptions, who come regularly every winter, lengthen their six weeks into ten or twelve, and go away at last because they can afford to stay no longer.'

'Well, other people must judge for themselves, and those who go to London may think nothing of Bath. But I, who live in a small retired village in the country, can never find greater sameness in such a place as this, than in my own home; for here are a variety of amusements, a variety of things to be seen and done all day long, which I can know nothing of there.'

'You are not fond of the country.'

'Yes, I am. I have always lived there, and always been very happy. But certainly there is much more sameness in a country life than in a Bath life. One day in the country is exactly like another.'

'But then you spend your time so much more rationally in the country.'

'Do I?'

'Do you not?'

'I do not believe there is much difference.'

'Here you are in pursuit only of amusement all day long.'

'And so I am at home – only I do not find so much of it. I walk about here, and so I do there; – but here I see a variety of people in every street, and there I can only go and call on Mrs Allen.'

Mr Tilney was very much amused. 'Only go and call on Mrs Allen!' he repeated. 'What a picture of intellectual poverty! However, when you sink into this abyss again, you will have more to say. You will be able to talk of Bath, and of all that you did here.'

'Oh! yes. I shall never be in want of something to talk of again to Mrs Allen, or any body else. I really believe I shall always be talking of Bath, when I am at home again – I *do* like it so very much. If I could but have papa and mamma, and the rest of them here. I suppose I should be too happy! James's coming (my eldest brother) is quite delightful – and especially as it turns out, that the very family we are just got so intimate with, are his intimate friends already. Oh! who can ever be tired of Bath?'

'Not those who bring such fresh feelings of every sort to it, as you do. But papas and mammas, and brothers and intimate friends are a good deal gone by, to most of the frequenters of Bath – and the honest relish of balls and plays, and every-day sights, is past with them.'

Here their conversation closed; the demands of the dance becoming now too importunate for a divided attention.

Soon after their reaching the bottom of the set, Catherine perceived herself to be earnestly regarded by a gentleman who stood among the lookers-on, immediately behind her partner. He was a very handsome man, of a commanding aspect, past the bloom, but not past the vigour of life; and with his eye still directed towards her, she saw him presently address Mr Tilney in a familiar whisper. Confused by his notice, and blushing from the fear of its being excited by something wrong in her appearance, she turned away her head. But while she did so, the gentleman retreated, and her partner coming nearer, said, 'I see that you guess what I have just been asked. That gentleman knows your name, and you have a right to know his. It is General Tilney, my father.'

Catherine's answer was only 'Oh!' – but it was an 'Oh!' expressing every thing needful; attention to his words, and perfect reliance on their truth. With real interest and strong admiration did her eye now follow the General, as he moved through the crowd, and 'How handsome a family they are!' was her secret remark.

In chatting with Miss Tilney before the evening concluded, a new source of felicity arose to her. She had never taken a country walk since her arrival in Bath. Miss Tilney, to whom all the commonly-frequented environs were familiar, spoke of them in terms which made her all eagerness to know them too; and on her openly fearing that she might find nobody to go with her, it was proposed by the brother and sister that they should join in a walk, some morning or other. 'I shall like it,' she cried, 'beyond any thing in the world; and do not let us put it off – let us go to-morrow.' This was readily agreed to, with only a proviso of Miss Tilney's, that it did not rain, which Catherine was sure it would not. At twelve o'clock, they were to call for her in Pulteney-street – and 'remember – twelve o'clock,' was her parting speech to her new friend. Of her other, her older, her more established friend, Isabella, of whose fidelity and worth she had enjoyed a fortnight's experience, she scarcely saw any thing during the evening. Yet, though longing to make her acquainted with her happiness, she cheerfully submitted to the wish of Mr Allen, which took them rather early away, and her spirits danced within her, as she danced in her chair all the way home.

CHAPTER ELEVEN

THE MORROW BROUGHT a very sober looking morning; the sun making only a few efforts to appear; and Catherine augured from it, every thing most favourable to her wishes. A bright morning so early in the year, she allowed would generally turn to rain, but a cloudy one foretold improvement as the day advanced. She applied to Mr Allen for confirmation of her hopes, but Mr Allen not having his own skies and barometer about him, declined giving any absolute promise of sunshine. She applied to Mrs Allen, and Mrs Allen's opinion was more positive. 'She had no doubt in the world of its being a very fine day, if the clouds would only go off, and the sun keep out.'

At about eleven o'clock however, a few specks of small rain upon the windows caught Catherine's watchful eye, and 'Oh! dear, I do believe it will be wet,' broke from her in a most desponding tone.

'I thought how it would be,' said Mrs Allen.

'No walk for me to-day,' sighed Catherine; – 'but perhaps it may come to nothing, or it may hold up before twelve.'

'Perhaps it may, but then, my dear, it will be so dirty.'

'Oh! that will not signify; I never mind dirt.'

'No,' replied her friend very placidly, 'I know you never mind dirt.'

After a short pause, 'It comes on faster and faster!' said Catherine, as she stood watching at a window.

'So it does indeed. If it keeps raining, the streets will be very wet.'

'There are four umbrellas up already. How I hate the sight of an umbrella!'

'They are disagreeable things to carry. I would much rather take a chair at any time.'

'It was such a nice looking morning! I felt so convinced it would be dry!'

'Any body would have thought so indeed. There will be very few people in the Pump-room, if it rains all the morning. I hope Mr Allen will put on his great coat when he goes, but I dare say he will not, for he had rather do any thing in the world than walk out in a great coat; I wonder he should dislike it, it must be so comfortable.'

The rain continued – fast, though not heavy. Catherine went every five minutes to the clock, threatening on each return that, if it still kept on raining another five minutes, she would give up the matter as hopeless. The clock struck twelve, and it still rained. – 'You will not be able to go, my dear.'

'I do not quite despair yet. I shall not give it up till a quarter after twelve. This is just the time of day for it to clear up, and I do think it looks a little lighter. There, it is twenty minutes after twelve, and now I *shall* give it up entirely. Oh! that we had such weather here as they had at Udolpho, or at least in Tuscany and the South of France! – the night that poor St Aubin died! – such beautiful weather!'

At half past twelve, when Catherine's anxious attention to the weather was over, and she could no longer claim any merit from its amendment, the sky began voluntarily to clear. A gleam of sunshine took her quite by surprize; she looked round; the clouds were parting, and she instantly returned to the window to watch over and encourage the happy appearance. Ten minutes more made it certain that a bright afternoon would succeed, and justified the opinion of Mrs Allen, who had 'always thought it would clear up.' But whether Catherine might still expect her friends, whether there had not been too much rain for Miss Tilney to venture, must yet be a question.

It was too dirty for Mrs Allen to accompany her husband to the Pump-room; he accordingly set off by himself, and Catherine had barely watched him down the street, when her notice was claimed by the approach of the same two open carriages, containing the same three people that had surprized her so much a few mornings back.

'Isabella, my brother, and Mr Thorpe, I declare! They are coming for me perhaps – but I shall not go – I cannot go indeed, for you know Miss Tilney may still call.' Mrs Allen agreed to it. John Thorpe was soon with them, and his voice was with them yet sooner, for on the stairs he was calling out to Miss Morland to be quick. 'Make haste! make haste!' as he threw open the door – 'put on your hat this moment – there is no time to be lost – we are going to Bristol. – How d'ye do, Mrs Allen?'

'To Bristol! Is not that a great way off? – But, however, I cannot go with you today, because I am engaged, I expect some friends every moment.' This was of course vehemently talked down as no reason at all; Mrs Allen was called on to second him, and the two others walked in, to give their assistance. 'My sweetest Catherine, is not this delightful? We shall have a most heavenly drive. You are to thank your brother and me for the scheme; it darted into our heads at breakfast-time, I verily believe at the same instant; and we should have been off two hours ago if it had not been for this detestable rain. But it does not signify, the nights are moonlight, and we shall do delightfully. Oh! I am in such extasies at the thoughts of a little country air and quiet! – so much better than going to the Lower Rooms. We shall drive directly to Clifton and dine there; and, as soon as dinner is over, if there is time for it, go on to Kingsweston.'

'I doubt our being able to do so much,' said Morland.

'You croaking fellow!' cried Thorpe, 'we shall be able to do ten times more. Kingsweston! aye, and Blaize Castle too, and any thing else we can hear of; but here is your sister says she will not go.'

'Blaize Castle!' cried Catherine; 'what is that?'

'The finest place in England – worth going fifty miles at any time to see.'

'What, is it really a castle, an old castle?'

'The oldest in the kingdom.'

'But is it like what one reads of?'

'Exactly – the very same.'

'But now really – are there towers and long galleries?'

'By dozens.'

'Then I should like to see it; but I cannot – I cannot go.'

'Not go! – my beloved creature, what do you mean?'

'I cannot go, because' – (looking down as she spoke, fearful of Isabella's smile) 'I expect Miss Tilney and her brother to call on me to take a country walk. They promised to come at twelve, only it rained; but now, as it is so fine, I dare say they will be here soon.'

'Not they indeed,' cried Thorpe; 'for, as we turned into Broad-street, I saw them – does he not drive a phaeton with bright chestnuts?'

'I do not know indeed.'

'Yes, I know he does; I saw him. You are talking of the man you danced with last night, are not you?'

'Yes.'

'Well, I saw him at that moment turn up the Lansdown Road, – driving a smart-looking girl.'

'Did you indeed?'

'Did upon my soul; knew him again directly, and he seemed to have got some very pretty cattle too.'

'It is very odd! but I suppose they thought it would be too dirty for a walk.'

'And well they might, for I never saw so much dirt in my life. Walk! you could no more walk than you could fly! it has not been so dirty the whole winter; it is ancle-deep every where.'

Isabella corroborated it: – 'My dearest Catherine, you cannot form an idea of the dirt; come, you must go; you cannot refuse going now.'

'I should like to see the castle; but may we go all over it? may we go up every staircase, and into every suite of rooms?'

'Yes, yes, every hole and corner.'

'But then, – if they should only be gone out for an hour till it is drier, and call by and bye?'

'Make yourself easy, there is no danger of that, for I heard Tilney hallooing to a man who was just passing by on horseback, that they were going as far as Wick Rocks.'

'Then I will. Shall I go, Mrs Allen?'

'Just as you please, my dear.'

'Mrs Allen, you must persuade her to go,' was the general cry. Mrs Allen was not inattentive to it: – 'Well, my dear,' said she, 'suppose you go.' – And in two minutes they were off.

Catherine's feelings, as she got into the carriage, were in a very unsettled state; divided between regret for the loss of one great pleasure, and the hope of soon enjoying another, almost its equal in degree, however unlike in kind. She could not think the Tilneys had acted quite well by her, in so readily giving up their engagement, without sending her any message of excuse. It was now but an hour later than the time fixed on for the beginning of their walk; and, in spite of what she had heard of the prodigious accumulation of dirt in the course of that hour, she could not from her own observation help thinking, that they might have gone with very little inconvenience. To feel herself slighted by them was very painful. On the other hand, the delight of exploring an edifice like Udolpho, as her fancy represented Blaize Castle to be, was such a counterpoise of good, as might console her for almost any thing.

They passed briskly down Pulteney-street, and through Laura-place, without the exchange of many words. Thorpe talked to his horse, and she meditated, by turns, on broken promises and broken arches, phaetons and false hangings, Tilneys and trap-doors. As they entered Argyle-buildings, however, she was roused by this address from her companion, 'Who is that girl who looked at you so hard as she went by?'

'Who? – where?'

'Stop, stop, Mr Thorpe.'

'On the right-hand pavement – she must be almost out of sight now.' Catherine looked round and saw Miss Tilney leaning on her brother's arm, walking slowly down the street. She saw them both looking back at her. 'Stop, stop, Mr Thorpe,' she impatiently cried, 'it is Miss Tilney; it is indeed. – How could you tell me they were gone? – Stop, stop, I will get out this moment and go to them.' But to what purpose did she speak?: – Thorpe only lashed his horse into a brisker trot; the Tilneys, who had soon ceased to look after her, were in a moment out of sight round the corner of Laura-place, and in another moment she was herself whisked into the Marketplace. Still, however, and during the length of another street, she intreated him to stop. 'Pray, pray stop, Mr Thorpe. – I cannot go on. – I will not go on. – I must go back to Miss Tilney.' But Mr Thorpe only laughed, smacked his whip, encouraged his horse, made odd noises, and drove on; and Catherine, angry and vexed as she was, having no power of getting away, was obliged to give up the point and submit. Her reproaches, however, were not spared. 'How could you deceive me so, Mr Thorpe? – How could you say, that you saw them driving up the Lansdown-road? – I would not have had it happen so for the world. – They must think it so strange; so rude of me! to go by them, too, without saying a word! You do not know how vexed I am – I shall have no pleasure at Clifton, nor in any thing else. I had rather, ten thousand times rather get out now, and walk back to them. How could you say, you saw them driving out in a phaeton?' Thorpe defended himself very stoutly, declared he had never seen two men so much alike in his life, and would hardly give up the point of its having been Tilney himself.

Their drive, even when this subject was over, was not likely to be very agreeable. Catherine's complaisance was no longer what it had been in their former airing. She listened reluctantly, and her replies were short. Blaize Castle remained her only comfort; towards *that*, she still looked at intervals with pleasure; though rather than be disappointed of the promised walk, and especially rather than be thought ill of by the Tilneys, she would willingly have given up all the happiness which its walls could supply – the happiness of a progress through a long suite of lofty rooms, exhibiting the remains of magnificent furniture, though now for many years deserted – the happiness of being stopped in their way along narrow, winding vaults, by a low, grated door; or even of having their lamp, their only lamp, extinguished by a sudden gust of wind, and of being left in total darkness. In the meanwhile, they proceeded on their journey without any mischance; and were within view of the town of Keynsham, when a halloo from Morland, who was behind them, made his friend pull up to know what the matter. The others then came close enough for conversation, and Morland said, 'We had better go back, Thorpe; it is too late to go on to-day; your sister thinks so as well I. We have been exactly an hour coming from Pulteney-street, very little more than seven miles; and, I suppose, we have at least eight more to go. It will never do. We set out a great deal too late. We had much better put it off another day, and turn round.'

'It is all one to me,' replied Thorpe rather angrily; and instantly turning his horse, they were on their way back to Bath.

'If your brother had not got such a d— beast to drive,' said he soon afterwards, 'we might have done it very well. My horse would have trotted to Clifton within the hour, if left to himself, and I have almost broke my arm with pulling him in to that cursed broken-winded jade's pace. Morland is a fool for not keeping a horse and gig of his own.'

'No, he is not,' said Catherine warmly, 'for I am sure he could not afford it.'

'And why cannot he afford it?'

'Because he has not money enough.'

'And whose fault is that?'

'Nobody's, that I know of.' Thorpe then said something in the loud, incoherent way to which he had often recourse, about its being a d— thing to be miserly; and that if people who rolled in money could not afford things; he did not know who could; which Catherine did not even endeavour to understand. Disappointed of what was to have been the consolation for her first disappointment, she was less and less disposed either to be agreeable herself, or to find her companion so; and they returned to Pulteney-street without her speaking twenty words.

As she entered the house, the footman told her, that a gentleman and lady had called and enquired for her a few minutes after her setting off; that, when he told them she was gone out with Mr Thorpe, the lady had asked whether any message had been left for her; and on his saying no, had felt for a card, but said she had none about her, and went away. Pondering over these heart-rending tidings, Catherine walked slowly up stairs. At the head of them she was met by Mr Allen, who, on hearing the reason of their speedy return, said 'I am glad your brother had so much sense, I am glad you are come back. It was a strange, wild scheme.'

They all spent the evening together at Thorpe's. Catherine was disturbed and out of spirits; but Isabella seemed to find a pool of commerce, in the fate of which she shared, by private partnership with Morland, a very good equivalent for the quiet and country air of an inn at Clifton. Her satisfaction too, in not being at the Lower Rooms, was spoken more than once. 'How I pity the poor creatures that are going there! How glad I am that I am not amongst them! I wonder whether it will be a full ball or not! They have not begun dancing yet. I would not be there for all the world. It is so delightful to have an evening now and then to one-self. I dare say, Mr Morland, you long to be at it, do not you? I am sure you do. Well, pray do not let any body here be a restraint on you. I dare say we could do very well without you; but you men think yourselves of such consequence.'

Catherine could almost have accused Isabella of being wanting in tenderness towards herself and her sorrows; so very little did they appear to dwell on her mind, and so very inadequate was the comfort she offered. 'Do not be so dull, my dearest creature,' she whispered. 'You will quite break my heart. It was amazingly shocking to be sure; but the Tilneys were entirely to blame. Why were not they more punctual? It was dirty, indeed, but what did that signify? I am sure John and I should not have minded it. I never mind going through any thing, where a friend is concerned; this is my disposition, and John is just the same; he has amazing strong feelings. Good heavens! what a delightful hand you have got! Kings, I vow! I never was so happy in my life! I would fifty times rather you should have them than myself.'

And now I may dismiss my heroine to the sleepless couch, which is the true heroine's portion; to a pillow strewed with thorns and wet with tears. And lucky may she think herself, if she get another good night's rest in the course of the next three months.

CHAPTER TWELVE

'MRS ALLEN,' SAID CATHERINE the next morning, 'will there be any harm in my calling on Miss Tilney to-day? I shall not be easy till I have explained every thing.'

'Go by all means, my dear; only put on a white gown, Miss Tilney always wears white.'

Catherine cheerfully complied; and being properly equipped, was more impatient than ever to be at the Pump-room, that she might inform herself of General Tilney's lodging, for though she believed they were in Milsom-street, she was not certain of the house, and Mrs Allen's wavering convictions only made it more doubtful. To Milsom-street she was directed: and having made herself perfect in the number, hastened away with eager steps and a beating heart to pay her visit, explain her conduct, and be forgiven; tripping lightly through the church-yard, and resolutely turning away her eyes, that she might not be obliged to see her beloved Isabella and her dear family, who, she had reason to believe, were in a shop hard by. She reached the house without any impediment, looked at the number, knocked at the door, and inquired for Miss Tilney. The man believed

Miss Tilney to be at home, but was not quite certain. Would she be pleased to send up her name? She gave her card. In a few minutes the servant returned, and with a look which did not quite confirm his words, said he had been mistaken, for that Miss Tilney was walked out. Catherine, with a blush of mortification, left the house. She felt almost persuaded that Miss Tilney *was* at home, and too much offended to admit her; and as she retired down the street, could not withhold one glance at the drawing-room windows, in expectation of seeing her there, but no one appeared at them. At the bottom of the street, however, she looked back again, and then, not at a window, but issuing from the door, she saw Miss Tilney herself. She was followed by a gentleman, whom Catherine believed to be her father, and they turned up towards Edgar's-buildings. Catherine, in deep mortification, proceeded on her way. She could almost be angry herself at such angry incivility; but she checked the resentful sensation; she remembered her own ignorance. She knew not how much an offence as her's might be classed by the laws of worldly politeness, to what a degree of unforgivingness it might with propriety lead, nor to what rigours of rudeness in return it might justly make her amenable.

Dejected and humbled, she had even some thoughts of not going with the others to the theatre that night; but it must be confessed that they were not of long continuance: for she soon recollected, in the first place, that she was without any excuse for staying at home; and, in the second, that it was a play she wanted very much to see. To the theatre accordingly they all went; no Tilneys appeared to plague or please her; she feared that, amongst the many perfections of the family, a fondness for plays was not to be ranked; but perhaps it was because they were habituated to the finer performances of the London stage, which she knew, on Isabella's authority, rendered ever thing else of the kind 'quite horrid.' She was not deceived in her own expectation of pleasure; the comedy so well suspended her care, that no one, observing her during the first four acts, would have supposed she had any wretchedness about her. On the beginning of the fifth, however, the sudden view of Mr Henry Tilney and his father, joining a party in the opposite box, recalled her to anxiety and distress. The stage could no longer excite genuine merriment – no longer keep her whole attention. Every other look upon an average was directed towards the opposite box; and, for the space of two entire scenes, did she thus watch Henry Tilney, without being once able to catch his eye. No longer could he be suspected of indifference for a play; his notice was never withdrawn from the stage during two whole scenes. At length, however, he did look towards her, and he bowed – but such a bow! no smile, no continued observance attended it; his eyes were immediately returned to their former direction. Catherine was restlessly miserable; she could almost have run round to the box in which he sat, and forced him to hear her explanation. Feelings rather natural than heroic possessed her; instead of considering her own dignity injured by this ready condemnation – instead of proudly resolving, in conscious innocence, to shew her resentment towards him who could harbour a doubt of it, to leave to him all the trouble of seeking an explanation, and to enlighten him on the past only by avoiding his sight, or flirting with somebody else, she took to herself all the shame of misconduct, or at least of its appearance, and was only eager for an opportunity of explaining its cause.

The play concluded – the curtain fell – Henry Tilney was no longer to be seen where he had hitherto sat, but his father remained, and perhaps he might be now coming round to their box. She was right; in a few minutes he appeared, and, making his way through the then thinning rows, spoke with like calm politeness to Mrs Allen and her friend. – Not with such calmness was he answered by the latter: 'Oh! Mr Tilney, I have been quite wild to speak to you, and make my apologies. You must have thought me so rude; but indeed it was not my own fault, – was it, Mrs Allen? Did not they tell me that Mr Tilney and his sister were gone out in a phaeton together? and then what could I do? But I had ten thousand times rather have been with you; now had not I, Mrs Allen?'

'My dear, you tumble my gown,' was Mrs Allen's reply.

Her assurance, however, standing sole as it did, was not thrown away; it brought a more cordial, more natural smile into his countenance, and he replied in a tone which retained only a little affected reserve: – 'We were much obliged to you at any rate for wishing us a pleasant walk after our passing you in Argyle-street; you were so kind as to look back on purpose.'

'But indeed I did not wish you a pleasant walk; I never thought of such a thing; but I begged Mr Thorpe so earnestly to stop; I called out to him as soon as ever I saw you; now, Mrs Allen, did not – Oh! you were not there; but indeed I did; and, if Mr Thorpe would only have stopped, I would have jumped out and run after you.'

Is there a Henry in the world who could be insensible to such a declaration? Henry Tilney at least was not. With a yet sweeter smile, he said every thing that need be said of his sister's concern, regret, and dependence on Catherine's honour. – 'Oh! do not say Miss Tilney was not angry,' cried Catherine, 'because I know she was;

for she would not see me this morning when I called; I saw her walk out of the house the next minute after my leaving it; I was hurt, but I was not affronted. Perhaps you did not know I had been there.'

'I was not within at the time; but I heard of it from Eleanor, and she has been wishing ever since to see you, to explain the reason of such incivility; but perhaps I can do it as well. It was nothing more than that my father – they were just preparing to walk out, and he being hurried for time, and not caring to have it put off, made a point of her being denied. That was all, I do assure you. She was very much vexed, and meant to make her apology as soon as possible.'

Catherine's mind was greatly eased by this information, yet a something of solicitude remained, from which sprang the following question, thoroughly artless in itself, though rather distressing to the gentleman: – 'But, Mr Tilney, why were *you* less generous than your sister? If she felt such confidence in my good intentions, and could suppose it to be only a mistake, why should *you* be so ready to take offence?'

'Me! – I take offence!'

'Nay, I am sure by your look, when you came into the box, you were angry.'

'I angry! I could have no right.'

'Well, nobody would have thought you had no right who saw your face.' He replied by asking her to make room for him, and talking of the play.

He remained with them some time, and was only too agreeable for Catherine to be contented when he went away. Before they parted, however, it was agreed that the projected walk should be taken as soon as possible; and, setting aside the misery of his quitting their box, she was, upon the whole, left one of the happiest creatures in the world.

While talking to each other, she had observed with some surprize, that John Thorpe, who was never in the same part of the house for ten minutes together, was engaged in conversation with General Tilney; and she felt something more than surprize, when she thought she could perceive herself the object of their attention and discourse. What could they have to say of her? She feared General Tilney did not like her appearance: she found it was implied in his preventing her admittance to his daughter, rather than postpone his own walk a few minutes. 'How came Mr Thorpe to know your father?' was her anxious inquiry, as she pointed them out to her companion. He knew nothing about it; but his father, like every military man, had a very large acquaintance.

When the entertainment was over, Thorpe came to assist them in getting out. Catherine was the immediate object of his gallantry; and, while they waited in the lobby for a chair, he prevented the inquiry which had travelled from her heart almost to the tip of her tongue, by asking, in a consequential manner, whether she had seen him talking with General Tilney: – 'He is a fine old fellow, upon my soul! – stout, active – looks as young as his son. I have a great regard for him, I assure you: a gentlemanlike, good sort of fellow as ever lived.'

'But how came you to know him?'

'Know him! – There are few people much about town that I do not know. I have met him for ever at the Bedford; and I knew his face again to-day the moment he came into the billiard-room. One

The same kind of delicate flattery.

of the best players we have, by the bye; and we had a little touch together, though I was almost afraid of him at first: the odds were five to four against me; and, if I had not made one of the cleanest strokes that perhaps ever was made in his world – I took his ball exactly – but I could not make you understand it without a table; – however I *did* beat him. A very fine fellow; as rich as a Jew. I should like to dine with him; I dare say he gives famous dinners. But what do you think we have been talking of? – You. Yes, by heavens! – and the General thinks you the finest girl in Bath.'

'Oh! nonsense! how can you say so?'

'And what do you think I said?' (lowering his voice) 'Well done, General, said I, I am quite of your mind.'

Here Catherine, who was much less gratified by his admiration than by General Tilney's, was not sorry to be called away by Mr Allen. Thorpe, however, would see her to her chair, and, till she entered it, continued the same kind of delicate flattery, in spite of her entreating him to have done.

That General Tilney, instead of disliking, should admire her, was very delightful; and she joyfully thought, that there was not one of the family whom she need now fear to meet. – The evening had done more, much more, for her, than could have been expected.

CHAPTER THIRTEEN

MONDAY, TUESDAY, WEDNESDAY, Thursday, Friday and Saturday have now passed in review before the reader; the events of each day, its hopes and fears, mortifications and pleasures have been separately stated, and the pangs of Sunday only now remain to be described and close the week. The Clifton scheme had been deferred, not relinquished, and on the afternoon's Crescent of this day, it was brought forward again. In a private consultation between Isabella and James, the former of whom had particularly set her heart upon going, and the latter no less anxiously placed his upon pleasing her, it was agreed that, provided the weather were fair, the party should take place on the following morning; and they were to set off very early, in order to be at home in good time. The affair thus determined, and Thorpe's approbation secured, Catherine only remained to be apprized of it. She had left them for a few minutes to speak to Miss Tilney. In that interval the plan was completed, and as soon as she came again, her agreement was demanded; but instead of the gay acquiescence expected by Isabella, Catherine looked grave, was very sorry, but could not go. The engagement which ought to have kept her from joining in the former attempt, would make it impossible for her to accompany them now. She had that moment settled with Miss Tilney to take their promised walk to-morrow; it was quite determined, and she would not, upon any account, retract. But that she *must* and *should* retract, was instantly the eager cry of both the Thorpes; they must go to Clifton to-morrow, they would not go without her, it would be nothing to put off a mere walk for one day longer, and they would not hear of a refusal. Catherine was distressed, but not subdued. 'Do not urge me, Isabella. I am engaged to Miss Tilney. I cannot go.' This availed nothing. The same arguments assailed her again; she must go, she should go, and they would not hear of a refusal. 'It would be so easy to tell Miss Tilney that you had just been reminded of a prior engagement, and must only beg to put off the walk till Tuesday.'

'No, it would not be easy. I could not do it. There has been no prior engagement.' But Isabella became only more and more urgent; calling on her in the most affectionate manner; addressing her by the most endearing names. She was sure her dearest, sweetest Catherine would not seriously refuse such a trifling request to a friend who loved her so dearly. She knew her beloved Catherine to have so feeling a heart, so sweet a temper, to be so easily persuaded by those she loved. But all in vain; Catherine felt herself to be in the right, and though pained by such tender, such flattering supplication, could not allow it to influence her. Isabeela then tried another method. She reproached her with having more affection for Miss Tilney, though she had known her so little a while, than for her best and oldest friends; with being grown cold and indifferent, in short, towards herself. 'I cannot help being jealous, Catherine, when I see myself slighted for strangers, I, who love you so excessively! When once my affections are placed, it is not in the power of any thing to change them. But I believe my feelings are stronger than any body's; I am sure they are too strong for my own peace; and to see myself supplanted in your friendship by strangers, does cut me to the quick, I own. These Tilneys seem to swallow up every thing else.'

Catherine thought this reproach equally strange and unkind. Was it the part of a friend thus to expose her feelings to the notice of others? Isabella appeared to her ungenerous and selfish, regardless of every thing but her own gratification. These painful ideas crossed her mind, though she said nothing. Isabella, in the meanwhile, had applied her handkerchief to her eyes; and Morland, miserable at such a sight, could not help saying, 'Nay, Catherine. I think you cannot stand out any longer now. The sacrifice is not much; and to oblige such a friend – I shall think you quite unkind, if you will refuse.'

This was the first time of her brother's openly siding against her, and anxious to avoid his displeasure, she proposed a compromise. If they would only put off their scheme till Tuesday, which they might easily do, as it depended only on themselves, she could go with them, and every body might then be satisfied. But 'No, no, no!' was the immediate answer; 'that could not be, for Thorpe did not know that he might not go to town on Tuesday.' Catherine was sorry, but could do no more; and a short silence ensued, which was broken by Isabella; who in a voice of cold resentment said, 'Very well, then there is an end of the party. If Catherine does not go, I cannot. I cannot be the only woman. I would not, upon any account in the world, do so improper a thing.'

'Catherine, you must go,' said James.

'But why cannot Mr Thorpe drive one of his other sisters? I dare say either of them would like to go.'

'Thank ye,' cried Thorpe, 'but I did not come to Bath to drive my sisters about, and look like a fool. No, if you do not go, d— me if I do. I only go for the sake of driving you.'

'That is a compliment which gives me no pleasure.' But her words were lost on Thorpe, who had turned abruptly away.

The three others still continued together, walking in a most uncomfortable manner to poor Catherine; sometimes not a word was said, sometimes she was again attacked with supplications or reproaches, and her arm was still linked within Isabella's, though their hearts were at war. At one moment she was softened, at another irritated; always distressed, but always steady.

'I did not think you had been so obstinate, Catherine,' said James; 'you were not used to be so hard to persuade; you once were the kindest, best-tempered of my sisters.'

'I hope I am not less so now,' she replied, very feelingly; 'but indeed I cannot go. If I am wrong, I am doing what I believe to be right.'

'I suspect,' said Isabella, in a low voice, 'there is no great struggle.'

Catherine's heart swelled; she drew away her arm, and Isabella made no opposition. Thus passed a long ten minutes, till they were again joined by Thorpe, who coming to them with a gayer look, said, 'Well, I have settled the matter, and now we may all go to-morrow with a safe conscience. I have been to Miss Tilney, and made your excuses.'

'You have not!' cried Catherine.

'I have, upon my soul. Left her this moment. Told her you had sent me to say, that having just recollected a prior engagement of going to Clifton with us to-morrow, you could not have the pleasure of walking with her till Tuesday. She said very well, Tuesday was just as convenient to her; so there is an end of all our difficulties. – A pretty good thought of mine – hey?'

Isabella's countenance was once more all smiles and good-humour, and James too looked happy again.

'A most heavenly thought indeed! Now, my sweet Catherine, all our distresses are over; you are honourably acquitted, and we shall have a most delightful party.'

'This will not do,' said Catherine; 'I cannot submit to this. I must run after Miss Tilney directly and set her right.'

Isabella, however, caught hold of one hand; Thorpe of the other; and remonstrances poured in from all three. Even James was quite angry. When every thing was settled, when Miss Tilney herself said that Tuesday would suit her as well, it was quite ridiculous, quite absurd to make any further objection.

'I do not care. Mr Thorpe had no business to invent any such message. If I had thought it right to put if off, I could have spoken to Miss Tilney myself. This is only doing it in a ruder way; and how do I know that Mr Thorpe has – he may be mistaken again perhaps; he led me into one act of rudeness by the mistake on Friday. Let me go, Mr Thorpe; Isabella, do not hold me.'

Thorpe told her it would be in vain to go after the Tilneys; they were turning the corner into Brock-street, when he had overtaken them, and were at home by this time.

'Then I will go after them,' said Catherine; 'wherever they are I will go after them. It does not signify talking. If I could not be persuaded into doing what I thought wrong, I never will be tricked into it.' And with these words she broke away and hurried off. Thorpe would have darted after her, but Morland withheld him. 'Let her go, let her go, if she will go.'

'She is as obstinate as – '

Thorpe never finished the simile, for it could hardly have been a proper one.

Away walked Catherine in great agitation, as fast as the crowd would permit her, fearful of being pursued, yet determined to persevere. As she walked, she reflected on what had passed. It was painful to her to disappoint and displease them, particularly to displease her brother; but she could not repent her resistance. Setting her own inclination apart, to have failed a second time in her engagement to Miss Tilney, to have retracted a promise voluntarily made

'Let me go, Mr Thorpe.'

only five minutes before, and on a false pretence too, must have been wrong. She had not been withstanding them on selfish principles alone, she had not consulted merely her own gratification; *that* might have been ensured in some degree by the excursion itself, by seeing Blaize Castle; no, she had attended to what was due to others, and to her own character in their opinion. Her conviction of being right however was not enough to restore her composure, till she had spoken to Miss Tilney she could not be at ease; and quickening her pace when she got clear of the Crescent, she almost ran over the remaining ground till she gained the top of Milsom-street. So rapid had been her movements, that in spite of the Tilneys' advantage in the outset, they were but just turning into their lodgings as she came within view of them; and the servant still remaining at the open door, she used only the ceremony of saying that she must speak with Miss Tilney that moment, and hurrying by him proceeded up stairs. Then, opening the first door before her, which happened to be the right, she immediately found herself in the drawing-room with General Tilney, his son and daughter. Her explanation, defective only in being – from her irritation of nerves and shortness of breath – no explanation at all, was instantly given. 'I am come in a great hurry – It was all a mistake – I never promised to go – I told them from the first I could not go. – I ran away in a great hurry to explain it. – I did not care what you thought of me. – I would not stay for the servant.'

The business however, though not perfectly elucidated by this speech, soon ceased to be a puzzle. Catherine found that John Thorpe *had* given the message; and Miss Tilney had no scruple in owning herself greatly surprized by it. But whether her brother had still exceeded her in resentment, Catherine, though she instinctively addressed herself as much to one as to the other in her vindication, had no means of knowing. Whatever might have been felt before her arrival, her eager declarations immediately made every look and sentence as friendly as she could desire.

The affair thus happily settled, she was introduced by Miss Tilney to her father, and received by him with such ready, such solicitous politeness as recalled Thorpe's information to her mind, and made her think with pleasure that he might be sometimes depended on. To such anxious attention was the general's civility carried, that not aware of her extraordinary swiftness in entering the house, he was quite angry with the servant whose neglect had reduced her to open the door of the apartment herself. 'What did William mean by it? He should make a point of inquiring into the matter.' And if Catherine had not most warmly asserted his innocence, it seemed likely that William would lose the favour of his master for ever, if not his place, by her rapidity.

After sitting with them a quarter of an hour, she rose to take leave, and was then most agreeably surprized by General Tilney's asking her if she would do his daughter the honour of dining and spending the rest of the day with her. Miss Tilney added her own wishes. Catherine was greatly obliged; but it was quite out of her power. Mr and Mrs Allen would expect her back every moment.

The general declared he could say no more; the claims of Mr and Mrs Allen were not to be superseded; but on some other day he trusted, when longer notice could be given, they would not refuse to spare her to her friend. 'Oh, no; Catherine was sure they would not have the least objection, and she should have great pleasure in coming.' The general attended her himself to the street-door, saying every thing gallant as they went down stairs, admiring the elasticity of her walk, which corresponded exactly with the spirit of her dancing, and making her one of the most graceful bows she had ever beheld, when they parted.

Catherine, delighted by all that had passed, proceeded gaily to Pulteney-street; walking, as she concluded, with great elasticity, though she had never thought of it before. She reached home without seeing any thing more of the offended party; and now that she had been triumphant throughout, had carried her point and was secure of her walk, she began (as the flutter of her spirits subsided) to doubt whether she had been perfectly right. A sacrifice was always noble; and if she had given way to their entreaties, she should have been spared the distressing idea of a friend displeased, a brother angry, and a scheme of great happiness to both destroyed, perhaps through her means. To ease her mind, and ascertain by the opinion of an unprejudiced person what her own conduct had really been, she took occasion to mention before Mr Allen the half-settled scheme of her brother and the Thorpes for the following day. Mr Allen caught at it directly. 'Well,' said he, 'and do you think of going too?'

'No; I had just engaged myself to walk with Miss Tilney before they told me of it; and therefore you know I could not go with them, could I?'

'No, certainly not; and I am glad you do not think of it. These schemes are not at all the thing. Young men and women driving about the country in open carriages! Now and then it is very well; but going to inns and public places together! It is not right; and I wonder Mrs Thorpe should allow it. I am glad you do not think of going; I am sure Mrs Morland would not be pleased. Mrs Allen, are not you of my way of thinking? Do not you think these kind of projects objectionable?'

'Yes, very much so indeed. Open carriages are nasty things. A clean gown is not five minutes wear in them. You are splashed getting in and getting out; and the wind takes your hair and your bonnet in every direction. I hate an open carriage myself.'

'I know you do; but that is not the question. Do not you think it has an odd appearance, if young ladies are frequently driven about in them by young men, to whom they are not even related?'

'Yes, my dear, a very odd appearance indeed. I cannot bear to see it.'

'Dear madam,' cried Catherine, 'then why did not you tell me so before? I am sure if I had known it to be improper, I would not have gone with Mr Thorpe at all; but I always hoped you would tell me, if you thought I was doing wrong.'

'And so I should, my dear, you may depend on it; for as I told Mrs Morland at parting, I would always do the best for you in my power. But one must not be over particular. Young people *will* be young people, as your good mother says herself. You know I wanted you, when we first came, not to buy that sprigged muslin, but you would. Young people do not like to be always thwarted.'

'But this was something of real consequence; and I do not think you would have found me hard to persuade.'

'As far as it has gone hitherto, there is no harm done,' said Mr Allen; 'and I would only advise you, my dear, not to go out with Mr Thorpe any more.'

'That is just what I was going to say,' added his wife.

Catherine, relieved for herself, felt uneasy for Isabella; and after a moment's thought, asked Mr Allen whether it would not be both proper and kind in her to write to Miss Thorpe, and explain the indecorum of which she must be as insensible as herself; for she considered that Isabella might otherwise perhaps be going to Clifton the next day, in spite of what had passed. Mr Allen however discouraged her from doing any such thing. 'You had better leave her alone, my dear, she is old enough to know what she is about; and if not, has a mother to advise her. Mrs Thorpe is too indulgent beyond a doubt; but however you had better not interfere. She and your brother chuse to go, and you will be only getting ill-will.'

Catherine submitted; and though sorry to think that Isabella should be doing wrong, felt greatly relieved by Mr Allen's approbation of her own conduct, and truly rejoiced to be preserved by his advice from the danger of falling into such an error herself. Her escape from being one of the party of Clifton was now an escape indeed; for what would the Tilneys have thought of her, if she had broken her promise to them in order to do what was wrong in itself? if she had been guilty of one breach of propriety, only to enable her to be guilty of another?

CHAPTER FOURTEEN

THE NEXT MORNING WAS fair, and Catherine almost expected another attack from the assembled party. With Mr Allen to support her, she felt no dread of the event: but she would gladly be spared a contest, where victory itself was painful; and was heartily rejoiced therefore at neither seeing nor hearing any thing of them. The Tilneys called for her at the appointed time; and no new difficulty arising, no sudden recollection, no unexpected summons, no impertinent intrusion to disconcert their measures, my heroine was most unnaturally able to fulfil her engagement, though it was made with the hero himself. They determined on walking round Beechen Cliff, that noble hill, whose beautiful verdure and hanging coppice render it so striking an object from almost every opening in Bath.

'I never look at it,' said Catherine, as they walked along the side of the river, 'without thinking of the south of France.'

'You have been abroad then?' said Henry, a little surprized.

'Oh! no, I only mean what I have read about. It always puts me in mind of the country that Emily and her father travelled through, in the "Mysteries of Udolpho." But you never read novels, I dare say?'

'Why not?'

'Because they are not clever enough for you – gentlemen read better books.'

'The person, be it gentleman or lady, who has not pleasure in a good novel, must be intolerably stupid. I have read all Mrs Radcliffe's works, and most of them with great pleasure. The Mysteries of Udolpho, when I had once begun it, I could not lay down again; – I remember finishing it in two days – my hair standing on end the whole time.'

'Yes,' added Miss Tilney, 'and I remember that you undertook to read it aloud to me, and that when I was called away for only five minutes to answer a note, instead of waiting for me, you took the volume into the Hermitage-walk, and I was obliged to stay till you had finished it.'

'Thank you, Eleanor; – a most honourable testimony. You see, Miss Morland, the injustice of your suspicions. Here was I, in my eagerness to get on, refusing to wait only five minutes for my sister; breaking the promise I had made of reading it aloud, and keeping her in suspense at a most interesting part, by running away with the volume, which, you are to observe, was her own, particularly her own. I am proud when I reflect on it, and I think it must establish me in your good opinion.'

'I am very glad to hear it indeed, and now I shall never be ashamed of liking Udolpho myself. But I really thought before, young men despised novels amazingly.'

'It is *amazingly*; it may well suggest *amazement* if they do – for they read nearly as many as women. I myself have read hundreds and hundreds. Do not imagine that you can cope with me in a knowledge of Julias and Louisas. If we proceed to particulars, and engage in the never-ceasing inquiry of "Have you read this?" and "Have you read that?" I shall soon leave you as far behind me as – what shall I say – I want an appropriate simile; – as far as your friend Emily herself left poor Valancourt when she went with her aunt into Italy. Consider how many years I have had the start of you. I had entered on my studies at Oxford, while you were a good little girl working your sampler at home!'

'Not very good I am afraid. But now really do not you think Udolpho the nicest book in the world?'

'The nicest; – by which I suppose you mean the neatest. That must depend upon the binding.'

'Henry,' said Miss Tilney, 'you are very impertinent. Miss Morland, he is treating you exactly as he does his sister. He is for ever finding fault with me, for some incorrectness of language, and now he is taking the same liberty with you. The word "nicest," as you used it, did not suit him; and you had better change it as soon as you can, or we shall be overpowered with Johnson and Blair all the rest of the way.'

'I am sure,' cried Catherine, 'I did not mean to say any thing wrong; but it *is* a nice book, and why should not I call it so?'

'Very true,' said Henry, 'and this is a very nice day, and we are taking a very nice walk, and you are two very nice young ladies. Oh! it is a very nice word indeed! – it does for every thing. Originally perhaps it was applied only to express neatness, propriety, delicacy, or refinement; – people were nice in their dress, in their sentiments, or their choice. But now every commendation on every subject is comprised in that one word.'

'While, in fact,' cried his sister, 'it ought only to be applied to you, without any commendation at all. You are more nice than wise. Come, Miss Morland, let us leave him to meditate over our faults in the utmost propriety of diction, while we praise Udolpho in whatever terms we like best. It is a most interesting work. You are fond of that kind of reading?'

'To say the truth, I do not much like any other.'

'Indeed!

'That is, I can read poetry and plays, and things of that sort, and do not dislike travels. But history, real solemn history, I cannot be interested in. Can you?'

'Yes, I am fond of history.'

'I wish I were too. I read it a little as a duty, but it tells me nothing that does not either vex or weary me. The quarrels of popes and kings, with wars or pestilences, in every page; the men all so good for nothing, and hardly any women at all – it is very tiresome: and yet I often think it odd that it should be so dull, for a great deal of it must be invention. The speeches that are put into the heroes' mouths, their thoughts and designs – the chief of all this must be invention, and invention is what delights me in other books.'

'Historians, you think,' said Miss Tilney, 'are not happy in their flights of fancy. They display imagination without raising interest. I am fond of history – and am very well contented to take the false with the true. In the principal facts they have sources of intelligence in former histories and records, which may be as much depended on, I conclude, as any thing that does not actually pass under one's own observation; and as for the little embellishments you speak of, they are embellishments, and I like them as such. If a speech be well drawn up, I read it with pleasure, by whomsoever it may be made – and probably with much greater, if the production of Mr Hume or Mr Robertson, than if the genuine words of Caractacus, Agricola, or Alfred the Great.'

'You are fond of history! – and so are Mr Allen and my father; and I have two brothers who do not dislike it. So many instances within my small circle of friends is remarkable! At this rate, I shall not pity the writers of history any longer. If people like to read their books, it is all very well, but to be at so much trouble in filling great volumes, which, as I used to think, nobody would willingly ever look into, to be labouring only for the torment of little boys and girls, always struck me as a hard fate; and though I know it is all very right and necessary, I have often wondered at the person's courage that could sit down on purpose to do it.'

'That little boys and girls should be tormented,' said Henry, 'is what no one at all acquainted with human nature in a civilized state can deny; but in behalf of our most distinguished historians, I must observe, that they might well be offended at being supposed to have no higher aim; and that by their method and style, they are perfectly well qualified to torment readers of the most advanced reason and mature time of life. I use the verb "to torment", as I observed to be your own method, instead of "to instruct", supposing them to be now admitted as synonimous.'

'You think me foolish to call instruction a torment, but if you had been as much used as myself to hear poor little children first learning their letters and then learning to spell, if you had ever seen how stupid they can be for a whole morning together, and how tired my poor mother is at the end of it, as I am in the habit of seeing almost every day of my life at home, you would allow that to *torment* and to *instruct* might sometimes be used as synonimous words.'

'Very probably. But historians are not accountable for the difficulty of learning to read; and even you yourself, who do not altogether seem particularly friendly to very severe, very intense application, may perhaps be brought to acknowledge that it is very well worth while to be tormented for two or three years of one's life, for the sake of being able to read all the rest of it. Consider – if reading had not been taught, Mrs Radcliffe would have written in vain – or perhaps might not have written at all.'

Catherine assented – and a very warm panegyric from her on that lady's merits, closed the subject. – The Tilneys were soon engaged in another on which she had nothing to say. They were viewing the country with the eyes of persons accustomed to drawing, and decided on its capability of being formed into pictures, with all the eagerness of real taste. Here Catherine was quite lost. She knew nothing of drawing – nothing of taste: – and she listened to them with an attention which brought her little profit, for they talked in phrases which conveyed scarcely any idea to her. The little which she could understand however appeared to contradict the very few notions she had entertained on the matter before. It seemed as if a good view were no longer to be taken from the top of an high hill, and that a clear blue sky was no longer a proof of a fine day. She was heartily ashamed of her ignorance. A misplaced shame. Where people wish to attach, they should always be ignorant. To come with a well-informed mind is to come with an inability of administering to the vanity of others, which a sensible person would always wish to avoid. A woman especially, if she have the misfortune of knowing any thing, should conceal it as well as she can.

The advantages of natural folly in a beautiful girl have been already set forth by the capital pen of a sister author; – and to her treatment of the subject I will only add in justice to men, that though to the larger and more trifling part of the sex, imbecility in females is a great enhancement of their personal charms, there is a portion of them too reasonable and too well informed themselves to desire any thing more in woman than ignorance. But Catherine did not know her own advantages – did not know that a good-looking girl, with an affectionate heart and a very ignorant mind, cannot fail of attracting a clever young man, unless circumstances are particularly untoward. In the present instance, she confessed and lamented her want of knowledge; declared that she would give any thing in the world to be able to draw; and a lecture on the picturesque immediately followed, in which his instructions were so clear that she soon began to see beauty in every thing admired by him, and her attention was so earnest, that he became perfectly satisfied of her having a great deal of natural taste. He talked of fore-grounds, distances, and second distances – side-screens and perspectives – lights and shades; – and Catherine was so hopeful a scholar, that when they gained the top of Beechen Cliff, she voluntarily rejected the whole city of Bath, as unworthy to make part of a landscape. Delighted with her progress, and fearful of wearying her with too much wisdom at once, Henry suffered the subject to decline, and by an easy transition from a piece of rocky fragment and the withered oak which he had placed near its summit, to oaks in general, to forests, the inclosure of them, waste lands, crown lands and government, he shortly found himself arrived at politics; and from politics, it was an easy step to silence. The general pause which succeeded his short disquisition on the state of the nation, was put an end to by Catherine, who, in rather a solemn tone of voice, uttered these words, 'I have heard that something very shocking indeed, will soon come out in London.'

Miss Tilney, to whom this was chiefly addressed, was startled, and hastily replied, 'Indeed! – and of what nature?'

'That I do not know, nor who is the author. I have only heard that it is to be more horrible than any thing we have met with yet.'

'Good heaven! – Where could you hear of such a thing?'

'A particular friend of mine had an account of it in a letter from London yesterday. It is to be uncommonly dreadful. I shall expect murder and every thing of the kind.'

'You speak with astonishing composure! But I hope your friend's accounts have been exaggerated; – and if such a design is known beforehand, proper measures will undoubtedly be taken by government to prevent its coming to effect.'

'Government,' said Henry, endeavouring not to smile, 'neither desires nor dares to interfere in such matters. There must be murder; and government cares not how much.'

The ladies stared. He laughed, and added, 'Come, shall I make you understand each other, or leave you to puzzle out an explanation as you can? No – I will be noble. I will prove myself a man, no less by the generosity of my soul than the clearness of my head. I have no patience with such of my sex as disdain to let themselves sometimes down to the comprehension of yours. Perhaps the abilities of women are neither sound nor acute – neither vigorous nor keen. Perhaps they may want observation, discernment, judgment, fire, genius, and wit.'

Knocked off his horse by a brickbat.

'Miss Morland, do not mind what he says; – but have the goodness to satisfy me as to this dreadful riot.'

'Riot! – what riot?'

'My dear Eleanor, the riot is only in your own brain. The confusion there is scandalous. Miss Morland has been talking of nothing more dreadful than a new publication which is shortly to come out, in three duodecimo volumes, two hundred and seventy-six pages in each, with a frontispiece to the first of two tombstones and a lantern – do you understand? – And you, Miss Morland – my stupid sister has mistaken all your clearest expressions. You talked of expected horrors in London – and instead of instantly conceiving, as any rational creature would have done, that such words could relate only to a circulating library, she immediately pictured to herself a mob of three thousand men assembling in St George's Fields; the Bank attacked, the Tower threatened, the streets of London flowing with blood, a detachment of the 12th Light Dragoons, (the hopes of the nation), called up from Northampton to quell the insurgents, and the gallant Capt. Frederick Tilney, in the moment of charging at the head of his troop, knocked off his horse by a brickbat from an upper window. Forgive her stupidity. The fears of the sister have added to the weakness of the woman; but she is by no means a simpleton in general.'

Catherine looked grave. 'And now, Henry,' said Miss Tilney. 'that you have made us understand each other you may as well make Miss Morland understand yourself – unless you mean to have her think you intolerably rude to your sister, and a great brute in your opinion of women in general. Miss Morland is not used to your odd ways.'

'I shall be most happy to make her better acquainted with them.'

'No doubt; – but that is no explanation of the present.'

'What am I to do?'

'You know what you ought to do. Clear your character handsomely before her. Tell her that you think very highly of the understanding of women.'

'Miss Morland, I think very highly of the understanding of all the women in the world – especially of those – whoever they may be – with whom I happen to be in company.'

'That is not enough. Be more serious.'

'Miss Morland, no one can think more highly of the understanding of women than I do. In my opinion, nature has given them so much, that they never find it necessary to use more than half.'

'We shall get nothing more serious from him now, Miss Morland. He is not in a sober mood. But I do assure you that he must be entirely misunderstood, if he can ever appear to say an unjust thing of any woman at all, or an unkind one of me.'

It was no effort to Catherine to believe that Henry Tilney could never be wrong. His manner might sometimes surprize, but his meaning must always be just: – and what she did not understand, she was almost as ready to admire, as what she did. The whole walk was delightful, and though it ended too soon, its conclusion was delightful too; – her friends attended her into the house, and Miss Tilney, before they parted, addressing herself with respectful form, as much to Mrs Allen as to Catherine, petitioned for the pleasure of her company to dinner on the day after the next. No difficulty was made on Mrs Allen's side – and the only difficulty on Catherine's was in concealing the excess of her pleasure.

The morning had passed away so charmingly as to banish all her friendship and natural affection; for no thought of Isabella or James had crossed her during their walk. When the Tilneys were gone, she became amiable again, but she was amiable for some time to little effect; Mrs Allen had no intelligence to give that could relieve her anxiety, she had heard nothing of any of them. Towards the end of the morning however, Catherine having occasion for some indispensable yard of ribbon which must be bought without a moment's delay, walked out into the town, and in Bond-street overtook the second Miss Thorpe, as she was loitering towards Edgar's Buildings between two of the sweetest girls in the world, who had been her dear friends all the morning. From her, she soon learned that the party to Clifton had taken place. 'They set off at eight this morning,' said Miss Anne, 'and I am sure I do not envy them their drive. I think you and I are very well off to be out of the scrape. – It must be the dullest thing in the world, for there is not a soul at Clifton at this time of year. Belle went with your brother, and John drove Maria.'

Catherine spoke the pleasure she really felt on hearing this part of the arrangement.

'Oh! yes,' rejoined the other, 'Maria is gone. She was quite wild to go. She thought it would be something very fine. I cannot say I admire her taste; and for my part I was determined from the first not to go, if they pressed me ever so much.'

Catherine, a little doubtful of this, could not help answering, 'I wish you could have gone too. It is a pity you could not all go.'

'Thank you; but it is quite a matter of indifference to me. Indeed, I would not have gone on any account, I was saying so to Emily and Sophia when you overtook us.'

Catherine was still unconvinced; but glad that Anne should have the friendship of an Emily and a Sophia to console her, she bade her adieu without much uneasiness, and returned home, pleased that the party had not been prevented by her refusing to join it, and very heartily wishing that it might be too pleasant to allow either James or Isabella to resent her resistance any longer.

CHAPTER FIFTEEN

EARLY THE NEXT DAY, A note from Isabella, speaking peace and tenderness in every line, and entreating the immediate presence of her friend on a matter of the utmost importance, hastened Catherine, in the happiest state of confidence and curiosity, to Edgar's Buildings. – The two youngest Miss Thorpes were by themselves in the parlour; and, on Anne's quitting it to call her sister, Catherine took the opportunity of asking the other for some particulars of their yesterday's party. Maria desired no greater pleasure than to speak of it; and Catherine immediately learnt that it had been altogether the most delightful scheme in the world; that nobody could imagine how charming it had been, and that it had been more delightful than any body could conceive. Such was the information of the first five minutes; the second unfolded thus much in detail, – that they had driven directly to the York Hotel, ate some soup, and bespoke an early dinner, walked down to the Pump-room, tasted the water, and laid out some shillings in purses and spars; thence adjourned to eat ice at a pastry-cook's, and hurrying back to the Hotel, swallowed their dinner in haste, to prevent being in the dark; and then had a delightful drive back, only the moon was not up, and it rained a little, and Mr Morland's horse was so tired he could hardly get it along.

Catherine listened with heartfelt satisfaction. It appeared that Blaize Castle had never been thought of; and, as for all the rest, there was nothing to regret for half an instant. – Maria's intelligence concluded with a tender effusion of pity for her sister Anne, whom she represented as insupportably cross, from being excluded the party.

'She will never forgive me, I am sure; but, you know, how could I help it? John would have me go, for he vowed he would not drive her, because she had such thick ancles. I dare say she will not be in good humour again this month; but I am determined I will not be cross; it is not a little matter that puts me out of temper.'

Isabella now entered the room with so eager a step, and a look of such happy importance, as engaged all her friend's notice. Maria was without ceremony sent away, and Isabella, embracing Catherine, thus began: – 'Yes, my dear Catherine, it is so indeed; your penetration has not deceived you. – Oh! that arch eye of yours! – It sees through every thing.'

Catherine replied only by a look of wondering ignorance.

'Nay, my beloved, sweetest friend,' continued the other, 'compose yourself. – I am amazingly agitated, as you perceive. Let us sit down and talk in comfort. Well, and so you guessed it the moment you had my note? – Sly creature! – Oh! my dear Catherine, you alone who know my heart can judge of my present happiness. Your brother is the most charming of men. I only wish I were more worthy of him. – But what will your excellent father and mother say? – Oh! heavens! when I think of them I am so agitated!'

Catherine's understanding began to awake: an idea of the truth suddenly darted into her mind; and, with the natural blush of so new an emotion, she cried out, 'Good heaven! – my dear Isabella, what do you mean? Can you – can you really be in love with James?'

This bold surmise, however, she soon learnt comprehended but half the fact. The anxious affection, which she was accused of having continually watched in Isabella's every look and action, had, in the course of their yesterday's party, received the delightful confession of an equal love. Her heart and faith were alike engaged to James. – Never had Catherine listened to any thing so full of interest, wonder, and joy. Her brother and her friend engaged! – New to such circumstances, the importance of it appeared unspeakably great, and she contemplated it as one of those grand events, of which the ordinary course of life can hardly afford a return. The strength of her feelings she could not express; the nature of them, however, contented her friend. The happiness of having such a sister was their first effusion, and the fair ladies mingled in embraces and tears of joy.

Delighting, however, as Catherine sincerely did in the prospect of the connexion, it must be acknowledged that Isabella far surpassed her in tender anticipations. – 'You will be so infinitely dearer to me, my Catherine, than either Anne or Maria: I feel that I shall be so much more attached to my dear Morland's family than to my own.'

This was a pitch of friendship beyond Catherine.

'You are so like your dear brother,' continued Isabella, 'that I quite doated on you the first moment I saw you. But so it always is with me; the first moment settles every thing. The very first day that Morland came to us last Christmas – the very first moment I beheld him – my heart was irrecoverably gone. I remember I wore my yellow gown, with my hair done up in braids; and when I came into the drawing-room, and John introduced him, I thought I never saw any body so handsome before.'

Here Catherine secretly acknowledged the power of love; for, though exceedingly fond of her brother, and partial to all his endowments, she had never in her life thought him handsome.

'I remember too, Miss Andrews drank tea with us that evening, and wore her puce-coloured sarsenet; and she looked so heavenly, that I thought your brother must certainly fall in love with her; I could not sleep a wink all night for thinking of it. Oh! Catherine, the many sleepless nights I have had on your brother's account! – I would not have you suffer half what I have done! I am grown wretchedly thin I know; but I will not pain you by describing my anxiety; you have seen enough of it. I feel that I have betrayed myself perpetually; – so unguarded in speaking of my partiality for the church! – But my secret I was always sure would be safe with *you*.'

Catherine felt that nothing could have been safer; but ashamed of an ignorance little expected, she dared no longer contest the point, nor refuse to have been as full of arch penetration and affectionate sympathy as Isabella chose to consider her. Her brother she found was preparing to set off with all speed to Fullerton, to make known his situation and ask consent; and here was a source of some real agitation to the mind of Isabella. Catherine endeavoured to persuade her, as she was herself persuaded, that her father and mother would never oppose their son's wishes. – 'It is impossible,' said she, 'for parents to be more kind, or more desirous of their children's happiness; I have no doubt of their consenting immediately.'

'Morland says exactly the same,' replied Isabella; 'and yet I dare not expect it; my fortune will be so small; they never can consent to it. Your brother, who might marry any body!'

Here Catherine again discerned the force of love.

'Indeed, Isabella, you are too humble. – The difference of fortune can be nothing to signify.'

'Oh! my sweet Catherine, in *your* generous heart I know it would signify nothing; but we must not expect such disinterestedness in many. As for myself, 'I am sure I only wish our situations were reversed. Had I the command of millions, were I mistress of the whole world, your brother would be my only choice.'

This charming sentiment, recommended as much by sense as novelty, gave Catherine a most pleasing remembrance of all the heroines of her acquaintance; and she thought her friend never looked more lovely than in uttering the grand idea. – 'I am sure they will consent,' was her frequent declaration; 'I am sure they will be delighted with you.'

'For my own part,' said Isabella, 'my wishes are so moderate, that the smallest income in nature would be enough for me. Where people are really attached, poverty itself is wealth: grandeur I detest: I would not settle in London for the universe. A cottage in some retired village would be extasy. There are some charming little villas about Richmond.'

'Richmond!' cried Catherine. – 'You must settle near Fullerton. You must be near us.'

'I am sure I shall be miserable if we do not. If I can but be near *you*, I shall be satisfied. But this is idle talking! I will not allow myself to think of such things, till we have your father's answer. Morland says that by sending it to-night to Salisbury, we may have it to-morrow. – To-morrow? – I know I shall never have courage to open the letter. I know it will be the death of me.'

A reverie succeeded this conviction – and when Isabella spoke again, it was to resolve on the quality of her wedding-gown.

Their conference was put an end to by the anxious young lover himself, who came to breathe his parting sigh before he set off for Wiltshire. Catherine wished to congratulate him, but knew not what to say, and her eloquence was only in her eyes. From them however the eight parts of speech shone out most expressively, and James could combine them with ease. Impatient for the realization of all that he hoped at home, his adieus were not long; and they would have been yet shorter, had he not been frequently detained by the urgent entreaties of his fair one that he would go. Twice was he called almost from the door by her eagerness to have him gone. 'Indeed, Morland, I must drive you away. Consider how far you have to ride. I cannot bear to see you linger so. For Heaven's sake, waste no more time. There, go, go – I insist on it.'

The two friends, with hearts now more united than ever, were inseparable for the day; and in schemes of sisterly happiness the hours flew along. Mrs Thorpe and her son, who were acquainted with every thing, and who seemed only to want Mr Morland's consent, to consider Isabella's engagement as the most famous circumstance imaginable for their family, were allowed to join their counsels, and add their quota of significant looks and mysterious expressions to fill up the measure of curiosity to be raised in the unprivileged younger sisters. To Catherine's simple feelings, this odd sort of reserve seemed neither kindly meant, nor consistently supported; and its unkindness she would hardly have forborn pointing out, had its inconsistency been less their friend; – but Anne and Maria soon set her heart at ease by the sagacity of their 'I know what;' and the evening was spent in a sort of war of wit, a display of family ingenuity; on one side in the mystery of an affected secret, on the other of undefined discovery, all equally acute.

Catherine was with her friend again the next day, endeavouring to support her spirits, and while away the many tedious hours before the delivery of the letters; a needful exertion, for as the time of reasonable expectation drew near, Isabella became more and more desponding, and before the letter arrived, had worked herself into a state of real distress. But when it did come, where could distress be found? 'I have had no difficulty in gaining the consent of my kind parents, and am promised that every thing in their power shall be done to forward my happiness,' were the first three lines, and in one moment all was joyful security. The brightest glow was instantly spread over Isabella's features, all care and anxiety seemed removed, her spirits became almost too high for controul, and she called herself without scruple the happiest of mortals.

Mrs Thorpe, with tears of joy, embraced her daughter, her son, her visitor, and could have embraced half the inhabitants of Bath with satisfaction. Her heart was overflowing with tenderness. It was 'dear John,' and 'dear Catherine' at every word; – 'dear Anne and dear Maria' must immediately be made sharers in their felicity; and two 'dears' at once before the name of Isabella were not more than that beloved child had now well earned. John himself was no skulker in joy. He not only bestowed on Mr Morland the high commendation of being one of the finest fellows in the world, but swore off many sentences in his praise.

The letter, whence sprang all this felicity, was short, containing little more than this assurance of success; and every particular was deferred till James could write again. But for particulars Isabella could well afford to wait. The needful was comprised in Mr Morland's promise; his honour was pledged to make every thing easy; and by what means their income was to be formed, whether landed property were to be resigned, or funded money made over, was a matter in which her disinterested spirit took no concern. She knew enough to feel secure of an honourable and speedy establishment, and her imagination took a rapid flight over its attendant felicities. She saw herself at the end of a few weeks, the gaze and admiration of every new acquaintance at Fullerton, the envy of every valued old friend in Putney, with a carriage at her command, a new name on her tickets, and a brilliant exhibition of hoop rings on her finger.

When the contents of the letter were ascertained, John Thorpe, who had only waited its arrival to begin his journey to London, prepared to set off. 'Well, Miss Morland,' said he, on finding her alone in the parlour, 'I am come to bid you good bye.' Catherine wished him a good journey. Without appearing to hear her, he walked to the window, fidgetted about, hummed a tune, and seemed wholly self-occupied.

'Shall not you be late at Devizes?' said Catherine. He made no answer; but after a minute's silence burst out with, 'A famous good thing this marrying scheme, upon my soul! A clever fancy of Morland's and Belle's. What do you think of it, Miss Morland? *I* say it is no bad notion.'

'I am sure I think it a very good one.'

'Do you? – that's honest, by heavens! I am glad you are no enemy to matrimony however. Did you ever hear the old song, "Going to one wedding brings on another." I say, you will come to Belle's wedding, I hope.'

'Yes; I have promised your sister to be with her, if possible.'

'And then you know' – twisting himself about and forcing a foolish laugh – 'I say, than you know, we may try the truth of this same old song.'

'May we? – but I never sing. Well, I wish you a good journey. I dine with Miss Tilney to-day, and must now be going home.'

'Nay, but there is no such confounded hurry. – Who knows when we may be together again? – Not but that I shall be down again by the end of a fortnight, and a devilish long fortnight it will appear to me.'

'Then why do you stay away so long?' replied Catherine – finding that he waited for an answer.

'That is kind of you, however – kind and good-natured. – I shall not forget it in a hurry. – But you have more good-nature and all that, than any body living I believe. A monstrous deal of good-nature, and it is not only good-nature, but you have so much, so much of every thing; and then you have such – upon my soul I do not know any body like you.'

'Oh! dear, there are a great many people like me. I dare say, only a great deal better. Good morning to you.'

'But I say, Miss Morland, I shall come and pay my respects at Fullerton before it is long, if not disagreeable.'

'Pray do. – My father and mother will be very glad to see you.'

'And I hope – I hope, Miss Morland, *you* will not be sorry to see me.'

'Oh! dear, not at all. There are very few people I am sorry to see. Company is always cheerful.'

'That is just my way of thinking. Give me but a little cheerful company, let me only have the company of the people I love, let me only be where I like and with whom I like, and the devil take the rest, say I. – And I am heartily glad to hear you say the same. But I have a notion, Miss Morland, you and I think pretty much alike upon most matters.'

'Perhaps we may; but it is more than I ever thought of. And as to *most matters*, to say the truth, there are not many that I know my own mind about.'

'By Jove, no more do I. It is not my way to bother my brains with what does not concern me. My notion of things is simple enough. Let me only have the girl I like, say I, with a comfortable house over my head, and what care I for all the rest? Fortune is nothing. I am sure of a good income of my own; and if she had not a penny, why so much the better.'

'Very true. I think like you there. If there is a good fortune on one side, there can be no occasion for any on the other. No matter which has it, so that there is enough. I hate the idea of one great fortune looking out for another. And to marry for money I think the wickedest thing in existence. – Good day. – We shall be very glad to see you at Fullerton, whenever it is convenient.' And away she went. It was not in the power of all his gallantry to detain her longer. With such news to communicate, and such a visit to prepare for, her departure was not to be delayed by any thing in his nature to urge; and she hurried away, leaving him to the undivided consciousness of his own happy address, and her explicit encouragement.

The agitation which she had herself experienced on first learning her brother's engagement, made her expect to raise no inconsiderable emotion in Mr and Mrs Allen, by the communication of the wonderful event. How great was her disappointment! The important affair, which many words of preparation ushered in, had been foreseen by them both ever since her brother's arrival; and all that they felt on the occasion was comprehended in a wish for the young people's happiness, with a remark, on the gentleman's side, in favour of Isabella's beauty, and on the lady's, of her great good luck. It was to Catherine the most surprizing insensibility. The disclosure however of the great secret of James's going to Fullerton the day before, did raise some emotion in Mrs Allen. She could not listen to that with perfect calmness; but repeatedly regretted the necessity of its concealment, wished she could have known his intention, wished she could have seen him before he went, as she should certainly have troubled him with her best regards to his father and mother, and her kind compliments to all the Skinners.

CHAPTER SIXTEEN

CATHERINE'S EXPECTATIONS OF pleasure from her visit in Milsom-street were so very high, that disappointment was inevitable; and accordingly, though she was most politely received by General Tilney, and kindly welcomed by his daughter, though Henry was at home, and no one else of the party, she found, on her return, without spending many hours in the examination of her feelings, that she had gone to her appointment preparing for happiness which it had not afforded. Instead of finding herself improved in acquaintance with Miss Tilney, from the intercourse of the day, she seemed hardly so intimate with her as before; instead of seeing Henry Tilney to greater advantage than ever, in the ease of a family party, he had never said so little, nor been so little agreeable; and, in spite of their father's great civilities to her – in spite of his thanks, invitations, and compliments – it had been a release to get away from him. It puzzled her to account for all this. It could not be General Tilney's fault. That he was perfectly agreeable and good-natured, and altogether a very charming man, did not admit of a doubt, for he was tall and handsome, and Henry's father. *He* could not be accountable for his children's want of spirits, or for her want of enjoyment in his company. The former she hoped at last might have been accidental, and the latter she could only attribute to her own stupidity. Isabella, on hearing the particulars of the visit, gave a different explanation: 'It was all pride, pride, insufferable haughtiness and pride! She had long suspected the family to be very high, and this made it certain. Such insolence of behaviour as Miss Tilney's she had never heard of in her life! Not to the honours of her house with common good-breeding! – To behave to her guest with such superciliousness! – Hardly even to speak to her!'

'But it was not so bad as that, Isabella; there was no superciliousness; she was very civil.'

'Oh! don't defend her! And then the brother, he, who had appeared so attached to you! Good heavens! well, some people's feelings are incomprehensible. And so he hardly looked once at you the whole day?'

'I do not say so; but he did not seem in good spirits.'

'How contemptible! Of all things in the world inconstancy is my aversion. Let me entreat you never to think of him again, my dear Catherine; indeed he is unworthy of you.'

'Unworthy! I do not suppose he ever thinks of me.'

'That is exactly what I say; he never thinks of you. – Such fickleness! Oh! how different to your brother and to mine! I really believe John has the most constant heart.'

'But as for General Tilney, I assure you it would be impossible for any body to behave to me with greater civility and attention; it seemed to be his only care to entertain and make me happy.'

'Oh! I know no harm of him; I do not suspect him of pride. I believe he is a very gentleman-like man. John thinks very well of him, and John's judgment – '

'Well, I shall see how they behave to me this evening; we shall meet them at the rooms.'

'And must I go?'

'Do not you intend it? I thought it was all settled.'

'Nay, since you make such a point of it, I can refuse you nothing. But do not insist upon my being very agreeable, for my heart, you know, will be some forty miles off. And as for dancing, do not mention it I beg; *that* is quite out of the question. Charles Hodges will plague me to death I dare say; but I shall cut him very short. Ten to one but he guesses the reason, and that is exactly what I want to avoid, so I shall insist on his keeping his conjecture to himself.'

Isabella's opinion of the Tilneys did not influence her friend; she was sure there had been no insolence in the manners either of brother or sister; and she did not credit there being any pride in their hearts. The evening rewarded her confidence; she was met by one with the same kindness, and by the other with the same attention as heretofore: Miss Tilney took pains to be near her, and Henry asked her to dance.

Having heard the day before in Milsom-street, that their elder brother, Captain Tilney, was expected almost every hour, she was at no loss for the name of a very fashionable-looking, handsome young man, whom she had never seen before, and who now evidently belonged to their party. She looked at him with great admiration, and even supposed it possible, that some people might think him handsomer than his brother, though, in her eyes, his air was more assuming, and his countenance less prepossessing. His taste and manners were beyond a doubt decidedly inferior; for, within her hearing, he not only protested against every thought of

The three villains in horsemen's greatcoats.

dancing himself, but even laughed openly at Henry for finding it possible. From the latter circumstance it may be presumed, that, whatever might be our heroine's opinion of him, his admiration of her was not of a very dangerous kind; not likely to produce animosities between the brothers, nor persecutions to the lady. *He* cannot be the instigator of the three villains in horsemen's great coats, by whom she will hereafter be forced into a travelling-chaise and four, which will drive off with incredible speed. Catherine, meanwhile, undisturbed by presentiments of such an evil, or of any evil at all, except that of having but a short set to dance down, enjoyed her usual happiness with Henry Tilney, listening with sparkling eyes to every thing he said; and, in finding him irresistible, becoming so herself.

At the end of the first dance, Captain Tilney came towards them again, and, much to Catherine's dissatisfaction, pulled his brother away. They retired whispering together; and, though her delicate sensibility did not take immediate alarm, and lay it down as fact, that Captain Tilney must have heard some malevolent misrepresentation of her, which he now hastened to communicate to his brother, in the hope of separating them for ever, she could not have her partner conveyed from her sight without very uneasy sensations. Her suspense was of full five minutes' duration; and she was beginning to think it a very long quarter of an hour, when they both returned, and an explanation was given, by Henry's requesting to know, if she thought her friend, Miss Thorpe, would have any objection to dancing, as his brother would be most happy to be introduced to her. Catherine, without hesitation, replied, that she was very sure Miss Thorpe did not mean to dance at all. The cruel reply was passed on to the other, and he immediately walked away.

'Your brother will not mind it I know,' said she, 'because I heard him say before, that he hated dancing; but it was very good-natured in him to think of it. I suppose he saw Isabella sitting down and fancied she might wish for a partner, but he is quite mistaken, for she would not dance upon any account in the world.'

Henry smiled, and said, 'How very little trouble it can give you to understand the motive of other people's actions.'

'Why? – What do you mean?'

'With you, it is not, How is such a one likely to be influenced? What is the inducement most likely to act upon such a person's feelings, age, situation, and probable habits of life considered? – but, how should *I* be influenced, what would be *my* inducement in acting so and so?'

'I do not understand you.'

'Then we are on very unequal terms, for I understand you perfectly well.'

'Me? – yes; I cannot speak well enough to be unintelligible.'

'Bravo! – an excellent satire on modern language.'

'But pray tell me what you mean.'

'Shall I indeed? – Do you really desire it? – But you are not aware of the consequences; it will involve you in a very cruel embarrassment, and certainly bring on a disagreement between us.'

'No, no; it shall not do either; I am not afraid.'

'Well then, I only meant that your attributing my brother's wish of dancing with Miss Thorpe to good-nature alone, convinced me of your being superior in good-nature yourself to all the rest of the world.'

Catherine blushed and disclaimed, and the gentleman's predictions were verified. There was something, however, in his words which repaid her for the pain of confusion; and that something occupied her mind so much, that she drew back for some time, forgetting to speak or to listen, and almost forgetting where she was; till, roused by the voice of Isabella, she looked up and saw her with Captain Tilney preparing to give them hands across.

Isabella shrugged her shoulders and smiled, the only explanation of this extraordinary change which could at that time be given; but as it was not quite enough for Catherine's comprehension, she spoke her astonishment in very plain terms to her partner.

'I cannot think how it could happen! Isabella was so determined not to dance.'

'And did Isabella never change her mind before?'

'Oh! but, because – and your brother! – After what you told him from me, how could he think of going to ask her?'

'I cannot take surprize to myself on that head. You bid me be surprized on your friend's account, and therefore I am; but as for my brother, his conduct in the business, I must own, has been no more than I believed him perfectly equal to. The fairness of your friend was an open attraction; her firmness, you know, could only be understood by yourself.'

'You are laughing; but, I assure you, Isabella is very firm in general.'

'It is as much as should be said of any one. To be always firm must be to be often obstinate. When properly to relax is the trial of judgment; and, without reference to my brother, I really think Miss Thorpe has by no means chosen ill in fixing on the present hour.'

The friends were not able to get together for any confidential discourse till all the dancing was over; but then, as they walked about the room arm in arm, Isabella thus explained herself: – 'I do not wonder at your surprize and I am really fatigued to death. He is such a rattle! – Amusing enough, if my mind had been disengaged; but I would have given the world to sit still.'

'Then why did not you?'

'Oh! my dear! it would have looked so particular; and you know how I abhor doing that. I refused him as long as I possibly could, but he would take no denial. You have no idea how he pressed me.

I begged him to excuse me, and get some other partner – but no, not he; after aspiring to my hand, there was nobody else in the room he could bear to think of; and it was not that he wanted merely to dance, he wanted to be with *me*. Oh! such nonsense! – I told him he had taken a very unlikely way to prevail upon me; for, of all things in the world, I hated fine speeches and compliments – and so – and so then I found there would be no peace if I did not stand up. Besides, I thought Mrs Hughes, who introduced him, might take it ill if I did not: and your dear brother, I am sure he would have been miserable if I had sat down the whole evening. I am glad it is over! My spirits are quite jaded with listening to his nonsense: and then, – being such a smart young fellow, I saw every eye was upon us.'

'He is very handsome indeed.'

'Handsome! – Yes, I suppose he may. I dare say people would admire him in general; but he is not at all in my style of beauty. I hate a florid complexion and dark eyes in a man. However, he is very well. Amazingly conceited, I am sure. I took him down several times you know in my way.'

When the young ladies next met, they had a far more interesting subject to discuss. James Morland's second letter was then received, and the kind intentions of his father fully explained. A living, of which Mr Morland was himself patron and incumbent, of about four hundred pounds yearly value, was to be resigned to his son as soon as he should be old enough to take it; no trifling deduction from the family income, no niggardly assignment to one of ten children. An estate of at least equal value, moreover, was assured as his future inheritance.

James expressed himself on the occasion with becoming gratitude; and the necessity of waiting between two and three years before they could marry, being, however unwelcome, no more than he had expected, was born by him without discontent. Catherine, whose expectations had been as unfixed as her ideas of her father's income, and whose judgment was now entirely led by her brother, felt equally well satisfied, and heartily congratulated Isabella on having every thing so pleasantly settled.

'It is very charming indeed,' said Isabella, with a grave face. 'Mr Morland has behaved vastly handsome indeed,' said the gentle Mrs Thorpe, looking anxiously at her daughter. 'I only wish I could do as much. One could not expect more from him you know. If he find he *can* do more by and bye, I dare say he will, for I am sure he must be an excellent good hearted man. Four hundred is but a small income to begin on indeed, but your wishes, my dear Isabella, are so moderate, you do not consider how little you ever want, my dear.'

'It is not on my own account I wish for more; but I cannot bear to be the means of injuring my dear Morland, making him sit down upon an income hardly enough to find one in the common necessaries of life. For myself, it is nothing; I never think of myself.'

'I know you never do, my dear; and you will always find your reward in the affection it makes every body feel for you. There never was a young woman so beloved as you are by every body that knows you; and I dare say when Mr Morland sees you, my dear child – but do not let us distress our dear Catherine by talking of such things. Mr Morland has behaved so very handsome you know. I always heard he was a most excellent man; and you know, my dear, we are not to suppose but what, if you had had a suitable fortune, he would have come down with something more, for I am sure he must be a most liberal-minded man.'

'Nobody can think better of Mr Morland than I do, I am sure. But every body has their failing you know, and every body has a right to do what they like with their own money.' Catherine was hurt by these insinuations. 'I am very sure,' said she, 'that my father has promised to do as much as he can afford.'

Isabella recollected herself. 'As to that, my sweet Catherine, there cannot be a doubt, and you know me well enough to be sure that a much smaller income would satisfy me. It is not the want of more money that makes me just at present a little out of spirits; I hate money; and if our union could take place now upon only fifty pounds a year, I should not have a wish unsatisfied. Ah! my Catherine, you have found me out. There's the sting. The long, long, endless two years and half that are to pass before your brother can hold the living.'

'Yes, yes, my darling Isabella,' said Mrs Thorpe, 'we perfectly see into your heart. You have no disguise. We perfectly understand the present vexation; and every body must love you the better for such a noble honest affection.'

Catherine's uncomfortable feelings began to lessen. She endeavoured to believe that the delay of the marriage was the only source of Isabella's regret; and when she saw her at their next interview as cheerful and amiable as ever, endeavoured to forget that she had for a minute thought otherwise. James soon followed his letter, and was received with the most gratifying kindness.

CHAPTER SEVENTEEN

THE ALLENS HAD NOW entered on the sixth week of their stay in Bath; and whether it should be the last, was for some time a question, to which Catherine listened with a beating heart. To have her acquaintance with the Tilneys end so soon, was an evil which nothing could counterbalance. Her whole happiness seemed at stake, while the affair was in suspense, and every thing secured when it was determined that the lodgings should be taken for another fortnight. What this additional fortnight was to produce to her beyond the pleasure of sometimes seeing Henry Tilney, made but a small part of Catherine's speculation. Once or twice indeed, since James's engagement had taught her what *could* be done, she had got so far as to indulge in a secret 'perhaps', but in general the felicity of being with him for the present bounded her views: the present was now comprised in another three weeks, and her happiness being certain for that period, the rest of her life was at such a distance as to excite but little interest. In the course of the morning which saw this business arranged, she visited Miss Tilney, and poured forth her joyful feelings. It was doomed to be a day of trial. No sooner had she expressed her delight in Mr Allen's lengthened stay, than Miss Tilney told her of her father's having just determined upon quitting Bath by the end of another week. Here was a blow! The past suspense of the morning had been ease and quiet to the present disappointment. Catherine's countenance fell, and in a voice of most sincere concern she echoed Miss Tilney's concluding words, 'By the end of another week!'

'Yes, my father can seldom be prevailed on to give the waters what I think a fair trial. He has been disappointed of some friends' arrival whom he expected to meet here, and as he is now pretty well, is in a hurry to get home.'

'I am very sorry for it,' said Catherine dejectedly, 'if I had know this before – '

'Perhaps,' said Miss Tilney in an embarrassed manner, you would be so good – it would make me very happy if – '

The entrance of her father put a stop to the civility, which Catherine was beginning to hope might introduce a desire of their corresponding. After addressing her with his usual politeness, he turned to his daughter and said, 'Well, Eleanor, may I congratulate you on being successful in your application to your fair friend?'

'I was just beginning to make the request, sir, as you came in.'

'Well proceed by all means. I know how much your heart is in it. My daughter, Miss Morland,' he continued, without leaving his daughter time to speak, 'has been forming a very bold wish. We leave Bath, as she has perhaps told you, on Saturday se'nnight. A letter from my steward tells me that my presence is wanted at home; and being disappointed in my hope of seeing the Marquis of Longtown and General Courteney here, some of my very old friends, there is nothing to detain me longer in Bath. And could we carry our selfish point with you, we should leave it without a single regret. Can you, in short, be prevailed on to quit this scene of public triumph and oblige your friend Eleanor with your company in Gloucestershire? I am almost ashamed to make the request, though its presumption would certainly appear greater to every creature in Bath than yourself. Modesty such as your's – but not for the world would I pain it by open praise. If you can be induced to honour us with a visit, you will make us happy beyond expression. 'Tis true, we can offer you nothing like the gaieties of this lively place; we can tempt you neither by amusement nor splendour, for our mode of living, as you see, is plain and unpretending; yet no endeavours shall be wanting on our side to make Northanger Abbey not wholly disagreeable.'

Northanger Abbey! – These were thrilling words, and wound up Catherine's feelings to the highest point of extasy. Her grateful and gratified heart could hardly restrain its expressions within the language of tolerable calmness. To receive so flattering an invitation! To have her company so warmly solicited! Every thing honourable and soothing, every present enjoyment, and every future hope was contained in it; and her acceptance, with only the saving clause of papa and mamma's approbation was eagerly given. – 'I will write home directly,' said she, 'and if they do not object, as I dare say they will not' –

General Tilney was not less sanguine, having already waited on her excellent friends in Pulteney-street, and obtained their sanction of his wishes. 'Since they can consent to part with you,' said he, 'we may expect philosophy from all the world.'

Miss Tilney was earnest, though gentle, in her secondary civilities, and the affair became in a few minutes as nearly settled, as this necessary reference to Fullerton would allow.

The circumstances of the morning had led Catherine's feelings through the varieties of suspense, security, and disappointment; but they were now safely lodged in perfect bliss; and with spirits elated to rapture, with Henry at her heart, and Northanger Abbey on her lips, she hurried home to write her letter. Mr and Mrs Morland, relying on the discretion of the friends to whom they had already entrusted their daughter, felt no doubt of the propriety of an acquaintance which had been formed under their eye, and sent therefore by return of post their ready consent to her visit in Gloucestershire. This indulgence, though not more than Catherine had hoped for, completed her conviction of being favoured beyond every other human creature, in friends and fortune, circumstance and chance. Every thing seemed to co-operate for her advantage. By the kindness of her first friends the Allens, she had been introduced into scenes, where pleasure of every kind had met her. Her feelings, her preferences had each known the happiness of a return. Wherever she felt attachment, she had been able to create it. The affection of Isabella was to be secured to her in a sister. The Tilneys, they, by whom above all, she desired to be favourably thought of, outstripped even her wishes in the flattering measures by which their intimacy was to be continued. She was to be their chosen visitor, she was to be for weeks under the same roof with the person whose society she mostly prized – and, in addition to all the rest, this roof was to be the roof of an abbey! – Her passion for ancient edifices was next in degree to her passion for Henry Tilney – and castles and abbies made usually the charm of those reveries which his image did not fill. To see and explore either the ramparts and keep of the one, or the cloisters of the other, had been for many weeks a darling wish, though to be more than the visitor of an hour, had seemed too nearly impossible for desire. And yet, this was to happen. With all the chances against her of house, hall, place, park, court, and cottage, Northanger turned up an abbey, and she was to be its inhabitant. Its long, damp passages, its narrow cells and ruined chapel, were to be within her daily reach, and she could not entirely subdue the hope of some traditional legends, some awful memorials of an injured and ill-fated nun.

It was wonderful that her friends should seem so little elated by the possession of such a home; that the consciousness of it should be so meekly born. The power of early habit only could account for it. A distinction to which they had been born gave no pride. Their superiority of abode was no more to them than their superiority of person.

Many were the inquiries she was eager to make of Miss Tilney; but so active were her thoughts, that when these inquiries were answered, she was hardly more assured than before, of Northanger

Abbey having been a richly-endowed convent at the time of the Reformation, of its having fallen into the hands of an ancestor of the Tilneys on its dissolution, of a large portion of the ancient building still making a part of the present dwelling although the rest was decayed, or of its standing low in a valley, sheltered from the north and east by rising woods of oak.

CHAPTER EIGHTEEN

WITH A MIND THUS FULL of happiness, Catherine was hardly aware that two or three days had passed away, without her seeing Isabella for more than a few minutes together. She began first to be sensible of this, and to sigh for her conversation, as she walked along the Pump-room one morning, by Mrs Allen's side, without any thing to say or to hear; and scarcely had she felt a five minutes' longing of friendship, before the object of it appeared, and inviting her to a secret conference, led the way to a seat. 'This is my favourite place,' said she, as they sat down on a bench between the doors, which commanded a tolerable view of every body entering at either, 'it is so out of the way.'

Catherine, observing that Isabella's eyes were continually bent towards one door or the other, as in eager expectation, and remembering how often she had been falsely accused of being arch, thought the present a fine opportunity for being really so; and therefore gaily, said, 'Do not be uneasy, Isabella. James will soon be here.'

'Psha! my dear creature,' she replied, 'do not think me such a simpleton as to be always wanting to confine him to my elbow. It would be hideous to be always together; we should be the jest of the place. And so you are going to Northanger! – I am amazingly glad of it. It is one of the finest places in England, I understand. I shall depend upon a most particular description of it.'

'You shall certainly have the best in my power to give. But who are you looking for? Are your sisters coming?'

'I am not looking for any body. One's eyes must be somewhere, and you know what a foolish trick I have of fixing mine, when my thoughts are an hundred miles off. I am amazingly absent, I believe I am the most absent creature in the world. Tilney says it is always the case with minds of a certain stamp.'

'But I thought, Isabella, you had something in particular to tell me?'

'Oh! yes, and so I have. But here is a proof of what I was saying. My poor head! I had quite forgot it. Well, the thing is this, I have just had a letter from John; – you can guess the contents.'

'No, indeed, I cannot.'

'My sweet love, do not be so abominably affected. What can he write about, but yourself? You know he is over head and ears in love with you.'

'With *me*, dear Isabella!'

'Nay, my sweetest Catherine, this is being quite absurd! Modesty, and all that, is very well in its way, but really a little common honesty is sometimes quite as becoming. I have no idea of being so overstrained! It is fishing for compliments. His attentions were such as a child must have noticed. And it was but half an hour before he left Bath, that you gave him the most positive encouragement. He says so in this letter, says that he as good as made you an offer, and that you received his advances in the kindest way; and now he wants me to urge his suit, and say all manner of pretty things to you. so it is in vain to affect ignorance.'

Catherine, with all the earnestness of truth, expressed her astonishment at such a charge, protesting her innocence of every thought of Mr Thorpe's being in love with her, and the consequent impossibility of her having ever intended to encourage him. 'As to any attentions on his side, I do declare, upon my honour, I never was sensible of them for a moment – except just his asking me to dance the first day of his coming. And as to making me an offer, or any thing like it, there must be some unaccountable mistake. I could not have misunderstood a thing of that kind, you know! – and, as I ever wish to be believed, I solemnly protest that no syllable of such a nature ever passed between us. The last half hour before he went away! – It must be all and completely a mistake – for I did not see him once that whole morning.'

'But *that* you certainly did, for you spent the whole morning in Edgar's Buildings – it was the day your father's consent came – and I am pretty sure that you and John were alone in the parlour, some time before you left the house.'

'Are you? – Well, if you say it, it was so, I dare say – but for the life of me, I cannot recollect it – I *do* remember now being with you, and seeing him as well as the rest – but that we were ever alone for five minutes – However, it is not worth arguing about, for whatever might pass on his side, you must be convinced, by my having no recollection of it, that I never thought, nor expected, nor wished for any thing of the kind from him. I am excessively concerned that he should have any regard for me – but indeed it has been quite unintentional on my side, I never had the smallest idea of it. Pray undeceive him as soon as you can, and tell him I beg his pardon – that is – I do not know what I ought to say – but make him understand what I mean, in the properest way. I would not speak disresepctfully of a brother of your's, Isabella, I am sure; but you know very well that if I could think of one man more than another – *he* is not the person.' Isabella was silent. 'My dear friend, you must not be angry with me. I cannot suppose your brother cares so very much about me. And, you know, we shall still be sisters.'

'Yes, yes,' (with a blush) 'there are more ways than one of our being sisters. – But where am I wandering to? – Well, my dear Catherine, the case seems to be, that you are determined against poor John – is not it so?'

'I certainly cannot return his affection, and as certainly never meant to encourage it.'

'Since that is the case, I am sure I shall not tease you any further. John desired me to speak to you on the subject, and therefore I have. But I confess, as soon as I read his letter, I thought it a very foolish, imprudent business, and not likely to promote the good of either; for what were you to live upon, supposing you came together? You have both of you something to be sure, but it is not a trifle that will support a family now-a-days; and after all that romancers may say, there is no doing without money. I only wonder John could think of it, he could not have received my last.'

'You *do* acquit me then of any thing wrong? – You are convinced that I never meant to deceive your brother, never suspected him of liking me till this moment?'

'Oh! as to that,' answered Isabella laughingly, 'I do not pretend to determine what your thoughts and designs in time past may have been. All that is best known to yourself. A little harmless flirtation or so will occur, and one is often drawn on to give more encouragement than one wishes to stand by. But you may be assured that I am the last person in the world to judge you severely. All those things should be allowed for in youth and high spirits. What one means one day, you know, one may not mean the next. Circumstances change, opinions alter.'

'But my opinion of your brother never did alter; it was always the same. You are decribing what never happened.'

'My dearest Catherine,' continued the other without at all listening to her, 'I would not for all the world be the means of hurrying you into an engagement before you knew what you were about. I do not think any thing would justify me in wishing you to sacrifice all your happiness merely to oblige my brother, because he is my brother, and who perhaps after all, you know, might be just as happy without you, for people seldom know what they would be at, young men especially, they are so amazingly changeable and inconstant. What I say is, why should a brother's happiness be dearer to me than a friend's? You know I carry my notions of friendship pretty high. But, above all things, my dear Catherine, do not be in a hurry. Take my word for it, that if you are in too great a hurry, you will certainly live to repent it. Tilney says, there is nothing people are so often deceived in, as the state of their own affections, and I believe he is very right. Ah! here he comes; never mind, he will not see us, I am sure.'

Catherine, looking up, perceived Captain Tilney, and Isabella, earnestly fixing her eye on him as she spoke, soon caught his notice. He approached immediately, and took the seat to which her movements invited him. His first address made Catherine start. Though spoken low, she could distinguish, 'What! always to be watched, in person or by proxy!'

'Psha, nonsense!' was Isabella's answer in the same half whisper. Why do you put such things into my head? If I could believe it – my spirit, you know is pretty independent.'

'I wish your heart were independent. That would be enough for me.'

'My heart, indeed! What can you have to do with hearts? You men have none of you any hearts.'

'If we have not hearts, we have eyes; and they give us torment enough.'

'Do they? I am sorry for it; I am sorry they find any thing so disagreeable in me. I will look another way. I hope this pleases you, (turning her back on him,) I hope your eyes are not tormented now.'

'Never more so; for the edge of a blooming cheek is still in view – at once too much and too little.'

Catherine heard all this, and quite out of countenance could listen no longer. Amazed that Isabella could endure it, and jealous for her brother, she rose up, and saying she should join Mrs Allen, proposed their walking. But for this Isabella shewed no inclination. She was so amazingly tired, and it was so odious to parade about the Pump-room; and if she moved from her seat she should miss her sisters, she was expecting her sisters every moment; so that her dearest Caherine must excuse her, and must sit quietly down again. But Catherine could be stubborn too; and Mrs Allen just then coming up to propose their returning home, she joined her and walked out of the Pump-room, leaving Isabella still sitting with Captain Tilney. With much uneasiness did she thus leave them. It seemed to her that Captain Tilney was falling in love with Isabella, and Isabella unconsciously encouraging him, unconsciously it must be, for Isabella's attachment to James was a certain and well acknowledged as her engagement. To doubt her truth or good intentions was impossible; and yet, during the whole of their conversation her manner had been odd. She wished Isabella had talked more like her usual self, and not so much about money; and had not looked so well pleased at the sight of Captain Tilney. How strange that she should

'The edge of a blooming cheek is still in view.'

not perceive his admiration! Catherine longed to give her a hint of it, to put her on her guard, and prevent all the pain which her too lively behaviour might otherwise create both for him and her brother.

The compliment of John Thorpe's affection did not make amends for this thoughtlessness in his sister. She was almost as far from believing as from wishing it to be sincere; for she had not forgotten that he could mistake, and his assertion of the offer and of her encouragement convinced her that his mistakes could sometimes be very egregious. In vanity therefore she gained but little, her chief profit was in wonder. That he should think it worth his while to fancy himself in love with her, was a matter of lively astonishment. Isabella talked of his attention; *she* had never been sensible of any; but Isabella had said many things which she hoped had been spoken in haste, and would never be said again; and upon this she was glad to rest altogether for present ease and comfort.

CHAPTER NINETEEN

A FEW DAYS PASSED AWAY, and Catherine, though not allowing herself to suspect her friend, could not help watching her closely. The result of her observations was not agreeable. Isabella seemed an altered creature. When she saw her indeed surrounded only by their immediate friends in Edgar's Buildings or Pulteney-street, her change of manners was so trifling that, had it gone no farther, it might have passed unnoticed. A something of languid indifference, or of that boasted absence of mind which Catherine had never heard of before, would occasionally come across her; but had nothing worse appeared, *that* might only have spread a new grace and inspired a warmer interest. But when Catherine saw her in public, admitting Captain Tilney's attentions as readily as they were offered, and allowing him almost an equal share with James in her notice and smiles, the alteration became too positive to be past over. What could be meant by such unsteady conduct, what her friend could be at, was beyond her comprehension. Isabella could not be aware of the pain she was inflicting; but it was a degree of wilful thoughtlessness which Catherine could not but resent. James was the sufferer. She saw him grave and uneasy; and however careless of his present comfort the woman might be who had given him her heart, to *her* it was always an object. For poor Captain Tilney too she was greatly concerned. Though his looks did not please her, his name was a passport to her good will, and she thought with sincere compassion of his approaching disappointment; for, in spite of what she had believed herself to overhear in the Pump-room, his behaviour was so incompatible with a knowledge of Isabella's engagement, that she could not, upon reflection, imagine him aware of it. He might be jealous of her brother as a rival, but if more had seemed implied, the fault must have been in her misapprehension. She wished, by a gentle remonstrance, to remind Isabella of her situation, and make her aware of this double unkindness; but for remonstrance, either opportunity or comprehension was always against her. If able to suggest a hint, Isabella could never understand it. In this distress, the intended departure of the Tilney family became her chief consolation, their journey into Gloucestershire was to take place within a few days, and Captain Tilney's removal would at least restore peace to every heart but his own. But Captain Tilney had at present no intention of removing; he was not to be of the party to Northanger, he was to continue at Bath. When Catherine knew this, her resolution was directly made. She spoke to Henry Tilney on the subject, regretting his brother's evident partiality for Miss Thorpe, and entreating him to make know her prior engagement.

'My brother does know it,' was Henry's answer.

'Does he? – then why does he stay here?'

He made no reply, and was beginning to talk of something else; but she eagerly continued, 'Why do not you persuade him to go away? The longer he stays, the worse it will be for him at last. Pray advise him for his own sake, and for every body's sake, to leave Bath directly. Absence will in time make him comfortable again; but he can have no hope here, and it is only staying to be miserable.' Henry smiled and said, 'I am sure my brother would not wish to do that.'

'Then you will persuade him to go away?'

'Persuasion is not at command; but pardon me, if I cannot even endeavour to persuade him. I have myself told him that Miss Thorpe is engaged. He knows what he is about, and must be his own master.'

'No, he does not know what he is about,' cried Catherine, 'he does not know the pain he is giving my brother. Not that James has ever told me so, but I am sure he is very uncomfortable.'

'And are you sure it is my brother's doing?'

'Yes, very sure.'

'Is it my brother's attention to Miss Thorpe, or Miss Thorpe's admission of them, that gives the pain?'

'Is not it the same thing?'

'I think Mr Morland would acknowledge a difference. No man is offended by another man's admiration of the woman he loves; it is the woman only who can make it a torment.'

Catherine blushed for her friend, and said, 'Isabella is wrong. But I am sure she cannot mean to torment, for she is very much attached to my brother. She has been in love with him ever since they first met, and while my father's consent was uncertain, she fretted herself almost into a fever. You know she must be attached to him.'

'I understand: she is in love with James, and flirts with Frederick.'

'Oh! no, not flirts. A woman in love with one man cannot flirt with another.'

'It is probable that she will neither love so well, nor flirt so well, as she might do either singly. The gentlemen must each give up a little.'

After a short pause, Catherine resumed with 'Then you do not believe Isabella so very much attached to my brother?'

'I can have no opinion on that subject.'

'But what can your brother mean? If he knows her engagement, what can he mean by his behaviour?'

'You are a very close questioner.'

'Am I? – I only ask what I want to be told.'

'But do you only ask what I can be expected to tell?'

'Yes, I think so; for you must know your brother's heart.'

'My brother's heart, as you term it, on the present occasion, I assure you I can only guess at.'

'Well?'

'Well! – Nay, if it is to be guess-work, let us all guess for ourselves. To be guided by second-hand conjecture is pitiful. The premises are before you. My brother is a lively, and perhaps sometimes a thoughtless young man; he has had about a week's acquaintance with your friend, and he has known her engagement almost as long as he has known her.'

'Well,' said Catherine, after some moments' consideration, '*you* may be able to guess at your brother's intentions from all this; but I am sure I cannot. But is not your father uncomfortable about it? – Does not he want Captain Tilney to go away? – Sure, if your father were to speak to him, he would go.'

'My dear Miss Morland,' said Henry, 'in this amiable solicitude for your brother's comfort, may you not be a little mistaken? Are you not carried a little too far? Would he thank you, either on his own account or Miss Thorpe's, for supposing that her affection, or at least her good-behaviour, is only to be secured by her seeing

'The mess-room will drink Isabella Thorpe for a fortnight.'

nothing of Captain Tilney? Is he safe only in solitude? – or, is her heart constant to him only when unsolicited by any one else? – He cannot think this – and you may be sure that he would not have you think it. I will not say, "Do not be uneasy," because I know that you are so, at this moment; but be as little uneasy as you can. You have no doubt of the mutual attachment of your brother and your friend; depend upon it therefore, that real jealousy never can exist between them; depend upon it that no disagreement between them can be of any duration. Their hearts are open to each other, as neither heart can be to you; they know exactly what is required and what can be borne; and you may be certain, that one will never tease the other beyond what is known to be pleasant.'

Perceiving her still to look doubtful and grave, he added, 'Though Frederick does not leave Bath with us, he will probably remain but a very short time, perhaps only a few days behind us. His leave of absence will soon expire, and he must return to his regiment. – And what will then be their acquaintance? – The mess-room will drink Isabella Thorpe for a fortnight, and she will laugh with your brother over poor Tilney's passion for a month.'

Catherine would contend no longer against comfort. She had resisted its approaches during the whole length of a speech, but it now carried her captive. Henry Tilney must know best. She blamed herself for the extent of her fears, and resolved never to think so seriously on the subject again.

Her resolution was supported by Isabella's behaviour in their parting interview. The Thorpes spent the last evening of Catherine's stay in Pulteney-street, and nothing passed between the lovers to excite her uneasiness, or make her quit them in apprehension. James was in excellent spirits, and Isabella most engagingly placid. Her tenderness for her friend seemed rather the first feeling of her heart; but that at such a moment was allowable; and once she gave her lover a flat contradiction, and once she drew back her hand; but Catherine remembered Henry's instructions, and placed it all to judicious affection. The embraces, tears, and promises of the parting fair ones may be fancied.

CHAPTER TWENTY

Mr and Mrs Allen were sorry to lose their young friend, whose good-humour and cheerfulness had made her a valuable companion, and in the promotion of whose enjoyment their own had been gently increased. Her happiness in going with Miss Tilney, however, prevented their wishing it otherwise; and, as they were to remain only one more week in Bath themselves, her quitting them now would not long be felt. Mr Allen attended her to Milsom-street, where she was to breakfast, and saw her seated with the kindest welcome among her new friends; but so great was her agitation in finding herself as one of the family, and so fearful was she of not doing exactly what was right, and of not being able to preserve their good opinion, that, in the embarrassment of the first five minutes, she could almost have wished to return with him to Pulteney-street.

Miss Tilney's manner and Henry's smile soon did away some of her unpleasant feelings; but still she was far from being at ease; nor could the incessant attentions of the General himself entirely reassure her. Nay, perverse as it seemed, she doubted whether she might not have felt less, had she been less attended to. His anxiety for her comfort – his continual solicitations that she would eat, and his often-expressed fears of her seeing nothing to her taste – though never in her life before had she beheld half such variety on a breakfast-table – made it impossible for her to forget for a moment that she was a visitor. She felt utterly unworthy of such respect, and knew not how to reply to it. Her tranquillity was not improved by the General's impatience for the appearance of his eldest son, nor by the displeasure he expressed at his laziness when Captain Tilney at last came down. She was quite pained by the severity of his father's reproof, which seemed disproportionate to the offence; and much was her concern increased, when she found herself the principal cause of the lecture; and that his tardiness was chiefly resented from being disrespectful to her. This was placing her in a very uncomfortable situation, and she felt great compassion for Captain Tilney, without being able to hope for his good-will.

He listened to his father in silence, and attempted not any defence, which confirmed her in fearing, that the inquietude of his mind, on Isabella's account, might, by keeping him long sleepless, have been the real cause of his rising late. – It was the first time of her being decidedly in his company, and she had hoped to be now able to form her opinion of him; but she scarcely heard his voice while his father remained in the room; and even afterwards, so much were his spirits affected, she could distinguish nothing but these words, in a whisper to Eleanor, 'How glad I shall be when you are all off.'

The bustle of going was not pleasant. – The clock struck ten while the trunks were carrying down, and the General had fixed to be out of Milsom-street by that hour. His great coat, instead of being brought for him to put on directly, was spread out in the curricle in which he was to accompany his son. The middle seat of the chaise was not drawn out, though there were three people to go in it, and his daughter's maid had so crowded it with parcels, that Miss Morland would not have room to sit; and, so much was he influenced by this apprehension when he handed her in, that she had some difficulty in saving her own new writing-desk from being thrown out into the street. – At last, however, the door was closed upon the three females, and they set off at the sober pace in which the handsome, highly-fed four horses of a gentleman usually perform a journey of thirty miles: such was the distance of Northanger from Bath, to be now divided into two equal stages. Catherine's spirits revived as they drove from the door; for with Miss Tilney she felt no restraint; and, with the interest of a road entirely new to her, of an abbey before, and a curricle behind, she caught the last view of Bath without any regret, and met with every mile-stone before she expected it. The tediousness of a two hours' bait at Petty-France, in which there was nothing to be done but to eat without being hungry, and loiter about without any thing to see, next followed – and her admiration of the style in which they travelled, of the fashionable chaise-and-four – postilions handsomely liveried, rising so regularly in their stirrups, and numerous out-riders properly mounted, sunk a little under this consequent inconvenience. Had their party been perfectly agreeable, the delay would have been nothing; but General Tilney, though so charming a man, seemed always a check upon his children's spirits, and scarcely any thing was said but by himself; the observation of which, with his discontent at whatever the inn afforded, and his angry impatience at the waiters, made Catherine grow every moment more in awe of him, and appeared to lengthen the two hours into four. – At last, however, the order of release was given; and much was Catherine then surprized by the General's proposal of her taking his place in his son's curricle for the rest of the journey: – 'the day was fine, and he was anxious for her seeing as much of the country as possible.'

The remembrance of Mr Allen's opinion, respecting young men's open carriages; made her blush at the mention of such a plan, and her first thought was to decline it; but her second was of greater deference for General Tilney's judgment; he could not propose any thing improper for her; and, in the course of a few minutes, she found herself with Henry in the curricle, as happy a being as ever existed. A very short trial convinced her that a curricle was the prettiest equipage in the world; the chaise-and-four wheeled off with some grandeur, to be sure, but it was a heavy and troublesome business, and she could not easily forget its having stopped two hours at Petty-France. Half the time would have been enough for the curricle, and so nimbly were the light horses disposed to move, that, had not the General chosen to have his own carriage lead the way, they could have passed it with ease in half a minute. But the merit of the curricle did not all belong to the horses; – Henry drove so well, – so quietly – without making any disturbance, without parading to her, or swearing at them; so different from the only gentleman-coachman whom it was in her power to compare him with! – And then his hat sat so well, and the innumerable capes of his great coat looked so becomingly important! – To be driven by him, next to being dancing with him, was certainly the greatest happiness in the world. In addition to every other delight, she had now that of listening to her own praise; of being thanked at least, on his sister's account, for her kindness in thus becoming her visitor; of hearing it ranked as real friendship, and described as creating real gratitude. His sister, he said was uncomfortably circumstanced – she had no female companion – and, in the frequent absence of her father, was sometimes without any companion at all.

'But how can that be?' said Catherine, 'are not you with her?'

'Northanger is not more than half my home; I have an establishment at my own house in Woodston, which is nearly twenty miles from my father's, and some of my time is necessarily spent there.'

'How sorry you must be for that!'

'I am always sorry to leave Eleanor.'

'Yes, but besides your affection for her, you must be so fond of the abbey! – After being used to such a home as the abbey, an ordinary parsonage-house must be very disagreeable.'

He smiled, and said, 'You have formed a very favourable idea of the abbey.'

'To be sure I have. Is not it a fine old place, just like what one reads about?'

'And are you prepared to encounter all the horrors that a building such as "what one reads about" may produce? – Have you a stout heart? – Nerves fit for sliding panels and tapestry?'

'Oh! yes – I do not think I should be easily frightened, because there would be so many people in the house – and besides, it has never been uninhabited and left deserted for years, and then the family come back to it unawares, without giving any notice, as generally happens.'

'No, certainly. – We shall not have to explore our way into a hall dimly lighted by the expiring embers of a wood fire – nor be obliged to spread our beds on the floor of a room without windows, doors, or furniture. But you must be aware that when a young lady is (by whatever means) introduced into a dwelling of this kind, she is always lodged apart from the rest of the family. While they snugly repair to their own end of the house, she is formally conducted by Dorothy the ancient housekeeper up a different staircase, and along many gloomy passages, into an apartment never used since some cousin or kin died in it about twenty years before. Can you stand such a ceremony as this? Will not your mind misgive you, when you find yourself in this gloomy chamber – too lofty and extensive for you, with only the feeble rays of a single lamp to take in its size – its walls hung with tapestry exhibiting figures as large as life, and the bed, of dark green stuff or purple velvet, presenting even a funereal appearance. Will not your heart sink within you?'

'Oh! but this will not happen to me, I am sure.'

'How fearfully will you examine the furniture of your apartment! – And what will you discern? – Not tables, toilettes, wardrobes, or drawers, but on one side perhaps the remains of a broken lute, on the other a ponderous chest which no efforts can open, and over the fire-place the portrait of some handsome warrior, whose features will so incomprehensibly strike you, that you will not be able to withdraw your eyes from it. Dorothy meanwhile, no less struck by your appearance, gazes on you in great agitation, and drops a few unintelligible hints. To raise your spirits, moreover, she gives you reason to suppose that the part of the abbey you inhabit is undoubtedly haunted, and informs you that you will not have a single domestic within call. With this parting cordial she curtseys off – you listen to the sound of her receding footsteps as long as the last echo can reach you – and when, with fainting spirits, you attempt to fasten your door, you discover, with increased alarm, that it has no lock.'

'Oh! Mr Tilney, how frightful! – This is just like a book! – But it cannot really happen to me. I am sure your housekeeper is not really Dorothy. – Well, what then?'

'Nothing further to alarm perhaps may occur the first night. After surmounting your *unconquerable* horror of the bed, you will retire to rest, and get a few hours' unquiet slumber. But on the second, or at farthest the *third* night after your arrival, you will probably have a violent storm. Peals of thunder so loud as to seem to shake the edifice to its foundation will roll round the neighbouring mountains – and during the frightful gusts of wind which accompany it, you will probably think you discern (for your lamp is not extinguished) one part of the hanging more violently agitated than the rest. Unable of course to repress your curiosity in so favourable a moment for indulging it, you will instantly arise, and throwing your dressing-gown around you, proceed to examine this mystery. After a very short search, you will discover a diversion in the tapestry so artfully constructed as to defy the minutest inspection, and on opening it, a door will immediately appear – which door being only secured by massy bars and a padlock, you will, after a few efforts, succeed in opening, – and, with your lamp in your hand, will pass through it into a small vaulted room.'

'No, indeed; I should be too much frightened to do any such thing.'

'What! not when Dorothy has given you to understand that there is a secret subterraneous communication between your apartment and the chapel of St Anthony, scarcely two miles off – Could you shrink from so simple an adventure? No, no, you will proceed into this small vaulted room, and through this into several others, without perceiving any thing very remarkable in either. In one perhaps there may be a dagger, in another a few drops of blood, and in a third the remains of some instrument of torture; but there being nothing in all this out of the common way, and your lamp being nearly exhausted, you will return towards your own apartment. In repassing through the small vaulted room, however, your eyes will be attracted towards a lage, old-fashioned cabinet of ebony and gold, which, though narrowly examining the furniture before, you had passed unnoticed. Impelled by an irresistible presentiment, you will eagerly advance to it, unlock its folding doors, and search into every drawer; – but for some time without discovering any thing of importance – perhaps nothing but a considerable hoard of diamonds. At last, however, by touching a secret spring, an inner compartment will open – a roll of paper appears: you seize it – it contains many sheets of manuscript – you hasten with the precious treasure into your own chamber, but scarcely have you been able to decipher "Oh! thou – whomsoever thou mayst be, into whose hands these memoirs of the wretched Matilda may fall" – when your lamp suddenly expires in the socket, and leaves you in total darkness.'

'Oh – no, no – do not say so. Well, go on.'

But Henry was too much amused by the interest he had raised, to be able to carry it farther; he could no longer command solemnity either of subject or voice, and was obliged to entreat her to use her own fancy in the perusal of Matilda's woes. Catherine, recollecting herself, grew ashamed of her eagerness, and began earnestly to assure him that her attention had been fixed without the smallest apprehension of really meeting with what he related. 'Miss Tilney, she was sure, would never put her into such a chamber as he had described! – She was not at all afraid.'

As they drew near the end of their journey, her impatience for a sight of the abbey – for some time suspended by his conversation on subjects very different – returned in full force, and every bend in the road was expected with solemn awe to afford a glimpse of its massy walls of grey stone, rising amidst a grove of ancient oaks, with the last beams of the sun playing in beautiful splendour on its high Gothic windows. But so low did the building stand, that she found herself passing through the great gates of the lodge into the very grounds of Northanger, without having discerned even an antique chimney.

She knew not that she had any right to be surprized, but there was a something in this mode of approach which she certainly had not expected. To pass between lodges of a modern appearance, to find herself with such ease in the very precincts of the abbey, and driven so rapidly along a smooth, level road of fine gravel, without obstacle, alarm or solemnity of any kind, struck her as odd and inconsistent. She was not long at leisure however for such considerations. A sudden scud of rain driving full in her face, made it impossible for her to observe any thing further, and fixed all her thoughts on the welfare of her new straw bonnet: – and she was actually under the Abbey walls, was springing, with Henry's assistance, from the carriage, was beneath the shelter of the old porch, and had even passed on to the hall, where her friend and the General were waiting to welcome her, without feeling one aweful foreboding of future misery to herself, or one moment's suspicion of any past scenes of horror being acted within the solemn edifice. The breeze had not seemed to waft the sighs of the murdered to her; it had wafted nothing worse than a thick mizzling rain; and having given a good shake to her habit, she was ready to be shewn into the common drawing-room, and capable of considering where she was.

An abbey! – yes, it was delightful to be really in an abbey! – but she doubted, as she looked round the room, whether any thing within her observation, would have given her the consciousness. The furniture was in all the profusion and elegance of modern taste. The fire-place, where she had expected the ample width and ponderous carving of former times, was contracted to a Rumford, with slabs of plain though handsome marble, and ornaments over it of the prettiest English china. The windows, to which she looked with peculiar dependence, from having heard the General talk of his preserving them in their Gothic form with reverential care, were yet less what her fancy had portrayed. To be sure, the pointed arch was preserved – the form of them was Gothic – they might be even casements – but every pane was so large, so clear, so light! To an imagination which had hoped for the smallest divisions, and the heaviest stone-work, for painted glass, dirt and cobwebs, the difference was very distressing.

The General, perceiving how her eye was employed, began to talk of the smallness of the room and simplicity of the furniture, where every thing being for daily use, pretended only to comfort, &c.; flattering himself however that there were some apartments in the Abbey not unworthy of her notice – and was proceeding to mention the costly gilding of one in particular, when taking out his watch, he stopped short to pronounce it with surprize within twenty minutes of five! This seemed the word of separation, and Catherine found herself hurried away by Miss Tilney in such a manner as convinced her that the strictest punctuality to the family hours would be expected at Northanger.

Returning through the large and lofty hall, they ascended a broad staircase of shining oak, which, after many flights and many landing-places, brought them upon a long wide gallery. On one side it had a range of doors, and it was lighted on the other by windows which Catherine had only time to discover looked into a quadrangle, before Miss Tilney led the way into a chamber, and scarcely staying to hope she would find it comfortable, left her with an anxious entreaty that she would make as little alteration as possible in her dress.

CHAPTER TWENTY-ONE

A MOMENT'S GLANCE WAS enough to satisfy Catherine that her apartment was very unlike the one which Henry had endeavoured to alarm her by the description of. – It was by no means unreasonably large, and contained neither tapestry nor velvet. – The walls were papered, the floor was carpeted; the windows were neither less perfect, nor more dim than those of the drawing-room below; the furniture, though not of the latest fashion, was handsome and comfortable, and the air of the room altogether far from uncheerful. Her heart instantaneously at ease on this point, she resolved to lose no time in particular examination of any thing, as she greatly dreaded disobliging the General by any delay. Her habit therefore was thrown off with all possible haste, and she was preparing to unpin the linen package, which the chaise-seat had conveyed for her immediate accommodation, when her eye suddenly fell on a large high chest, standing back in a deep recess on one side of the fire-place. The sight of it made her start; and, forgetting everything else, she stood gazing on it in motionless wonder, while these thoughts crossed her: –

'This is strange indeed! I did not expect such a sight as this! – An immense heavy chest! – What can it hold? – Why should it be placed here? – Pushed back too, as if meant to be out of sight! – I will look into it – cost me what it may, I will look into it – and directly too – by day-light. – If I stay till evening my candle may go out.' She advanced and examined it closely: it was of cedar, curiously inlaid with some darker wood, and raised, about a foot from the ground, on a carved stand of the same. The lock was silver, though tarnished from age; at each end were the imperfect remains of handles also of silver, broken perhaps prematurely by some strange violence; and, on the centre of the lid, was a mysterious cypher, in the same metal. Catherine bent over it intently, but without being able to distinguish any thing with certainty. She could not, in whatever direction she took it, believe the last letter to be a T; and yet that it should be any thing else in that house was a circumstance to raise no common degree of astonishment. If not originally their's, by what strange events could it have fallen into the Tilney family?

Her fearful curiosity was every moment growing greater; and seizing, with trembling hands, the hasp of the lock, she resolved at all hazards to satisfy herself at least as to its contents. With difficulty, for something seemed to resist her efforts, she raised the lid a few inches; but at that moment a sudden knocking at the door of the room made her, starting, quit her hold, and the lid closed with alarming violence. This ill-timed intruder was Miss Tilney's maid, sent by her mistress to be of use to Miss Morland; and though Catherine immediately dismissed her, it recalled her to the sense of what she ought to be doing, and forced her, in spite of her anxious desire to penetrate this mystery, to proceed in her dressing without further delay. Her progress was not quick, for her thoughts and her eyes were still bent on the object so well calculated to interest and alarm; and though she dared not waste a moment upon a second attempt, she could not remain many paces from the chest. At length, however, having slipped one arm into her gown, her toilette seemed so nearly finished, that the impatience of her curiosity might safely be indulged. One moment surely might be spared; and, so desperate should the exertion of her strength, that, unless secured by supernatural means, the lid in one moment should be thrown back. With this spirit she sprang forward, and her confidence did not deceive her. Her resolute effort threw back the lid, and gave to her astonished eyes the view of a white cotton counterpane, properly folded, reposing at one end of the chest in undisputed possession!

She was gazing on it with the first blush of surprize, when Miss Tilney, anxious for her friend's being ready, entered the room, and to the rising shame of having harboured for some minutes an absurd expectation, was then added the shame of being caught in so idle a search. 'That is a curious old chest, is not it?' said Miss Tilney, as Catherine hastily closed it and turned away to the glass. 'It is impossible to say how many generations it has been here. How it came to be first put in this room I know not, but I have not had it moved, because I thought it might sometimes be of use in holding hats and bonnets. The worse of it is that its weight makes it difficult to open. In that corner, however, it is at least out of the way.'

Catherine had no leisure for speech, being at once blushing, tying her gown, and forming wise resolutions with the most violent dispatch. Miss Tilney gently hinted for her fear of being late; and in half a minute they ran down stairs together, in an alarm not wholly unfounded, for General Tilney was pacing the drawing-

General Tilney was pacing the drawing-room.

room, his watch in his hand, and having, on the very instant of their entering, pulled the bell with violence, ordered 'Dinner to be on table *directly!*'

Catherine trembled at the emphasis with which he spoke, and sat pale and breathless, in a most humble mood, concerned for his children, and detesting old chests; and the General recovering his politeness as he looked at her, spent the rest of his time in scolding his daughter, for so foolishly hurrying her fair friend, who was absolutely out of breath from haste, when there was not the least occasion for hurry in the world: but Catherine could not at all get over the double distress of having involved her friend in a lecture and been a great simpleton herself, till they were happily seated at the dinner-table, when the General's complacent smiles, and a good appetite of her own, restored her to peace. The dining-parlour was a noble room, suitable in its dimensions to a much larger drawing-room than the one in common use, and fitted up in a style of luxury and expense which was almost lost on the unpractised eye of Catherine, who saw little more than its spaciousness and the number of their attendants. Of the former, she spoke aloud her admiration; and the General, with a very gracious countenance, acknowledged that it was by no means an ill-sized room; and further confessed, that, though as careless on such subjects as most people, he did look upon a tolerably large eating-room as one of the necessaries of life; he supposed, however, 'that she must have been used to much better sized apartments at Mr Allen's?'

'No, indeed,' was Catherine's honest assurance; 'Mr Allen's dining-parlour was not more than half as large:' and she had never seen so large a room as this in her life. The General's good-humour increased. – Why, as he *had* such rooms, he thought it would be simple not to make use of them; but, upon his honour, he believed there might be more comfort in rooms of only half their size. Mr Allen's house, he was sure, must be exactly of the true size for rational happiness.

The evening passed without any further disturbance, and, in the occasional absence of General Tilney, with much positive cheerfulness. It was only in his presence that Catherine felt the smallest fatigue from her journey; and even then, even in moments of languor or restraint, a sense of general happiness preponderated, and she could think of her friends in Bath without one wish of being with them.

The night was stormy; the wind had been rising at intervals the whole afternoon; and by the time the party broke up, it blew and rained violently. Catherine, as she crossed the hall, listened to the tempest with sensations of awe; and, when she heard it rage round a corner of the ancient building and close with sudden fury a distant door, felt for the first time that she was really in an Abbey. – Yes, these were characteristic sounds; – they brought to her recollection a countless variety of dreadful situations and horrid scenes, which such buildings had witnessed, and such storms ushered in; and most heartily did she rejoice in the happier circumstances attending her entrance within walls so solemn! – *She* had nothing to dread from midnight assassins or drunken gallants. Henry had certainly been only in jest in what he had told her that morning. In a house so furnished, and so guarded, she could have nothing to explore or to suffer; and might go to her bedroom as securely as if it had been her own chamber at Fullerton. Thus wisely fortifying her mind, as she proceeded up stairs, she was enabled, especially on perceiving that Miss Tilney slept only two doors from her, to enter her room with a tolerably stout heart; and her spirits were immediately assisted by the cheerful blaze of a wood fire. 'How much better this is,' said she, as she walked to the fender – 'how much better to find a fire ready lit, than to have to wait shivering in the cold till all the family are in bed, as so many poor girls have been obliged to do, and then to have a faithful old servant frightening one by coming in with a faggot! How glad I am that Northanger is what it is! If it had been like some other places, I do not know that, in such a night as this, I could have answered for my courage: – but now, to be sure, there is nothing to alarm one.'

She looked round the room. The window curtains seemed in motion. It could be nothing but the violence of the wind penetrating through the divisions of the shutters; and she stept boldly forward, carelessly humming a tune, to assure herself of its being so, peeped courageously behind each curtain, saw nothing on either low window seat to scare her, and on placing a hand against the shutter, felt the strongest conviction of the wind's force. A glance at the old chest, as she turned away from this examination, was not without its use; she scorned the causeless fears of an idle fancy, and began with a most happy indifference to prepare herself for bed. 'She should take her time; she should not hurry herself; she did not care if she were the last person up in the house. But she would not make up her fire; *that* would seem cowardly, as if she wished for the protection of light after she were in bed.' The fire therefore died away, and Catherine, having spent the best part of an hour in her arrangements, was beginning to think of stepping into bed, when, on giving a parting glance round the room, she was struck by the appearance of a high, old-fashioned black cabinet, which, though in a situation conspicuous enough, had never caught her notice before. Henry's words, his description of the ebony cabinet which was to escape her observation at first, immediately rushed across her; and though there could be nothing really in it, there was something whimsical, it was certainly a very remarkable coincidence! She took her candle and looked closely at the cabinet. It was not absolutely ebony and gold; but it was Japan, black and yellow Japan of the handsomest kind; and as she held her candle, the yellow had very much the effect of gold. The key was in the door, and she had a strange fancy to look into it; not however with the smallest expectation of finding any thing, but it was so very odd, after what Henry had said. In short, she could not sleep till she had examined it. So, placing the candle with great caution on a chair, she seized the key with a very tremulous hand and tried to turn it; but it resisted her utmost strength. Alarmed, but not discouraged, she tried it another way; a bolt flew, and she believed herself successful; but how strangely mysterious! – the door was still immoveable. She paused a moment in breathless wonder. The wind roared down the chimney, the rain beat in torrents against the windows, and every thing seemed to speak the awfulness of her situation. To retire to bed, however, unsatisfied on such a point, would be vain, since sleep must be impossible with the consciousness of a cabinet so mysteriously closed in her immediate vicinity. Again therefore she applied herself to the key, and after moving it in every possible way for some instants with the determined celerity of hope's last effort, the door suddenly yielded to her hand: her heart leaped with exultation at such a victory, and having thrown open each folding door, the second being secured only by bolts of less wonderful construction than the lock, though that her eye could not discern any thing unusual, a double range of small drawers appeared in view, with some larger drawers above and below them; and in the centre, a small door, closed also with a lock and key, secured in all probability a cavity of importance.

Catherine's heart beat quick, but her courage did not fail her. With a cheek flushed by hope, and an eye straining with curiosity, her fingers grasped the handle of a drawer and drew it forth. It was entirely empty. With less alarm and greater eagerness she seized a second, a third, a fourth; each was equally empty. Not one was left unsearched, and in not one was any thing found. Well read in the art of concealing a treasure, the possibility of false lining to the drawers did not escape her, and she felt round each with anxious acuteness in vain. The place in the middle alone remained now unexplored; and though she had 'never from the first had the smallest idea of finding any thing in any part of the cabinet, and was not in the least disappointed at her ill success thus far, it would be foolish not to examine it thoroughly while she was about it.' It was some time however before she could unfasten the door, the same difficulty occurring in the management of this inner lock as of the outer; but at length it did open; and not vain, as hitherto, was her search; her quick eyes directly fell on a roll of paper pushed back into the further part of the cavity, apparently for concealment, and her feelings at that moment were indescribable. Her heart fluttered, her knees trembled, and her cheeks grew pale. She seized, with an unsteady hand, the precious manuscript, for half a glance sufficed to ascertain written characters; and while she acknowledged with awful sensations this striking exemplification of what Henry had foretold, resolved instantly to peruse every line before she attempted to rest.

The dimness of the light her candle emitted made her turn to it with alarm; but there was no danger of its sudden extinction, it had yet some hours to burn; and that she might not have any greater difficulty in distinguishing the writing than what its ancient date might occasion, she hastily snuffed it. Alas! it was snuffed and extinguished in one. A lamp could not have expired with more awful effect. Catherine, for a few moments, was motionless with horror. It was done completely; not a remnant of light in the wick could give hope to the rekindling breath. Darkness impenetrable and immoveable filled the room. A violent gust of wind, rising with sudden fury, added fresh horror to the moment. Catherine trembled from head to foot. In the pause which succeeded, a sound like receding footsteps and the closing of a distant door struck on her affrighted ear. Human nature could support no more. A cold sweat stood on her forehead, the manuscript fell from her hand, and groping her way to the bed, she jumped hastily in, and sought some suspension of agony by creeping far underneath the clothes. To close her eyes in sleep that night, she felt must be entirely out of the question. With a curiosity so justly awakened, and feelings in every way so agitated, repose must be absolutely impossible. The storm too abroad so dreadful! – She had not been used to feel alarm from wind, but now every blast seemed fraught with awful intelligence. The manuscript so wonderfully found, so wonderfully accomplishing the morning's prediction, how was it to be accounted for? – What could it contain? – to whom could it relate? – by what means could it have been so long concealed? – and how singularly strange that it should fall to her lot to discover it! Till she had made herself mistress of its contents, however, she could have neither repose nor comfort; and with the sun's first rays she was determined to peruse it. But many were the tedious hours which must yet intervene. She shuddered, tossed about in her bed, and envied every quiet sleeper. The storm still raged and various were the noises, more terrific even than the wind, which struck at intervals on her startled ear. The very curtain of her bed seemed at one moment in motion, and at another the lock of her door was agitated, as if by the attempt of somebody to enter. Hollow murmurs seemed to creep along the gallery, and more than once her blood was chilled by the sound of distant moans. Hour after hour passed away, and the wearied Catherine had heard three proclaimed by all the clocks in the house, before the tempest subsided, or she unknowingly fell fast asleep.

CHAPTER TWENTY-TWO

THE HOUSEMAID'S FOLDING back her window-shutters at eight o'clock the next day, was the sound which first roused Catherine; and she opened her eyes, wondering that they could ever have been closed, on objects of cheerfulness; her fire was already burning, and a bright morning had succeeded the tempest of the night. Instantaneously with the consciousness of existence, returned her recollection of the manuscript; and springing from the bed in the very moment of the maid's going away, she eagerly collected every scattered sheet which had burst from the roll on its falling to the ground, and flew back to enjoy the luxury of their perusal on her pillow. She now plainly saw that she must not expect a manuscript of equal length with the generality of what she had shuddered over in books, for the roll, seeming to consist entirely of small disjointed sheets, was altogether but of trifling size, and much less than she had supposed it to be at first.

Her greedy eye glanced rapidly over a page. She started at its import. Could it be possible, or did not her senses play her false? – An inventory of linen, in coarse and modern characters, seemed all that was before her! If the evidence of sight might be trusted, she held a washing-bill in her hand. She seized another sheet, and saw the same articles with little variation; a third, a fourth, and a fifth presented nothing new. Shirts, stockings, cravats and waistcoats faced her in each. Two others, penned by the same hand, marked an expenditure scarcely more interesting, in letters, hair-powder, shoe-string and breeches-ball. And the larger sheet, which had inclosed the rest, seemed by its first cramp line, 'To poultice chestnut mare,' – a farrier's bill! Such was the collection papers, (left perhaps, as she could then suppose, by the negligence of a servant in the place whence she had taken them,) which had filled her with expectation and alarm, and robbed her of half her night's rest! She felt humbled to the dust. Could not the adventure of the chest have taught her wisdom? A corner of it catching her eye as she lay, seemed to rise up in judgment against her. Nothing could now be clearer than the absurdity of her recent fancies. To suppose that a manuscript of many generations back could have remained undiscovered in a room such as that, so modern, so habitable! – or that she should be the first to possess the skill of unlocking a cabinet, the key of which was open to all!

How could she have so imposed on herself? – Heaven forbid that Henry Tilney should ever know her folly! And it was in a great measure his own doing, for had not the cabinet appeared so exactly to agree with his description of her adventures, she should never have felt the smallest curiosity about it. This was the only comfort that occurred. Impatient to get rid of those hateful evidences of her folly, those detestable papers then scattered over the bed, she rose directly, and folding them up as nearly as possible in the same shape as before, returned them to the same spot within the cabinet, with a very hearty wish that no untoward accident might ever bring them forward again, to disgrace her even with herself.

Why the locks should have been so difficult to open however, was still something remarkable, for she could now manage them with perfect ease. In this there was surely something mysterious, and she indulged in the flattering suggestion for half a minute, till the possibility of the door's having been at first unlocked, and of being herself its fastener, darted into her head, and cost her another blush.

She got away as soon as she could from a room in which her conduct produced such unpleasant reflections, and found her way with all speed to the breakfast-parlour, as it had been pointed out to her by Miss Tilney the evening before. Henry was alone in it; and his immediate hope of her having been undisturbed by the tempest, with an arch reference to the character of the building they inhabited, was rather distressing. For the world would she not have her weakness suspected; and yet, unequal to an absolute falsehood, was constrained to acknowledge that the wind had kept her awake a little. 'But we have a charming morning after it,' she added, desiring to get rid of the subject; 'and storms and sleeplessness are nothing when they are over. What beautiful hyacinths! – I have just learnt to love a hyacinth.'

'And how might you learn? – By accident or argument?'

'Your sister taught me; I cannot tell how. Mrs Allen used to take pains, year after year, to make me like them; but I never could till I saw them the other day in Milsom-street; I am naturally indifferent about flowers.'

'But now you love a hyacinth. So much the better. You have gained a new source of enjoyment, and it is well to have as many holds upon happiness as possible. Besides, a taste for flowers is always desirable in your sex, as a means of getting you out of doors, and tempting you to more frequent exercise than you would otherwise take. And though the love of a hyacinth may be rather domestic, who can tell, the sentiment once raised, but you may in time come to love a rose?'

'But I do not want any such pursuit to get me out of doors. The pleasure of walking and breathing fresh air is enough for me, and in fine weather I am out more than half my time. – Mamma says, I am never within.'

'At any rate, however, I am pleased that you have learnt to love a hyacinth. The mere habit of learning to love is the thing; and a teachableness of disposition in a young lady is a great blessing. – Has my sister a pleasant mode of instruction?'

Catherine was saved the embarrassment of attempting an answer, by the entrance of the General, whose smiling compliments announced a happy state of mind, but whose gentle hint of sympathetic early rising did not advance her composure.

The elegance of the breakfast set forced itself on Catherine's notice when they were seated at table; and, luckily, it had been the General's choice. He was enchanted by her approbation of his taste, confessed it to be neat and simple, thought it right to encourage the manufacture of his country; and for his part, to his uncritical palate, the tea was as well flavoured from the clay of Staffordshire, as from that of Dresden or Sêve. But this was quite an old set, purchased two years ago. The manufacture was much improved since that time; he had seen some beautiful specimens when last in town, and had he not been perfectly without vanity of that kind, might have been tempted to order a new set. He trusted, however, that an opportunity might ere long occur of selecting one – though not for himself. Catherine was probably the only one of the party who did not understand him.

Shortly after breakfast Henry left them for Woodston, where business required and would keep him two or three days. They all

They all attended in the hall to see him mount.

attended in the hall to see him mount his horse, and immediately on re-entering the breakfast room, Catherine walked to a window in the hope of catching another glimpse of his figure. 'This is a somewhat heavy call upon your brother's fortitude,' observed the General to Eleanor. 'Woodston will make but a sombre appearance today.'

'Is it a pretty place?' asked Catherine.

'What say you, Eleanor? – speak your opinion, for ladies can best tell the taste of ladies in regard to places as well as men. I think it would be acknowledged by the most impartial eye to have many recommendations. The house stands among fine meadows facing the south-east, with an excellent kitchen-garden in the same aspect; the walls surrounding which I built and stocked myself about ten years ago, for the benefit of my son. It is a family living, Miss Morland; and the property in the place being chiefly my own, you may believe I take care that it shall not be a bad one. Did Henry's income depend solely on this living, he would not be ill provided for. Perhaps it may seem odd, that with only two younger children, I should think any profession necessary for him; and certainly there are moments when we could all wish him disengaged from every tie of business. But though I may not exactly make converts of you young ladies, I am sure your father, Miss Morland, would agree with me in thinking it expedient to give every young man some employment. The money is nothing, it is not an object, but employment is the thing. Even Frederick, my eldest son, you see, who will perhaps inherit as considerable a landed property as any private man in the county, has his profession.'

The imposing effect of this last argument was equal to his wishes. The silence of the lady proved it to be unanswerable.

Something had been said the evening before of her being shewn over the house, and he now offered himself as her conductor; and though Catherine had hoped to explore it accompanied only by his daughter, it was a proposal of too much happiness in itself, under any circumstances, not to be gladly accepted; for she had been already eighteen hours in the Abbey, and had seen only a few of its rooms. The netting-box, just leisurely drawn forth, was closed with joyful haste, and she was ready to attend him in a moment. 'And when they had gone over the house, he promised himself moreover the pleasure of accompanying her into the shrubberies and garden.' She curtsied her acquiescence. 'But perhaps it might be more agreeable to her to make those her first object. The weather was at present favourable, and at this time of year the uncertainty was very great of its continuing so. – Which would she prefer? He was equally at her service. – Which did his daughter think would most accord with her fair friend's wishes? – But he thought he could discern. – Yes, he certainly read in Miss Morland's eyes a judicious desire of making use of the present smiling weather. – But when did she judge amiss? – The Abbey would be always safe and dry. – He yielded implicitly, and would fetch his hat and attend them in a moment.' He left the room, and Catherine, with a disappointed, anxious face, began to speak of her unwillingness that he should be taking them out of doors against his own inclination, under a mistaken idea of pleasing her; but she was stopt by Miss Tilney's saying, with a little confusion, 'I believe it will be wisest to take the morning while it is so fine; and do not be uneasy on my father's account, he always walks out at this time of day.'

Catherine did not exactly know how this was to be understood. Why was Miss Tilney embarrassed? Could there be any unwillingness on the General's side to shew her over the Abbey? The proposal was his own. And was not it odd that he should *always* take his walk so early? Neither her father nor Mr Allen did so. It was certainly very provoking. She was all impatience to see the house, and had scarcely any curiosity about the grounds. If Henry had been with them indeed! – but now she should not know what was picturesque when she saw it. Such were her thoughts, but she kept them to herself, and put on her bonnet in patient discontent.

She was struck however, beyond her expectation, by the grandeur of the Abbey, as she saw it for the first time from the lawn. The whole building enclosed a large court; and two sides of the quadrangle, rich in Gothic ornaments, stood forward for admiration. The remainder was shut off by knolls of old trees, or luxuriant plantations, and the steep woody hills rising behind to give it shelter, were beautiful even in the leafless month of March. Catherine had seen nothing to compare with it; and her feelings of delight were so strong, that without waiting for any better authority, she boldly burst forth in wonder and praise. The General listened with assenting gratitude; and it seemed as if his own estimation of Northanger had waited unfixed till that hour.

The kitchen-garden was to be next admired, and he led the way to it across a small portion of the park.

The number of acres contained in this garden was such as Catherine could not listen to without dismay, being more than double the extent of all Mr Allen's, as well as her father's, including church-yard and orchard. The walls seemed countless in number, endless in length; a village of hot-houses seemed to arise among them, and a whole parish to be at work within the inclosure. The General was flattered by her looks of surprize, which told him almost as plainly, as he soon forced her to tell him in words, that she had never seen any gardens at all equal to them before; – and he then modestly owned that, 'without any ambition of that sort himself – without any solicitude about it, – he did believe them to be unrivalled in the kingdom. If he had a hobby-horse, it was *that*. He loved a garden. Though careless enough in most matters of eating, he loved good fruit – or if he did not, his friends and children did. There were great vexations however attending such a garden as his. The utmost care could not always secure the most valuable fruits. The pinery had yielded only one hundred in the last year. Mr Allen, he supposed, must feel these inconveniences as well as himself.

'No, not at all. Mr Allen did not care about the garden, and never went into it.'

With a triumphant smile of self-satisfaction, the General wished he could do the same, for he never entered his, without being vexed in some way or other, by its falling short of his plan.

'How were Mr Allen's succession-houses worked?' describing the nature of his own as they entered them.

'Mr Allen had only one small hot-house, which Mrs Allen had the use of for her plants in winter, and there was a fire in it now and then.'

'He is a happy man!' said the General, with a look of very happy contempt.

Having taken her into every division, and led her under every wall, till she was heartily weary of seeing and wondering, he suffered the girls at last to seize the advantage of an outer door, and then expressing his wish to examine the effect of some recent alterations about the tea-house, proposed it as no unpleasant extension of their walk, if Miss Morland were not tired. 'But where are you going, Eleanor? – Why do you chuse that cold, damp path to it? Miss Morland will get wet. Our best way is across the park.'

'This is so favourite a walk of mine,' said Miss Tilney, 'that I always think it the best and nearest way. But perhaps it may be damp.'

It was a narrow winding path through a thick grove of old Scotch firs; and Catherine, struck by its gloomy aspect, and eager to enter it, could not, even by the General's disapprobation, be kept from stepping forward. He perceived her inclination, and having again urged the plea of health in vain, was too polite to make further opposition. He excused himself however from attending them: – 'The rays of the sun were not too cheerful for him, and he would meet them by another course.' He turned away; and Catherine was shocked to find how much her spirits were relieved by the separation. The shock however being less real than the relief, offered it no injury; and she began to talk with easy gaiety of the delightful melancholy which such a grove inspired.

'I am particularly fond of this spot,' said her companion, with a sigh. 'It was my mother's favourite walk.'

Catherine had never heard Mrs Tilney mentioned in the family before, and the interest excited by this tender remembrance, shewed itself directly in her altered countenance, and in the attentive pause with which she waited for something more.

'I used to walk here so often with her!' added Eleanor; 'though I never loved it then, as I have loved it since. At that time indeed I used to wonder at her choice. But her memory endears it now.'

'And ought it not,' reflected Catherine, 'to endear it to her husband? Yet the General would not enter it.' Miss Tilney continuing silent, she ventured to say, 'Her death must have been a great affliction.'

'A great and increasing one,' replied the other, in a low voice. 'I was only thirteen when it happened; and though I felt my loss perhaps as strongly as one so young could feel it, I did not, I could not know what a loss it was.' She stopped for a moment, and then added, with great firmness, 'I have no sister, you know – and though Henry – though my brothers are very affectionate, and Henry is a great deal here, which I am most thankful for, it is impossible for me not to be often solitary.'

'To be sure you must miss him very much.'

'A mother would have been always present. A mother would have been a constant friend; her influence would have been beyond all other.'

'Was she a very charming woman? Was she handsome? Was there any picture of her in the Abbey? And why had she been so partial to that grove? Was it from dejection of spirits?' – were questions now eagerly poured forth; – the first three received a ready affirmative, the two others were passed by; and Catherine's interest in the deceased Mrs Tilney augmented with every question, whether answered or not. Of her unhappiness in marriage, she felt persuaded. The General certainly had been an unkind husband. He did not love her walk: – could he therefore have loved her? And besides, handsome as he was, there was a something in the turn of his features which spoke his not having behaved well to her.

'Her picture, I suppose,' blushing at the consummate art of her own question, 'hangs in your father's room?'

'No; – it was intended for the drawing-room; but my father was dissatisfied with the painting, and for some time it had no place. Soon after her death I obtained it for my own, and hung it in my bed-chamber – where I shall be happy to shew it you; – it is very like.' – Here was another proof. A portrait – very like – of a departed wife, not valued by the husband! – He must have been dreadfully cruel to her!

Catherine attempted no longer to hide from herself the nature of the feelings which, in spite of all his attentions, he had previously excited; and what had been terror and dislike before, was now absolute aversion. Yes, aversion! His cruelty to such a charming woman made him odious to her. She had often read of such characters; characters, which Mr Allen had been used to call unnatural and overdrawn; but here was proof positive of the contrary.

She had just settled this point, when the end of the path brought them directly upon the General; and in spite of all her virtuous indignation, she found herself again obliged to walk with him, listen to him, and even to smile when he smiled. Being no longer able however to receive pleasure from the surrounding objects, she soon began to walk with lassitude; the General perceived it, and with a concern for her health, which seemed to reproach her for her opinion of him, was most urgent for returning with his daughter to the house. He would follow them in a quarter of an hour. Again they parted – but Eleanor was called back in half a minute to receive a strict charge against taking her friend round the Abbey till his return. This second instance of his anxiety to delay what she so much wished for, struck Catherine as very remarkable.

CHAPTER TWENTY-THREE

AN HOUR PASSED AWAY before the General came in, spent, on the part of his young guest, in no very favourable consideration of his character. – 'This lengthened absence, these solitary rambles, did not speak a mind at ease, or a conscience void of reproach.' – At length he appeared; and, whatever might have been the gloom of his meditations, he could still smile with *them*. Miss Tilney, understanding in part her friend's curiosity to see the house, soon revived the subject; and her father being, contrary to Catherine's expectations, unprovided with any pretence for further delay, beyond that of stopping five mintues to order refreshments to be in the room by their return, was at last ready to escort them.

They set forward; and, with a grandeur of air, a dignified step, which caught the eye, but could not shake the doubts of the well-read Catherine, he led the way across the hall, through the common drawing-room and one useless anti-chamber, into a room magnificent both in size and furniture – the real drawing-room, used only with company of consequence. – It was very noble – very grand – very charming! – was all that Catherine had to say, for her indiscriminating eye scarcely discerned the colour of the satin; and all minuteness of praise, all praise that had much meaning, was supplied by the General, the costliness or elegance of any room's fitting-up could be nothing to her; she cared for no furniture of a more modern date than the fifteenth century. When the General had satisfied his own curiosity, in a close examination of every well-known ornament, they proceeded into the library, an apartment, in its way, of equal magnificence, exhibiting a collection of books, on which an humble man might have looked with pride. – Catherine heard, admired, and wondered with more genuine feeling than before – gathered all that she could from this storehouse of knowledge, by running over the titles of half a shelf, and was ready to proceed. But suites of apartments did not spring up with her wishes. – Large as was the building, she had already visited the greatest part; though, on being told that, with the addition of the kitchen, the six or seven rooms she had now seen surrounded three sides of the court, she could scarcely believe it, or overcome the suspicion of there being many chambers secreted. It was some relief, however, that they were to return to the rooms in common use, by passing through a few of less importance, looking into the court, which, with occasional passages, not wholly unintricate, connected the different sides; – and she was further soothed in her progress, by being told, that she was treading what had once been a cloister, having traces of cells pointed out, and observing several doors, that were neither opened nor explained to her; – by finding herself successively in a billiard-room, and in the General's private apartment, without comprehending their connexion, or being able to turn aright when she left them; and lastly, by passing through a dark little room, owning Henry's authority, and strewed with his litter of books, guns, and great coats.

From the dining-room of which, though already seen, and always to be seen at five o'clock, the General could not forego the pleasure of pacing out the length, for the more certain information of Miss Morland, as to what she neither doubted nor cared for, they proceeded by quick communication to the kitchen – the ancient kitchen of the convent, rich in the massy walls and smoke of former days, and in the stoves and hot closets of the present. The General's improving hand had not loitered here: every modern invention to facilitate the labour of the cooks, had been adopted within this, their spacious theatre; and, when the genius of others had failed, his own had often produced the perfection wanted. His endowments of this spot alone might at any time have placed him high among the benefactors of the convent.

With the walls of the kitchen ended all the antiquity of the Abbey; the fourth side of the quadrangle having, on account of its decaying state, been removed by the General's father, and the present erected in its place. All that was venerable ceased here. The new building was not only new, but declared itself to be so; intended only for offices, and enclosed behind by stable-yards, no uniformity of architecture had been thought necessary. Catherine could have raved at the hand which had swept away what must have been beyond the value of all the rest, for the purposes of mere domestic economy; and would willingly have been spared the mortification of a walk through scenes so fallen, had the General allowed it; but if he had a vanity, it was in the arrangement of his offices; and as he was convinced, that, to a mind like Miss Morland's, a view of the accommodations and comforts, by which the labours of her inferiors were softened, must always be gratifying, he should make no apology for leading her on. They took a slight survey of all; and Catherine was impressed, beyond her expectation, by their multiplicity and their convenience. The purposes for which a few shapeless pantries and a comfortless scullery were deemed sufficient at Fullerton, were here carried on in appropriate divisions, commodious and roomy. The number of servants continually appearing, did not strike her less than the number of their offices. Wherever they went, some pattened girl stopped to curtsey, or some footman in dishabille sneaked off. Yet this was an Abbey! – How inexpressibly different in these domestic arrangements from such as she had read about – from abbeys and castles, in which, though certainly larger than Northanger, all the dirty work of the house was to be done by two pair of female hands at the utmost. How they could get through it all, had often amazed Mrs Allen; and, when Catherine saw what was necessary here, she began to be amazed herself.

They returned to the hall, that the chief stair-case might be ascended, and the beauty of its wood, and ornaments of rich carving might be pointed out: having gained the top, they turned in an opposite direction from the gallery in which her room lay, and shortly entered one on the same plan, but superior in length and breadth. She was here shewn successively into three large bedchambers, with their dressing-rooms, most completely and handsomely fitted up; every thing that money and taste could do, to give comfort and elegance to apartments, had been bestowed on these; and being furnished within the last five years, they were perfect in all that would be geneerally pleasing, and wanting in all that could give pleasure to Catherine. As they were surveying the last, the

General, after slightly naming a few of the distinguished characters, by whom they had at times been honoured, turned with a smiling countenance to Catherine, and ventured to hope, that henceforward some of their earliest tenants might be 'our friends from Fullerton.' She felt the unexpected compliment, and deeply regretted the impossibility of thinking well of a man so kindly disposed towards herself, and so full of civility to all her family.

The gallery was terminated by folding doors, which Miss Tilney advancing, had thrown open, and passed through, and seemed on the point of doing the same by the first door to the left, in another long reach of gallery, when the General, coming forwards called her hastily, and, as Catherine thought, rather angrily back, demanding whither she was going? – And what was there more to be seen? – Had not Miss Morland already seen all that could be worth her notice? – And did she not suppose her friend might be glad of some refreshment after so much exercise? Miss Tilney drew back directly, and the heavy doors were closed upon the mortified Catherine, who, having seen, in a momentary glance beyond them, a narrower passage, more numerous openings, and symptoms of a winding stair-case, believed herself at last within the reach of something worth her notice; and felt, as she unwillingly paced back the gallery, that she would rather be allowed to examine that end of the house, than see all the finery of all the rest. – The General's evident desire of preventing such an examination was an additional stimulant. Something was certainly to be concealed; her fancy, though it had trespassed once or twice, could not mislead her here; and what that something was, a short sentence of Miss Tilney's, as they followed the General at some distance down stairs, seemed to point out: – 'I was going to take you into what was my mother's room – the room in which she died – ' were all the words; but few as they were, they conveyed pages of intelligence to Catherine. It was no wonder that the General should shrink from the sight of such objects as that room must contain; a room in all probability never entered by him since the dreadful scene had passed, which released his suffering wife, and left him to the stings of conscience.

She ventured, when next alone with Eleanor, to express her wish of being permitted to see it, as well as all the rest of that side of the house; and Eleanor promised to attend her there, whenever they should have a convenient hour. Catherine understood her: – the General must be watched from home, before that room could be entered. 'It remains as it was, I suppose?' said she, in a tone of feeling.

'Yes, entirely.'

'And how long ago may it be that your mother died?'

'She has been dead these nine years.' And nine years, Catherine knew was a trifle of time, compared with what generally elapsed after the death of an injured wife, before her room was put to rights.

'You were with her, I suppose, to the last?'

'No,' said Miss Tilney, sighing; 'I was unfortunately from home. – Her illness was sudden and short; and before I arrived it was all over.'

Catherine's blood ran cold with the horrid suggestions which naturally sprang from these words. Could it be possible? – Could Henry's father? – And yet how many were the examples to justify even the blackest suspicions! – And, when she saw him in the evening, while she worked with her friend, slowly pacing the drawing-room for an hour together in silent thoughtfulness, with downcast eyes and contracted brow, she felt secure from all possibility of wronging him. It was the air and attitude of a Montoni! – What could more plainly speak the gloomy workings of a mind not wholly dead to every sense of humanity, in its fearful review of past scenes of guilt? Unhappy man! – And the anxiousness of her spirits directed her eyes towards his figure so repeatedly, as to catch Miss Tilney's notice. 'My father,' she whispered, 'often walks about the room in this way; it is nothing unusual.'

'So much the worse!' thought Catherine; such ill-timed exercise was of a piece with the strange unseasonableness of his morning walks, and boded nothing good.

After an evening, the little variety and seeming length of which made her peculiarly sensible of Henry's importance among them, she was heartily glad to be dismissed; though it was a look from the General not designed for her observation which sent his daughter to the bell. When the butler would have lit his master's candle, however, he was forbidden. The latter was not going to retire. 'I have many pamphlets to finish,' said he to Catherine, 'before I can close my eyes; and perhaps may be poring over the affairs of the nation for hours after you are asleep. Can either of us be more meetly employed? *My* eyes will be blinding for the good of others; and *yours* preparing by rest for future mischief.'

But neither the business alleged, nor the magnificent compliment, could win Catherine from thinking, that some very different object must occasion so serious a delay of proper repose. To be kept up for hours, after the family were in bed, by stupid pamphlets, was not very likely. There must be some deeper cause: something was to be done which could be done only while the household slept; and the probability that Mrs Tilney yet lived, shut up for causes unknown, and receiving from the pitiless hands of her husband a nightly supply of coarse food, was the conclusion which necessarily followed. Shocking as was the idea, it was at least better than a death unfairly hastened, as, in the natural course of things, she must ere long be released. The suddenness of her reputed illness; the absence of her daughter, and probably of her other children, at the time – all favoured the supposition of her imprisonment. – Its origin – jealousy perhaps, or wanton cruelty – was yet to be unravelled.

In revolving these matters, while she undressed, it suddenly struck her as not unlikely, that she might that morning have passed nearly the very spot of this unfortunate woman's confinement – might have been within a few paces of the cell in which she languished out her days; for what part of the Abbey could be more fitted for the purpose than that which yet bore the traces of monastic division? In the high-arched passage, paved with stone, which already she had trodden with peculiar awe, she well remembered the doors of which the General had given no account. To what might not those doors lead? In support of the plausibility of this conjecture, it further occurred to her, that the forbidden gallery, in which lay the apartments of the unfortunate Mrs Tilney, must be, as certainly as her memory could guide her, exactly over this suspected range of cells, and the stair-case by the side of those apartments of which she had caught a transient glimpse, communicating by some secret means with those cells, might well have favoured the barbarous proceedings of her husband. Down that stair-case she had perhaps been conveyed in a state of well-prepared insensibility!

Catherine sometimes started at the boldness of her own surmises, and sometimes hoped or feared that she had gone too far; but they were supported by such appearances as made their dismissal impossible.

The side of the quadrangle, in which she supposed the guilty scene to be acting, being, according to her belief, just opposite her own, it struck her that, if judiciously watched, some rays of light from the General's lamp might glimmer through the lower windows, as he passed to the prison of his wife; and, twice before she stepped into bed, she stole gently from her room to the corresponding window in the gallery, to see if it appeared; but all abroad was dark, and it must yet be too early. The various ascending noises convinced her that the servants must still be up. Till midnight, she supposed it would be in vain to watch; but then, when the clock had struck twelve, and all was quiet, she would, if not quite appalled by darkness, steal out and look once more. The clock struck twelve – and Catherine had been half an hour asleep.

CHAPTER TWENTY-FOUR

THE NEXT DAY AFFORDED no opportunity for the proposed examination of the mysterious apartments. It was Sunday, and the whole time between morning and afternoon service was required by the General in exercise abroad or eating cold meat at home; and great as was Catherine's curiosity, her courage was not equal to a wish of exploring them after dinner, either by the fading light of the sky between six and seven o'clock, or by the yet more partial though stronger illumination of a treacherous lamp. The day was unmarked therefore by any thing to interest her imagination beyond the sight of a very elegant momument to the memory of Mrs Tilney, which immediately fronted the family pew. By that her eye was instantly caught and long retained; and the perusal of the highly-strained epitaph, in which every virtue was ascribed to her by the inconsolable husband, who must have been in some way or other her destroyer, affected her even to tears.

That the General, having erected such a monument, should be able to face it, was not perhaps very strange, and yet that he could sit so boldly collected within its view, maintain so elevated an air, look so fearlessly around, nay, that he should even enter the church, seemed wonderful to Catherine. Not however that many instances of being equally hardened in guilt might not be produced. She could remember dozens who had persevered in every possible vice, going on from crime to crime, murdering whomsoever they chose, without any feeling of humanity or remorse; till a violent death or a religious retirement closed their black career. The erection of the monument itself could not in the smallest degree affect her doubts of Mrs Tilney's actual decease. Were she even to descend into the family vault where her ashes were supposed to slumber, were she to behold the coffin in which they were said to be enclosed – what could it avail in such a case? Catherine had read too much not to be perfectly aware of the ease with which a waxen figure might be introduced, and a suppositious funeral carried on.

The succeeding morning promised something better. The General's early walk, ill-timed as it was in every other view, was favourable here; and when she knew him to be out of the house, she directly proposed to Miss Tilney the accomplishment of her promise. Eleanor was ready to oblige her; and Catherine reminding her as they went of another promise, their first visit in consequence was to the portrait in her bed-chamber. It represented a very lovely woman, with a mild and pensive countenance, justifying, so far, the expectations of its new observer; but they were not in every respect answered, for Catherine had depended upon meeting with features, air, complexion that should be the very counterpart, the very image, if not of Henry's, of Eleanor's; – the only portraits of which she had been in the habit of thinking, bearing always an equal resemblance of mother and child. A face once taken was taken for generations. But here she was obliged to look and consider and study for a likeness. She contemplated it, however, in spite of this drawback, with much emotion; and, but for a yet stronger interest, would have left it unwillingly.

Her agitation as they entered the great gallery was too much for any endeavour of discourse; she could only look at her companion. Eleanor's countenance was dejected, yet sedate; and its composure spoke her enured to all the gloomy objects to which they were advancing. Again she passed through the folding-doors, again her hand was upon the important lock, and Catherine, hardly able to breathe, was turning to close the former with fearful caution, when the figure, the dreaded figure of the General himself at the further end of the gallery, stood before her! The name of 'Eleanor' at the same moment, in his loudest tone, resounded through the building, giving to his daughter the first intimation of his presence, and to Catherine terror upon terror. An attempt at concealment had been her first instinctive movement on perceiving him, yet she could scarcely hope to have escaped his eye; and when her friend, who with an apologizing look darted hastily by her, had joined and disappeared with him, she ran for safety to her own room, and, locking herself in, believed that she should never have courage to go down again. She remained there at least an hour, in the greatest agitation, deeply commiserating the state of her poor friend, and expecting a summons herself from the angry General to attend him in his own apartment. No summons however arrived; and at last, on seeing a carriage drive up to the Abbey, she was emboldened to descend and meet him under the protection of visitors. The breakfast-room was gay with company; and she was named to them by the General, as the friend of his daughter, in a complimentary style, which so well concealed his resentful ire, as to make her feel secure at least of life for the present. And Eleanor, with a command of countenance which did honour to her concern for his character, taking an early occasion of saying to her, 'My father only wanted me to answer a note,' she began to hope that she had either been unseen by the General, or that from some consideration of policy she should be allowed to suppose herself so. Upon this trust she dared still to remain in his presence, after the company left them, and nothing occurred to disturb it.

In the course of this morning's reflections, she came to a resolution of making her next attempt on the forbidden door alone. It would be much better in every respect that Eleanor should know nothing of the matter. To involve her in the danger of a second detection, to court her into an apartment which must wring her heart, could not be the office of a friend. The General's utmost anger could not be to herself what it might be to a daughter; and, besides, she thought the examination itself would be more satisfactory if made without any companion. It would be impossible to explain to Eleanor the suspicions, from which the other had, in all likelihood, been hitherto happily exempt; nor could she therefore, in *her* presence, search for those proofs of the General's cruelty, which however they might yet have escaped discovery, she felt confident of somewhere drawing forth, in the shape of some fragmented journal, continued to the last gasp. Of the way to the apartment she was now perfectly mistress; and as she wished to get it over before Henry's return, who was expected on the morrow, there was no time to be lost. The day was bright, her courage high; at four o'clock, the sun was now two hours above the horizon, and it would be only her retiring to dress half an hour earlier than usual.

It was done, and Catherine found herself alone in the gallery before the clocks had ceased to strike. It was no time for thought; she hurried on, slipped with the least possible noise through the folding doors, and without stopping to look or breathe, rushed forward to the one in question. The lock yielded to her hand, and, luckily, with no sullen sound that could alarm a human being. On tip-toe she entered; the room was before her; but it was some minutes before she could advance another step. She beheld what fixed her to the spot and agitated every feature. – She saw a large, well-proportioned apartment, an handsome dimity bed, arranged as unoccupied with an housemaid's care, a bright Bath stove, mahogany wardrobes and neatly-painted chairs on which the warm beams of a western sun gaily poured through two sash windows! Catherine had expected to have her feelings worked, and worked they were. Astonishment and doubt first seized them; and a shortly succeeding ray of common sense added some bitter emotions of shame. She could not be mistaken as to the room; but how grossly mistaken in every thing else! – in Miss Tilney's meaning, in her own calculation! This apartment, to which she had given a date so ancient, a position so awful, proved to be one end of what the General's father had built. There were two other doors in the chamber, leading probably into dressing-closets; but she had no inclination to open either. Would the veil in which Mrs Tilney had last walked, or the volume in which she had last read, remain to tell what nothing else was allowed to whisper? No: whatever might have been the General's crimes, he had certainly too much wit to let them sue for detection. She was sick of exploring, and desired but to be safe in

'Mr Tilney!' she exclaimed.

her own room, with her own heart only privy to its folly; and she was on the point of retreating as softly as she had entered, when the sound of footsteps, she could hardly tell where, made her pause and tremble. To be found there, even by a servant, would be unpleasant; but by the General, (and he seemed always at hand when least wanted,) much worse! – She listened – the sound had ceased; and resolving not to lose a moment, she passed through and closed the door. At that instant a door underneath was hastily opened; some one seemed with swift steps to ascend the stairs, by the head of which she had to pass before she could gain the gallery. She had no power to move. With a feeling of terror not very definable, she fixed her eyes on the staircase, and in a few moments it gave Henry to her view. 'Mr Tilney!' she exlaimed in a voice of more than common astonishment. He looked astonished too. 'Good God!' she continued, not attending to his address, 'how came you here? – how came you up that staircase?'

'How came I up that staircase!' he replied, greatly surprized. 'Because it is my nearest way from the stable-yard to my own chamber; and why should I not come up it?'

Catherine recollected herself, blushed deeply, and could say no more. He seemed to be looking in her countenance for that explanation which her lips did not afford. She moved on towards the gallery. 'And may I not, in my turn,' said he, as he pushed back the folding doors, ask how *you* came here? – This passage is at least as extraordinary a road from the breakfast-parlour to your apartment, as that staircase can be from the stables to mine.'

'I have been,' said Catherine, looking down, 'to see your mother's room.'

'My mother's room! – Is there any thing extraordinary to be seen there?'

'No, nothing at all. – I thought you did not mean to come back till tomorrow.'

'I did not expect to be able to return sooner, when I went away; but three hours ago I had the pleasure of finding nothing to detain me. – You look pale. – I am afraid I alarmed you by running so fast up those stairs. Perhaps you did not know – you were not aware of their leading from the offices in common use?'

'No, I was not. – You have had a very fine day for your ride.'

'Very; – and does Eleanor leave you to find your way into all the rooms in the house by yourself?'

'Oh! no; she shewed me over the greatest part on Sunday – and we were coming here to these rooms – but only – (dropping her voice) – your father was with us.'

'And that prevented you;' said Henry, earnestly regarding her. – 'Have you looked into all the rooms in that passage?'

'No, I only wanted to see – Is not it very late? I must go and dress.'

'It is only a quarter past four, (shewing his watch) and you are not now in Bath. No theatre, no rooms to prepare for. Half an hour at Northanger must be enough.'

She could not contradict it, and therefore suffered herself to be detained, though her dread of further questions made her, for the first time in their acquaintance, wish to leave him. They walked slowly up the gallery. 'Have you had any letter from Bath since I saw you?'

'No, and I am very much surprized. Isabella promised so faithfully to write directly.'

'Promised so faithfully! – A faithful promise! – That puzzles me. – I have heard of a faithful performance. But a faithful promise – the fidelity of promising! It is a power little worth knowing however, since it can deceive and pain you. My mother's room is very commodious, is it not? Large and cheerful-looking, and the dressing closets so well disposed! It always strikes me as the most comfortable apartment in the house, and I rather wonder that Eleanor should not take it for her own. She sent you to look at it, I suppose?'

'No.'

'It has been your own doing entirely?' – Catherine said nothing. – After a short silence, during which he had closely observed her, he added, 'As there is nothing in the room in itself to raise curiosity, this must have proceeded from a sentiment of respect for my mother's character, as described by Eleanor, which does honour to her memory. The world, I believe, never saw a better woman. But it is not often that virtue can boast an interest such as this. The domestic, unpretending merits of a person never known, do not often create that kind of fervent, venerating tenderness which would prompt a visit like yours. Eleanor, I suppose, has talked of her a great deal?'

'Yes, a great deal. That is – no, not much, but what she did say, was very interesting. Her dying so suddenly,' (slowly and with hesitation it was spoken,) 'and you – none of you being at home – and your father, I thought – perhaps had not been very fond of her.'

'And from these circumstances,' he replied, (his quick eye fixed on her's,) 'you infer perhaps the probability of some negligence – some – (involuntarily she shook her head) – or it may be – of something still less pardonable.' She raised her eyes towards him more fully than she had ever done before. 'My mother's illness,' he continued, 'the seizure which ended in her death *was* sudden. The malady itself, one from which she had often suffered, a bilious fever – its cause therefore constitutional. On the third day, in short as soon as she could be prevailed on, a physician attended her, a very respectable man, and one in whom she had always placed great confidence. Upon his opinion of her danger, two others were called in the next day, and remained in almost constant attendence for four-and-twenty-hours. On the fifth day she died. During the progress of her disorder, Frederick and I (*we* were both at home) saw her repeatedly; and from our own observation can bear witness to her having received every possible attention which could spring from the affection of those about her, or which her situation in life could command. Poor Eleanor *was* absent, and at such a distance as to return only to see her mother in her coffin.'

'But your father,' said Catherine, 'was *he* afflicted?'

'For a time, greatly so. You have erred in supposing him not attached to her. He loved her, I am persuaded, as well as it was possible for him to – We have not all, you know, the same tenderness of disposition – and I will not pretend to say that while she lived, she might not often have had much to bear, but though his temper injured her, his judgment never did. His value of her was sincere, and, if not permanently, he was truly afflicted by her death.'

'I am very glad of it,' said Catherine, 'it would have been very shocking!' –

'If I understand you rightly, you had formed a surmise of such horror as I have hardly words to – Dear Miss Morland, consider the dreadful nature of the suspicions you have entertained. What have you been judging from? Remember the country and the age in which we live. Remember that we are English, that we are Christians. Consult your own understanding, your own sense of the probable, your own observation of what is passing around you – Does our education prepare us for such atrocities? Do our laws connive at them? Could they be perpetrated without being known, in a country like this, where social and literary intercourse is on such a footing; where every man is surrounded by a neighbourhood of voluntary spies, and where roads and newspapers lay every thing open? Dearest Miss Morland, what ideas have you been admitting?'

They had reached the end of the gallery; and with tears of shame she ran off to her own room.

CHAPTER TWENTY-FIVE

THE VISIONS OF ROMANCE were over. Catherine was completely awakened. Henry's address, short as it had been, had more thoroughly opened her eyes to the extravagance of her late fancies than all their several disappointments had done. Most grievously was she humbled. Most bitterly did she cry. It was not only with herself that she was sunk – but with Henry. Her folly, which now seemed even criminal, was all exposed to him, and he must despise her for ever. The liberty which her imagination had dared to take with the character of his father, could he ever forgive it? The absurdity of her curiosity and her fears, could they ever be forgotten? She hated herself more than she could express. He had – she thought he had, once or twice before this fatal morning, shewn something like affection for her. – But now – in short, she made herself as miserable as possible for about half an hour, went down when the clock struck five, with a broken heart, and could scarcely give an intelligible answer to Eleanor's inquiry, if she was well. The formidable Henry soon followed her into the room, and the only difference in his behaviour to her, was that he paid her rather more attention than usual. Catherine had never wanted comfort more, and he looked as if he was aware of it.

The evening wore away with no abatement of this soothing politeness; and her spirits were gradually raised to a modest tranquillity. She did not learn either to forget or defend the past; but she learned to hope that it would never transpire farther, and that it might not cost her Henry's entire regard. Her thoughts being still chiefly fixed on what she had with such causeless terror felt and done, nothing could shortly be clearer, than that it had been all a voluntary, self-created delusion, each trifling circumstance receiving importance from an imagination resolved on alarm, and every thing forced to bend to one purpose by a mind which, before she entered the Abbey, had been craving to be frightened. She remembered with what feeling she had prepared for a knowledge of Northanger. She saw that the infatuation had been created, the mischief settled long before her quitting Bath, and it seemed as if the whole might be traced to the influence of that sort of reading which she had there indulged.

Charming as were all Mrs Radcliffe's works, and charming even as were the works of all her imitators, it was not in them perhaps that human nature, at least in the midland counties of England, was to be looked for. Of the Alps and Pyrenees, with their pine forests and their vices, they might give a faithful delineation; and Italy, Switzerland, and the South of France, might be as fruitful in horrors as they were there represented. Catherine dared not doubt beyond her own country, and even of that, if hard pressed, would have yielded the northern and western extremities. But in the central part of England there was surely some security for the existence even of a wife not beloved, in the laws of the land, and the manners of the age. Murder was not tolerated, servants were not slaves, and neither poison nor sleeping potions to be procured, like rhubarb, from every druggist. Among the Alps and Pyrenees, perhaps, there was no mixed characters. There, such as were not as spotless as an angel, might have the dispositions of a fiend. But in England it was not so; among the English, she believed, in their hearts and habits, there was a general though unequal mixture of good and bad. Upon this conviction, she would not be surprized if even in Henry and Eleanor Tilney, some slight imperfection might hereafter appear; and upon this conviction she need not fear to acknowledge some actual specks in the character of their father, who, though cleared from the grossly injurious suspicions which she must ever blush to have entertained, she did believe, upon serious consideration, to be not perfectly amiable.

Her mind made up on these several points, and her resolution formed, of always judging and acting in future with the greatest good sense, she had nothing to do but to forgive herself and be happier than ever; and the lenient hand of time did much for her by insensible gradations in the course of another day. Henry's astonishing generosity and nobleness of conduct, in never alluding in the slightest way to what had passed, was of the greatest assistance to her; and sooner than she could have supposed it possible in the beginning of her distress, her spirits became absolutely comfortable, and capable, as heretofore, of continual improvement by any thing he said. There were still some subjects indeed, under which she believed they must always tremble – the mention of a chest or a cabinet, for instance – and she did not love the sight of japan in any shape: but even *she* could allow, that an occasional memento of past folly, however painful, might not be without use.

The anxieties of common life began soon to succeed to the alarms of romance. Her desire of hearing from Isabella grew every day greater. She was quite impatient to know how the Bath world went on, and how the Rooms were attended; and especially was she anxious to be assured of Isabella's having matched some fine netting-cotton, on which she had left her intent; and of her continuing on the best terms with James. Her only dependence for information of any kind was on Isabella. James had protested against writing to her till his return to Oxford; and Mrs Allen had given her no hopes of a letter till she had got back to Fullerton. – But Isabella had promised and promised again; and when she promised a thing, she was so scrupulous in performing it! this made it so particularly strange!

For nine successive mornings, Catherine wondered over the repetition of a disappointment, which each morning became more severe; but, on the tenth, when she entered the breakfast-room, her first object was a letter, held out by Henry's willing hand. She thanked him as heartily as if he had written it himself. ' 'Tis only from James, however,' as she looked at the direction. She opened it; it was from Oxford; and to this purpose:-

Dear Catherine,

'Though, God knows, with little inclination for writing, I think it my duty to tell you, that every thing is at an end between Miss Thorpe and me. – I left her and Bath yesterday, never to see either again. I shall not enter into particulars, they would only pain you more. You will soon hear enough from another quarter to know where lies the blame; and I hope will acquit your brother of every thing but the folly of too easily thinking his affection returned. Thank God! I am undeceived in time! But it is a heavy blow! – After my father's consent had been so kindly given – but no more of this. She has made me miserable for ever! Let me soon hear from you, dear Catherine; you are my only friend; your *love I do build upon. I wish your visit at Northanger may be over before Captain Tilney makes his engagement known, or you will be uncomfortably circumstanced. – Poor Thorpe is in town: I dread the sight of him; his honest heart would feel so much. I have written to him and my father. Her duplicity hurts me more than all; till the very last, if I reasoned with her, she declared herself as much attached to me as ever, and laughed at my fears. I am ashamed to think how long I bore with it; but if ever man had reason to believe himself loved, I was that man. I cannot understand even now what she would be at, for there could be no need of my being played off to make her secure of Tilney. We parted at last by mutual consent – happy for me had we never met! I can never expect to know such another woman! Dearest Catherine, beware how you give your heart.*

'Believe me,' &c.

Catherine had not read three lines before her sudden change of countenance, and short exclamations of sorrowing wonder, declared her to be receiving unpleasant news; and Henry, earnestly watching her through the whole letter, saw plainly that it ended no better than it began. He was prevented, however, from even looking his surprize by his father's entrance. They went to breakfast directly; but Catherine could hardly eat any thing. Tears filled her eyes, and even ran down her cheeks as she sat. The letter was one moment in her hand, then in her lap, and then in her pocket; and she looked as if she knew not what she did. The General, between his cocoa and his newspaper, had luckily no leisure for noticing her; but to the other two her distress was equally visible. As soon as she dared leave the table she hurried away to her own room; but the house-maids were busy in it, and she was obliged to come down again. She turned into the drawing-room for privacy, but Henry and Eleanor had likewise retreated thither, and were at that moment deep in consultation about her. She drew back, trying to beg their pardon, but was, with gentle violence, forced to return; and the others withdrew, after Eleanor had affectionately expressed a wish of being of use or comfort to her.

After half an hour's free indulgence of grief and reflection, Catherine felt equal to encountering her friends, but whether she should make her distress known to them was another consideration. Perhaps, if particularly questioned, she might just give an idea – just distantly hint at it – but not more. To expose a friend, such a friend as Isabella had been to her – and then their own brother so closely concerned in it! – She believed she must wave the subject altogether. Henry and Eleanor were by themselves in the breakfast-room; and each, as she entered it, looked at her anxiously. Catherine took her place at the table, and, after a short silence, Eleanor said, 'No bad news from Fullerton, I hope? Mr and Mrs Morland – your brothers and sisters – I hope they are none of them ill?'

'No, I thank you,' (sighing as she spoke,) 'they are all very well. My letter was from my brother at Oxford.'

Nothing further was said for a few minutes; and then speaking through her tears, she added, 'I do not think I shall ever wish for a letter again!'

'I am sorry,' said Henry, closing the book he had just opened; 'if I had suspected the letter of containing any thing unwelcome, I should have given it with very different feelings.'

'It contained something worse than any body could suppose! – Poor James is so unhappy! – You will soon know why.'

'To have so kind-hearted, so affectionate a sister,' replied Henry, warmly, 'must be a comfort to him under any distress.'

'I have one favour to beg,' said Catherine, shortly afterwards, in an agitated manner, 'that, if your brother should be coming here, you will give me notice of it, that I may go away.'

'Our brother! – Frederick!'

'Yes; I am sure I should be very sorry to leave you so soon, but something has happened that would make it very dreadful for me to be in the same house with Captain Tilney.'

Eleanor's work was suspended while she gazed with increasing astonishment; but Henry began to suspect the truth, and something, in which Miss Thorpe's name was included, passed his lips.

'How quick you are!' cried Catherine: 'you have guessed it, I declare! – And yet, when we talked about it in Bath, you little thought of its ending so. Isabella – no wonder *now* I have not heard from her – Isabella has deserted my brother, and is to marry your's! Could you have believed there had been such inconstancy and fickleness, and every thing that is bad in the world?'

'I hope, so far as concerns my brother, you are misinformed. I hope he has not had any material share in bringing on Mr Morland's disappointment. His marrying Miss Thorpe is not probable. I think you must be decieved so far. I am very sorry for Mr Morland – sorry that any one you love should be unhappy, but my surprize would be greater at Frederick's marrying her, than at any other part of the story.'

'It is very true, however; you shall read James's letter yourself. – Stay – there is one part – ' recollecting with a blush the last line.

'Will you take the trouble of reading to us the passages which concern my brother?'

'No, read it yourself,' cried Catherine, whose second thoughts were clearer. 'I do not know what I was thinking of,' (blushing again that she had blushed before,) – 'James only means to give me good advice.'

He gladly received the letter; and, having read it through, with close attention, returned it saying, 'Well, if it is to be so, I can only say that I am sorry for it. Frederick will not be the first man who has chosen a wife with less sense than his family expected. I do not envy his situation, either as a lover or a son.'

Miss Tilney, at Catherine's invitation, now read the letter likewise; and, having expressed also her concern and surprize, began to inquire into Miss Thorpe's connections and fortune.

'Her mother is a very good sort of woman,' was Catherine's answer.

'What was her father?'

'A lawyer, I believe. – They live at Putney.'

'Are they a wealthy family?'

'No, not very. I do not believe Isabella has any fortune at all; but that will not signify in your family. – Your father is so very liberal! He told me the other day, that he only valued money as it allowed him to promote the happiness of his children.' The brother and sister looked at each other. 'But,' said Eleanor, after a short pause, 'would it be to promote his happiness, to enable him to marry such a girl? – She must be an unprincipled one, or she could not have used your brother so. – And how strange an infatuation on Frederick's side! A girl who, before his eyes, is violating an engagement voluntarily entered into with another man! Is not it inconceivable, Henry? Frederick too, who always wore his heart so proudly! who found no woman good enough to be loved!'

'That is the most unpromising circumstance, the strongest presumption against him. When I think of his past declarations, I give him up. – Moreover, I have too good an opinion of Miss Thorpe's prudence, to suppose that she would part with one gentleman before the other was secured. It is all over with Frederick indeed! He is a deceased man – defunct in understanding. Prepare for your sister-in-law, Eleanor, and such a sister-in-law as you must delight in! – Open, candid, artless, guileless, with affections strong but simple, forming no pretensions, and knowing no disguise.'

'Such a sister-in-law, Henry, I should delight in,' said Eleanor, with a smile.

'But perhaps,' observed Catherine, 'though she has behaved so ill by our family, she may behave better by your's. Now she has really got the man she likes, she may be constant.'

'Indeed I am afraid she will,' replied Henry; 'I am afraid she will be very constant, unless a baronet should come in her way; that is Frederick's only chance. – I will get the Bath paper, and look over the arrivals.'

'You think it is all for ambition then? – And, upon my word, there are some things that seem very like it. I cannot forget, that, when she first knew what my father would do for them, she seemed quite disappointed that it was not more. I never was so deceived in any one's character in my life before.'

'Among all the great variety that you have known and studied.'

'My own disappointment and loss in her is very great; but, as for poor James, I suppose he will hardly ever recover it.'

'Your brother is certainly very much to be pitied at present, but we must not, in our concern for his sufferings, undervalue your's.

You feel, I suppose, that, in losing Isabella, you lose half yourself; you feel a void in your heart which nothing else can occupy. Society is becoming irksome; and as for the amusements in which you were wont to share at Bath, the very idea of them without her is abhorrent. You would not, for instance, now go to a ball for the world. You feel that you have no longer any friend to whom you can speak with unreserve, on whose regard you can place dependence; or whose counsel, in any difficulty, you could rely on. You feel all this?'

'No,' said Catherine, after a few moment's reflection, 'I do not – ought I? To say the truth, though I am hurt and grieved, that I cannot still love her, that I am never to hear from her, perhaps never to see her again, I do not feel so very, very much afflicted as one would have thought.'

'You feel, as you always do, what is most to the credit of human nature. – Such feelings ought to be investigated, that they may know themselves.'

Catherine, by some chance or other, found her spirits so very much relieved by this conversation, that she could not regret her being led on, though so unaccountably, to mention the circumstance which had produced it.

CHAPTER TWENTY-SIX

FROM THIS TIME, THE subject was frequently canvassed by the three young people; and Catherine found, with some surprize, that her two young friends were perfectly agreed in considering Isabella's want of consequence and fortune as likely to throw great difficulties in the way of her marrying their brother. Their persuasion that the General would, upon this ground alone, independent of the objection that might be raised against her character, oppose the connexion, turned her feelings moreover with some alarm towards herself. She was as insignificant, and perhaps as portionless as Isabella; and if the heir of the Tilney property had not grandeur and wealth enough in himself, at what point of interest were the demands of his younger brother to rest? The very painful reflections to which this thought led, could only be dispersed by a dependence on the effect of that particular partiality, which, as she was given to understand by his words as well as his actions, she had from the first been so fortunate as to excite in the General; and by a recollection of some most generous and disinterested sentiments on the subject of money, which she had more than once heard him utter, and which tempted her to think his disposition in such matters misunderstood by his children.

They were so fully convinced, however, that their brother would not have the courage to apply in person for his father's consent, and so repeatedly assured her that he had never in his life been less likely to come to Northanger than at the present time, that she suffered her mind to be at ease as to the necessity of any sudden removal of her own. But as it was not to be supposed that Captain Tilney, whenever he made his application, would give his father any just idea of Isabella's conduct, it occurred to her as highly expedient that Henry should lay the whole business before him as it really was, enabling the General by that means to form a cool and impartial opinion, and prepare his objections on a fairer ground than inequality of situations. She proposed it to him accordingly; but he did not catch at the measure so eagerly as she had expected. 'No,' said he, 'my father's hands need not be strengthened, and Frederick's confession of folly need not be forestalled. He must tell his own story.'

'But he will tell only half of it.'

'A quarter would be enough.'

A day or two passed away and brought no tidings of Captain Tilney. His brother and sister knew not what to think. Sometimes it appeared to them as if his silence would be the natural result of the suspected engagement, and at others that it was wholly incompatible with it. The General, meanwhile, though offended every morning by Frederick's remissness in writing, was free from any real anxiety about him; and had no more pressing solicitude than that of making Miss Morland's time at Northanger pass pleasantly. He often expressed his uneasiness on this head, feared the sameness of every day's society and employments would disgust her with the place, wished the Lady Frasers had been in the country, talked every now and then of having a large party to dinner, and once or twice began even to calculate the number of young dancing people in the neighbourhood. But then it was such a dead time of year, no wild-fowl, no game, and the Lady Frasers were not in the country. And it all ended, at last, in his telling Henry one morning, that when he next went to Woodston, they would take him by surprize there some day or other, and eat their mutton with him. Henry was greatly honoured and very happy, and Catherine was quite delighted with the scheme. 'And when do you think, sir, I may look forward to this pleasure? – I must be at Woodston on

Monday to attend the parish meeting, and shall probably be obliged to stay two or three days.'

'Well, well, we will take our chance some one of those days. There is no need to fix. You are not to put yourself at all out of your way. Whatever you may happen to have in the house will be enough. I think I can answer for the young ladies making allowance for a bachelor's table. Let me see; Monday will be a busy day with you, we will not come on Monday; and Tuesday will be a busy one with me. I expect my surveyor from Brockham with his report in the morning; and afterwards I cannot in decency fail attending the club. I really could not face my acquaintance if I staid away now; for, as I am known to be in the country, it would be taken exceedingly amiss; and it is a rule with me, Miss Morland, never to give offence to any of my neighbours, if a small sacrifice of time and attention can prevent it. They are a set of very worthy men. They have half a buck from Northanger twice a year; and I dine with them whenever I can. Tuesday, therefore, we may say is out of the question. But on Wednesday, I think, Henry, you may expect us; and we shall be with you early, that we may have time to look about us. Two hours and three quarters will carry us to Woodston, I suppose; we shall be in the carriage by ten; so, about a quarter before one on Wednesday, you may look for us.'

A ball itself could not have been more welcome to Catherine than this little excursion, so strong was her desire to be acquainted with Woodston; and her heart was still bounding with joy, when Henry, about an hour afterwards, came booted and great coated into the room where she and Eleanor were sitting, and said, 'I am come, young ladies, in a very moralizing strain, to observe that our pleasures in this world are always to be paid for, and that we often purchase them at a great disadvantage, giving ready-monied actual happiness for a draft on the future, that may not be honoured. Witness myself, at this present hour. Because I am to hope for the satisfaction of seeing you at Woodston on Wednesday, which bad weather, or twenty other causes may prevent, I must go away directly, two days before I intended it.'

'Go away!' said Catherine, with a very long face; 'and why?'

'Why! – How can you ask the question? – Because no time is to be lost in frightening my old housekeeper out of her wits, – because I must go and prepare a dinner for you to be sure.'

'Oh! not seriously!'

'Aye, and sadly too – for I had much rather stay.'

'But how can you think of such a thing, after what the General said? when he so particularly desired you not to give yourself any trouble, because *any thing* would do.'

Henry only smiled. 'I am sure it is quite unnecessary upon your sister's account and mine. You must know it to be so; and the General made such a point of your providing nothing extraordinary: – besides, if he had not said half so much as he did, he had always such an excellent dinner at home, that sitting down to a middling one for one day could not signify.'

'I wish I could reason like you, for his sake and my own. Good bye. As to-morrow is Sunday, Eleanor, I shall not return.'

He went; and, it being at any time a much simpler operation to Catherine to doubt her own judgment than Henry's, she was very soon obliged to give him credit for being right, however disagreeable to her his going. But the inexplicability of the General's conduct dwelt much on her thoughts. That he was very particular in his eating, she had, by her own unassisted observation, already discovered; but why he should say one thing so positively, and mean another all the while, was most unaccountable! How were people, at that rate, to be understood? Who but Henry could have been aware of what his father was at?

From Saturday to Wednesday, however, they were now to be without Henry. This was the sad finale of every reflection: – and Captain Tilney's letter would certainly come in his absence; and Wednesday she was very sure would be wet. The past, present, and future, were all equally in gloom. Her brother so unhappy, and her loss in Isabella so great; and Eleanor's spirits always affected by Henry's absence! What was there to interest or amuse her? She was tired of the woods and the shrubberies – always so smooth and so dry; and the Abbey in itself was no more to her now than any other house. The painful remembrance of the folly it had helped to nourish and perfect, was the only emotion which could spring from a consideration of the building. What a revolution in her ideas! she, who had so longed to be in an abbey! Now, there was nothing so charming to her imagination as the unpretending comfort of a well-connected Parsonage, something like Fullerton, but better: Fullerton had its faults, but Woodston probably had none. – If Wednesday should ever come!

It did come, and exactly when it might be reasonably looked for. It came – it was fine – and Catherine trod on air. By ten o'clock, the chaise-and-four conveyed the trio from the Abbey; and, after an agreeable drive of almost twenty miles, they entered Woodston, a large and populous village, in a situation not unpleasant. Catherine was ashamed to say how pretty she thought it, as the General seemed

Henry and the friends of his solitude.

to think an apology necessary for the flatness of the country, and the size of the village; but in her heart she preferred it to any place she had ever been at, and looked with great admiration at every neat house above the rank of a cottage, and at all the little chandler's shops which they passed. At the further end of the village, and tolerably disengaged from the rest of it, stood the Parsonage, a new-built substantial stone house, with its semi-circular sweep and green gates; and, as they drove up to the door, Henry, with the friends of his solitude, a large Newfoundland puppy and two or three terriers, was ready to receive and make much of them.

Catherine's mind was too full, as she entered the house, for her either to observe or to say a great deal; and, till called on by the General for her opinion of it, she had very little idea of the room in which she was sitting. Upon looking round it then, she perceived in a moment that it was the most comfortable room in the world; but she was too guarded to say so, and the coldness of her praise disappointed him.

'We are not calling it a good house,' said he. – 'We are not comparing it with Fullerton and Northanger – We are considering it as a mere Parsonage, small and confined, we allow, but decent perhaps, and habitable; and altogether not inferior to the generality; – or, in other words, I believe there are few country parsonages in England half so good. It may admit of improvement, however. Far be it from me to say otherwise; and any thing in reason – a bow thrown out, perhaps – though, between ourselves, if there is one thing more than another my aversion, it is a patched-on bow.'

Catherine did not hear enough of this speech to understand or be pained by it; and other subjects being studiously brought forward and supported by Henry, at the same time that a tray full of refreshments was introduced by his servant, the General was shortly restored to his complacency, and Catherine to all her usual ease of spirits.

The room in question was of a commodious, well-proportioned size, and handsomely fitted up as a dining parlour; and on their quitting it to walk round the grounds, she was shewn, first into a smaller apartment, belonging peculiarly to the master of the house, and made unusually tidy on the occasion; and afterwards into what was to be the drawing-room, with the appearance of which, though unfurnished, Catherine was delighted enough even to satisfy the General. It was a prettily-shaped room, the windows reaching to the ground, and the view from them pleasant, though only over green meadows; and she expressed her admiration at the moment with all the honest simplicity with which she felt it. 'Oh! why do not you fit up this room, Mr Tilney? What a pity not to have it fitted up! It is the prettiest room I ever saw; – it is the prettiest room in the world!'

'I trust,' said the General, with a most satisfied smile, 'that it will very speedily be furnished: it waits only for a lady's taste!'

'Well, if it was my house, I should never sit any where else. Oh! what a sweet little cottage there is among the trees – apple trees too! It is the prettiest cottage!' –

'You like it – you approve it as an object; – it is enough. Henry, remember that Robinson is spoken to about it. The cottage remains.'

Such a compliment recalled all Catherine's consciousness, and silenced her directly; and, though pointedly applied to by the General for her choice of the prevailing colour of the paper and hangings, nothing like an opinion on the subject could be drawn from her. The influence of fresh objects and fresh air, however, was of great use in dissipating these embarrassing associations; and, having reached the ornamental part of the premises, consisting of a walk round two sides of a meadow, on which Henry's genius had begun to act about half a year ago, she was sufficiently recovered to think it prettier than any pleasure-ground she had ever been in before, though there was not a shrub in it higher than the green bench in the corner.

A saunter into other meadows, and through part of the village, with a visit to the stables to examine some improvements, and a charming game of play with a litter of puppies just able to roll about, brought them to four o'clock, when Catherine scarcely thought it could be three. At four they were to dine, and at six to set off on their return. Never had any day passed so quickly!

She could not but observe that the abundance of the dinner did not seem to create the smallest astonishment in the General; nay, that he was even looking at the side-table for cold meat which was not there. His son and daughter's observations were of a different kind. They had seldom seen him eat so heartily at any table but his own; and never before known him so little disconcerted by the melted butter's being oiled.

At six o'clock, the General having taken his coffee, the carriage again received them; and so gratifying had been the tenor of his conduct throughout the whole visit, so well assured was her mind on the subject of his expectations, that, could she have felt equally confident of the wishes of his son, Catherine would have quitted Woodston with little anxiety as to the How or the When she might return to it.

CHAPTER TWENTY-SEVEN

THE NEXT MORNING BROUGHT the following very unexpected letter from Isabella: –

Bath, April—

My dearest Catherine,

I received your two kind letters with the greatest delight, and have a thousand apologies to make for not answering them sooner. I really am quite ashamed of my idleness; but in this horrid place one can find time for nothing. I have had my pen in my hand to begin a letter to you almost every day since you left Bath, but have always been prevented by some silly trifler or other. Pray write to me soon, and direct to my own home. Thank God! we leave this vile place to-morrow. Since you went away, I have had no pleasure in it – the dust is beyond any thing; and every body one cares for is gone. I believe if I could see you I should not mind the rest, for you are dearer to me than any body can conceive. I am quite uneasy about your dear brother, not having heard from him since he went to Oxford; and am fearful of some misunderstanding. Your kind offices will set all right: – he is the only man I ever did or could love, and I trust you will convince him of it. The spring fashions are partly down; and the hats the most frightful you can imagine. I hope you spend your time pleasantly, but am afraid you never think of me. I will not say all that I could of the family you are with, because I would not be ungenerous, or set you against those you esteem; but it is very difficult to know whom to trust, and young men never know their minds two days together. I rejoice to say, that the young man whom, of all others, I particularly abhor, has left Bath. You will know, from this description, I must mean Captain Tilney, who, as you may remember, was amazingly disposed to follow and tease me, before you went away. Afterwards he got worse, and became quite my shadow. Many girls might have been taken in, for never were such attentions; but I knew the fickle sex too well. He went away to his regiment two days ago, and I trust I shall never be plagued with him again. He is the greatest coxcomb I ever saw, and amazingly disagreeable. The last two days he was always by the side of Charlotte Davis: I pitied his taste, but took no notice of him. The last time we met was in Bath-street, and I turned directly into a shop that he might not speak to me; – I would not even look at him. He went into the Pump-room afterwards; but I would not have followed him for all the world. Such a contrast between him and your brother! – pray send me some news of the latter – I am quite unhappy about him, he seemed so uncomfortable when he went away, with a cold, or something that affected his spirits. I would write to him myself, but have mislaid his direction; and, as I hinted above, am afraid he took something in my conduct amiss. Pray explain every thing to his satisfaction; or, if he still harbours any doubt, a line from himself to me, or a call at Putney when next in town, might set all to rights. I have not been to the Rooms this age, nor to the Play, except going in last night with the Hodges's, for a frolic, at half-price: they teased me into it; and I was determined they should not say I shut myself up because Tilney was gone. We happened to sit by the Mitchells, and they pretended to be quite surprized to see me out. I knew their spite: – at one time they could not be civil to me, but now they are all friendship; but I am not such a fool as to be taken in by them. You know I have a pretty good spirit of my own. Anne

Mitchell had tried to put on a turban like mine, as I wore it the week before at the Concert, but made wretched work of it – it happened to become my odd face I believe, at least Tilney told me so at the time, and said every eye was upon me; but he is the last man whose word I would take. I wear nothing but purple now: I know I look hideous in it, but no matter – it is your dear brother's favourite colour. Lose no time, my dearest, sweetest Catherine, in writing to him and to me,

Who ever am, &c.

Such a strain of shallow artifice could not impose even upon Catherine. Its inconsistencies, contradictions, and falsehood, struck her from the very first. She was ashamed of Isabella, and ashamed of having ever loved her. Her professions of attachment were now as disgusting as her excuses were empty, and her demands impudent. 'Write to James on her behalf! – No, James should never hear Isabella's name mentioned by her again.'

On Henry's arrival from Woodston, she made known to him and Eleanor their brother's safety, congratulating them with sincerity on it, and reading aloud the most material passages of her letter with strong indignation. When she had finished it, – 'So much for Isabella,' she cried, 'and for all our intimacy! She must think me an idiot, or she could not have written so; but perhaps this has served to make her character better known to me than mine is to her. I see what she has been about. She is a vain coquette, and her tricks have not answered. I do not believe she had ever any regard either for James or for me, and I wish I had never known her.'

'It will soon be as if you never had,' said Henry.

'There is but one thing that I cannot understand. I see that she has had designs on Captain Tilney, which have not succeeded; but I do not understand what Captain Tilney has been about all this time. Why should he pay her such attentions as to make her quarrel with my brother, and then fly off himself?'

'I have very little to say for Frederick's motives, such as I believe them to have been. He has his vanities as well as Miss Thorpe, and the chief difference is, that, having a stronger head, they have not yet injured himself. If the *effect* of his behaviour does not justify him with you, we had better not seek after the cause.'

'Then you do not suppose he ever really cared about her?'

'I am persuaded that he never did.'

'And only made believe to do so for mischief's sake?'

Henry bowed his assent.

'Well, then, I must say that I do not like him at all. Though it has turned out so well for us, I do not like him at all. As it happens, there is no great harm done, because I do not think Isabella has any heart to lose. But, suppose he had made her very much in love with him?'

'But we must first suppose Isabella to have had a heart to lose, – consequently to have been a very different creature; and, in that case, she would have met with very different treatment.'

'It is very right that you should stand by your brother.'

'And if you would stand by *your's*, you would not be much distressed by the disappointment of Miss Thorpe. But your mind is warped by an innate principle of general integrity, and therefore not accessible to the cool reasonings of family partiality, or a desire of revenge.'

Catherine was complimented out of further bitterness. Frederick could not be unpardonably guilty, while Henry made himself so agreeable. She resolved on not answering Isabella's letter; and tried to think no more of it.

CHAPTER TWENTY-EIGHT

SOON AFTER THIS, THE General found himself obliged to go to London for a week; and he left Northanger earnestly regretting that any necessity should rob him even for an hour of Miss Morland's company, and anxiously recommending the study of her comfort and amusement to his children as their chief object in his absence. His departure gave Catherine the first experimental conviction that a loss may be sometimes a gain. The happiness with which their time now passed, every employment voluntary, every laugh indulged, every meal a scene of ease and good-humour, walking where they liked and when they liked, their hours, pleasures and fatigues at their own command, made her thoroughly sensible of the restraint which the General's presence had imposed, and most thankfully feel their present release from it. Such ease and such delights made her love the place and the people more and more every day; and had it not been for a dread of its soon becoming expedient to leave the one, and an apprehension of not being equally beloved by the other, she would at each moment of each day have been perfectly happy; but she was now in the fourth week of her visit; before the General came home, the fourth week would be turned, and perhaps it might seem an intrusion if she staid much longer. This was a painful consideration whenever it occurred; and eager to get rid of such a weight on her mind, she very soon resolved to speak to Eleanor about it at once, propose going away, and be guided in her conduct by the manner in which her proposal might be taken.

Aware that if she gave herself much time, she might feel it difficult to bring forward so unpleasant a subject, she took the first opportunity of being suddenly alone with Eleanor, and of Eleanor's being in the middle of a speech about something very different, to start forth her obligation of going away very soon. Eleanor looked and declared herself much concerned. She had 'hoped for the pleasure of her company for a much longer time – had been misled (perhaps by her wishes) to suppose that a much longer visit had been promised – and could not but think that if Mr and Mrs Morland were aware of the pleasure it was to her to have her there, they would be too generous to hasten her return.' – Catherine explained. – 'Oh! as to *that*, papa and mamma were in no hurry at all. As long as she was happy, they would always be satisfied.'

'Then why, might she ask, in such a hurry herself to leave them?'

'Oh! because she had been there so long.'

'Nay, if you can use such a word, I can urge you no farther. If you think it long – '

'Oh! no, I do not indeed. For my own pleasure, I could stay with you as long again.' – And it was directly settled that, till she had, her leaving them was not even to be thought of. In having this cause of uneasiness so pleasantly removed, the force of the earnestness of Eleanor's manner in pressing her to stay, and Henry's gratified look on being told that her stay was determined, were such sweet proofs of her importance with them, as left her only just so much solicitude as the human mind can never do comfortably without. She did – almost always – believe that Henry loved her, and quite always that his father and sister loved and even wished her to belong to them; and believing so far, her doubts and anxieties were merely sportive irritations.

Henry was not able to obey his father's injunction of remaining wholly at Northanger in attendance on the ladies, during his absence in London; the engagements of his curate at Woodston obliging him to leave them on Saturday for a couple of nights. His loss was not now what it had been while the General was at home; it lessened their gaiety, but did not ruin their comfort; and the two girls agreeing in occupation, and improving in intimacy, found themselves so well-sufficient for the time to themselves, that it was eleven o'clock, rather a late hour at the Abbey, before they quitted the supper-room on the day of Henry's departure. They had just reached the head of the stairs, when it seemed, as far as the thickness of the walls would allow them to judge, that a carriage was driving up to the door, and the next moment confirmed the idea by the loud noise of the house-bell. After the first perturbation of surprize had passed away, in a 'Good Heaven! what can be the matter?' it was quickly decided by Eleanor to be her eldest brother, whose arrival was often as sudden, if not quite so unseasonable, and accordingly she hurried down to welcome him.

Catherine walked on to her chamber, making up her mind as well as she could, to a further acquaintance with Captain Tilney, and comforting herself under the unpleasant impression his conduct had given her, and the persuasion of his being by far too fine a gentleman to approve of her, that at least they should not meet under such circumstances as would make their meeting materially painful. She trusted he would never speak of Miss Thorpe; and indeed, as he must by this time be ashamed of the part he had acted, there could be no danger of it; and as long as all mention of Bath scenes were avoided, she thought she could behave to him very civilly. In such considerations time passed away, and it was certainly in his favour that Eleanor should be so glad to see him, and have so much to say, for half an hour was almost gone since his arrival, and Eleanor did not come up.

At that moment Catherine thought she heard her step in the gallery, and listened for its continuance; but all was silent. Scarcely, however, had she convicted her fancy of error, when the noise of something moving close to her door made her start; it seemed as if some one was touching the very doorway – and in another moment a slight motion of the lock proved that some hand must be on it. She trembled a little at the idea of any one's approaching so cautiously; but resolving not to be again overcome by trivial appearances of alarm, or misled by a raised imagination, she stepped quietly forward, and opened the door. Eleanor, and only Eleanor, stood there. Catherine's spirits however were tranquillized but for an instant, for Eleanor's cheeks were pale, and her manner greatly agitated. Though evidently intending to come in, it seemed an effort to enter the room, and a still greater to speak when there. Catherine, supposing some uneasiness on Captain Tilney's account, could only express her concern by silent attention; obliged her to be seated, rubbed her temples with lavender-water, and hung over her with affectionate solicitude. 'My dear Catherine, you must not – you must not indeed – ' were Eleanor's first connected words. 'I am quite well. This kindness distracts me – I cannot bear it – I come to you on such an errand!'

'Errand! – to me!'

'How shall I tell you! – Oh! how shall I tell you!'

A new idea now darted into Catherine's mind, and turning as pale as her friend, she exclaimed, ' 'Tis a messenger from Woodston!'

'You are mistaken, indeed,' returned Eleanor, looking at her most compassionately – 'it is no one from Woodston. It is my father himself.' Her voice faltered, and her eyes were turned to the ground as she mentioned his name. His unlooked-for return was enough in itself to make Catherine's heart sink, and for a few moments she hardly supposed there were any thing worse to be told. She said nothing; and Eleanor endeavouring to collect herself and speak with firmness, but with eyes still cast down, soon went on. 'You are too good, I am sure, to think the worse of me for the part I am obliged to perform. I am indeed a most unwilling messenger. After what has so lately passed, so lately been settled between us – how joyfully, how thankfully on my side! – as to your continuing here as I hoped for many, many weeks longer, how can I tell you that your kindness is not to be accepted – and that the happiness your company has hitherto given us is to be repaid by – but I must not trust myself with words. My dear Catherine, we are to part. My father had recollected an engagement that takes our whole family away on Monday. We are going to Lord Longtown's, near Hereford, for a fortnight. Explanation and apology are equally impossible. I cannot attempt either.'

'My dear Eleanor,' cried Catherine, suppressing her feelings as well as she could, 'do not be so distressed. A second engagement must give way to a first. I am very, very sorry we are to part – so soon, and so suddenly too; but I am not offended, indeed I am not. I can finish my visit here you know at any time; or I hope you will come to me. Can you, when you return from this lord's, come to Fullerton?'

'It will not be in my power, Catherine.'

'Come when you can, then.' –

Eleanor made no answer; and Catherine's thoughts recurring to something more directly interesting, she added, thinking aloud, 'Monday – so soon as Monday; – and you *all* go. Well, I am certain of – I shall be able to take leave however. I need not go till just before you do, you know. Do not be distressed, Eleanor, I can go on Monday very well. My father and mother's having no notice of it is of very little consequence. The General will send a servant with me, I dare say, half the way – and then I shall soon be at Salisbury, and then I am only nine miles from home.'

'Ah, Catherine! were it settled so, it would be somewhat less intolerable, though in such common attentions you would have received but half what you ought. But – how can I tell you? – To-morrow morning is fixed for your leaving us, and not even the hour is left to your choice; the very carriage is ordered, and will be here at seven o'clock, and no servant will be offered you.'

Catherine sat down, breathless and speechless. 'I could hardly believe my senses, when I heard it; – and no displeasure, no resentment that you can feel at this moment, however justly great, can be more than I myself – but I must not talk of what I felt. Oh! that I could suggest any thing in extenuation! Good God! what will your father and mother say! After courting you from the protection of real friends to this – almost double distance from your home, to have you driven out of the house, without the considerations even of decent civility! Dear, dear Catherine, in being the bearer of such a message, I seem guilty myself of all its insult; yet, I trust you will acquit me, for you must have been long enough in this house to see that I am but a nominal mistress of it, that my real power is nothing.'

'Have I offended the General?' said Catherine in a faltering voice.

'Alas! for my feelings as a daughter, all that I know, all that I answer for is, that you can have given him no just cause of offence. He certainly is greatly, very greatly discomposed; I have seldom seen him more so. His temper is not happy, and something has now occurred to ruffle it in an uncommon degree, some disappointment, some vexation, which just at this moment seems important; but which I can hardly suppose you to have any concern in, for how is it possible?'

It was with pain that Catherine could speak at all; and it was only for Eleanor's sake that she attempted it. 'I am sure,' said she, 'I am very sorry if I have offended him. It was the last thing I would willingly have done. But do not be unhappy, Eleanor. An engagement you know must be kept. I am only sorry it was not recollected sooner, that I might have written home. But it is of very little consequence.'

'I hope, I earnestly hope that to your real safety it will be of none; but to every thing else it is of the greatest consequence; to comfort, appearance, propriety, to your family, to the world. Were your friends, the Allens, still in Bath, you might go to them with comparative ease; a few hours would take you there; but a journey of seventy miles, to be taken post by you, at your age, alone, unattended!'

'Oh, the journey is nothing. Do not think about that. And if we are to part, a few hours sooner or later, you know, makes no difference. I can be ready by seven. Let me be called in time.'

Eleanor saw that she wished to be alone; and believing it better for each that they should avoid any further conversation, now left her with 'I shall see you in the morning.'

Catherine's swelling heart needed relief. In Eleanor's presence friendship and pride had equally restrained her tears, but no sooner was she gone than they burst forth in torrents. Turned from the house, and in such a way! – Without any reason that could justify, any apology that could atone for the abruptness, the rudeness, nay, the insolence of it. Henry at a distance – not able even to bid him farewell. Every hope, every expectation from him suspended, at least, and who could say how long? – Who could say when they might meet again? – And all this by such a man as General Tilney, so polite, so well-bred, and heretofore so particularly fond of her! It was as incomprehensible as it was mortifying and grievous. From what it could arise, and where it would end, were considerations of equal perplexity and alarm. The manner in which it was done so grossly uncivil; hurrying her away without any reference to her own convenience, or allowing her even the appearance of choice as to the time or mode of her travelling; of two days, the earliest fixed on, and of that almost the earliest hour, as if resolved to have her gone before he was stirring in the morning, that he might not be obliged even to see her. What could all this mean but an intentional affront? By some means or other she must have had the misfortune to offend him. Eleanor had wished to spare her from so painful a notion, but Catherine could not believe it possible that any injury or any misfortune could provoke such ill-will against a person not connected, or, at least, not supposed to be connected with it.

Heavily past the night. Sleep, or repose that deserved the name of sleep, was out of the question. That room, in which her disturbed imagination had tormented her on her first arrival, was again the scene of agitated spirits and unquiet slumbers. Yet how different now the source of her inquietude from what it had been then – how mournfully superior in reality and substance! Her anxiety had foundation in fact, her fears in probability; and with a mind so occupied in the contemplation of actual and natural evil, the solitude of her situation, the darkness of her chamber, the antiquity of the building were felt and considered without the smallest emotion; and though the wind was high, and often produced strange and sudden noises throughout the house, she heard it all as she lay awake, hour after hour, without curiosity or terror.

Soon after six Eleanor entered her room, eager to show attention or give assistance where it was possible, but very little remained to be done. Catherine had not loitered; she was almost dressed, and her packing almost finished. The possibility of some conciliatory message from the General occurred to her as his daughter appeared. What so natural, as that anger should pass away and repentance succeed it? and she only wanted to know how far, after what had passed, an apology might properly be received by her. But the knowledge would have been useless here, it was not called for; neither clemency nor dignity was put to the trial – Eleanor brought no message. Very little passed between them on meeting; each found her greatest safety in silence, and few and trivial were the sentences exchanged while they remained up stairs, Catherine in busy agitation completing her dress, and Eleanor with more good-will than experience intent upon filling the trunk. When every thing was done they left the room, Catherine lingering only half a minute behind her friend to throw a parting glance on every well-known cherished object, and went down to the breakfast-parlour, where breakfast was prepared. She tried to eat, as well to save herself from the pain of being urged, as to make her friend comfortable; but she had no appetite, and could not swallow many mouthfuls. The contrast between this and her last breakfast in that room, gave her fresh misery, and strengthened her distaste for every thing before her. It was not four-and-twenty hours ago since they had met there to the same repast, but in circumstances how different! With what cheerful ease, what happy, though false security, had she then looked around her, enjoying every thing present, and fearing little in future, beyond Henry's going to Woodston for a day! Happy, happy breakfast! for Henry had been there, Henry had sat by her and helped her. These reflections were long indulged undisturbed by any address from her companion, who sat as deep in thought as herself; and the appearance of the carriage was the first thing to startle and recall them to the present moment. Catherine's colour rose at the sight of it; and the indignity with which she was treated striking at that instant on her mind with peculiar force, made her for a short time sensible only of resentment. Eleanor seemed now impelled into resolution and speech.

'You *must* write to me, Catherine,' she cried, 'you *must* let me hear from you as soon as possible. Till I know you to be safe at home, I shall not have an hour's comfort. For *one* letter, at all risks, all hazards, I must entreat. Let me have the satisfaction of knowing that you are safe at Fullerton, and have found your family well, and then, till I can ask for your correspondence as I ought to do, I will not expect more. Direct to me at Lord Longtown's, and, I must ask it, under cover to Alice.'

'No, Eleanor, if you are not allowed to receive a letter from me,

I am sure I had better not write. There can be no doubt of my getting home safe.'

Eleanor only replied, 'I cannot wonder at your feelings. I will not importune you. I will trust to your own kindness of heart when I am at a distance from you.' But this, with the look of sorrow accompanying it, was enough to melt Catherine's pride in a moment, and she instantly said, 'Oh, Eleanor, I *will* write to you indeed.'

There was yet another point which Miss Tilney was anxious to settle, though somewhat embarrassed in speaking of. It had occurred to her, that after so long an absence from home, Catherine might not be provided with money enough for the expenses of her journey, and, upon suggesting it to her with most affectionate offers of accommodation, it proved to be exactly the case. Catherine had never thought on the subject till that moment; but, upon examining her purse, was convinced that but for this kindness of her friend, she might have been turned from the house without even the means of getting home; and the distress in which she must have been thereby involved filling the minds of both, scarcely another word was said by either during the time of their remaining together. Short, however, was that time. The carriage was soon announced to be ready; and Catherine, instantly rising, a long and affectionate embrace supplied the place of language in bidding each other adieu; and, as they entered the hall, unable to leave the house without some mention of one whose name had not yet been spoken by either, she paused a moment, and with quivering lips just made it intelligible that she left 'her kind remembrance for her absent friend.' But with this approach to his name ended all possibility of restraining her feelings; and, hiding her face as well as she could with her handkerchief, she darted across the hall, jumped into the chaise, and in a moment was driven from the door.

CHAPTER TWENTY-NINE

Catherine was too wretched to be fearful. The journey in itself had no terrors for her; and she began it without either dreading its length, or feeling its solitariness. Leaning back in one corner of the carriage, in a violent burst of tears, she was conveyed some miles beyond the walls of the Abbey before she raised her head; and the highest point of ground within the park was almost closed from her view before she was capable of turning her eyes towards it. Unfortunately, the road she now travelled was the same which only ten days ago she had so happily passed along in going to and from Woodston; and, for fourteen miles, every bitter feeling was rendered more severe by the review of objects on which she had first looked under impressions so different. Every mile, as it brought her nearer Woodston, added to her sufferings, and when within the distance of five, she passed the turning which led to it, and thought of Henry, so near, yet so unconscious, her grief and agitation were excessive.

The day which she had spent at that place had been one of the happiest of her life. It was there, it was on that day that the General had made use of such expressions with regard to Henry and herself, had so spoken and so looked as to give her the most positive conviction of his actually wishing their marriage. Yes, only ten days ago had he elated her by his pointed regard – had he even confused her by his too significant reference! And now – what had she done, or what had she omitted to do, to merit such a change?

The only offence against him of which she could accuse herself, had been such as was scarcely possible to reach his knowledge. Henry and her own heart only were privy to the shocking suspicions which she had so idly entertained; and equally safe did she believe her secret with each. Designedly, at least, Henry could not have betrayed her. If, indeed, by any strange mischance his father should have gained intelligence of what she had dared to think and look for, of her causeless fancies and injurious examinations, she could not wonder at any degree of his indignation. If aware of her having viewed him as a murderer, she could not wonder at his even turning her from his house. But a justification so full of torture to herself, she trusted would not be in his power.

Anxious as were all her conjectures on this point, it was not, however, the one on which she dwelt most. There was a thought yet nearer, a more prevailing, more impetuous concern. How Henry would think, and feel, and look, when he returned on the morrow to Northanger and heard of her being gone, was a question of force and interest to rise over every other, to be never ceasing, alternately irritating and soothing; it sometimes suggested the dread of his calm acquiescence, and at others was answered by the sweetest confidence in his regret and resentment. To the General, of course, he would not dare to speak; but to Eleanor – what might he not say to Eleanor about her?

In this unceasing recurrence of doubts and inquiries, on any one article of which her mind was incapable of more than momentary repose, the hours passed away, and her journey advanced much faster than she looked for. The pressing anxieties of thought, which prevented her from noticing any thing before her, when once beyond the neighbourhood of Woodston, saved her at the same time from watching her progress; and though no object on the road could engage a moment's attention, she found no stage of it tedious. From this, she was preserved too by another cause, by feeling no eagerness for her journey's conclusion; for to return in such a manner to Fullerton was almost to destroy the pleasure of a meeting with those she loved best, even after an absence such as her's – an eleven weeks absence. What had she to say that would not humble herself and pain her family; that would not increase her own grief by the confession of it, extend an useless resentment, and perhaps involve the innocent with the guilty in undistinguishing ill-will? She could never do justice to Henry and Eleanor's merit; she felt it too strongly for expression; and should a dislike be taken against them, should they be thought of unfavourably, on their father's account, it would cut her to the heart.

With these feelings, she rather dreaded than sought for the first view of that well-known spire which would announce her within twenty miles of home. Salisbury she had known to be her point on leaving Northanger; but after the first stage she had been indebted to the post-masters for the names of the places which were then to conduct her to it; so great had been her ignorance of her route. She met with nothing, however, to distress or frighten her. Her youth, civil manners and liberal pay, procured her all the attention that a traveller like herself could require; and stopping only to change horses, she travelled on for about eleven hours without accident or alarm, and between six and seven o'clock in the evening found herself entering Fullerton.

A heroine returning, at the close of her career, to her native village, in all the triumph of recovered reputation, and all the dignity of a countess, with a long train of noble relations in their several phaetons, and three waiting-maids in a travelling chaise-and-four, behind her, is an event on which the pen of the contriver may well delight to dwell; it gives credit to every conclusion, and the author must share in the glory she so liberally bestows. – But my affair is widely different; I bring back my heroine to her home in solitude and disgrace; and no sweet elation of spirits can lead me into minuteness. A heroine in a hack post-chaise, is such a blow upon sentiment, as no attempt at grandeur or pathos can withstand. Swiftly therefore shall her post-boy drive through the village, amid the gaze of Sunday groups, and speedy shall be her descent from it.

But, whatever might be the distress of Catherine's mind, as she thus advanced towards the Parsonage, and whatever the humiliation of her biographer in relating it, she was preparing enjoyment of no every-day nature for those to whom she went; first, in the appearance of her carriage – and secondly, in herself. The chaise of a traveller being a rare sight in Fullerton, the whole family were immediately at the window; and to have it stop at the sweep-gate was a pleasure to brighten every eye and occupy every fancy – a pleasure quite unlooked for by all but the two youngest children, a boy and girl of six and four years old, who expected a brother or sister in every carriage. Happy the glance that first distinguished Catherine! – Happy the voice that proclaimed the discovery! – But whether such happiness were the lawful property of George or Harriet could never be exactly understood.

Her father, mother, Sarah, George, and Harriet, all assembled at the door, to welcome her with affectionate eagerness, was a sight to awaken the best feelings of Catherine's heart; and in the embrace of each, as she stepped from the carriage, she found herself soothed beyond any thing that she had believed possible. So surrounded, so caressed, she was even happy! In the joyfulness of family love every thing for a short time was subdued, and the pleasure of seeing her, leaving them at first little leisure for calm curiosity, they were all seated round the tea-table, which Mrs Morland had hurried for the comfort of the poor traveller, whose pale and jaded looks soon caught her notice, before any inquiry so direct as to demand a positive answer was addressed to her.

Reluctantly, and with much hesitation, did she then begin what might perhaps, at the end of half an hour, be termed by the courtesy of her hearers, an explanation; but scarcely, within that time, could they at all discover the cause, or collect the particulars of her sudden return. They were far from being an irritable race; far from any quickness in catching, or bitterness in resenting affronts: – but here, when the whole was unfolded, was an insult not to be overlooked, nor, for the first half hour, to be easily pardoned. Without suffering any romantic alarm, in the consideration of their daughter's long and lonely journey, Mr and Mrs Morland could not but feel that it might have been productive of much unpleasantness to her; that it was what they could never have voluntarily suffered; and that, in forcing her on such a measure, General Tilney had acted neither honourably nor feelingly – neither as a gentleman nor as a parent. Why he had done it, what could have provoked him to such a breach of hospitality, and so suddenly turned all his partial regard for their daughter into actual ill-will, was a matter which they were at least as far from divining as Catherine herself; but it did not oppress them by any means so long; and, after a due course of useless conjecture, that, 'it was a strange business, and that he must be a very strange man,' grew enough for all their indignation and wonder; though Sarah indeed still indulged in the sweets of incomprehensibility, exclaiming and conjecturing with youthful ardour. – 'My dear, you give yourself a great deal of needless trouble,' said

Happy the voice that proclaimed the discovery!

her mother at last; 'depend upon it, it is something not at all worth understanding.'

'I can allow for his wishing Catherine away, when he recollected this engagement,' said Sarah, 'but why not do it civilly?'

'I am sorry for the young people,' returned Mrs Morland; 'they must have a sad time of it; but as for any thing else, it is no matter now; Catherine is safe at home, and our comfort does not depend upon General Tilney.' Catherine sighed. 'Well,' continued her philosophic mother, 'I am glad I did not know of your journey at the time; but now it is all over perhaps there is no great harm done. It is always good for young people to be put upon exerting themselves; and you know, my dear Catherine, you always were a sad little shatter-brained creature; but now you must have been forced to have your wits about you, with so much changing of chaises and so forth; and I hope it will appear that you have not left any thing behind you in any of the pockets.'

Catherine hoped so too, and tried to feel an interest in her own amendment, but her spirits were quite worn down; and, to be silent and alone becoming soon her only wish, she readily agreed to her mother's next counsel of going to bed. Her parents seeing nothing in her ill-looks and agitation but the natural consequence of mortified feelings, and of the unusual exertion and fatigue of such a journey, parted from her without any doubt of their being soon slept away; and though, when they all met the next morning, her recovery was not equal to their hopes, they were still perfectly unsuspicious of there being any deeper evil. They never once thought of her heart, which, for the parents of a young lady of seventeen, just returned from her first excursion from home, was odd enough!

As soon as breakfast was over, she sat down to fulfil her promise to Miss Tilney, whose trust in the effect of time and distance on her friend's disposition was already justified, for already did Catherine reproach herself with having parted from Eleanor coldly; with having never enough valued her merits or kindness; and never enough commiserated her for what she had been yesterday left to endure. The strength of these feelings, however, was far from assisting her pen; and never had it been harder for her to write than in addressing Eleanor Tilney. To compose a letter which might at once do justice to her sentiments and her situation, convey gratitude without servile regret, be guarded without coldness, and honest without resentment – a letter which Eleanor might not be pained by and perusal of – and, above all, which she might not blush herself, if Henry should chance to see, was an undertaking to frighten away all her powers of performance, and, after long thought and much perplexity, to be very brief was all that she could determine on with any confidence of safety. The money therefore which Eleanor had advanced was inclosed with little more than grateful thanks, and the thousand good wishes of a most affectionate heart.

'This has been a strange acquaintance,' observed Mrs Morland, as the letter was finished; 'soon made and soon ended. – I am sorry it happens so, for Mrs Allen thought them very pretty kind of young people; and you were sadly out of luck too in your Isabella. Ah! poor James! Well, we must live and learn; and the next few friends you make I hope will be better worth keeping.'

Catherine coloured as she warmly answered, 'No friend can be better worth keeping than Eleanor.'

'If so, my dear, I dare say you will meet again some time or other; do not be uneasy. It is ten to one but you are thrown together again in the course of a few years; and then what a pleasure it will be!'

Mrs Morland was not happy in her attempt at consolation. The hope of meeting again in the course of a few years could only put into Catherine's head what might happen within that time to make a meeting dreadful to her. She could never forget Henry Tilney, or think of him with less tenderness than she did at that moment; but he might forget her; and in that case to meet! – Her eyes filled with tears as she pictured her acquaintance so renewed; and her mother, perceiving her comfortable suggestions to have had no good effect, proposed, as another expedient for restoring her spirits, that they should call on Mrs Allen.

The two houses were only a quarter of a mile apart; and, as they walked, Mrs Morland quickly dispatched all that she felt on the score of James's disappointment. 'We are sorry for him,' said she, 'but otherwise there is no harm done in the match going off; for it could not be a desirable thing to have him engaged to a girl whom we had not the smallest acquaintance with, and who was so entirely without fortune; and now, after such behaviour, we cannot think at all well of her. Just at present it comes hard to poor James; but that will not last for ever; and I dare say he will be a discreeter man all his life, for the foolishness of his first choice.'

This was just such a summary view of the affair as Catherine could listen to; another sentence might have endangered her complaisance, and made her reply less rational; for soon were all her thinking powers swallowed up in the reflection of her own change of feelings and spirits since last she had trodden that well-known road. It was not three months ago since wild with joyful expectation, she had there run backwards and forwards some ten times a-day, with an heart light, gay, and independent; looking forward to pleasures untasted and unalloyed, and free from the apprehension of evil as from the knowledge of it. Three months ago had seen her all this, and now, how altered a being did she return!

She was received by the Allens with all the kindness which her unlooked-for appearance, acting on a steady affection, would naturally call forth; and great was their surprize, and warm their displeasure, on hearing how she had been treated, – though Mrs Morland's account of it was no inflated representation, no studied appeal to their passions. 'Catherine took us quite by surprize yesterday evening,' said she. 'She travelled all the way post by herself, and knew nothing of coming till Saturday night, for General Tilney, from some odd fancy or other, all of a sudden grew tired of having her there, and almost turned her out of the house. Very unfriendly, certainly; and he must be a very odd man; – but we are so glad to have her amongst us again! And it is a great comfort to find that she is not a poor helpless creature, but can shift very well for herself.'

Mr Allen expressed himself on the occasion with the reasonable resentment of a sensible friend; and Mrs Allen thought his expressions quite good enough to be immediately made use of again by herself. His wonder, his conjectures, and his explanations, became in succession her's, with the addition of this single remark – 'I really have not patience with the General' – to fill up every accidental pause, and, 'I really have not patience with the General,' was uttered twice after Mr Allen left the room, without any relaxation of anger, or any material digression of thought. A more considerable degree of wandering attended the third repetition, and, after completing the fourth, she immediately added, 'Only think, my dear, of my having got that frightful great rent in my best Mechlin so charmingly mended, before I left Bath, that one can hardly see where it was. I must shew it you some day or other. Bath is a nice place, Catherine, after all, I assure you I did not above half like coming away. Mrs Thorpe's being there was such a comfort to us, was not it? You know you and I were quite forlorn at first.'

'Yes, but *that* did not last long,' said Catherine, her eyes brightening at the recollection of what had first given spirit to her existence there.

'Very true: we soon met with Mrs Thorpe, and then we wanted for nothing. My dear, do not you think these silk gloves wear very well? I put them on new the first time of our going to the Lower

Rooms, you know, and I have worn them a great deal since. Do you remember that evening?'

'Do I! Oh! perfectly.'

'It was very agreeable, was not it? Mr Tilney drank tea with us, and I always thought him a great addition, he is so very agreeable. I have a notion you danced with him, but am not quite sure. I remember I had my favourite gown on.'

Catherine could not answer; and, after a short trial of other subjects, Mrs Allen again returned to – 'I really have not patience with the General! Such an agreeable, worthy man as he seemed to be! I do not suppose, Mrs Morland, you ever saw a better-bred man in your life. His lodgings were taken the very day after he left them. Catherine. But no wonder; Milsom-street you know.' –

As they walked home again, Mrs Morland endeavoured to impress on her daughter's mind the happiness of having such steady well-wishers as Mr and Mrs Allen, and the very little consideration which the neglect or unkindness of slight acquaintance like the Tilneys ought to have with her, while she could preserve the good opinion and affection of her earliest friends. There was a great deal of good sense in all this; but there are some situations of the human mind in which good sense has very little power; and Catherine's feelings contradicted almost every position her mother advanced. It was upon the behaviour of these very slight acquaintance that all her present happiness depended; and while Mrs Morland was successfully confirming her own opinions by the justness of her own representations, Catherine was silently reflecting that *now* Henry must have arrived at Northanger; *now* he must have heard of her departure; and *now*, perhaps they were all setting off for Hereford.

CHAPTER THIRTY

CATHERINE'S DISPOSITION was not naturally sedentary, nor had her habits been ever very industrious; but whatever might hitherto have been her defects of that sort, her mother could not but perceive them now to be greatly increased. She could neither sit still, nor employ herself for ten minutes together, walking round the garden and orchard again and again, as if nothing but motion was voluntary; and it seemed as if she could even walk about the house rather than remain fixed for any time in the parlour. Her loss of spirits was a yet greater alteration. In her rambling and her idleness she might only be a caricature of herself; but in her silence and sadness she was the very reverse of all that she had been before.

For two days Mrs Morland allowed it to pass even without a hint; but when a third night's rest had neither restored her cheerfulness, improved her in useful activity, nor given her a greater inclination for needle-work, she could no longer refrain from the gentle reproof of, 'My dear Catherine, I am afraid you are growing quite a fine lady. I do not know when poor Richard's cravats would be done, if he had no friend but you. Your head runs too much upon Bath; but there is a time for every thing – a time for balls and plays, and a time for work. You have had a long run of amusement, and now you must try to be useful.'

Catherine took up her work directly, saying, in a dejected voice, that 'her head did not run upon Bath – much.'

'Then you are fretting about General Tilney, and that is very simple of you; for ten to one whether you ever see him again. You should never fret about trifles.' After a short silence – 'I hope, my Catherine, you are not getting out of humour with home because it is not so grand as Northanger. That would be turning your visit into an evil indeed. Wherever you are you should always be contented, but especially at home, because there you must spend the most of your time. I did not quite like, at breakfast, to hear you talk so much about the French-bread at Northanger.'

'I am sure I do not care about the bread. It is all the same to me what I eat.'

'There is a very clever Essay in one of the books up stairs upon much such a subject, about young girls that have been spoilt for home by great acquaintance – "The Mirror," I think. I will look it out for you some day or other, because I am sure it will do you good.'

Catherine said no more, and, with an endeavour to do right, applied to her work; but, after a few minutes, sunk again, without knowing it herself, into languor and listlessness, moving herself in her chair, from the irritation of weariness, much oftener than she moved her needle. – Mrs Morland watched the progress of this relapse; and seeing, in her daughter's absent and dissatisfied look, the full proof of that repining spirit to which she had now begun to attribute her want of cheerfulness, hastily left the room to fetch the book in question, anxious to lose no time in attacking so dreadful a malady. It was some time before she could find what she looked for; and other family matters occurring to detain her, a quarter of an hour had elapsed ere she returned downstairs with the volume from which so much was hoped. Her avocations above having shut

It was some time before she could find what she looked for.

out all noise but what she created herself, she knew not that a visitor had arrived within the last few minutes, till, on entering the room, the first object she beheld was a young man who she had never seen before. With a look of much respect, he immediately rose, and being introduced to her by her conscious daughter as 'Mr Henry Tilney,' with the embarrassment of real sensibility began to apologise for his appearance there, acknowledging that after what had passed he had little right to expect a welcome at Fullerton, and stating his impatience to be assured of Miss Morland's having reached her home in safety, as the cause of his intrusion. He did not address himself to an uncandid judge or a resentful heart. Far from comprehending him or his sister in their father's misconduct, Mrs Morland had been always kindly disposed towards each, and instantly, pleased by his appearance, received him with the simple professions of unaffected benevolence; thanking him for such an attention to her daughter, assuring him that the friends of her children were always welcome there, and intreating him to say not another word of the past.

He was not ill inclined to obey this request, for, though his heart was greatly relieved by such unlooked-for mildness, it was not just at that moment in his power to say any thing to the purpose. Returning in silence to his seat, therefore, he remained for some minutes most civilly answering all Mrs Morland's common remarks about the weather and roads. Catherine meanwhile, – the anxious, agitated, happy, feverish Catherine, – said not a word; but her glowing cheek and brightened eye made her mother trust that this good-natured visit would at least set her heart at ease for a time, and gladly therefore did she lay aside the first volume of the Mirror for a future hour.

Desirous of Mr Morland's assistance, as well in giving encouragement, as in finding conversation for her guest, whose embarrassment on his father's account she earnestly pitied, Mrs Morland had very early dispatched one of the children to summon him; but Mr Morland was from home – and being thus without any support, at the end of a quarter of an hour she had nothing to say. After a couple of minutes unbroken silence, Henry, turning to Catherine for the first time since her mother's entrance, asked her, with sudden alacrity, if Mr and Mrs Allen were now at Fullerton? and on developing, from amidst all her perplexity of words in reply, the meaning, which one short syllable would have given, immediately expressed his intention of paying his respects to them, and, with a rising colour, asked her if she would have the goodness to shew him the way. 'You may see the house from this window, sir,' was information on Sarah's side, which produced only a bow of acknowledgment from the gentleman, and a silencing nod from her mother; for Mrs Morland, thinking it probable, as a secondary consideration in his wish of waiting on their worthy neighbours, that he might have some explanation to give of his father's behaviour, which it must be more pleasant for him to communicate only to Catherine, would not on any account prevent her accompanying him. They began their walk, and Mrs Morland was not entirely mistaken in his object in wishing it. Some explanation on his father's account he had to give; but his first purpose was to explain himself, and before they reached Mr Allen's grounds he had done it so well, that Catherine did not think it could ever be repeated too often. She was assured of his affection; and that heart in return was solicited, which, perhaps, they pretty equally knew was already entirely his own; for, though Henry was now sincerely attached to her, though he felt and delighted in all the excellencies of her character and truly loved her society, I must confess that his affection originated in nothing better than gratitude, or, in other words, that a persuasion of her partiality for him had been the only cause of giving her a serious thought. It is a new circumstance in romance, I acknowledge, and dreadfully derogatory of an heroine's dignity; but if it be as new in common life, the credit of a wild imagination will at least be all my own.

A very short visit to Mrs Allen, in which Henry talked at random, without sense or connection, and Catherine, wrapt in the contemplation of her own unutterable happiness, scarcely opened her lips, dismissed them to the extasies of another tête-à-tête; and before it was suffered to close, she was enabled to judge how far he was sanctioned by parental authority in his present application. On his return from Woodston, two days before, he had been met near the Abbey by his impatient father, hastily informed in angry terms of Miss Morland's departure, and ordered to think of her no more.

Such was the permission upon which he had now offered her his hand. The affrighted Catherine, amidst all the terrors of expectation, as she listened to this account, could not but rejoice in the kind caution with which Henry had saved her from the necessity of a conscientious rejection, by engaging her faith before he mentioned the subject, and as he proceeded to give the particulars, and explain the motives of his father's conduct, her feelings soon hardened into even a triumphant delight. The General had had nothing to accuse her of, nothing to lay to her charge, but her being the involuntary, unconscious object of a deception which his pride could not pardon, and which a better pride would have been ashamed to own. She was guilty only of being less rich than he had supposed her to be. Under a mistaken persuasion of her possessions and claims, he had courted her acquaintance in Bath, solicited her company at Northanger, and designed her for his daughter in law. On discovering his error, to turn her from the house seemed the best, though to his feelings an inadequate proof of his resentment towards herself, and his contempt of her family.

John Thorpe had first misled him. The General, perceiving his son one night at the theatre to be paying considerable attention to Miss Morland, had accidentally inquired of Thorpe, if he knew more of her than her name. Thorpe, most happy to be on speaking terms with a man of General Tilney's importance, had been joyfully and proudly communicative; – and being at that time not only in daily expectation of Morland's engaging Isabella, but likewise pretty well resolved upon marrying Catherine himself, his vanity induced him to represent the family as yet more wealthy than his vanity and avarice had made him believe them. With whomsoever he was, or was likely to be connected, his own consequence always required that theirs should be great, and as his intimacy with any acquaintance grew, so regularly grew their fortune. The expectations of his friend Morland, therefore, from the first over-rated, had ever since his introduction to Isabella, been gradually increasing; and by merely adding twice as much for the grandeur of the moment, by doubling what he chose to think the amount of Mr Morland's preferment, trebling his private fortune, bestowing a rich aunt, and sinking half the children, he was able to represent the whole family to the General in a most respectable light. For Catherine, however, the peculiar object of the General's curiosity, and his own speculations, he had yet something more in reserve, and the ten or fifteen thousand pounds which her father could give her, would be a pretty addition to Mr Allen's estate. Her intimacy there had made him seriously determine on her being handsomely legacied hereafter; and to speak of her therefore as the almost acknowledged future heiress of Fullerton naturally followed. Upon such intelligence the General had proceeded; for never had it occurred to him to doubt its authority. Thorpe's interest in the family, by his sister's approaching connection with one of its members, and his own views on another, (circumstances of which he boasted with almost equal openness,) seemed sufficient vouchers for his truth; and to these were added the absolute facts of the Allens being wealthy and childless, of Miss Morland's being under their care, and – as soon as his acquaintance allowed him to judge – of their treating her with parental kindness. His resolution was soon formed. Already had he discerned a liking towards Miss Morland in the countenance of his son; and thankful for Mr Thorpe's communication, he almost instantly determined to spare no pains in weakening his boasted interest and ruining his dearest hopes. Catherine herself could not be more ignorant at the time of all this, than his own children. Henry and Eleanor, perceiving nothing in her situation likely to engage their father's particular respect, had seen with astonishment the suddenness, continuance and extent of his attention; and though latterly, from some hints which had accompanied an almost positive command to his son of doing every thing in his power to attach her, Henry was convinced of his father's believing it to be an advantageous connection, it was not till the late explanation at Northanger that they had the smallest idea of the false calculations which had hurried him on. That they were false, the General had learnt from the very person who had suggested them, from Thorpe himself, whom he had chanced to meet again in town, and who, under the influence of exactly opposite feelings, irritated by Catherine's refusal, and yet more by the failure of a very recent endeavour to accomplish a reconciliation between Morland and Isabella, convinced that they were separated for ever, and spurning a friendship which could be no longer serviceable, hastened to contradict all that he had said before to the advantage of the Morlands; – confessed himself to have been totally mistaken in his opinion of their circumstances and character, misled by the rhodomontade of his friend to believe his father a man of substance and credit, whereas the transactions of the two or three last weeks proved him to be neither; for after coming eagerly forward on the first overture of a marriage between the families, with the most liberal proposals, he had, on being brought to the point by the shrewdness of the relator, been constrained to acknowledge himself incapable of giving the young people even a decent support. They were, in fact, a necessitous family, numerous too almost beyond example, by no means respected in their own neighbourhood, as he had lately had particular opportunities of discovering. aiming at a style of life which their fortune could not warrant. seeking to better themselves by wealthy connexions; a forward, bragging, scheming race.

The terrified General pronounced the name of Allen with an inquiring look; and here too Thorpe had learnt his error. The Allens, he believed, had lived near them too long, and he knew the young man on whom the Fullerton estate must devolve. The General needed no more. Enraged with almost every body in the world but himself, he set out the next day for the Abbey, where his performances have been seen.

I leave it to my readers' sagacity to determine how much of all this it was possible for Henry to communicate at this time to Catherine, how much of it he could have learnt from his father, in what points his own conjectures might assist him, and what portion must yet remain to be told in a letter from James. I have united for their ease what they must divide for mine. Catherine, at any rate, heard enough to feel, that in suspecting General Tilney of either murdering or shutting up his wife, she had scarcely sinned against his character, or magnified his cruelty.

Henry, in having such things to relate of his father, was almost as pitiable as in their first avowal to himself. He blushed for the narrow-minded counsel which he was obliged to expose. The conversation between them at Northanger had been of the most unfriendly kind. Henry's indignation on hearing how Catherine had been treated, on comprehending his father's views, and being ordered to acquiesce in them, had been open and bold. The General, accustomed on every ordinary occasion to give the law in his family, prepared for no reluctance but of feeling, no opposing desire that should dare to clothe itself in words, could ill brook the opposition of his son, steady as the sanction of reason and the dictate of conscience could make it. But, in such a cause, his anger, though it must shock, could not intimidate Henry, who was sustained in his purpose by a conviction of its justice. He felt himself bound as much in honour as in affection to Miss Morland, and believing that heart to be his own which he had been directed to gain, no unworthy retraction of a tacit consent, no reversing decree of unjustifiable anger, could shake his fidelity, or influence the resolutions it prompted.

He steadily refused to accompany his father into Herefordshire, an engagement formed almost at the moment, to promote the dismissal of Catherine, and as steadily declared his intention of offering her his hand. The General was furious in his anger, and they parted in dreadful disagreement. Henry, in an agitation of mind which many solitary hours were required to compose, had returned almost instantly to Woodston; and, on the afternoon of the following day, had begun his journey to Fullerton.

CHAPTER THIRTY-ONE

MR AND MRS MORLAND's surprize on being applied to by Mr Tilney, for their consent to his marrying their daughter, was, for a few minutes, considerable; it having never entered their heads, to suspect an attachment on either side; but as nothing, after all, could be more natural than Catherine's being beloved, they soon learnt to consider it with only the happy agitation of gratified pride, and, as far as they alone were concerned, had not a single objection to start. His pleasing manners and good sense were self-evident recommendations; and having never heard evil of him, it was not their way to suppose any evil could be told. Good-will supplying the place of experience, his character needed no attestation. 'Catherine would make a sad heedless young house-keeper to be sure,' was her mother's foreboding remark; but quick was the consolation of there being nothing like practice.

There was but one obstacle, in short, to be mentioned; but till that one was removed, it must be impossible for them to sanction the engagement. Their tempers were mild, but their principles were steady, and while his parent so expressly forbad the connexion, they could not allow themselves to encourage it. That the General should come forward to solicit the alliance, or that he should even very heartily approve it, they were not refined enough to make any parading stipulation; but the decent appearance of consent must be yielded, and that once obtained – and their own hearts made them trust that it could not be very long denied – their willing approbation was instantly to follow. His *consent* was all that they wished for. They were no more inclined than entitled to demand his *money*. Of a very considerable fortune, his son was, by marriage settlements, eventually secure; his present income was an income of independence and comfort, and under every pecuniary view, it was a match beyond the claims of their daughter.

The young people could not be surprized at a decision like this. They felt and they deplored – but they could not resent it; and they parted, endeavouring to hope that such a change in the General, as each believed almost impossible, might speedily take place, to unite them again in the fullness of privileged affection. Henry returned to what was now his only home, to watch over his young plantations, and extend his improvements for her sake, to whose share in them he looked anxiously forward; and Catherine remained at Fullerton to cry. Whether the torments of absence were softened by a clandestine correspondence, let us not inquire. Mr and Mrs Morland never did – they had been too kind to exact any promise; and whenever Catherine received a letter, as, at that time, happened pretty often, they always looked another way.

The anxiety, which in this state of their attachment must be the portion of Henry and Catherine, and of all who loved either, as to its final event, can hardly extend, I fear, to the bosom of my readers, who will see in the tell-tale compression of the pages before them, that we are all hastening together to perfect felicity. The means by which their early marriage was effected can be the only doubt: what probable circumstance could work upon a temper like the General's? The circumstance which chiefly availed, was the marriage of his daughter with a man of fortune and consequence, which took place in the course of the summer – an accession of dignity that threw him into a fit of good-humour, from which he did not recover till after Eleanor had obtained his forgiveness of Henry, and his permission for him 'to be a fool if he liked it!'

The marriage of Eleanor Tilney, her removal from all the evils of such a home as Northanger had been made by Henry's banishment, to the home of her choice and the man of her choice, is an event which I expect to give general satisfaction among all her acquaintance. My own joy on the occasion is very sincere. I know no one more entitled, by unpretending merit, or better prepared by habitual suffering, to receive and enjoy felicity. Her partiality for this gentleman was not of recent origin; and he had been long

They always looked another way.

withheld only by inferiority of situation from addressing her. His unexpected accession to title and fortune had removed all his difficulties; and never had the General loved his daughter so well in all her hours of companionship, utility, and patient endurance, as when he first hailed her, 'Your Ladyship!' Her husband was really deserving of her; independent of his peerage, his wealth, and his attachment, being to a precision the most charming young man in the world. Any further definition of his merits must be unnecessary; the most charming young man in the world is instantly before the imagination of us all. Concerning the one in question therefore I have only to add – (aware that the rules of composition forbid the introduction of a character not connected with my fable) – that this was the very gentleman whose negligent servant left behind him that collection of washing-bills, resulting from a long visit at Northanger, by which my heroine was involved in one of her most alarming adventures.

The influence of the Viscount and Viscountess in their brother's behalf was assisted by that right understanding of Mr Morland's circumstances which, as soon as the General would allow himself to be informed, they were qualified to give. It taught him that he had been scarcely more misled by Thorpe's first boast of the family wealth, than by his subsequent malicious overthrow of it; that in no sense of the word were they necessitous or poor, and that Catherine would have three thousand pounds. This was so material an amendment of his late expectations, that it greatly contributed to smooth the descent of his pride; and by no means without its effect was the private intelligence, which he was at some pains to procure, that the Fullerton estate, being entirely at the disposal of its present proprietor, was consequently open to every greedy speculation.

On the strength of this, the General, soon after Eleanor's marriage, permitted his son to return to Northanger, and thence made him the bearer of his consent, very courteously worded in a page full of empty professions to Mr Morland. The event which it authorized soon followed: Henry and Catherine were married, the bells rang and every body smiled; and, as this took place within a twelvemonth from the first day of their meeting, it will not appear, after all the dreadful delays occasioned by the General's cruelty, that they were essentially hurt by it. To begin perfect happiness at the respective ages of twenty-six and eighteen, is to do pretty well; and professing myself moreover convinced, that the General's unjust interference, so far from being really injurious to their felicity, was perhaps rather conducive to it, by improving their knowledge of each other, and adding strength to their attachment, I leave it to be settled by whomsoever it may concern, whether the tendency of this work be altogether to recommend parental tyranny, or reward filial disobedience.